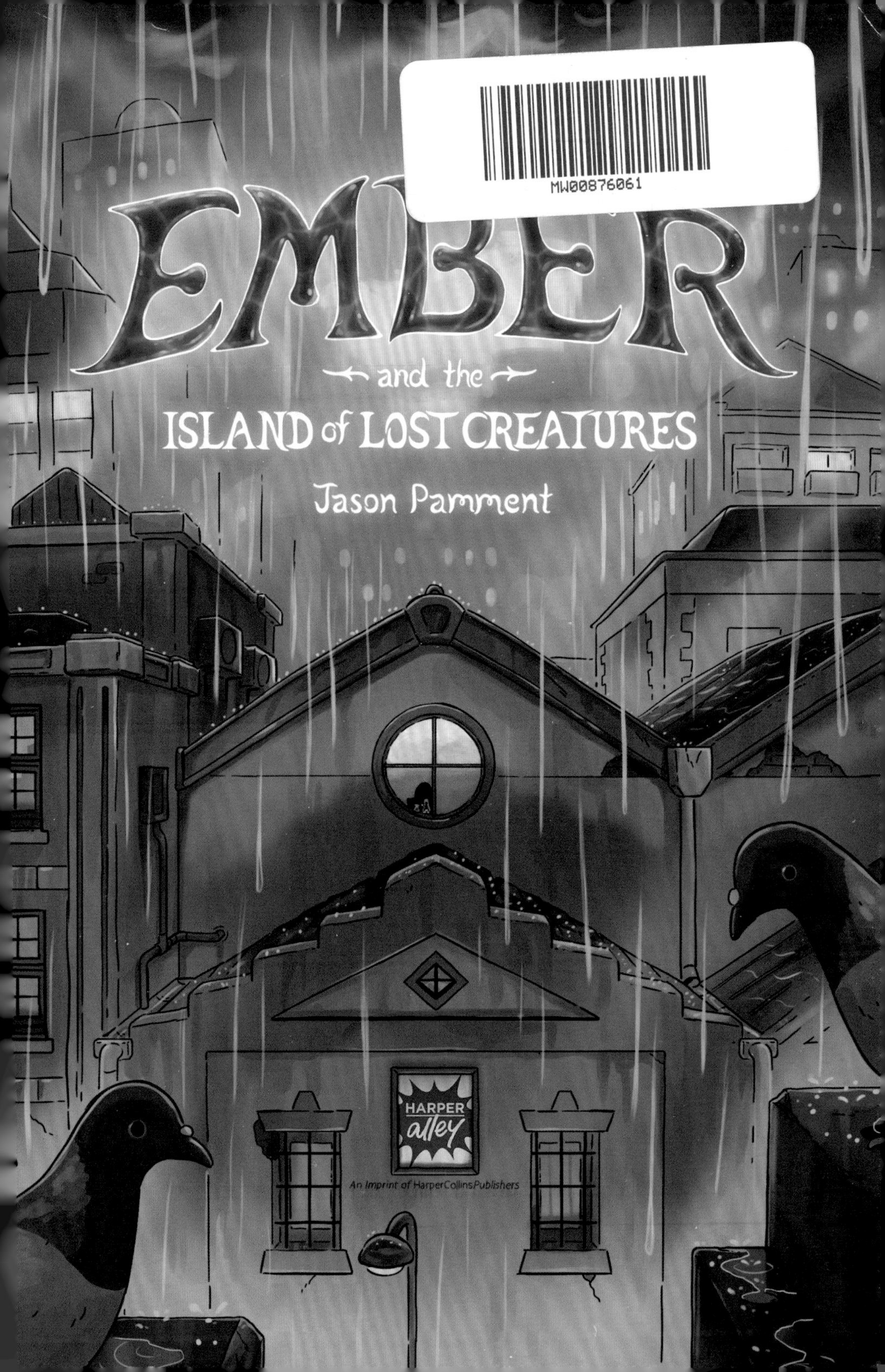
MW00876061
EMBER
and the
ISLAND of LOST CREATURES
Jason Pamment
HARPER alley
An Imprint of HarperCollinsPublishers

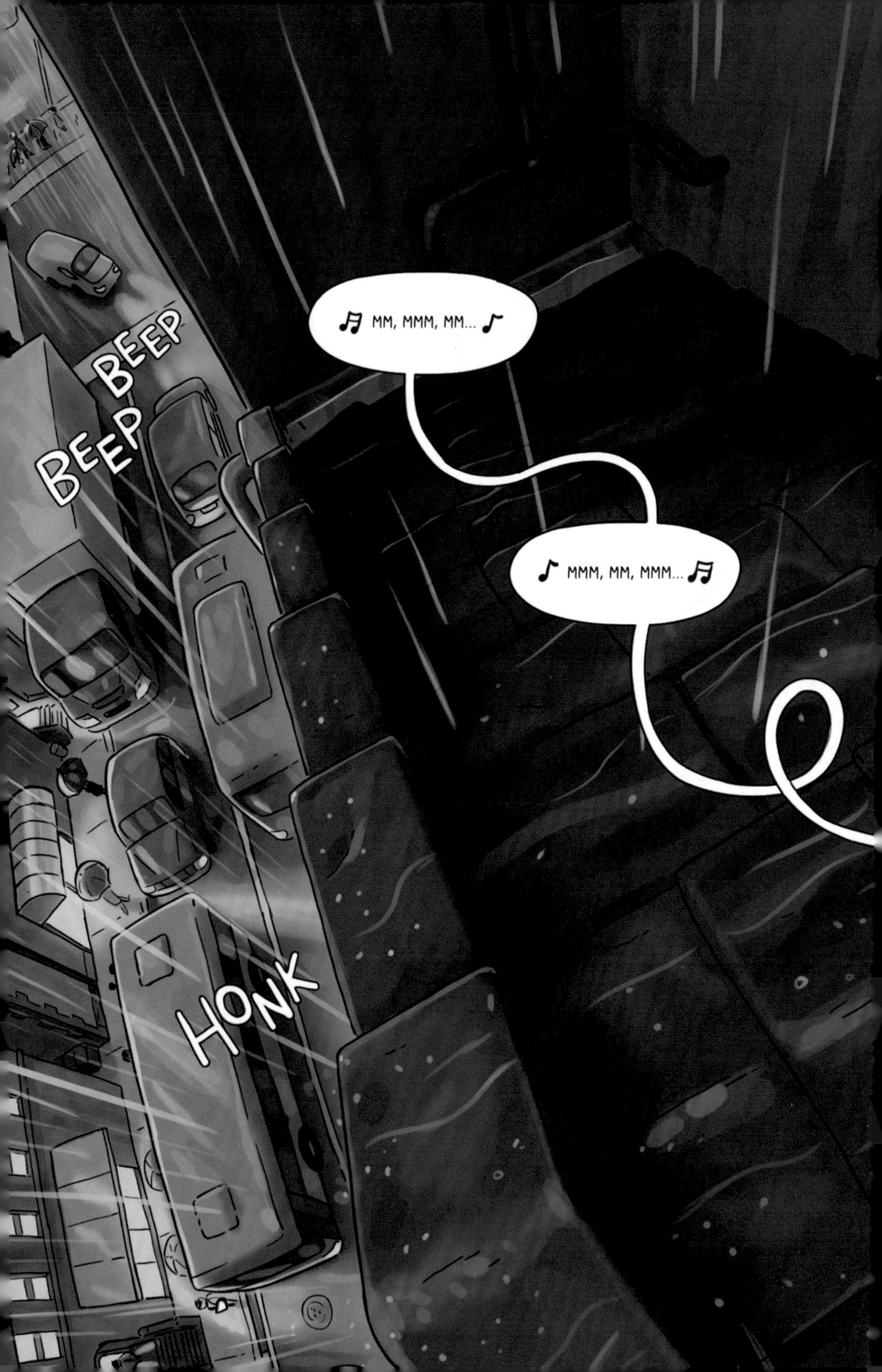BEEP BEEP
♬ MM, MMM, MM... ♪
♪ MMM, MM, MMM... ♬
HONK

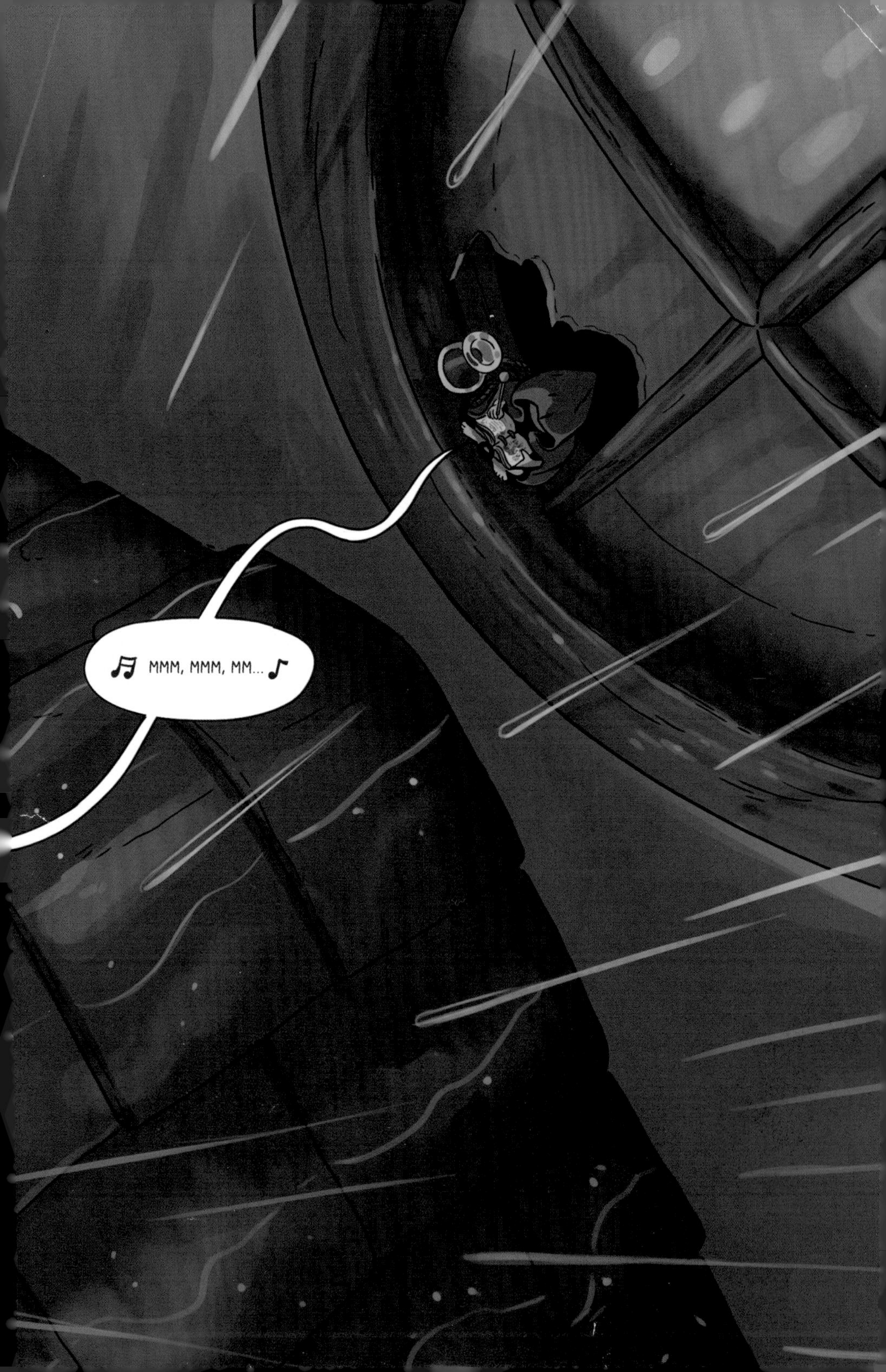
MMM, MMM, MM...

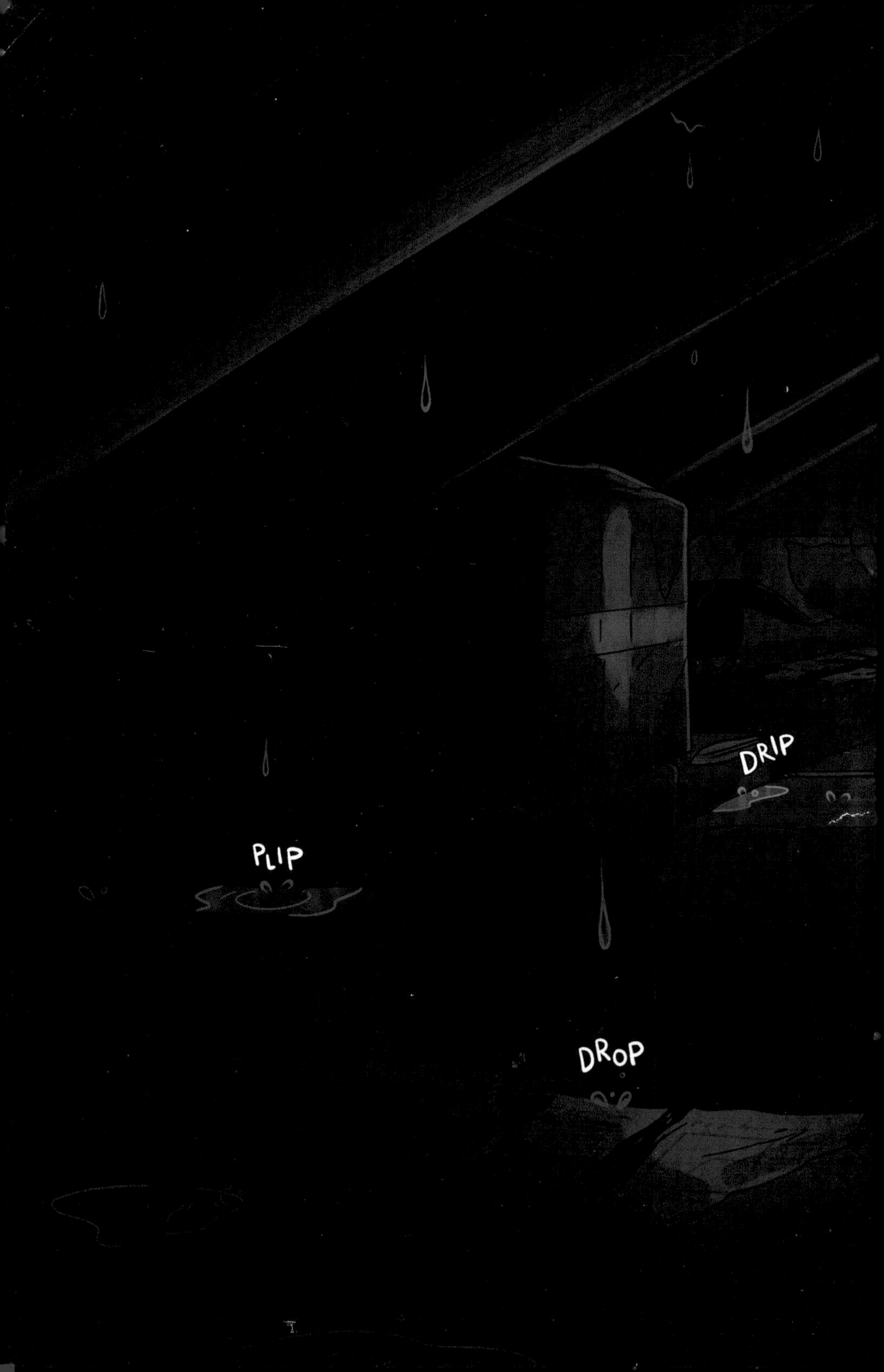
DRIP
PLIP
DROP

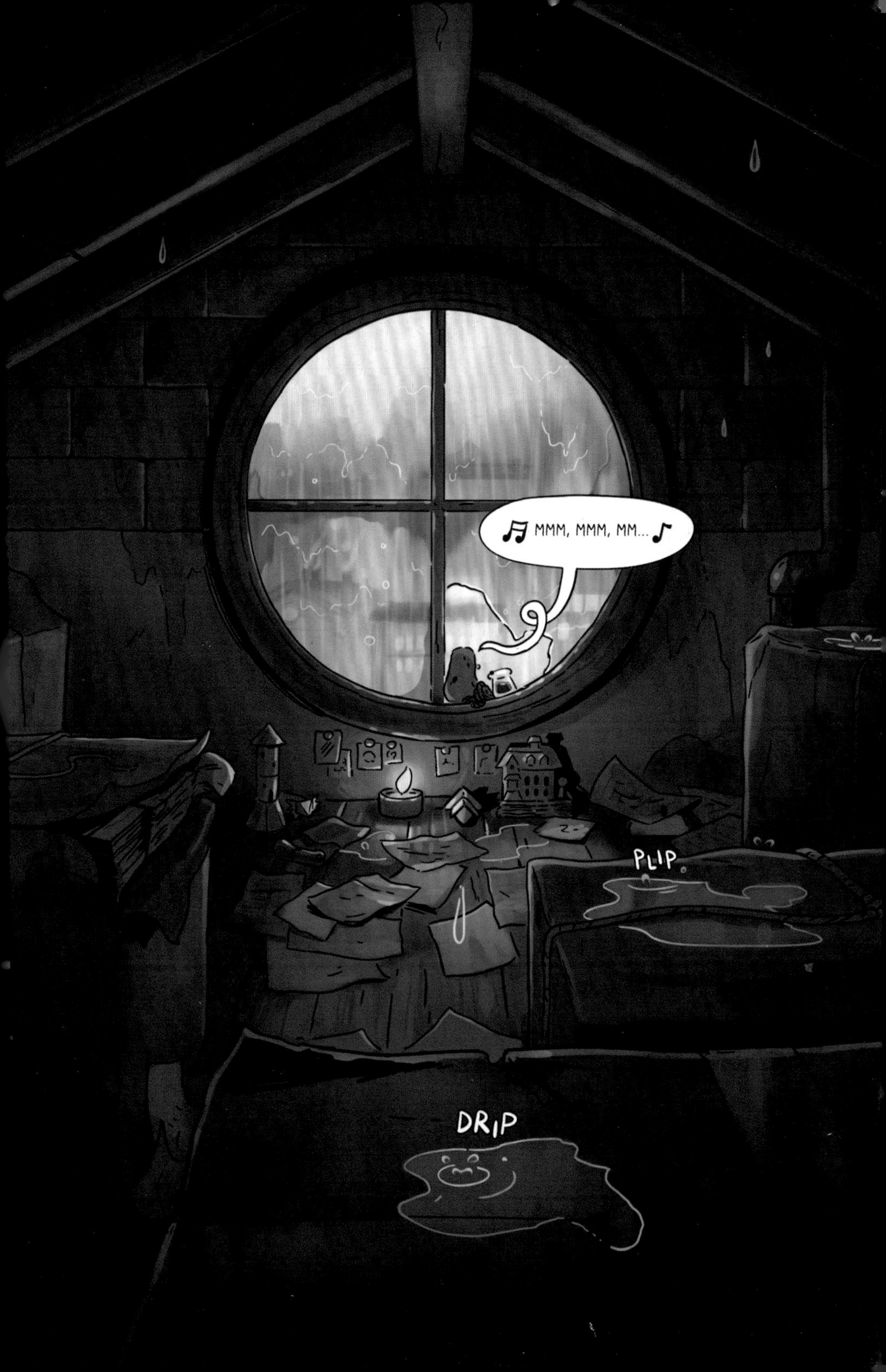
MMM, MMM, MM...
PLIP
DRIP

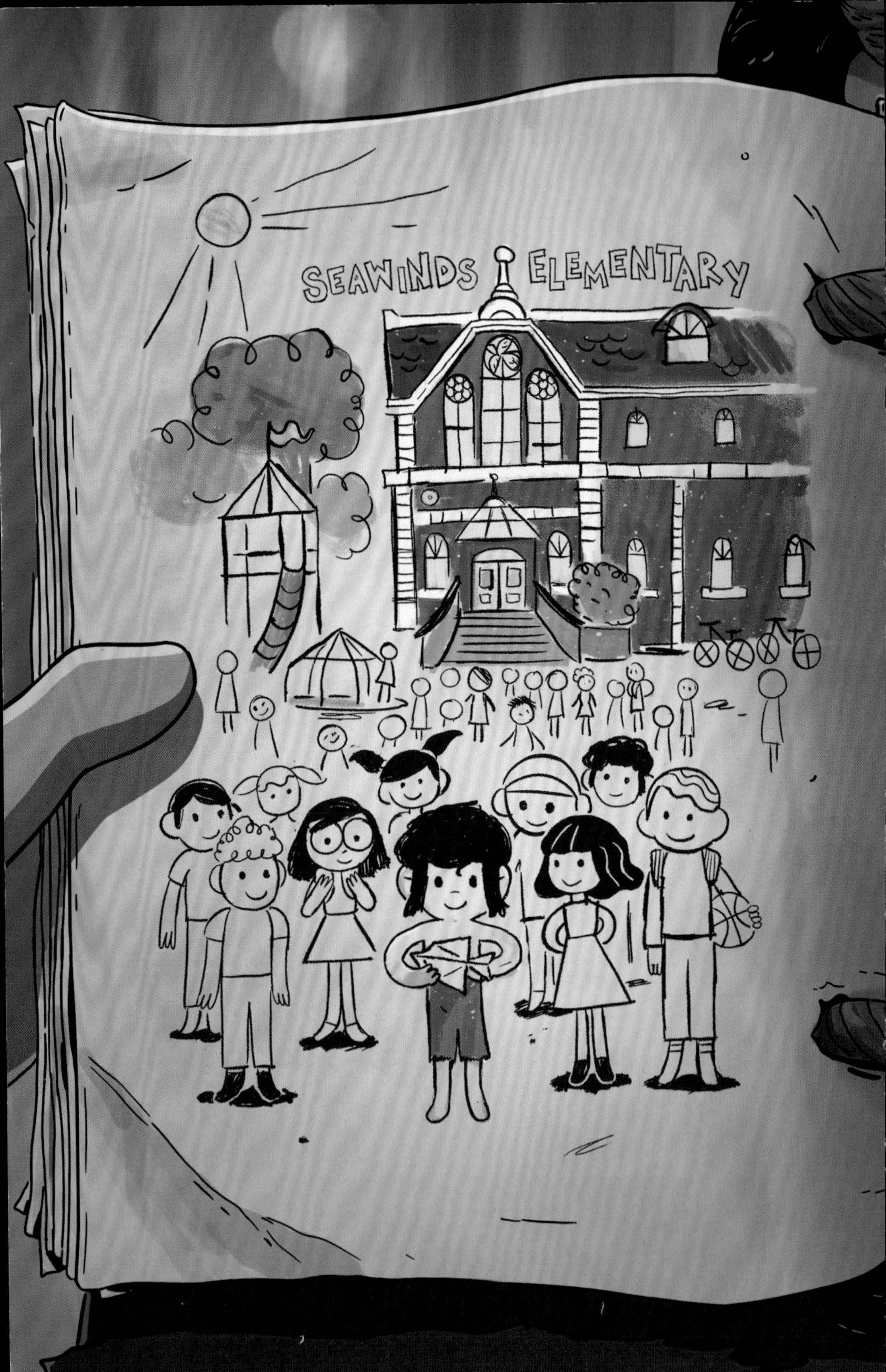
SEAWINDS ELEMENTARY

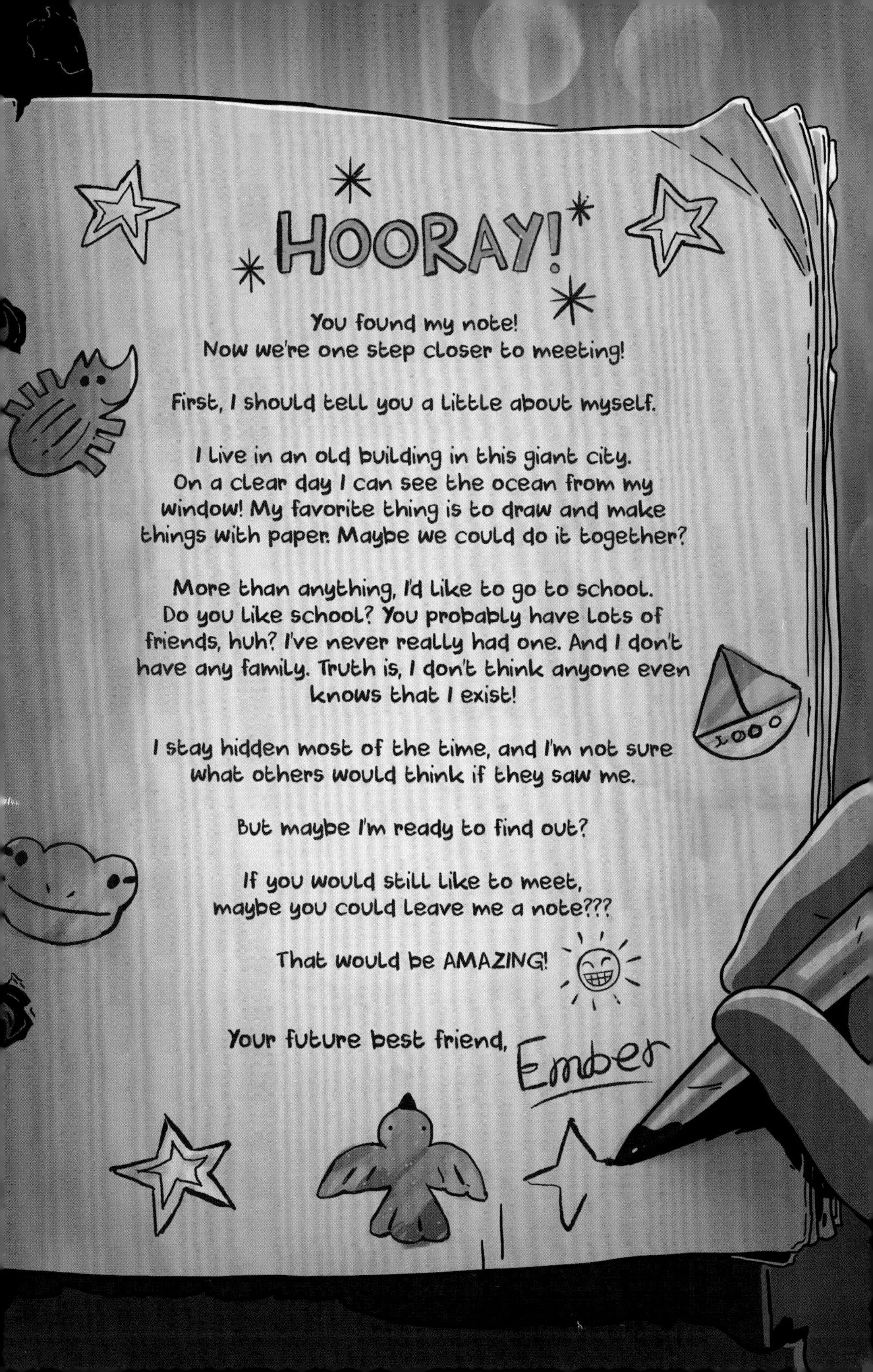

HOORAY!

You found my note!
Now we're one step closer to meeting!

First, I should tell you a little about myself.

I live in an old building in this giant city. On a clear day I can see the ocean from my window! My favorite thing is to draw and make things with paper. Maybe we could do it together?

More than anything, I'd like to go to school. Do you like school? You probably have lots of friends, huh? I've never really had one. And I don't have any family. Truth is, I don't think anyone even knows that I exist!

I stay hidden most of the time, and I'm not sure what others would think if they saw me.

But maybe I'm ready to find out?

If you would still like to meet, maybe you could leave me a note???

That would be AMAZING!

Your future best friend, Ember

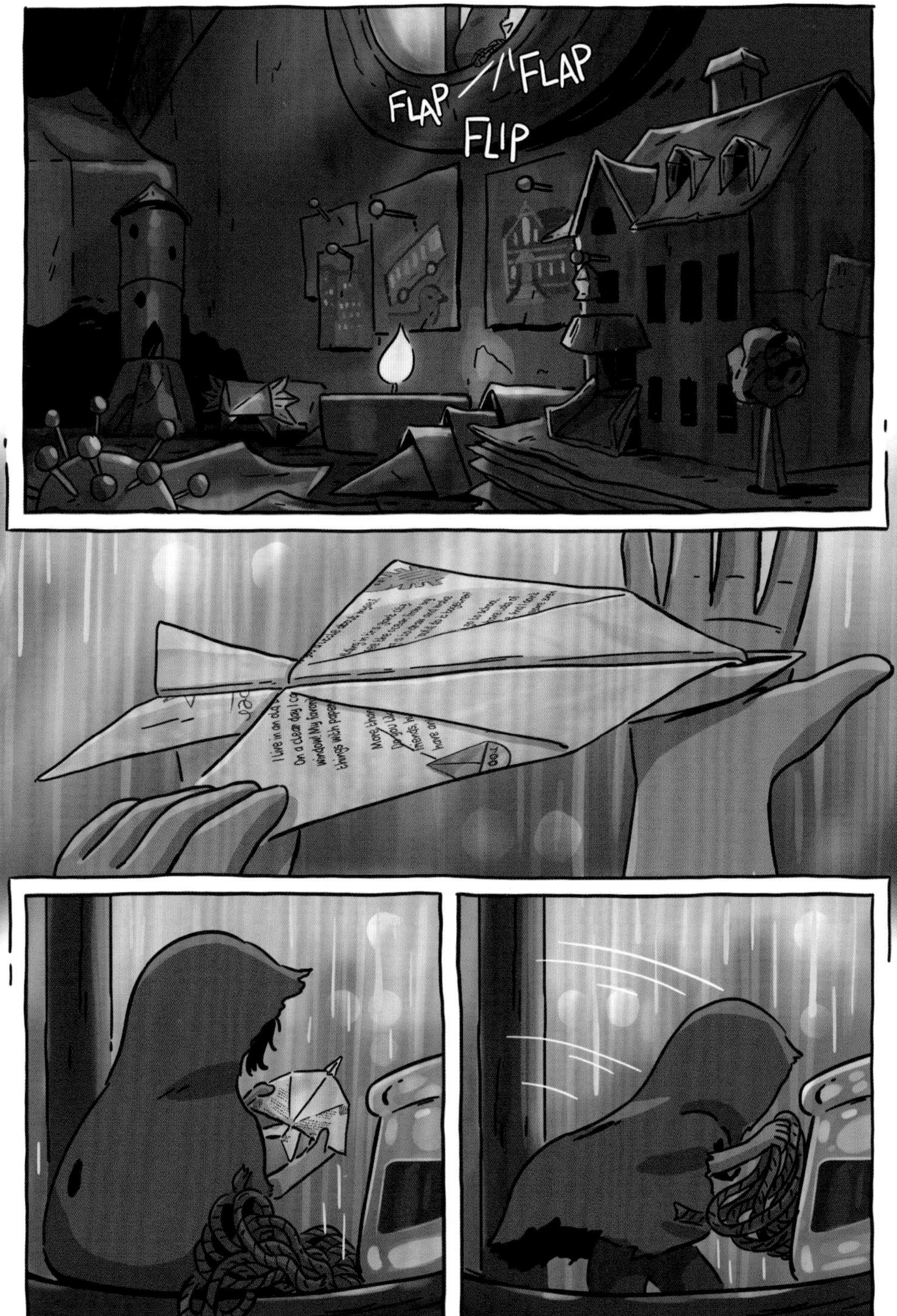
FLAP
FLAP
FLIP

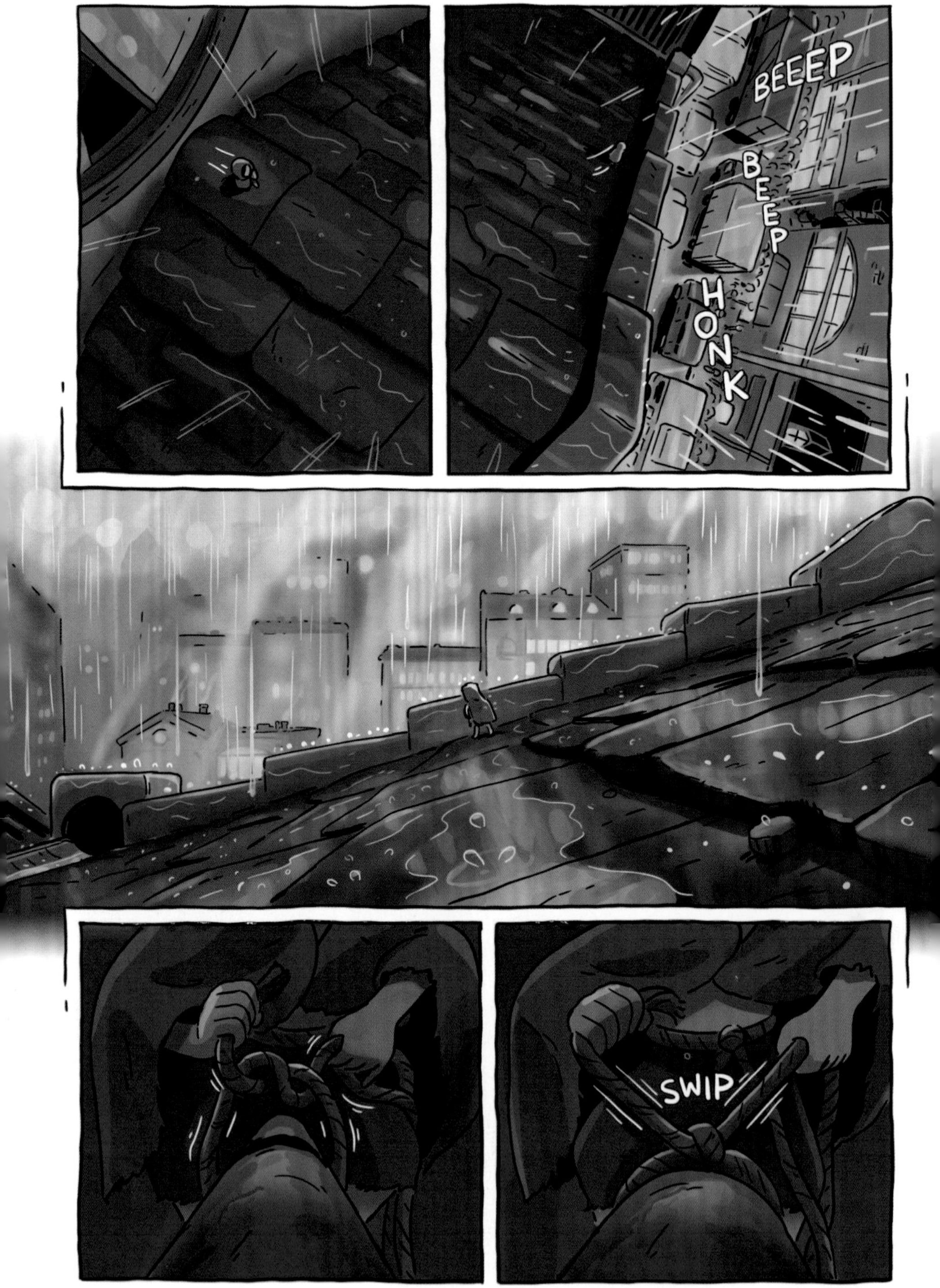
BEEEP
BEEP
HONK
SWIP

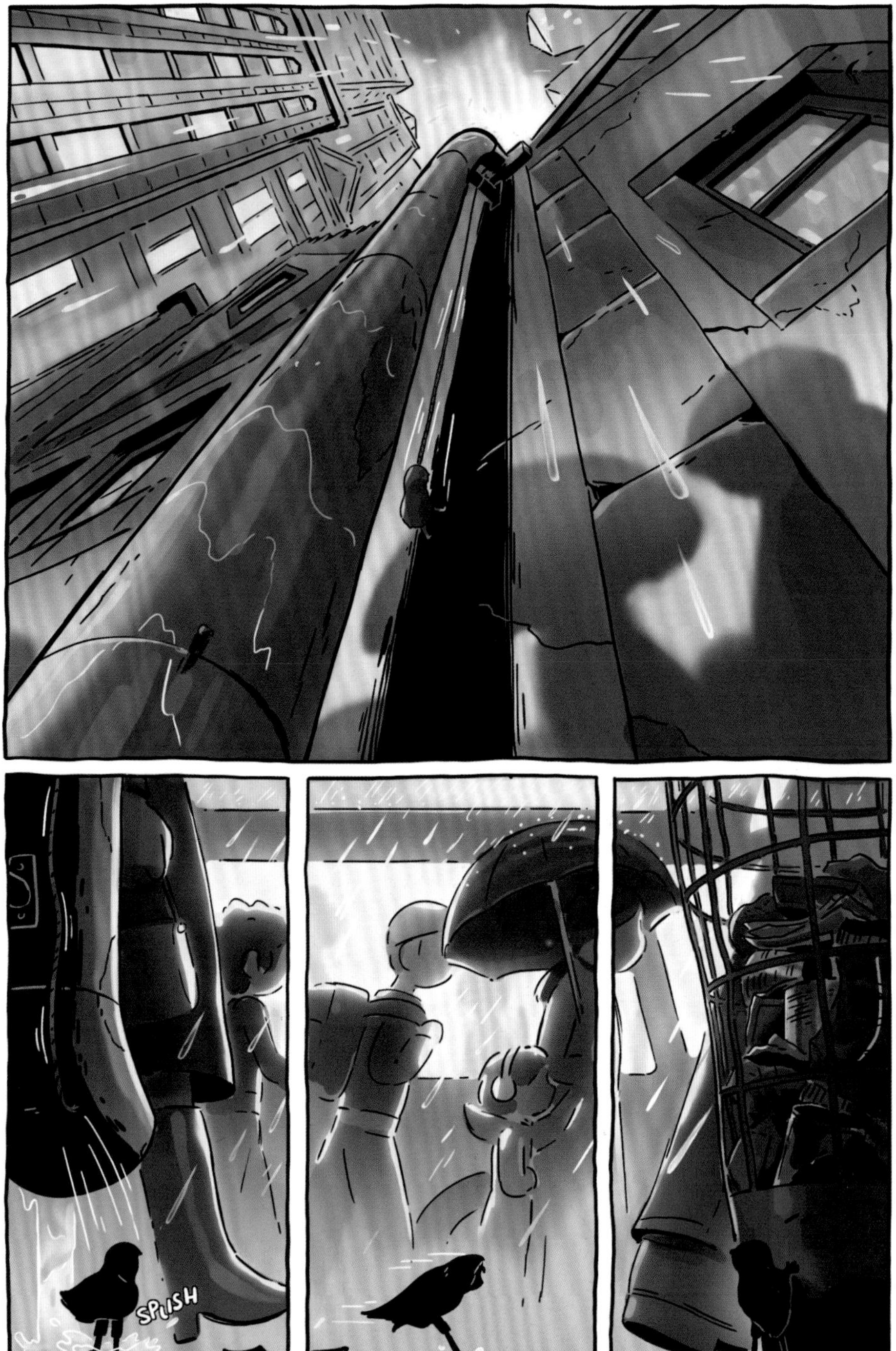
SPLISH

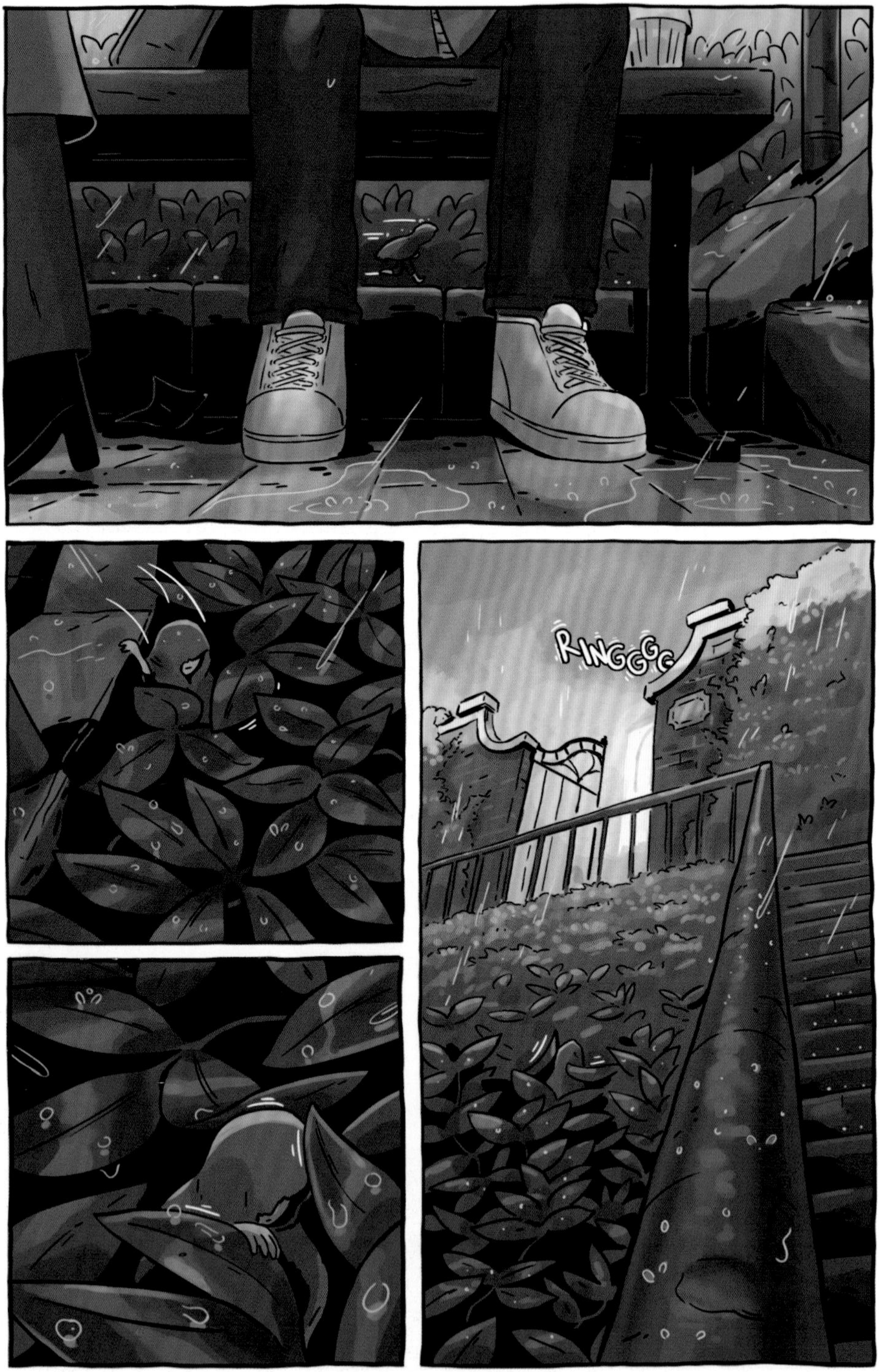
RINGGGG

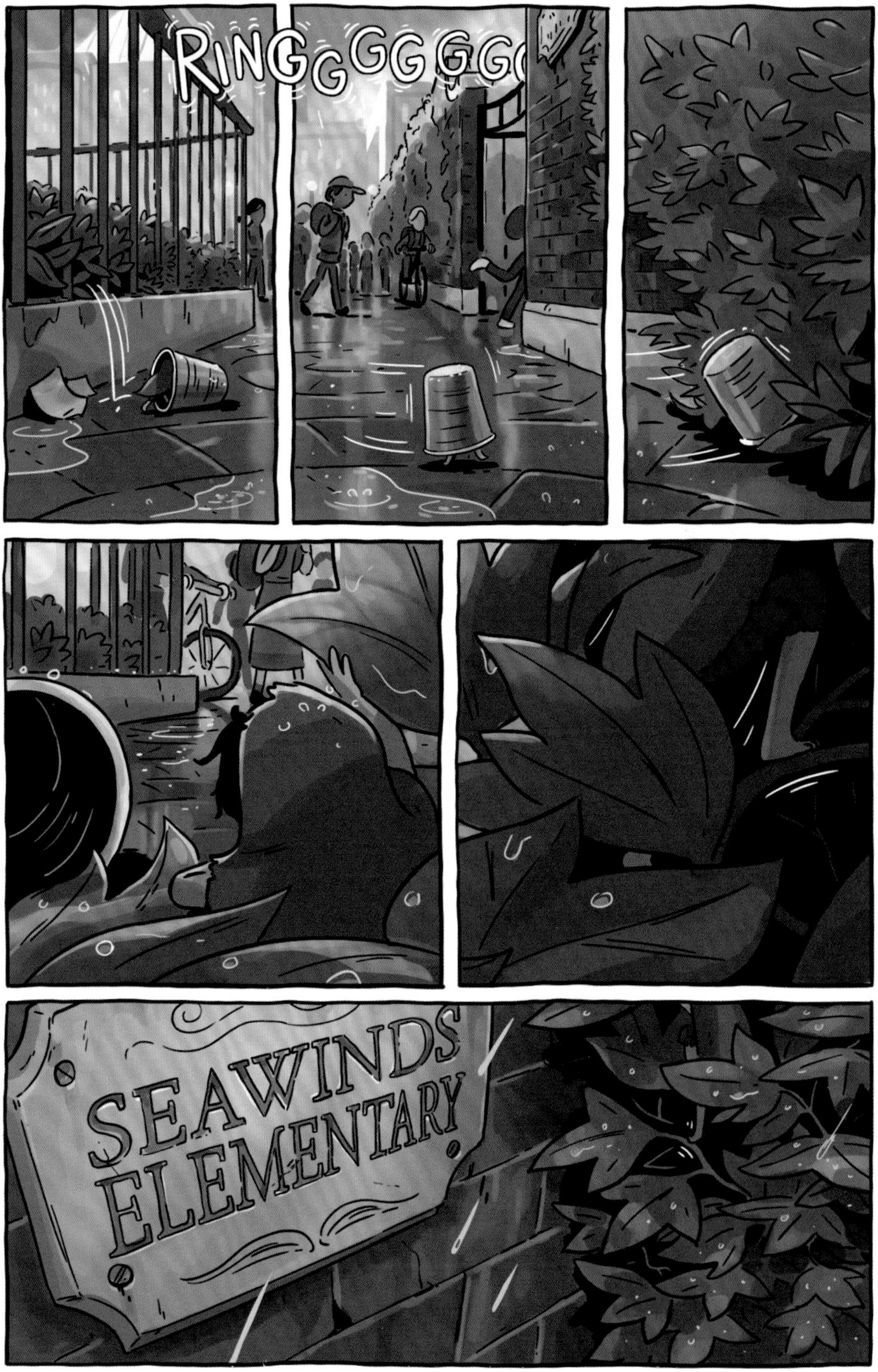
RINGGGGGGG
SEAWINDS ELEMENTARY

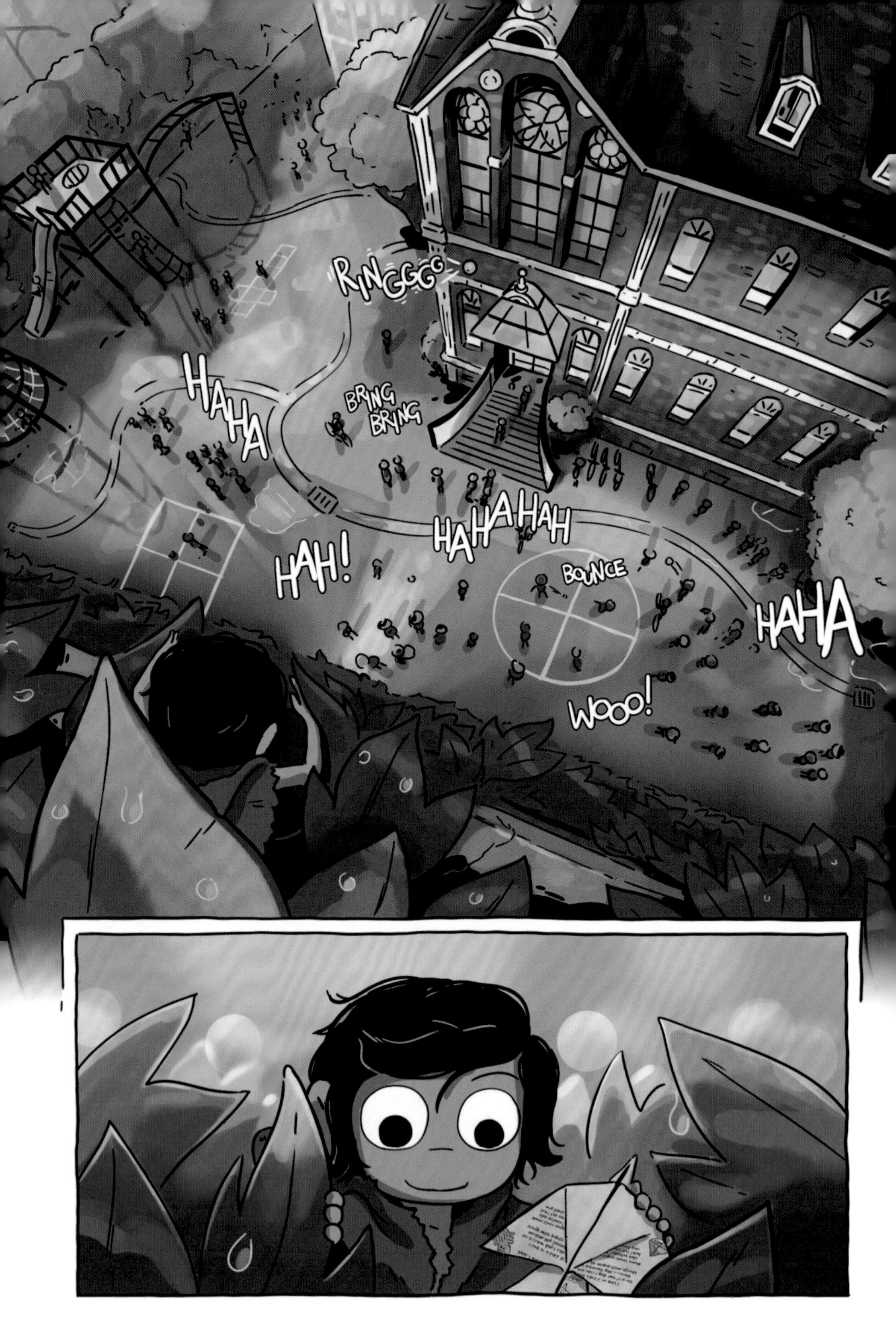
RINGGGG
HAHA
BRYNG BRYNG
HAHAHAHAH
HAH!
BOUNCE
HAHA
WOOO!

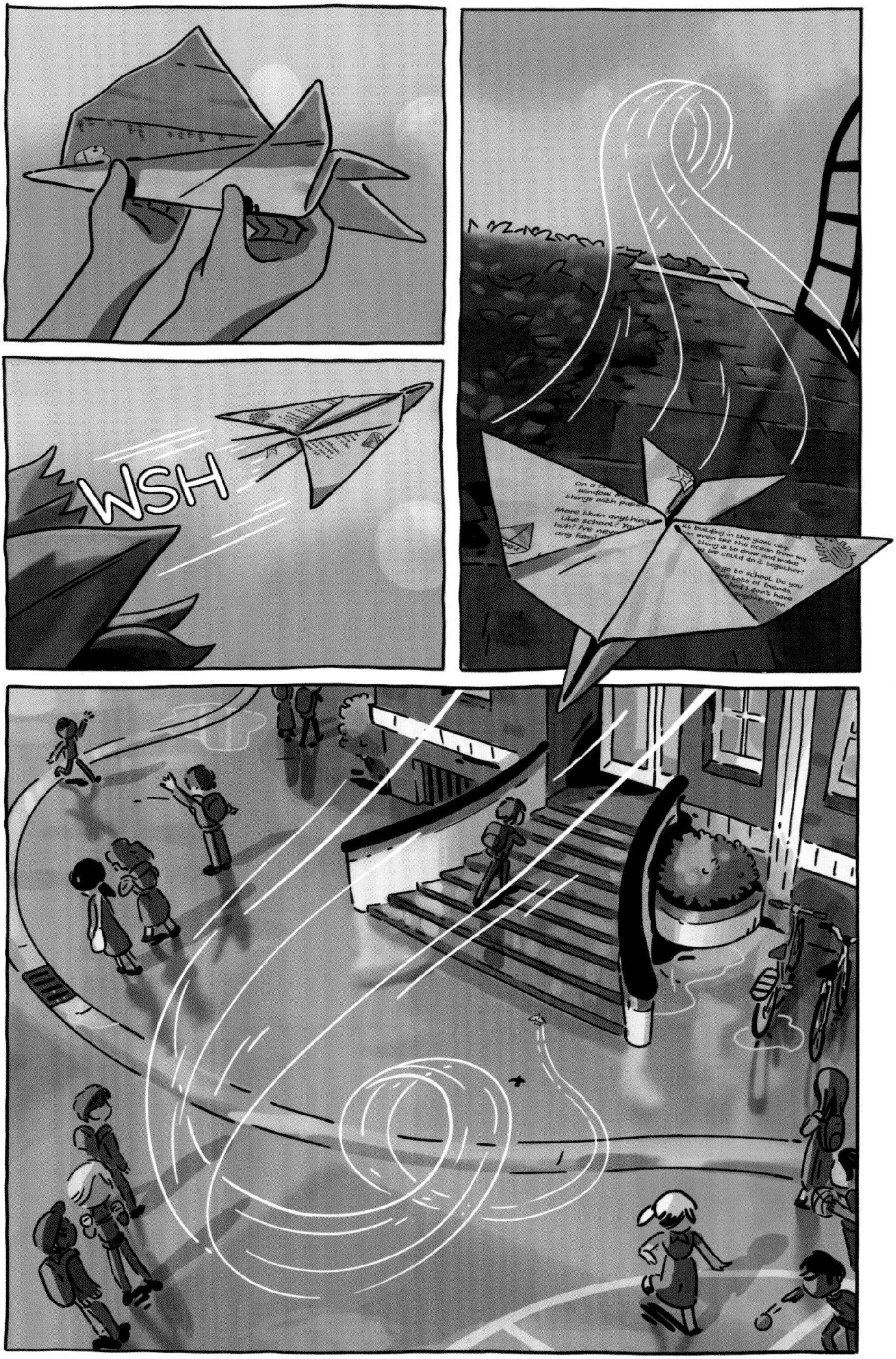
WSH
things with paper
More than anything
like school? You
huh? I've never
building in this giant city
even see the ocean from my
thing is to draw and make
we could do it together?
go to school. Do you
lots of friends,
And I don't have
anyone even

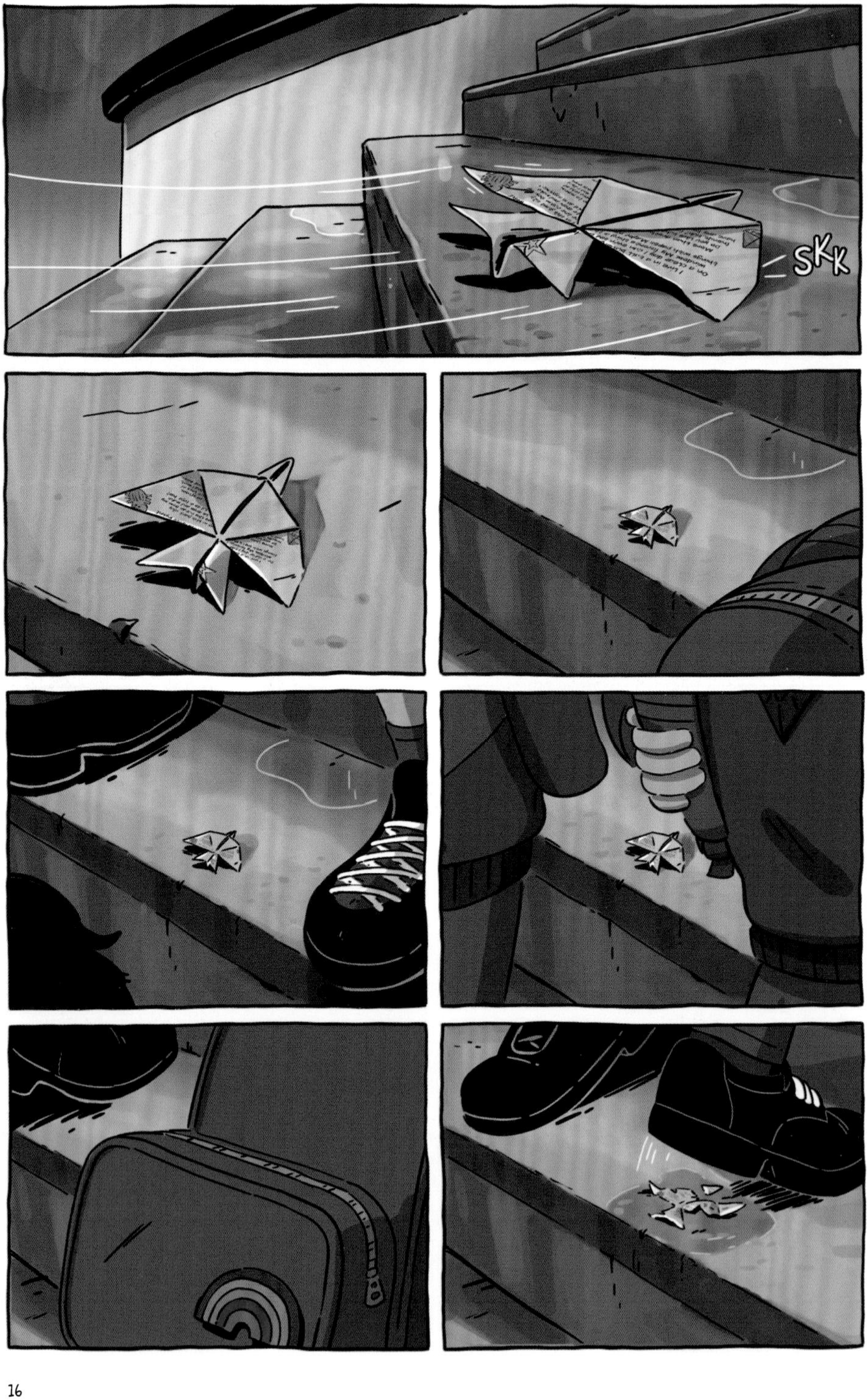
SKK

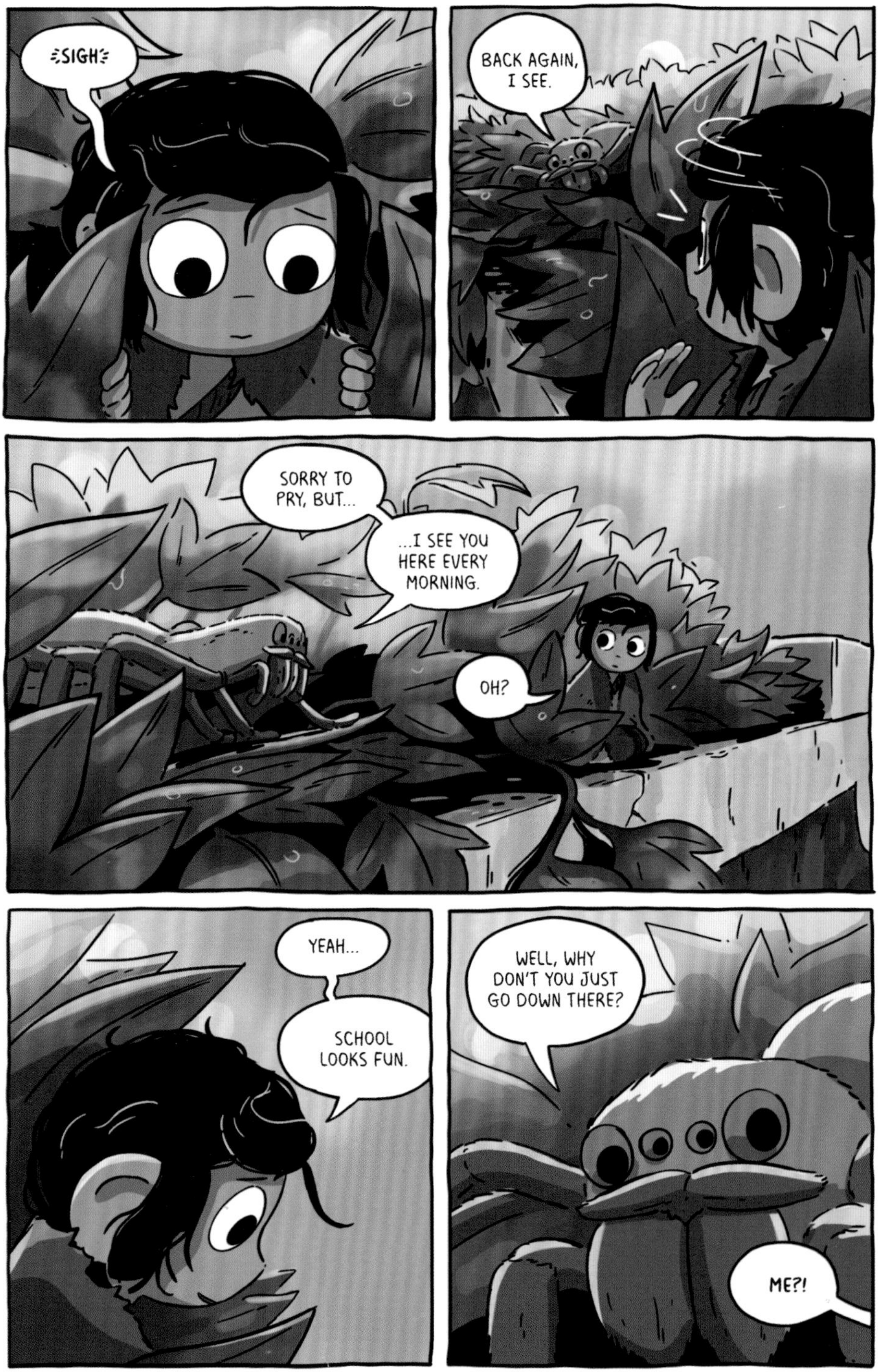

SIGH
BACK AGAIN, I SEE.
SORRY TO PRY, BUT...
...I SEE YOU HERE EVERY MORNING.
OH?
YEAH...
SCHOOL LOOKS FUN.
WELL, WHY DON'T YOU JUST GO DOWN THERE?
ME?!

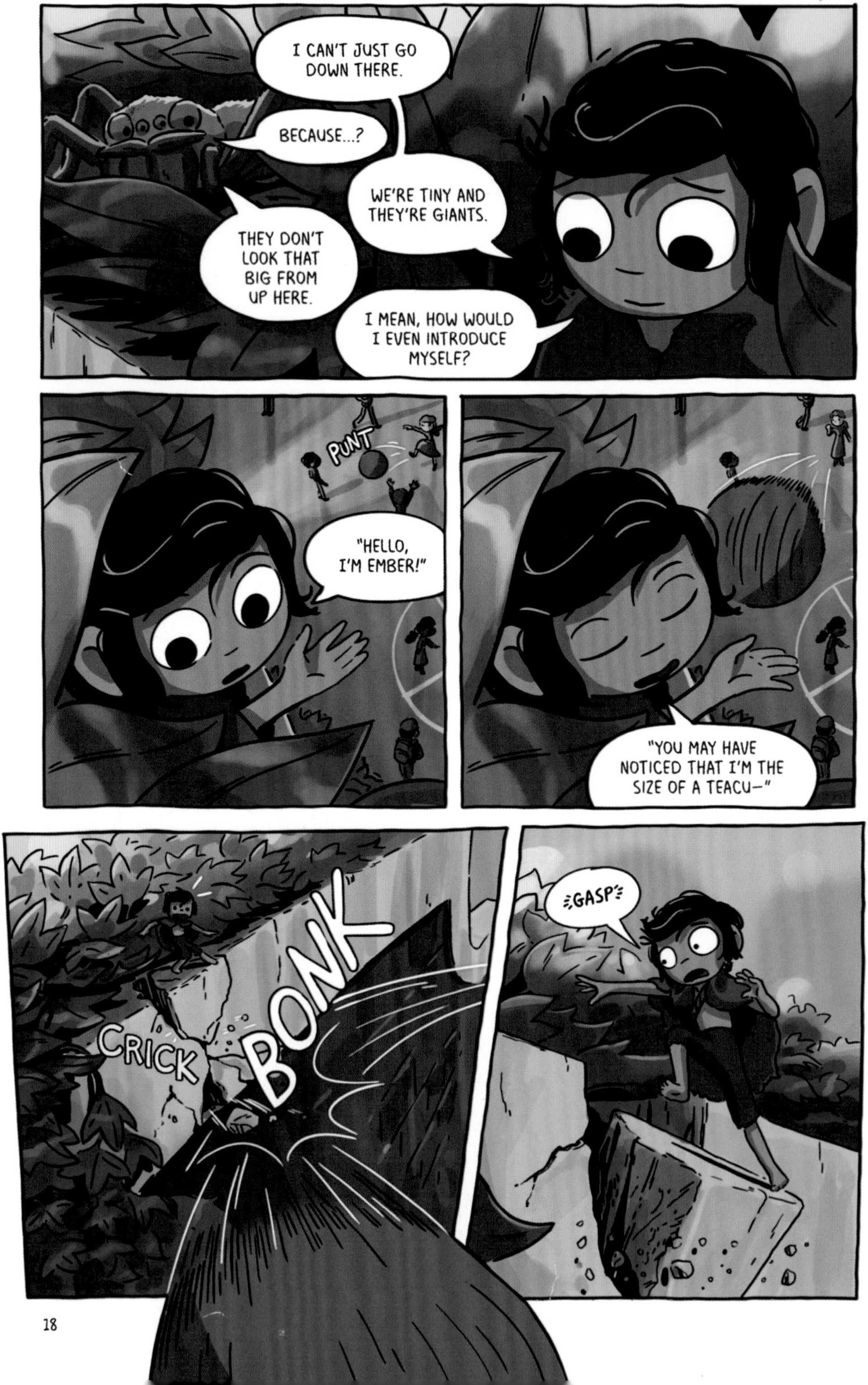
I CAN'T JUST GO DOWN THERE.
BECAUSE...?
WE'RE TINY AND THEY'RE GIANTS.
THEY DON'T LOOK THAT BIG FROM UP HERE.
I MEAN, HOW WOULD I EVEN INTRODUCE MYSELF?
PUNT
"HELLO, I'M EMBER!"
"YOU MAY HAVE NOTICED THAT I'M THE SIZE OF A TEACU—"
CRICK
BONK
GASP

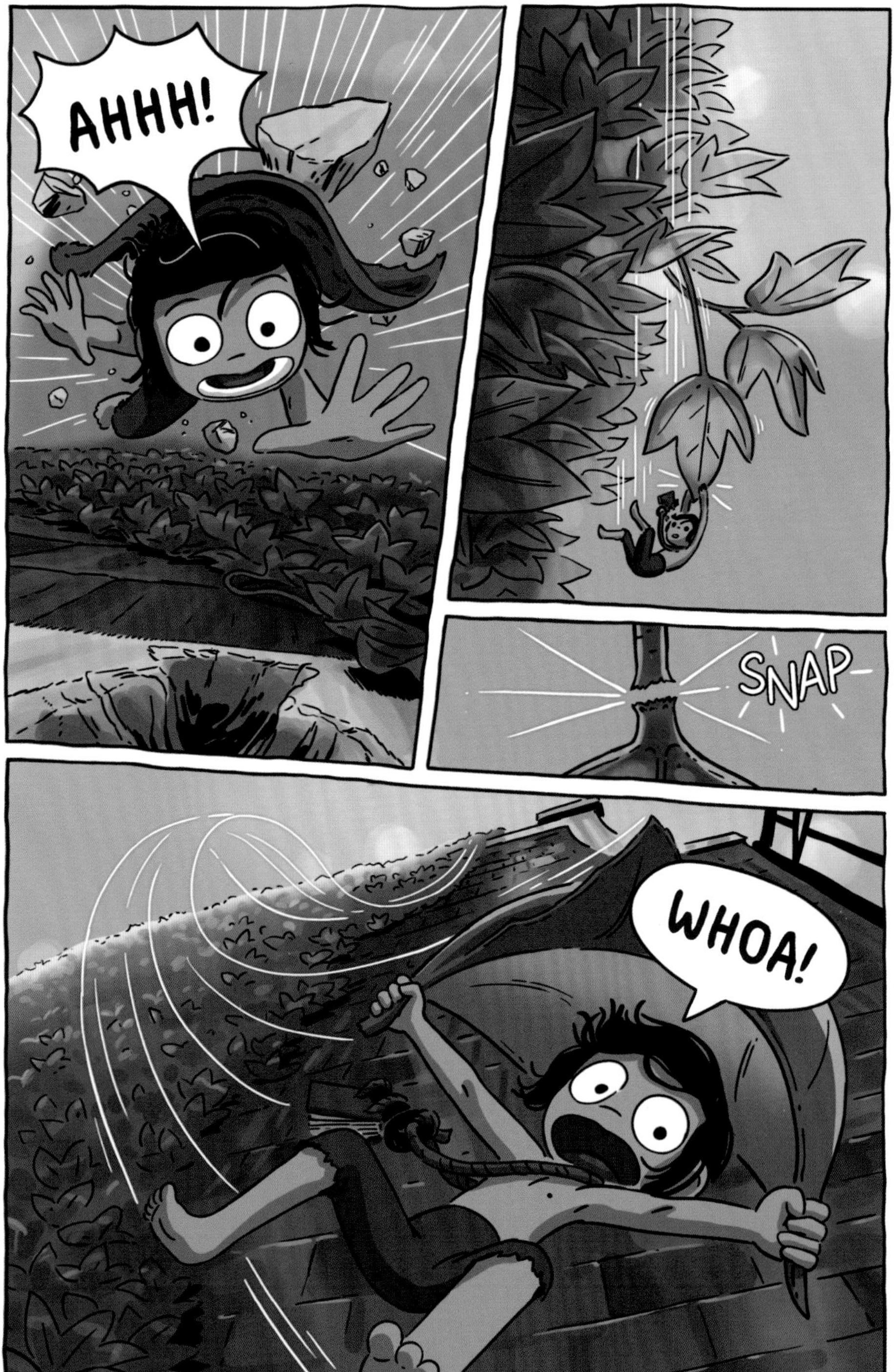
AHHH!
SNAP
WHOA!

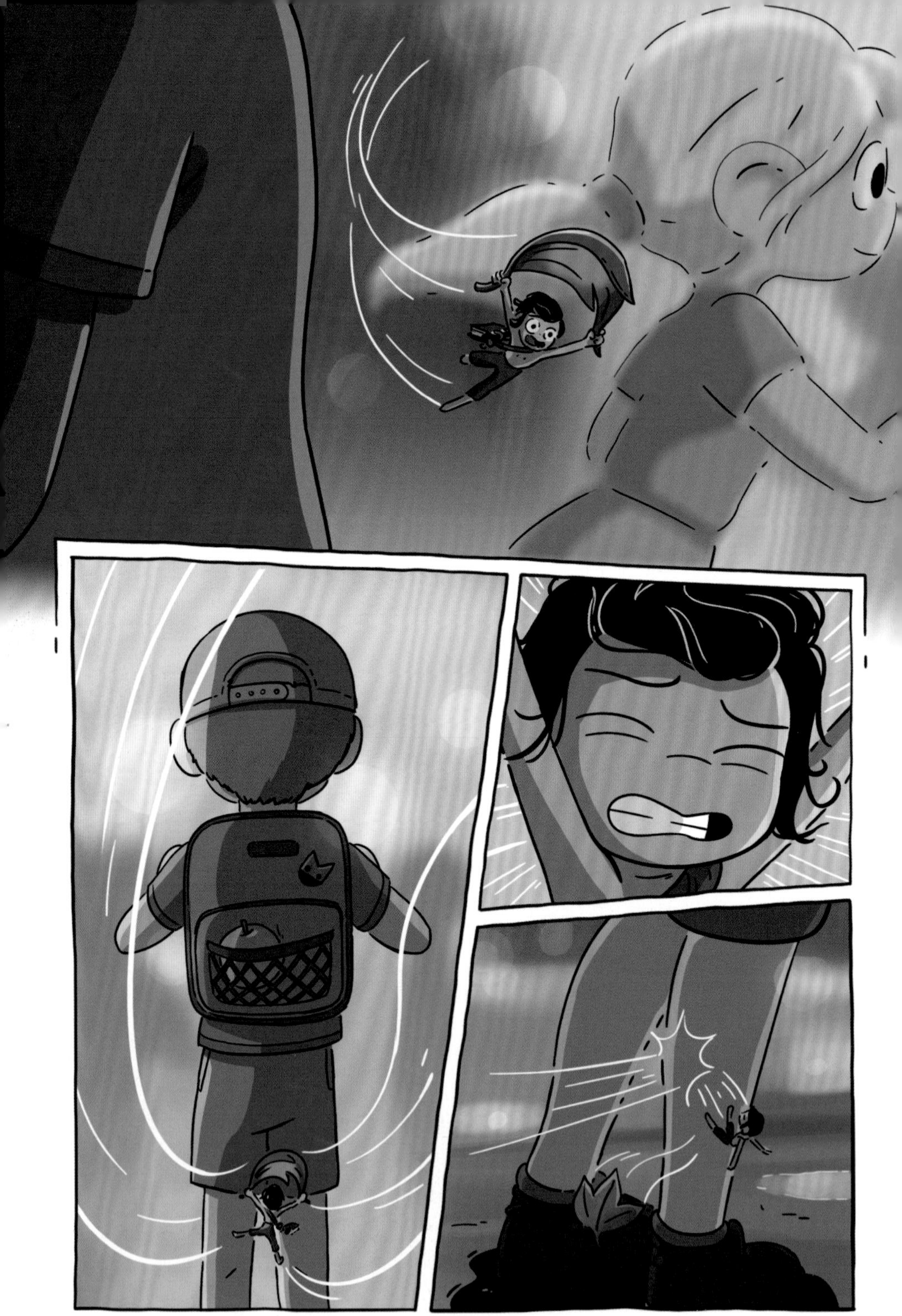

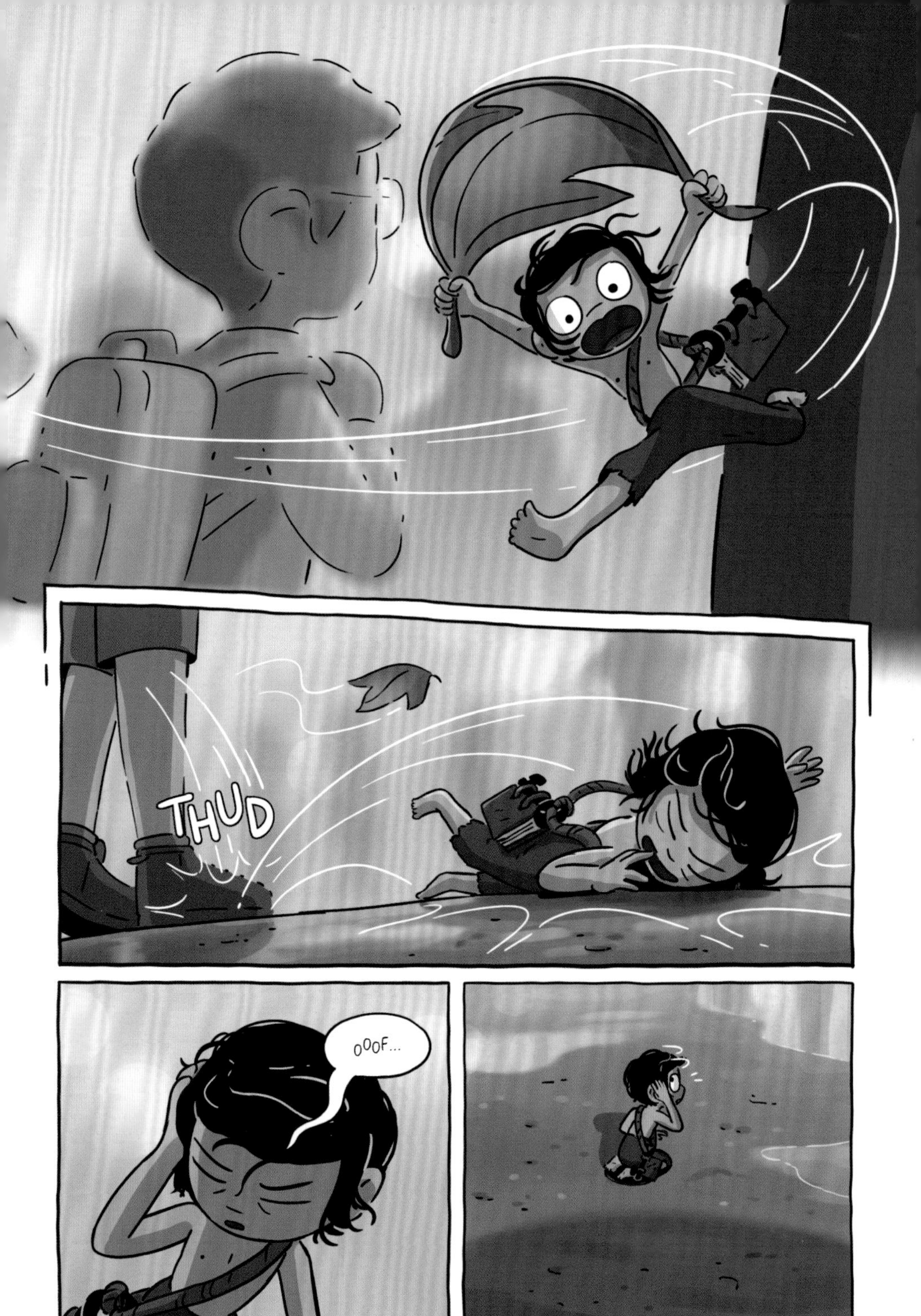
THUD
OOOF...

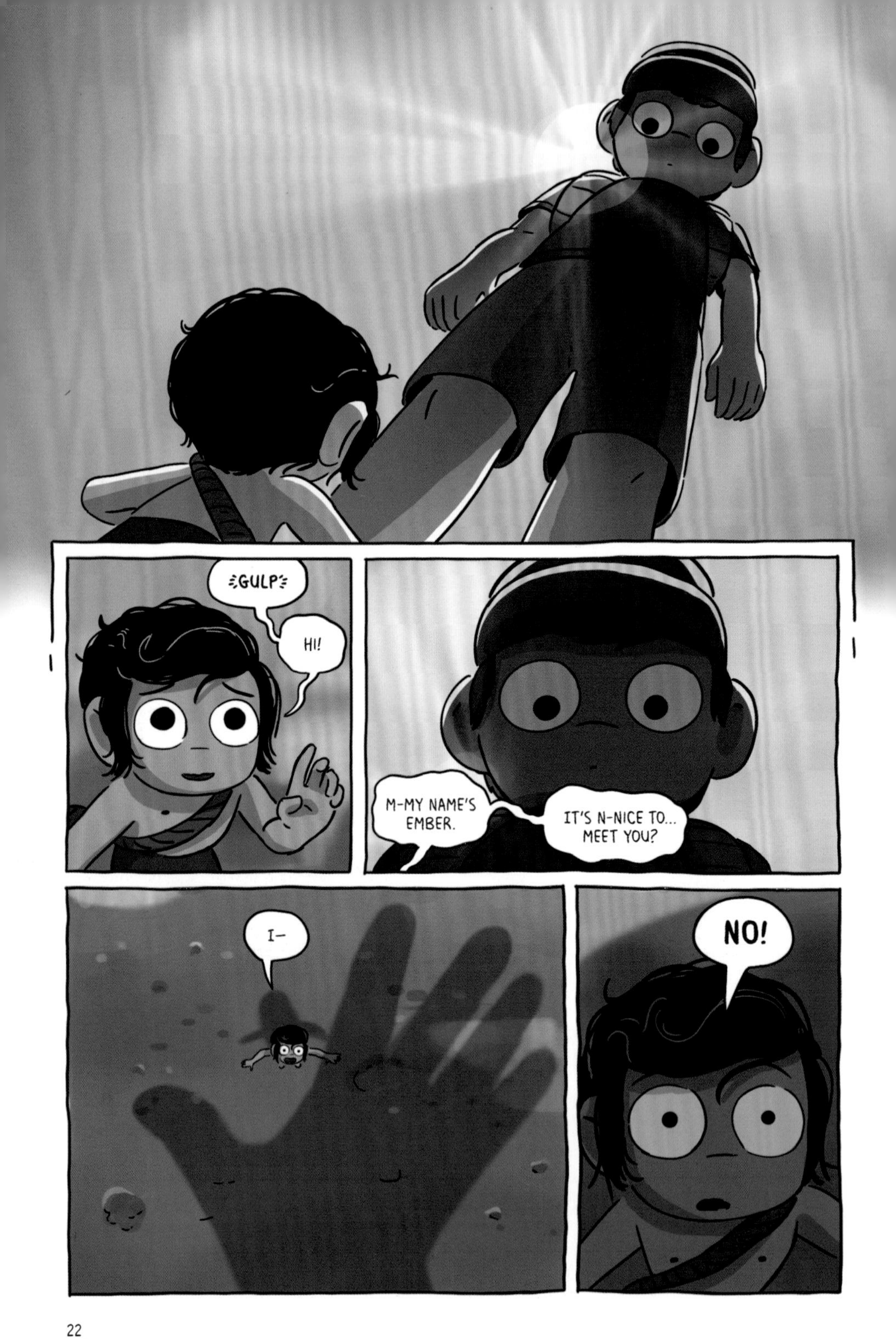
GULP
HI!
M-MY NAME'S EMBER.
IT'S N-NICE TO... MEET YOU?
I–
NO!

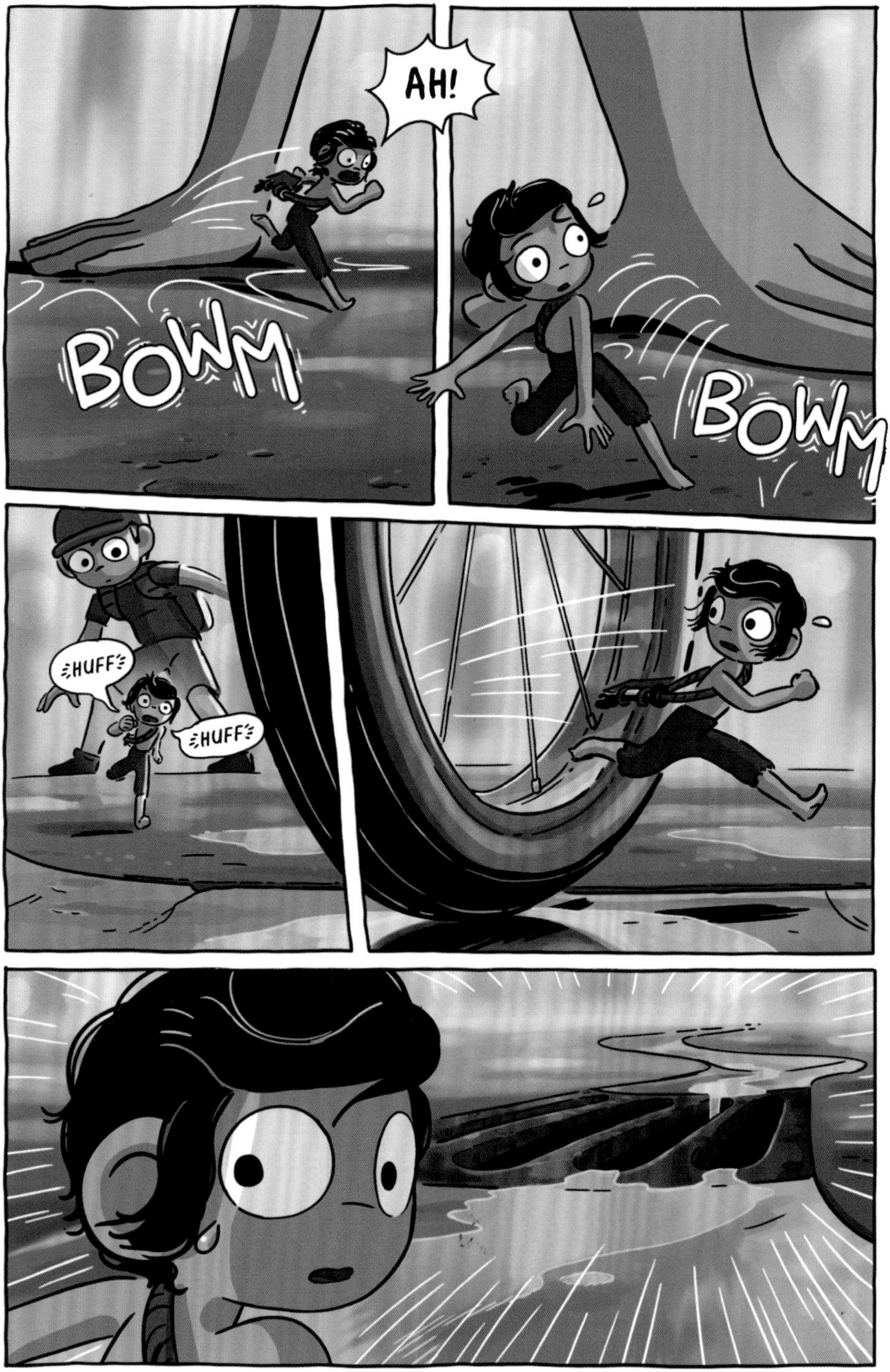
AH!
BOWM
BOWM
HUFF
HUFF

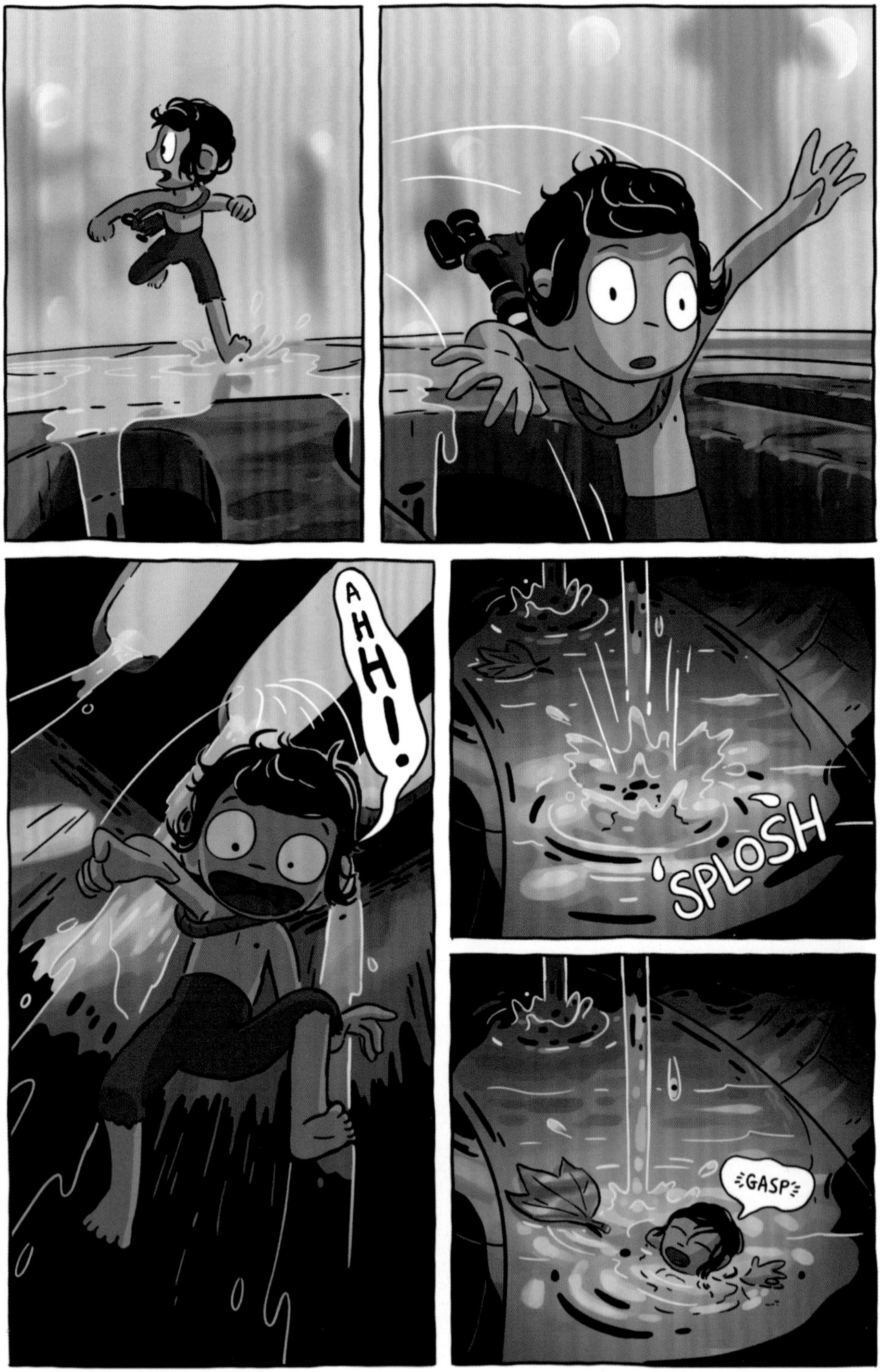
AHHH!
SPLOSH
GASP

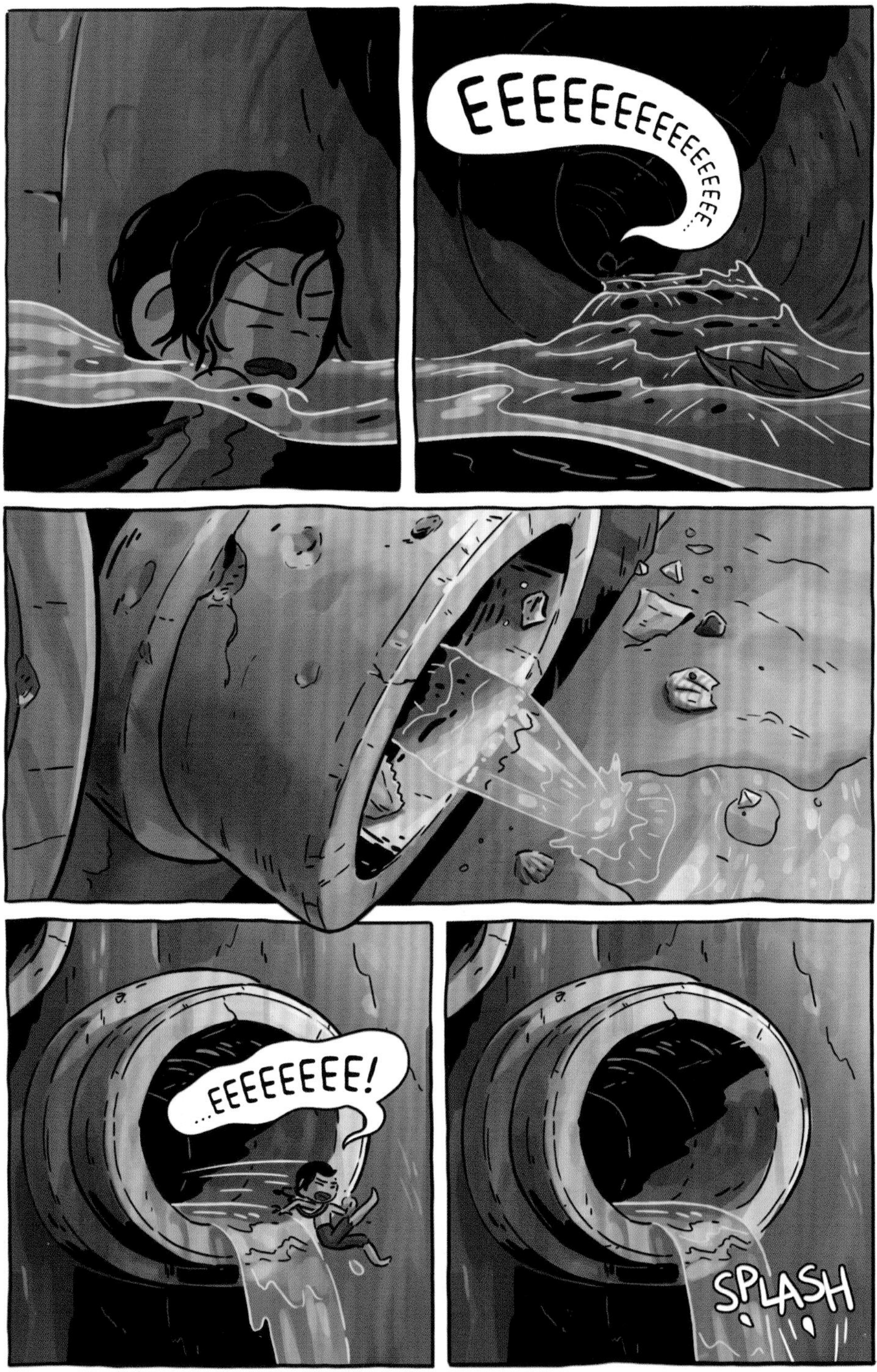
EEEEEEEEEEEEEEEEE...
...EEEEEEEE!
SPLASH

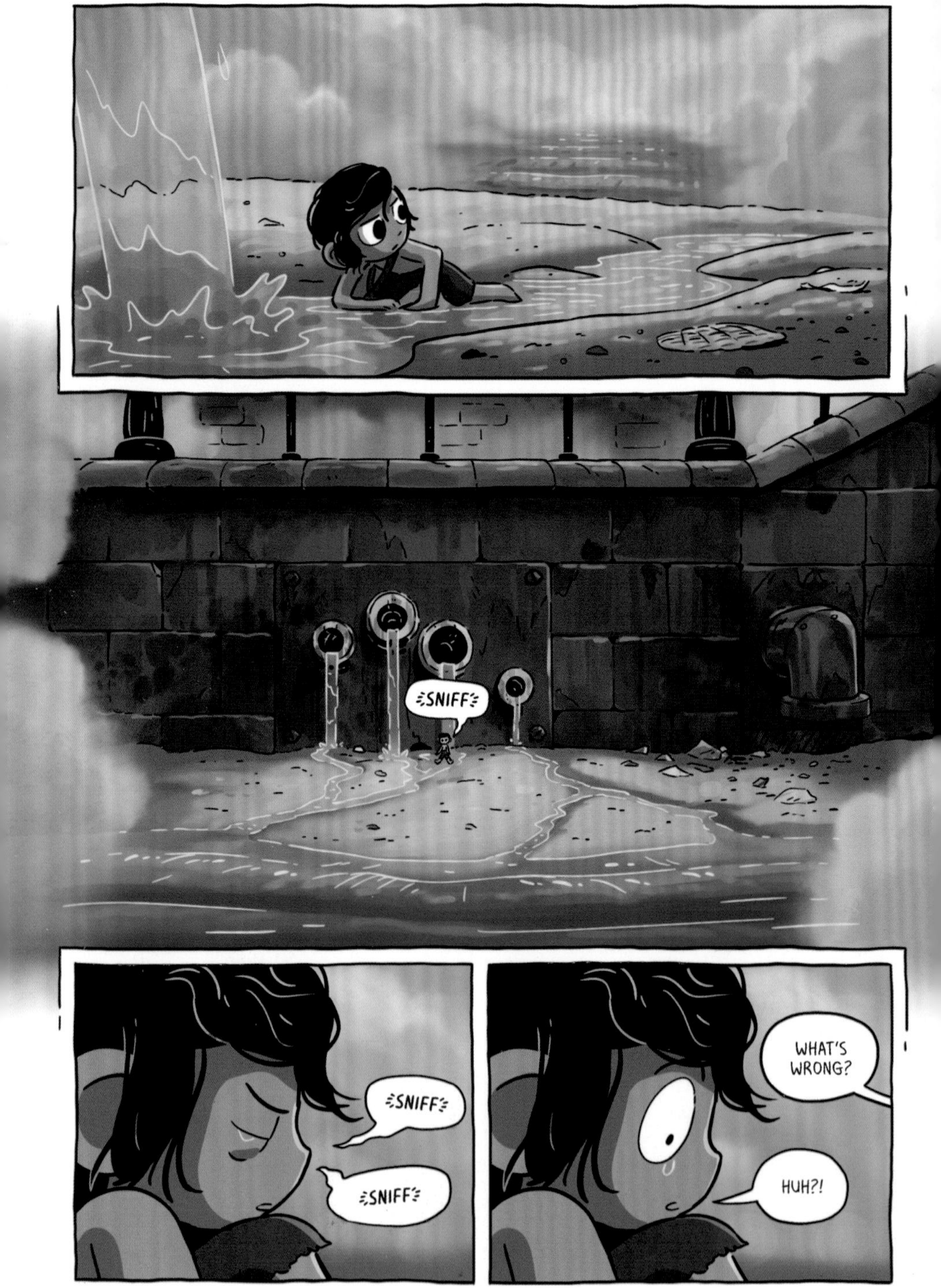
SNIFF
SNIFF
SNIFF
WHAT'S WRONG?
HUH?!

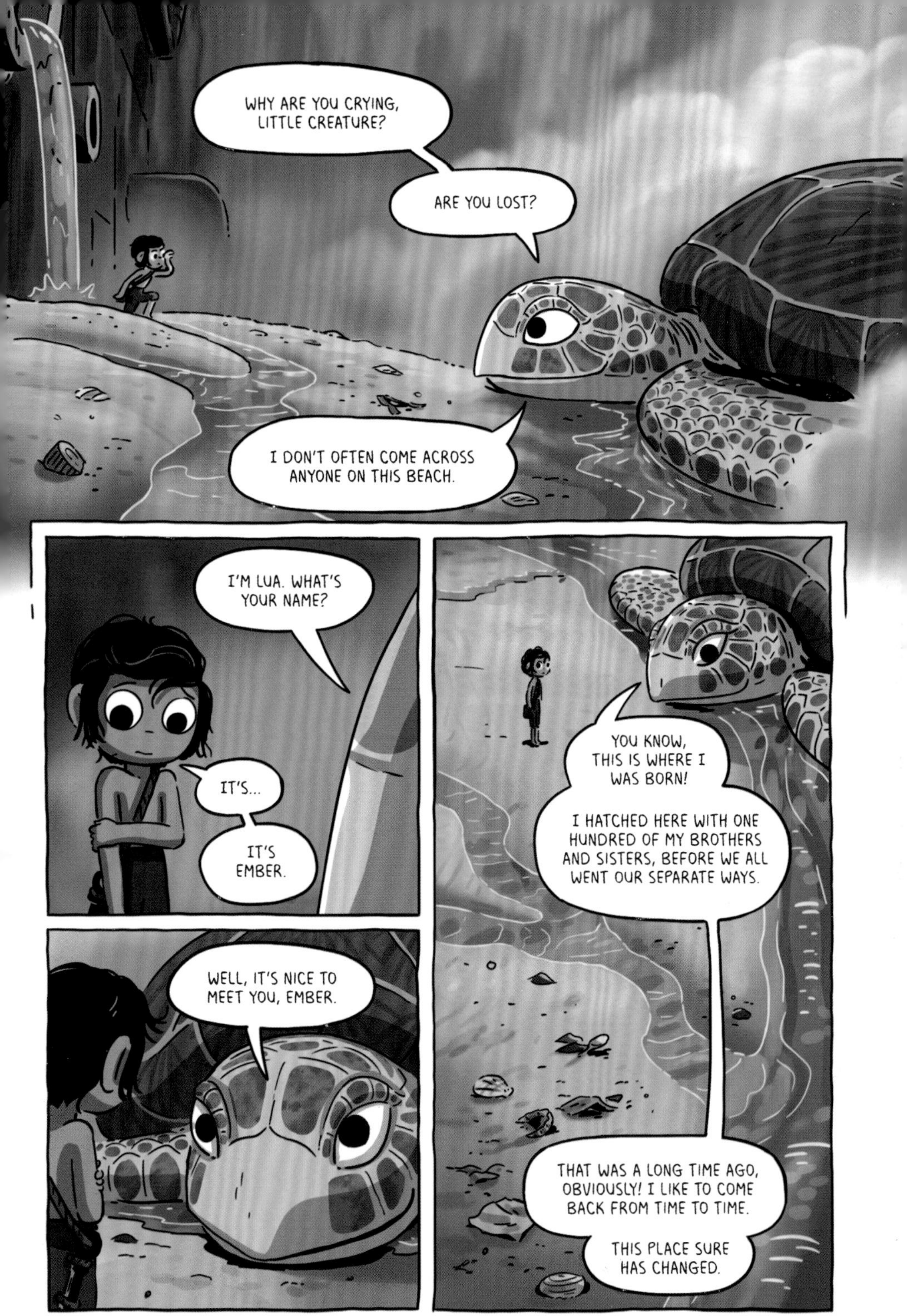
WHY ARE YOU CRYING, LITTLE CREATURE?
ARE YOU LOST?
I DON'T OFTEN COME ACROSS ANYONE ON THIS BEACH.
I'M LUA. WHAT'S YOUR NAME?
IT'S...
IT'S EMBER.
WELL, IT'S NICE TO MEET YOU, EMBER.
YOU KNOW, THIS IS WHERE I WAS BORN!
I HATCHED HERE WITH ONE HUNDRED OF MY BROTHERS AND SISTERS, BEFORE WE ALL WENT OUR SEPARATE WAYS.
THAT WAS A LONG TIME AGO, OBVIOUSLY! I LIKE TO COME BACK FROM TIME TO TIME.
THIS PLACE SURE HAS CHANGED.

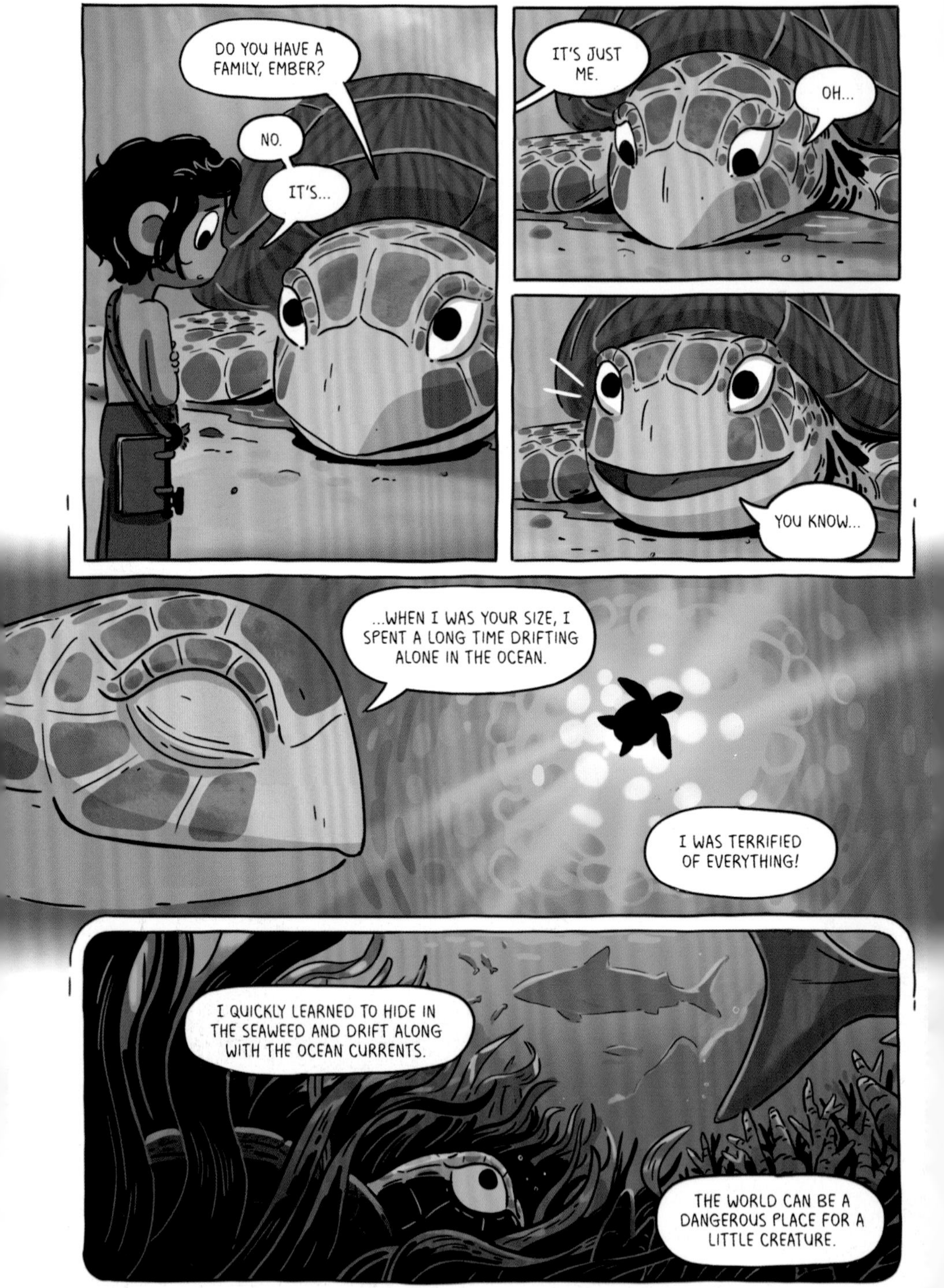
DO YOU HAVE A FAMILY, EMBER?
NO.
IT'S...
IT'S JUST ME.
OH...
YOU KNOW...
...WHEN I WAS YOUR SIZE, I SPENT A LONG TIME DRIFTING ALONE IN THE OCEAN.
I WAS TERRIFIED OF EVERYTHING!
I QUICKLY LEARNED TO HIDE IN THE SEAWEED AND DRIFT ALONG WITH THE OCEAN CURRENTS.
THE WORLD CAN BE A DANGEROUS PLACE FOR A LITTLE CREATURE.

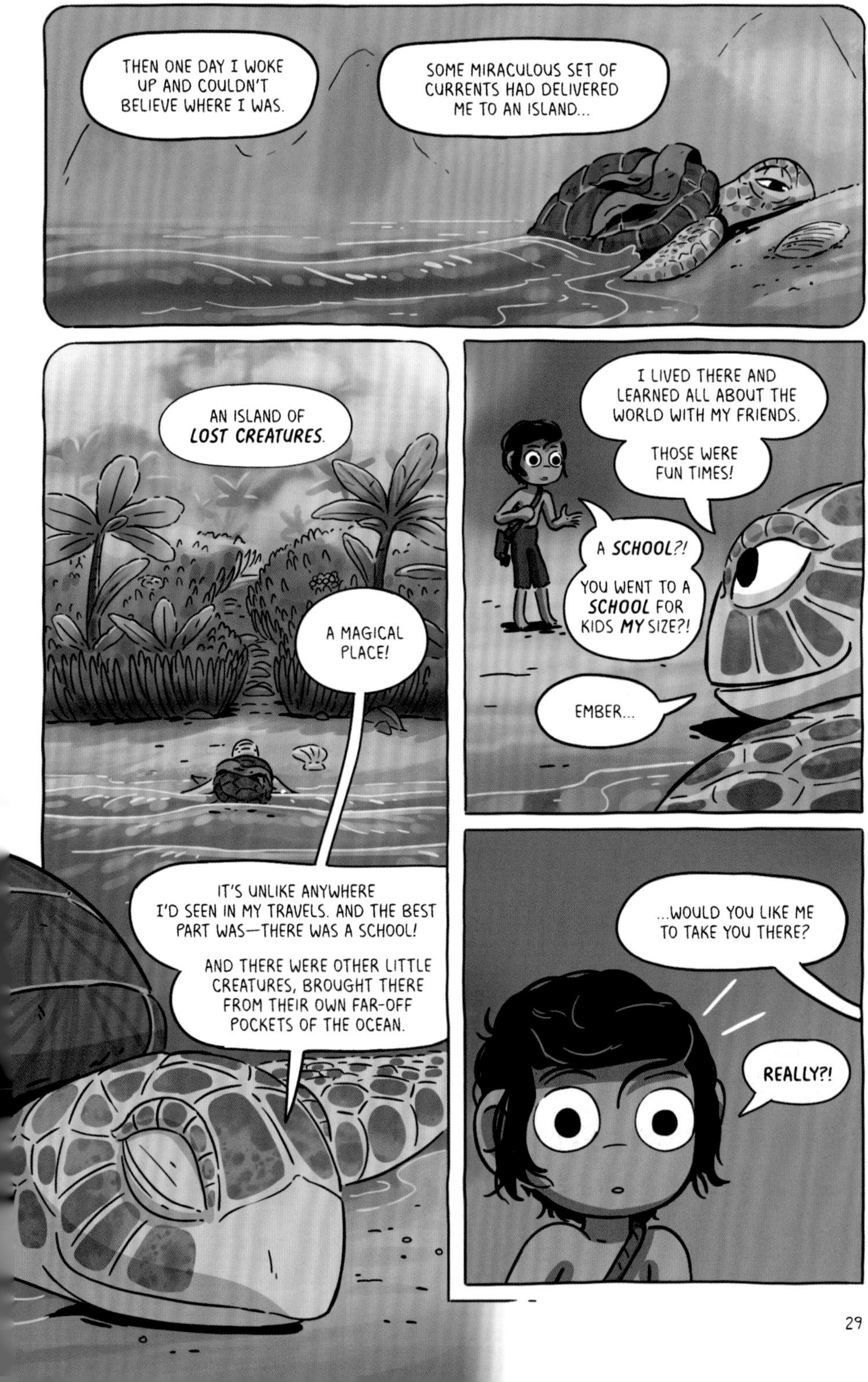
THEN ONE DAY I WOKE UP AND COULDN'T BELIEVE WHERE I WAS.
SOME MIRACULOUS SET OF CURRENTS HAD DELIVERED ME TO AN ISLAND...
AN ISLAND OF ***LOST CREATURES***.
A MAGICAL PLACE!
IT'S UNLIKE ANYWHERE I'D SEEN IN MY TRAVELS. AND THE BEST PART WAS—THERE WAS A SCHOOL!
AND THERE WERE OTHER LITTLE CREATURES, BROUGHT THERE FROM THEIR OWN FAR-OFF POCKETS OF THE OCEAN.
I LIVED THERE AND LEARNED ALL ABOUT THE WORLD WITH MY FRIENDS.
THOSE WERE FUN TIMES!
A ***SCHOOL***?!
YOU WENT TO A ***SCHOOL*** FOR KIDS ***MY*** SIZE?!
EMBER...
...WOULD YOU LIKE ME TO TAKE YOU THERE?
REALLY?!

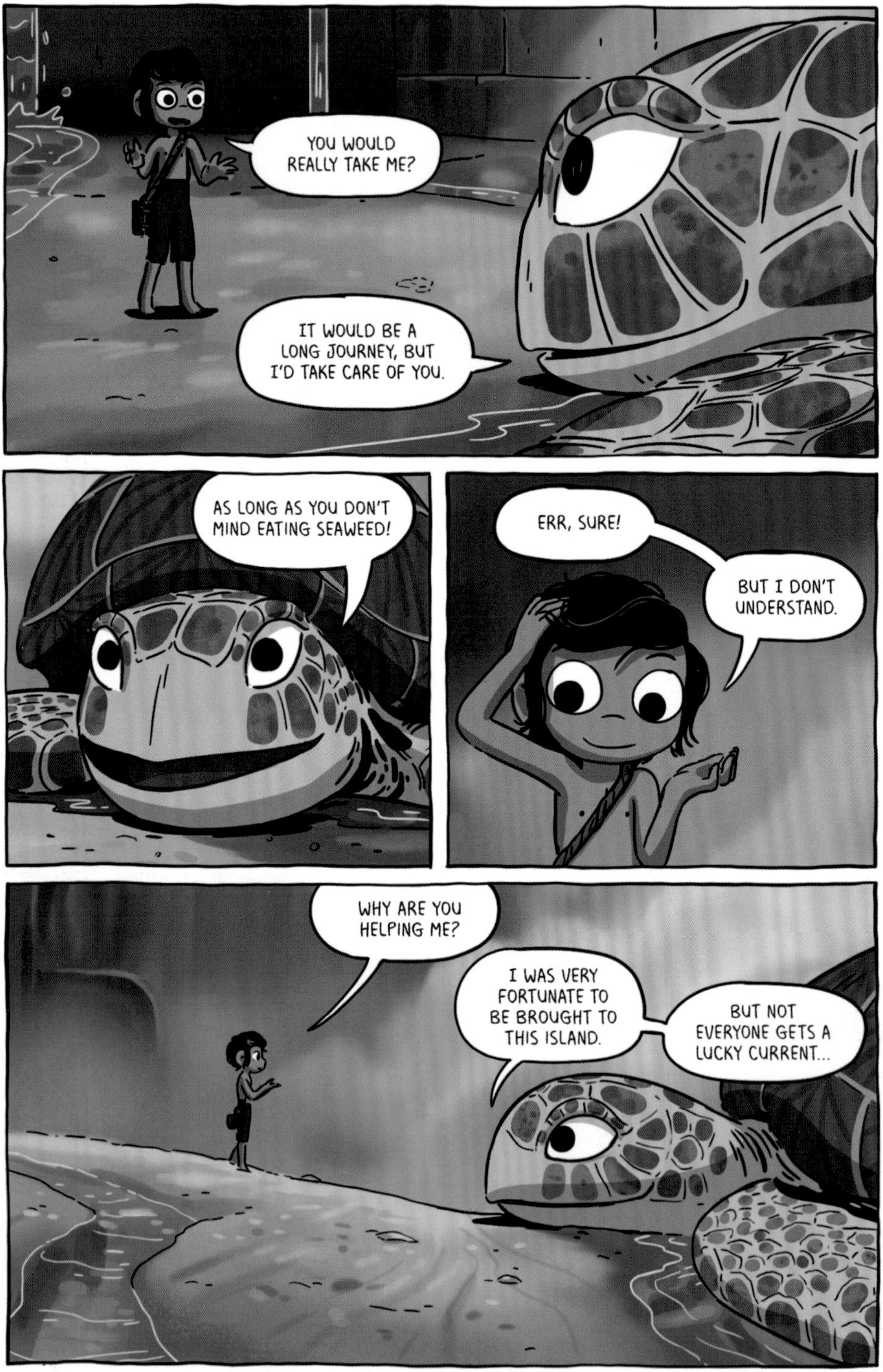
YOU WOULD REALLY TAKE ME?
IT WOULD BE A LONG JOURNEY, BUT I'D TAKE CARE OF YOU.
AS LONG AS YOU DON'T MIND EATING SEAWEED!
ERR, SURE!
BUT I DON'T UNDERSTAND.
WHY ARE YOU HELPING ME?
I WAS VERY FORTUNATE TO BE BROUGHT TO THIS ISLAND.
BUT NOT EVERYONE GETS A LUCKY CURRENT...

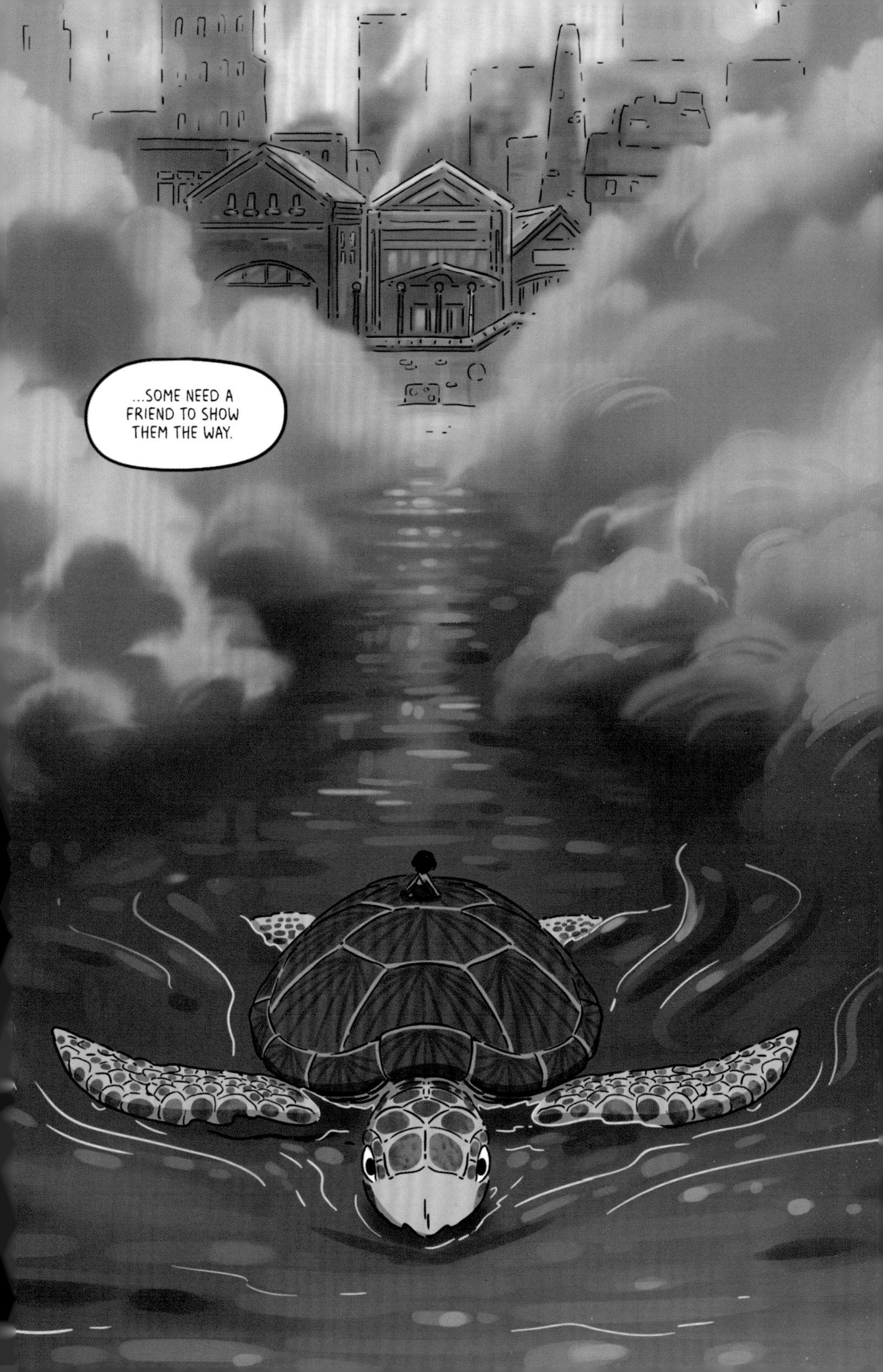
...SOME NEED A FRIEND TO SHOW THEM THE WAY.

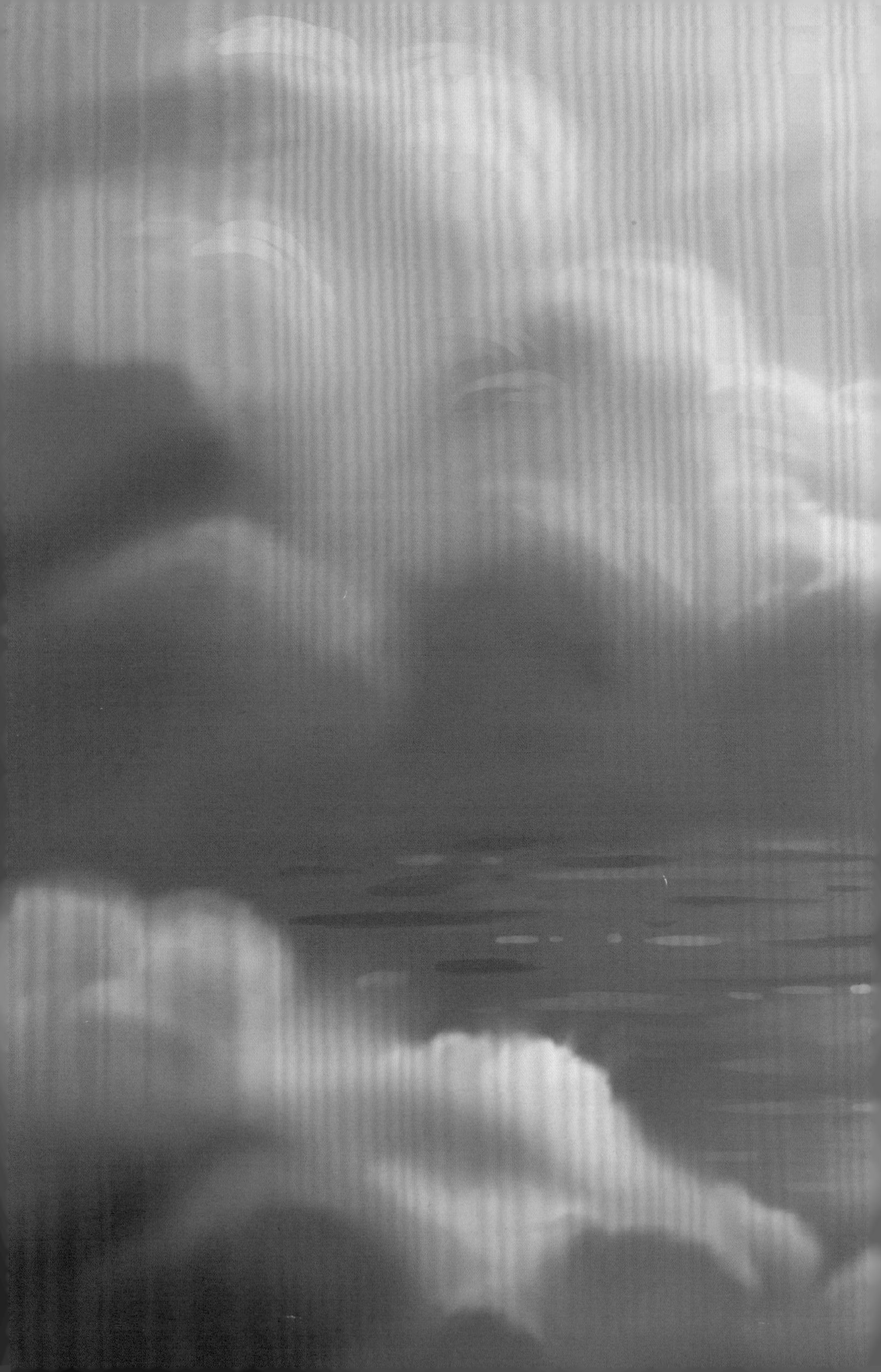

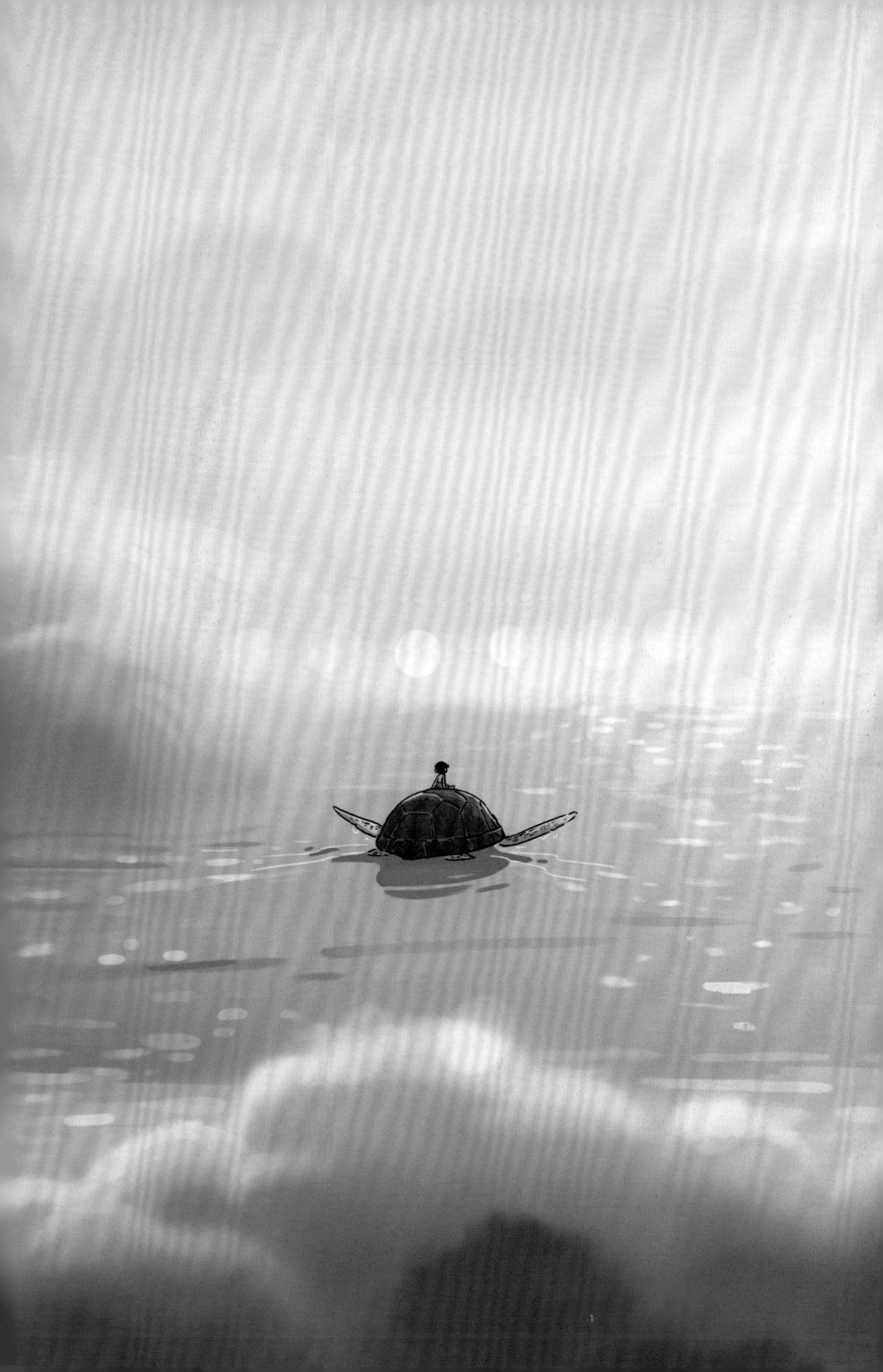

Lua took me far away across the ocean. I was a bit nervous at first and didn't say very much, so Lua did most of the talking.

She told me about all her travels. Volcano islands, icy glaciers, huge storms with giant waves. She's been pretty much everywhere!

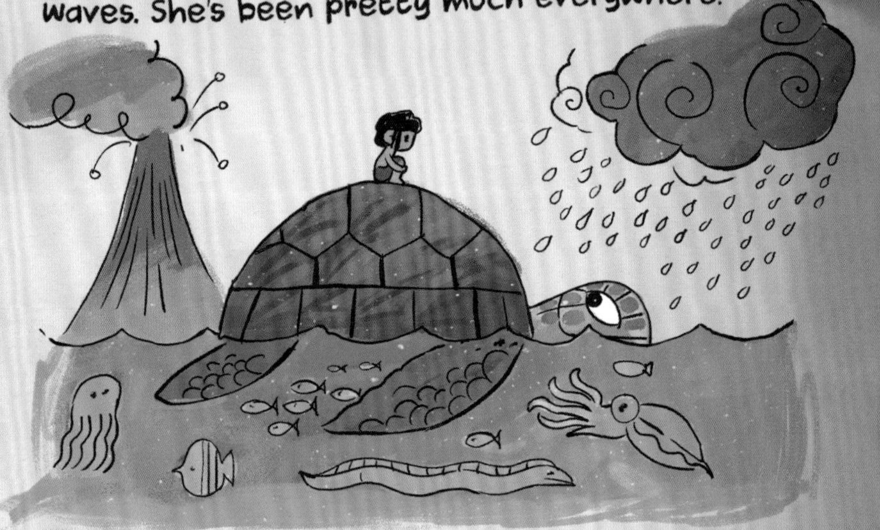

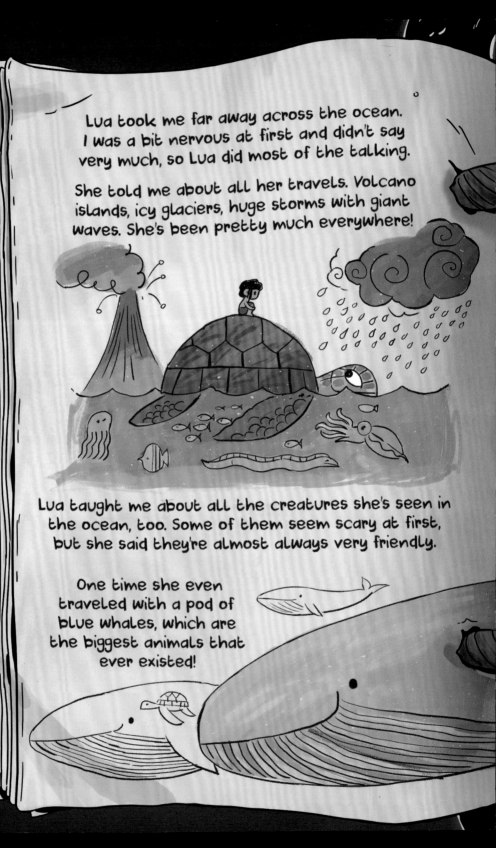

Lua taught me about all the creatures she's seen in the ocean, too. Some of them seem scary at first, but she said they're almost always very friendly.

One time she even traveled with a pod of blue whales, which are the biggest animals that ever existed!

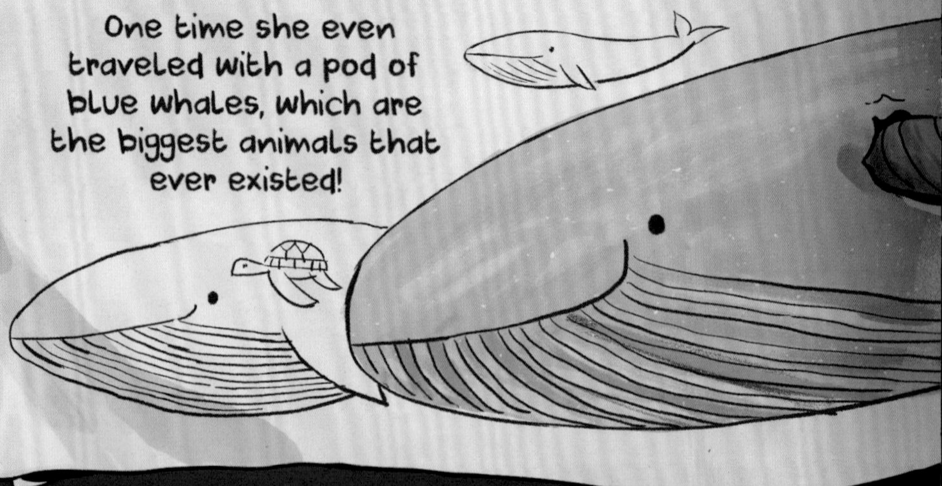

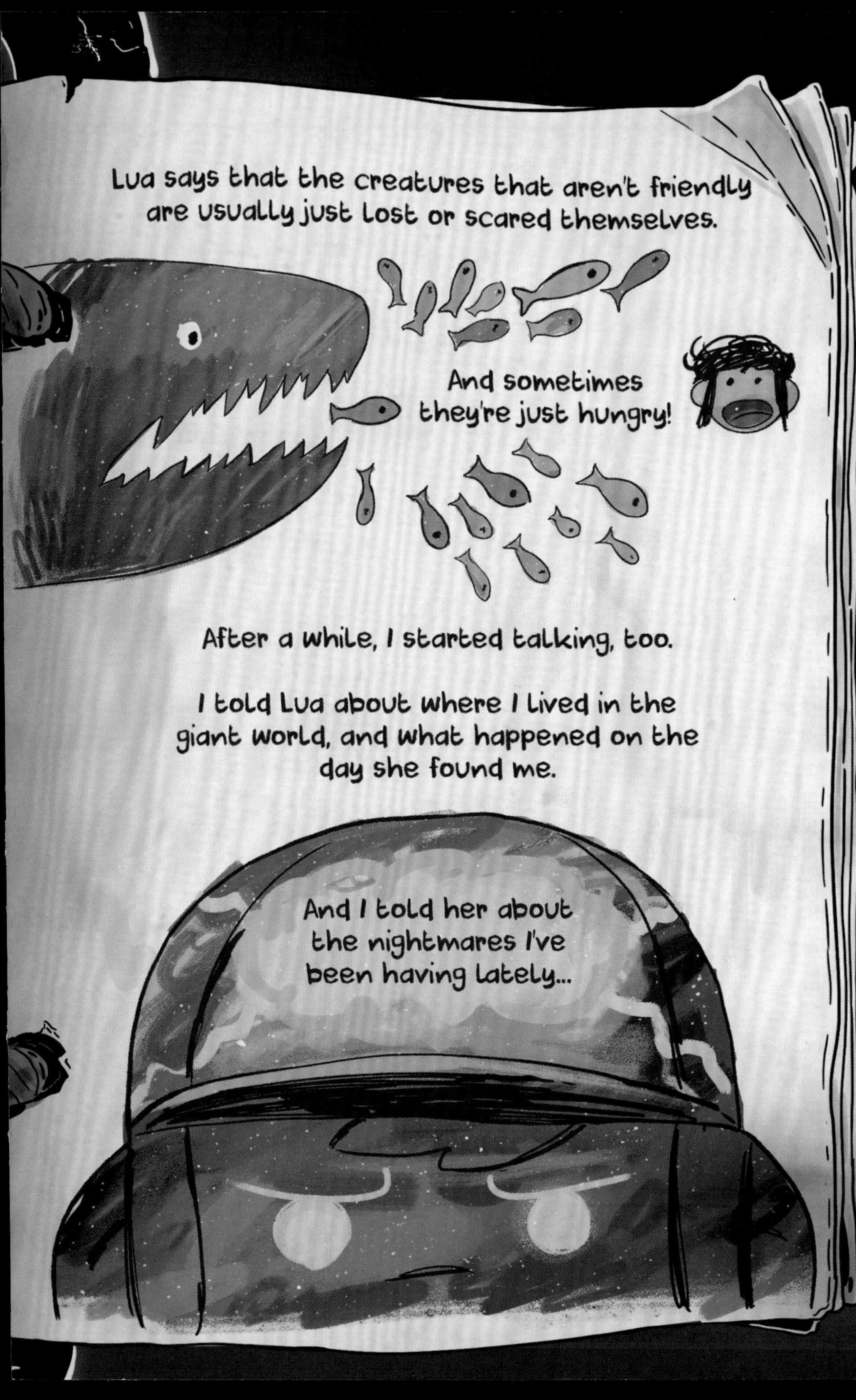
Lua says that the creatures that aren't friendly are usually just lost or scared themselves.
And sometimes they're just hungry!
After a while, I started talking, too.
I told Lua about where I lived in the giant world, and what happened on the day she found me.
And I told her about the nightmares I've been having lately...

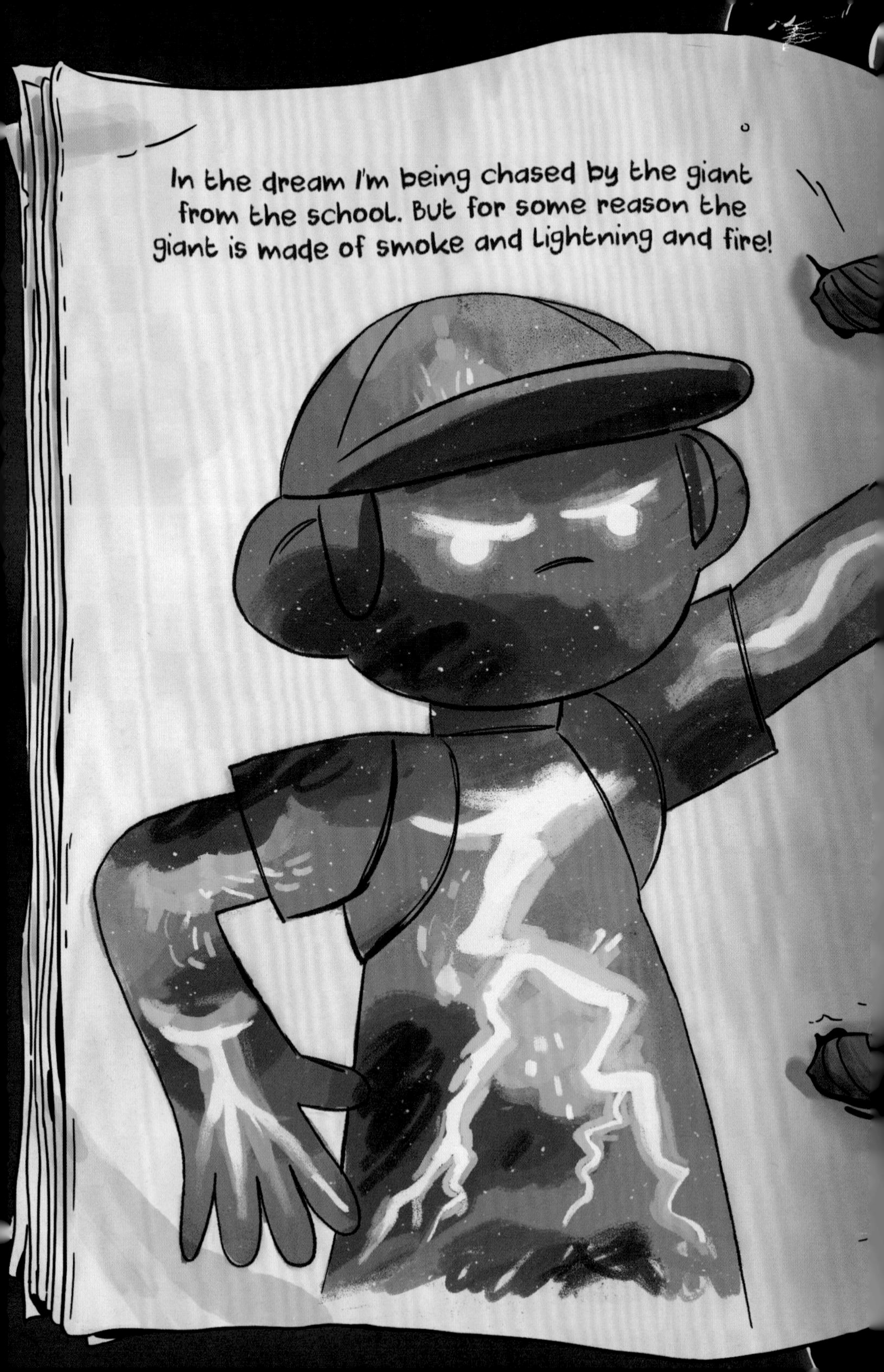
In the dream I'm being chased by the giant from the school. But for some reason the giant is made of smoke and lightning and fire!

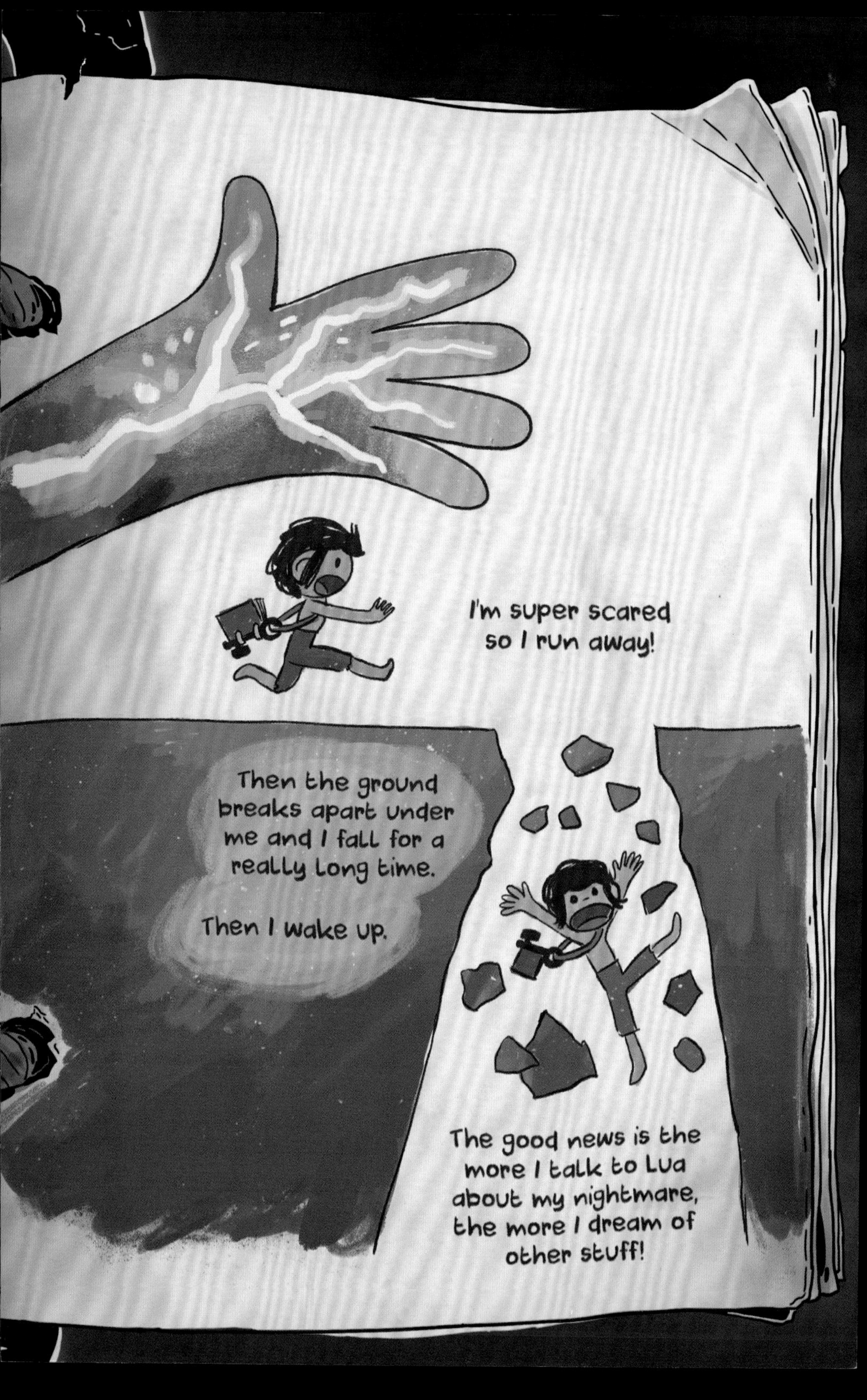
I'm super scared so I run away!
Then the ground breaks apart under me and I fall for a really long time.
Then I wake up.
The good news is the more I talk to Lua about my nightmare, the more I dream of other stuff!

Apart from creatures, it turns out the ocean is full of something else.

Floating giant junk!

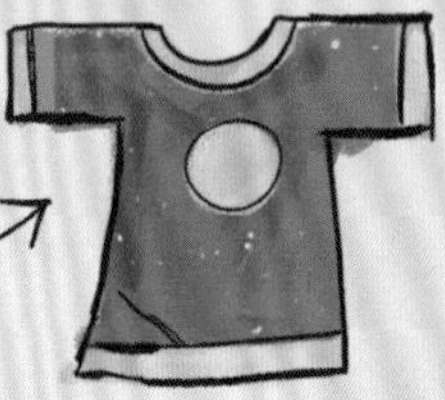
A giant's T-shirt

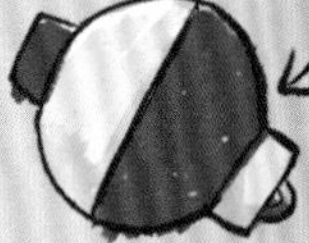
A fishing bobber

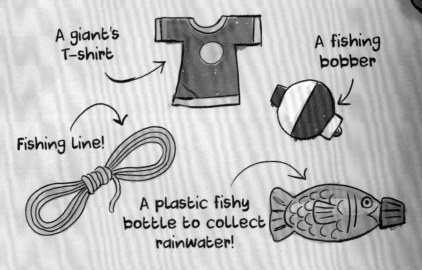

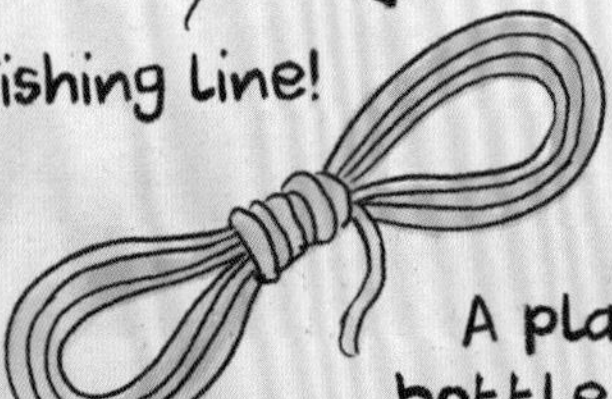
Fishing line!

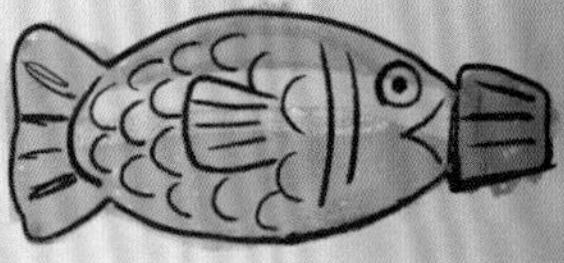
A plastic fishy bottle to collect rainwater!

The bobber and fishing line make a great satchel. And Lua helped me make a special cloak from the shirt to keep warm.

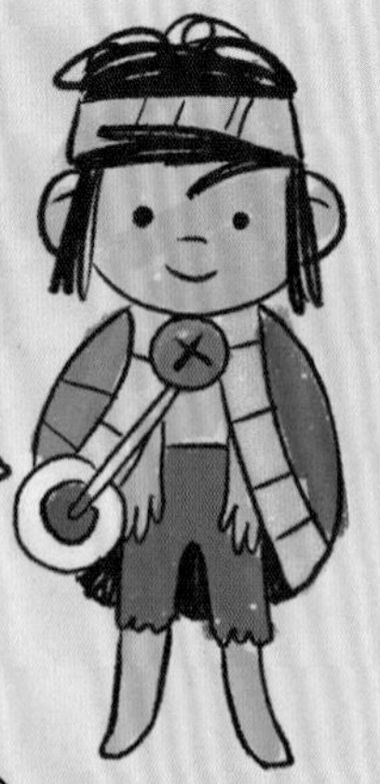
Satchel

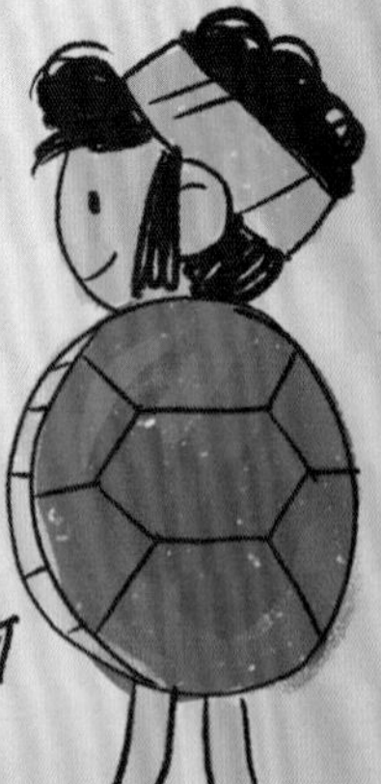
I even sewed in a turtle shell pattern, just like Lua's!

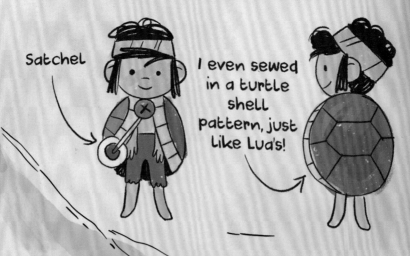

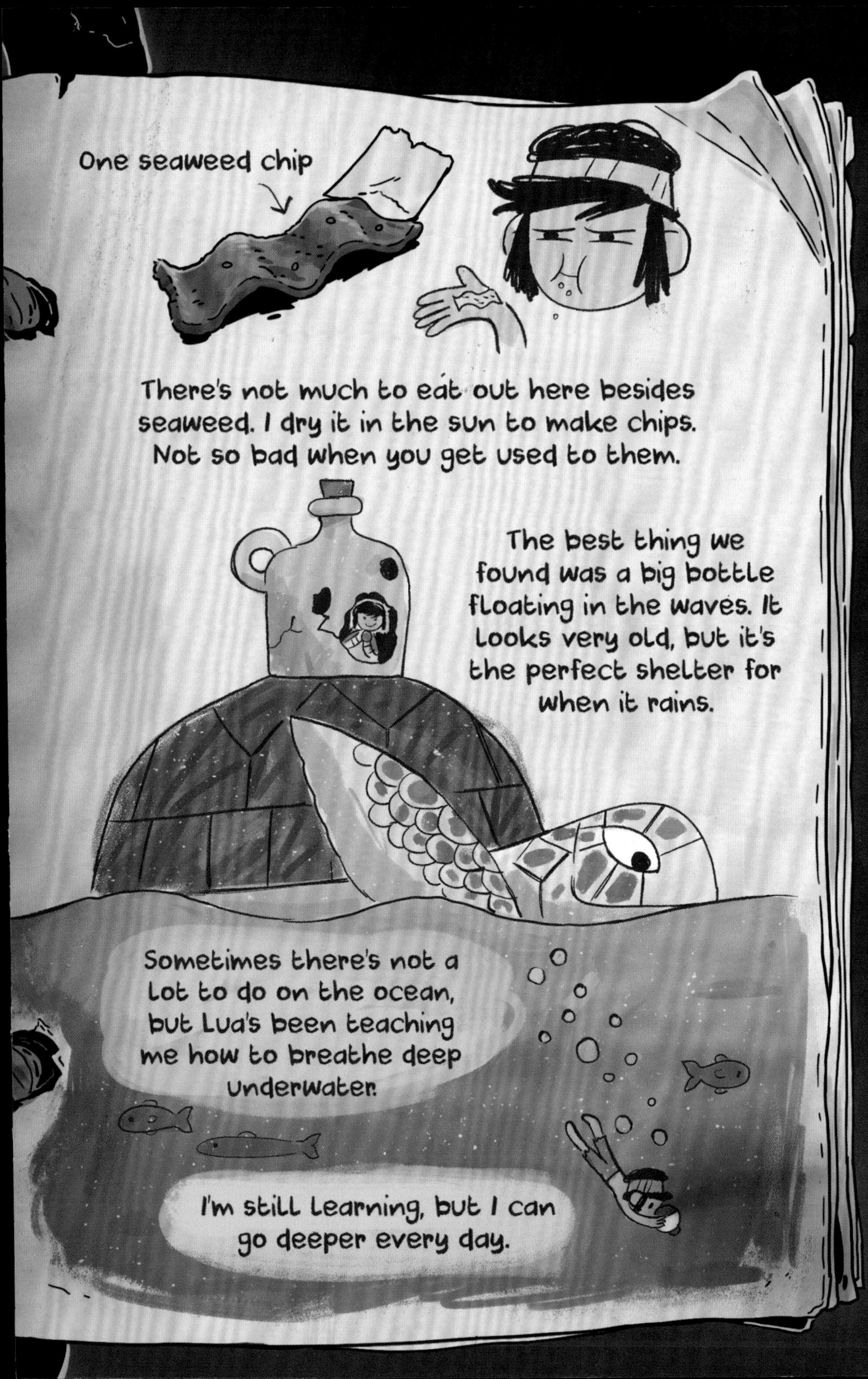

One seaweed chip
There's not much to eat out here besides seaweed. I dry it in the sun to make chips. Not so bad when you get used to them.
The best thing we found was a big bottle floating in the waves. It looks very old, but it's the perfect shelter for when it rains.
Sometimes there's not a lot to do on the ocean, but Lua's been teaching me how to breathe deep underwater.
I'm still learning, but I can go deeper every day.

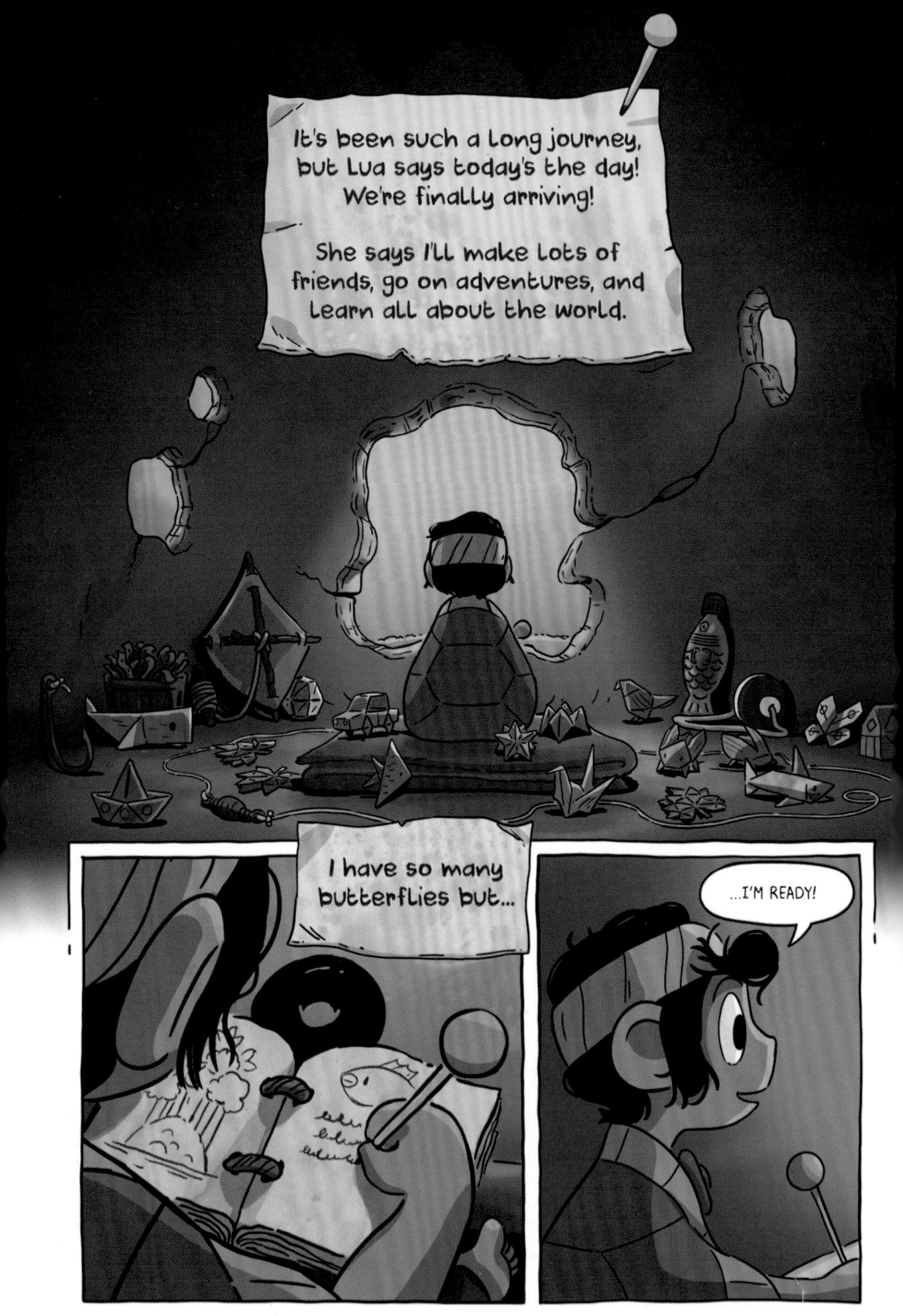
It's been such a long journey, but Lua says today's the day! We're finally arriving!
She says I'll make lots of friends, go on adventures, and learn all about the world.
I have so many butterflies but...
...I'M READY!

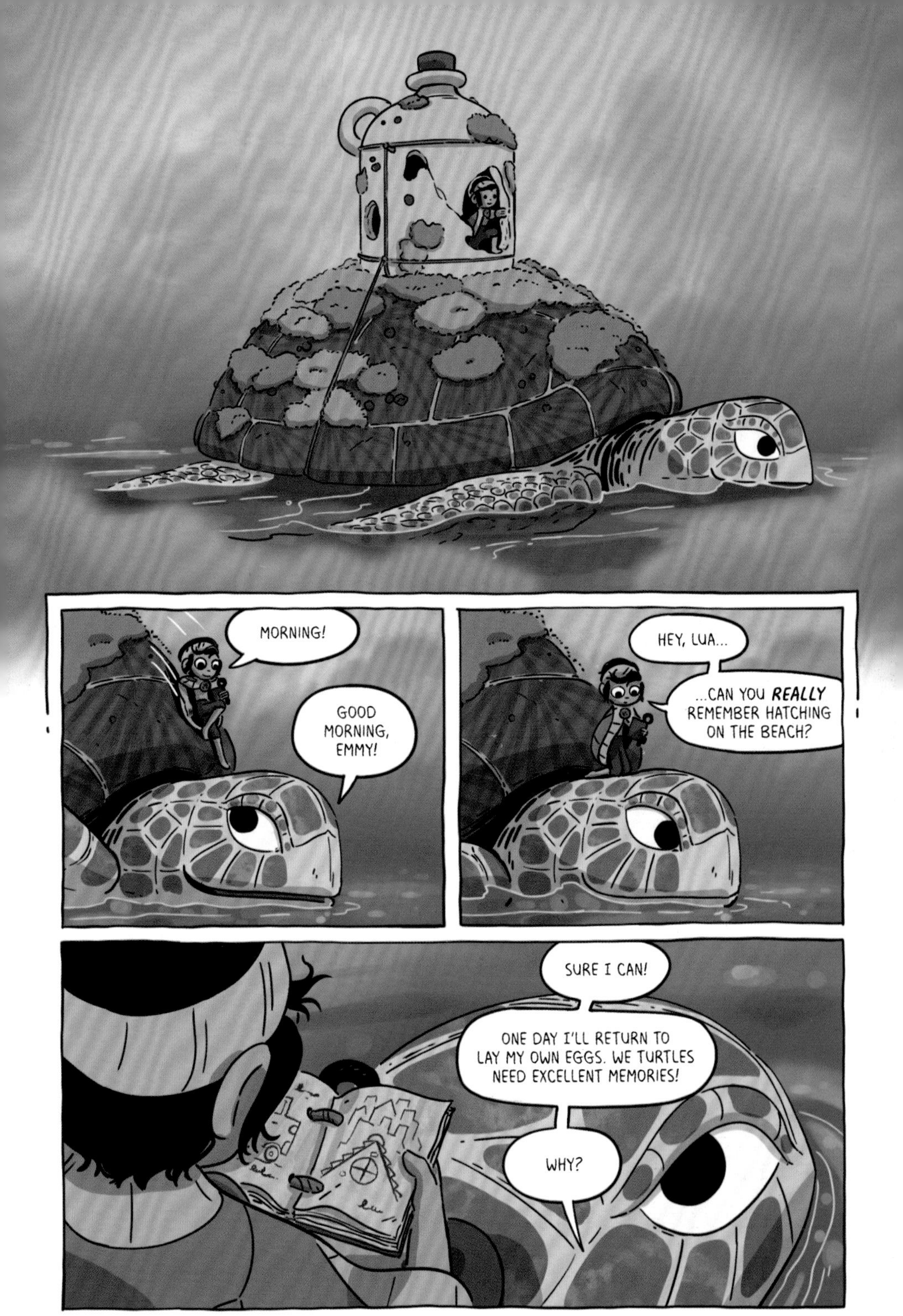
MORNING!
GOOD MORNING, EMMY!
HEY, LUA...
...CAN YOU **REALLY** REMEMBER HATCHING ON THE BEACH?
SURE I CAN!
ONE DAY I'LL RETURN TO LAY MY OWN EGGS. WE TURTLES NEED EXCELLENT MEMORIES!
WHY?

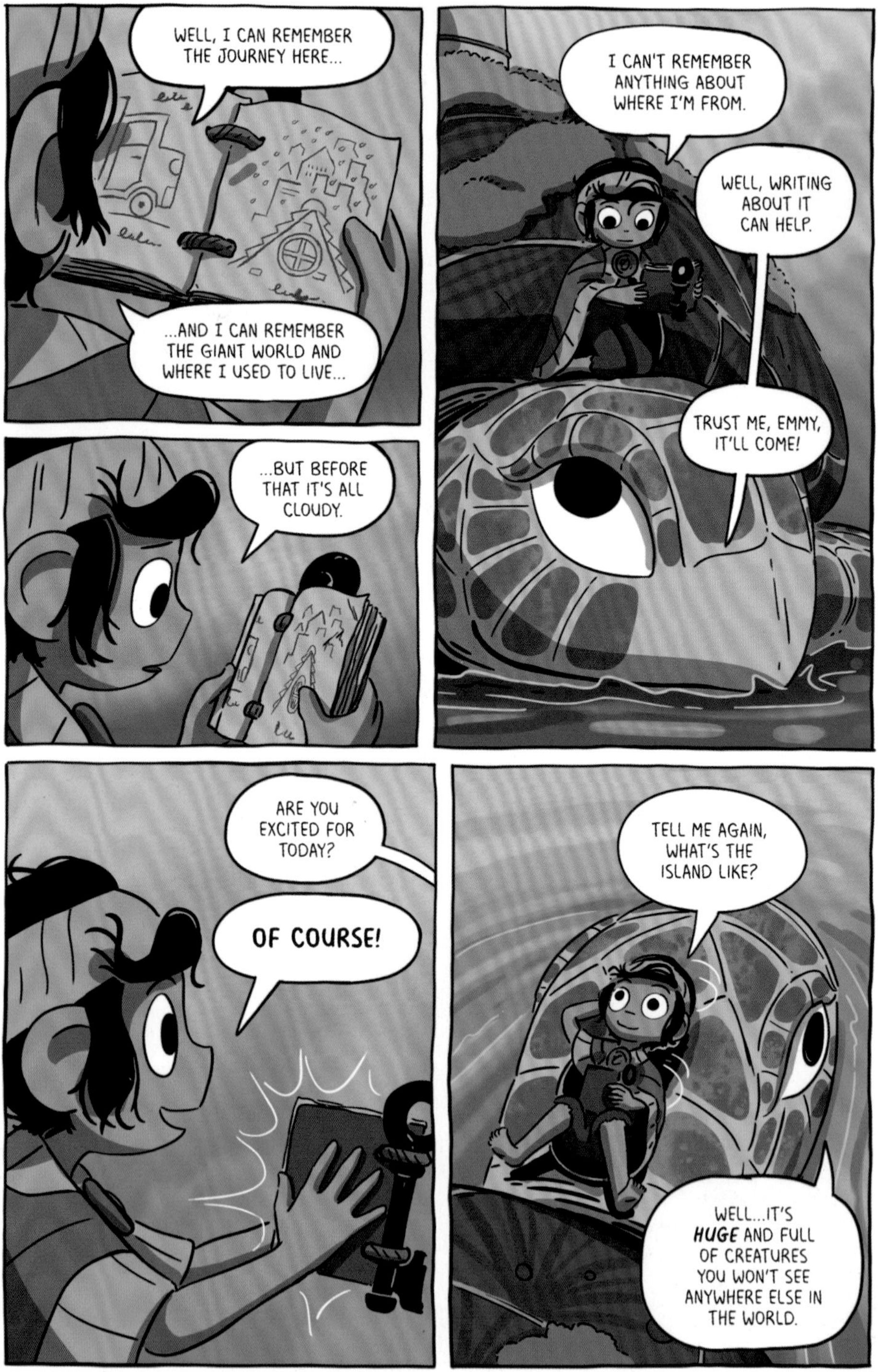
WELL, I CAN REMEMBER THE JOURNEY HERE...
...AND I CAN REMEMBER THE GIANT WORLD AND WHERE I USED TO LIVE...
...BUT BEFORE THAT IT'S ALL CLOUDY.
I CAN'T REMEMBER ANYTHING ABOUT WHERE I'M FROM.
WELL, WRITING ABOUT IT CAN HELP.
TRUST ME, EMMY, IT'LL COME!
ARE YOU EXCITED FOR TODAY?
OF COURSE!
TELL ME AGAIN, WHAT'S THE ISLAND LIKE?
WELL...IT'S **HUGE** AND FULL OF CREATURES YOU WON'T SEE ANYWHERE ELSE IN THE WORLD.

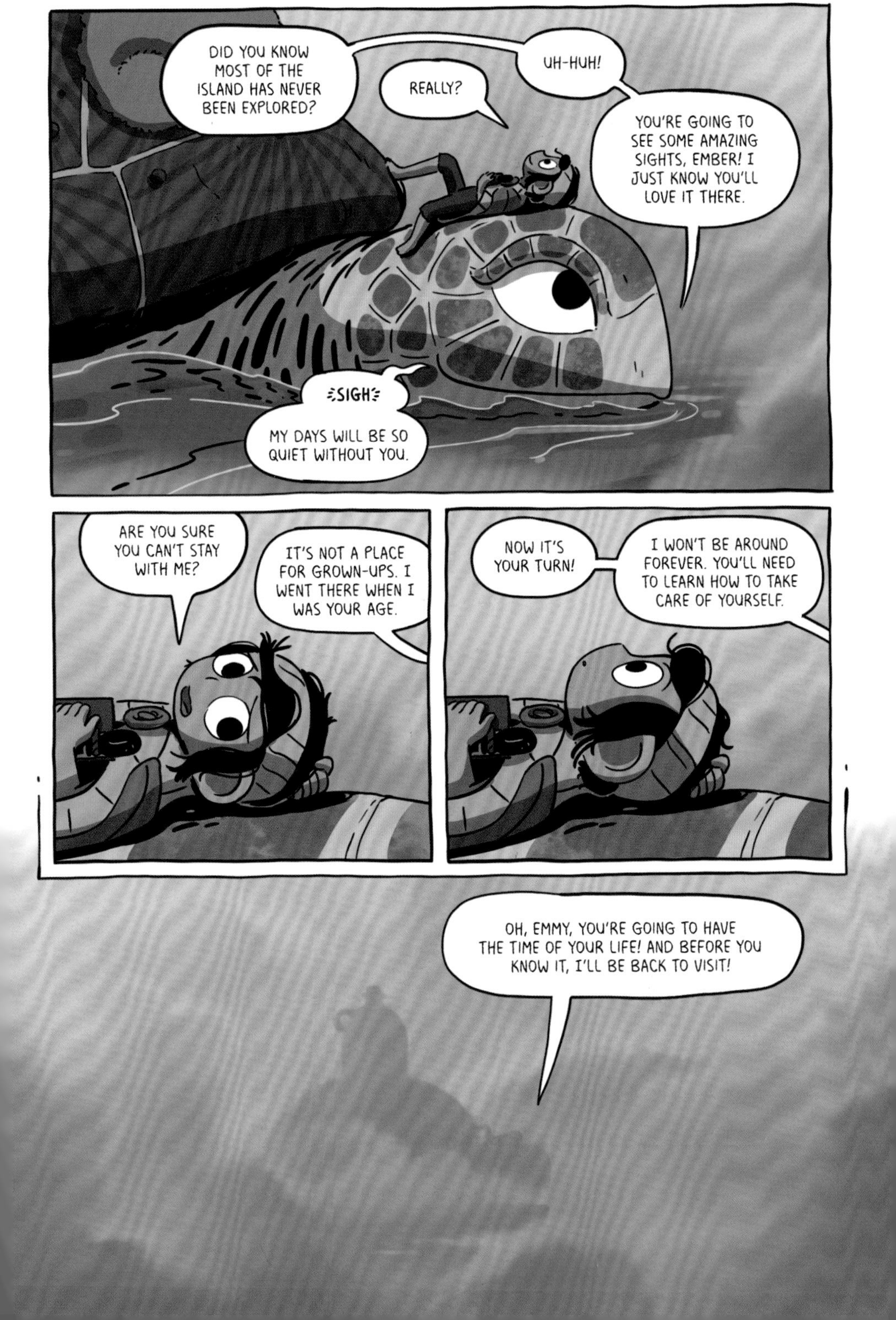
DID YOU KNOW MOST OF THE ISLAND HAS NEVER BEEN EXPLORED?
REALLY?
UH-HUH!
YOU'RE GOING TO SEE SOME AMAZING SIGHTS, EMBER! I JUST KNOW YOU'LL LOVE IT THERE.
SIGH
MY DAYS WILL BE SO QUIET WITHOUT YOU.
ARE YOU SURE YOU CAN'T STAY WITH ME?
IT'S NOT A PLACE FOR GROWN-UPS. I WENT THERE WHEN I WAS YOUR AGE.
NOW IT'S YOUR TURN!
I WON'T BE AROUND FOREVER. YOU'LL NEED TO LEARN HOW TO TAKE CARE OF YOURSELF.
OH, EMMY, YOU'RE GOING TO HAVE THE TIME OF YOUR LIFE! AND BEFORE YOU KNOW IT, I'LL BE BACK TO VISIT!

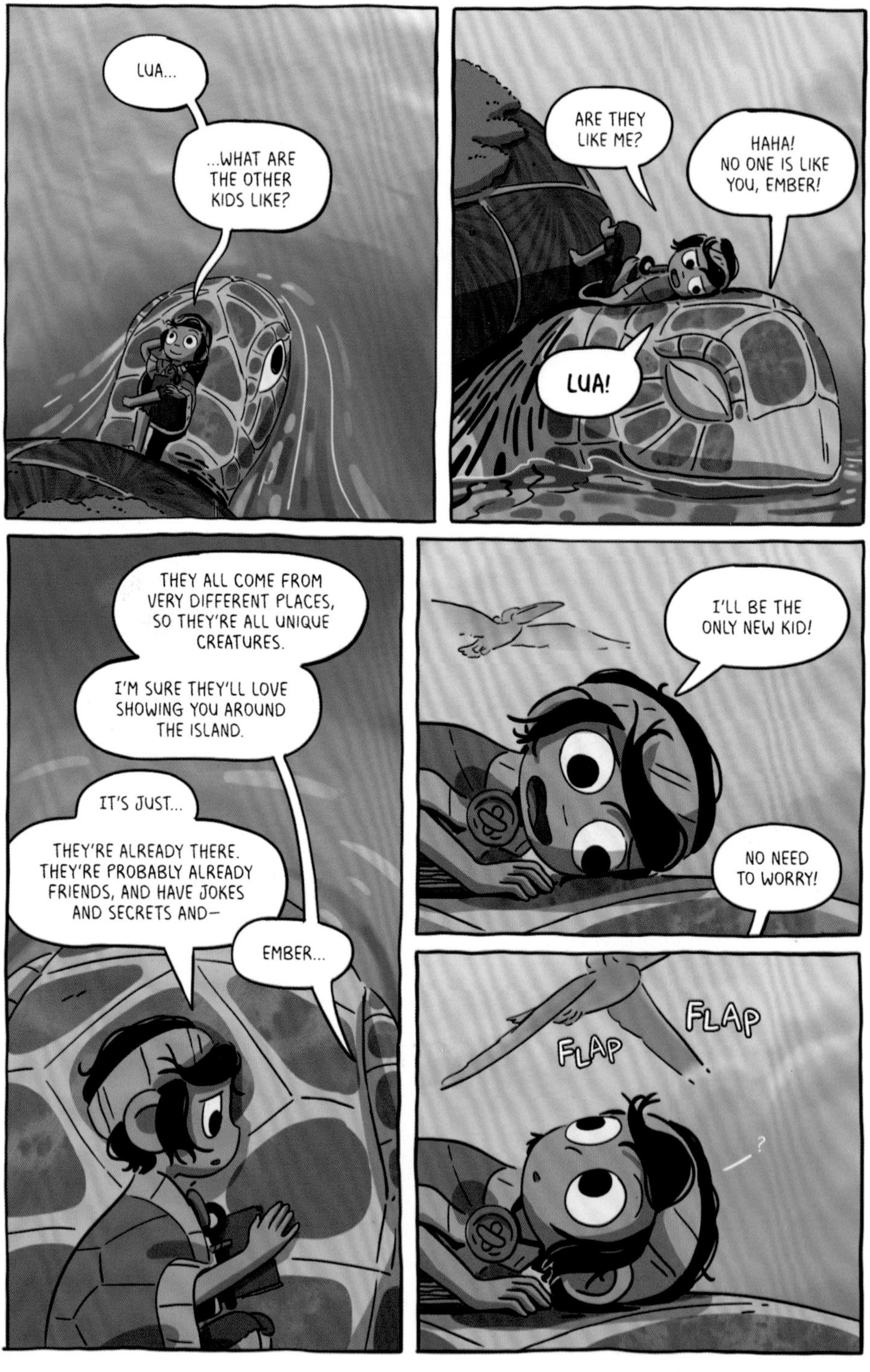
LUA...
...WHAT ARE THE OTHER KIDS LIKE?
ARE THEY LIKE ME?
HAHA! NO ONE IS LIKE YOU, EMBER!
LUA!
THEY ALL COME FROM VERY DIFFERENT PLACES, SO THEY'RE ALL UNIQUE CREATURES.
I'M SURE THEY'LL LOVE SHOWING YOU AROUND THE ISLAND.
IT'S JUST...
THEY'RE ALREADY THERE. THEY'RE PROBABLY ALREADY FRIENDS, AND HAVE JOKES AND SECRETS AND—
EMBER...
I'LL BE THE ONLY NEW KID!
NO NEED TO WORRY!
FLAP
FLAP
?

BE KIND.

INTRODUCE YOURSELF.

ASK WHAT THEIR NAMES ARE.

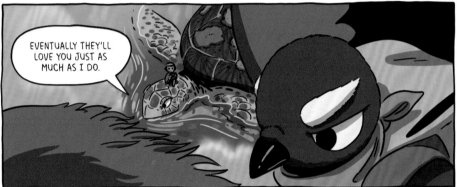

EVENTUALLY THEY'LL LOVE YOU JUST AS MUCH AS I DO.

EMMY, LOOK...

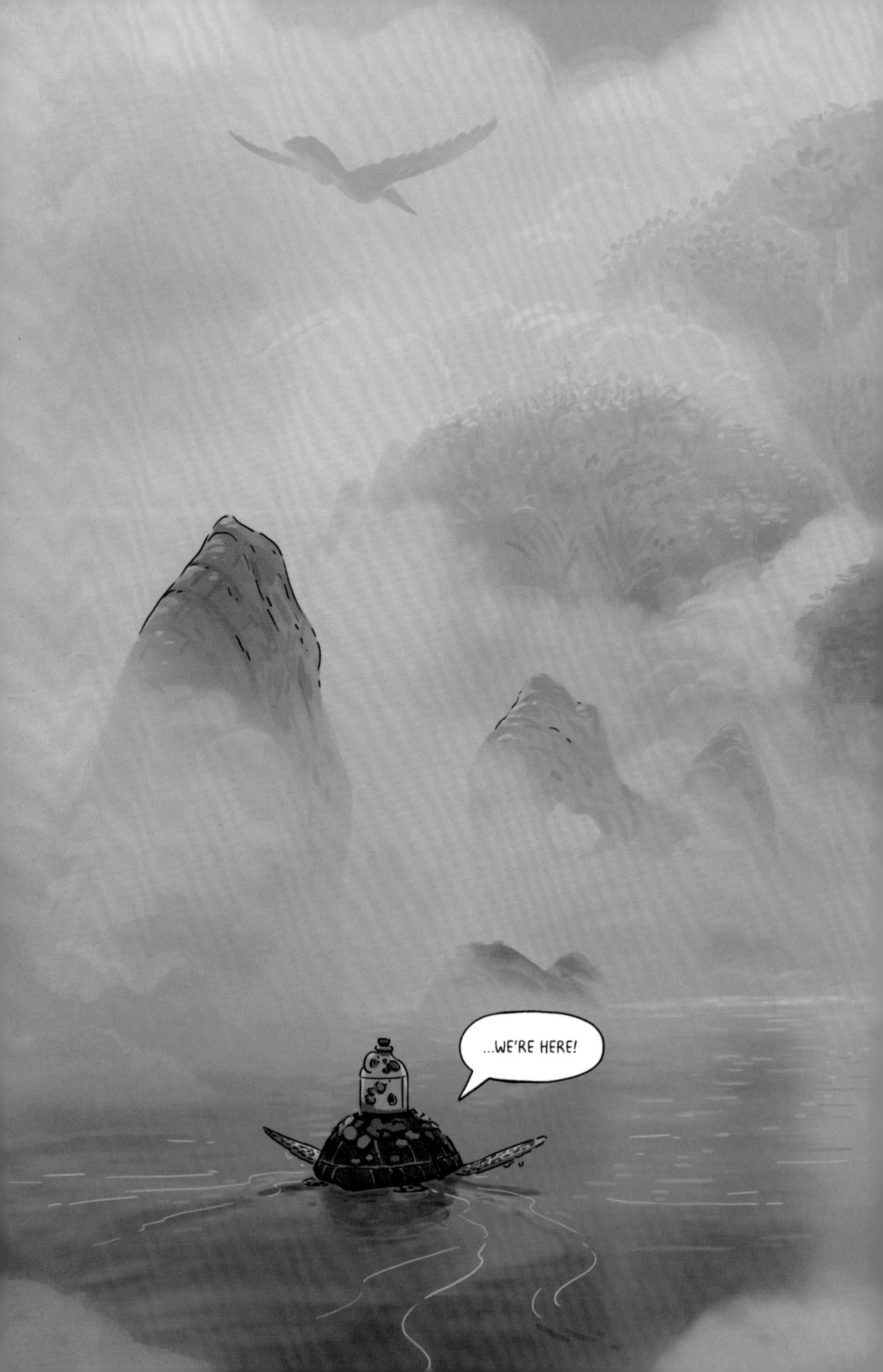
...WE'RE HERE!

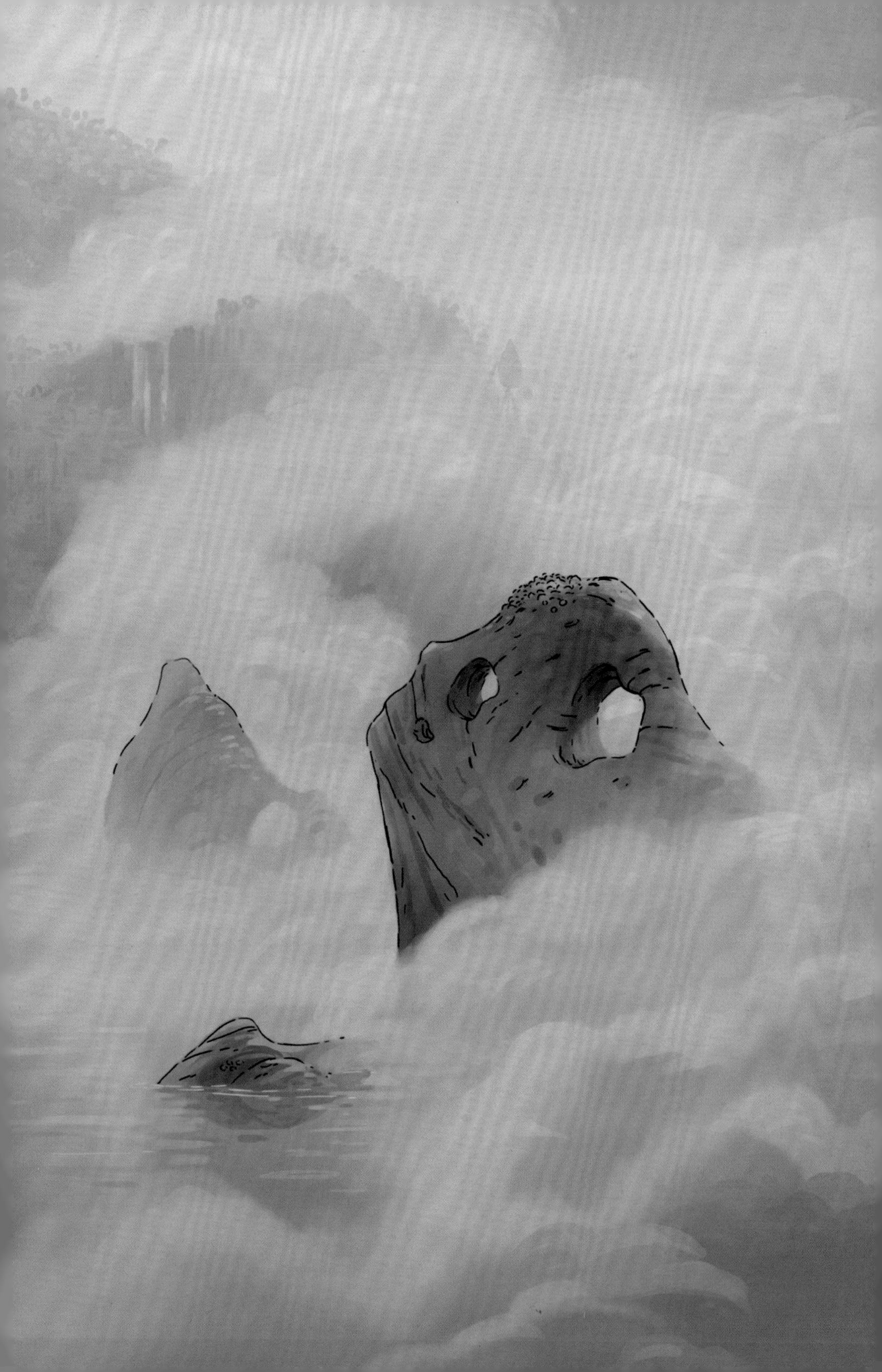

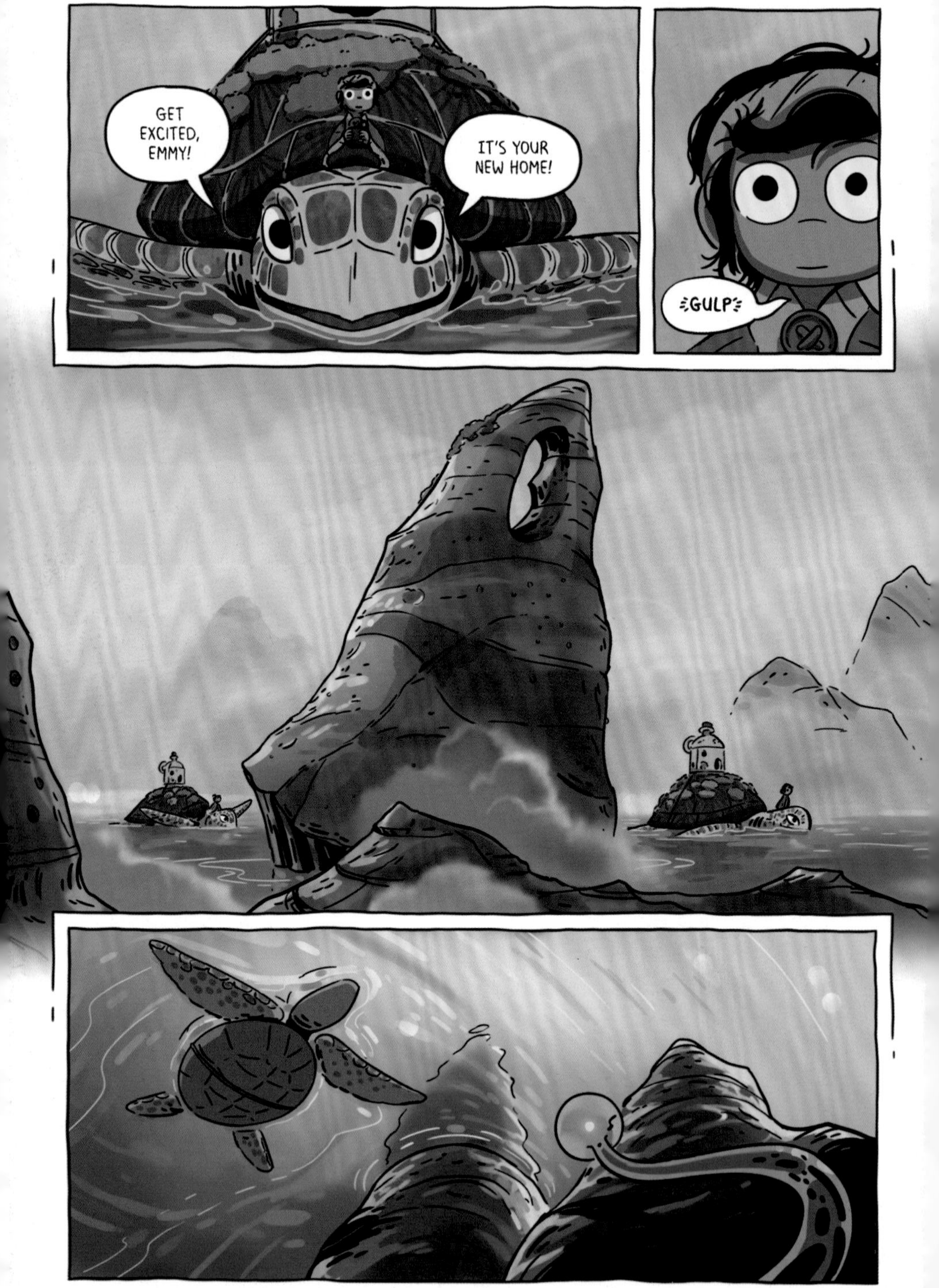
GET EXCITED, EMMY!
IT'S YOUR NEW HOME!
GULP

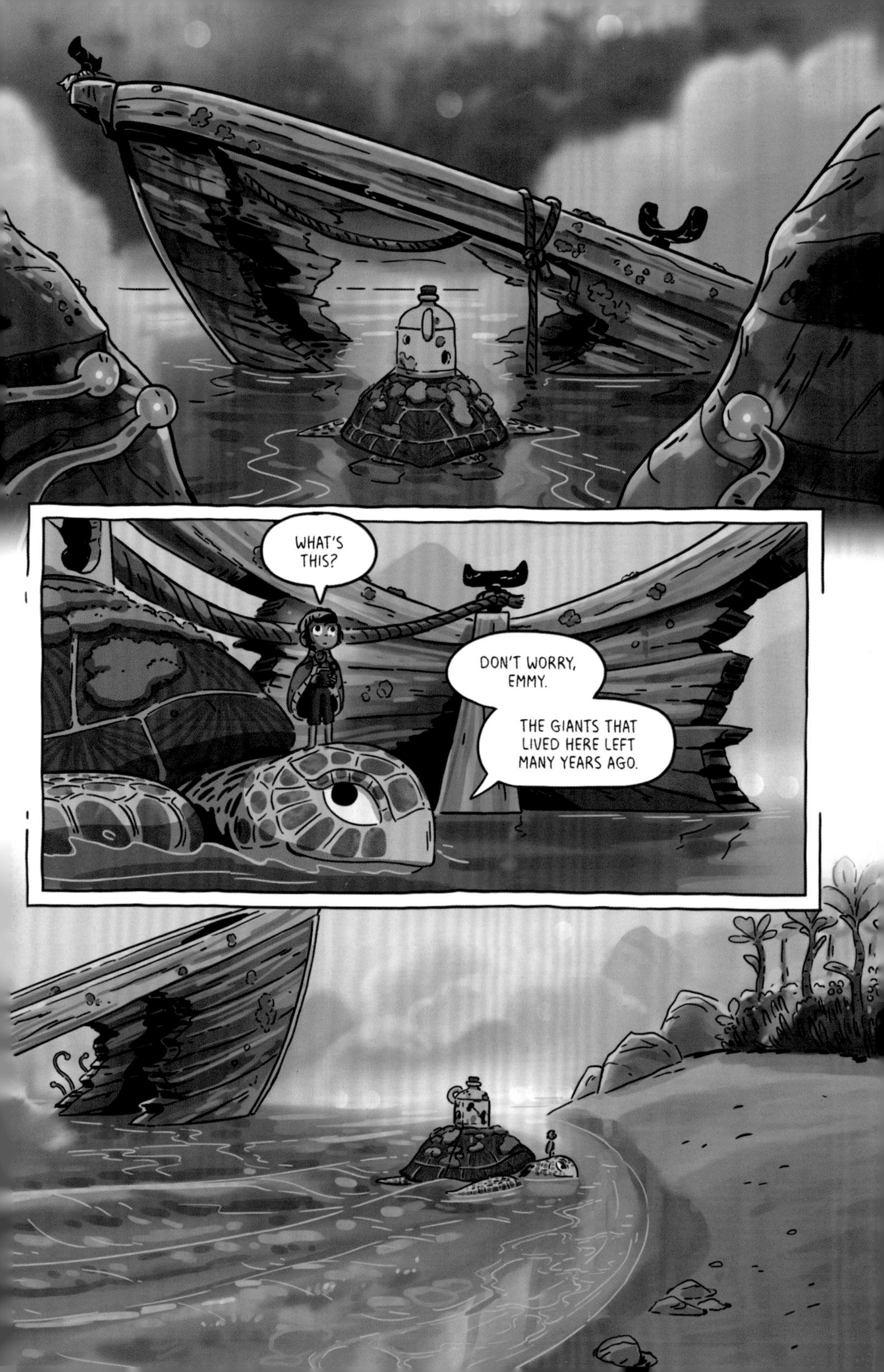
WHAT'S THIS?
DON'T WORRY, EMMY.
THE GIANTS THAT LIVED HERE LEFT MANY YEARS AGO.

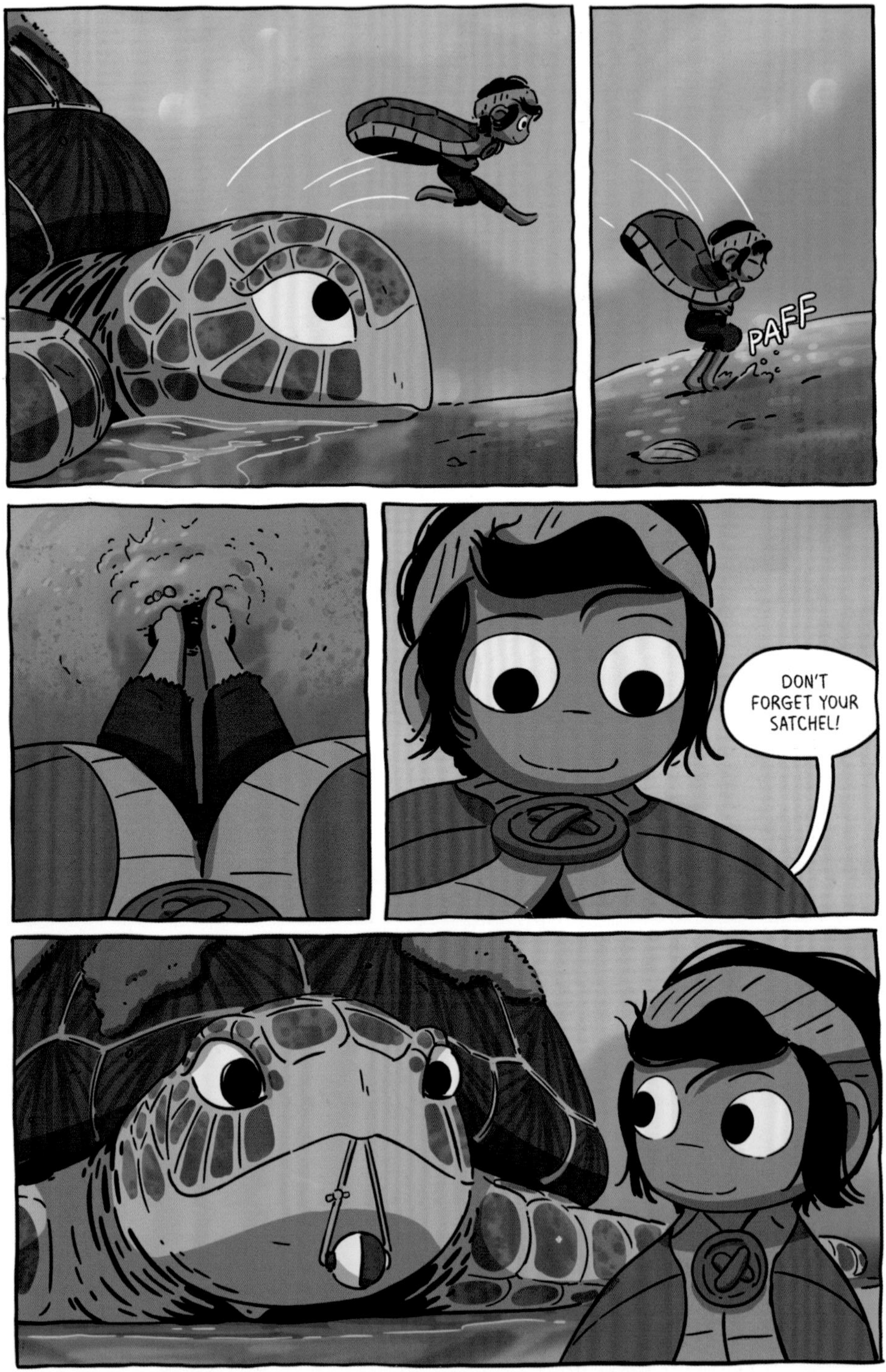
PAFF
DON'T FORGET YOUR SATCHEL!

THANKS.

LOOK INSIDE...

HM?

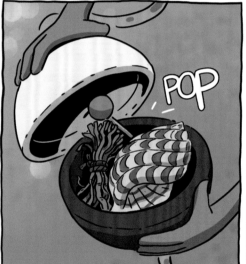

POP

...A SHELL?

IT'S CALLED A **CONCH** SHELL!

A KIND FRIEND GAVE IT TO ME WHEN I WAS A LITTLE TURTLE.

IT HELPED ME WHENEVER I WAS LOST AND FEELING LONELY...

OH!

AND YOU CAN HEAR THE OCEAN IN THERE, TOO!

KSHHH

COOOOL.

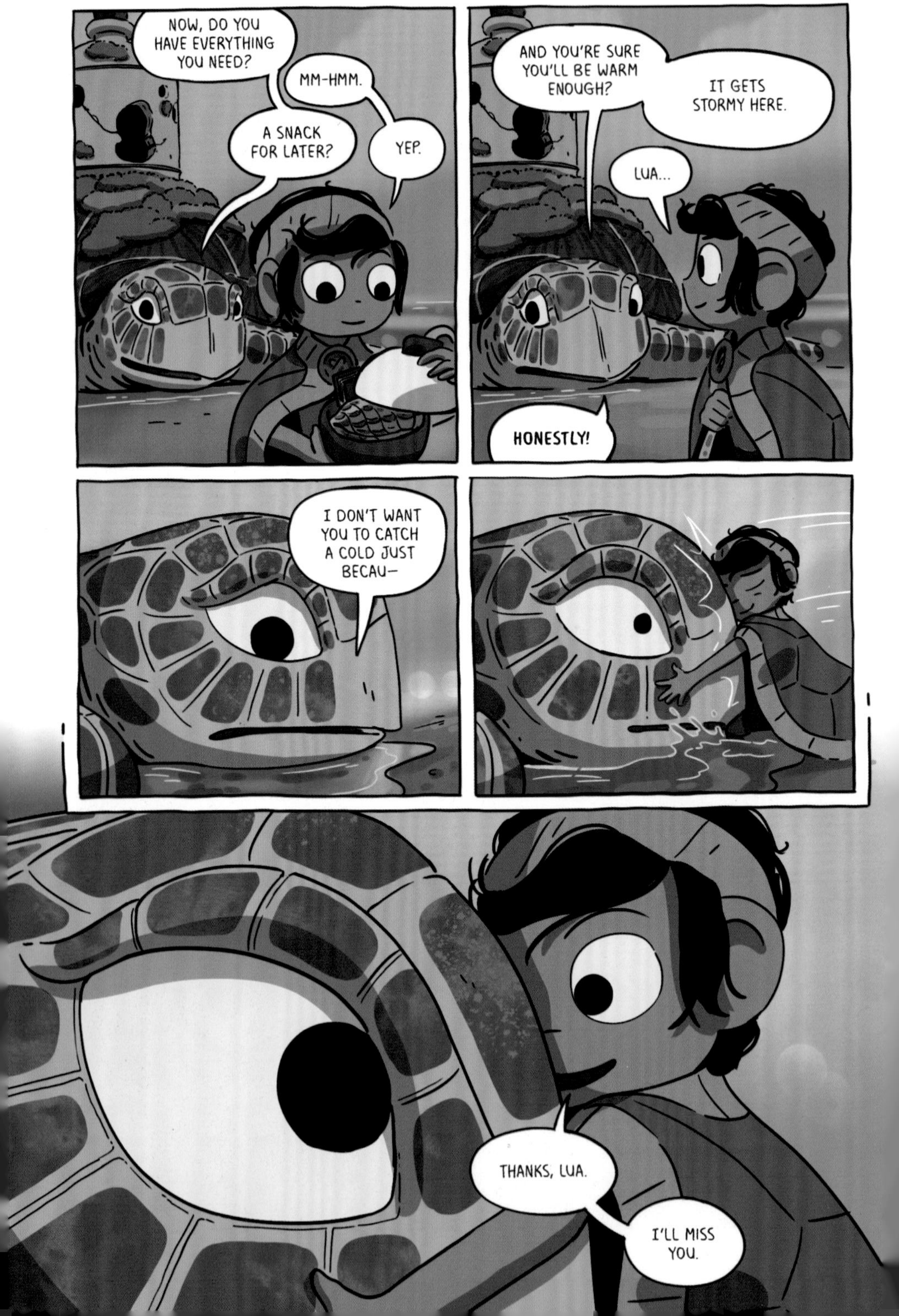
NOW, DO YOU HAVE EVERYTHING YOU NEED?
MM-HMM.
A SNACK FOR LATER?
YEP.
AND YOU'RE SURE YOU'LL BE WARM ENOUGH?
IT GETS STORMY HERE.
LUA...
HONESTLY!
I DON'T WANT YOU TO CATCH A COLD JUST BECAU—
THANKS, LUA.
I'LL MISS YOU.

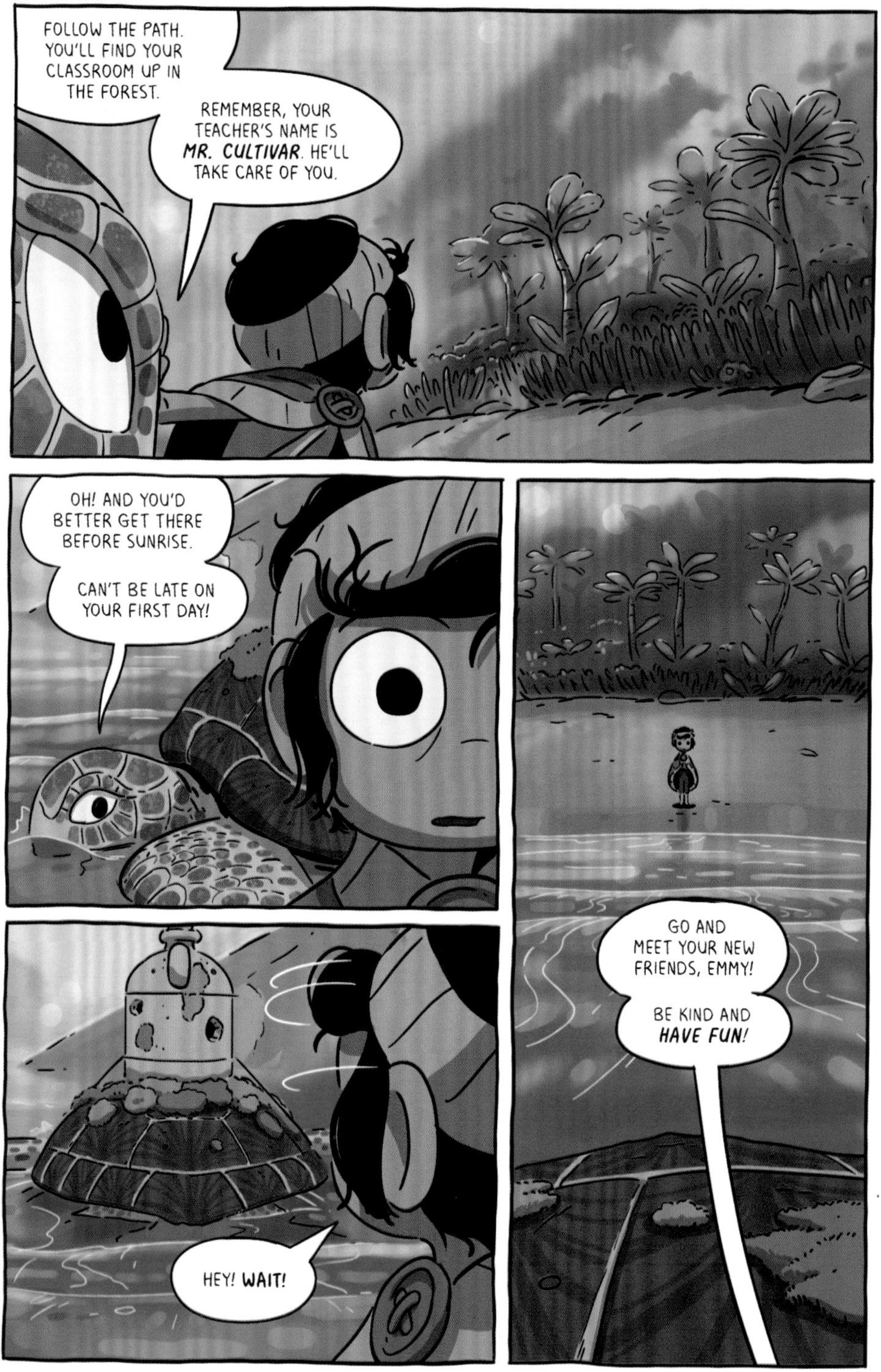
FOLLOW THE PATH. YOU'LL FIND YOUR CLASSROOM UP IN THE FOREST.
REMEMBER, YOUR TEACHER'S NAME IS **MR. CULTIVAR**. HE'LL TAKE CARE OF YOU.
OH! AND YOU'D BETTER GET THERE BEFORE SUNRISE.
CAN'T BE LATE ON YOUR FIRST DAY!
HEY! **WAIT!**
GO AND MEET YOUR NEW FRIENDS, EMMY!
BE KIND AND ***HAVE FUN!***

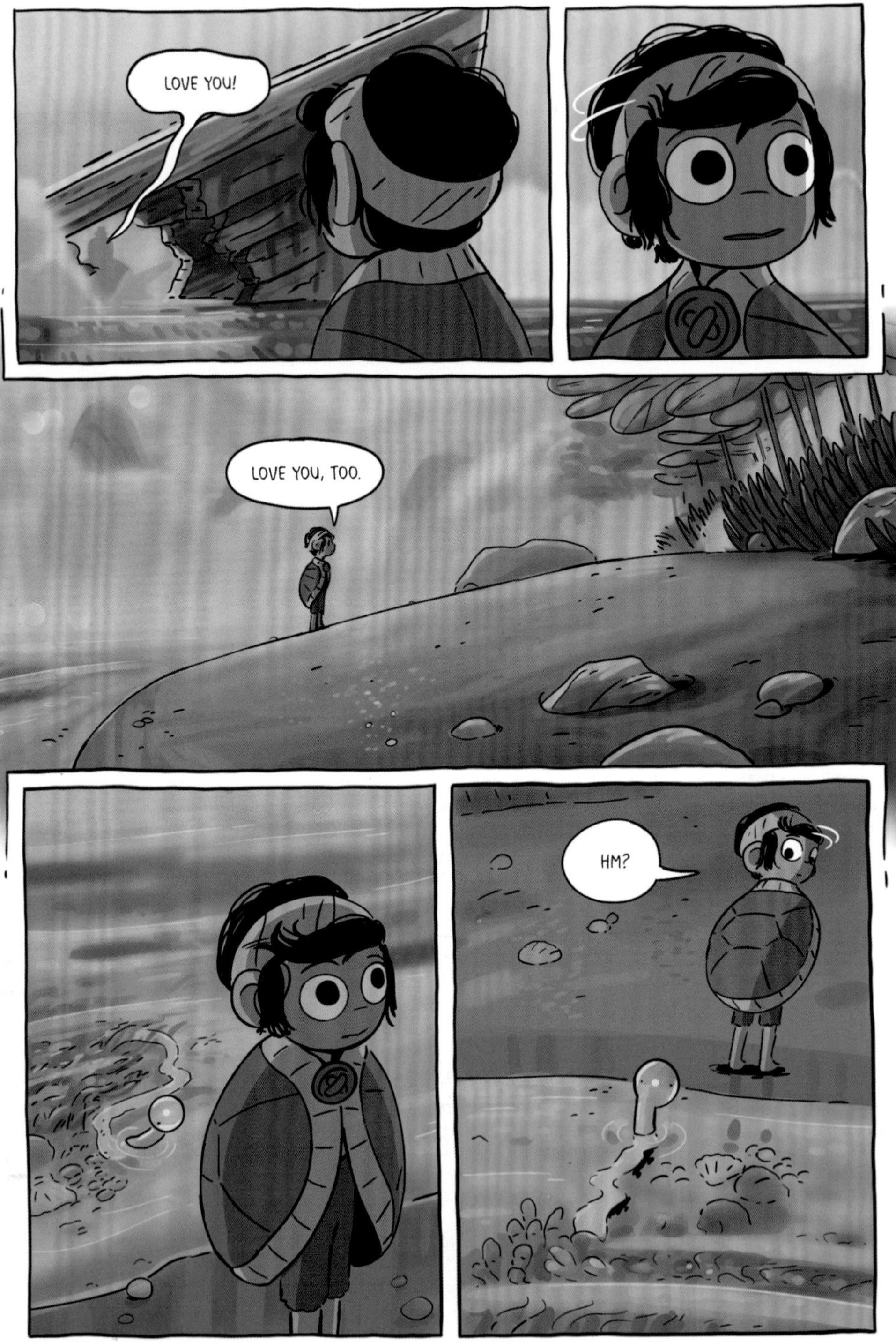
LOVE YOU!
LOVE YOU, TOO.
HM?

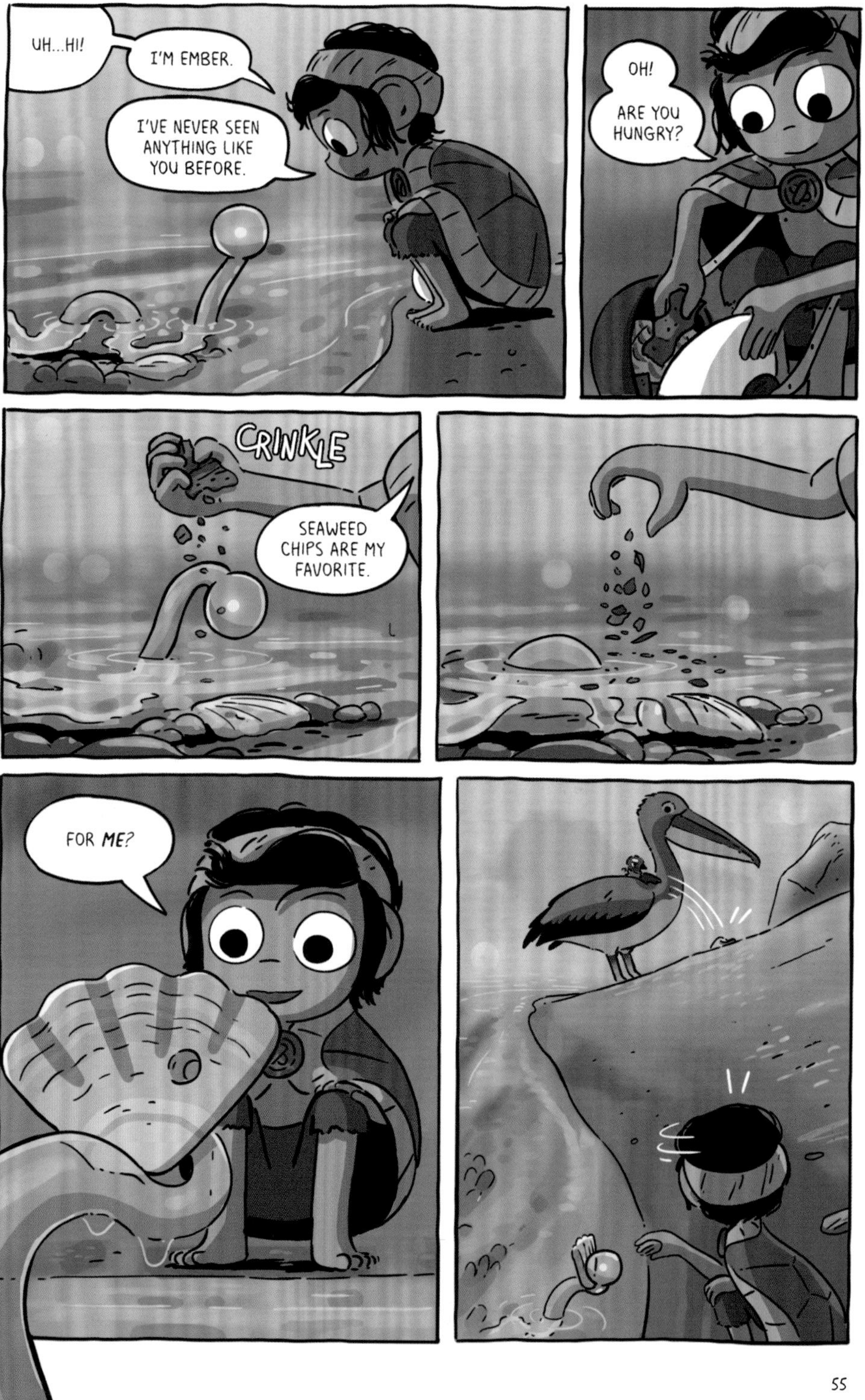
UH...HI!
I'M EMBER.
I'VE NEVER SEEN ANYTHING LIKE YOU BEFORE.
OH!
ARE YOU HUNGRY?
CRINKLE
SEAWEED CHIPS ARE MY FAVORITE.
FOR ME?

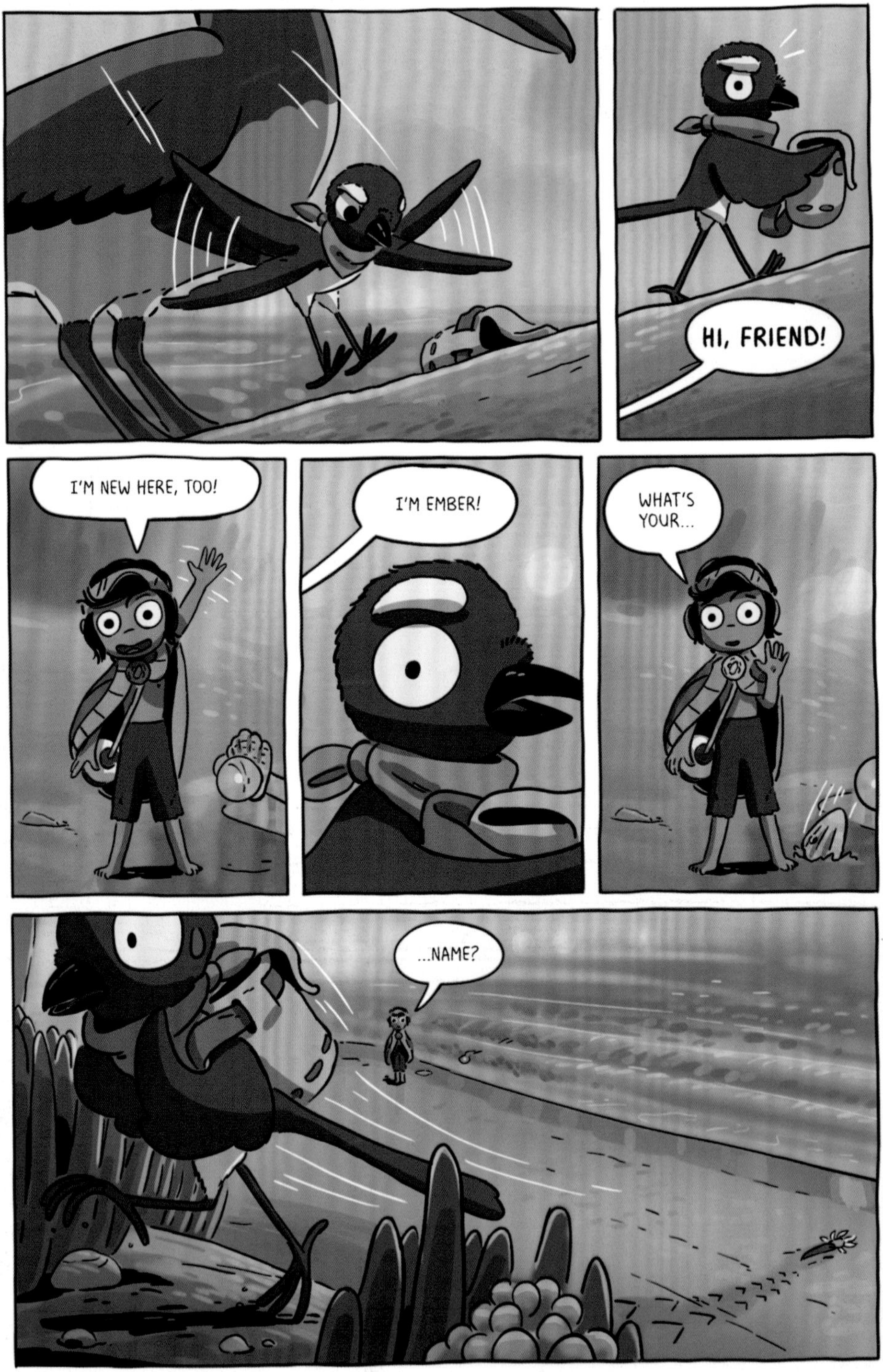
HI, FRIEND!
I'M NEW HERE, TOO!
I'M EMBER!
WHAT'S YOUR...
...NAME?

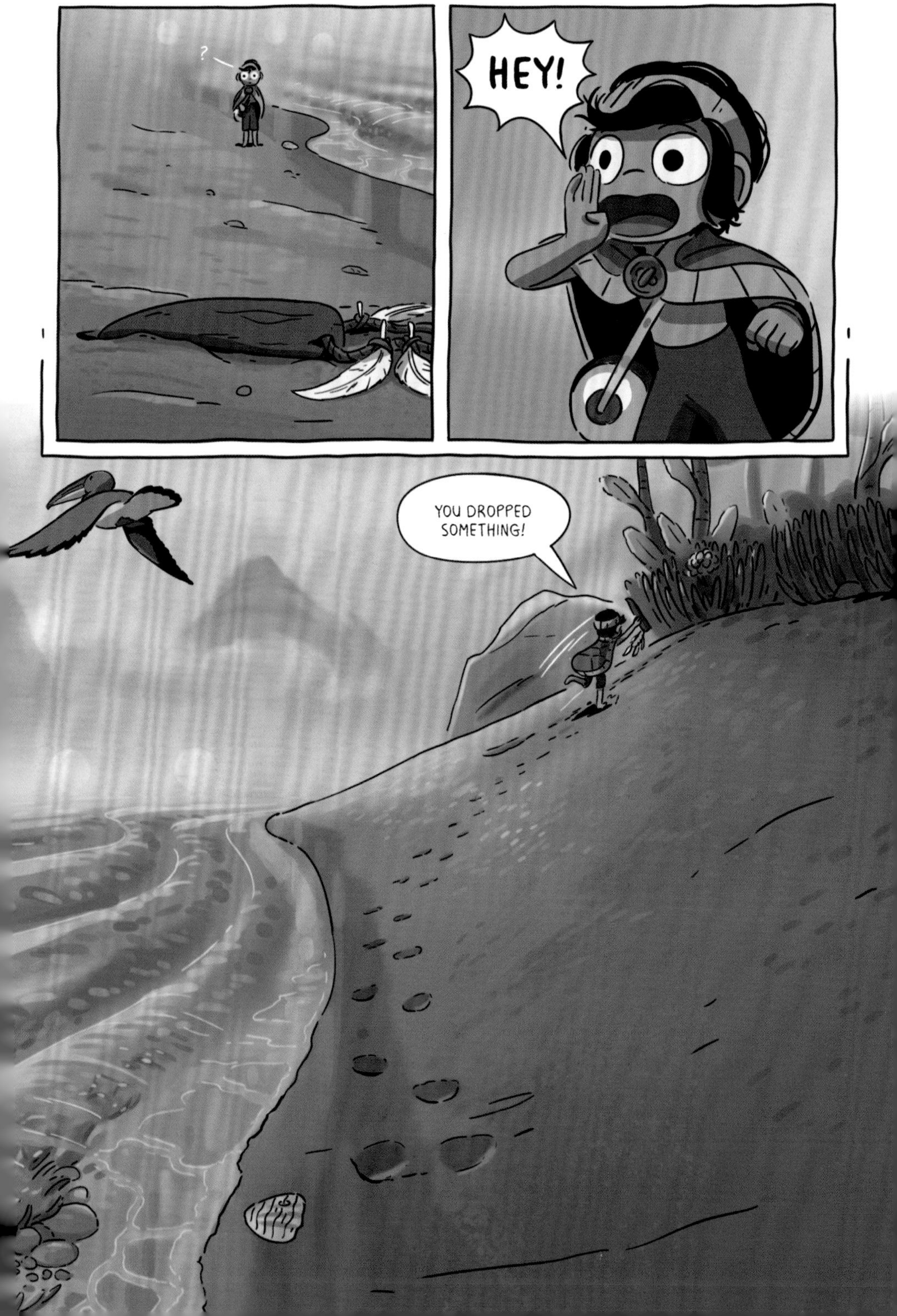
?
HEY!
YOU DROPPED SOMETHING!

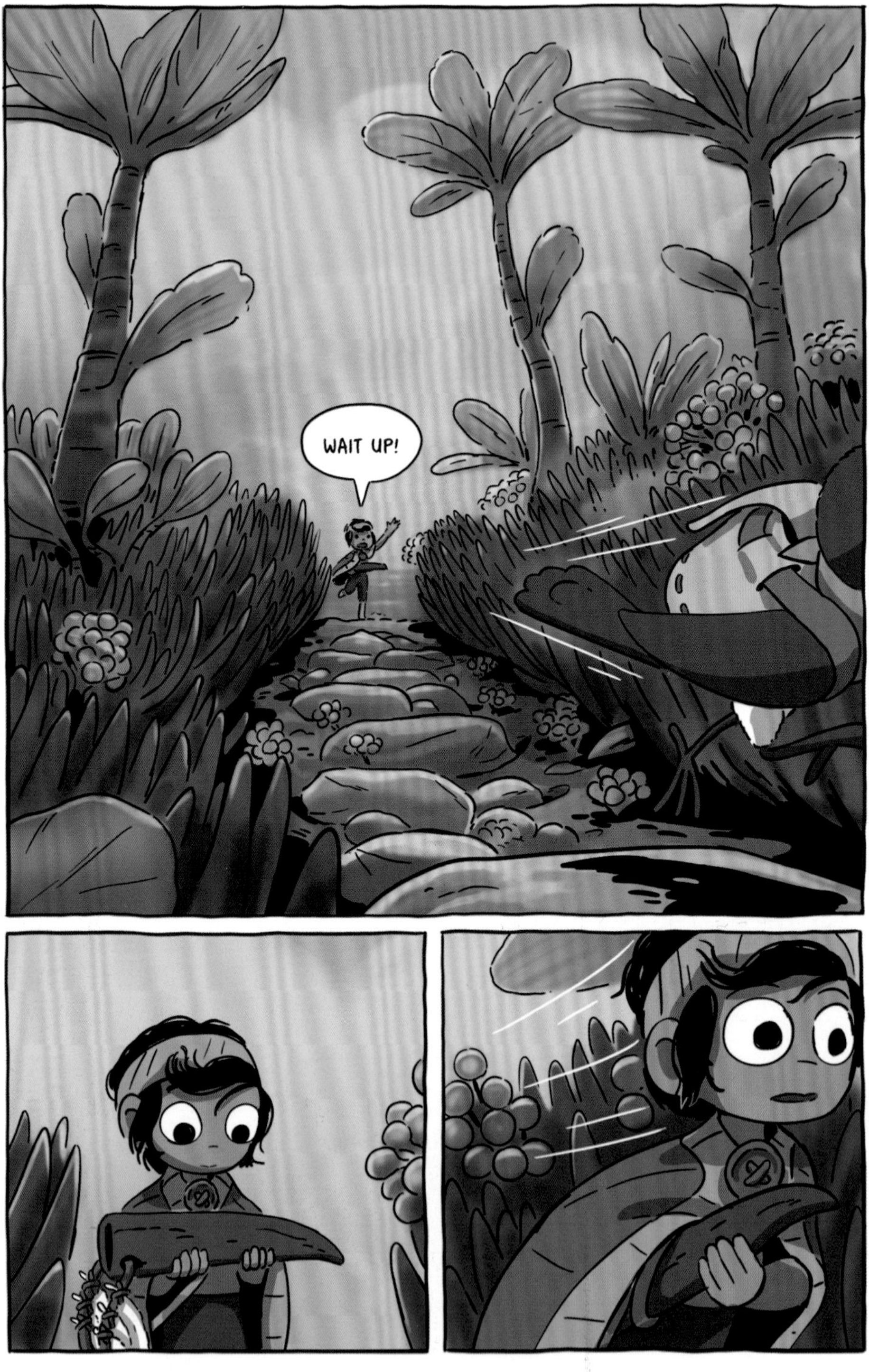
WAIT UP!

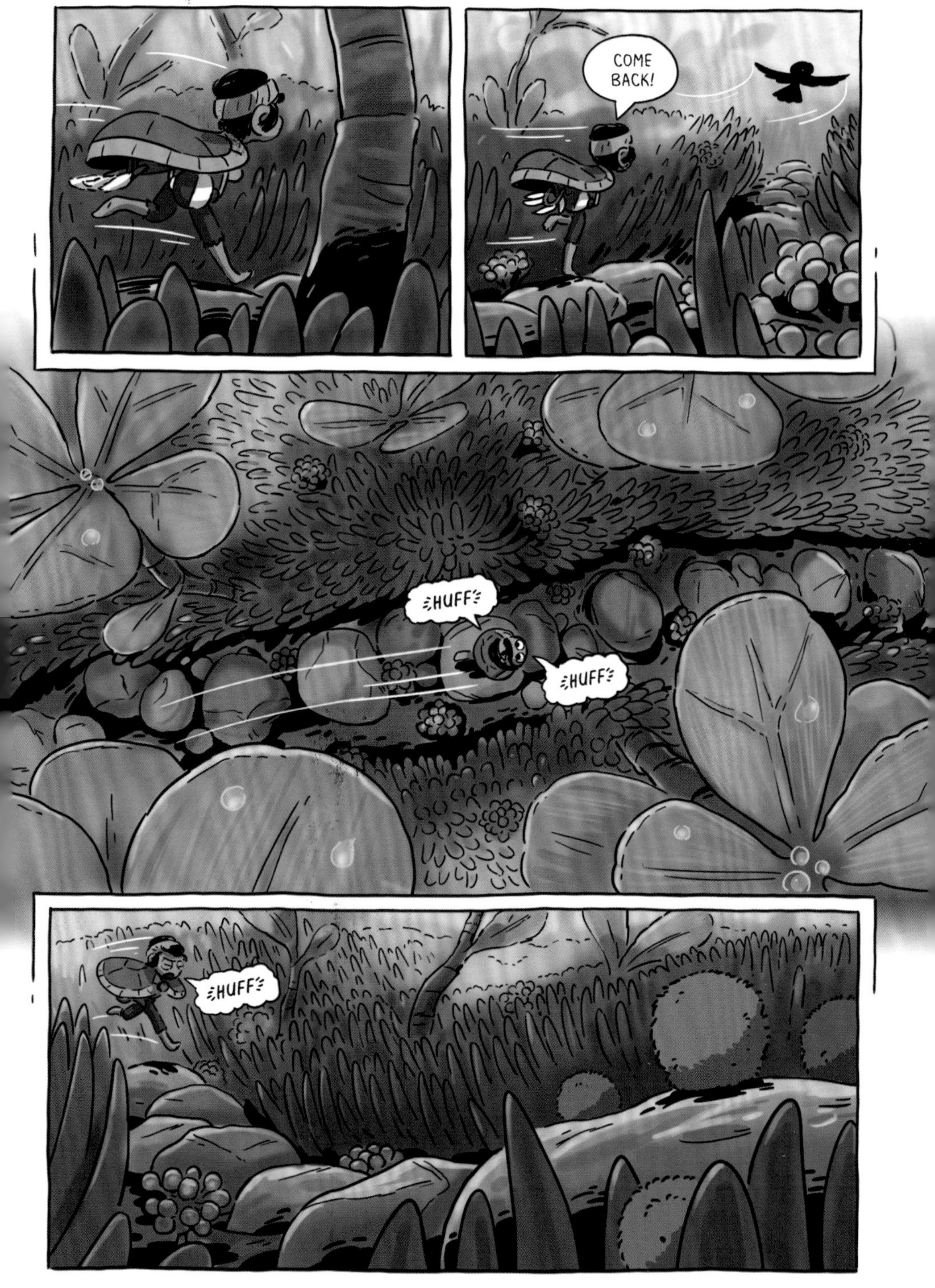
COME BACK!
HUFF
HUFF
HUFF

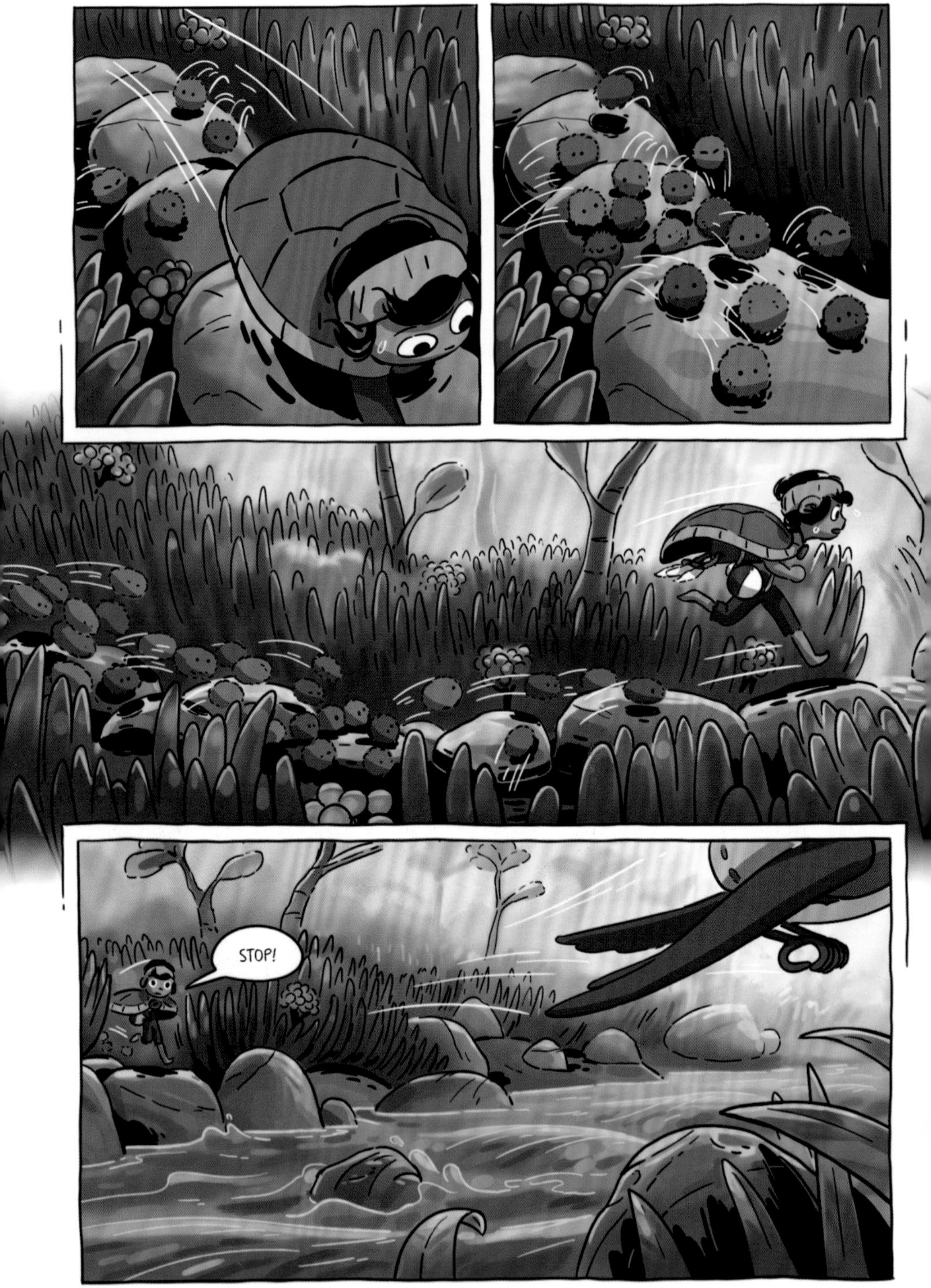
STOP!

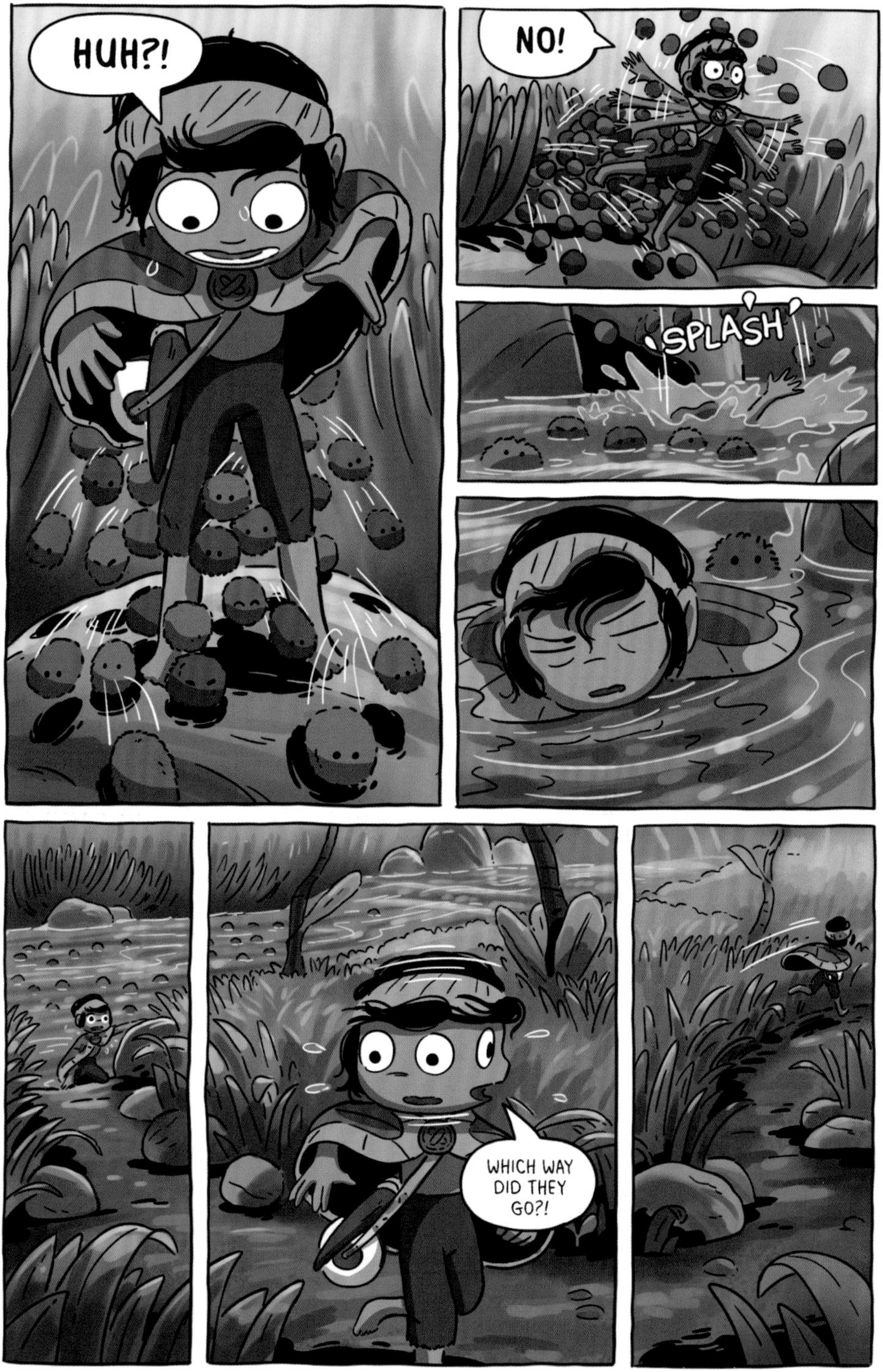
HUH?!
NO!
SPLASH
WHICH WAY DID THEY GO?!

UGH.

I'M *SO* LOST.

CLATTER

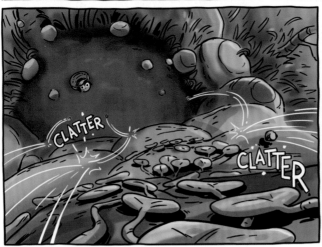

CLATTER

CLATTER

IS SOMEONE UP THERE...?

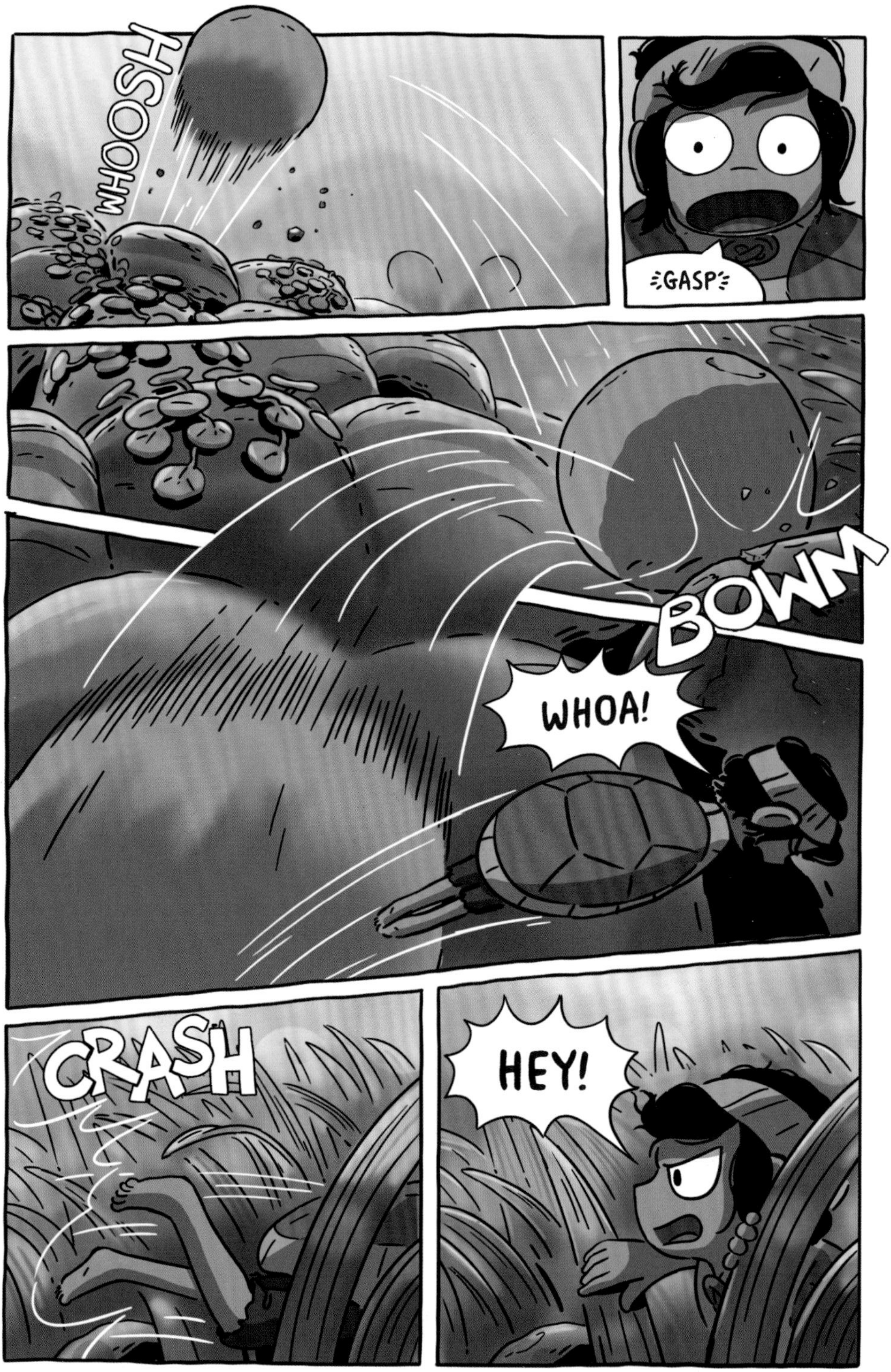
WHOOSH
GASP
BOWM
WHOA!
CRASH
HEY!

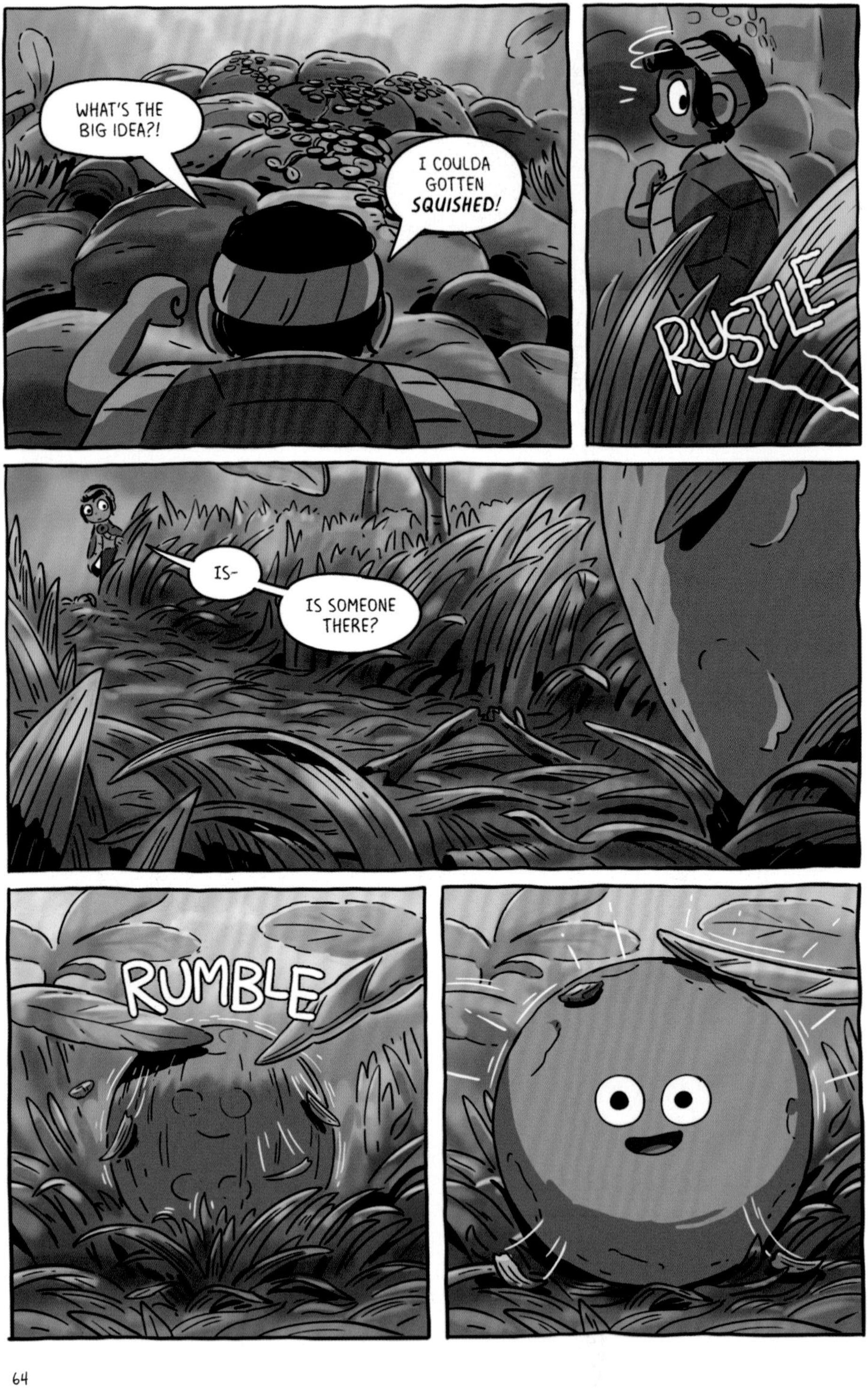
WHAT'S THE BIG IDEA?!
I COULDA GOTTEN **SQUISHED**!
RUSTLE
IS-
IS SOMEONE THERE?
RUMBLE

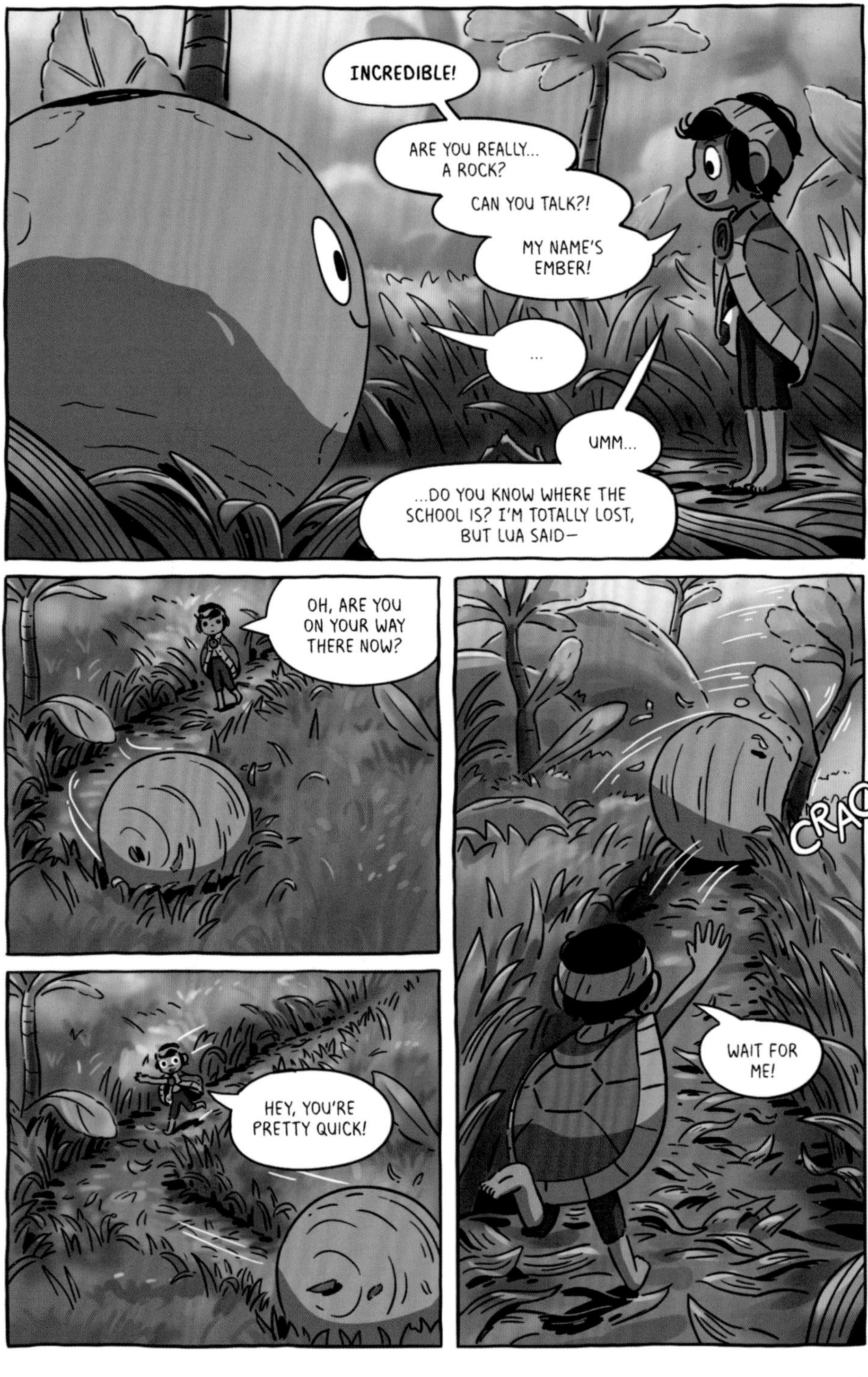
INCREDIBLE!
ARE YOU REALLY... A ROCK?
CAN YOU TALK?!
MY NAME'S EMBER!
...
UMM...
...DO YOU KNOW WHERE THE SCHOOL IS? I'M TOTALLY LOST, BUT LUA SAID—
OH, ARE YOU ON YOUR WAY THERE NOW?
HEY, YOU'RE PRETTY QUICK!
CRACK
WAIT FOR ME!

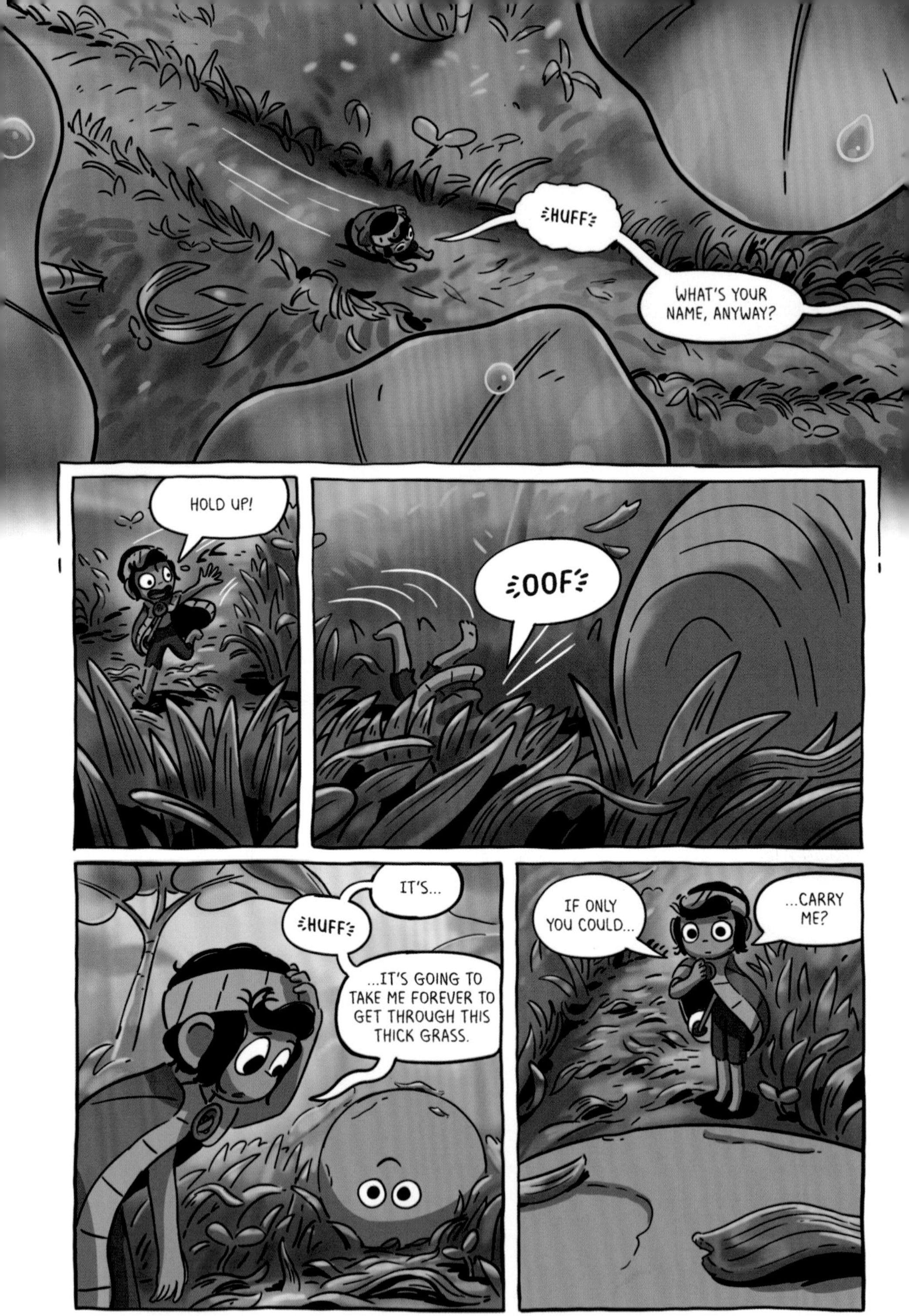
HUFF
WHAT'S YOUR NAME, ANYWAY?
HOLD UP!
OOF
IT'S...
HUFF
...IT'S GOING TO TAKE ME FOREVER TO GET THROUGH THIS THICK GRASS.
IF ONLY YOU COULD...
...CARRY ME?

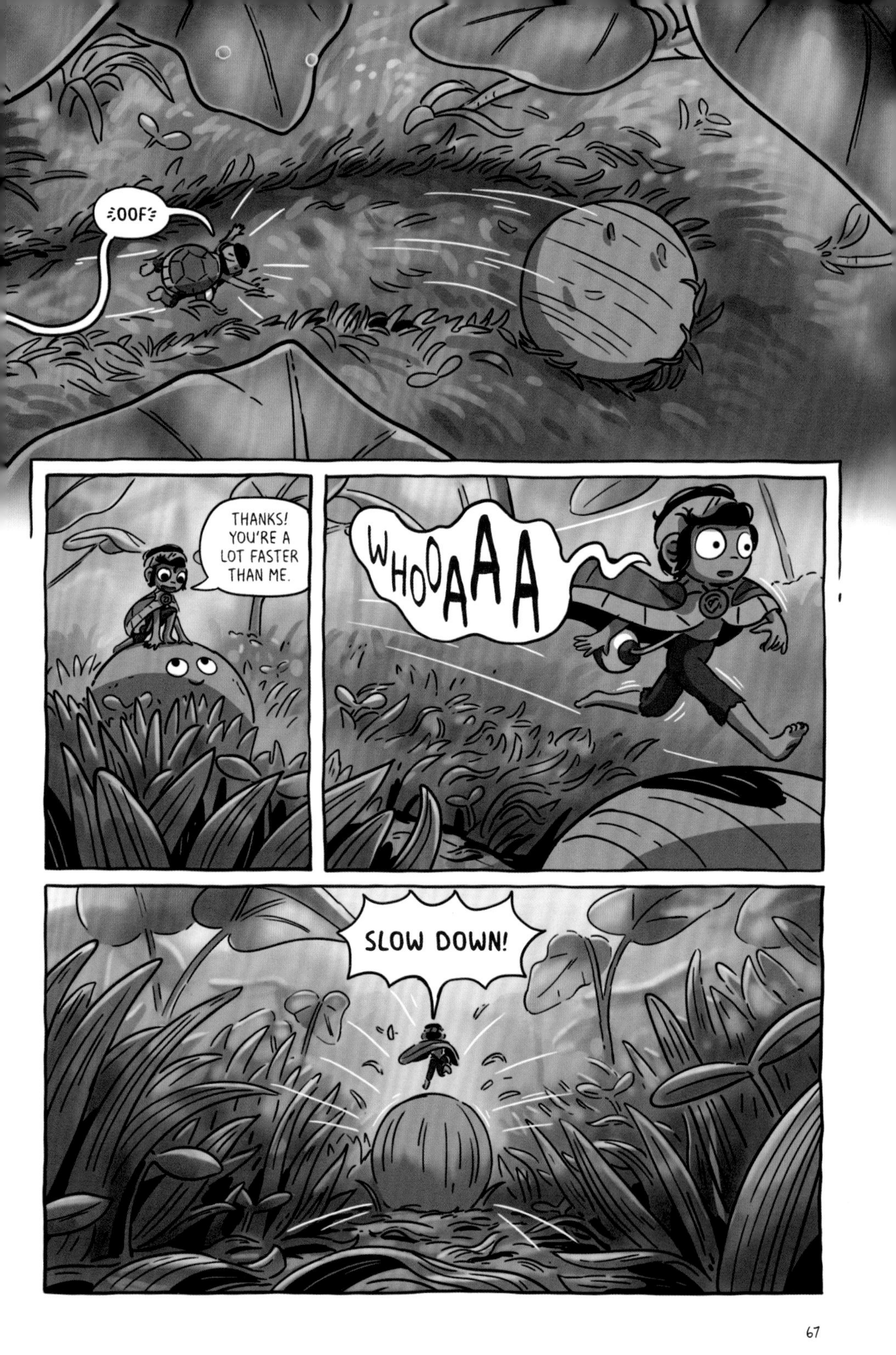
OOF
THANKS! YOU'RE A LOT FASTER THAN ME.
WHOOAAA
SLOW DOWN!

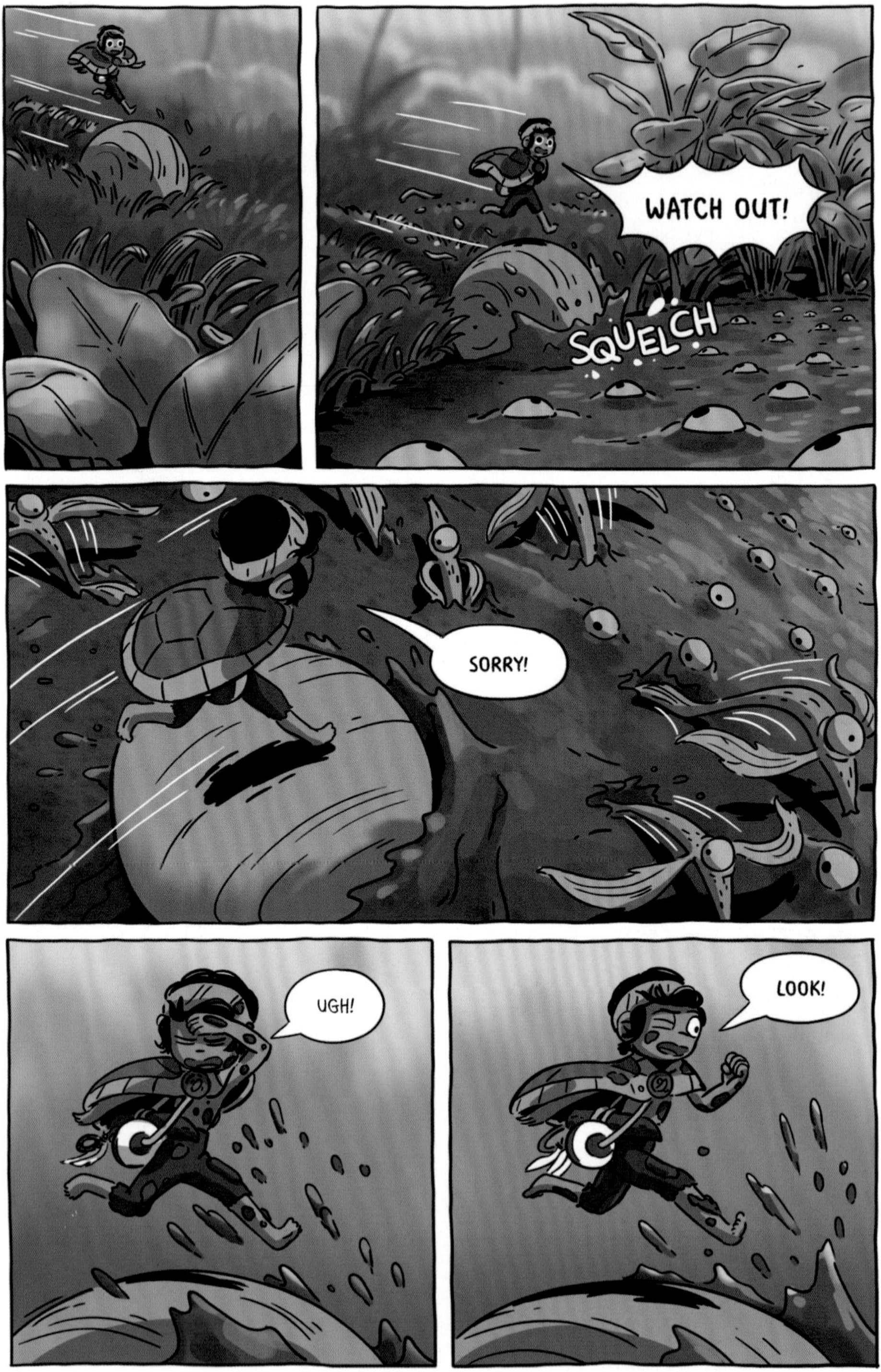
WATCH OUT!
SQUELCH
SORRY!
UGH!
LOOK!

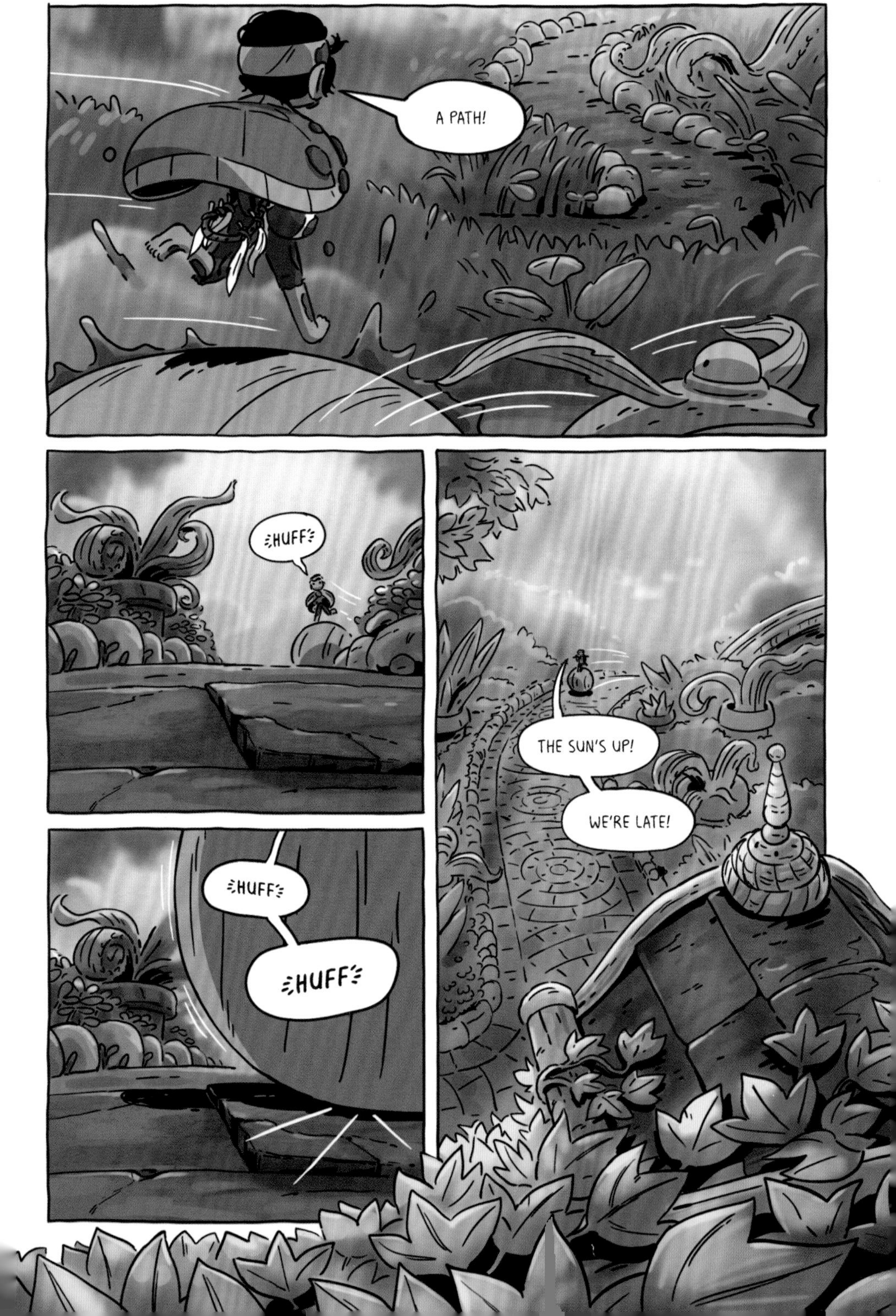
A PATH!
HUFF
THE SUN'S UP!
WE'RE LATE!
HUFF
HUFF

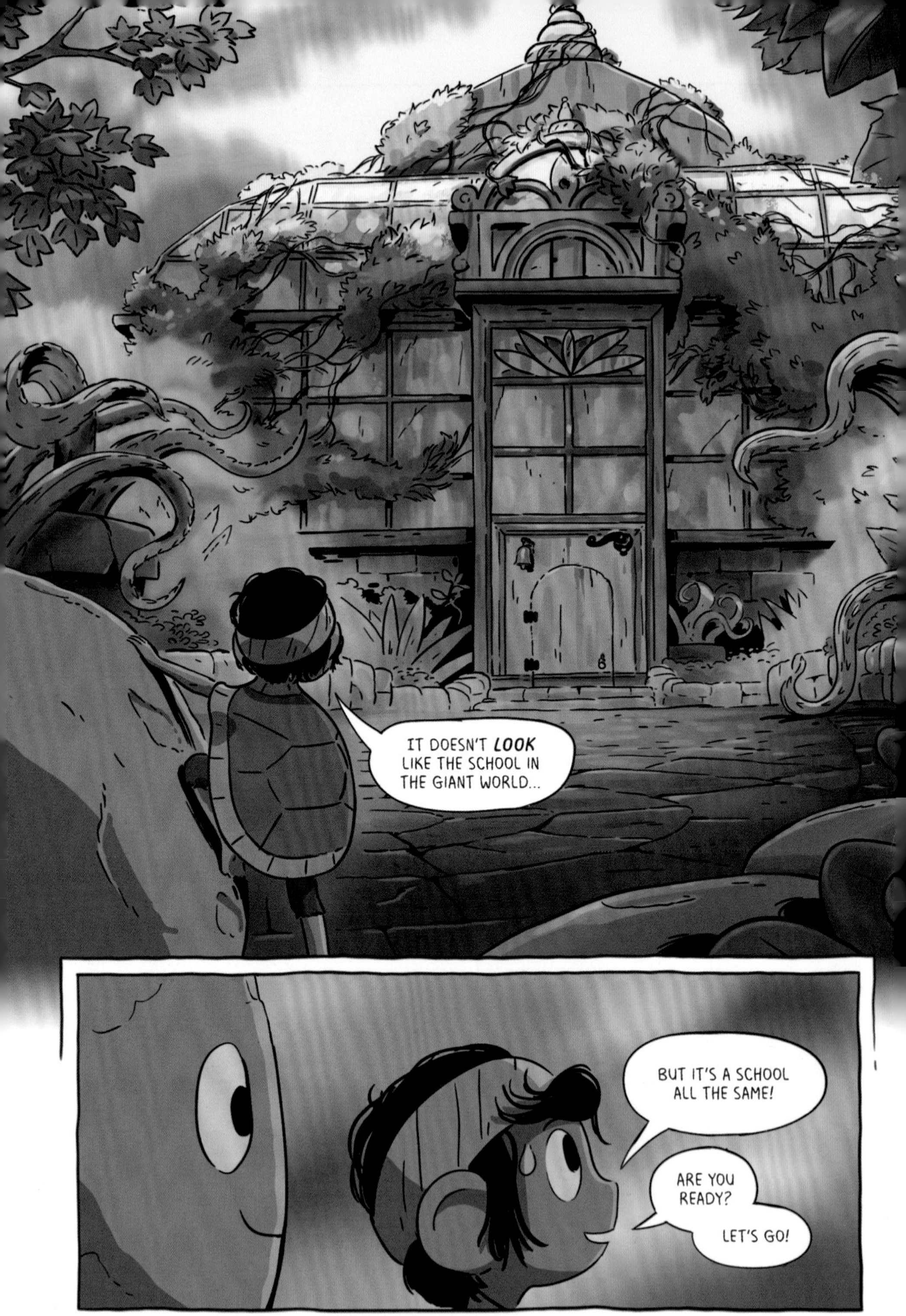
IT DOESN'T **LOOK** LIKE THE SCHOOL IN THE GIANT WORLD...
BUT IT'S A SCHOOL ALL THE SAME!
ARE YOU READY?
LET'S GO!

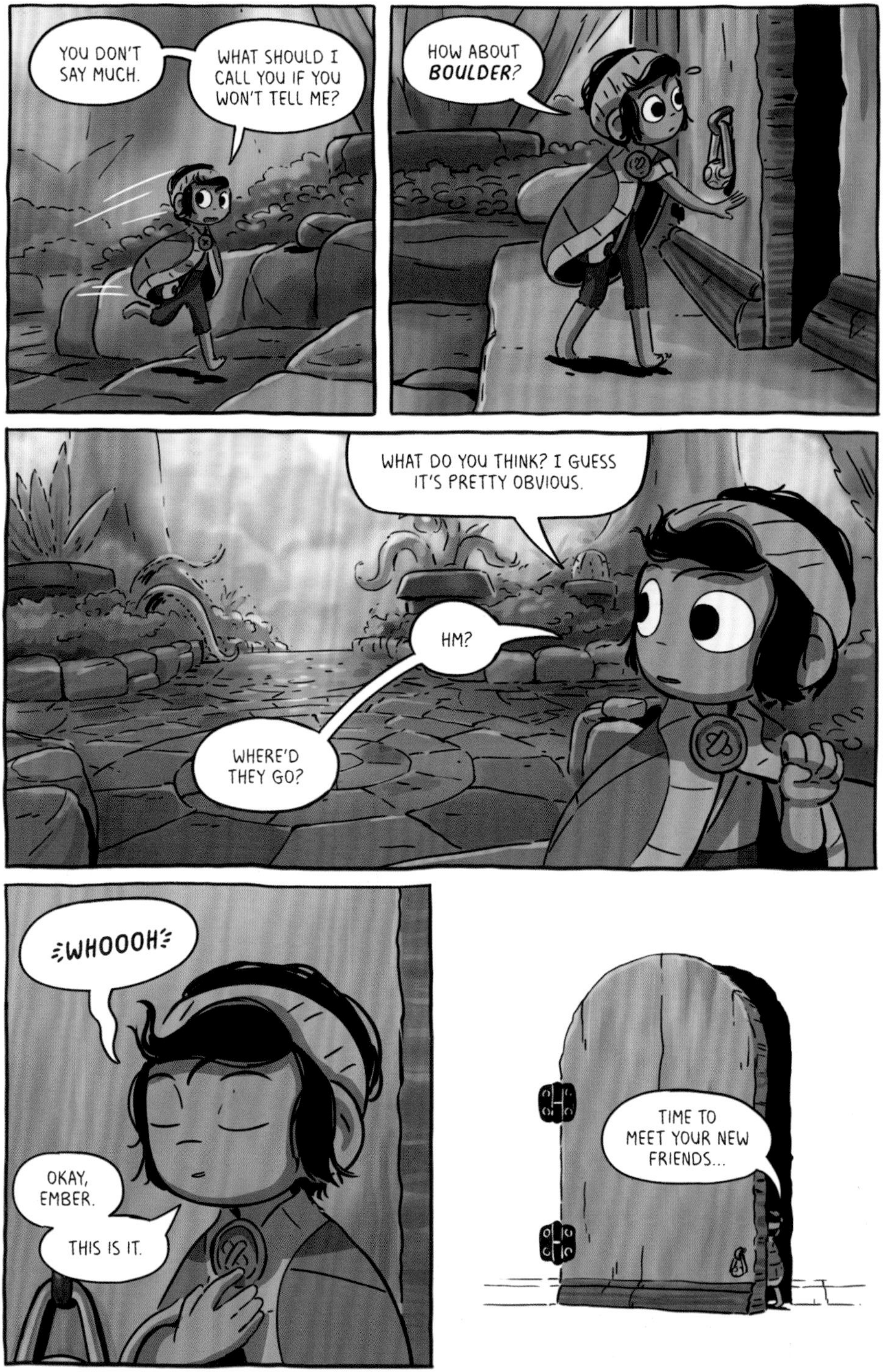
YOU DON'T SAY MUCH.
WHAT SHOULD I CALL YOU IF YOU WON'T TELL ME?
HOW ABOUT **BOULDER**?
WHAT DO YOU THINK? I GUESS IT'S PRETTY OBVIOUS.
HM?
WHERE'D THEY GO?
WHOOOH
OKAY, EMBER.
THIS IS IT.
TIME TO MEET YOUR NEW FRIENDS...

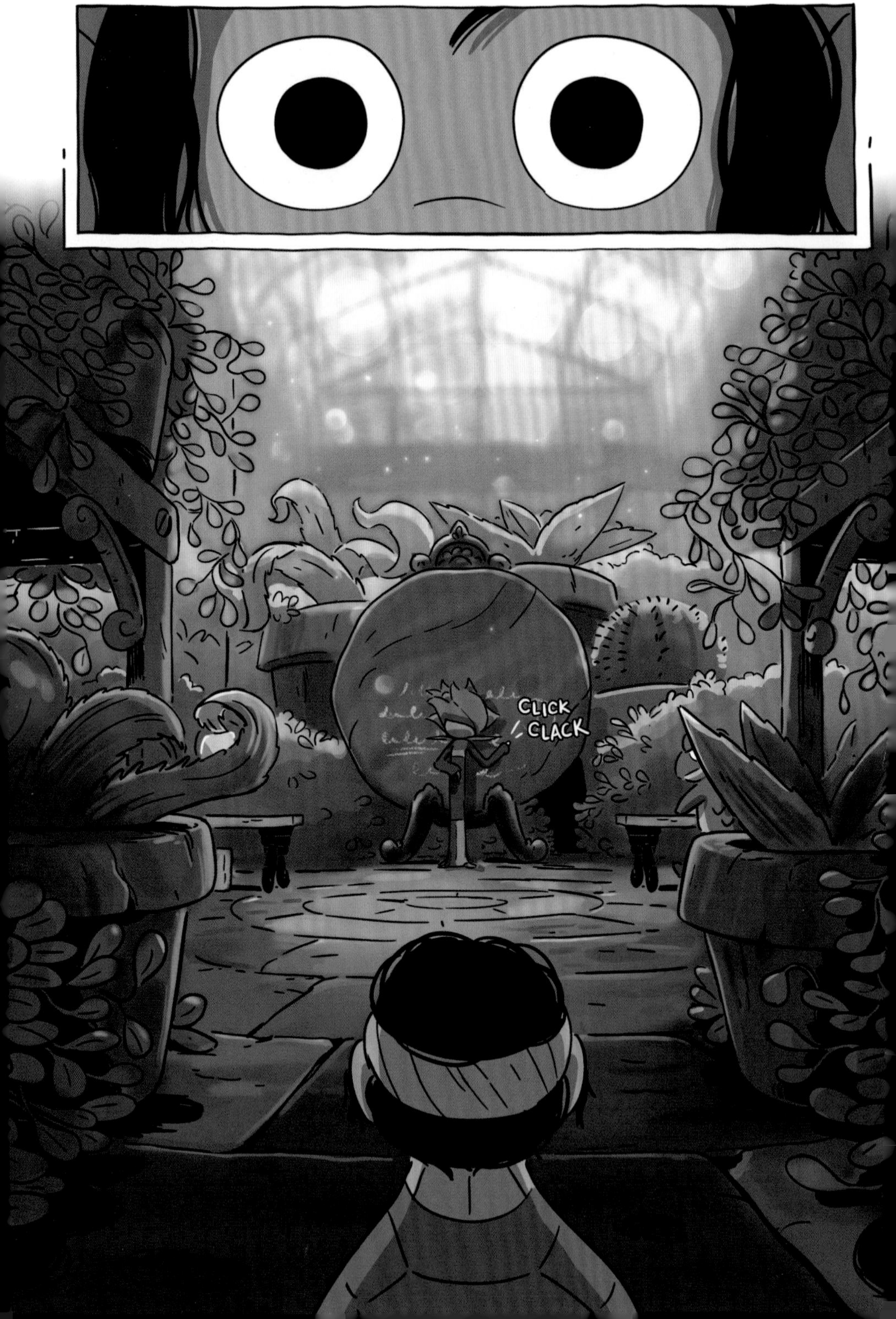
CLICK
CLACK

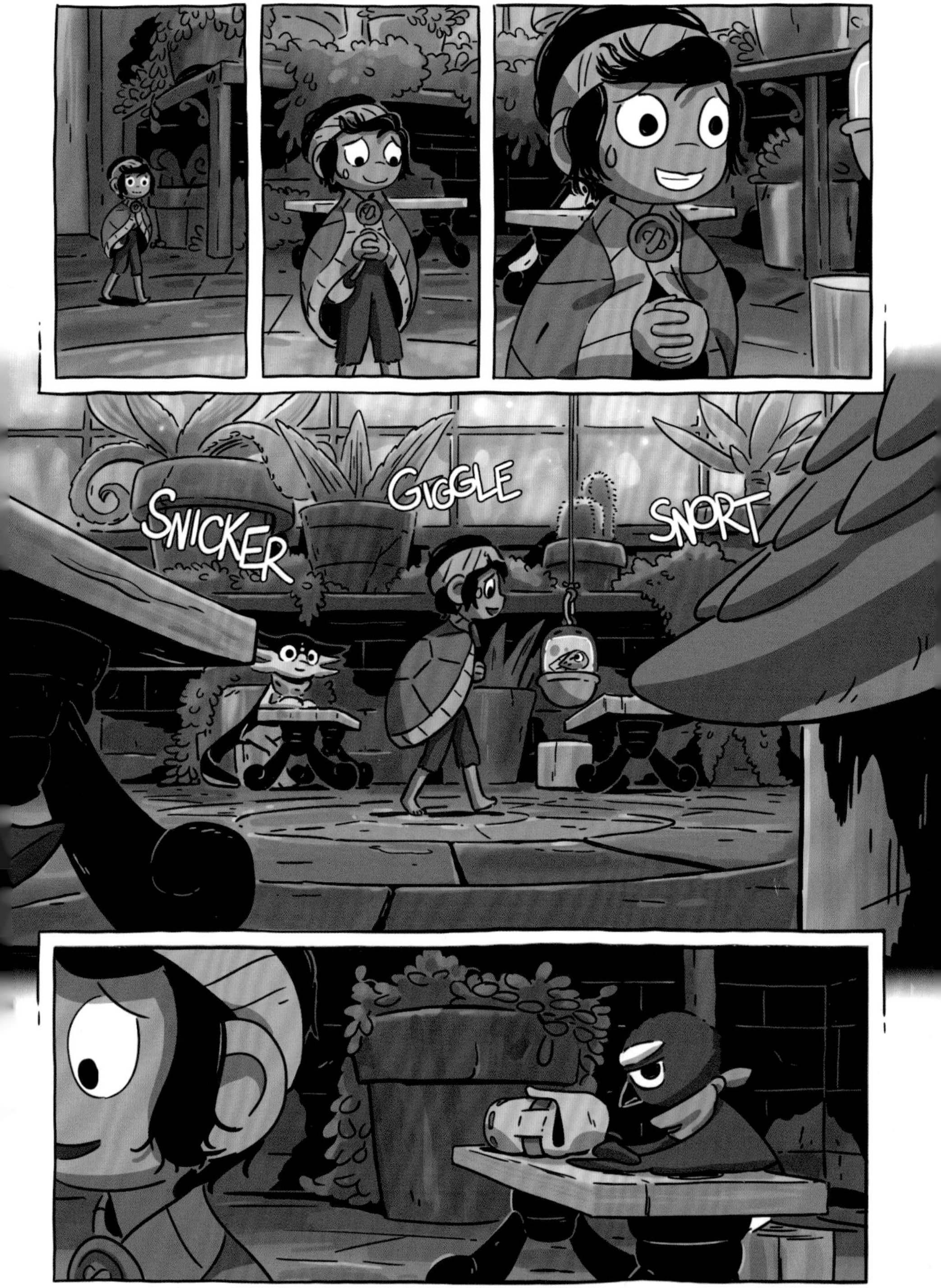
SNICKER
GIGGLE
SNORT

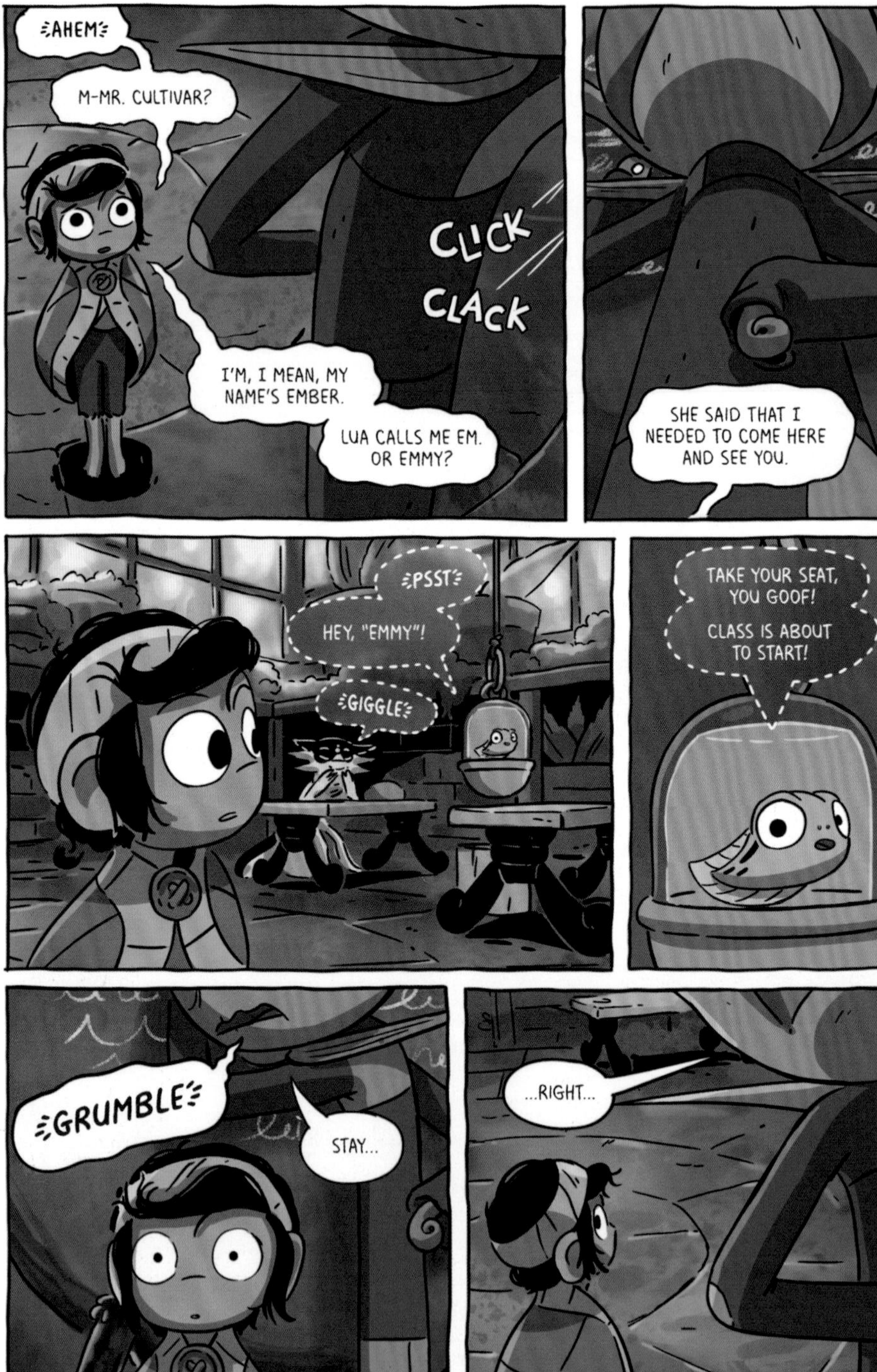
AHEM
M-MR. CULTIVAR?
I'M, I MEAN, MY NAME'S EMBER.
LUA CALLS ME EM. OR EMMY?
CLICK
CLACK
SHE SAID THAT I NEEDED TO COME HERE AND SEE YOU.
PSST
HEY, "EMMY"!
GIGGLE
TAKE YOUR SEAT, YOU GOOF!
CLASS IS ABOUT TO START!
GRUMBLE
STAY...
...RIGHT...

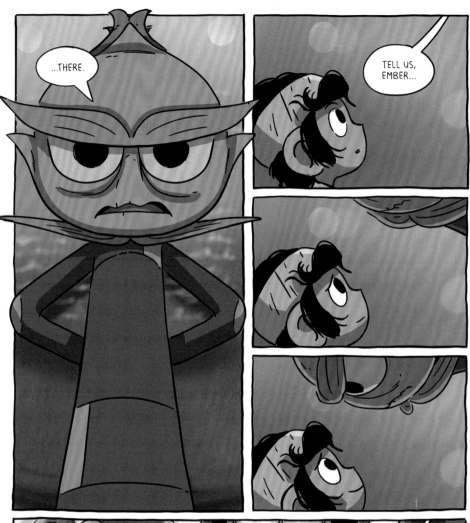

...THERE.

TELL US, EMBER...

WHICH **CRAB** HAS EIGHT **ARMS**, TWO **WINGS**...

...AND A **BEAK?**

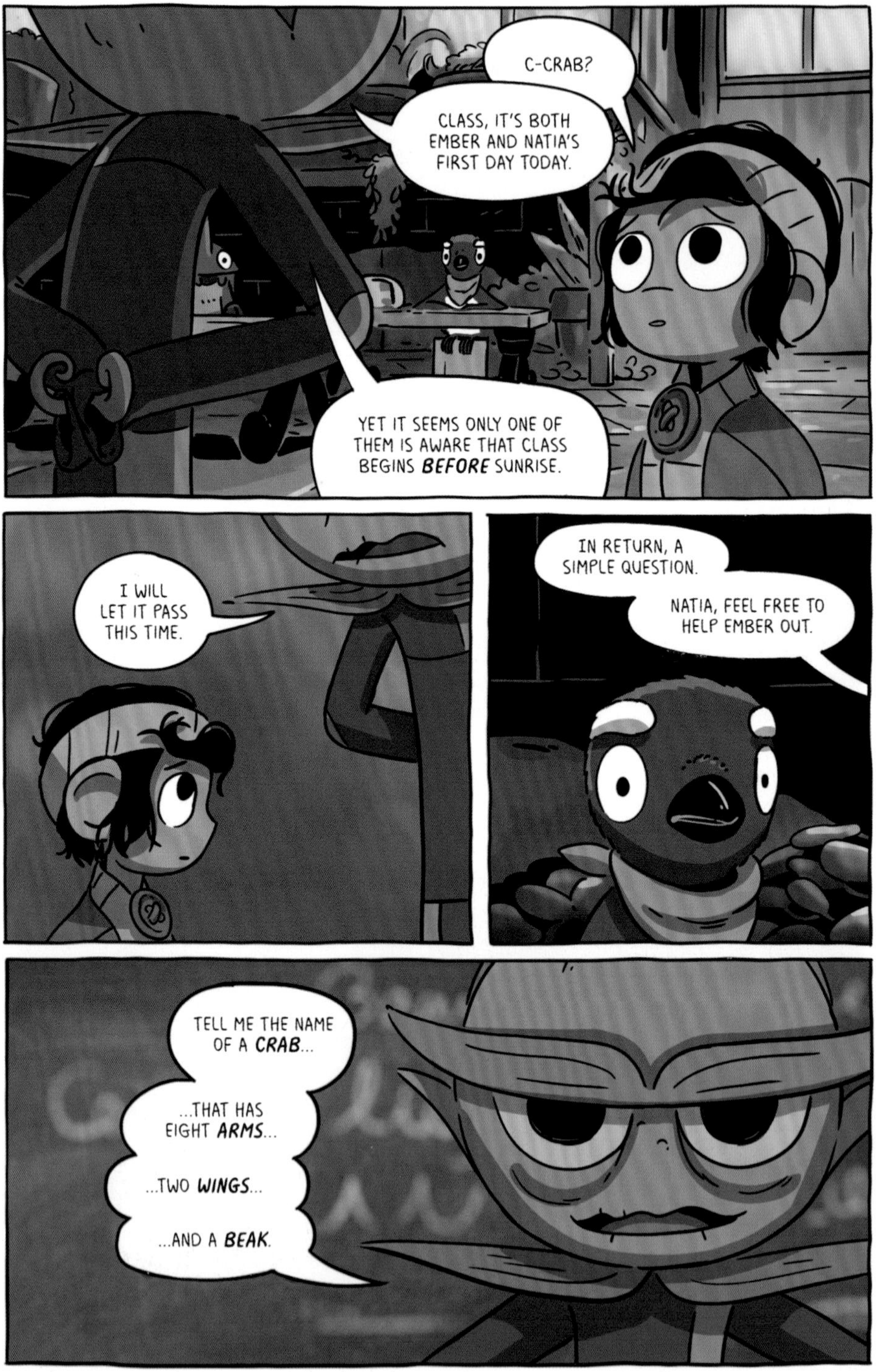
C-CRAB?
CLASS, IT'S BOTH EMBER AND NATIA'S FIRST DAY TODAY.
YET IT SEEMS ONLY ONE OF THEM IS AWARE THAT CLASS BEGINS **BEFORE** SUNRISE.
I WILL LET IT PASS THIS TIME.
IN RETURN, A SIMPLE QUESTION.
NATIA, FEEL FREE TO HELP EMBER OUT.
TELL ME THE NAME OF A **CRAB**...
...THAT HAS EIGHT **ARMS**...
...TWO **WINGS**...
...AND A **BEAK**.

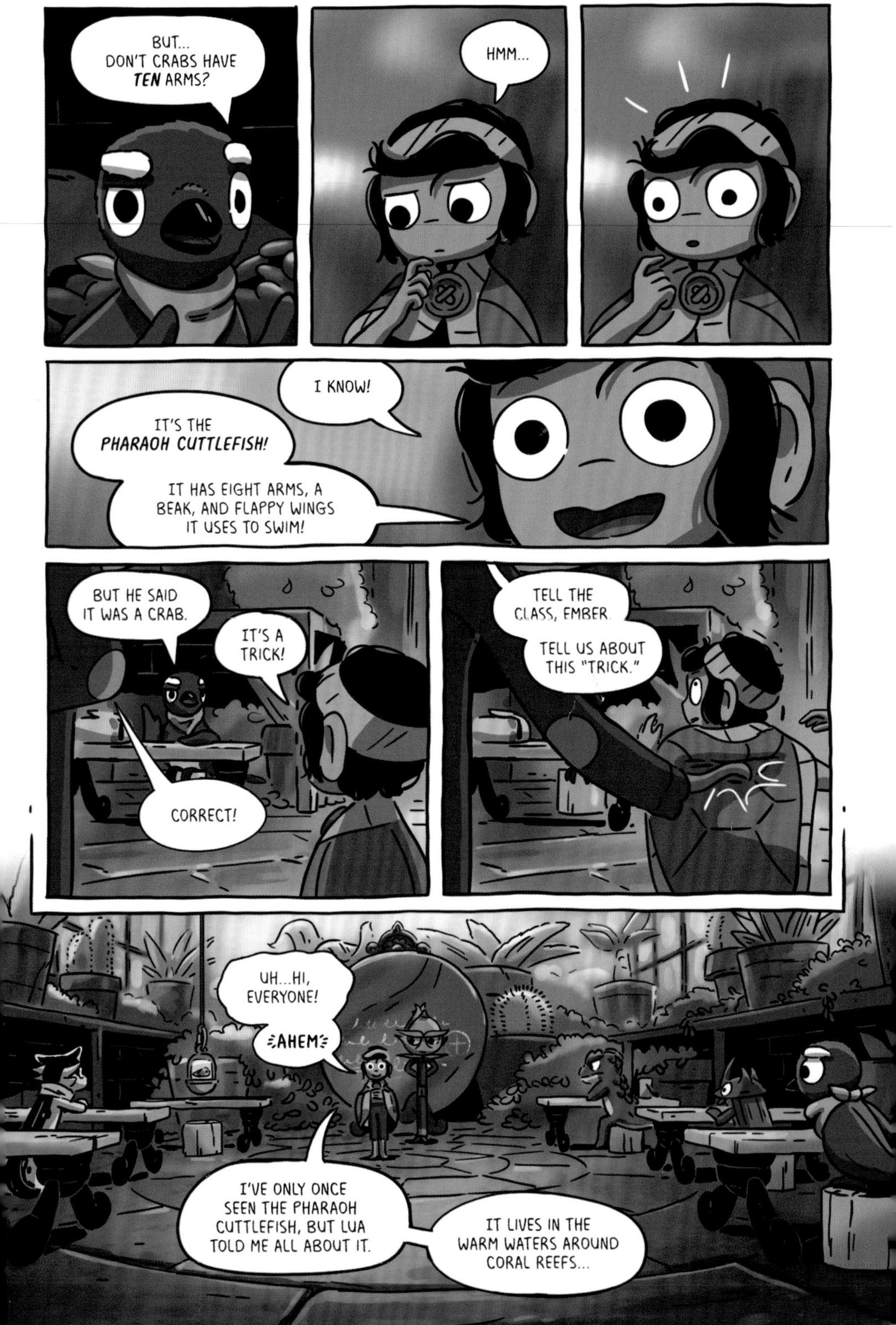

BUT... DON'T CRABS HAVE **TEN** ARMS?
HMM...
I KNOW!
IT'S THE **PHARAOH CUTTLEFISH!**
IT HAS EIGHT ARMS, A BEAK, AND FLAPPY WINGS IT USES TO SWIM!
BUT HE SAID IT WAS A CRAB.
IT'S A TRICK!
CORRECT!
TELL THE CLASS, EMBER.
TELL US ABOUT THIS "TRICK."
UH...HI, EVERYONE!
AHEM
I'VE ONLY ONCE SEEN THE PHARAOH CUTTLEFISH, BUT LUA TOLD ME ALL ABOUT IT.
IT LIVES IN THE WARM WATERS AROUND CORAL REEFS...

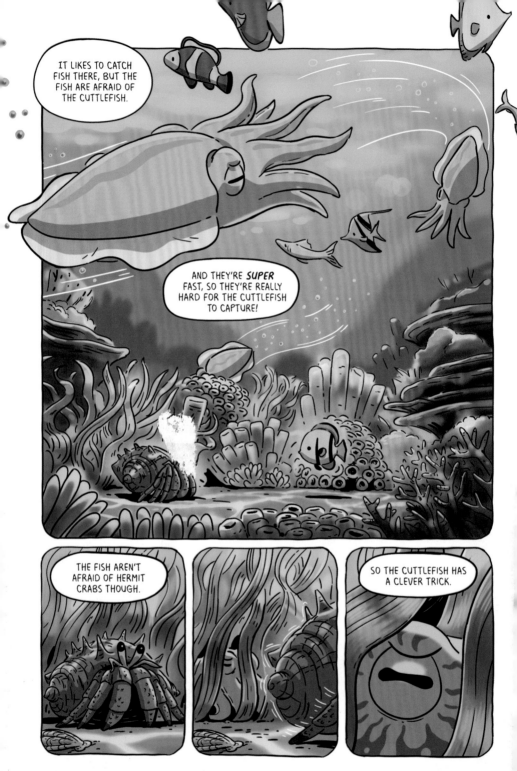

IT LIKES TO CATCH FISH THERE, BUT THE FISH ARE AFRAID OF THE CUTTLEFISH.

AND THEY'RE *SUPER* FAST, SO THEY'RE REALLY HARD FOR THE CUTTLEFISH TO CAPTURE!

THE FISH AREN'T AFRAID OF HERMIT CRABS THOUGH.

SO THE CUTTLEFISH HAS A CLEVER TRICK.

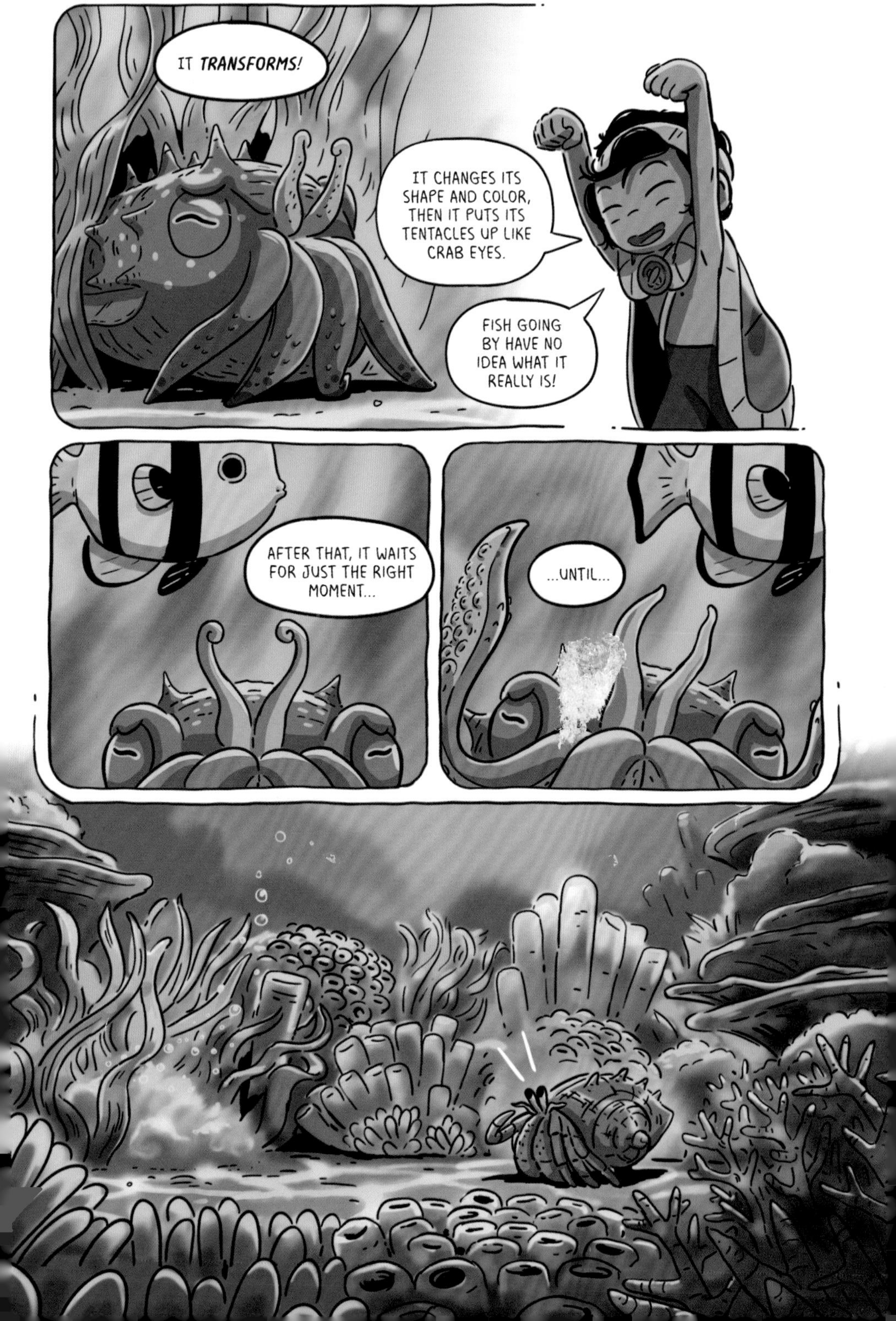
IT *TRANSFORMS!*
IT CHANGES ITS SHAPE AND COLOR, THEN IT PUTS ITS TENTACLES UP LIKE CRAB EYES.
FISH GOING BY HAVE NO IDEA WHAT IT REALLY IS!
AFTER THAT, IT WAITS FOR JUST THE RIGHT MOMENT...
...UNTIL...

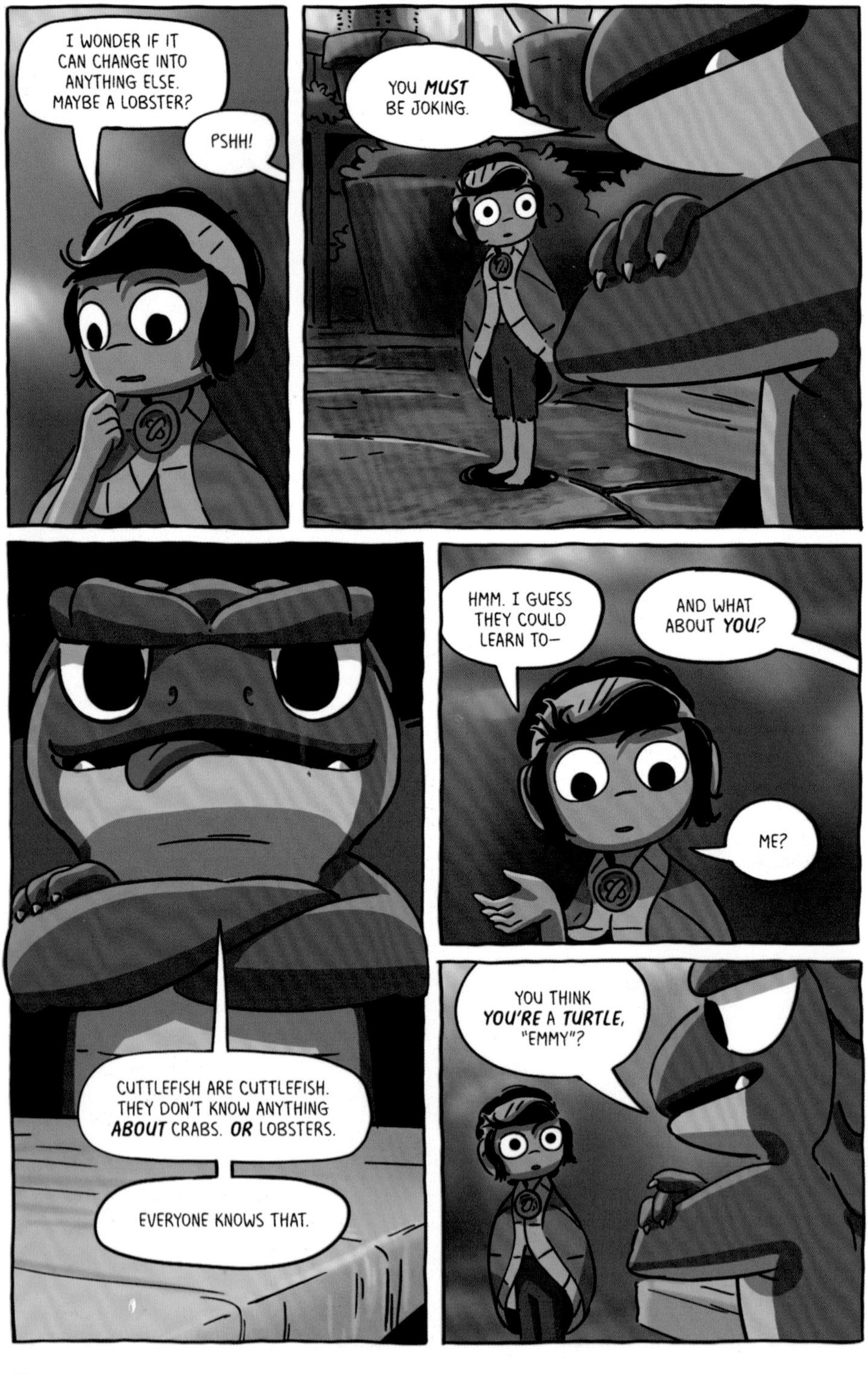
I WONDER IF IT CAN CHANGE INTO ANYTHING ELSE. MAYBE A LOBSTER?
PSHH!
YOU **MUST** BE JOKING.
CUTTLEFISH ARE CUTTLEFISH. THEY DON'T KNOW ANYTHING **ABOUT** CRABS. **OR** LOBSTERS.
EVERYONE KNOWS THAT.
HMM. I GUESS THEY COULD LEARN TO—
AND WHAT ABOUT **YOU?**
ME?
YOU THINK **YOU'RE** A **TURTLE,** "EMMY"?

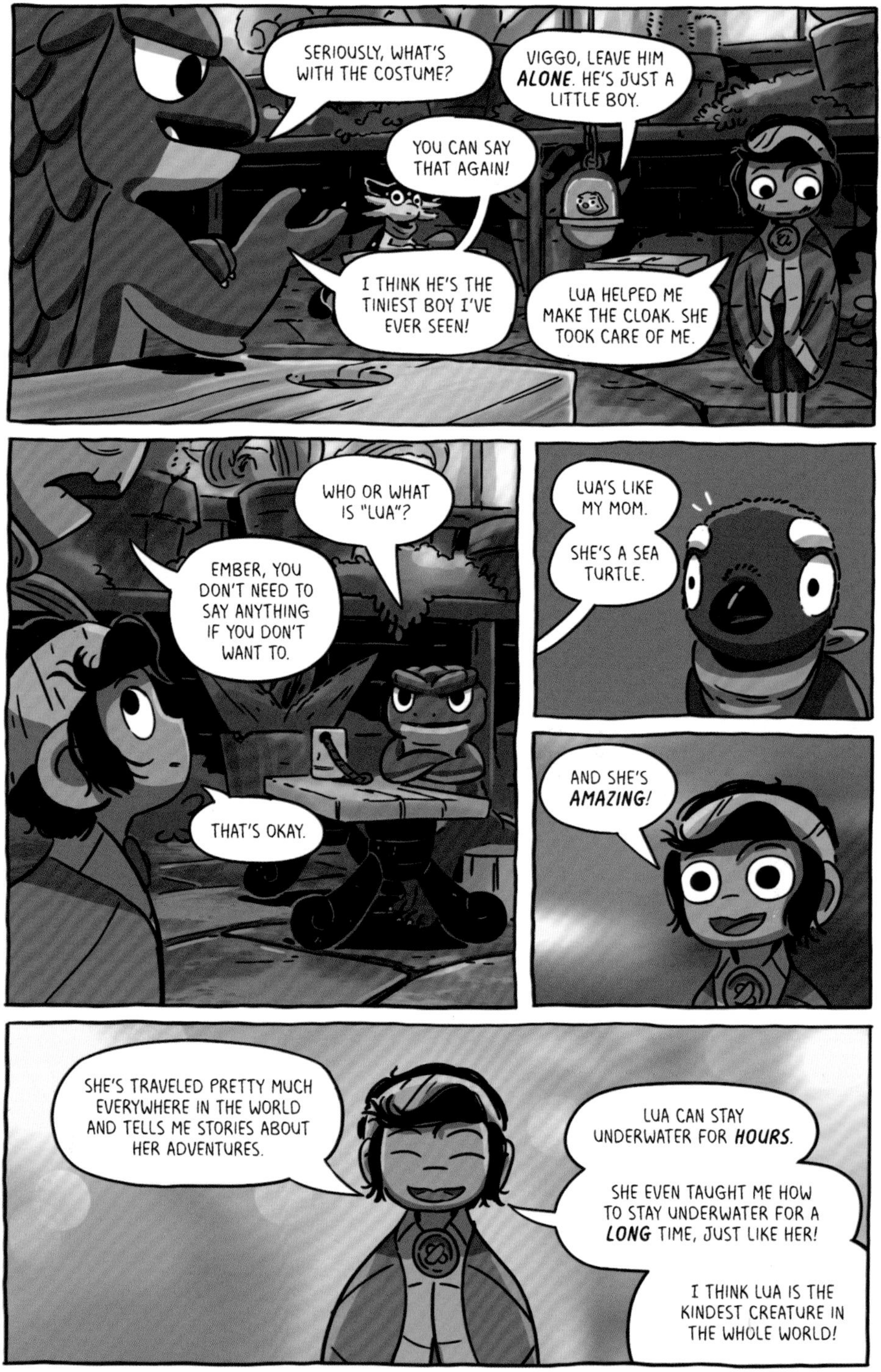
SERIOUSLY, WHAT'S WITH THE COSTUME?
VIGGO, LEAVE HIM ALONE. HE'S JUST A LITTLE BOY.
YOU CAN SAY THAT AGAIN!
I THINK HE'S THE TINIEST BOY I'VE EVER SEEN!
LUA HELPED ME MAKE THE CLOAK. SHE TOOK CARE OF ME.
WHO OR WHAT IS "LUA"?
EMBER, YOU DON'T NEED TO SAY ANYTHING IF YOU DON'T WANT TO.
THAT'S OKAY.
LUA'S LIKE MY MOM.
SHE'S A SEA TURTLE.
AND SHE'S AMAZING!
SHE'S TRAVELED PRETTY MUCH EVERYWHERE IN THE WORLD AND TELLS ME STORIES ABOUT HER ADVENTURES.
LUA CAN STAY UNDERWATER FOR HOURS.
SHE EVEN TAUGHT ME HOW TO STAY UNDERWATER FOR A LONG TIME, JUST LIKE HER!
I THINK LUA IS THE KINDEST CREATURE IN THE WHOLE WORLD!

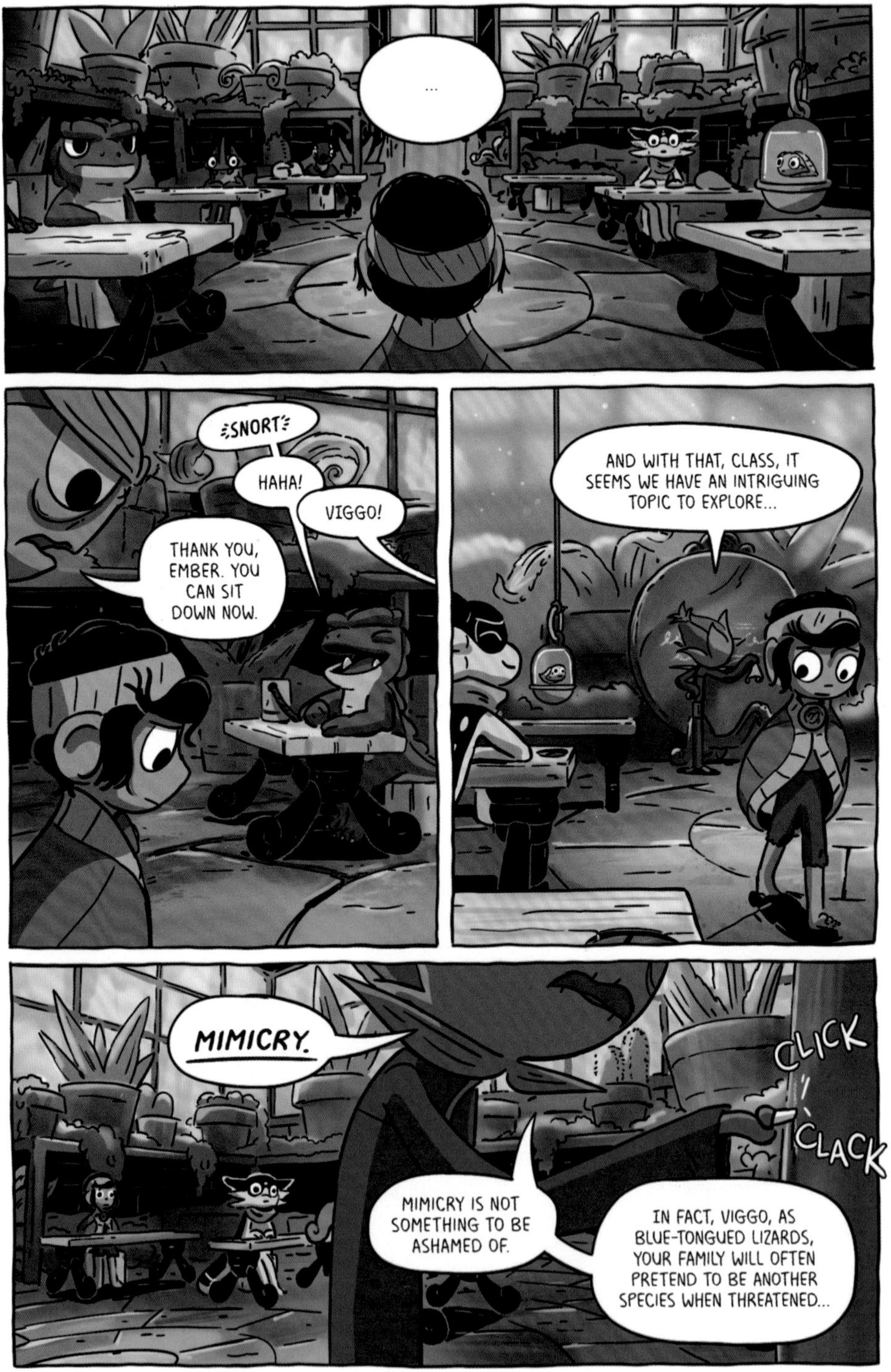
...
SNORT
HAHA!
VIGGO!
THANK YOU, EMBER. YOU CAN SIT DOWN NOW.
AND WITH THAT, CLASS, IT SEEMS WE HAVE AN INTRIGUING TOPIC TO EXPLORE...
MIMICRY.
CLICK
CLACK
MIMICRY IS NOT SOMETHING TO BE ASHAMED OF.
IN FACT, VIGGO, AS BLUE-TONGUED LIZARDS, YOUR FAMILY WILL OFTEN PRETEND TO BE ANOTHER SPECIES WHEN THREATENED...

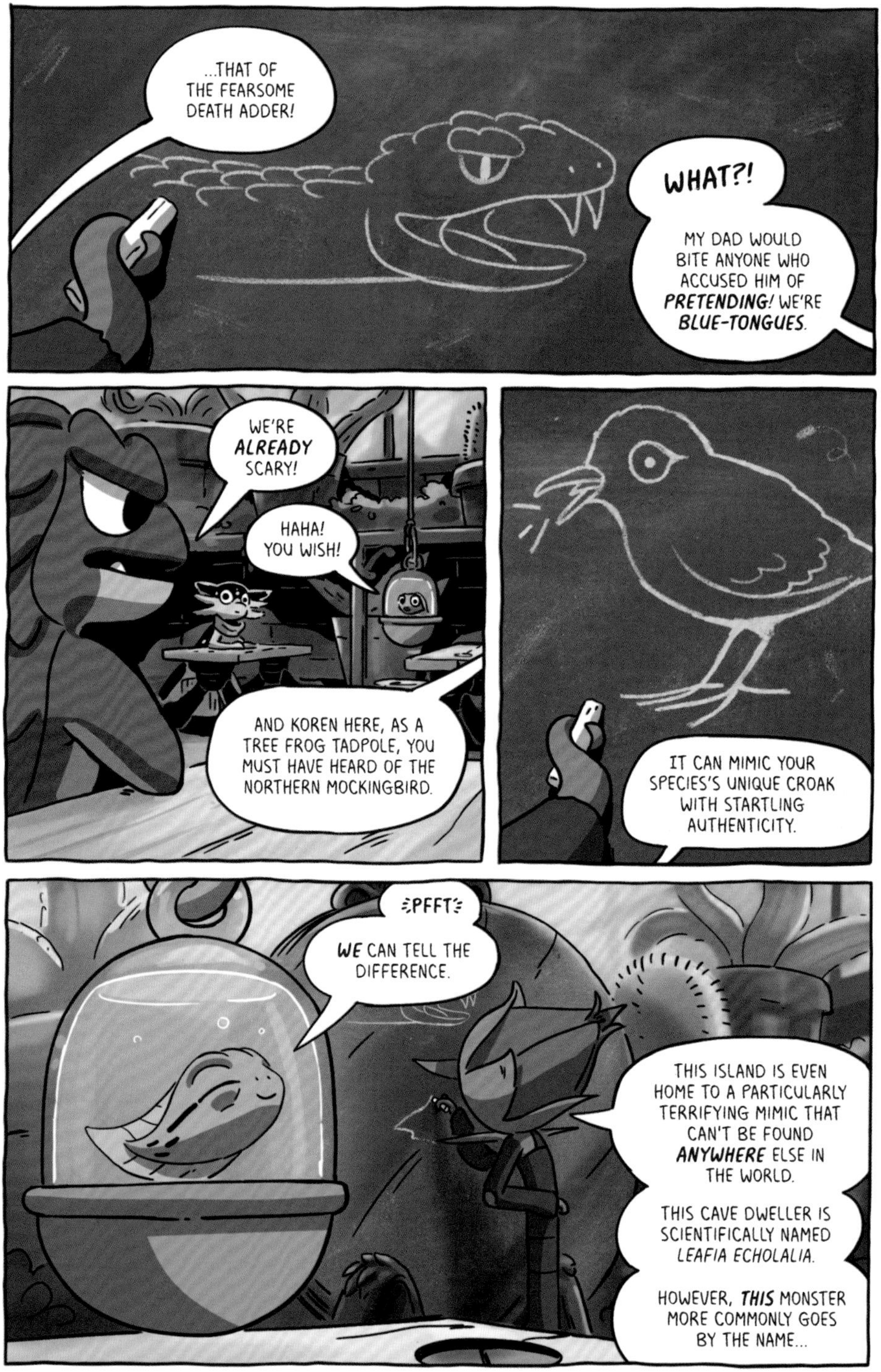
...THAT OF THE FEARSOME DEATH ADDER!
WHAT?!
MY DAD WOULD BITE ANYONE WHO ACCUSED HIM OF ***PRETENDING!*** WE'RE ***BLUE-TONGUES***.
WE'RE ***ALREADY*** SCARY!
HAHA! YOU WISH!
AND KOREN HERE, AS A TREE FROG TADPOLE, YOU MUST HAVE HEARD OF THE NORTHERN MOCKINGBIRD.
IT CAN MIMIC YOUR SPECIES'S UNIQUE CROAK WITH STARTLING AUTHENTICITY.
PFFT
WE CAN TELL THE DIFFERENCE.
THIS ISLAND IS EVEN HOME TO A PARTICULARLY TERRIFYING MIMIC THAT CAN'T BE FOUND ***ANYWHERE*** ELSE IN THE WORLD.
THIS CAVE DWELLER IS SCIENTIFICALLY NAMED *LEAFIA ECHOLALIA*.
HOWEVER, ***THIS*** MONSTER MORE COMMONLY GOES BY THE NAME...

...*SKIPLET*.

IT LIVES IN A PARTICULAR CAVERN IN THE SPINY CAVES, WHICH ARE NOT TOO FAR FROM HERE.

LIKE THE NORTHERN MOCKINGBIRD, THIS TERRIFYING CREATURE CAN MIMIC SOUND.

SO? IT DOESN'T LOOK VERY SCARY.

IT MAY BE TINY IN STATURE, VIGGO.

GRRRR

HOWEVER, WHEN THREATENED...

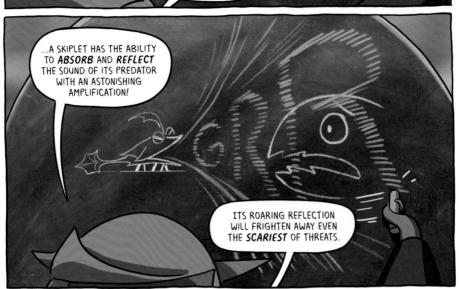

...A SKIPLET HAS THE ABILITY TO *ABSORB* AND *REFLECT* THE SOUND OF ITS PREDATOR WITH AN ASTONISHING AMPLIFICATION!

ITS ROARING REFLECTION WILL FRIGHTEN AWAY EVEN THE *SCARIEST* OF THREATS.

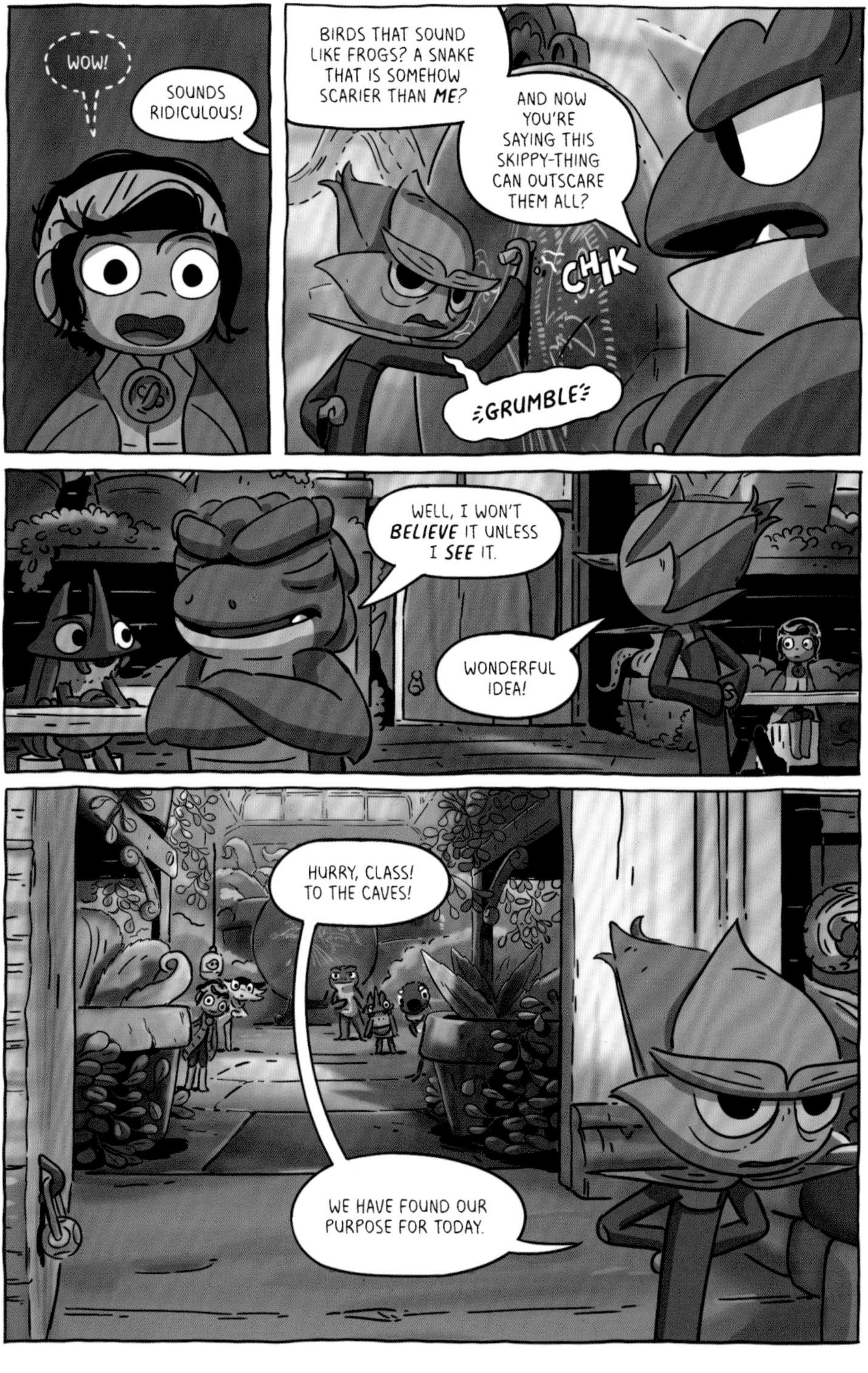
WOW!
SOUNDS RIDICULOUS!
BIRDS THAT SOUND LIKE FROGS? A SNAKE THAT IS SOMEHOW SCARIER THAN ME?
AND NOW YOU'RE SAYING THIS SKIPPY-THING CAN OUTSCARE THEM ALL?
CHIK
GRUMBLE
WELL, I WON'T BELIEVE IT UNLESS I SEE IT.
WONDERFUL IDEA!
HURRY, CLASS! TO THE CAVES!
WE HAVE FOUND OUR PURPOSE FOR TODAY.

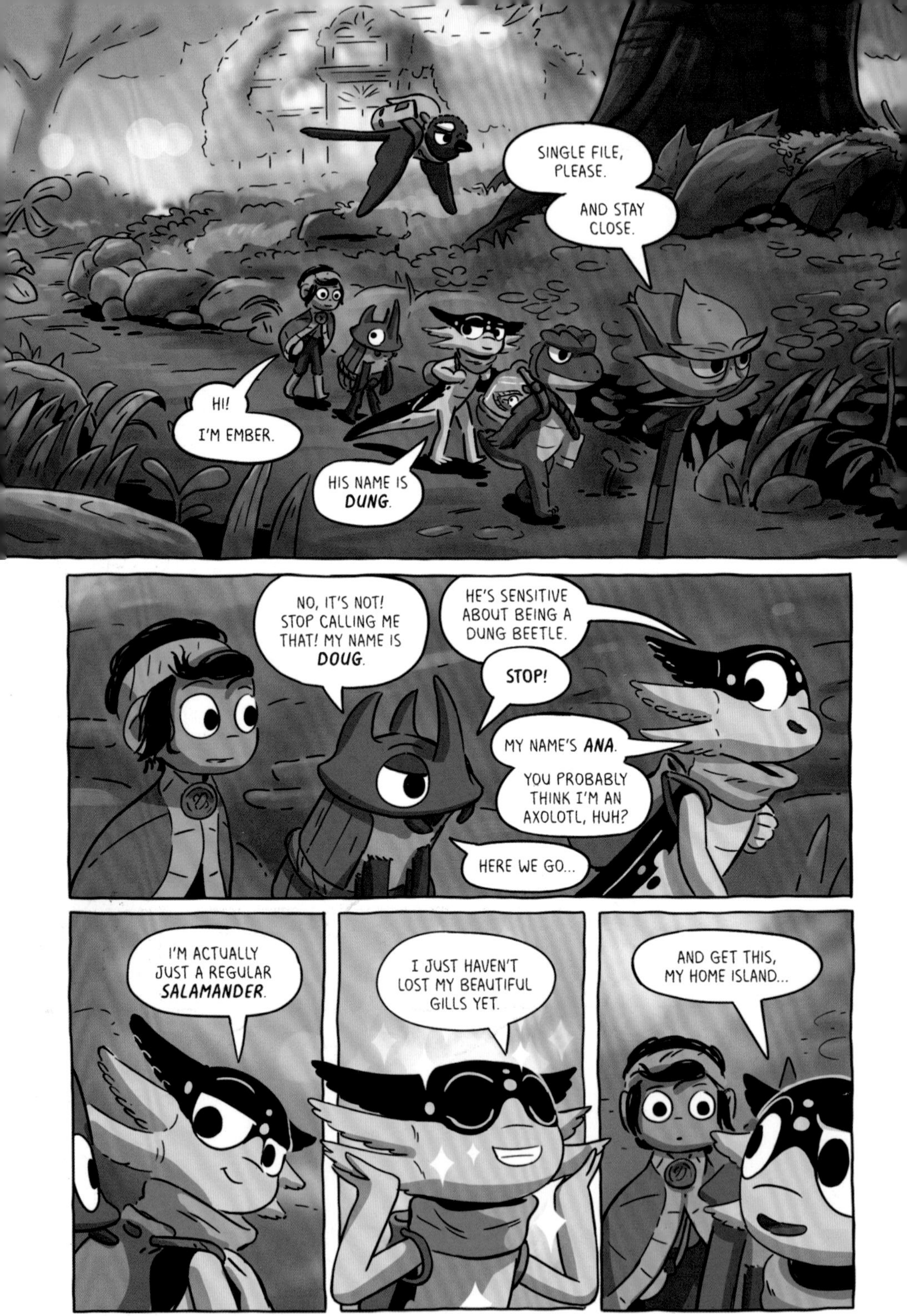
SINGLE FILE, PLEASE.
AND STAY CLOSE.
HI!
I'M EMBER.
HIS NAME IS **DUNG**.
NO, IT'S NOT! STOP CALLING ME THAT! MY NAME IS **DOUG**.
HE'S SENSITIVE ABOUT BEING A DUNG BEETLE.
STOP!
MY NAME'S **ANA**.
YOU PROBABLY THINK I'M AN AXOLOTL, HUH?
HERE WE GO...
I'M ACTUALLY JUST A REGULAR **SALAMANDER**.
I JUST HAVEN'T LOST MY BEAUTIFUL GILLS YET.
AND GET THIS, MY HOME ISLAND...

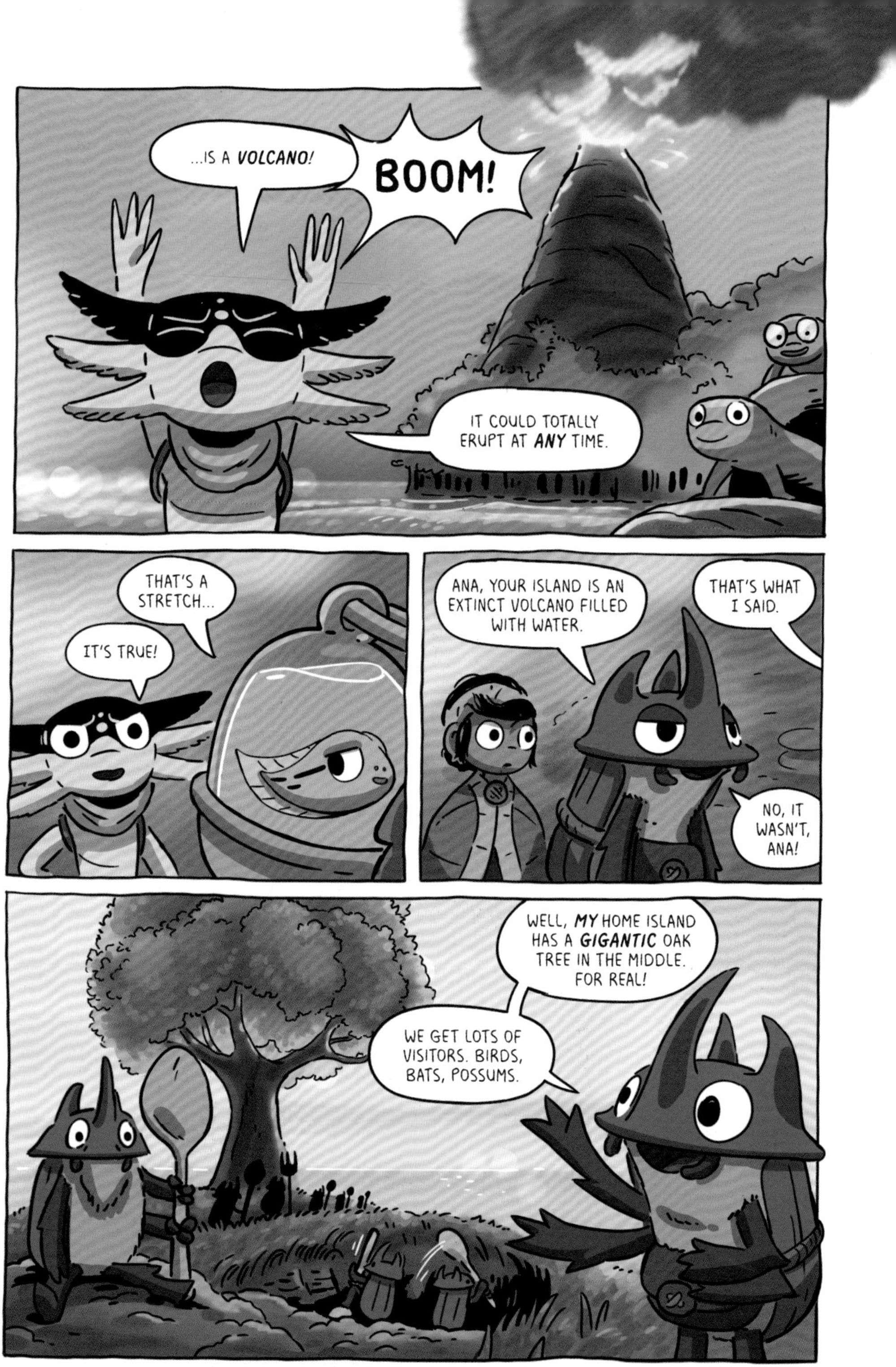
...IS A *VOLCANO!*
BOOM!
IT COULD TOTALLY ERUPT AT *ANY* TIME.
THAT'S A STRETCH...
IT'S TRUE!
ANA, YOUR ISLAND IS AN EXTINCT VOLCANO FILLED WITH WATER.
THAT'S WHAT I SAID.
NO, IT WASN'T, ANA!
WELL, *MY* HOME ISLAND HAS A *GIGANTIC* OAK TREE IN THE MIDDLE. FOR REAL!
WE GET LOTS OF VISITORS. BIRDS, BATS, POSSUMS.

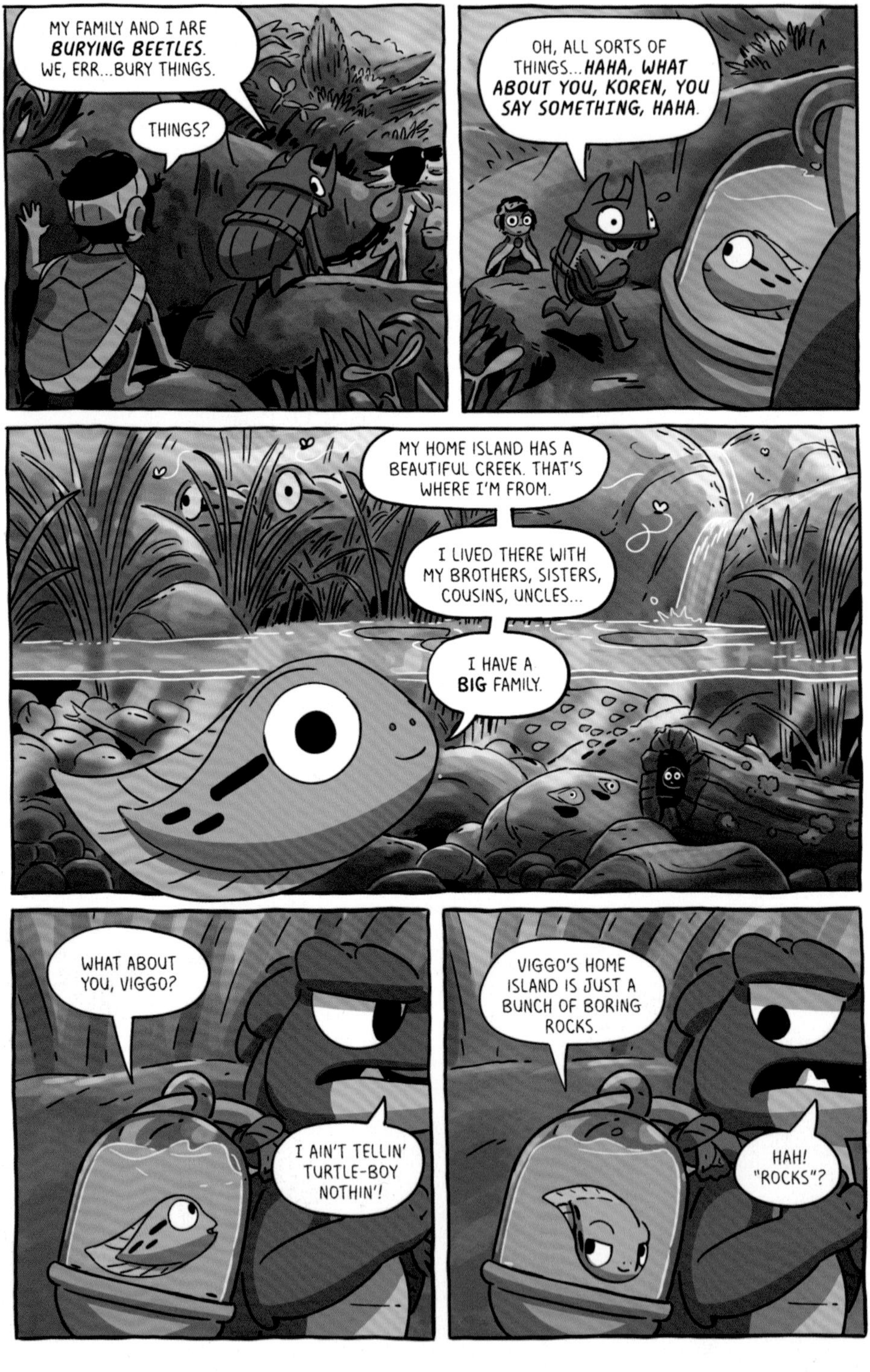
MY FAMILY AND I ARE **BURYING BEETLES**. WE, ERR...BURY THINGS.
THINGS?
OH, ALL SORTS OF THINGS... **HAHA, WHAT ABOUT YOU, KOREN, YOU SAY SOMETHING, HAHA**.
MY HOME ISLAND HAS A BEAUTIFUL CREEK. THAT'S WHERE I'M FROM.
I LIVED THERE WITH MY BROTHERS, SISTERS, COUSINS, UNCLES...
I HAVE A **BIG** FAMILY.
WHAT ABOUT YOU, VIGGO?
I AIN'T TELLIN' TURTLE-BOY NOTHIN'!
VIGGO'S HOME ISLAND IS JUST A BUNCH OF BORING ROCKS.
HAH! "ROCKS"?

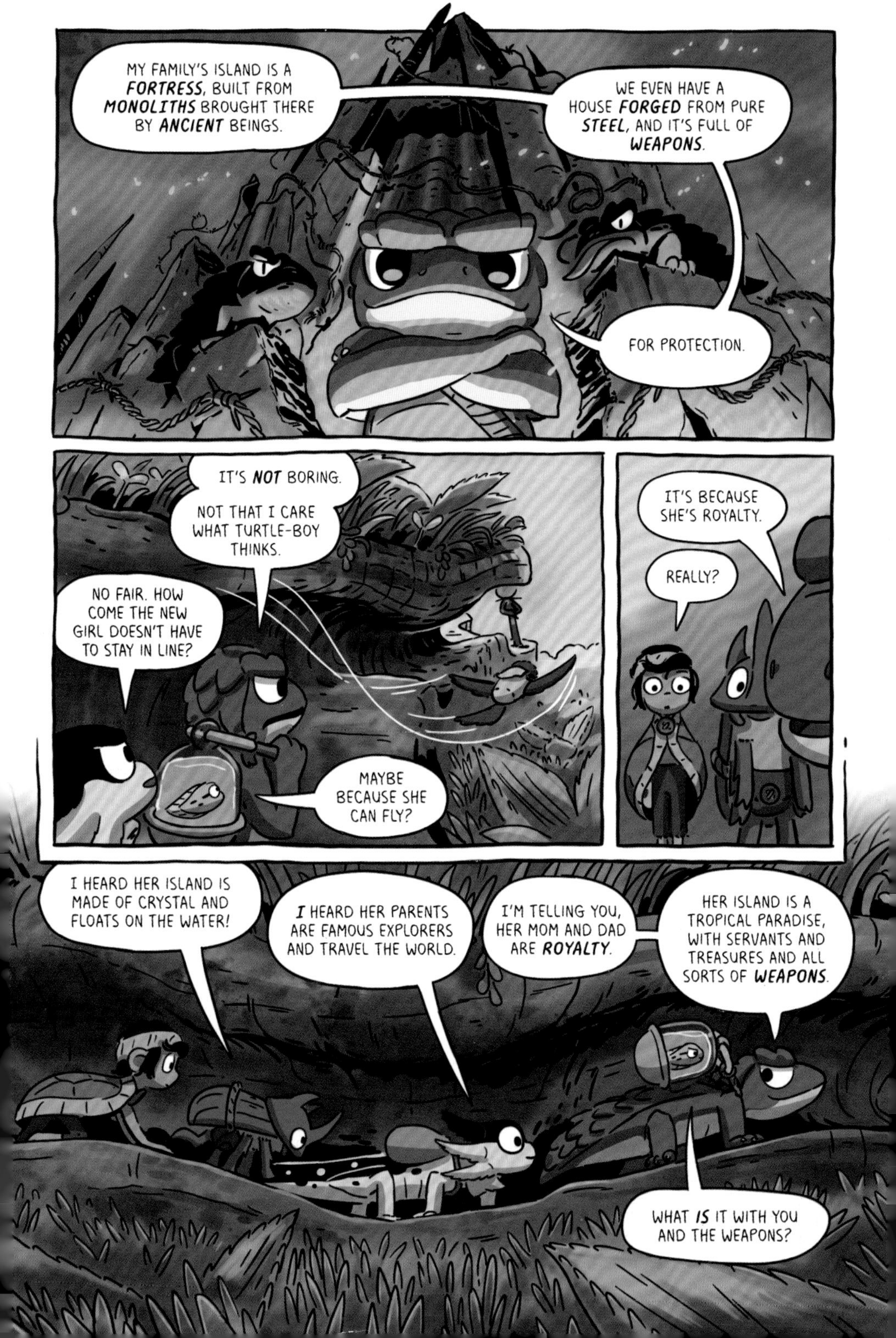
MY FAMILY'S ISLAND IS A FORTRESS, BUILT FROM MONOLITHS BROUGHT THERE BY ANCIENT BEINGS.
WE EVEN HAVE A HOUSE FORGED FROM PURE STEEL, AND IT'S FULL OF WEAPONS.
FOR PROTECTION.
IT'S NOT BORING.
NOT THAT I CARE WHAT TURTLE-BOY THINKS.
NO FAIR. HOW COME THE NEW GIRL DOESN'T HAVE TO STAY IN LINE?
MAYBE BECAUSE SHE CAN FLY?
IT'S BECAUSE SHE'S ROYALTY.
REALLY?
I HEARD HER ISLAND IS MADE OF CRYSTAL AND FLOATS ON THE WATER!
I HEARD HER PARENTS ARE FAMOUS EXPLORERS AND TRAVEL THE WORLD.
I'M TELLING YOU, HER MOM AND DAD ARE ROYALTY.
HER ISLAND IS A TROPICAL PARADISE, WITH SERVANTS AND TREASURES AND ALL SORTS OF WEAPONS.
WHAT IS IT WITH YOU AND THE WEAPONS?

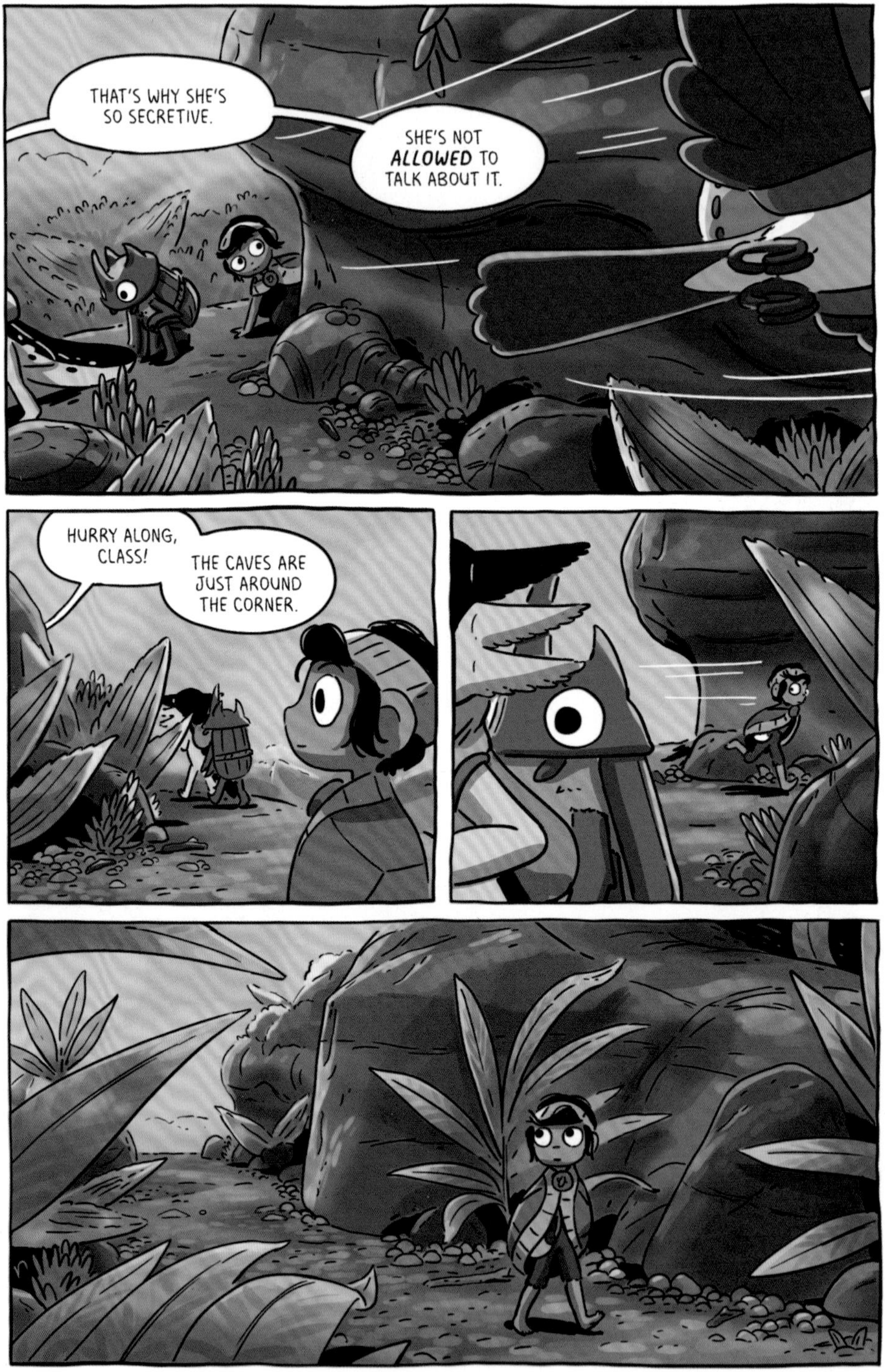
THAT'S WHY SHE'S SO SECRETIVE.
SHE'S NOT **ALLOWED** TO TALK ABOUT IT.
HURRY ALONG, CLASS!
THE CAVES ARE JUST AROUND THE CORNER.

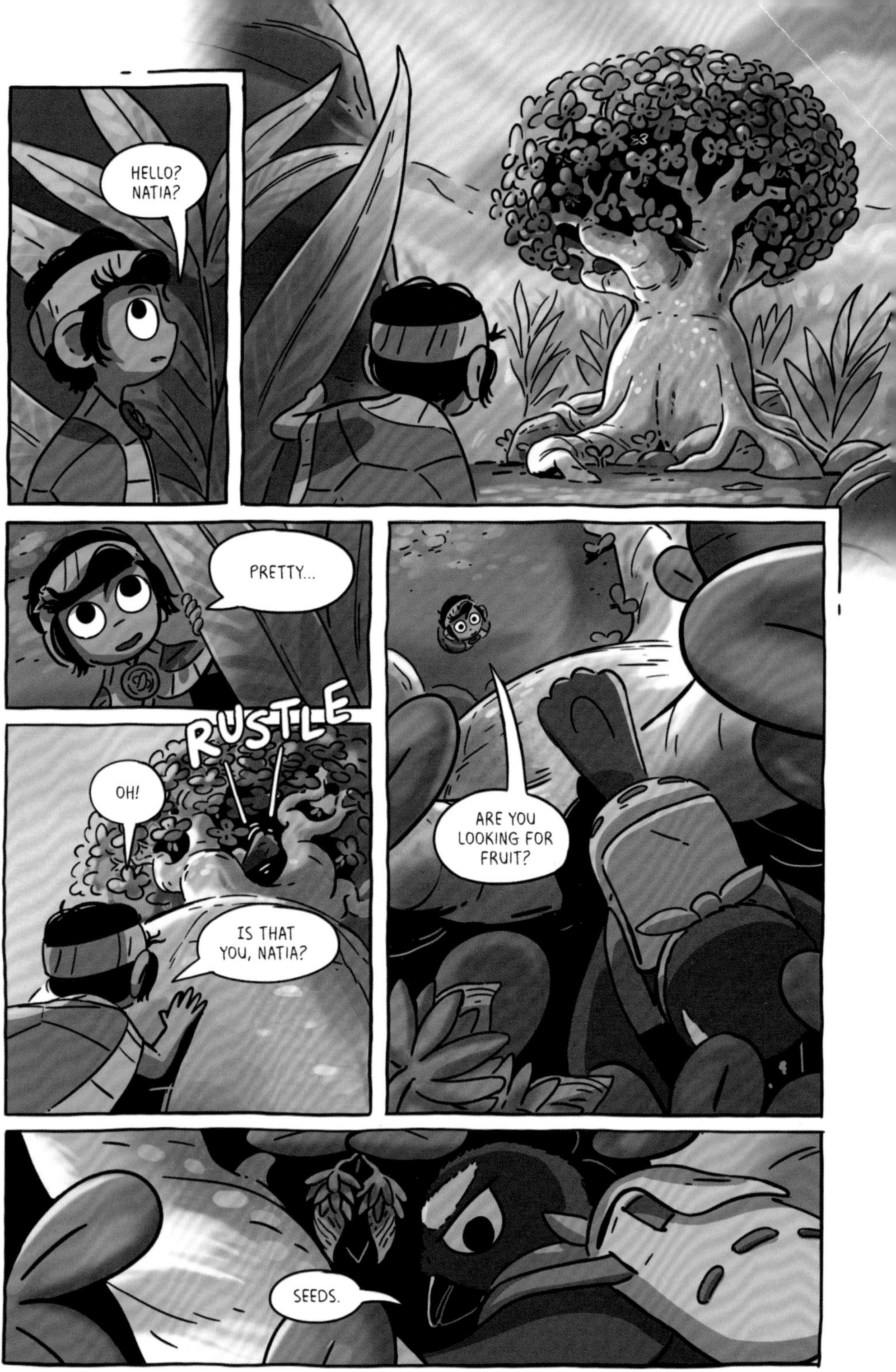
HELLO? NATIA?
PRETTY...
RUSTLE
OH!
IS THAT YOU, NATIA?
ARE YOU LOOKING FOR FRUIT?
SEEDS.

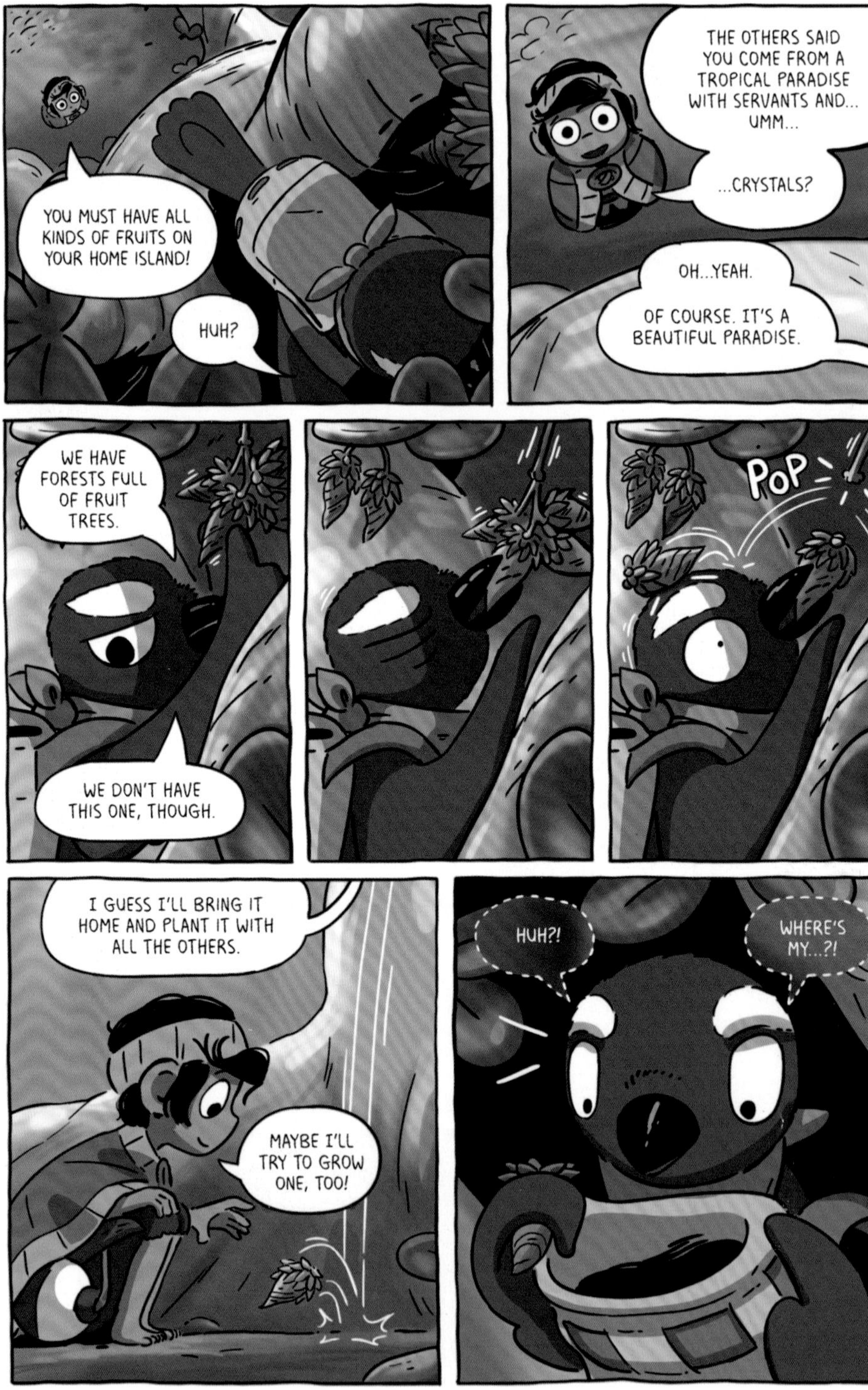
YOU MUST HAVE ALL KINDS OF FRUITS ON YOUR HOME ISLAND!
HUH?
THE OTHERS SAID YOU COME FROM A TROPICAL PARADISE WITH SERVANTS AND... UMM...
...CRYSTALS?
OH...YEAH.
OF COURSE. IT'S A BEAUTIFUL PARADISE.
WE HAVE FORESTS FULL OF FRUIT TREES.
WE DON'T HAVE THIS ONE, THOUGH.
POP
I GUESS I'LL BRING IT HOME AND PLANT IT WITH ALL THE OTHERS.
MAYBE I'LL TRY TO GROW ONE, TOO!
HUH?!
WHERE'S MY...?!

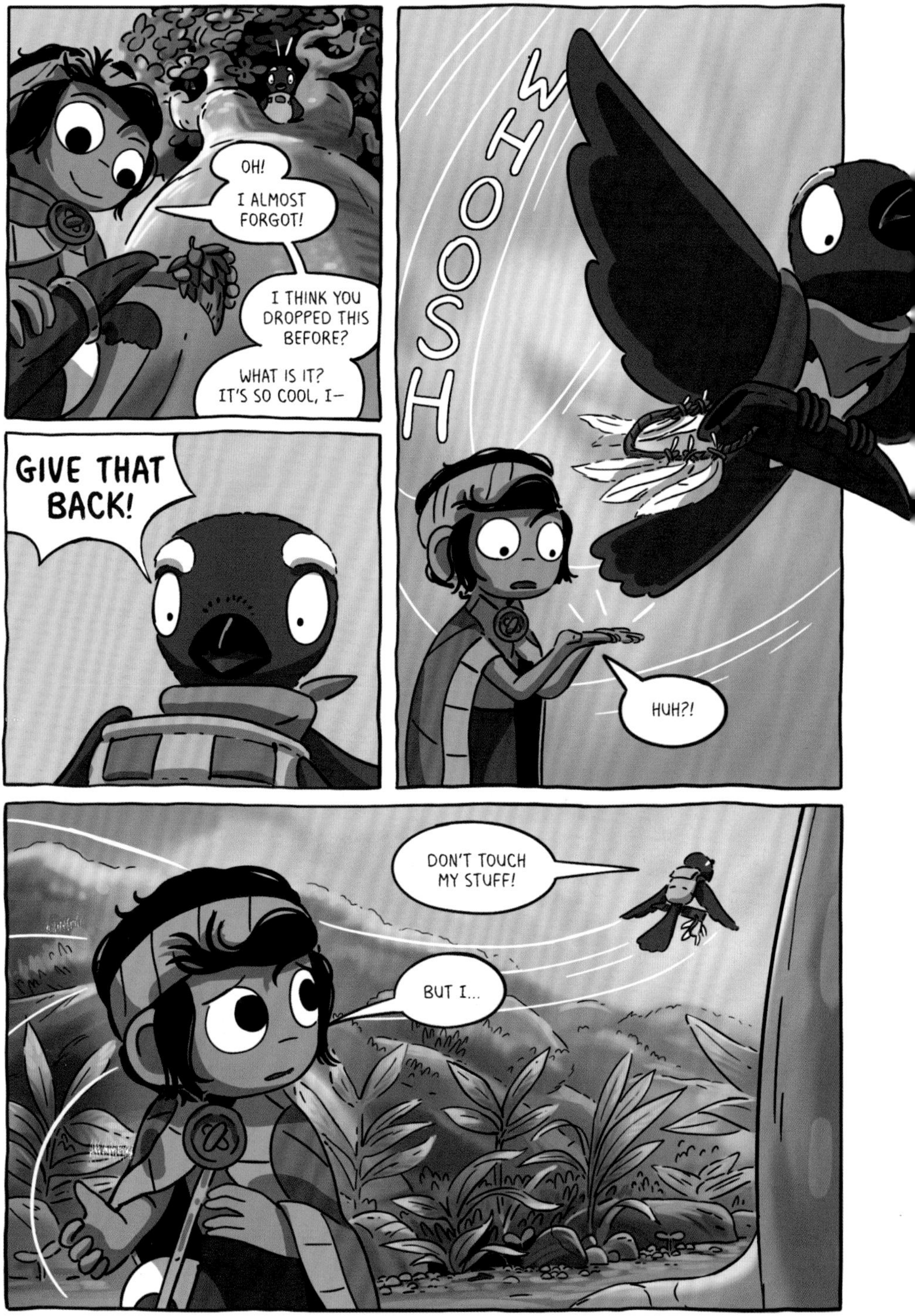
OH!
I ALMOST FORGOT!
I THINK YOU DROPPED THIS BEFORE?
WHAT IS IT? IT'S SO COOL, I—
WHOOSH
GIVE THAT BACK!
HUH?!
DON'T TOUCH MY STUFF!
BUT I...

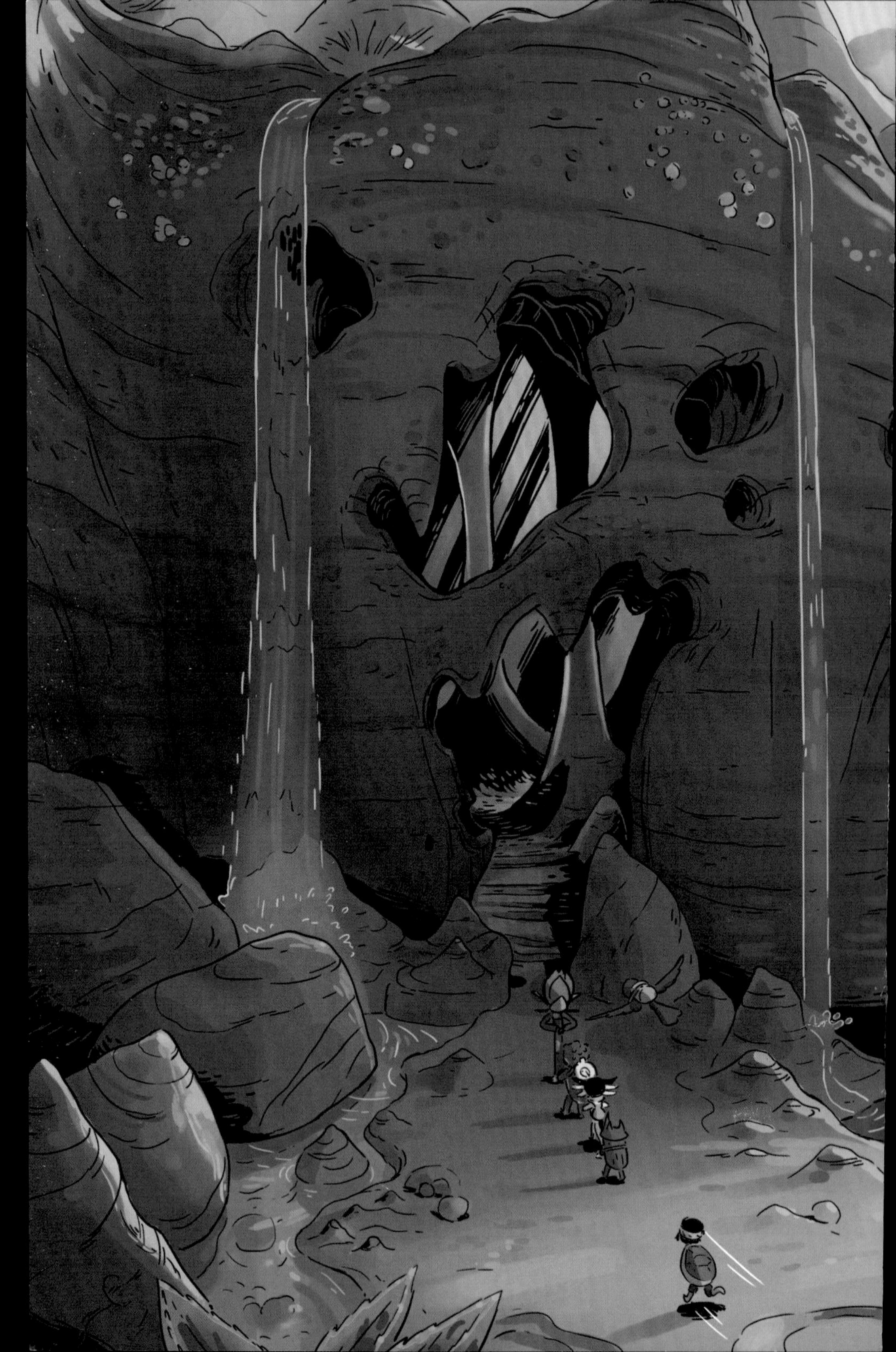

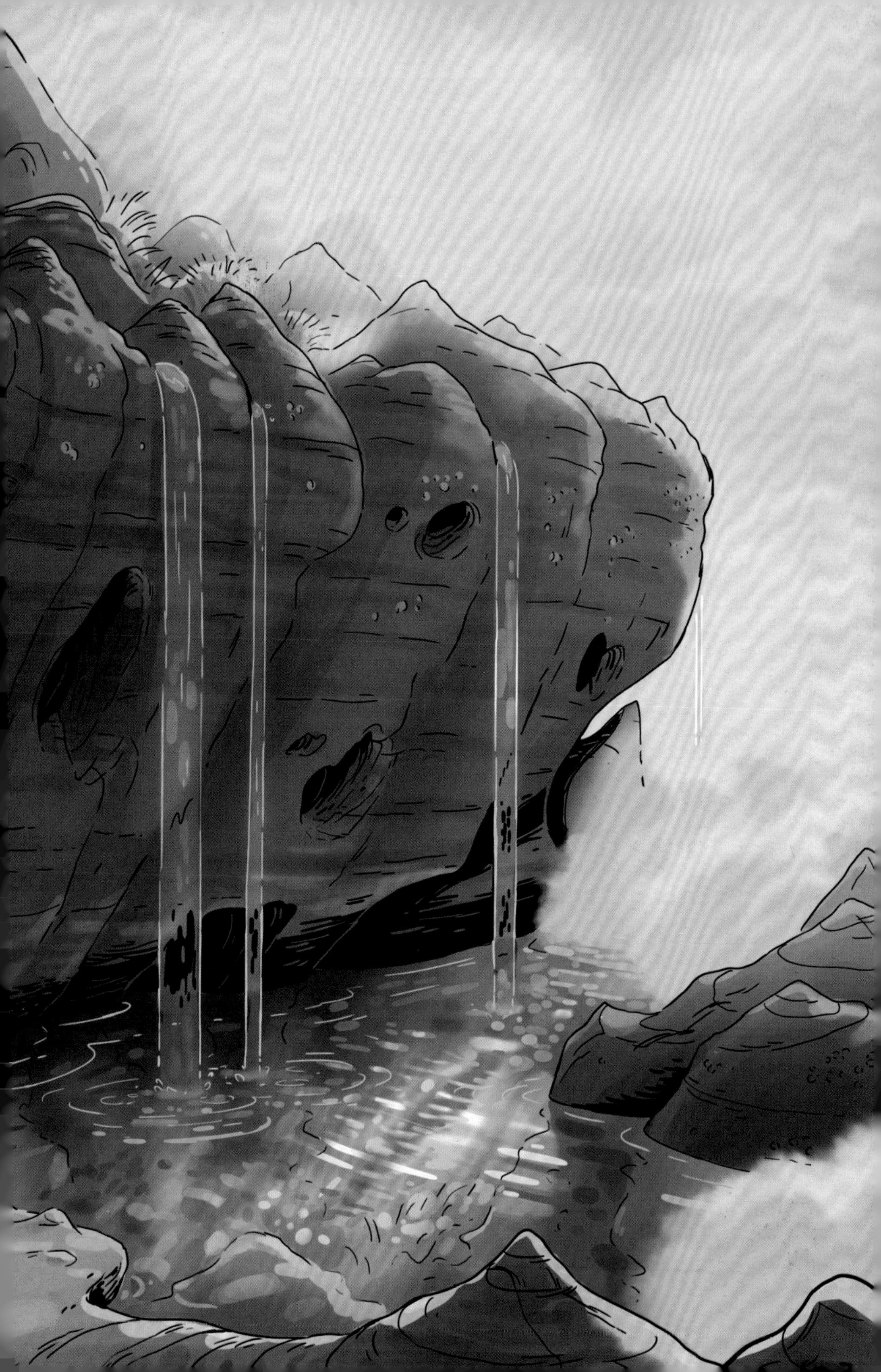

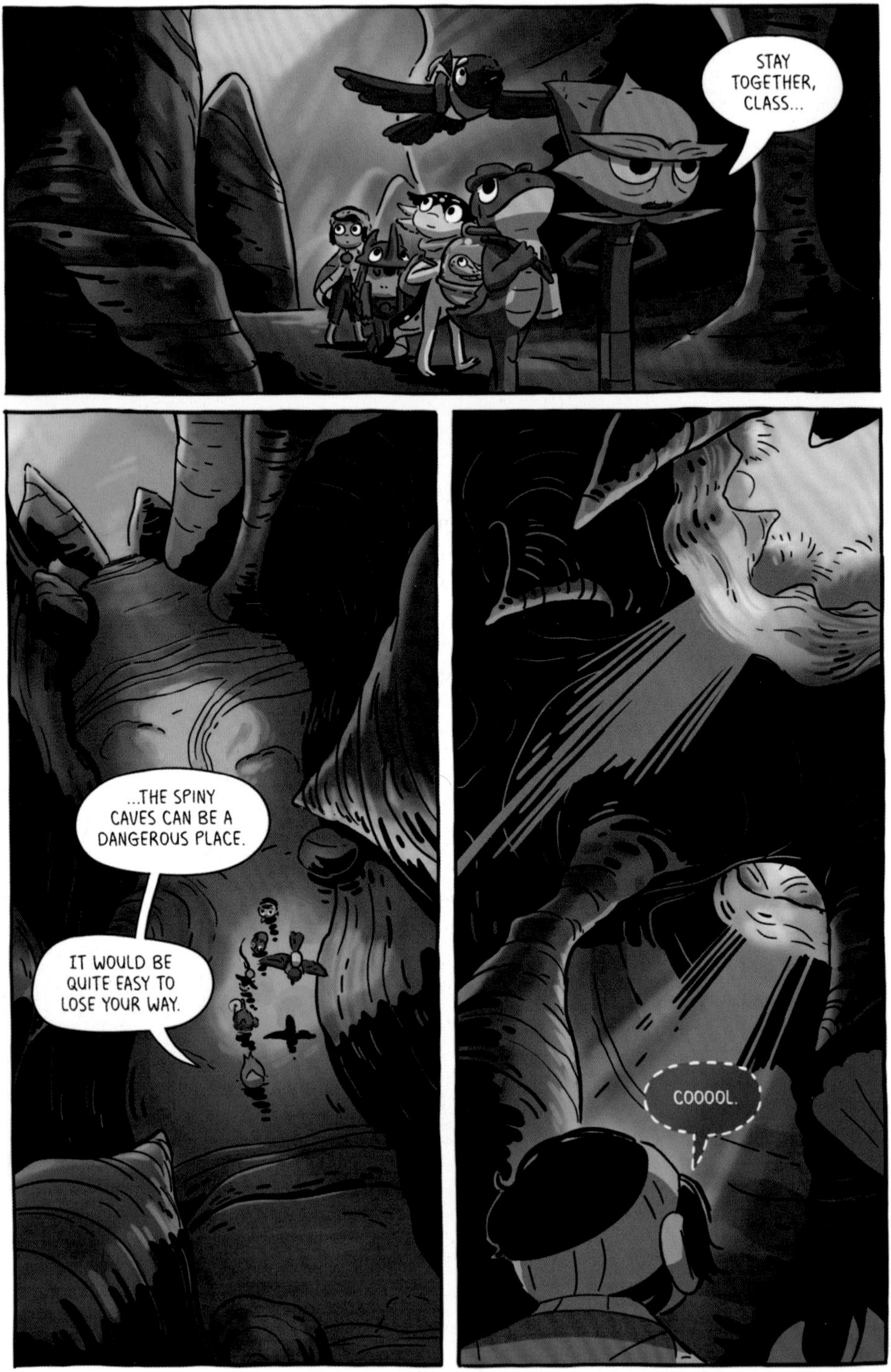
STAY TOGETHER, CLASS...
...THE SPINY CAVES CAN BE A DANGEROUS PLACE.
IT WOULD BE QUITE EASY TO LOSE YOUR WAY.
COOOOL.

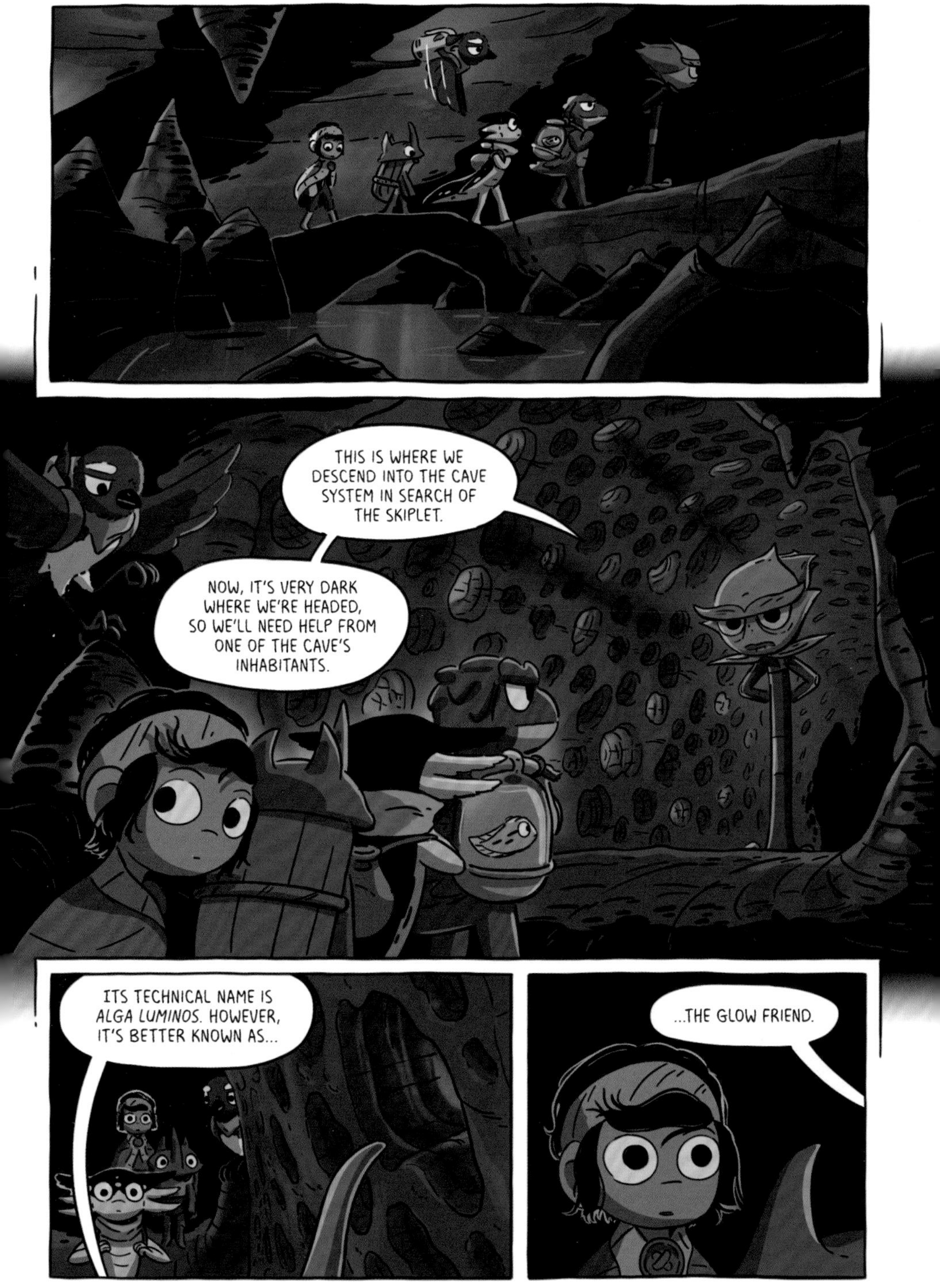
THIS IS WHERE WE DESCEND INTO THE CAVE SYSTEM IN SEARCH OF THE SKIPLET.
NOW, IT'S VERY DARK WHERE WE'RE HEADED, SO WE'LL NEED HELP FROM ONE OF THE CAVE'S INHABITANTS.
ITS TECHNICAL NAME IS *ALGA LUMINOS*. HOWEVER, IT'S BETTER KNOWN AS...
...THE GLOW FRIEND.

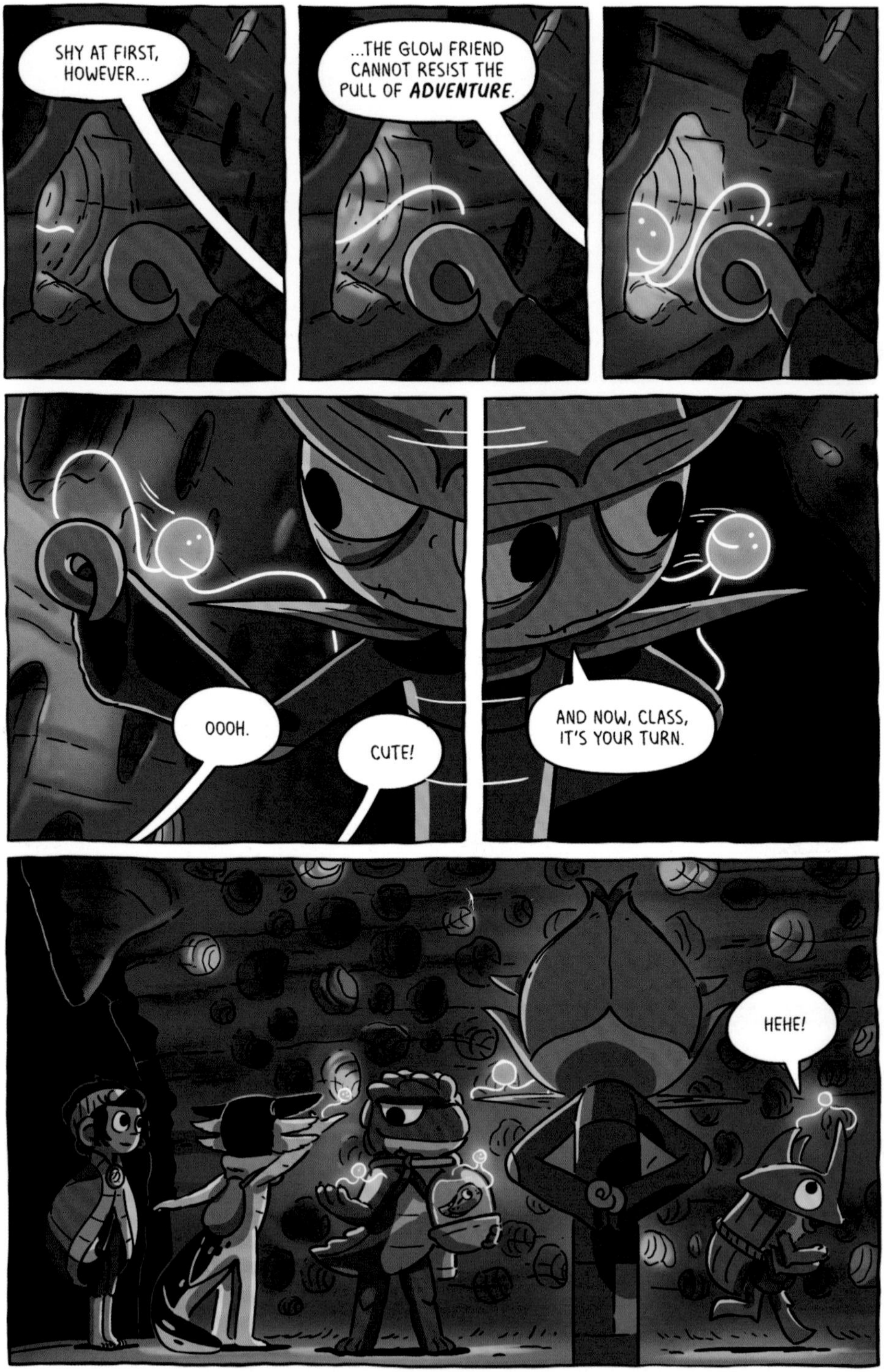
SHY AT FIRST, HOWEVER...
...THE GLOW FRIEND CANNOT RESIST THE PULL OF ADVENTURE.
OOOH.
CUTE!
AND NOW, CLASS, IT'S YOUR TURN.
HEHE!

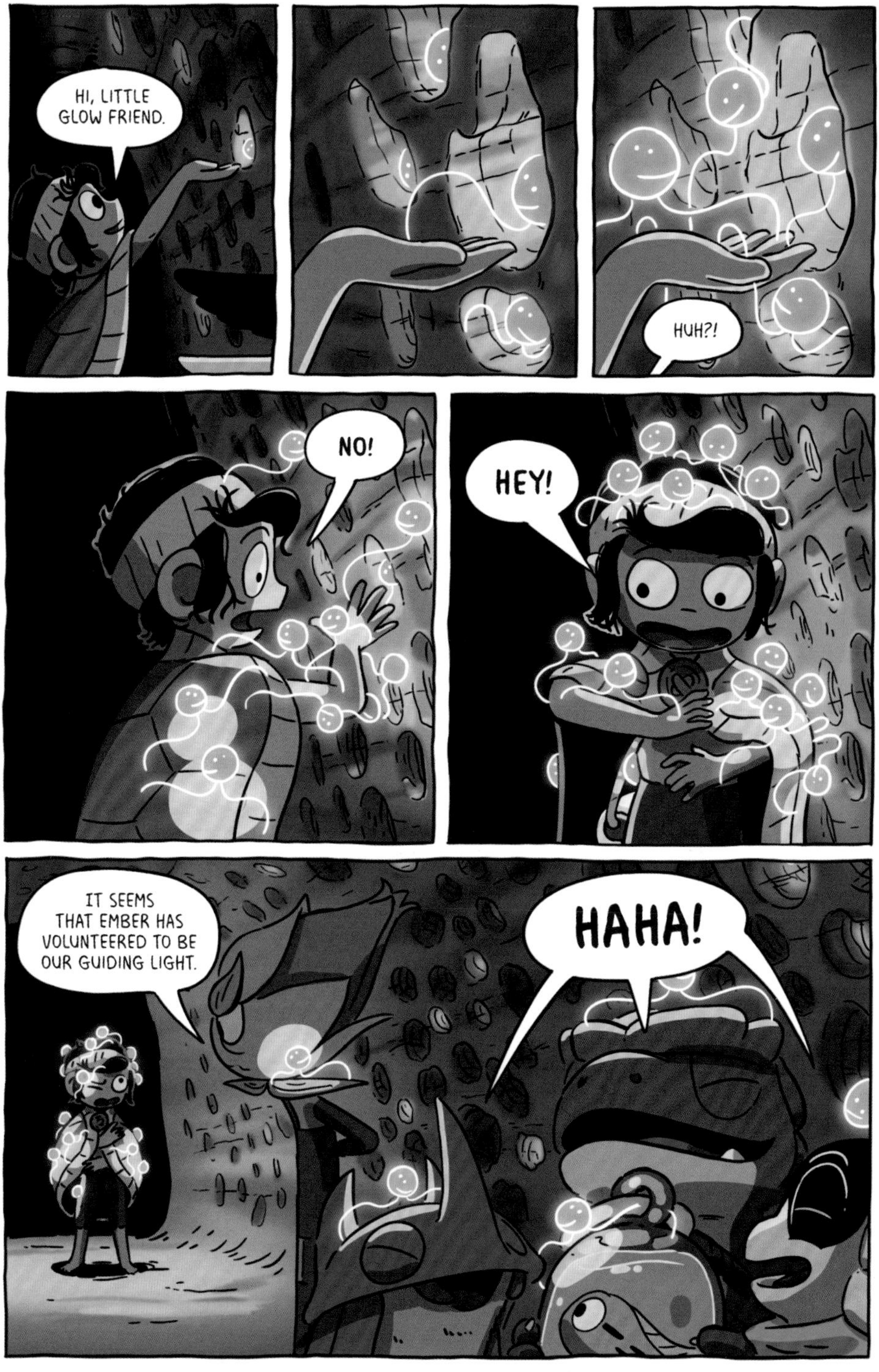
HI, LITTLE GLOW FRIEND.
HUH?!
NO!
HEY!
IT SEEMS THAT EMBER HAS VOLUNTEERED TO BE OUR GUIDING LIGHT.
HAHA!

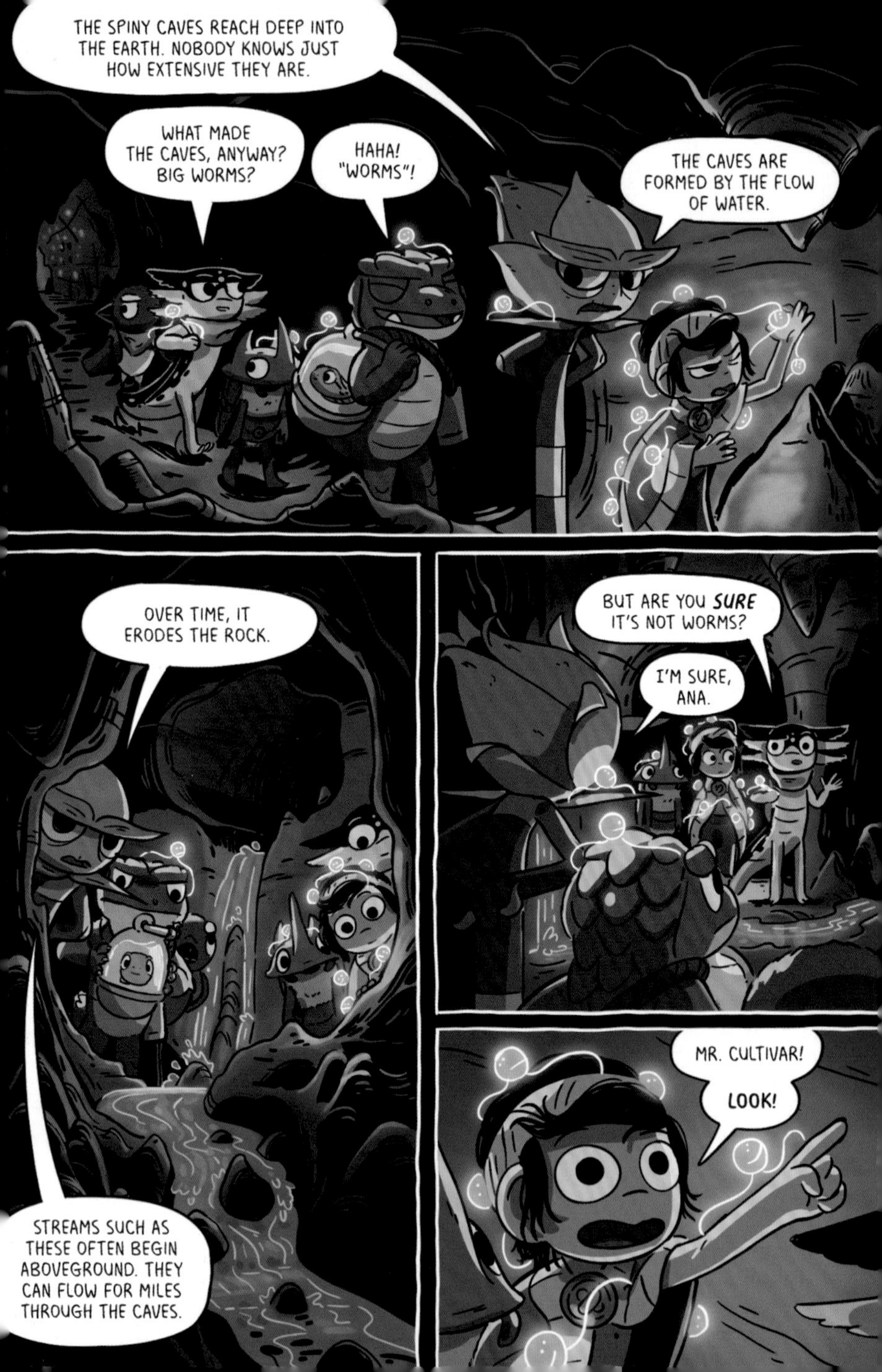
THE SPINY CAVES REACH DEEP INTO THE EARTH. NOBODY KNOWS JUST HOW EXTENSIVE THEY ARE.
WHAT MADE THE CAVES, ANYWAY? BIG WORMS?
HAHA! "WORMS"!
THE CAVES ARE FORMED BY THE FLOW OF WATER.
OVER TIME, IT ERODES THE ROCK.
STREAMS SUCH AS THESE OFTEN BEGIN ABOVEGROUND. THEY CAN FLOW FOR MILES THROUGH THE CAVES.
BUT ARE YOU *SURE* IT'S NOT WORMS?
I'M SURE, ANA.
MR. CULTIVAR!
LOOK!

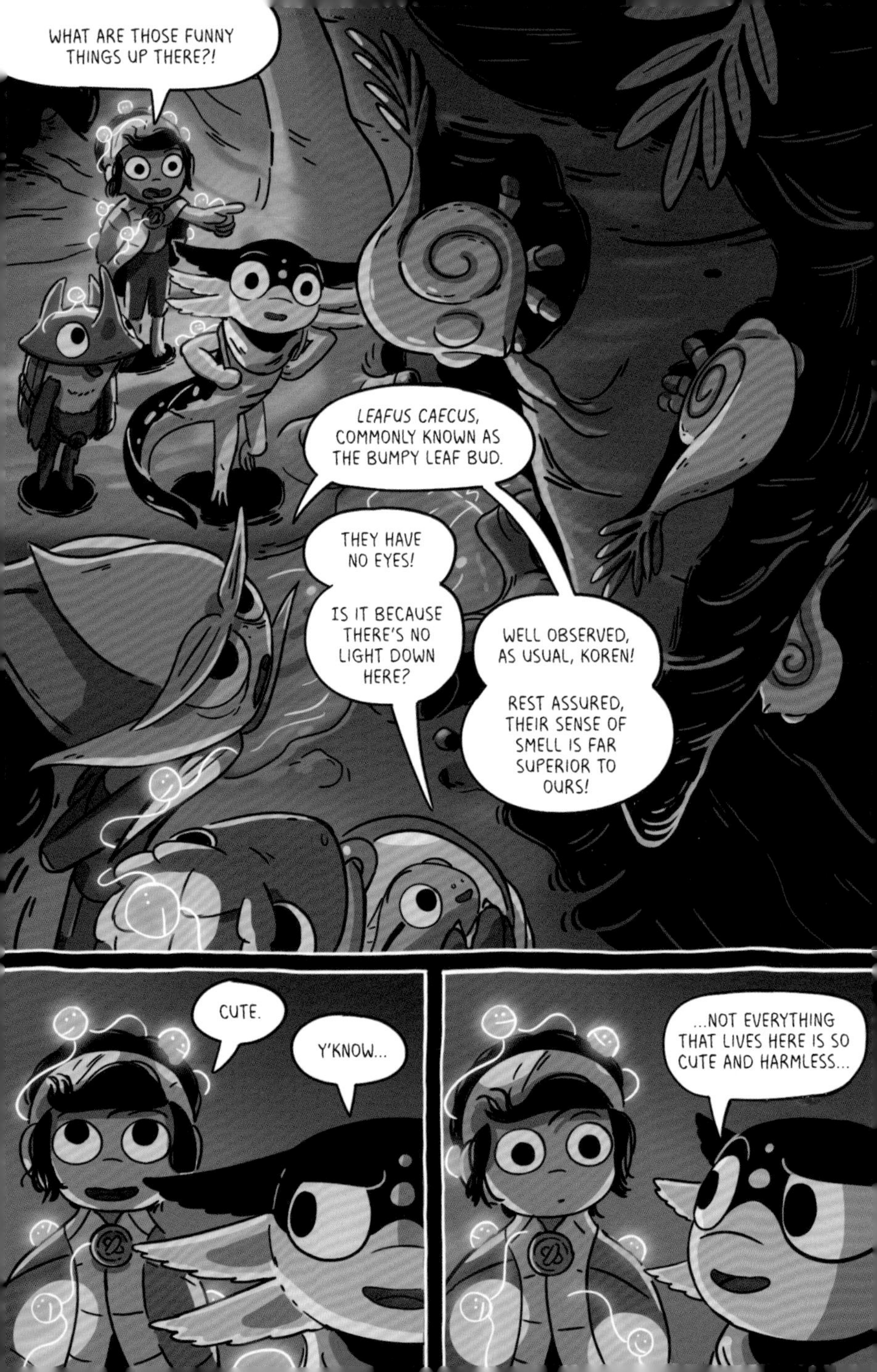
WHAT ARE THOSE FUNNY THINGS UP THERE?!
LEAFUS CAECUS, COMMONLY KNOWN AS THE BUMPY LEAF BUD.
THEY HAVE NO EYES!
IS IT BECAUSE THERE'S NO LIGHT DOWN HERE?
WELL OBSERVED, AS USUAL, KOREN!
REST ASSURED, THEIR SENSE OF SMELL IS FAR SUPERIOR TO OURS!
CUTE.
Y'KNOW...
...NOT EVERYTHING THAT LIVES HERE IS SO CUTE AND HARMLESS...

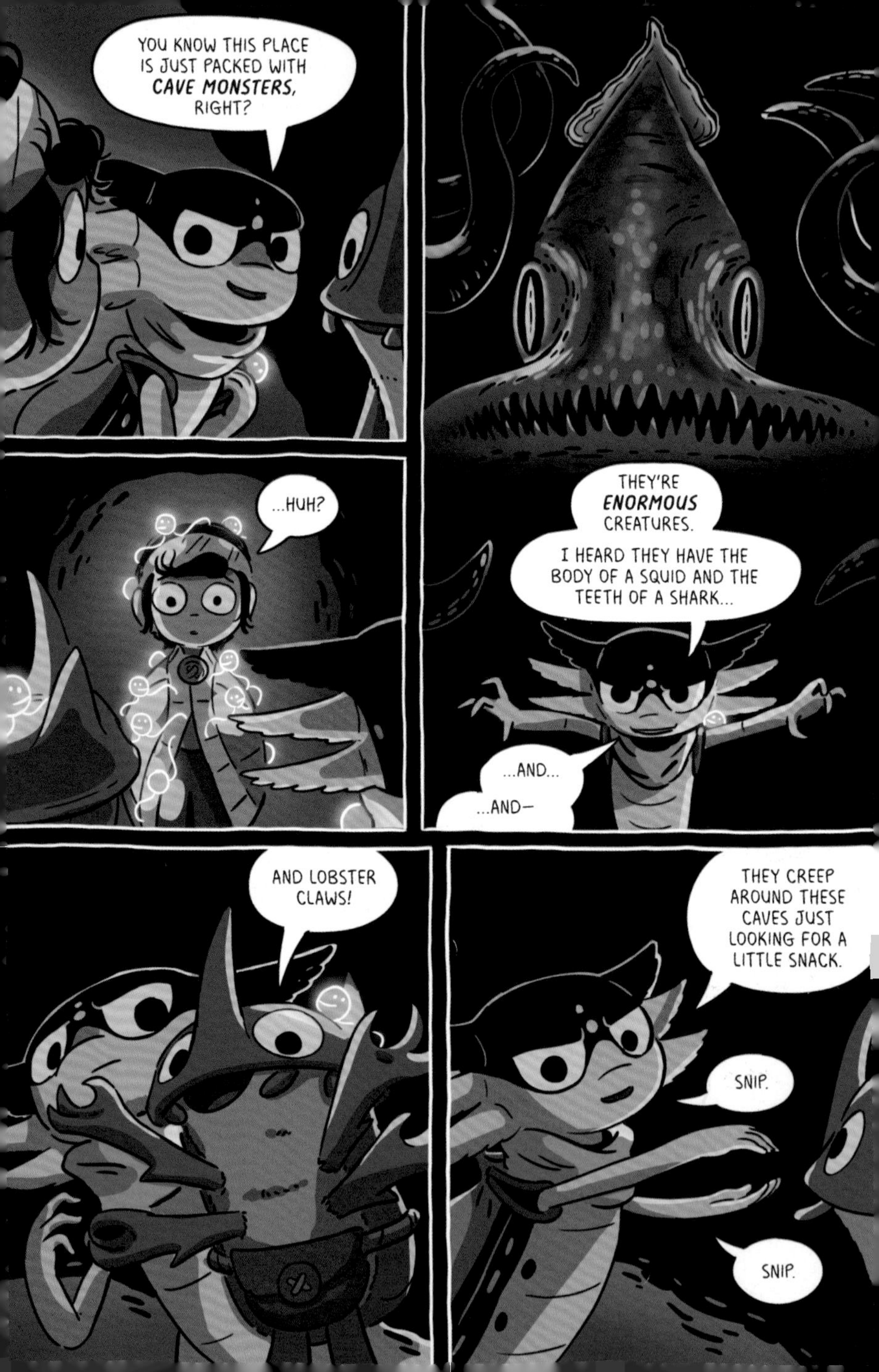
YOU KNOW THIS PLACE IS JUST PACKED WITH **CAVE MONSTERS,** RIGHT?
...HUH?
THEY'RE ***ENORMOUS*** CREATURES.
I HEARD THEY HAVE THE BODY OF A SQUID AND THE TEETH OF A SHARK...
...AND...
...AND—
AND LOBSTER CLAWS!
THEY CREEP AROUND THESE CAVES JUST LOOKING FOR A LITTLE SNACK.
SNIP.
SNIP.

SNAP

ANA?

CARE TO SHARE THIS DISCUSSION WITH THE REST OF THE CLASS?

I WAS *ONLY* TELLING "EMMY" ABOUT THE GIANT MONSTERS IN THE CAVE THAT EAT KIDS.

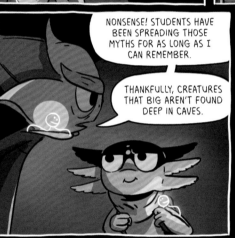

NONSENSE! STUDENTS HAVE BEEN SPREADING THOSE MYTHS FOR AS LONG AS I CAN REMEMBER.

THANKFULLY, CREATURES THAT BIG AREN'T FOUND DEEP IN CAVES.

THOSE THAT *DO* EXIST, YOU WOULD MORE LIKELY ENCOUNTER ON YOUR WAY TO CLASS.

COME ALONG, NOW.

I BELIEVE OUR SKIPLET IS JUST AROUND THE CORNER.

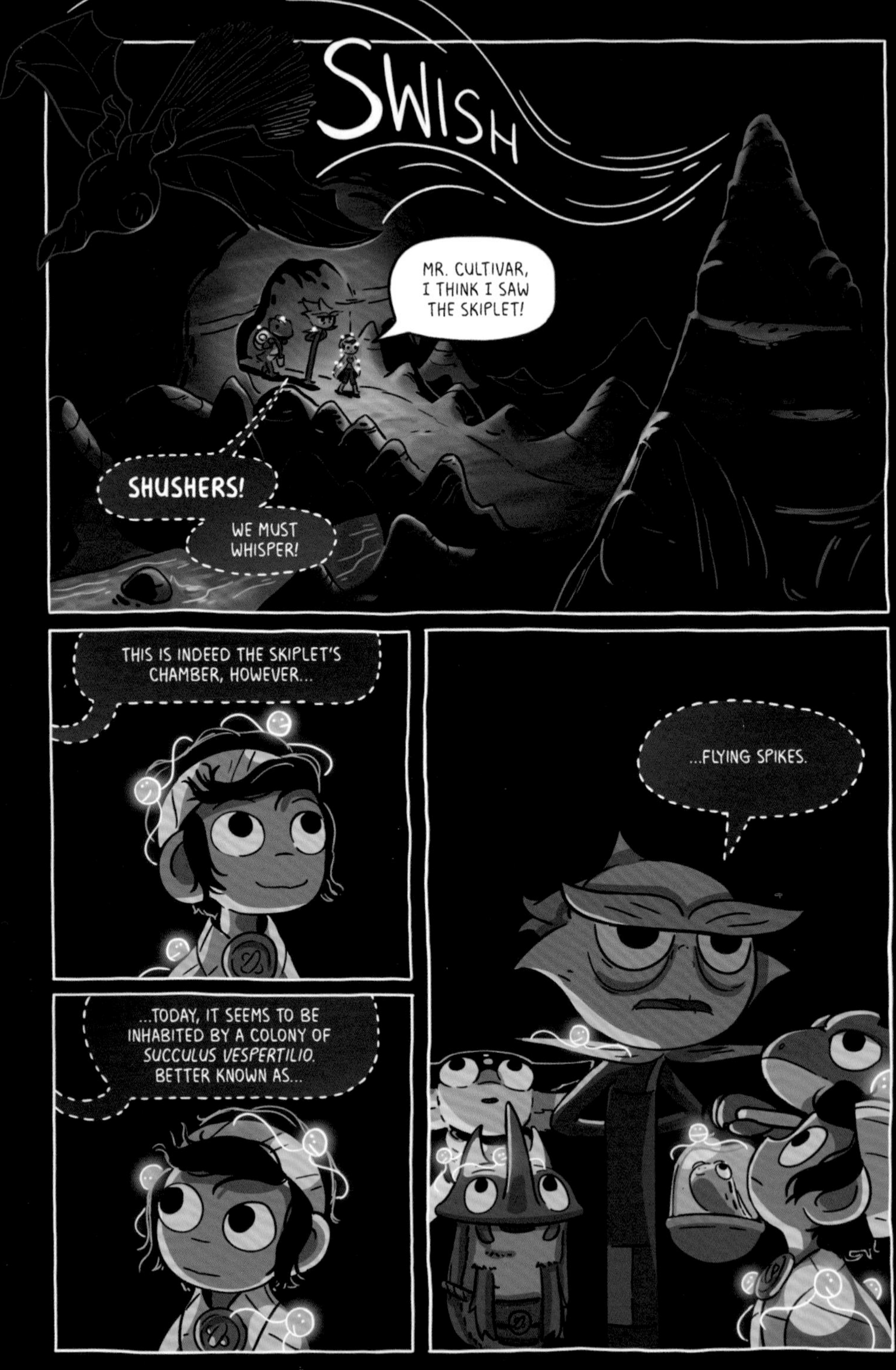
SWISH
MR. CULTIVAR, I THINK I SAW THE SKIPLET!
SHUSHERS!
WE MUST WHISPER!
THIS IS INDEED THE SKIPLET'S CHAMBER, HOWEVER...
...TODAY, IT SEEMS TO BE INHABITED BY A COLONY OF *SUCCULUS VESPERTILIO*. BETTER KNOWN AS...
...FLYING SPIKES.

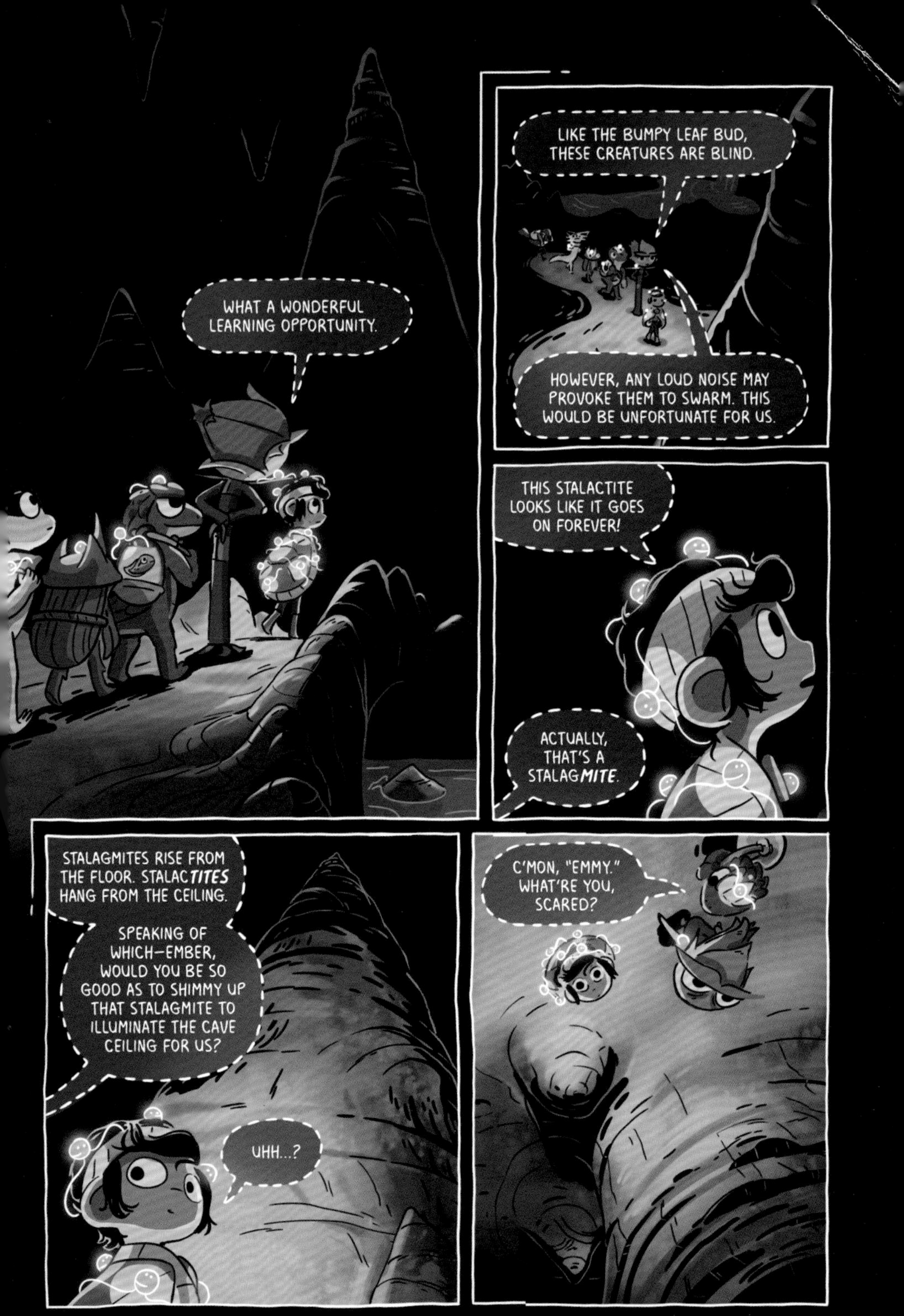
WHAT A WONDERFUL LEARNING OPPORTUNITY.
LIKE THE BUMPY LEAF BUD, THESE CREATURES ARE BLIND.
HOWEVER, ANY LOUD NOISE MAY PROVOKE THEM TO SWARM. THIS WOULD BE UNFORTUNATE FOR US.
THIS STALACTITE LOOKS LIKE IT GOES ON FOREVER!
ACTUALLY, THAT'S A STALAG*MITE*.
STALAGMITES RISE FROM THE FLOOR. STALAC*TITES* HANG FROM THE CEILING.
SPEAKING OF WHICH—EMBER, WOULD YOU BE SO GOOD AS TO SHIMMY UP THAT STALAGMITE TO ILLUMINATE THE CAVE CEILING FOR US?
UHH...?
C'MON, "EMMY." WHAT'RE YOU, SCARED?

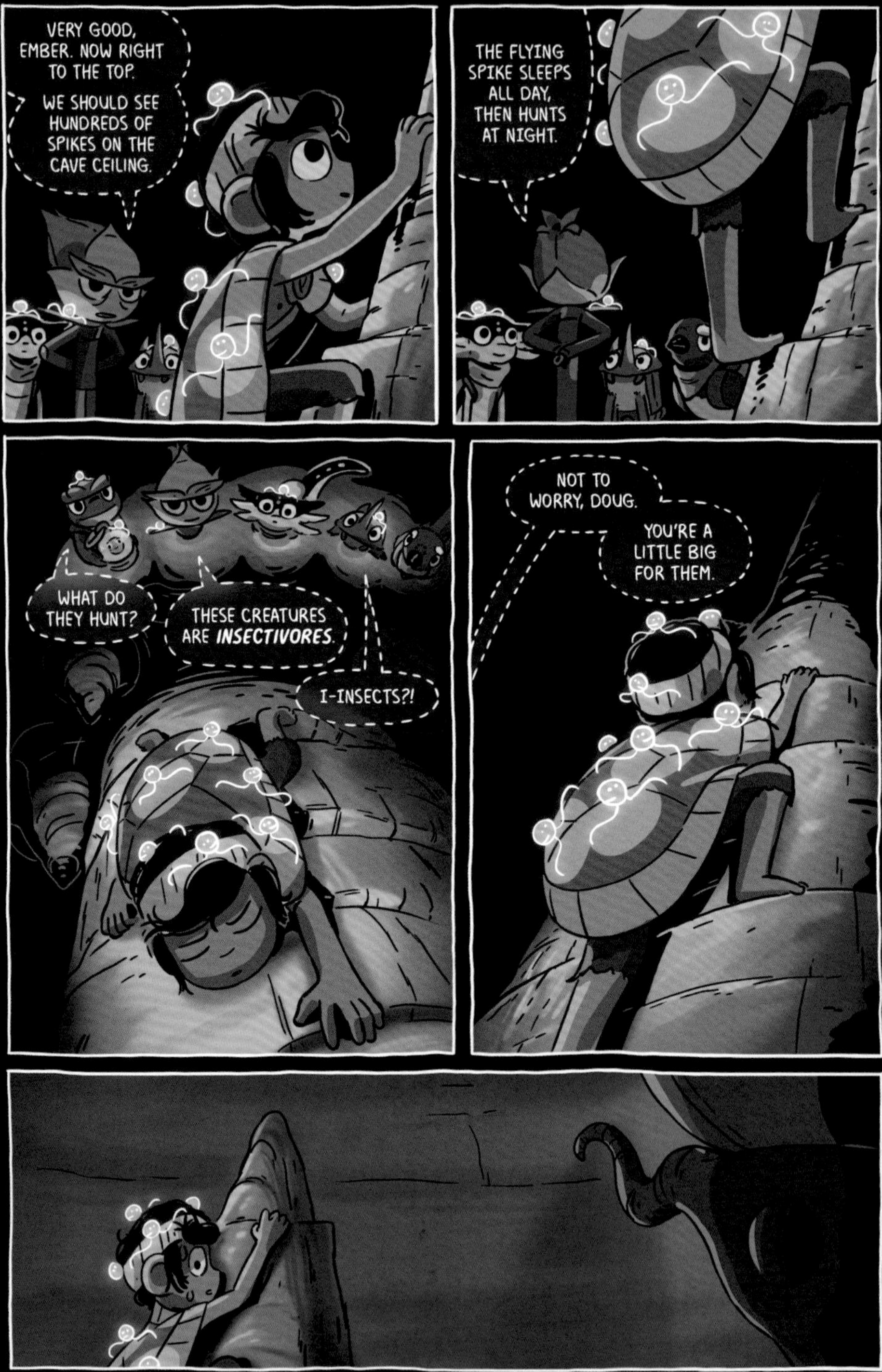
VERY GOOD, EMBER. NOW RIGHT TO THE TOP.
WE SHOULD SEE HUNDREDS OF SPIKES ON THE CAVE CEILING.
THE FLYING SPIKE SLEEPS ALL DAY, THEN HUNTS AT NIGHT.
WHAT DO THEY HUNT?
THESE CREATURES ARE *INSECTIVORES*.
I-INSECTS?!
NOT TO WORRY, DOUG.
YOU'RE A LITTLE BIG FOR THEM.

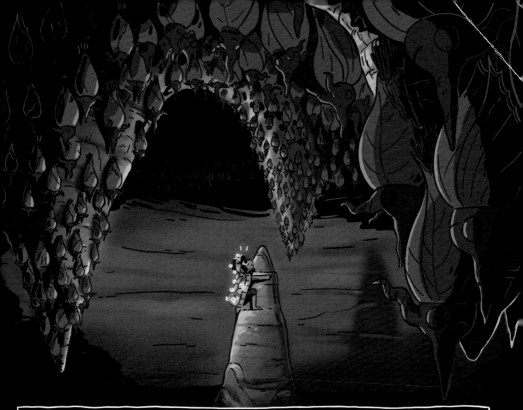

WOOOW!

HEY...

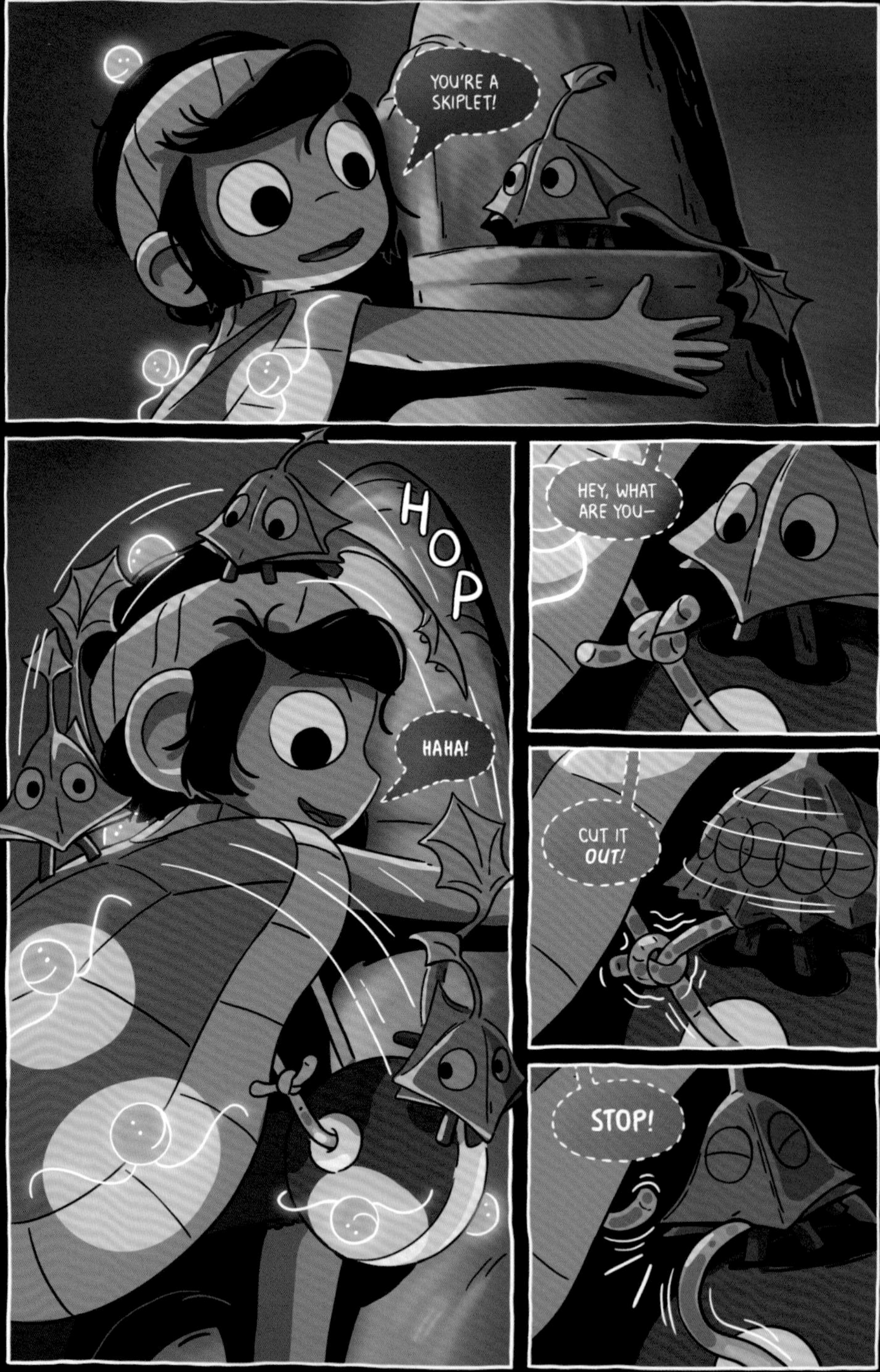

YOU'RE A SKIPLET!
HOP
HAHA!
HEY, WHAT ARE YOU–
CUT IT OUT!
STOP!

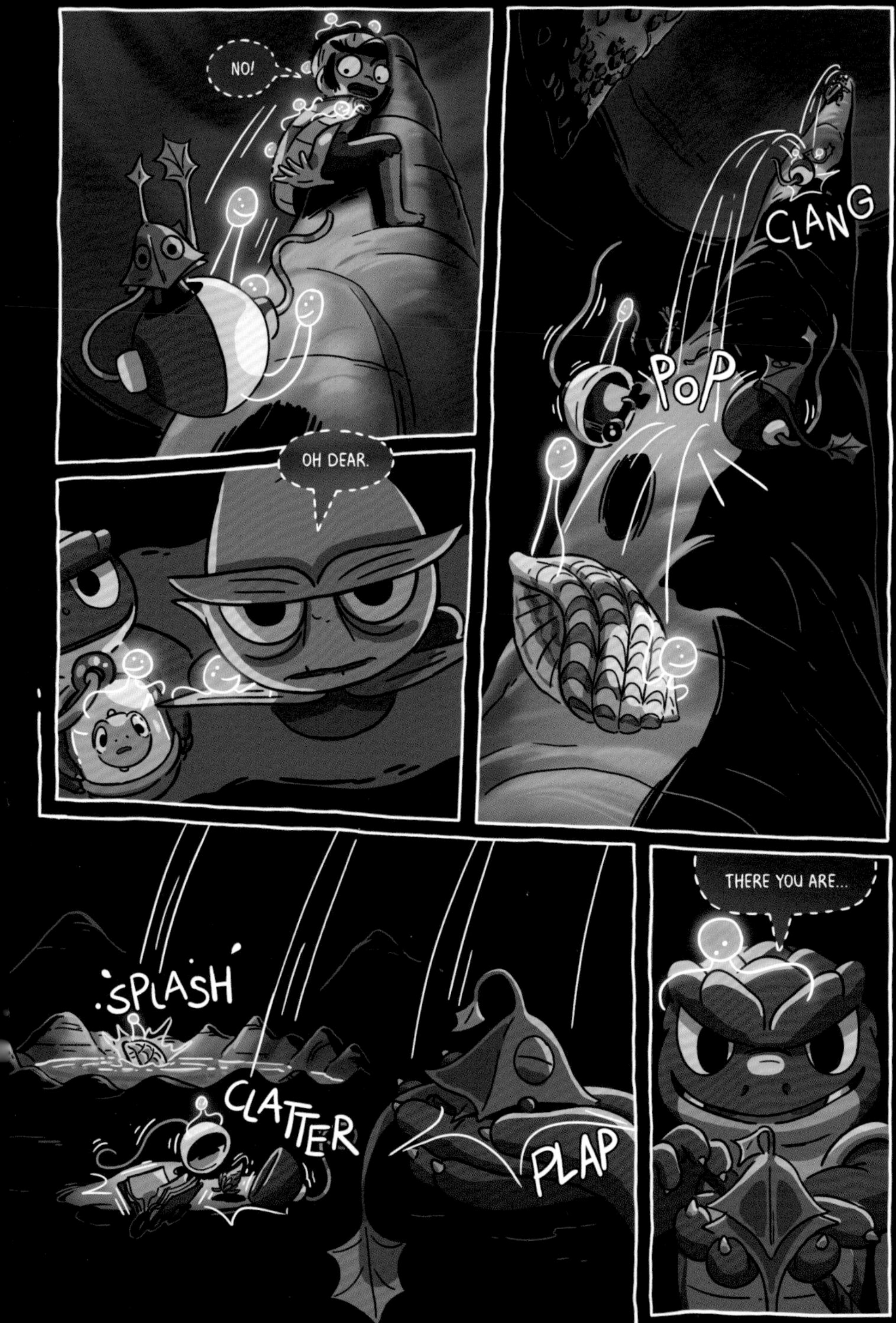
NO!
OH DEAR.
CLANG
POP
SPLASH
CLATTER
PLAP
THERE YOU ARE...

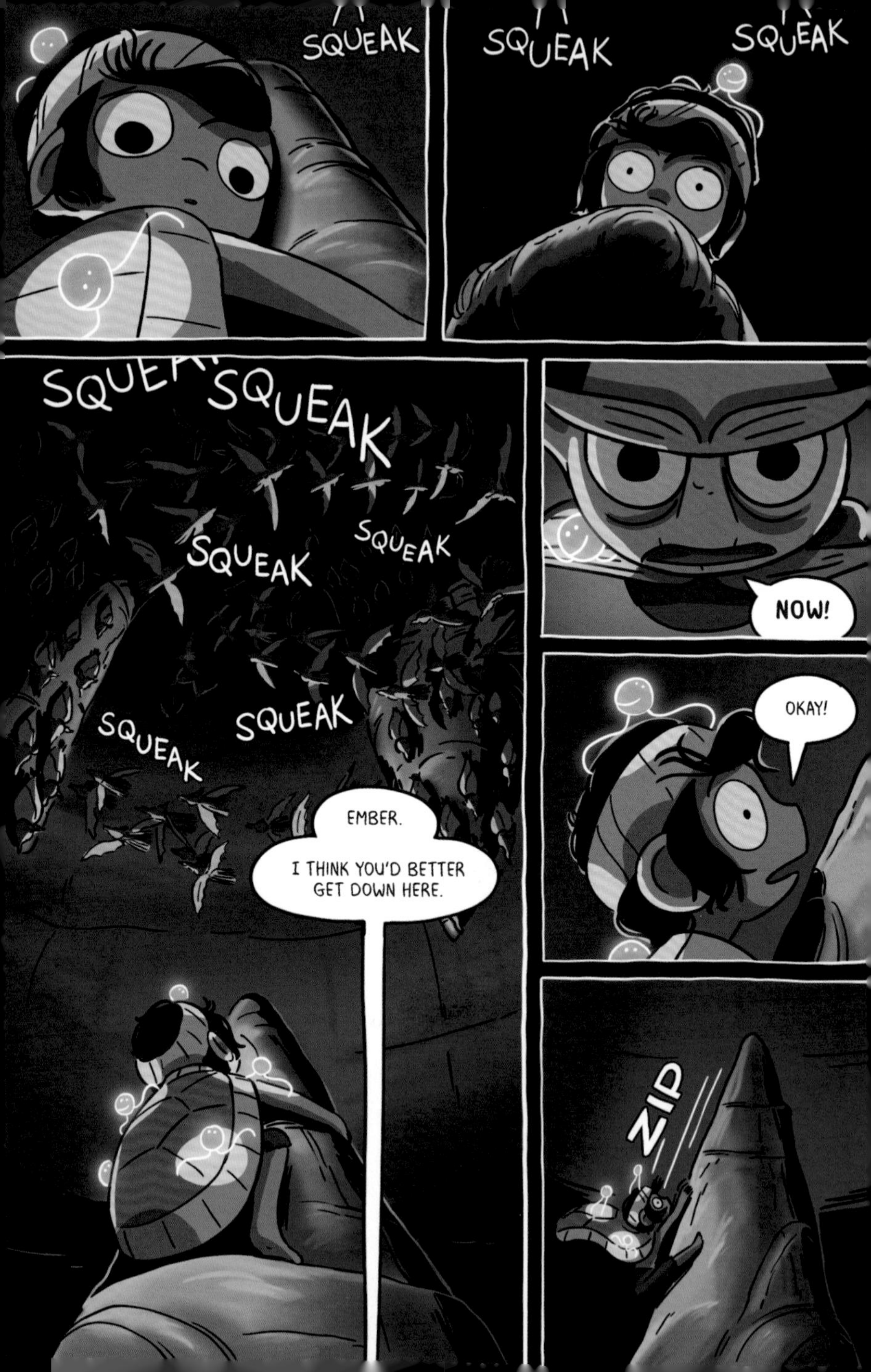
SQUEAK
SQUEAK
SQUEAK
SQUEAK
SQUEAK
SQUEAK
SQUEAK
SQUEAK
SQUEAK
EMBER.
I THINK YOU'D BETTER GET DOWN HERE.
NOW!
OKAY!
ZIP

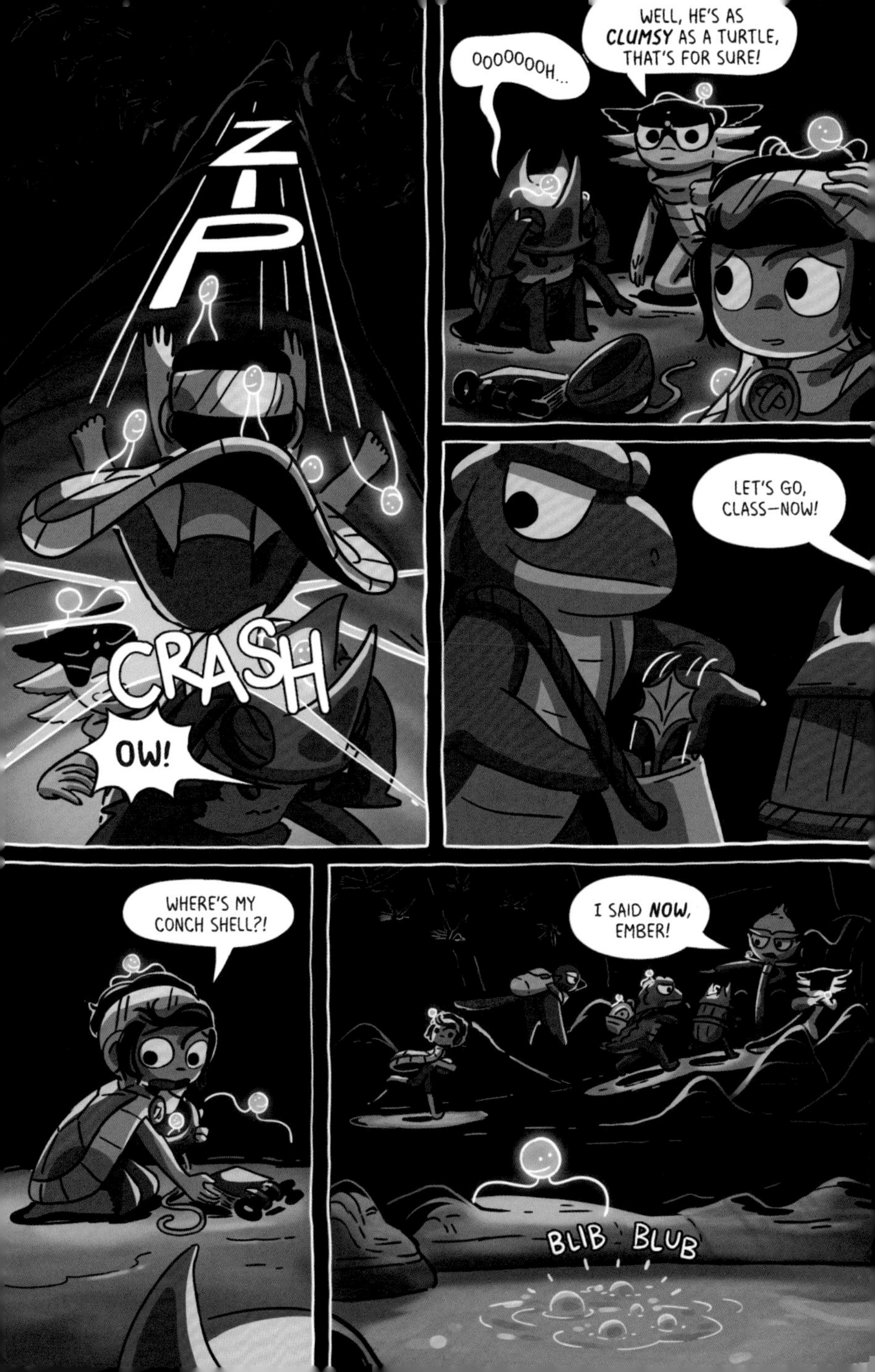
ZIP
CRASH
OW!
OOOOOOOH...
WELL, HE'S AS **CLUMSY** AS A TURTLE, THAT'S FOR SURE!
LET'S GO, CLASS—NOW!
WHERE'S MY CONCH SHELL?!
I SAID **NOW**, EMBER!
BLIB BLUB

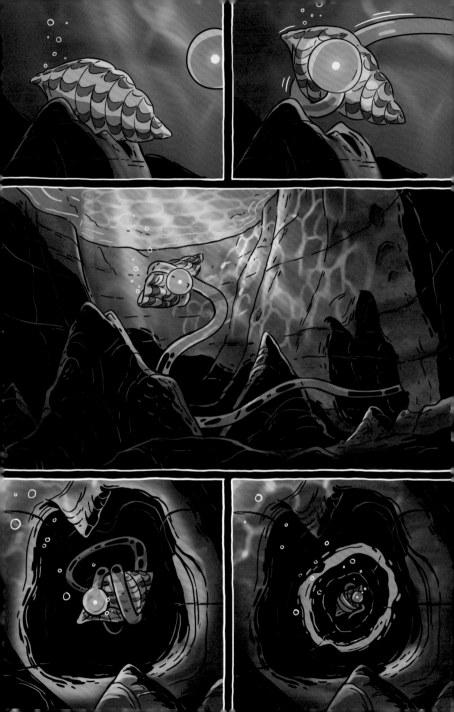

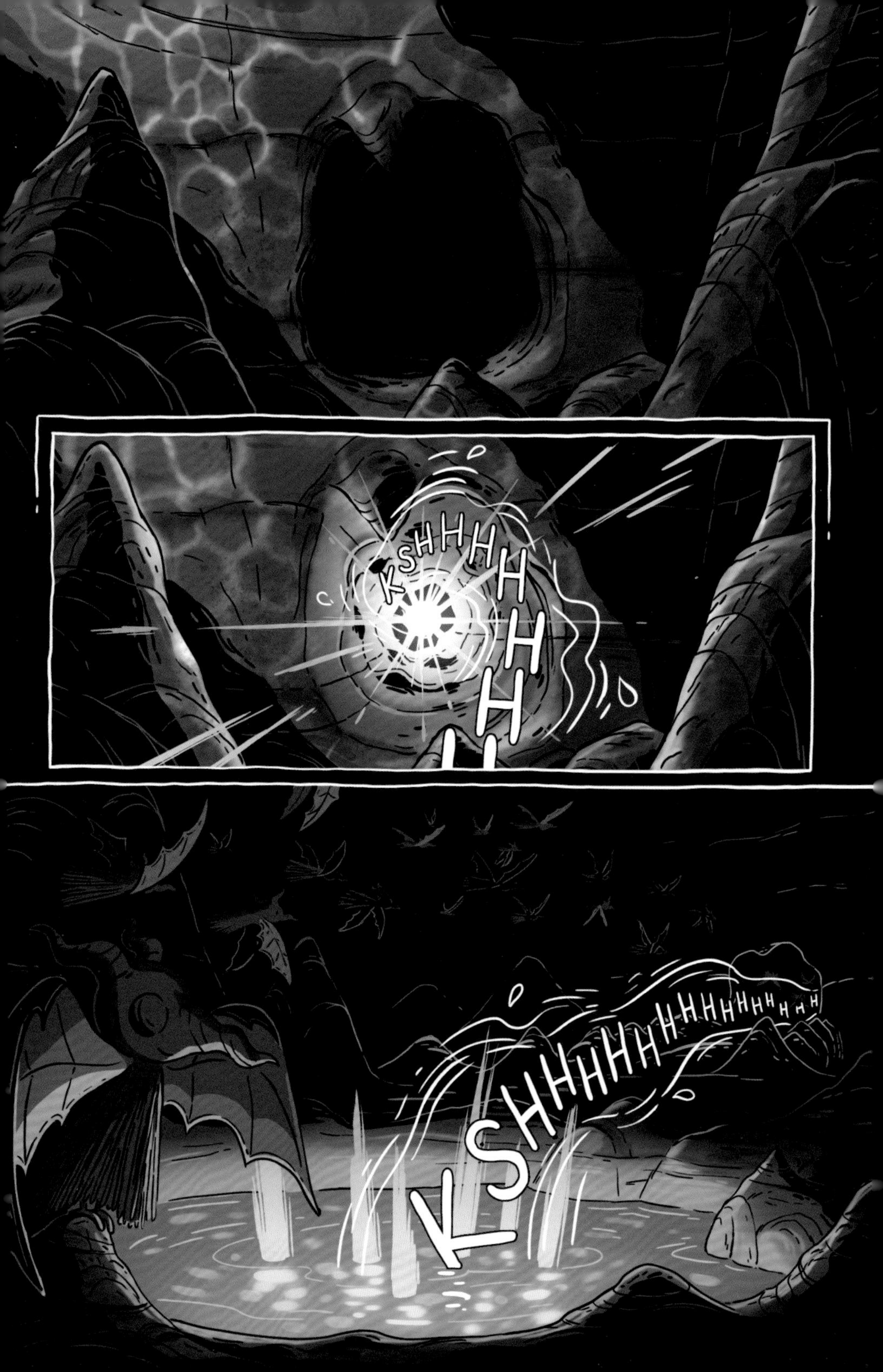
KSHHHHHHHH
KSHHHHHHHHHHHHHHHHHHHHH

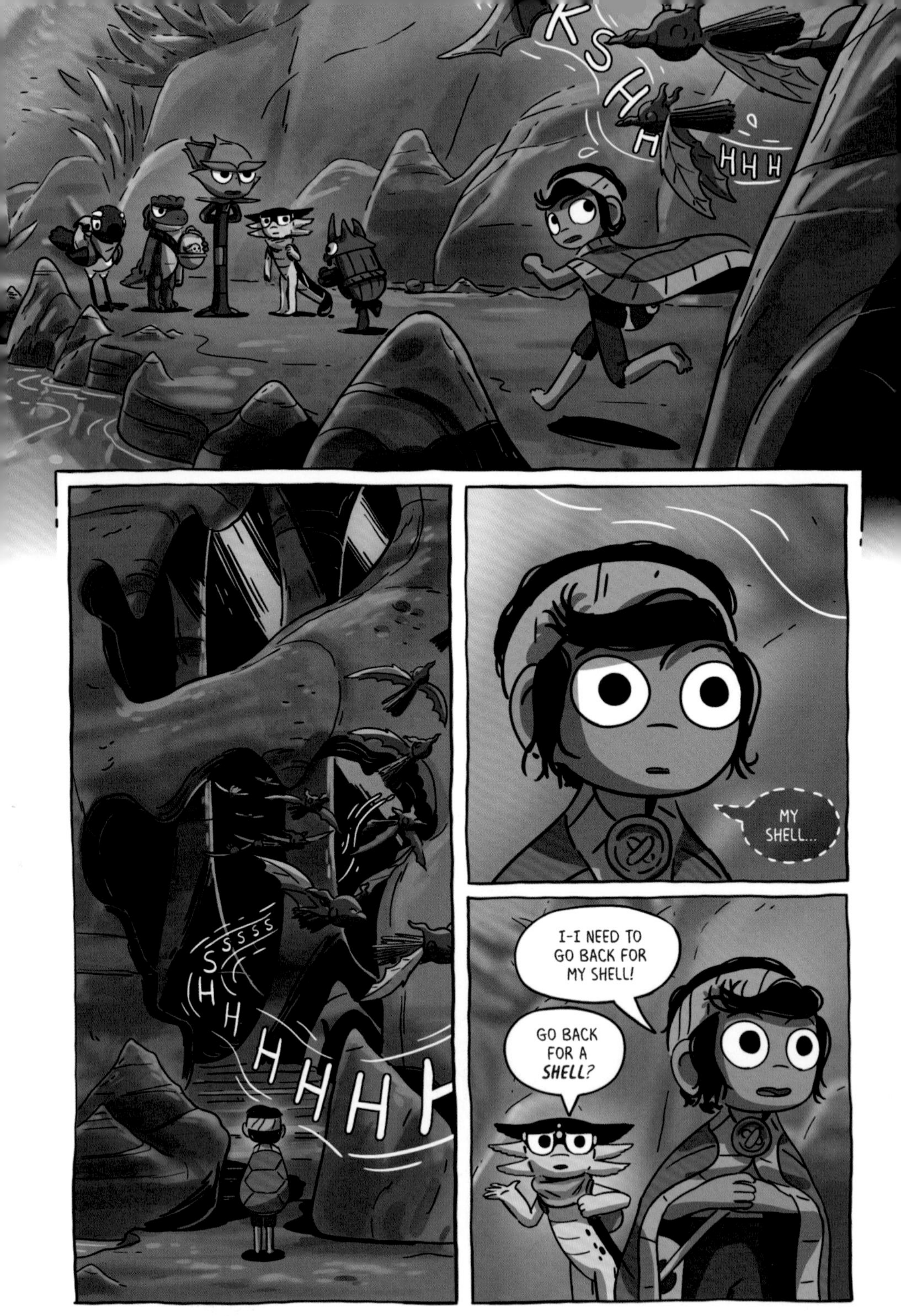
KSHHHHH
SSSSSS
HHHHHH
MY SHELL...
I-I NEED TO GO BACK FOR MY SHELL!
GO BACK FOR A *SHELL?*

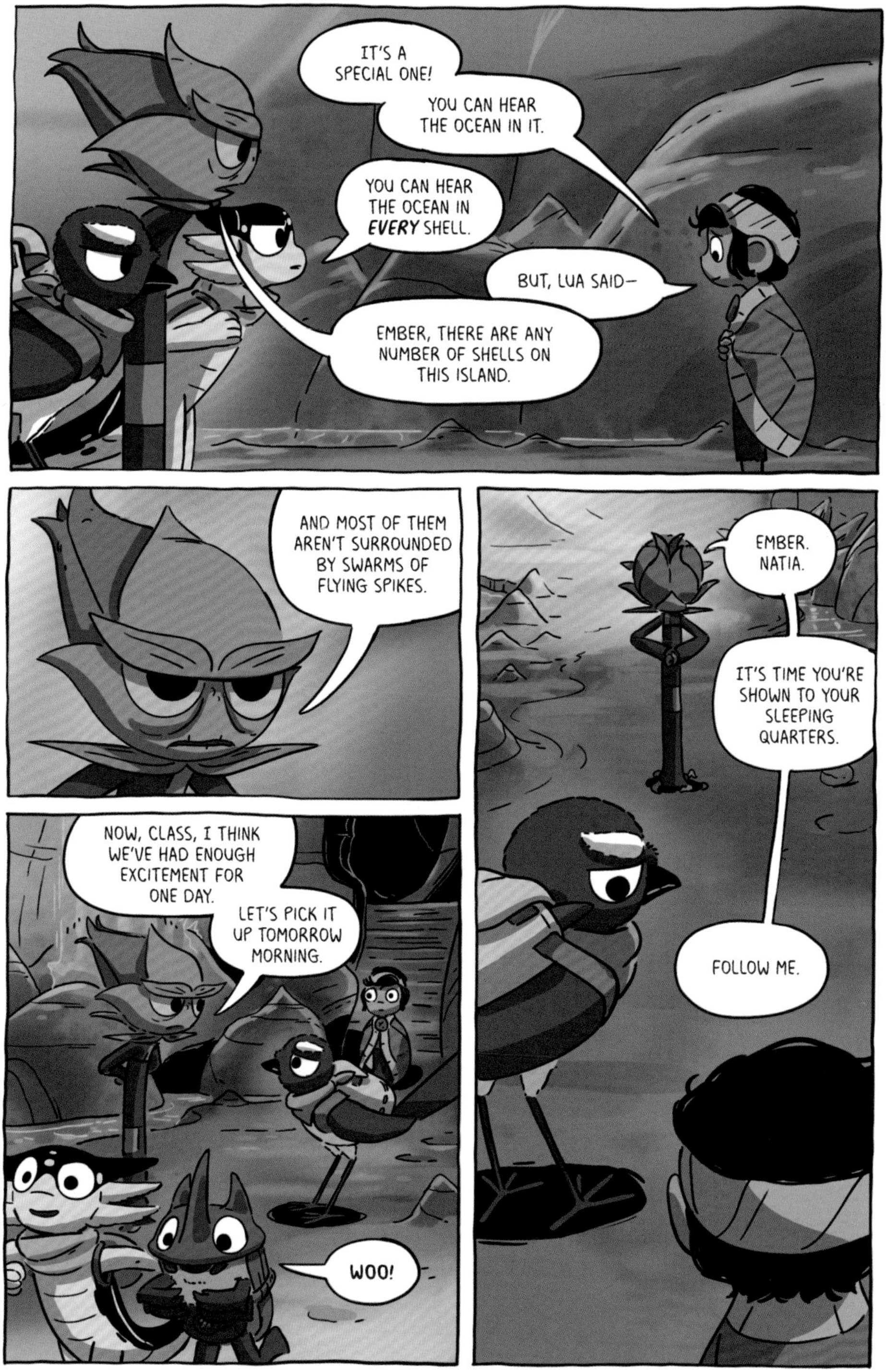
IT'S A SPECIAL ONE!
YOU CAN HEAR THE OCEAN IN IT.
YOU CAN HEAR THE OCEAN IN **EVERY** SHELL.
BUT, LUA SAID—
EMBER, THERE ARE ANY NUMBER OF SHELLS ON THIS ISLAND.
AND MOST OF THEM AREN'T SURROUNDED BY SWARMS OF FLYING SPIKES.
NOW, CLASS, I THINK WE'VE HAD ENOUGH EXCITEMENT FOR ONE DAY.
LET'S PICK IT UP TOMORROW MORNING.
WOO!
EMBER. NATIA.
IT'S TIME YOU'RE SHOWN TO YOUR SLEEPING QUARTERS.
FOLLOW ME.

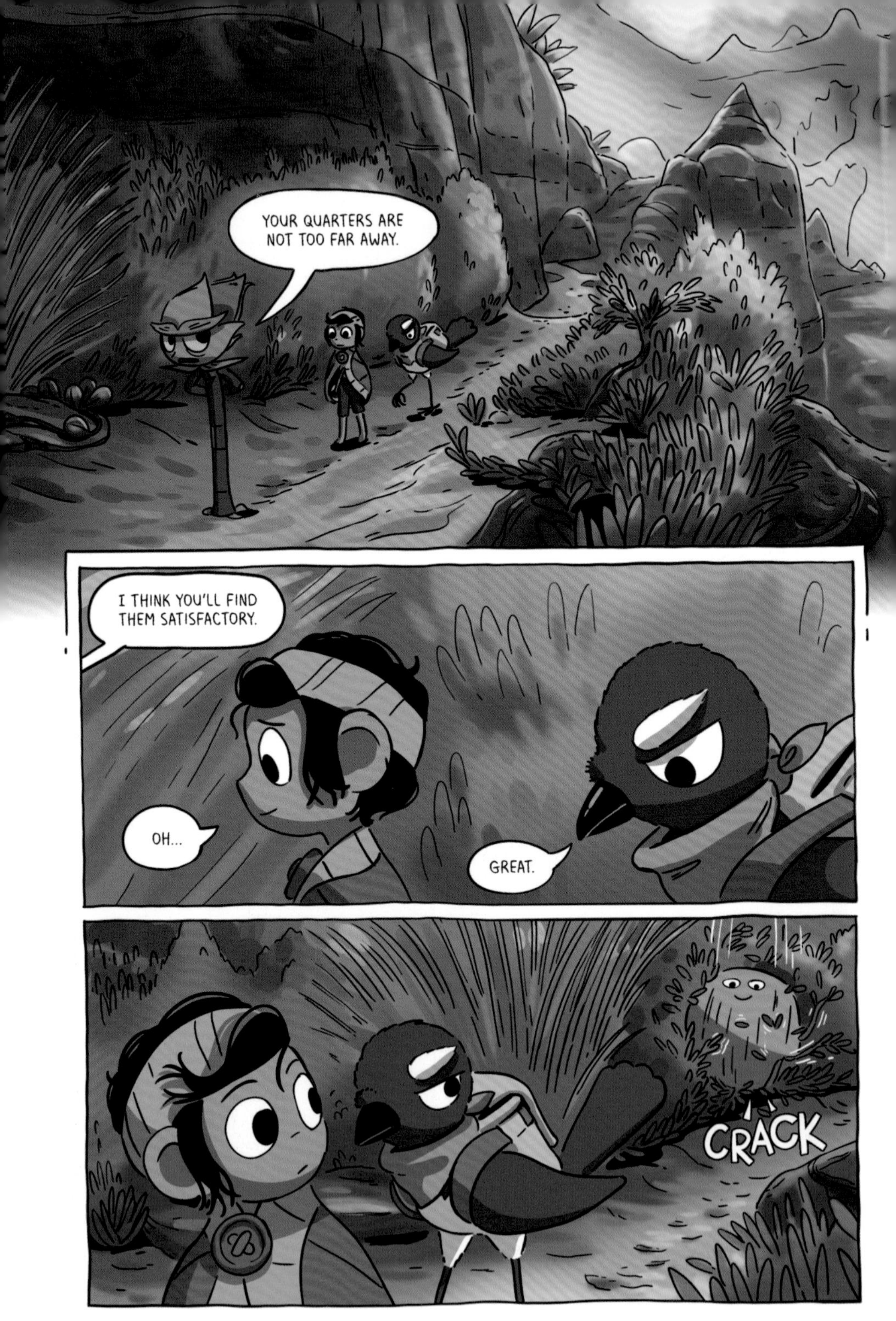
YOUR QUARTERS ARE NOT TOO FAR AWAY.
I THINK YOU'LL FIND THEM SATISFACTORY.
OH...
GREAT.
CRACK

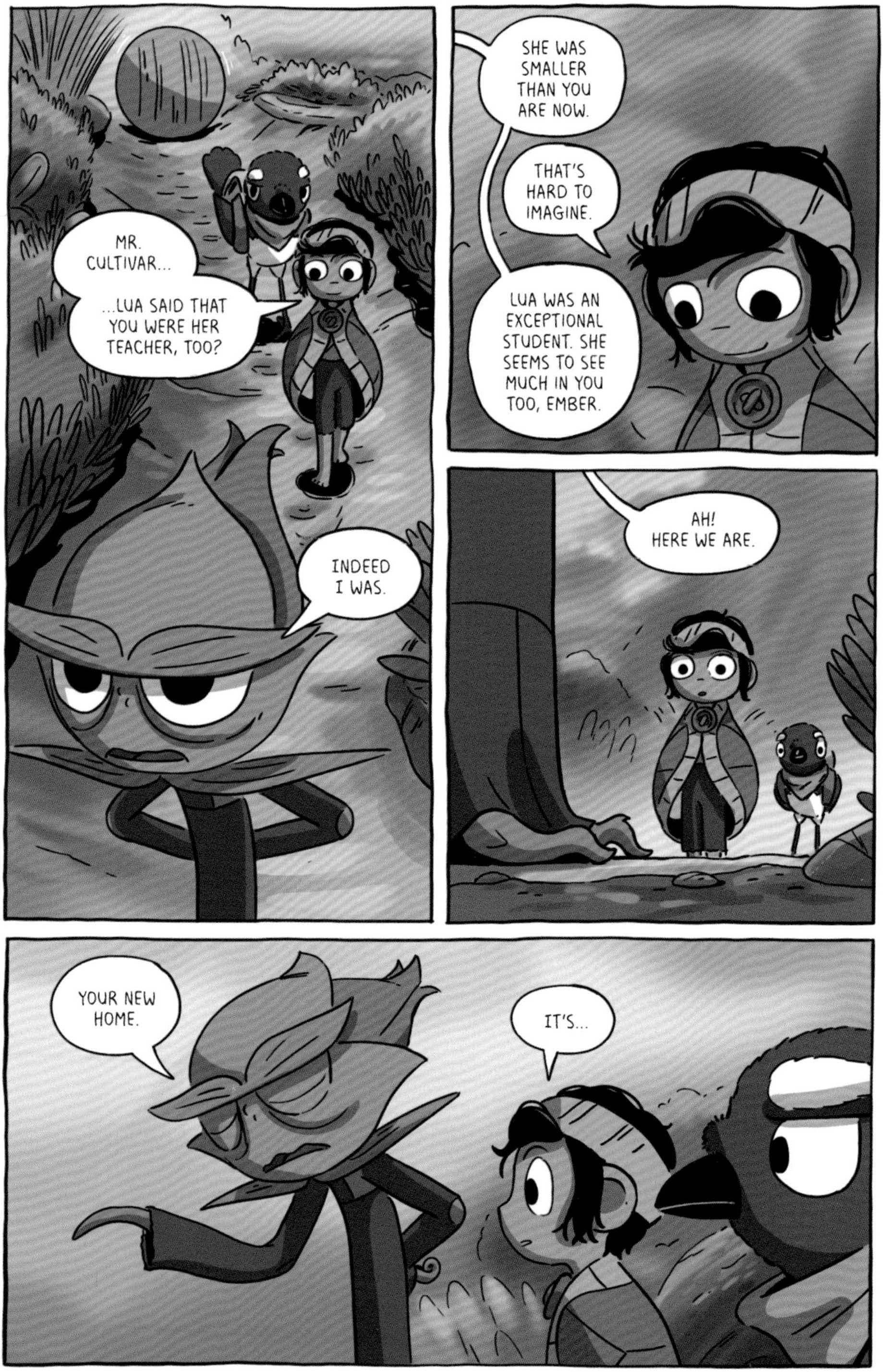
MR. CULTIVAR...
...LUA SAID THAT YOU WERE HER TEACHER, TOO?
INDEED I WAS.
SHE WAS SMALLER THAN YOU ARE NOW.
THAT'S HARD TO IMAGINE.
LUA WAS AN EXCEPTIONAL STUDENT. SHE SEEMS TO SEE MUCH IN YOU TOO, EMBER.
AH! HERE WE ARE.
YOUR NEW HOME.
IT'S...

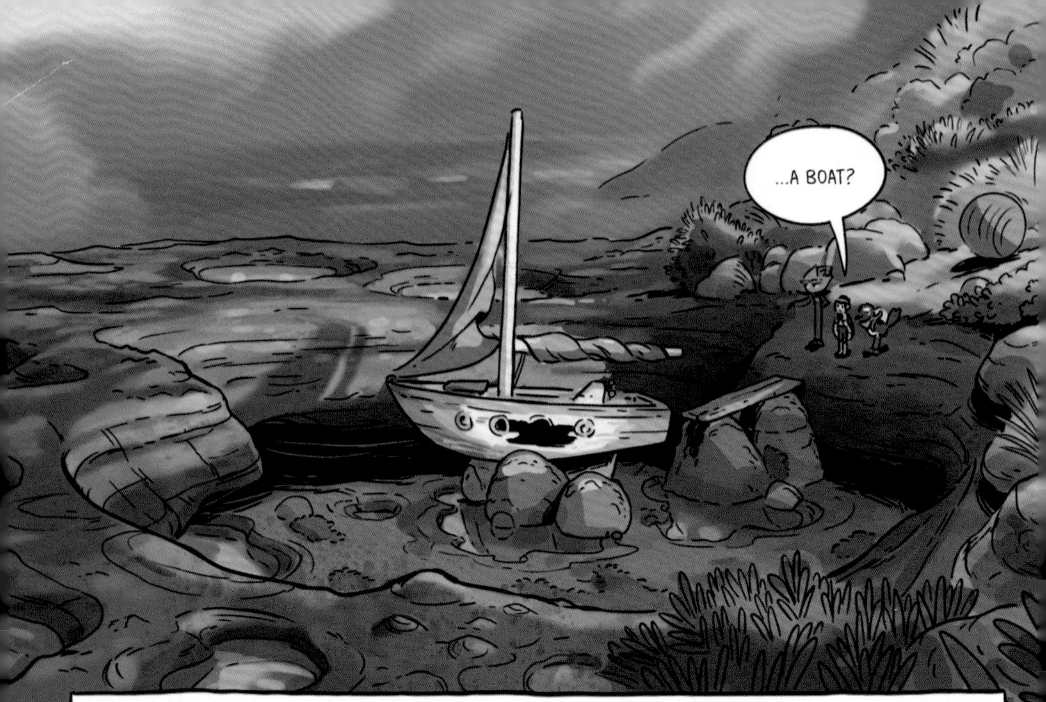
...A BOAT?

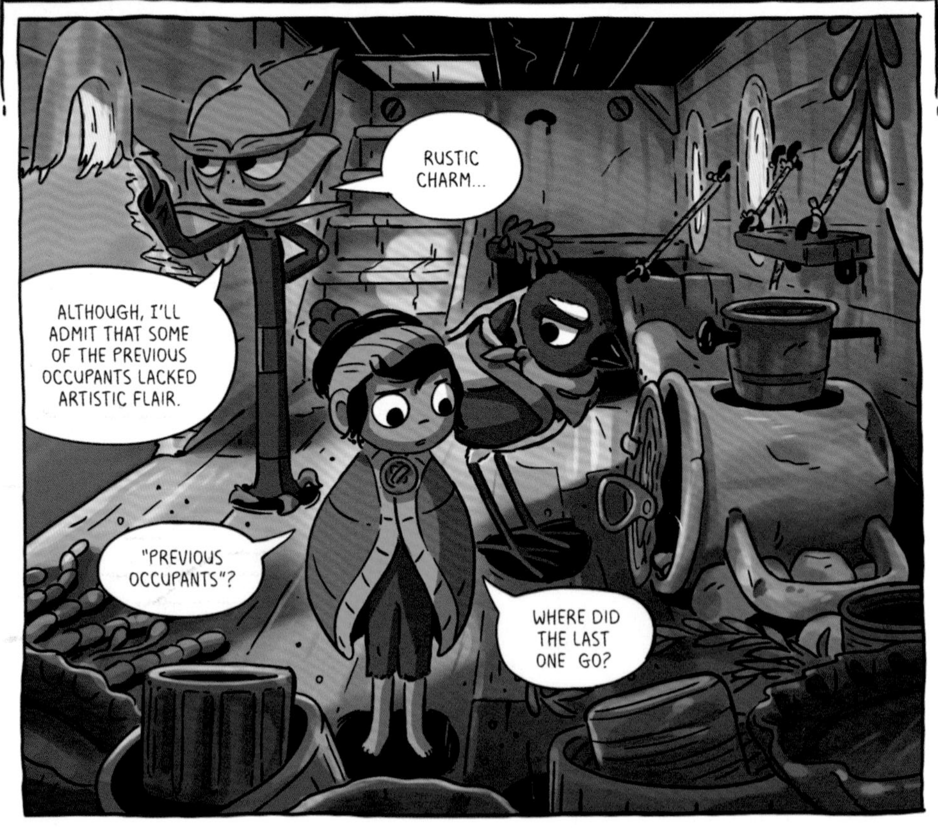
RUSTIC CHARM...
ALTHOUGH, I'LL ADMIT THAT SOME OF THE PREVIOUS OCCUPANTS LACKED ARTISTIC FLAIR.
"PREVIOUS OCCUPANTS"?
WHERE DID THE LAST ONE GO?

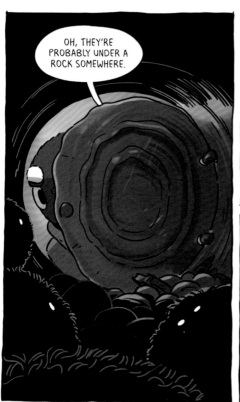

OH, THEY'RE PROBABLY UNDER A ROCK SOMEWHERE.

HMM. LOTS OF BOTTLE CAPS...

AH!

CLATTER

IS THERE REALLY NOWHERE ELSE?

AFRAID NOT!

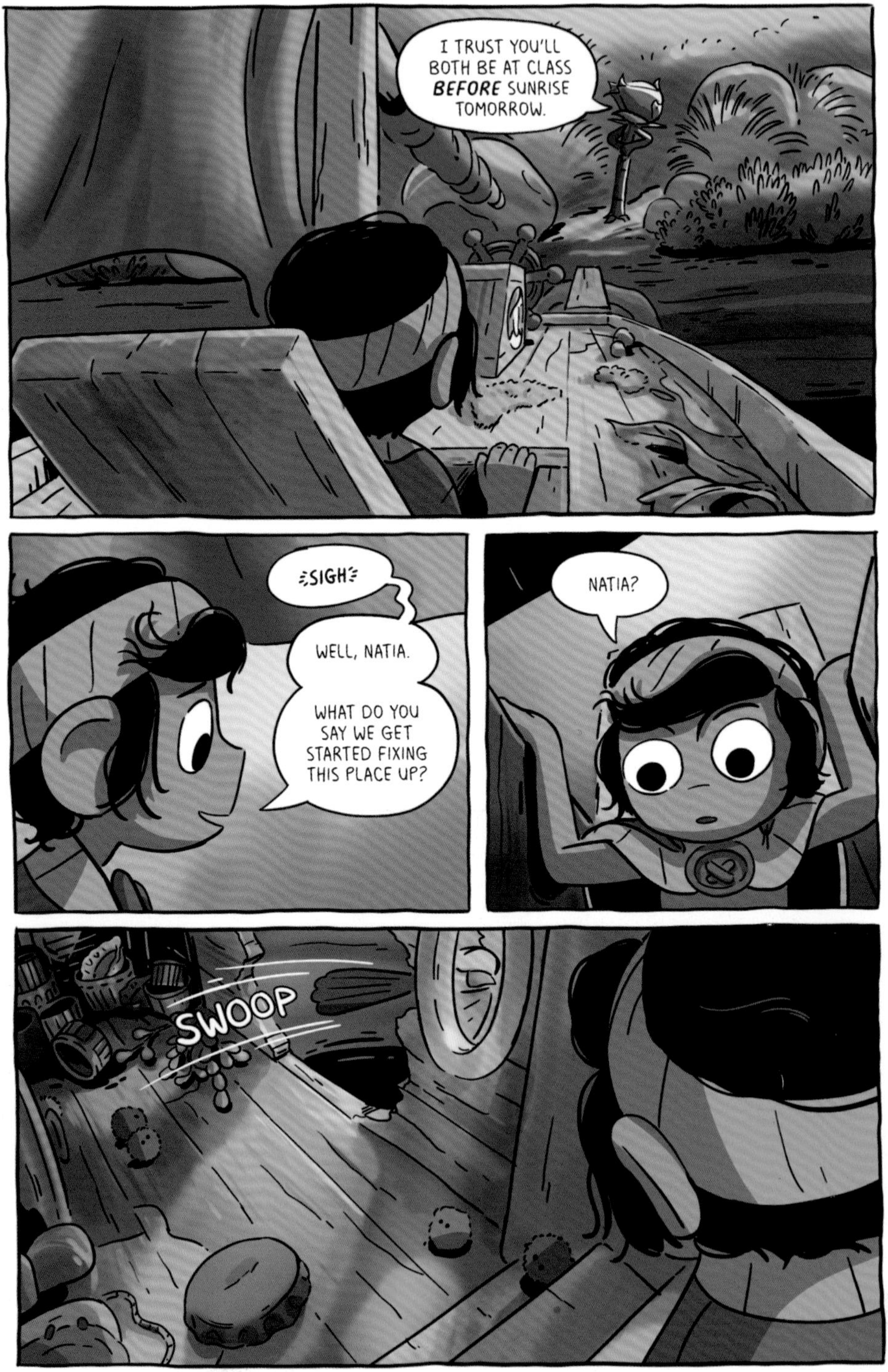
I TRUST YOU'LL BOTH BE AT CLASS BEFORE SUNRISE TOMORROW.
SIGH
WELL, NATIA.
WHAT DO YOU SAY WE GET STARTED FIXING THIS PLACE UP?
NATIA?
SWOOP

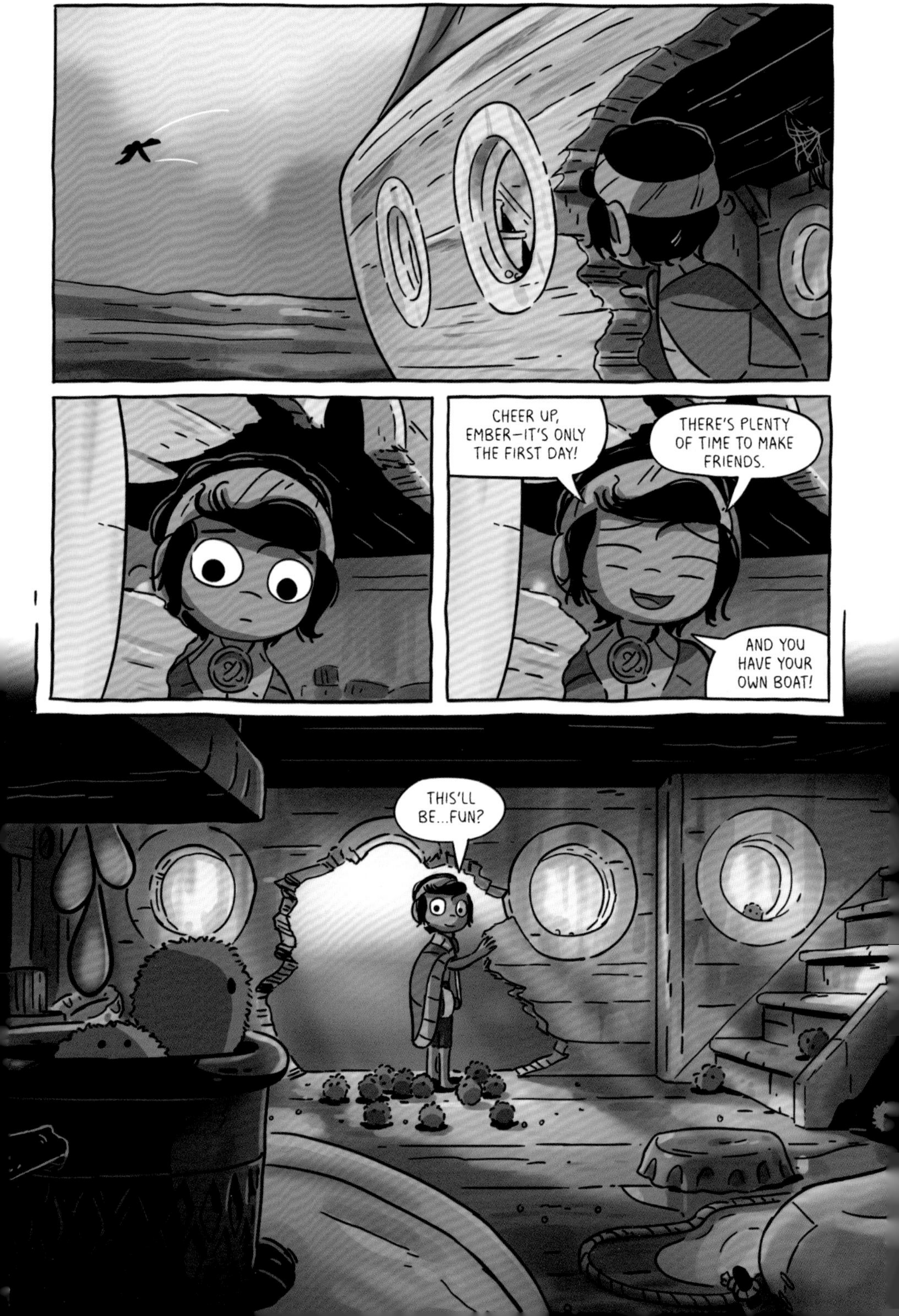
CHEER UP, EMBER—IT'S ONLY THE FIRST DAY!
THERE'S PLENTY OF TIME TO MAKE FRIENDS.
AND YOU HAVE YOUR OWN BOAT!
THIS'LL BE...FUN?

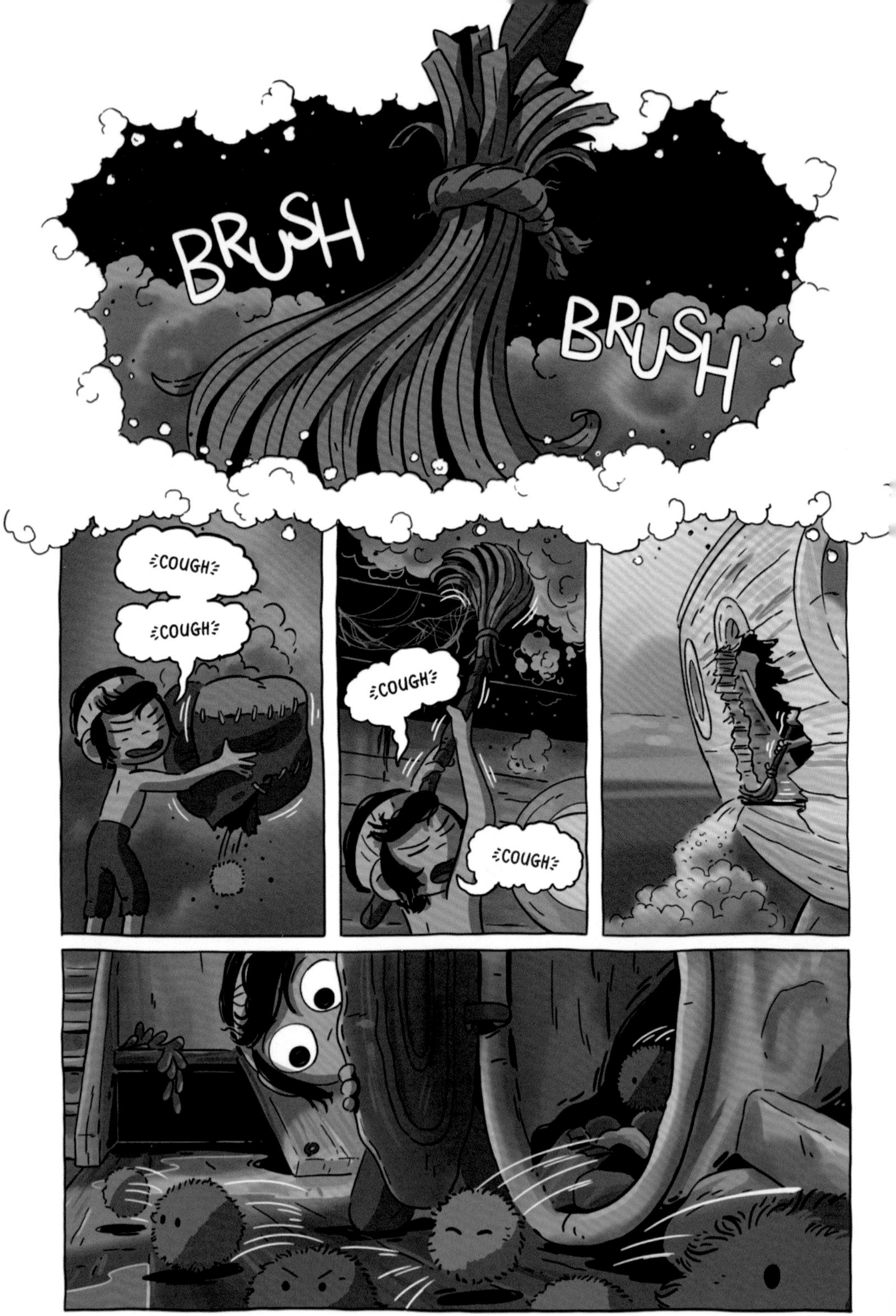
BRUSH
BRUSH
COUGH
COUGH
COUGH
COUGH

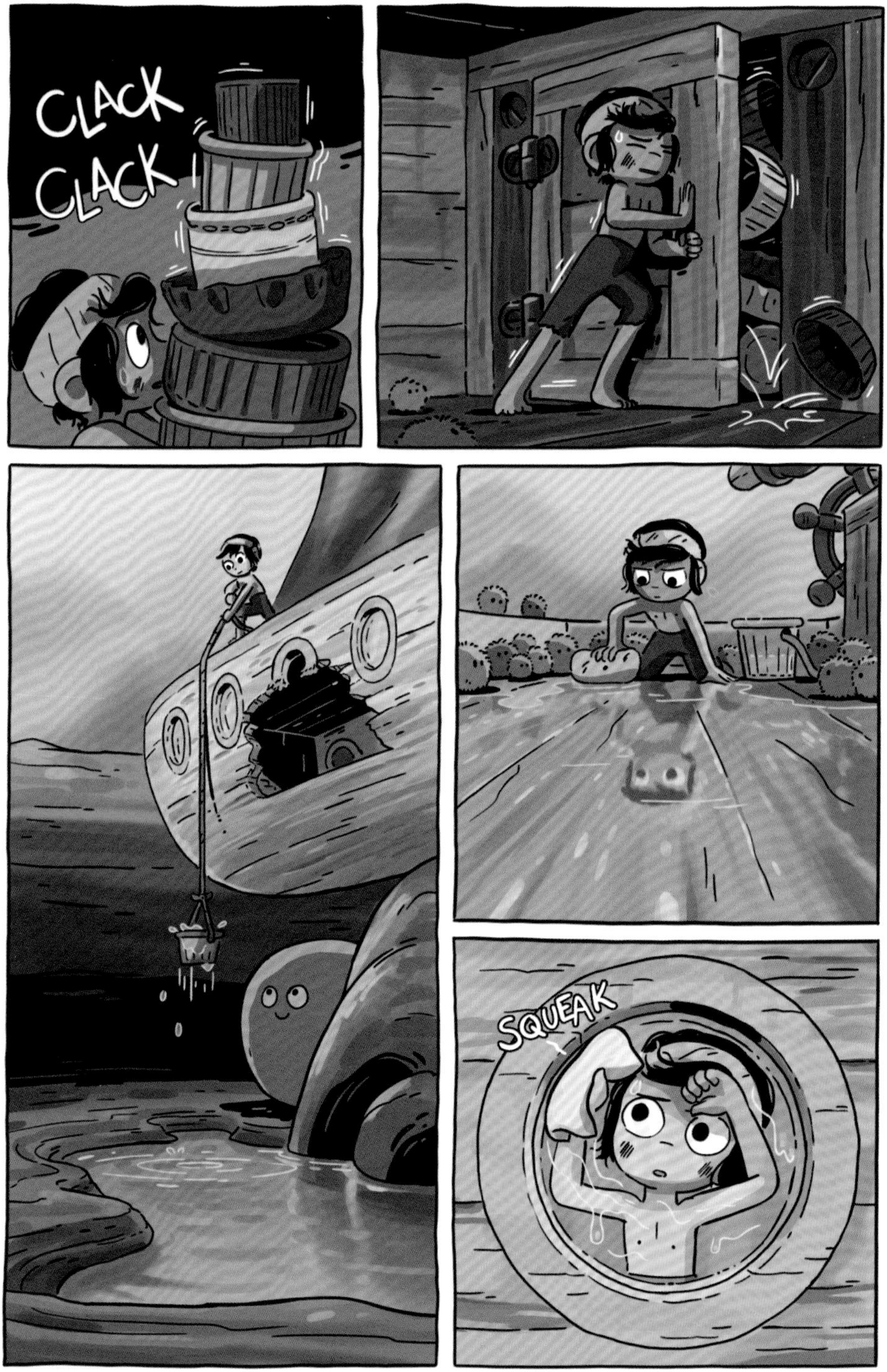
CLACK
CLACK
SQUEAK

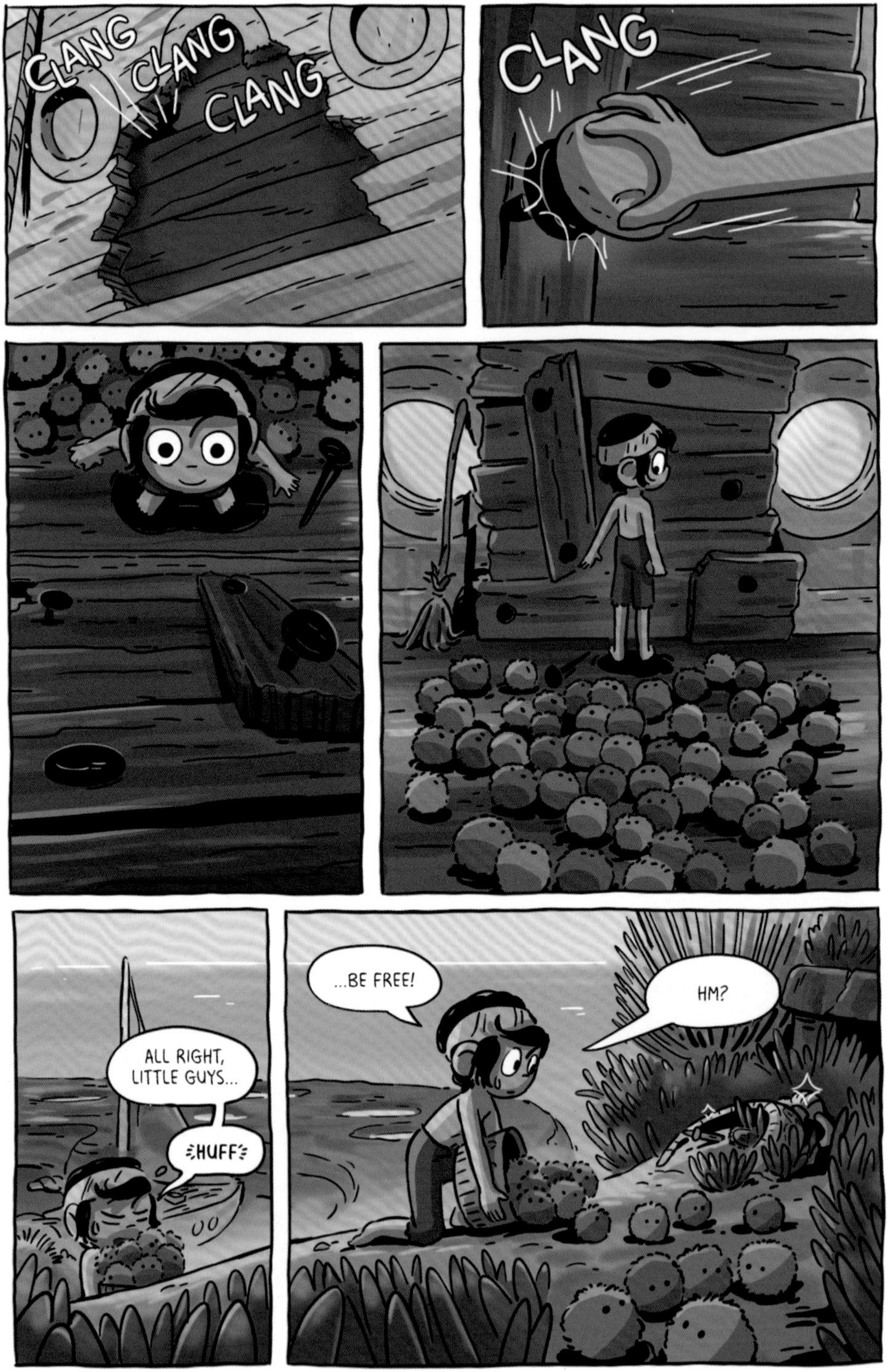
CLANG
CLANG
CLANG
CLANG
ALL RIGHT, LITTLE GUYS...
HUFF
...BE FREE!
HM?

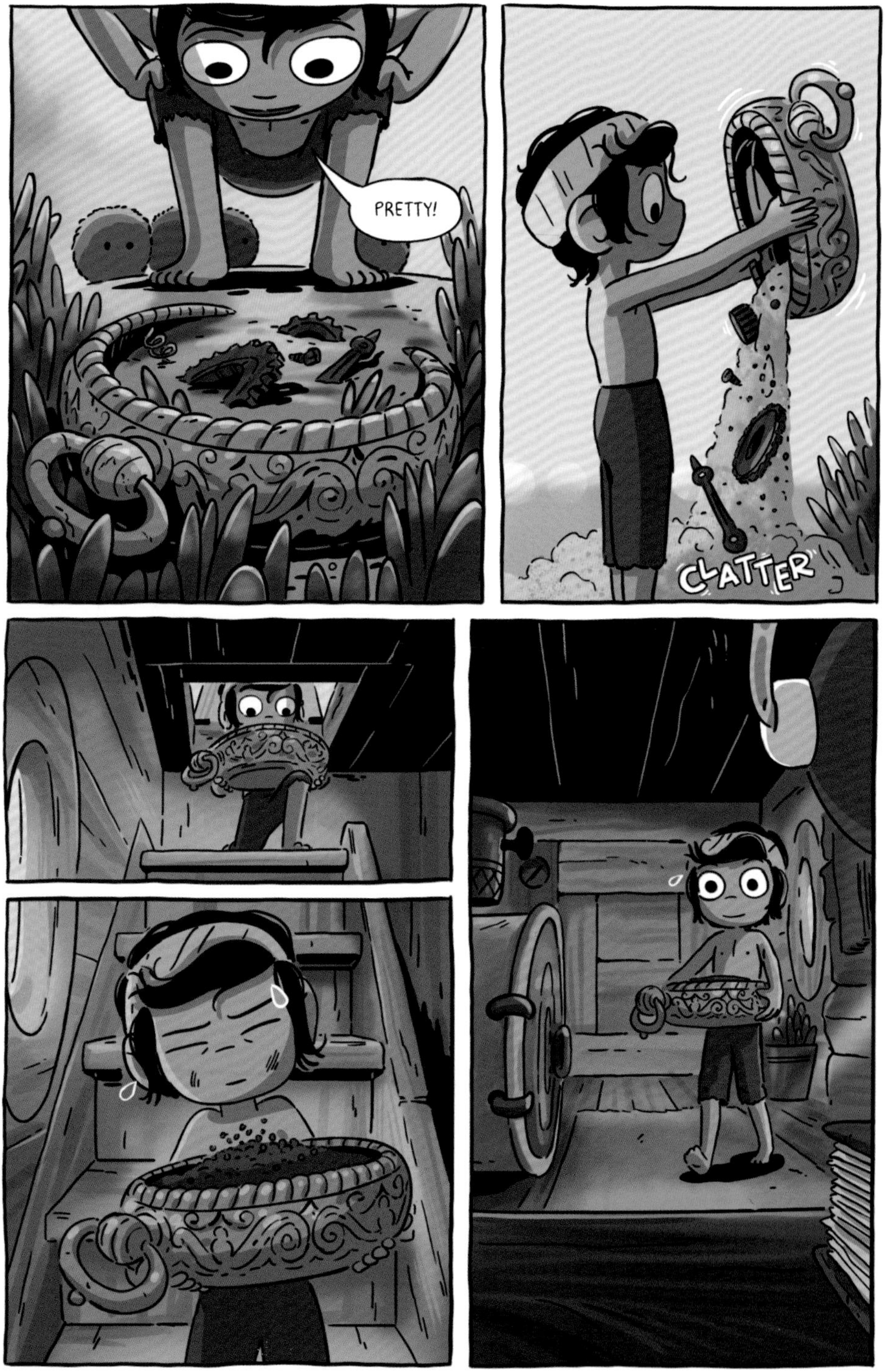
PRETTY!
CLATTER

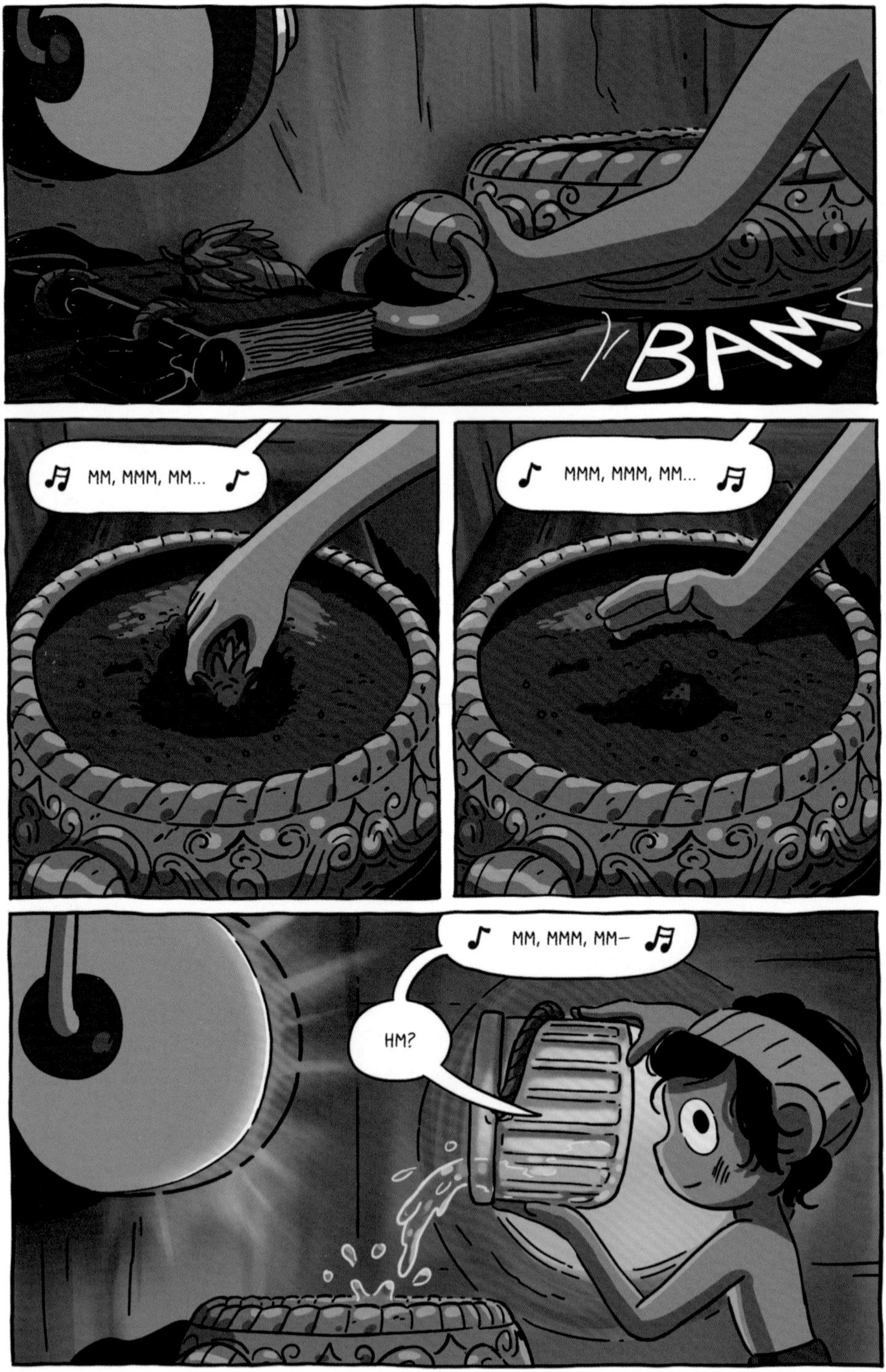
BAM
MM, MMM, MM...
MMM, MMM, MM...
MM, MMM, MM–
HM?

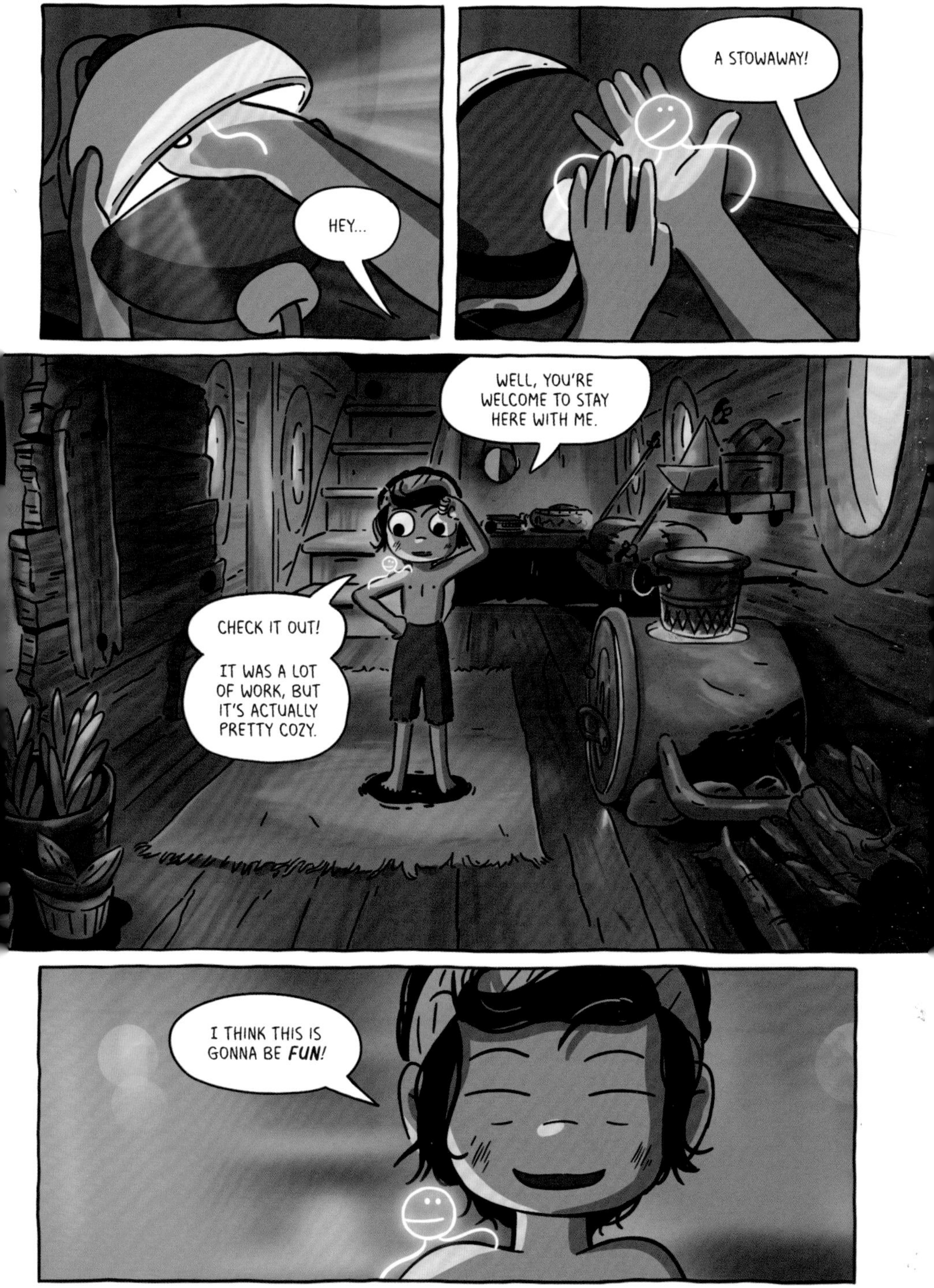
HEY...
A STOWAWAY!
WELL, YOU'RE WELCOME TO STAY HERE WITH ME.
CHECK IT OUT!
IT WAS A LOT OF WORK, BUT IT'S ACTUALLY PRETTY COZY.
I THINK THIS IS GONNA BE *FUN*!

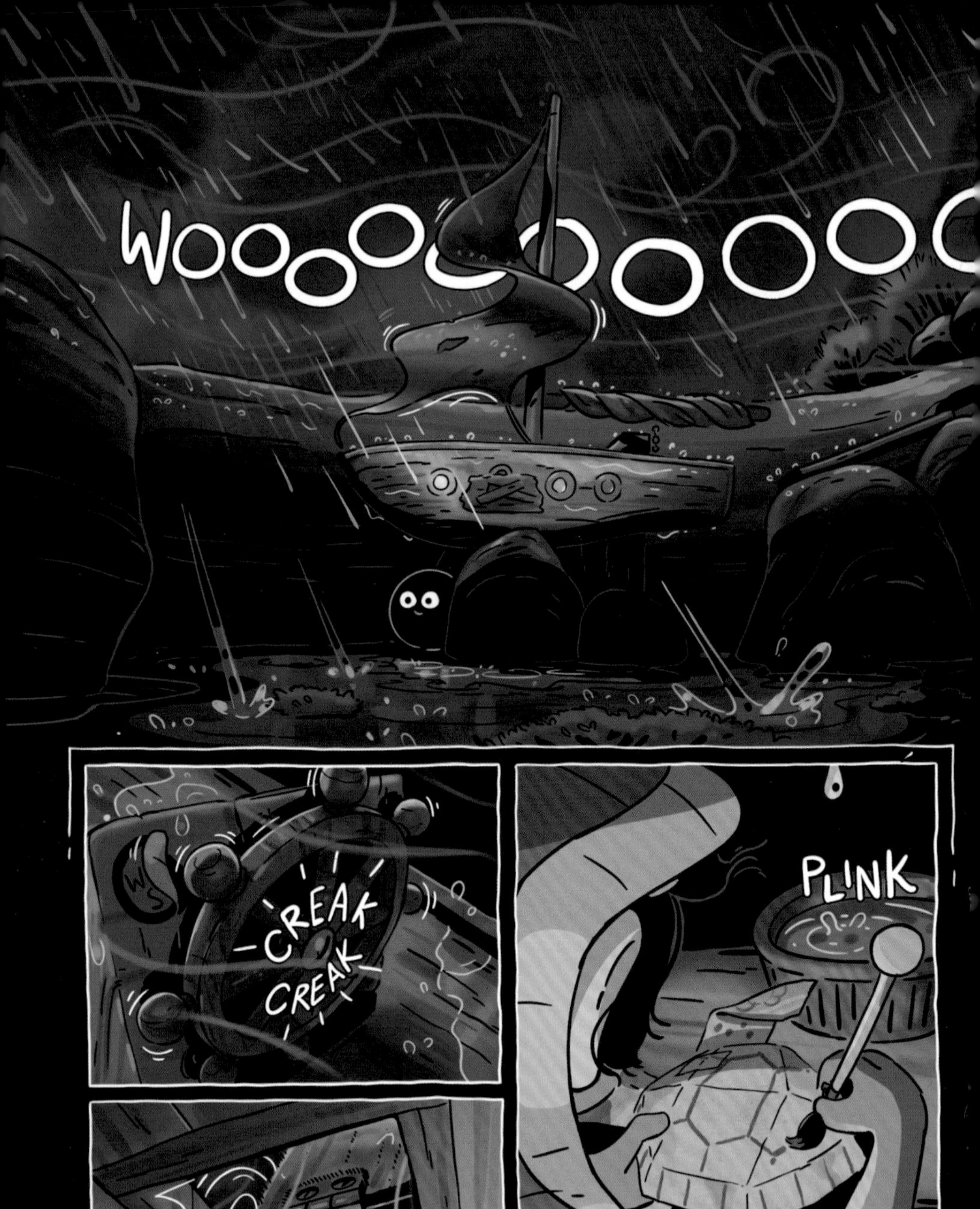
WOOOOOOOOOO
CREAK
CREAK
CLAP
CLAP
PLINK

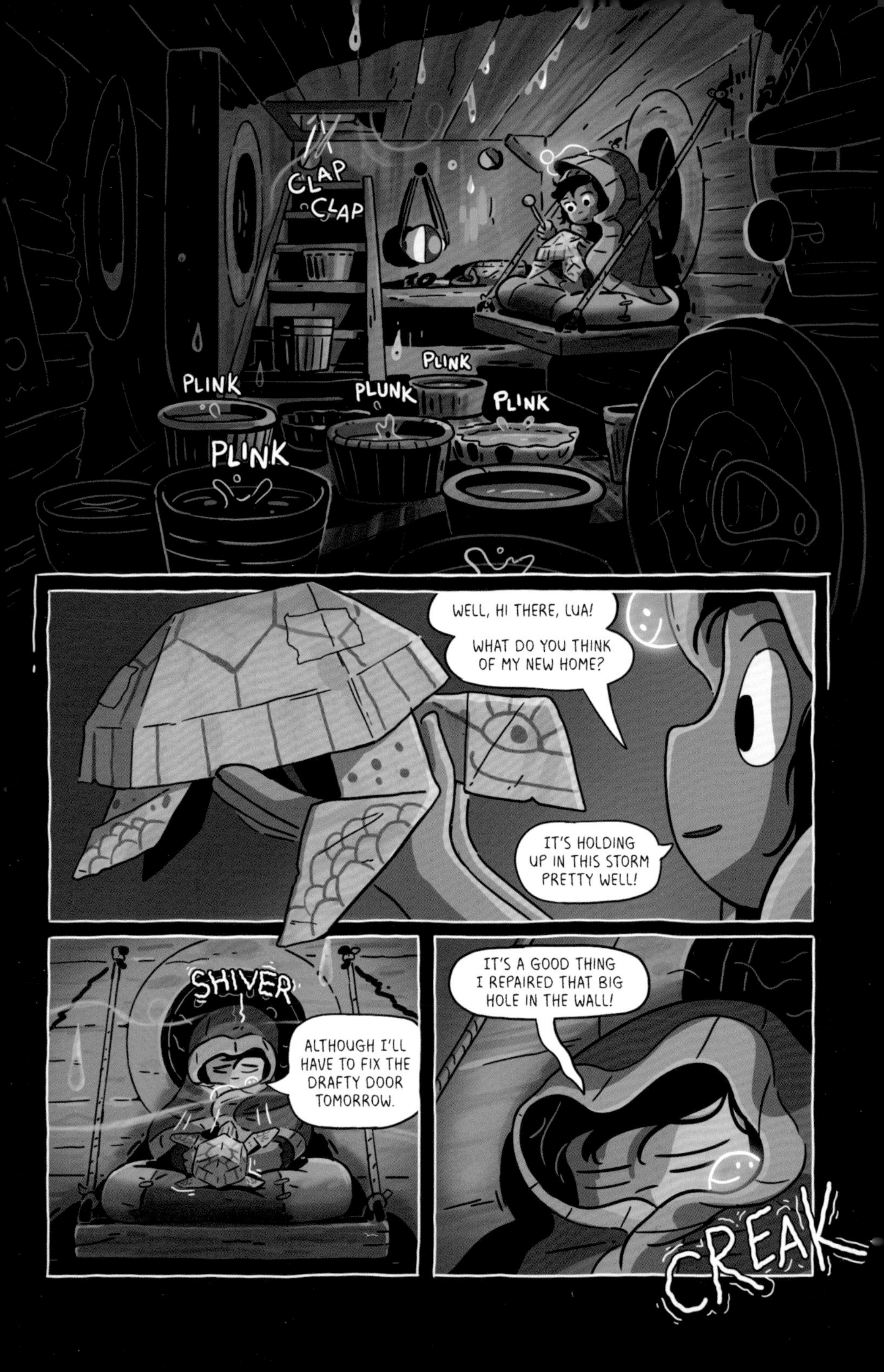
CLAP
CLAP
PLINK
PLUNK
PLINK
PLINK
PLINK
WELL, HI THERE, LUA!
WHAT DO YOU THINK OF MY NEW HOME?
IT'S HOLDING UP IN THIS STORM PRETTY WELL!
SHIVER
ALTHOUGH I'LL HAVE TO FIX THE DRAFTY DOOR TOMORROW.
IT'S A GOOD THING I REPAIRED THAT BIG HOLE IN THE WALL!
CREAK

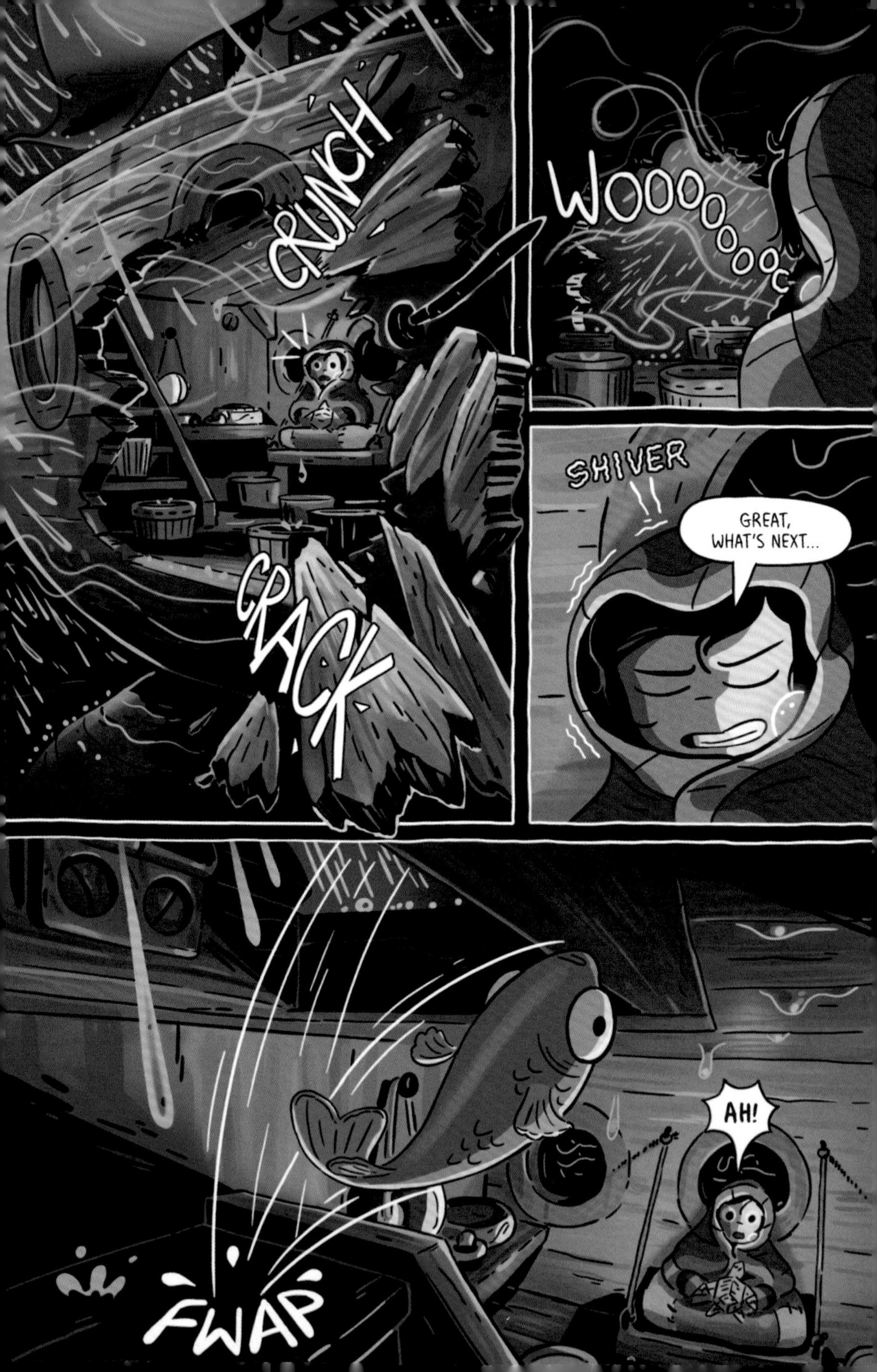
CRUNCH
CRACK
WOOOOOOOC
SHIVER
GREAT, WHAT'S NEXT...
FWAP
AH!

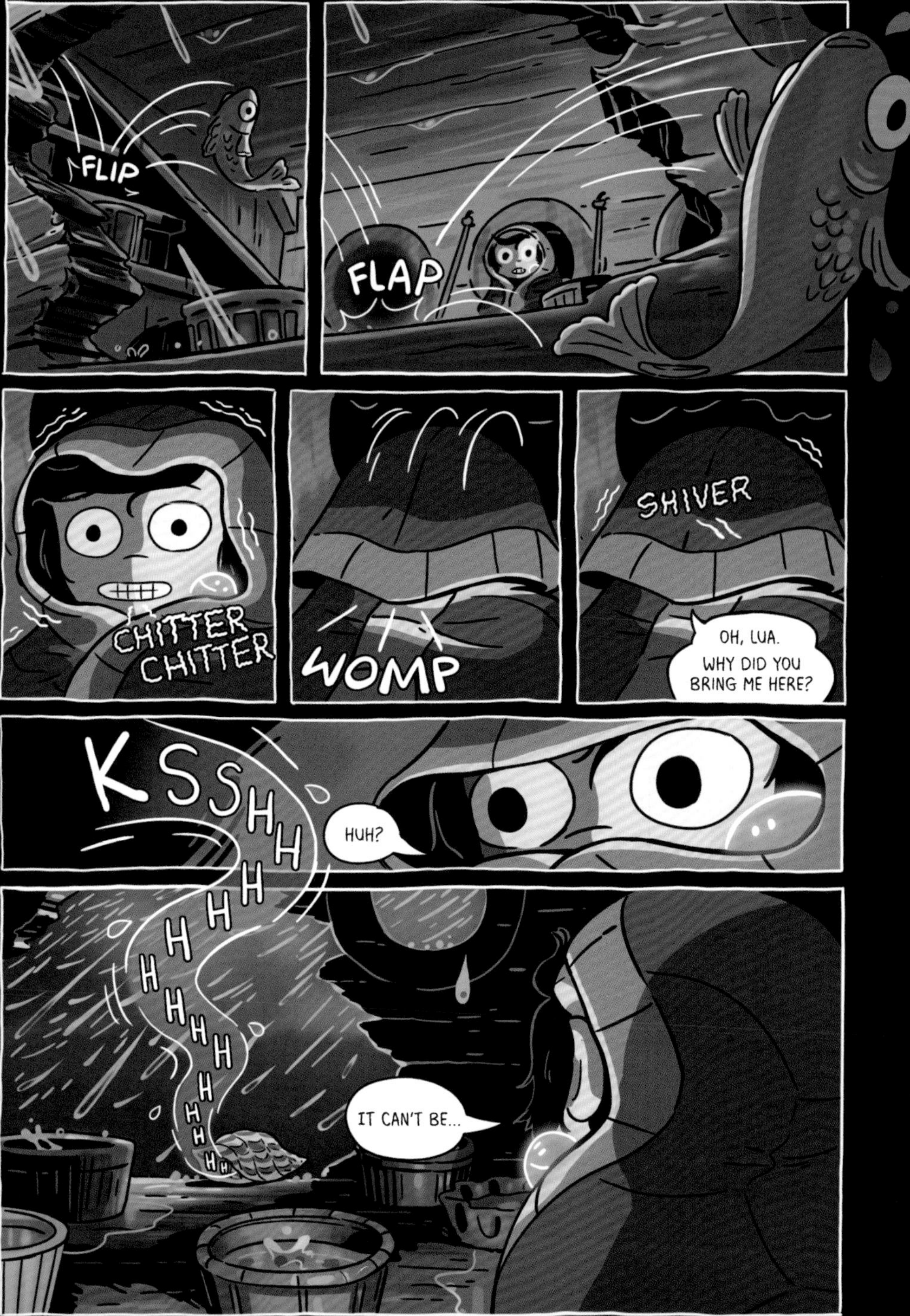
FLIP
FLAP
CHITTER CHITTER
WOMP
SHIVER
OH, LUA. WHY DID YOU BRING ME HERE?
KSSHHHHHHHHHHHHH
HUH?
IT CAN'T BE...

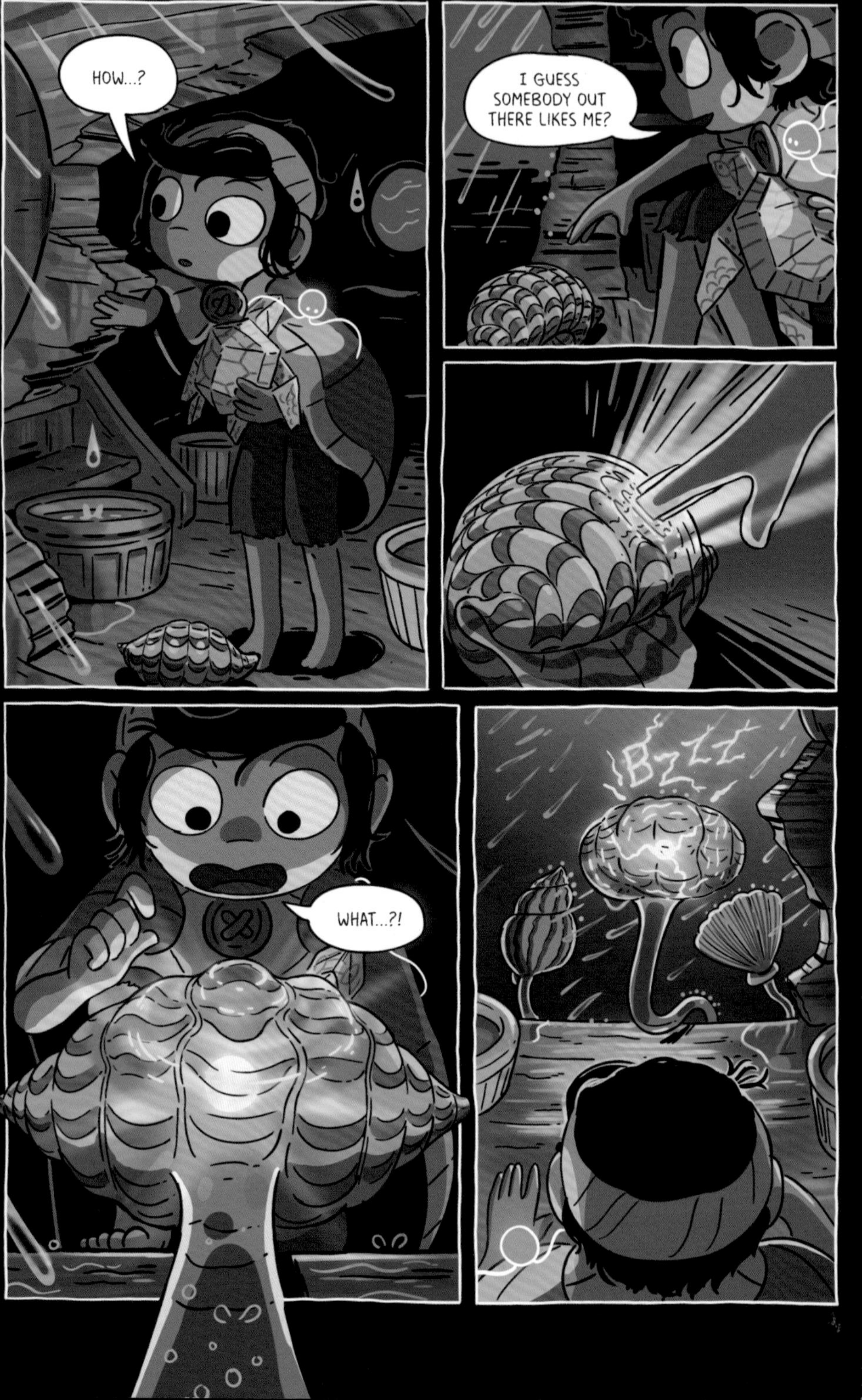
HOW...?
I GUESS SOMEBODY OUT THERE LIKES ME?
WHAT...?!
BZZZ

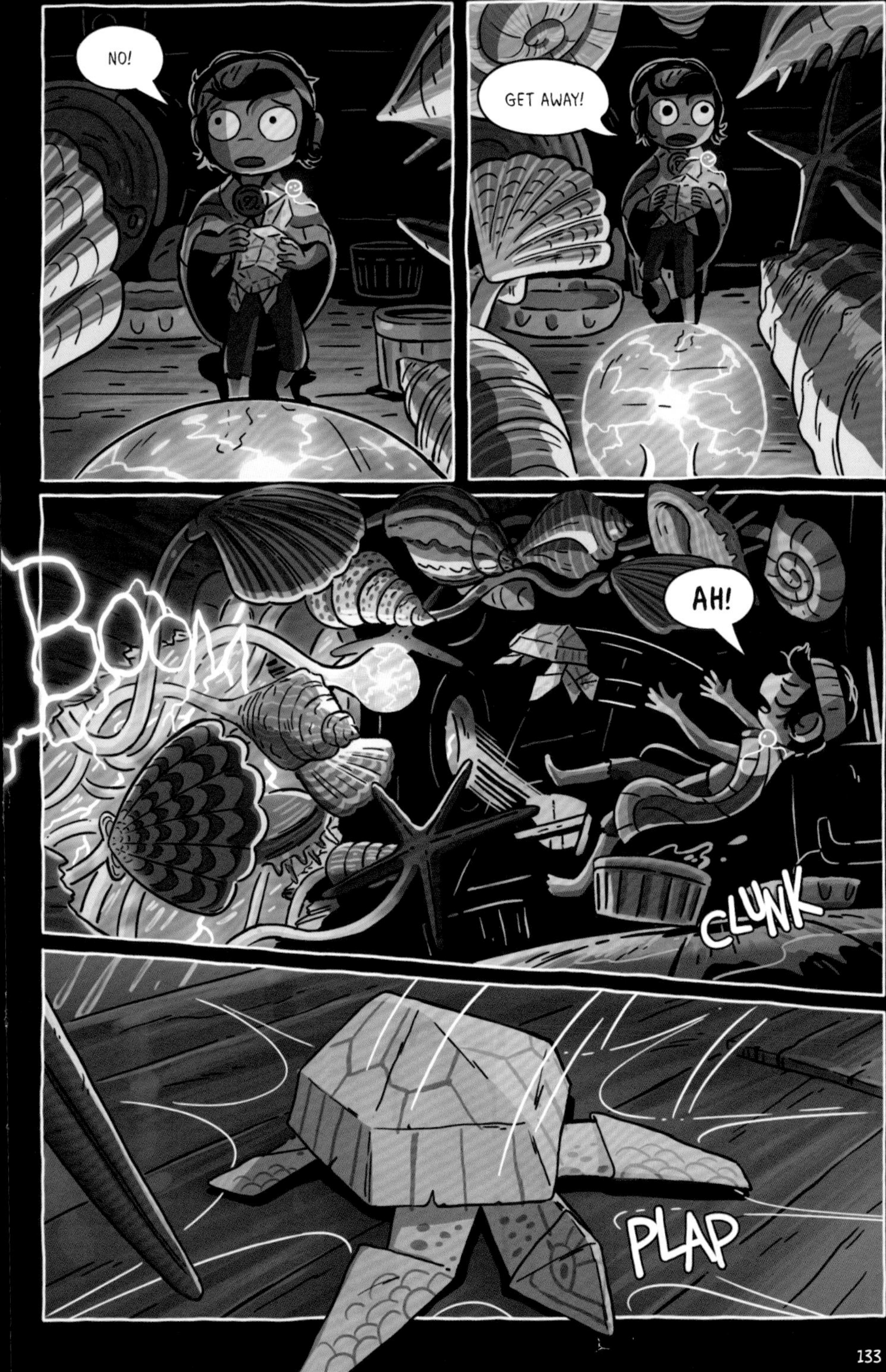
NO!
GET AWAY!
BOOM
AH!
CLUNK
PLAP

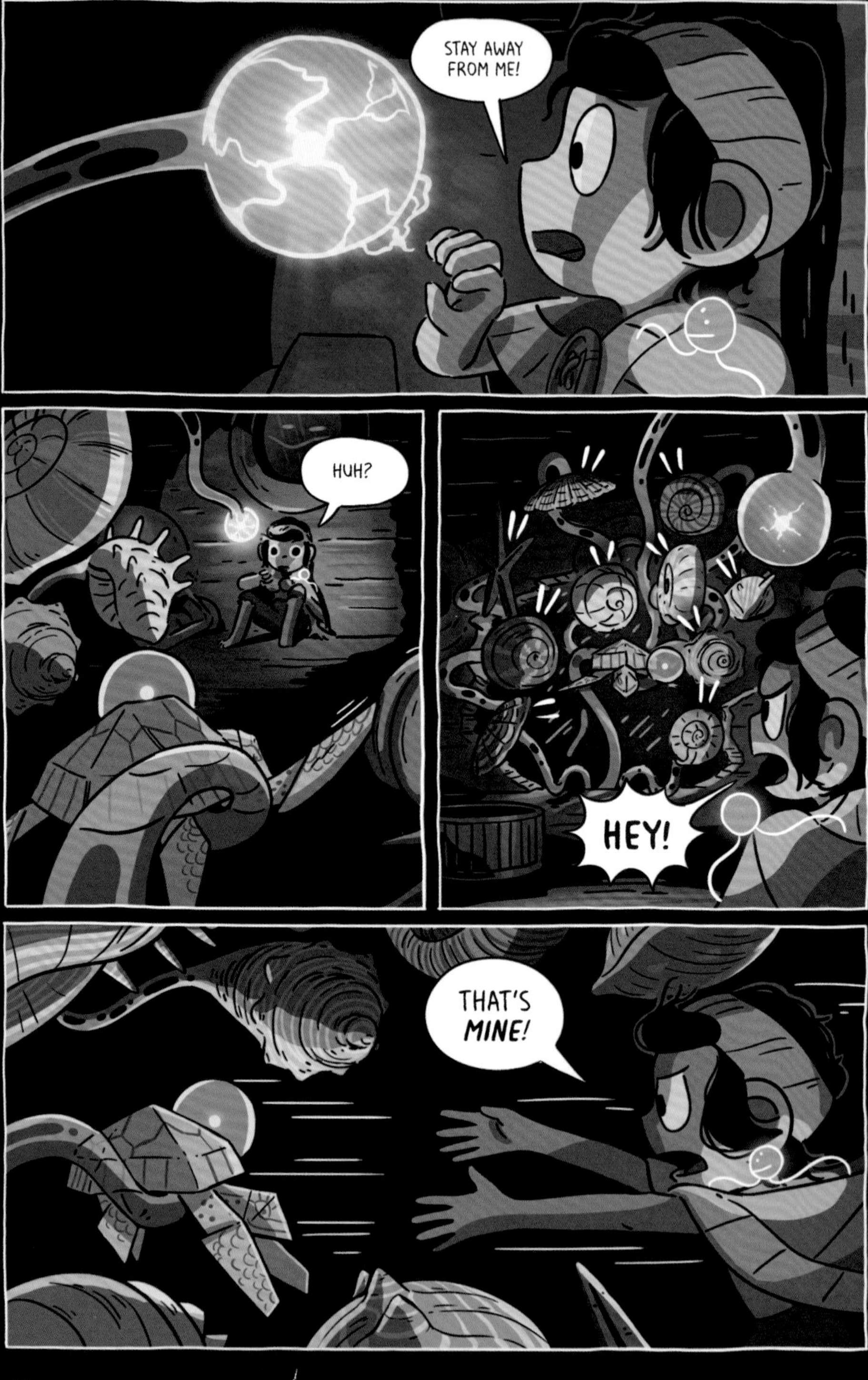
STAY AWAY FROM ME!
HUH?
HEY!
THAT'S MINE!

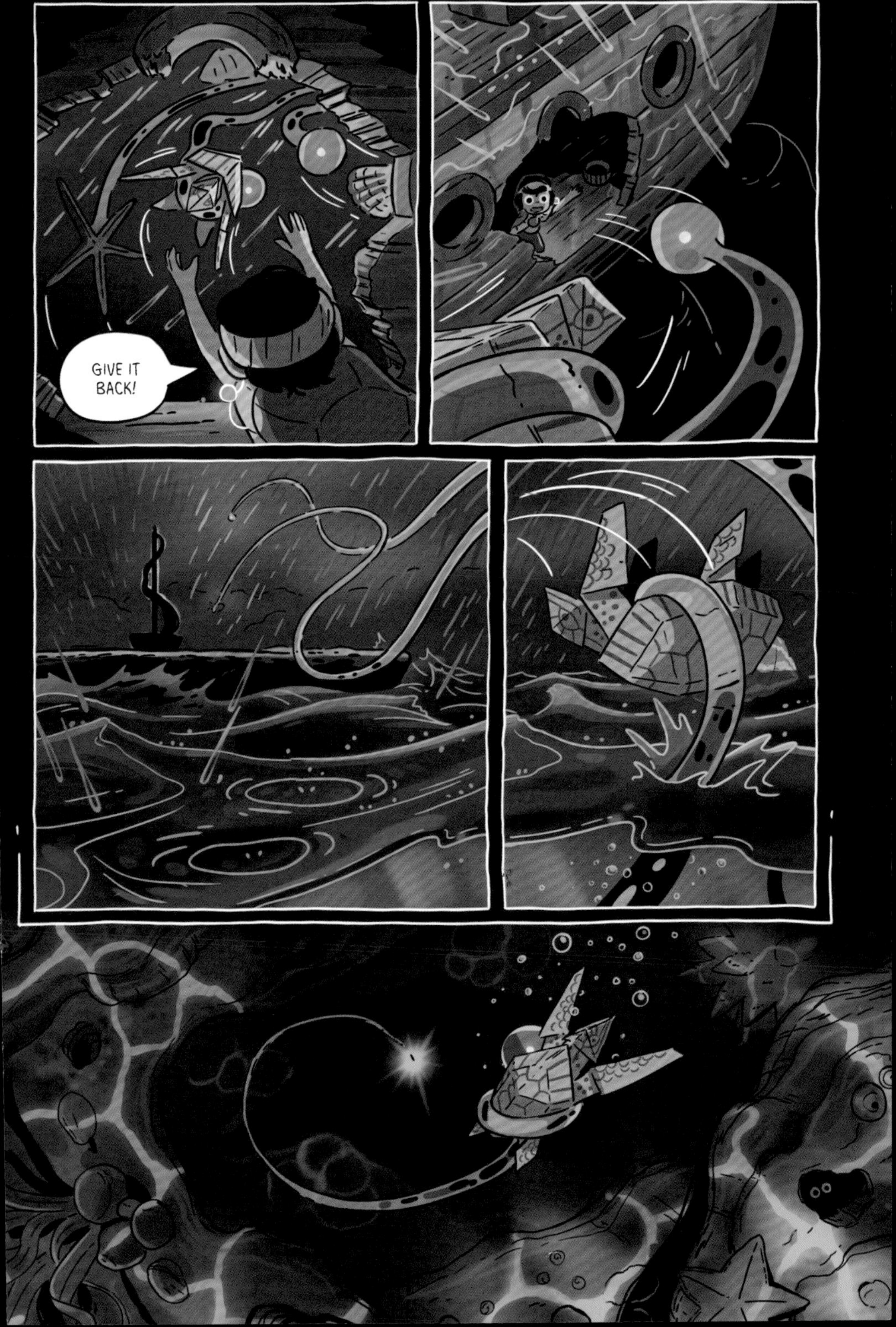
GIVE IT BACK!

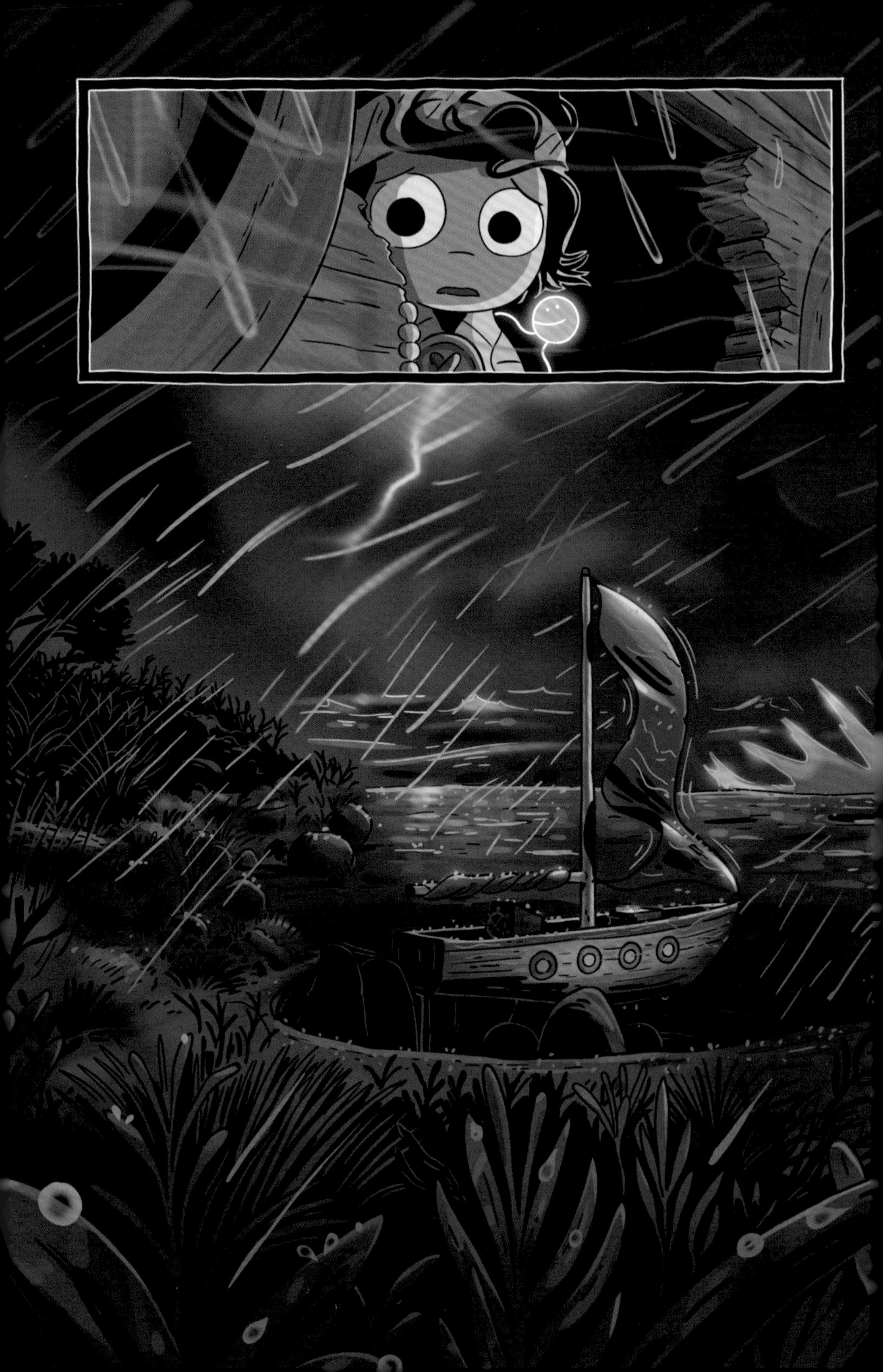

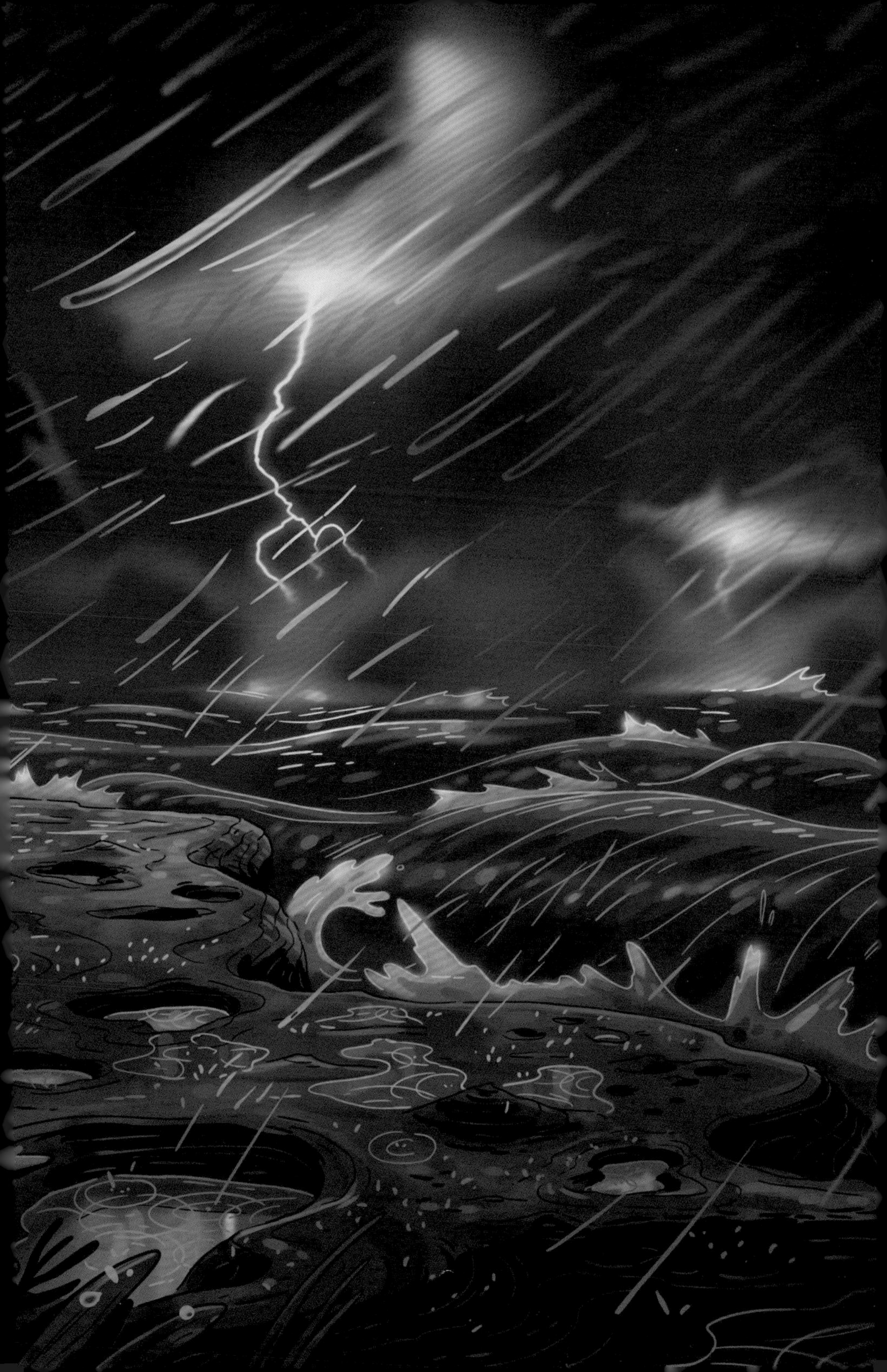

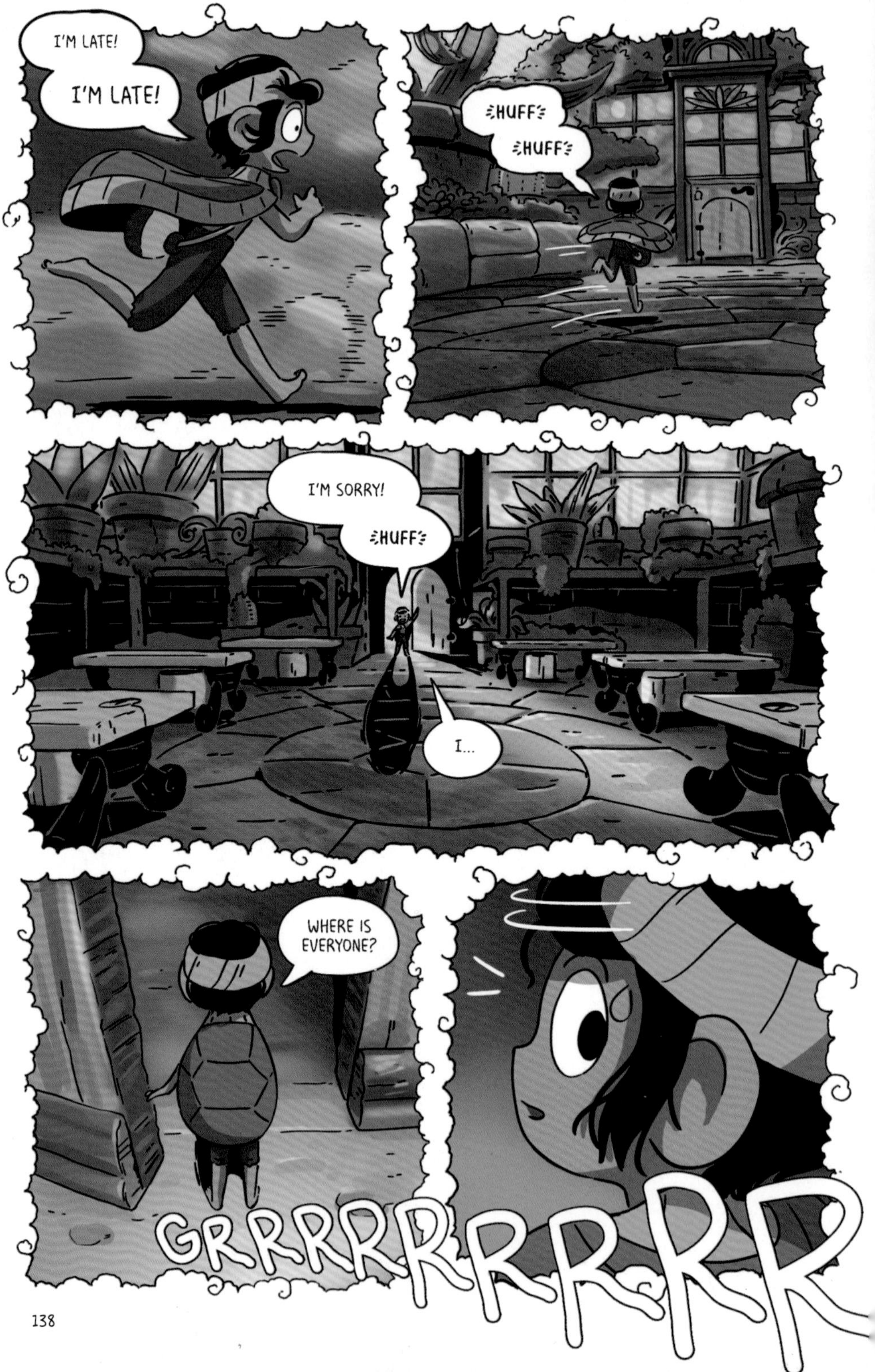

I'M LATE!
I'M LATE!
HUFF
HUFF
I'M SORRY!
HUFF
I...
WHERE IS EVERYONE?
GRRRRRRRRR

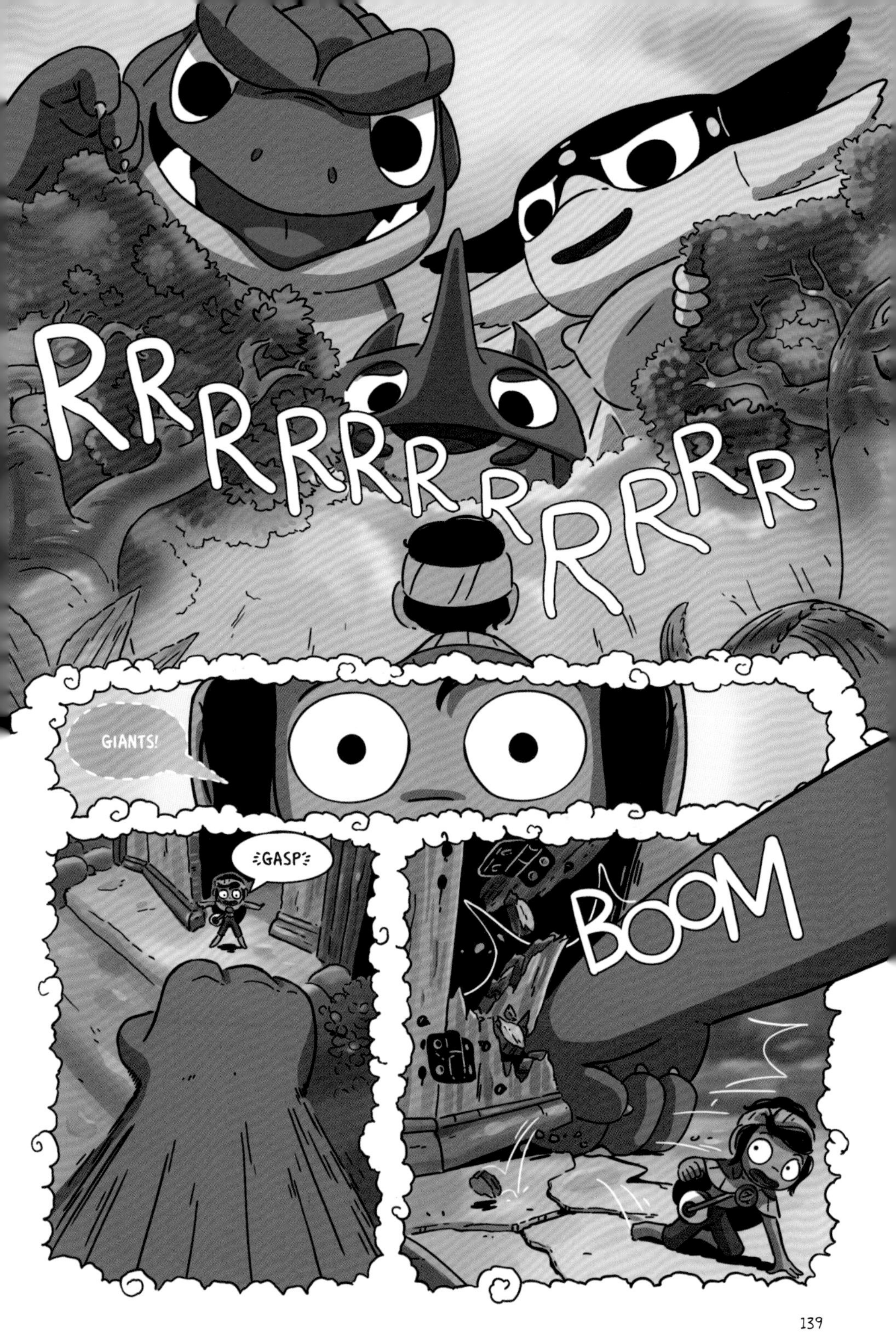
RRRRRRRRRRRRR
GIANTS!
GASP
BOOM

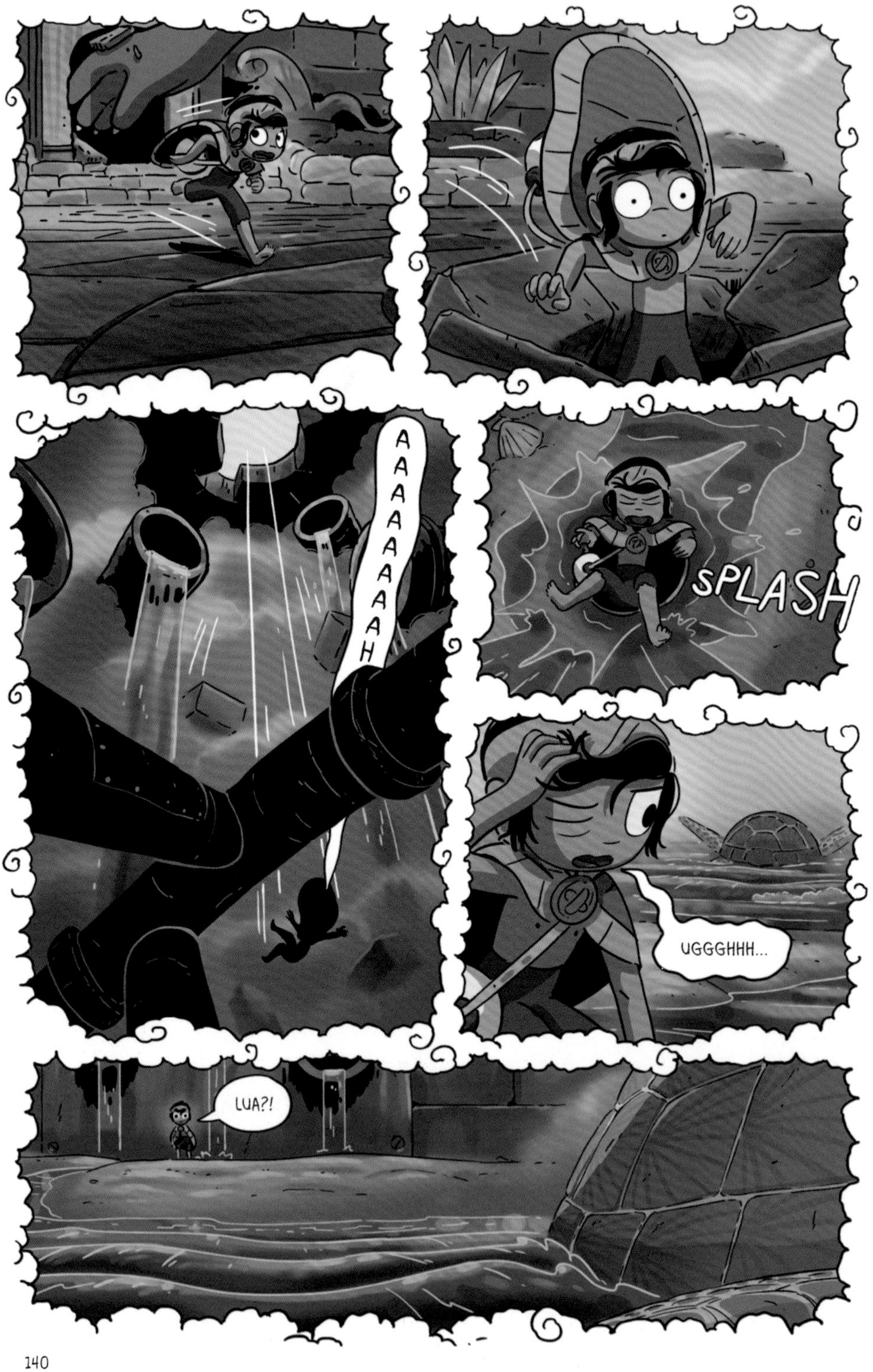
AAAAAAAAAH
SPLASH
UGGGHHH...
LUA?!

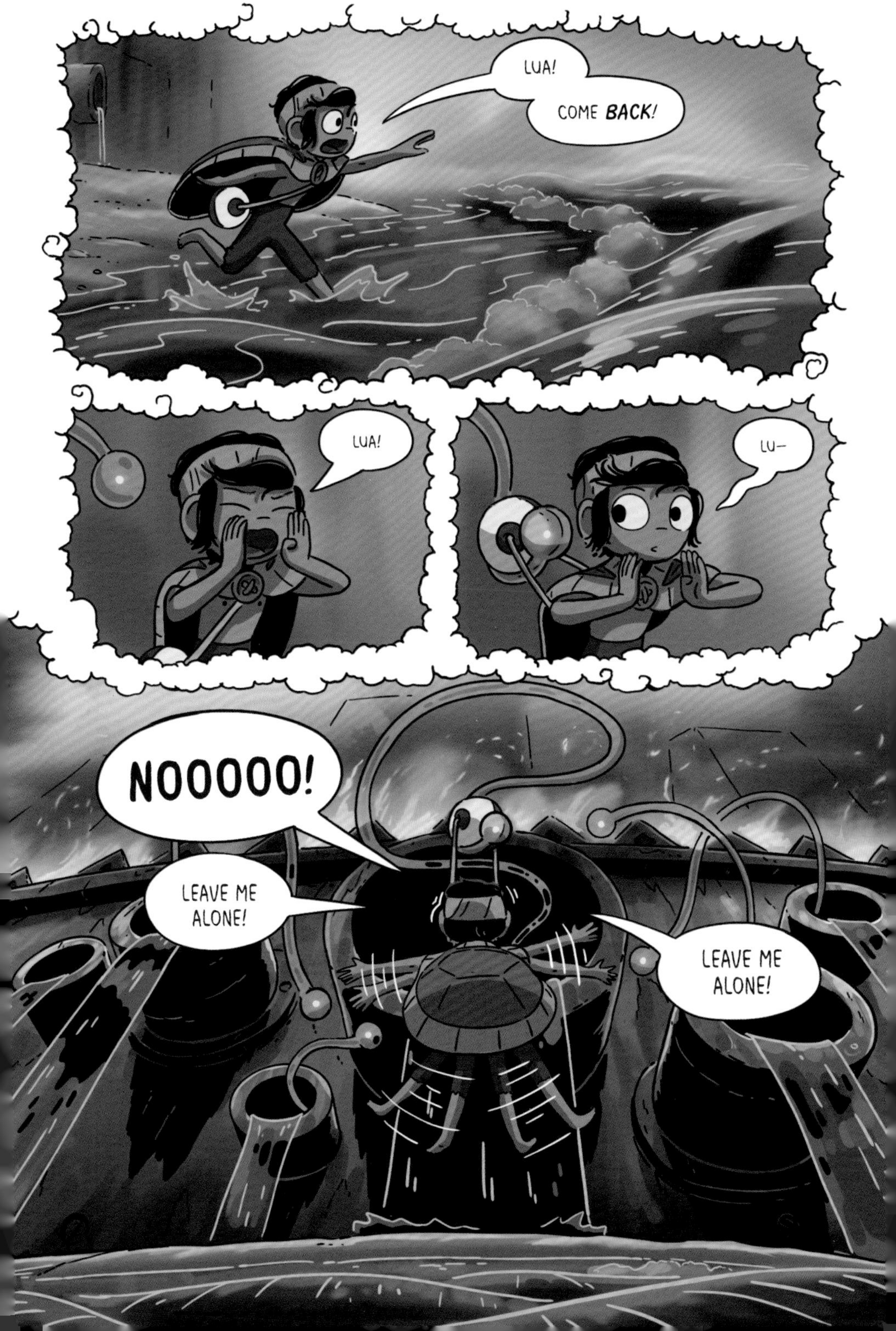
LUA!
COME **BACK**!
LUA!
LU–
NOOOOO!
LEAVE ME ALONE!
LEAVE ME ALONE!

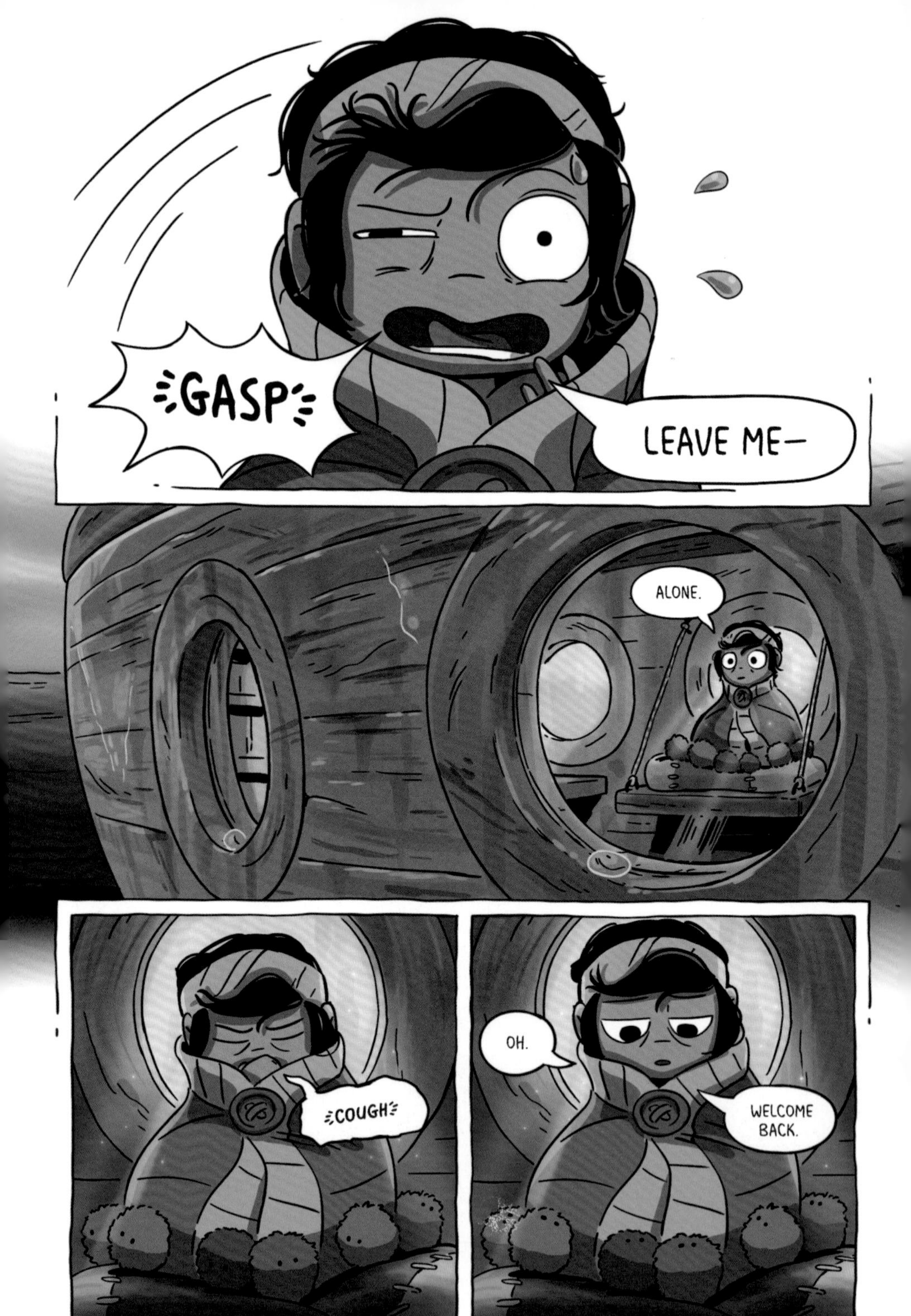
GASP
LEAVE ME–
ALONE.
COUGH
OH.
WELCOME BACK.

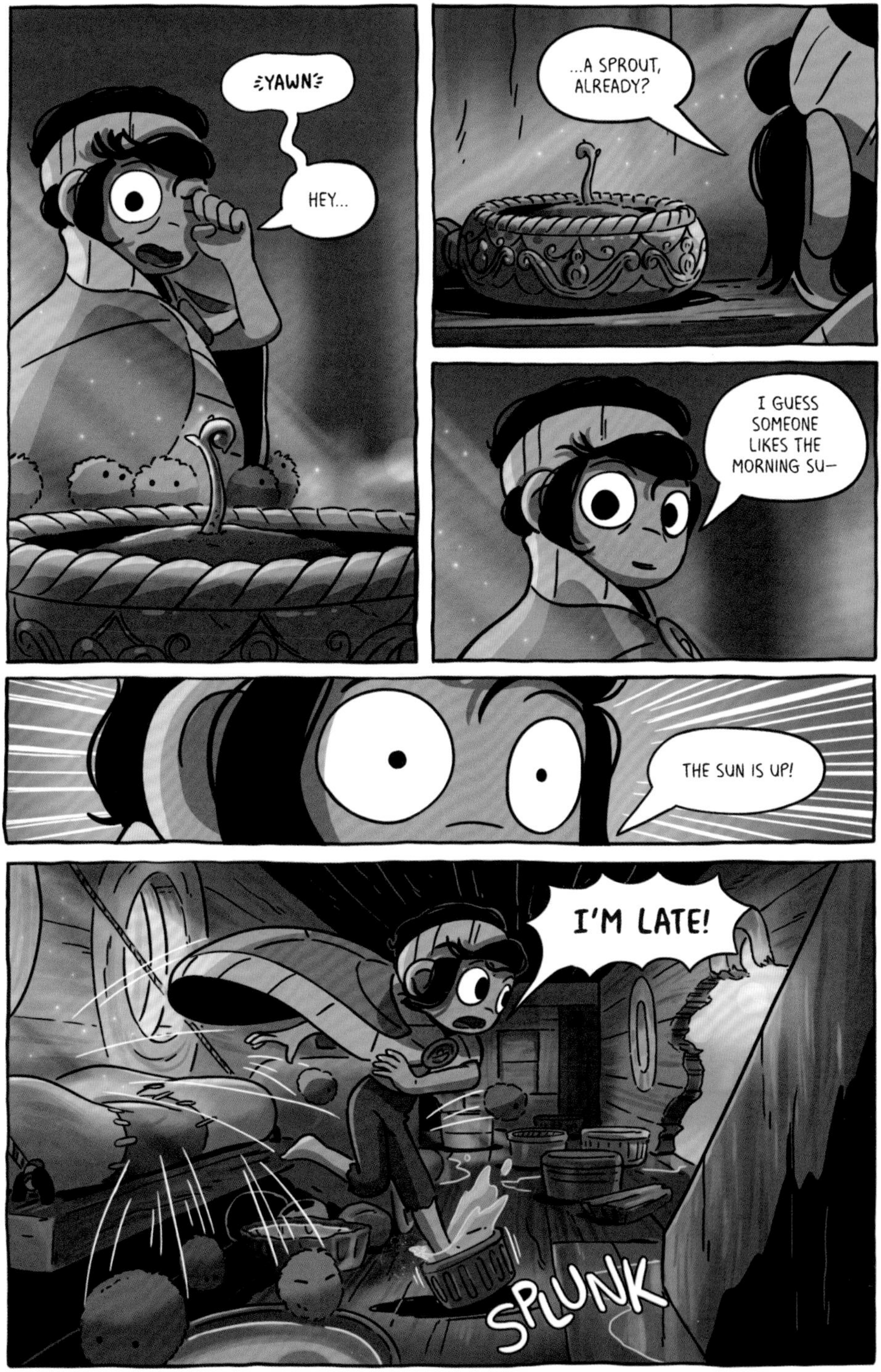
YAWN
HEY...
...A SPROUT, ALREADY?
I GUESS SOMEONE LIKES THE MORNING SU—
THE SUN IS UP!
I'M LATE!
SPLUNK

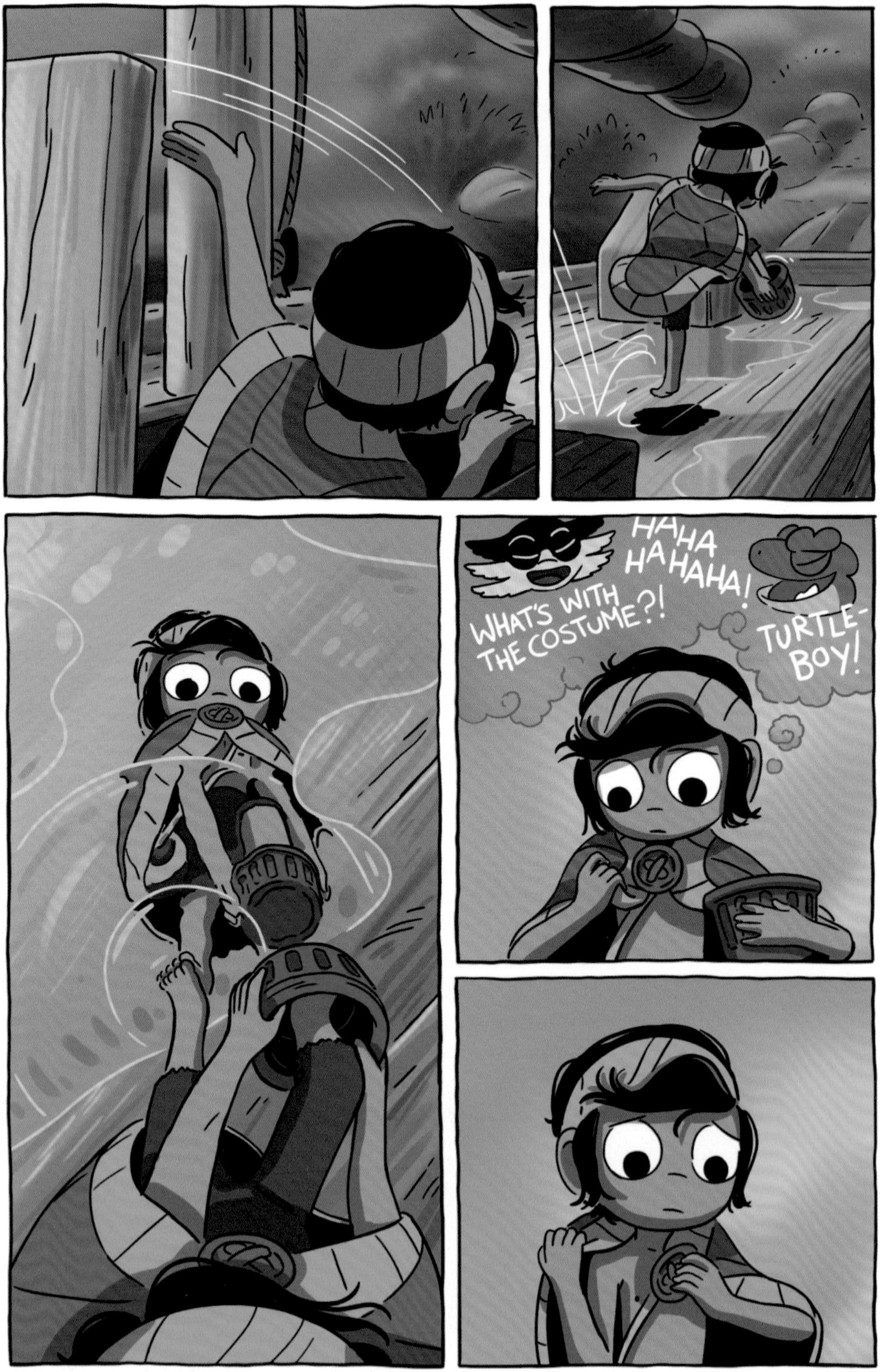
HAHA
HAHAHAHA!
WHAT'S WITH THE COSTUME?!
TURTLE-BOY!

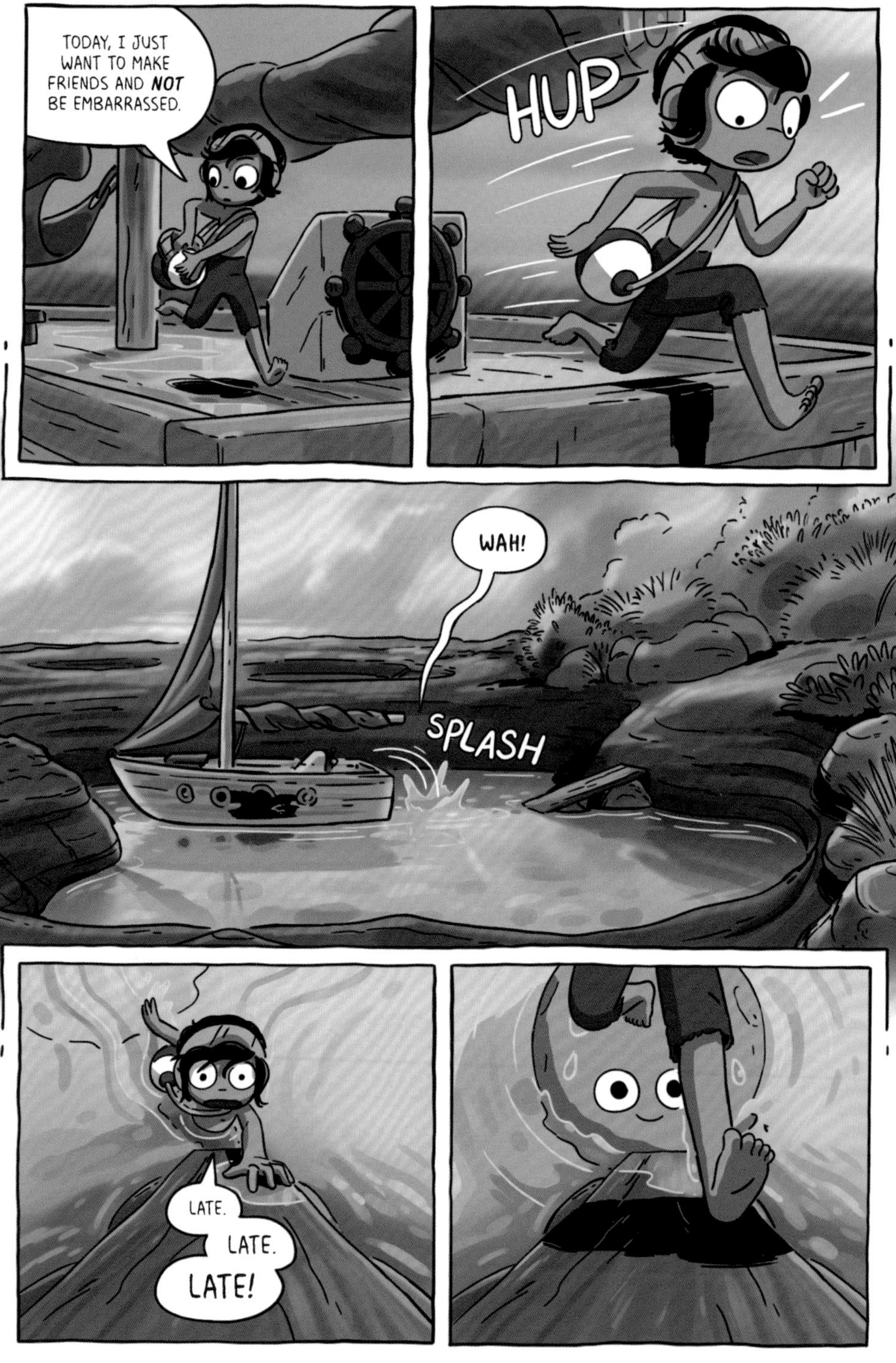

TODAY, I JUST WANT TO MAKE FRIENDS AND **NOT** BE EMBARRASSED.
HUP
WAH!
SPLASH
LATE.
LATE.
LATE!

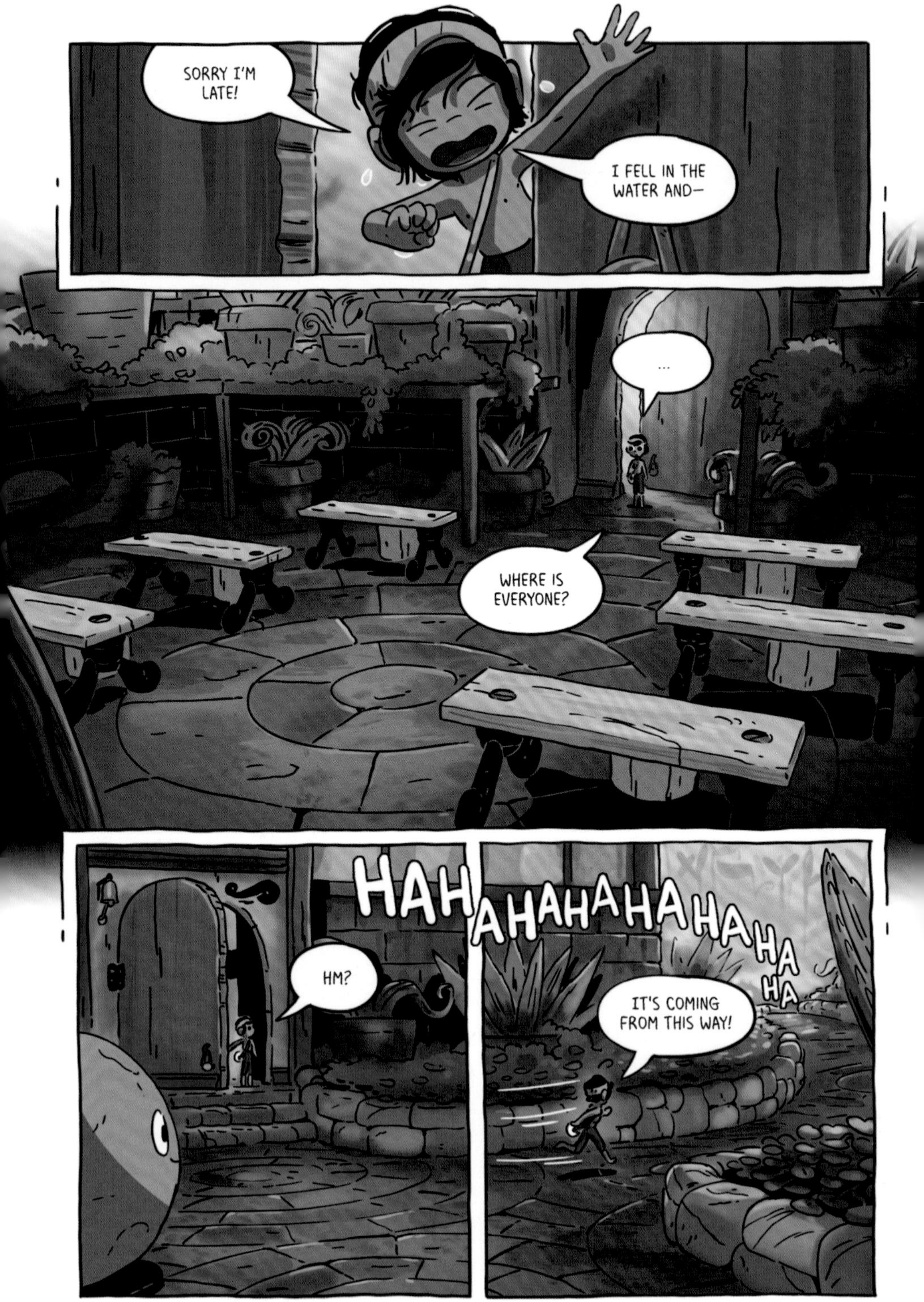
SORRY I'M LATE!
I FELL IN THE WATER AND—
...
WHERE IS EVERYONE?
HAHAHAHAHAHAHAHAHA
HM?
IT'S COMING FROM THIS WAY!

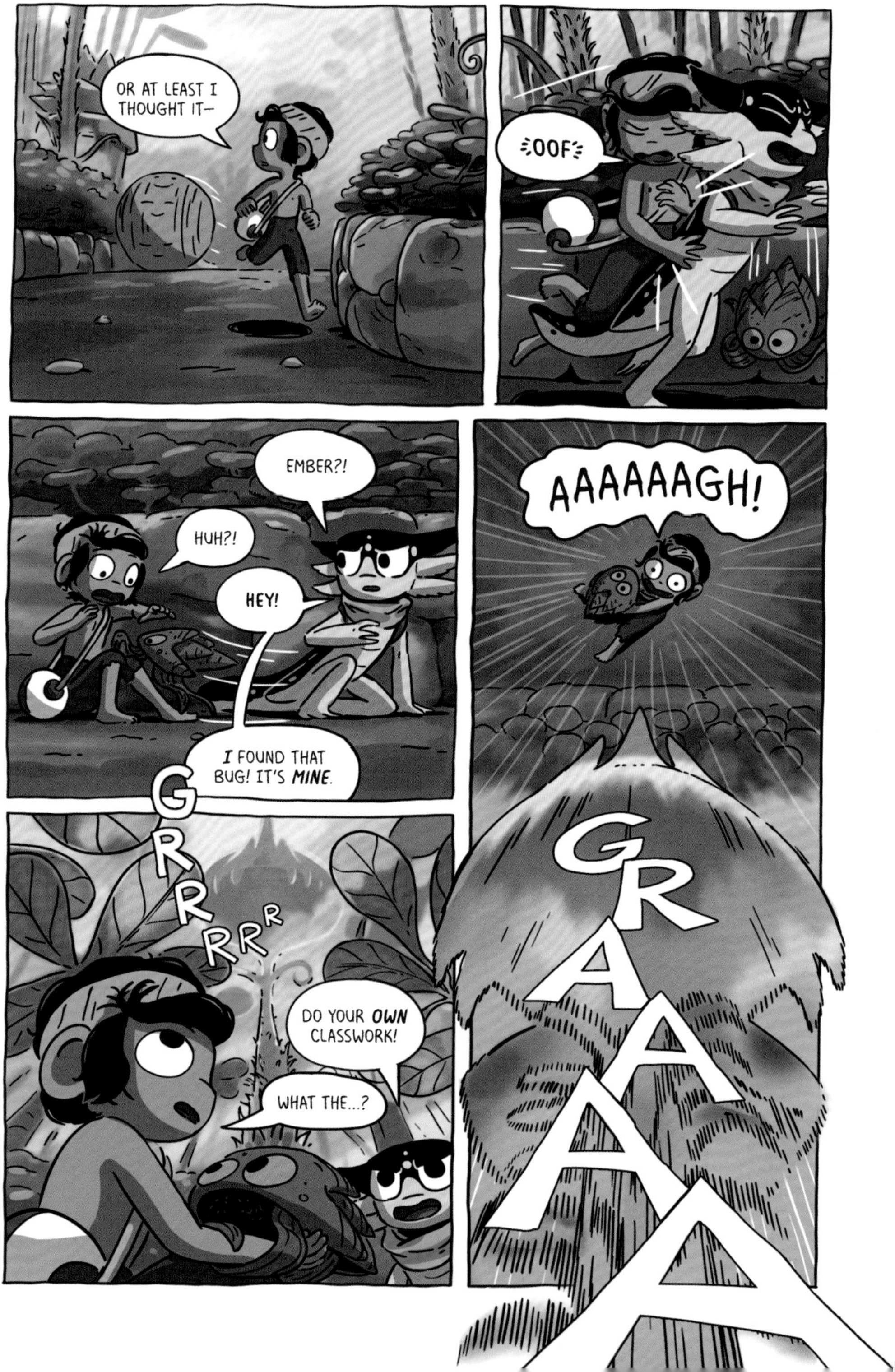
OR AT LEAST I THOUGHT IT—
OOF
EMBER?!
HUH?!
HEY!
I FOUND THAT BUG! IT'S MINE.
AAAAAAGH!
GRRRRR
DO YOUR OWN CLASSWORK!
WHAT THE...?
GRAAAA

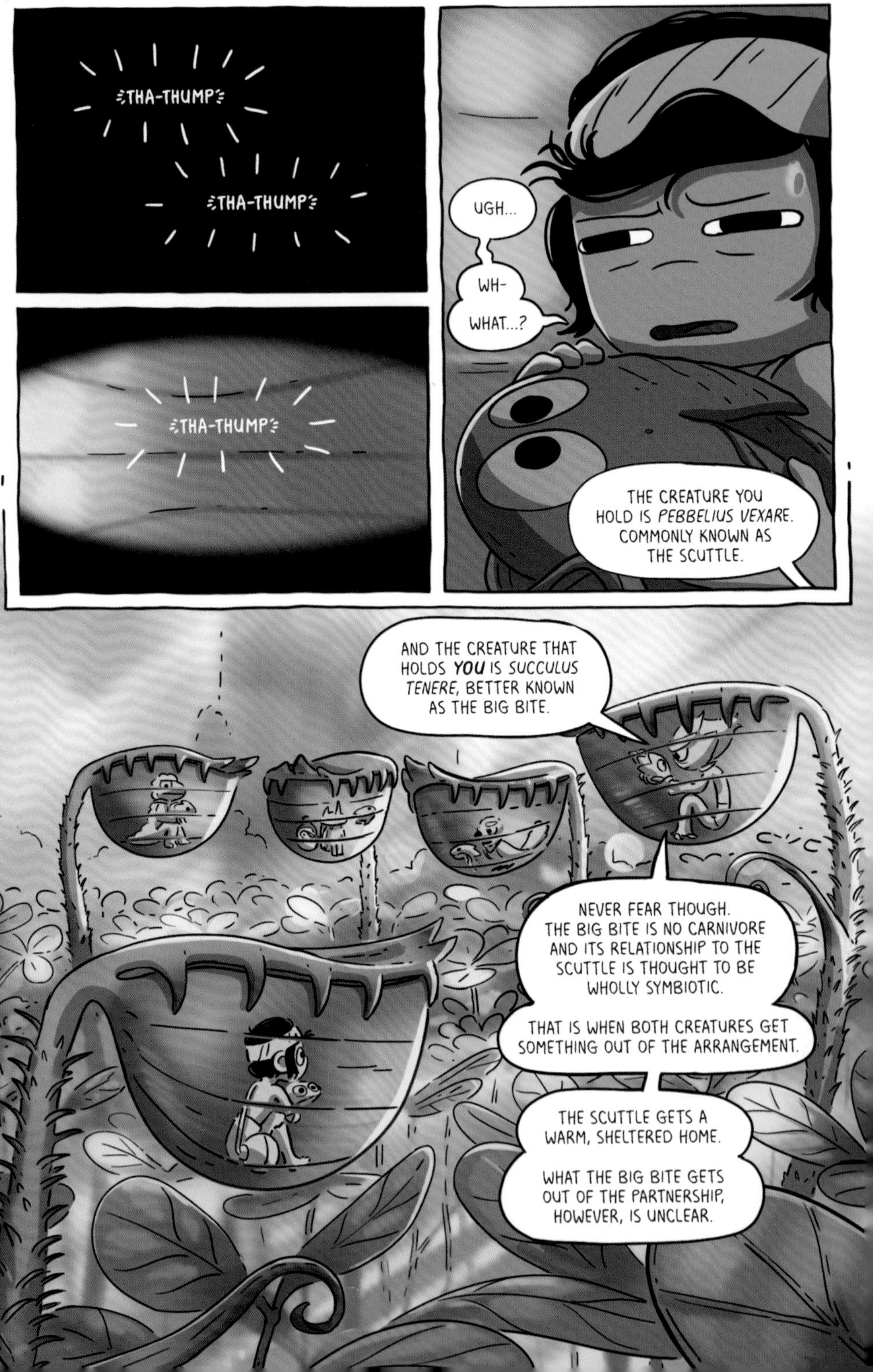
THA-THUMP
THA-THUMP
THA-THUMP
UGH...
WH-
WHAT...?
THE CREATURE YOU HOLD IS *PEBBELIUS VEXARE*. COMMONLY KNOWN AS THE SCUTTLE.
AND THE CREATURE THAT HOLDS ***YOU*** IS *SUCCULUS TENERE*, BETTER KNOWN AS THE BIG BITE.
NEVER FEAR THOUGH. THE BIG BITE IS NO CARNIVORE AND ITS RELATIONSHIP TO THE SCUTTLE IS THOUGHT TO BE WHOLLY SYMBIOTIC.
THAT IS WHEN BOTH CREATURES GET SOMETHING OUT OF THE ARRANGEMENT.
THE SCUTTLE GETS A WARM, SHELTERED HOME.
WHAT THE BIG BITE GETS OUT OF THE PARTNERSHIP, HOWEVER, IS UNCLEAR.

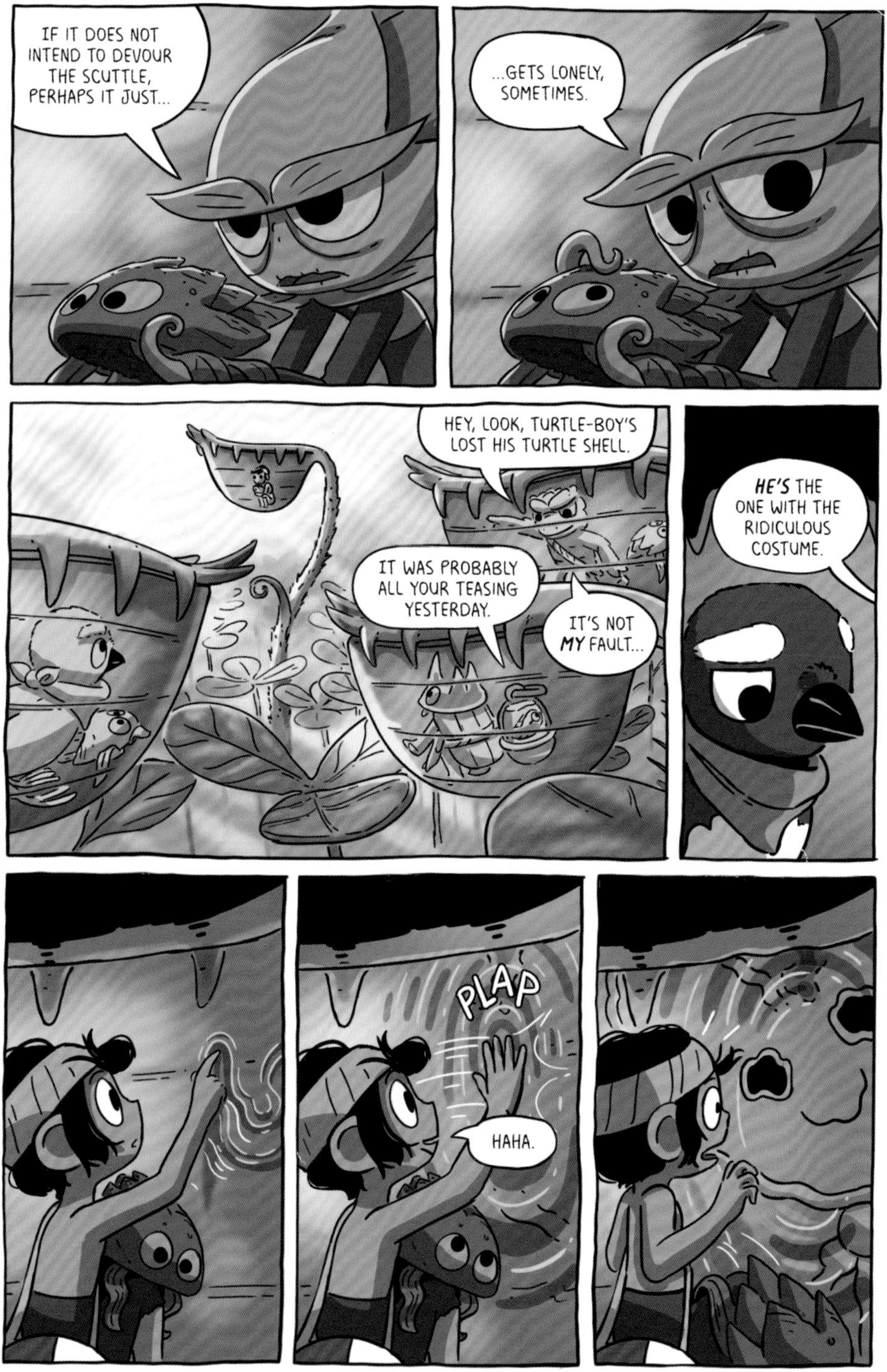
IF IT DOES NOT INTEND TO DEVOUR THE SCUTTLE, PERHAPS IT JUST...
...GETS LONELY, SOMETIMES.
HEY, LOOK, TURTLE-BOY'S LOST HIS TURTLE SHELL.
IT WAS PROBABLY ALL YOUR TEASING YESTERDAY.
IT'S NOT MY FAULT...
HE'S THE ONE WITH THE RIDICULOUS COSTUME.
PLAP
HAHA.

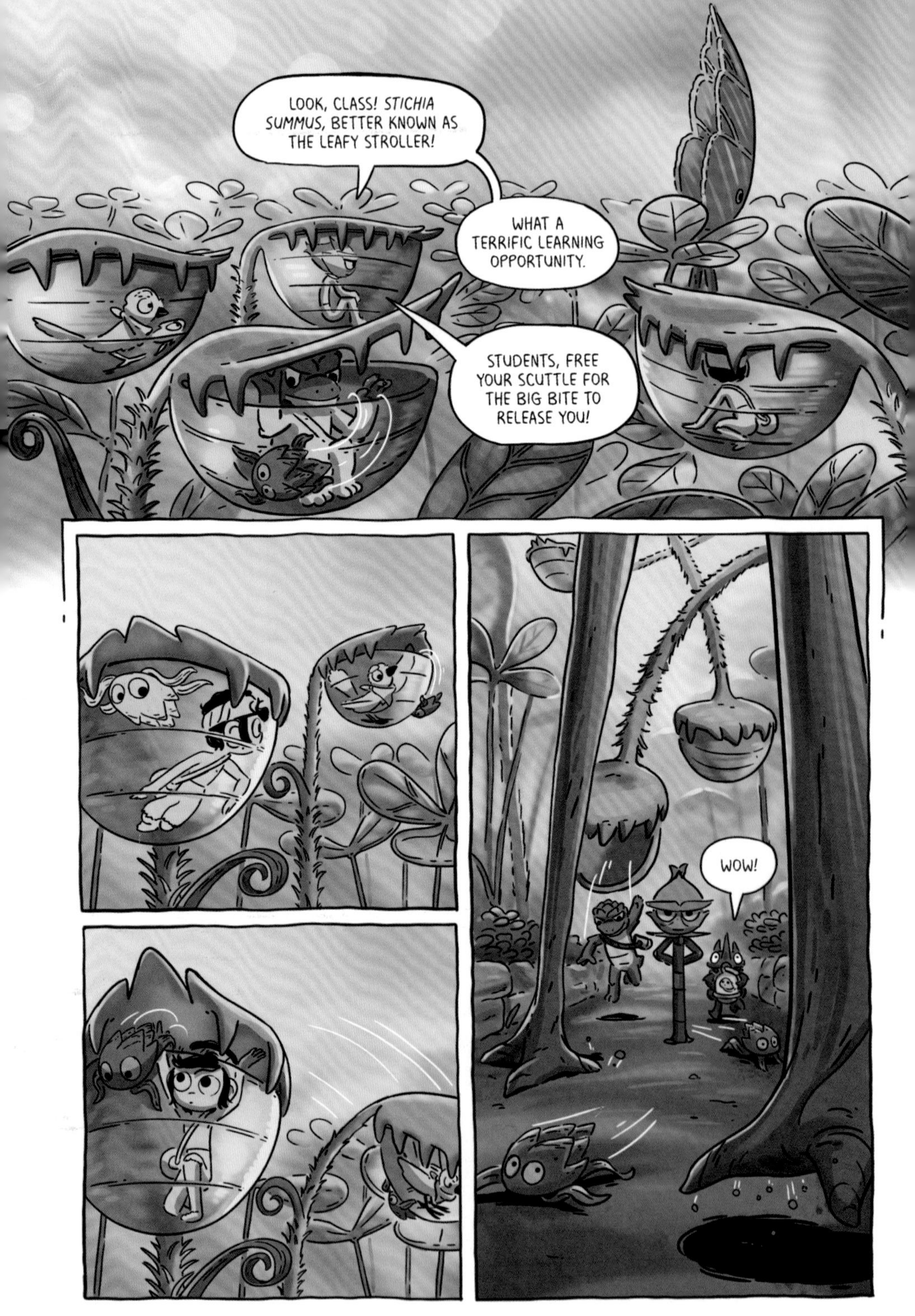
LOOK, CLASS! *STICHIA SUMMUS*, BETTER KNOWN AS THE LEAFY STROLLER!
WHAT A TERRIFIC LEARNING OPPORTUNITY.
STUDENTS, FREE YOUR SCUTTLE FOR THE BIG BITE TO RELEASE YOU!
WOW!

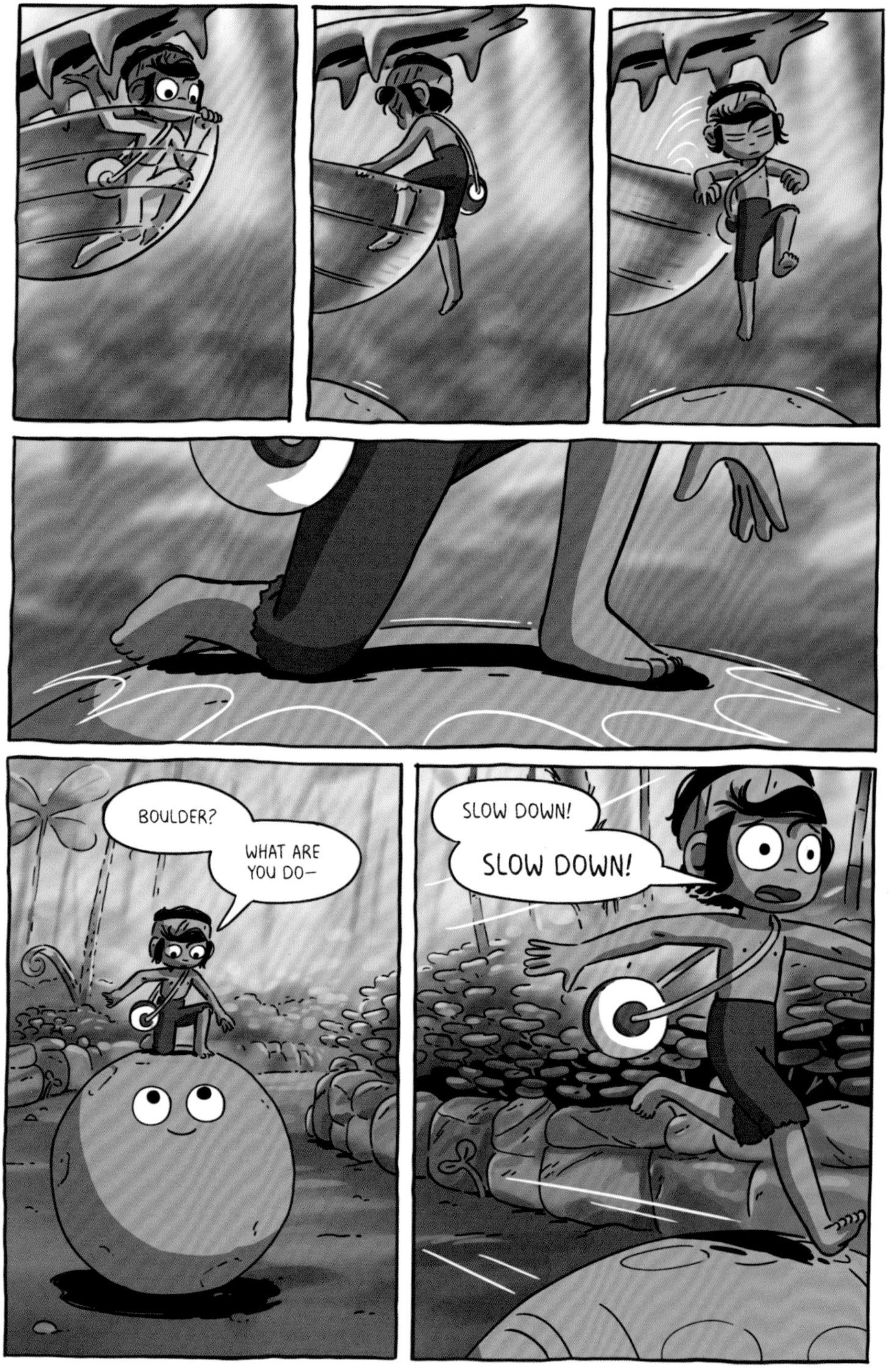
BOULDER?
WHAT ARE YOU DO—
SLOW DOWN!
SLOW DOWN!

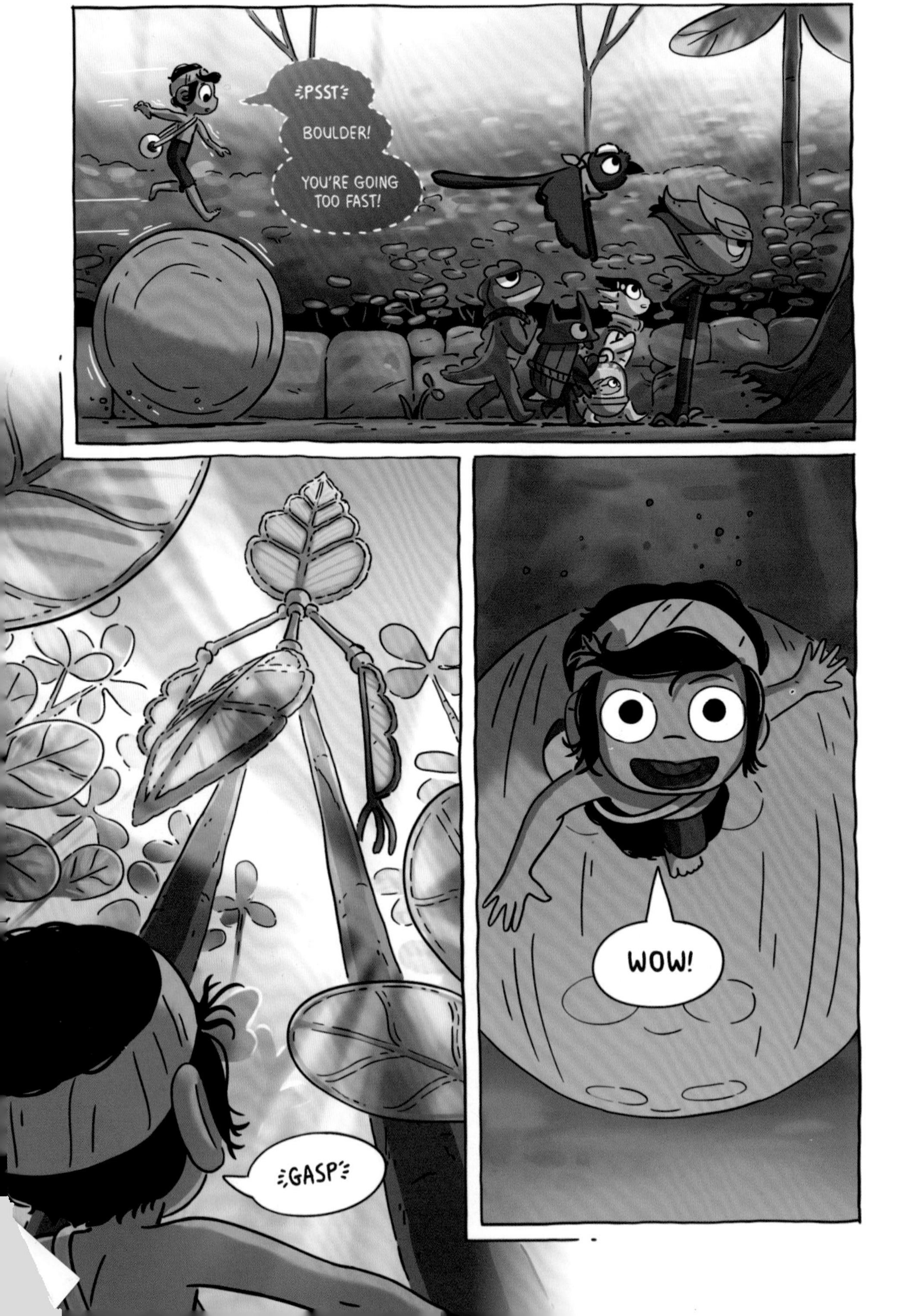
PSST
BOULDER!
YOU'RE GOING TOO FAST!
GASP
WOW!

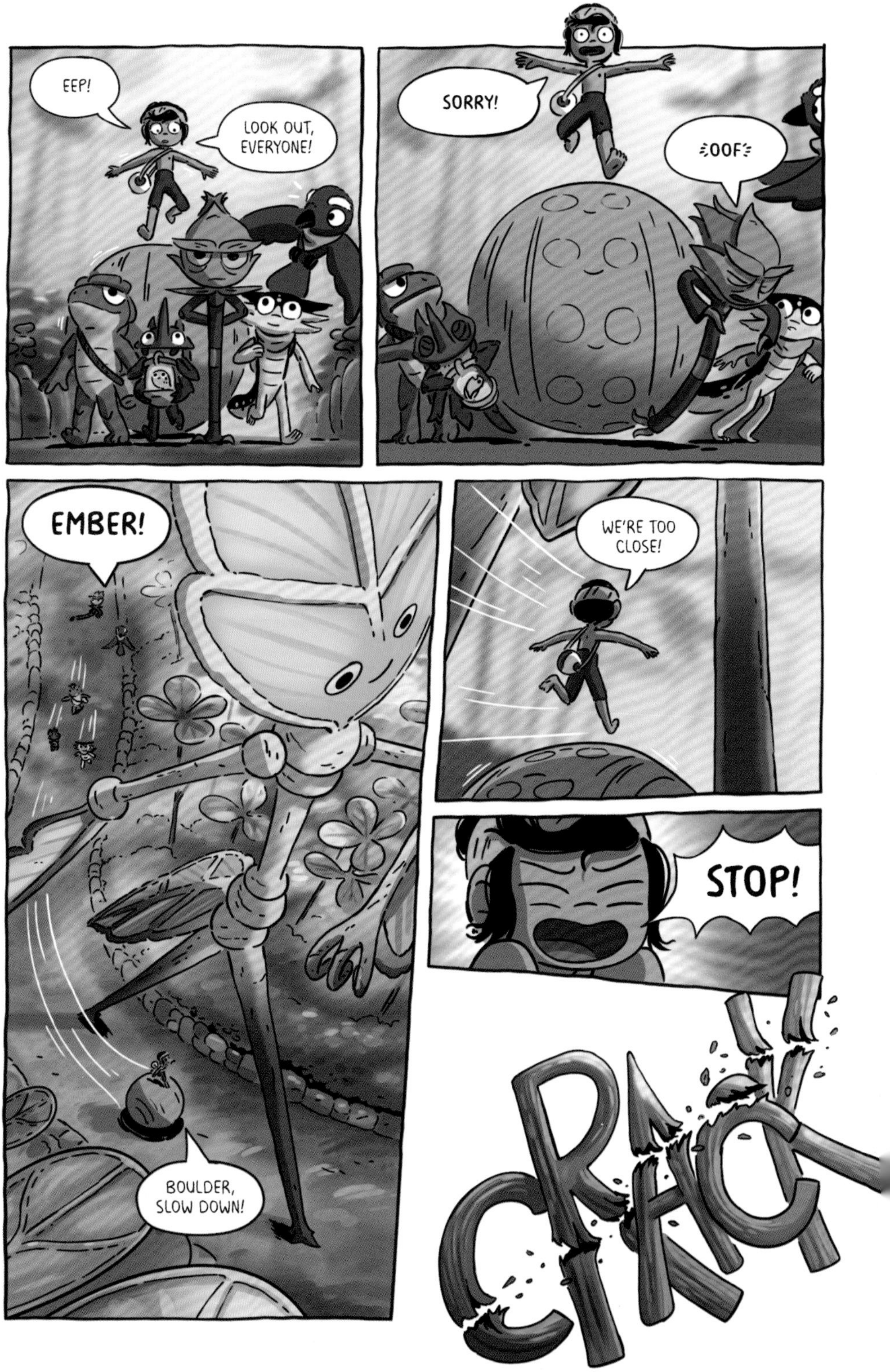
EEP!
LOOK OUT, EVERYONE!
SORRY!
OOF
EMBER!
BOULDER, SLOW DOWN!
WE'RE TOO CLOSE!
STOP!
CRACK

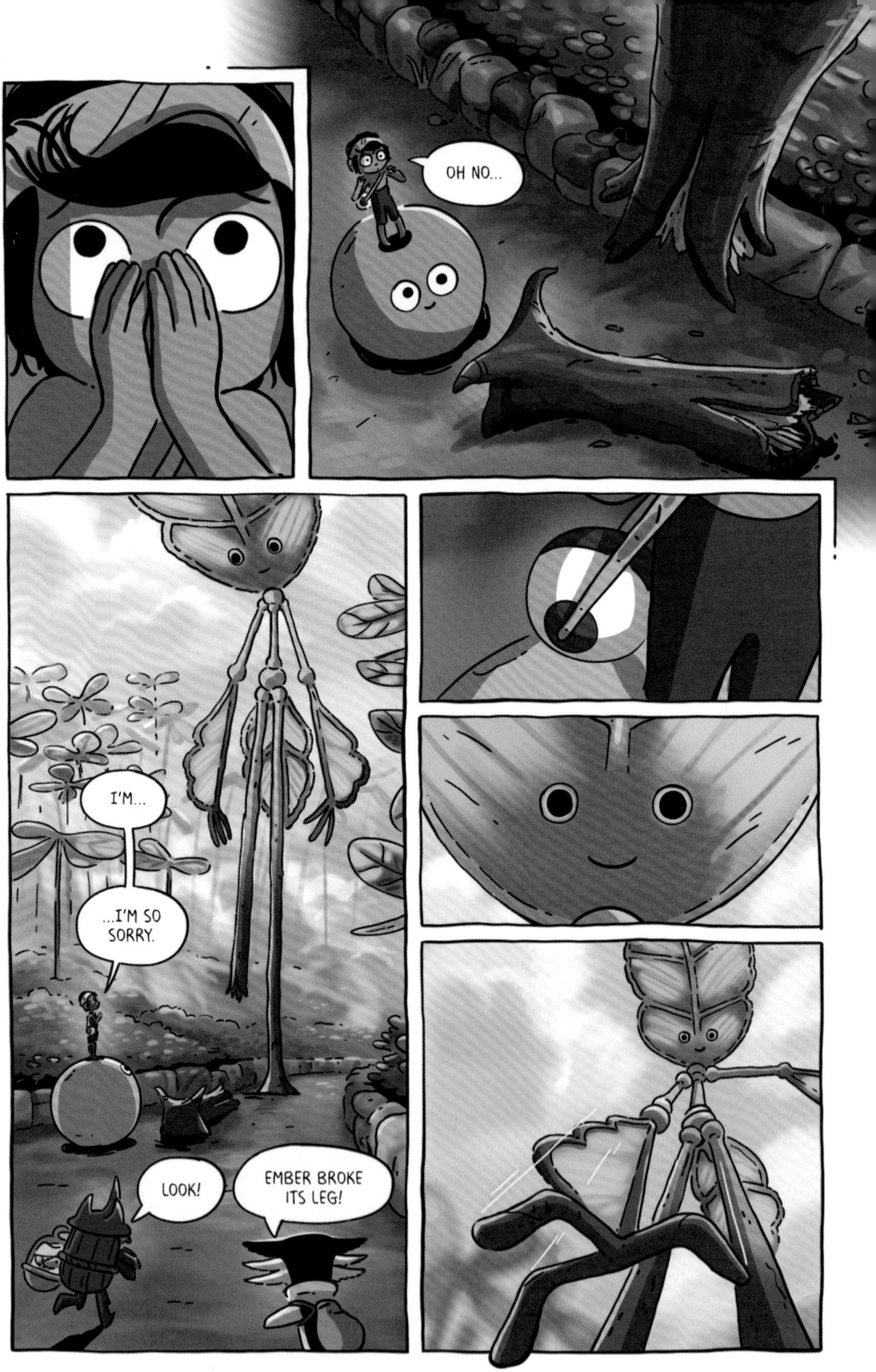
OH NO...
I'M...
...I'M SO SORRY.
LOOK!
EMBER BROKE ITS LEG!

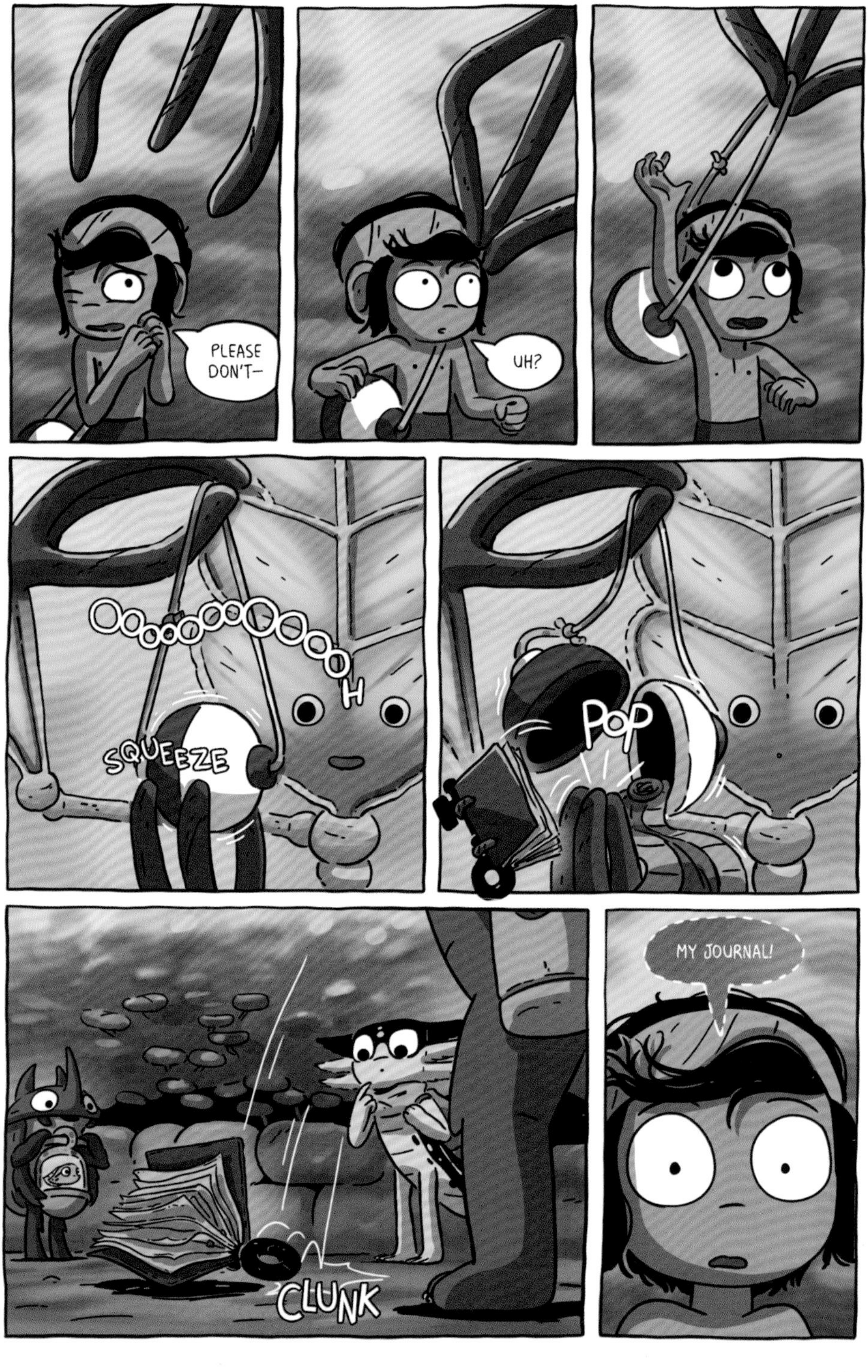
PLEASE DON'T—
UH?
OOOOOOOOOOOOOH
SQUEEZE
POP
CLUNK
MY JOURNAL!

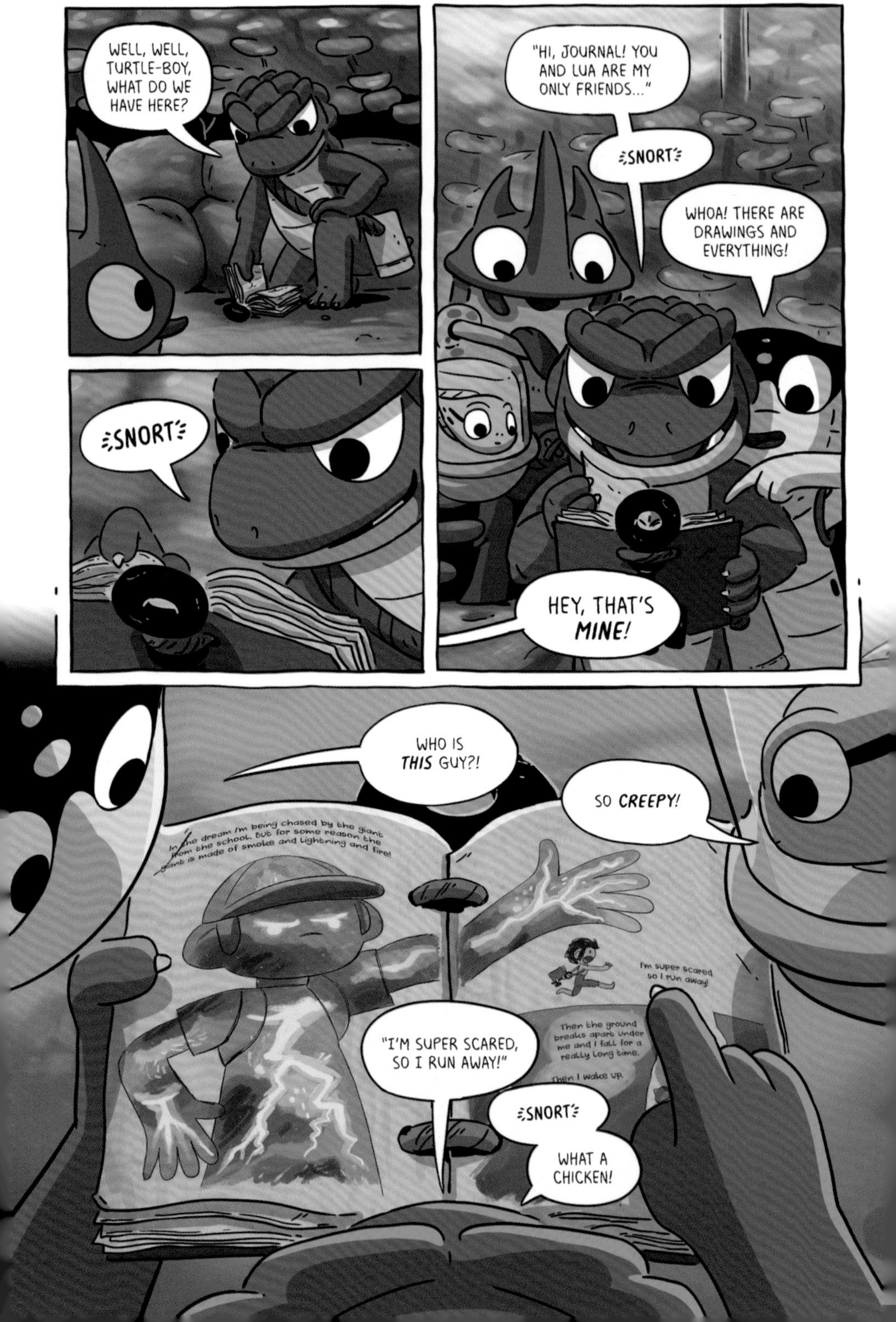
WELL, WELL, TURTLE-BOY, WHAT DO WE HAVE HERE?
SNORT
"HI, JOURNAL! YOU AND LUA ARE MY ONLY FRIENDS..."
SNORT
WHOA! THERE ARE DRAWINGS AND EVERYTHING!
HEY, THAT'S *MINE*!
WHO IS *THIS* GUY?!
SO *CREEPY*!
In the dream I'm being chased by the giant from the school. But for some reason the giant is made of smoke and lightning and fire!
I'm super scared so I run away!
Then the ground breaks apart under me and I fall for a really long time.
Then I wake up.
"I'M SUPER SCARED, SO I RUN AWAY!"
SNORT
WHAT A CHICKEN!

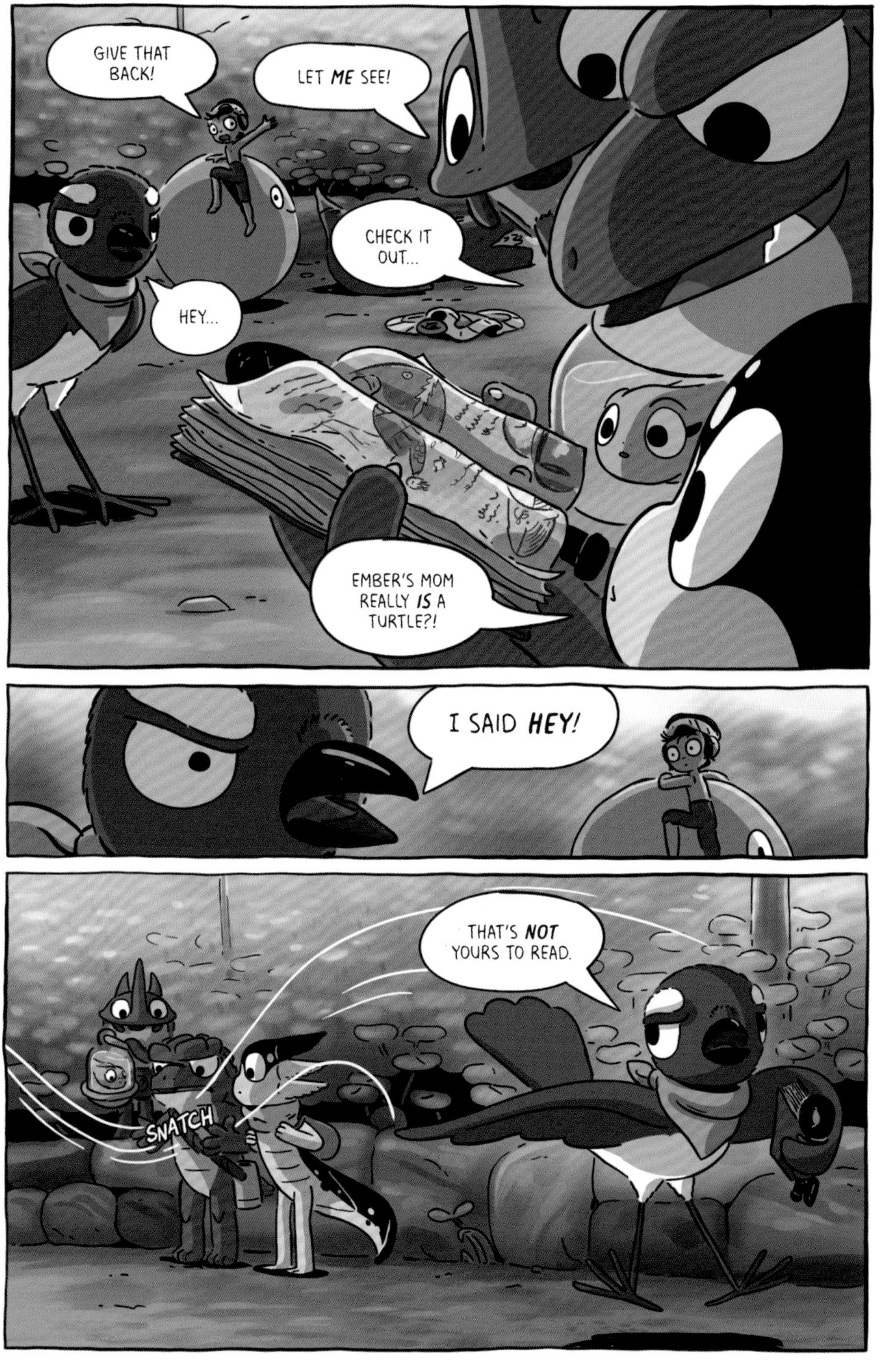
GIVE THAT BACK!
LET ME SEE!
CHECK IT OUT...
HEY...
EMBER'S MOM REALLY IS A TURTLE?!
I SAID HEY!
THAT'S NOT YOURS TO READ.
SNATCH

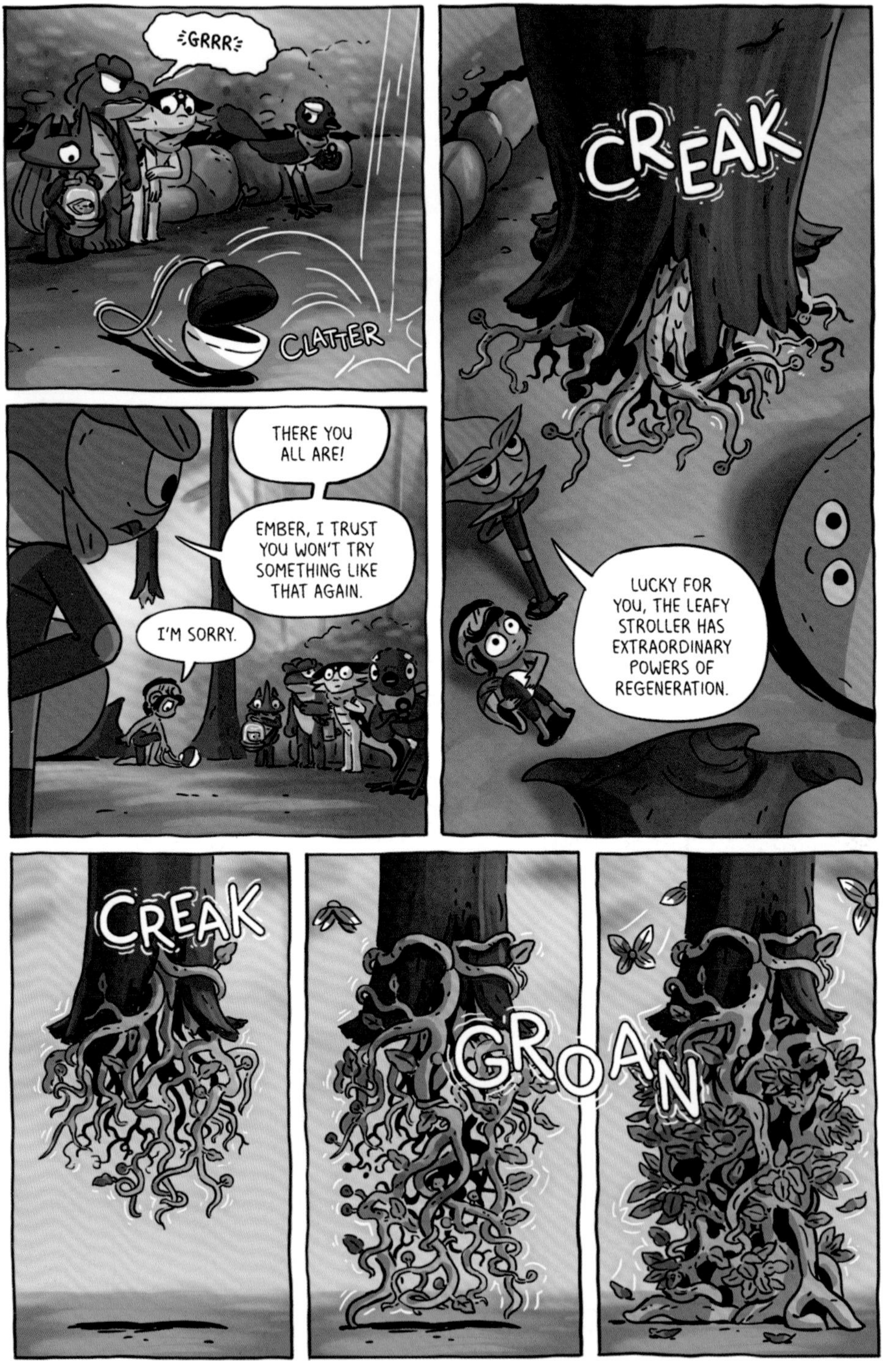
GRRR
CLATTER
CREAK
THERE YOU ALL ARE!
EMBER, I TRUST YOU WON'T TRY SOMETHING LIKE THAT AGAIN.
I'M SORRY.
LUCKY FOR YOU, THE LEAFY STROLLER HAS EXTRAORDINARY POWERS OF REGENERATION.
CREAK
GROAN

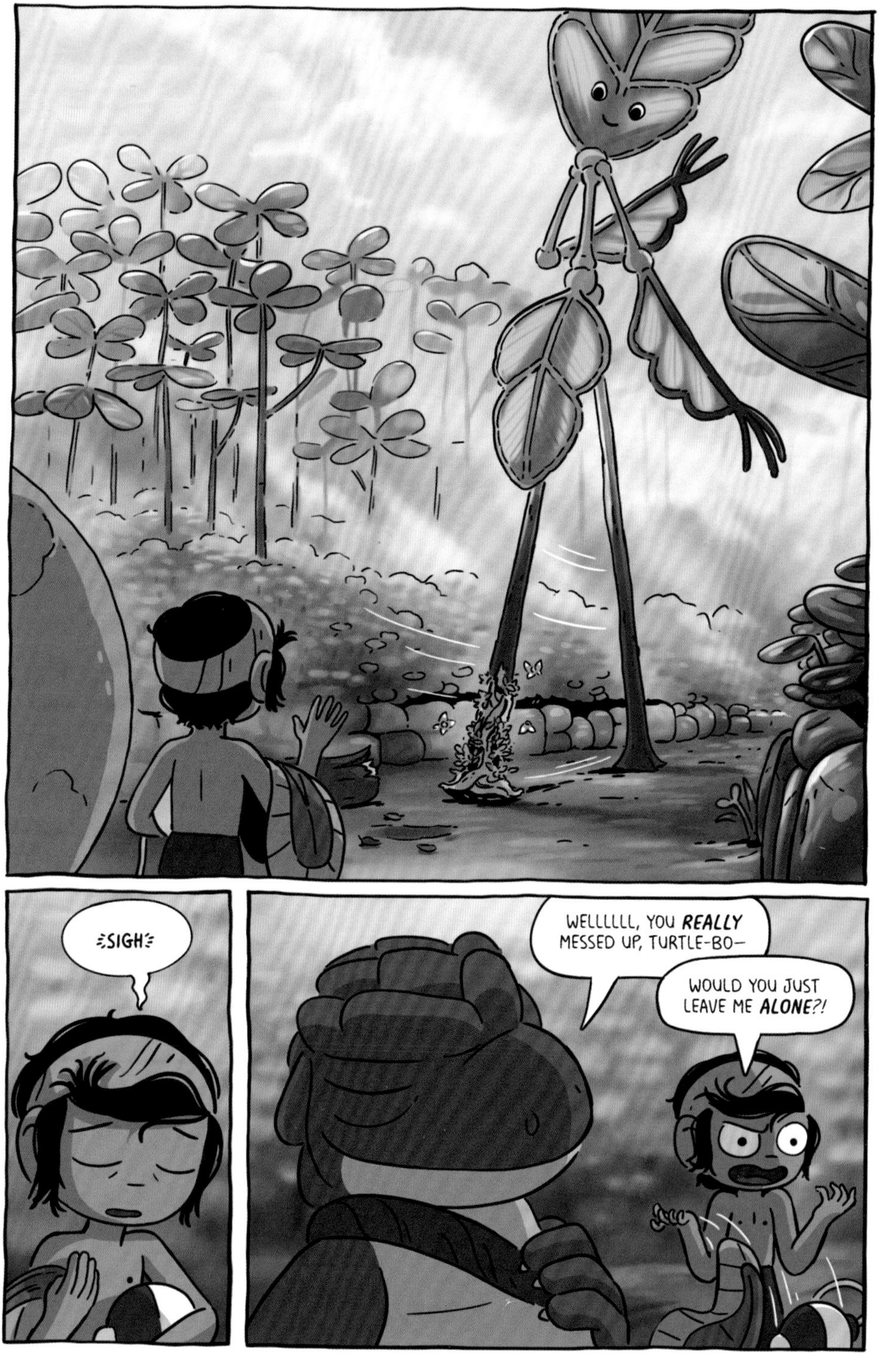
SIGH
WELLLLLLL, YOU REALLY MESSED UP, TURTLE-BO—
WOULD YOU JUST LEAVE ME ALONE?!

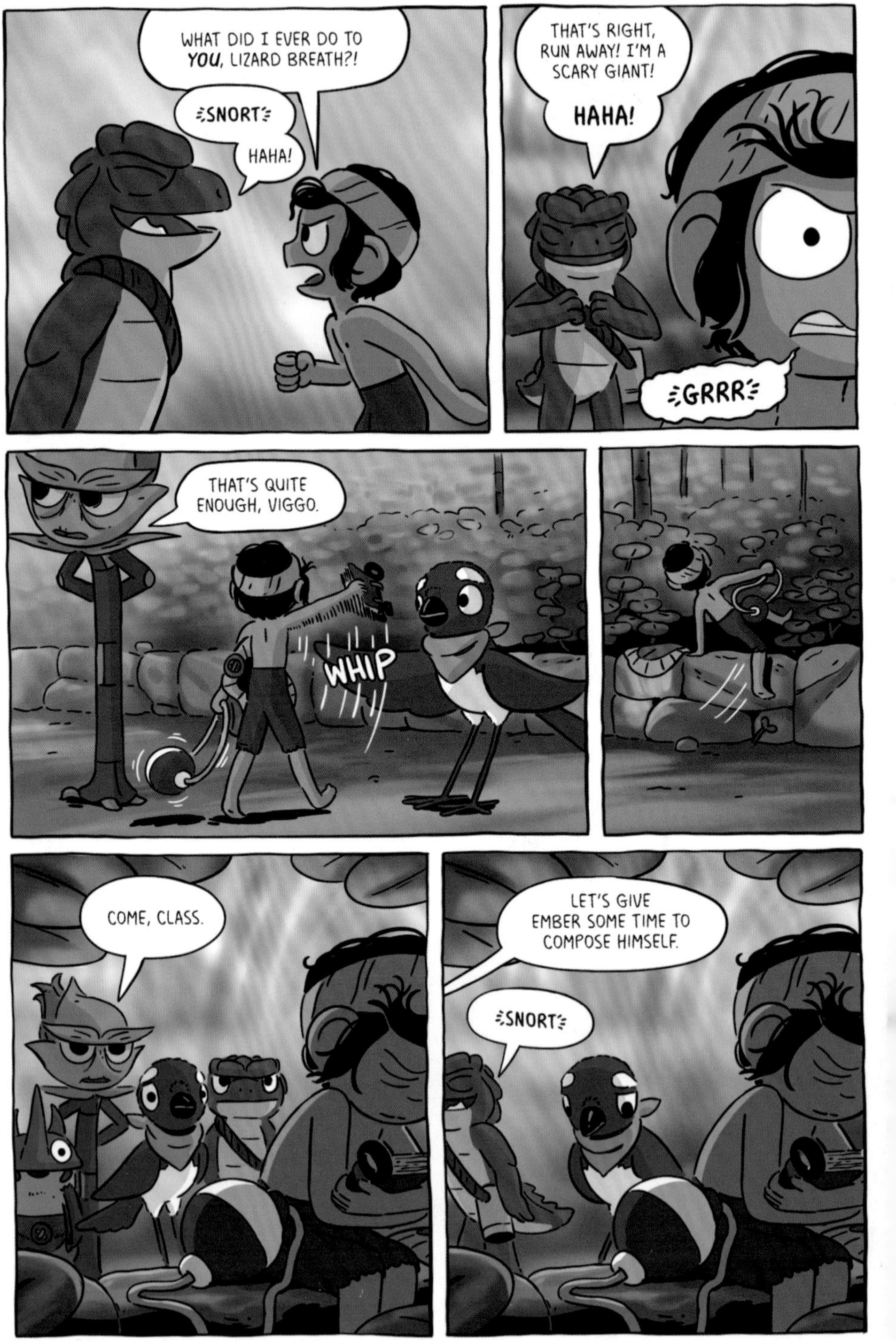
WHAT DID I EVER DO TO *YOU*, LIZARD BREATH?!
SNORT
HAHA!
THAT'S RIGHT, RUN AWAY! I'M A SCARY GIANT!
HAHA!
GRRR
THAT'S QUITE ENOUGH, VIGGO.
WHIP
COME, CLASS.
LET'S GIVE EMBER SOME TIME TO COMPOSE HIMSELF.
SNORT

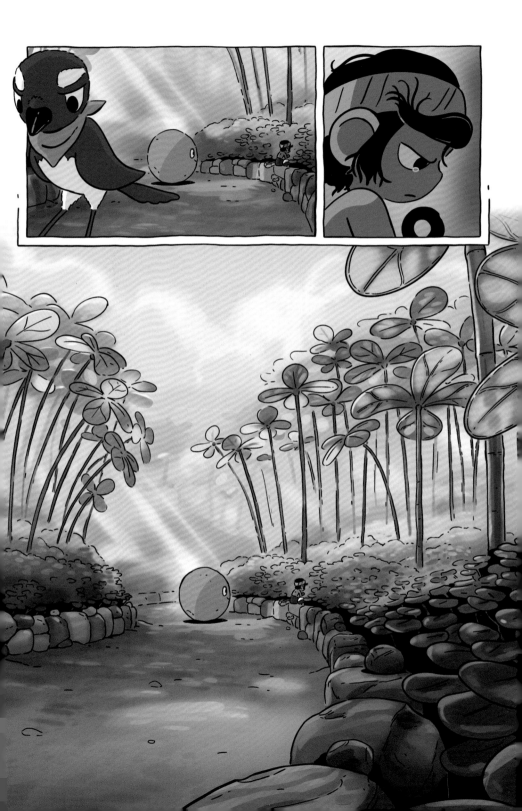

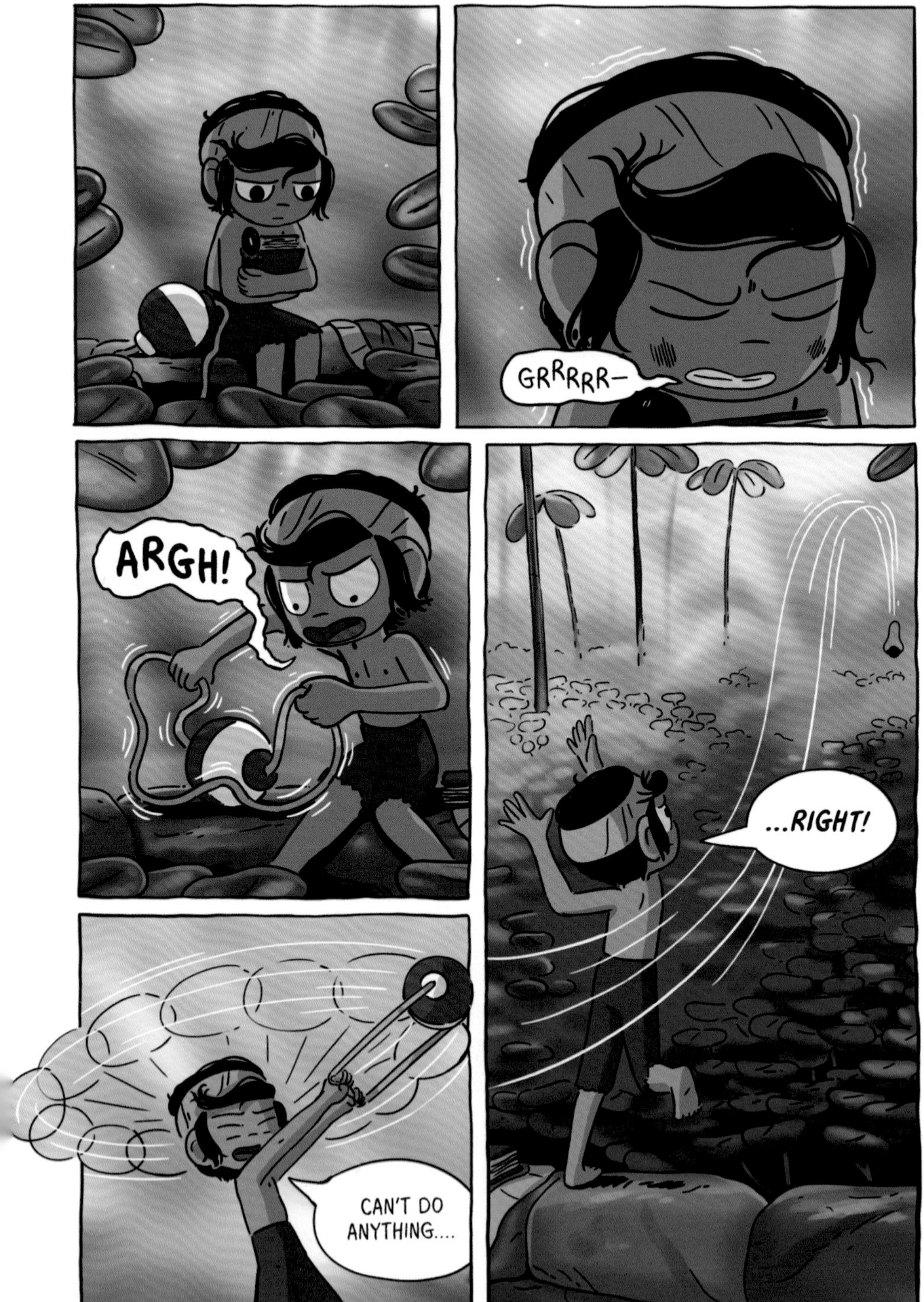
GRRRRR–
ARGH!
...RIGHT!
CAN'T DO ANYTHING....

SPLASH

?

SIGH

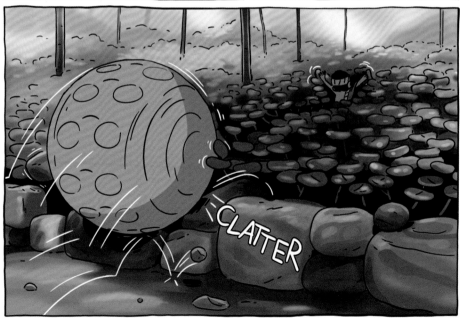

CLATTER

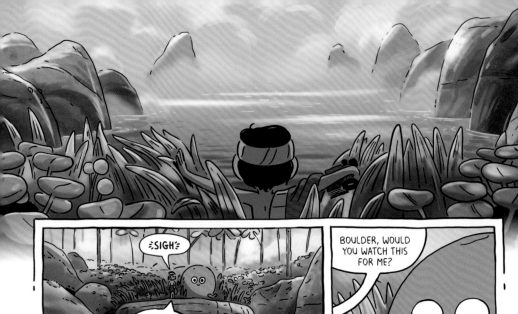

SIGH

GREAT.

JUST MY LUCK.

BOULDER, WOULD YOU WATCH THIS FOR ME?

I DON'T WANT IT TO GET WET WHEN I—

HEY...

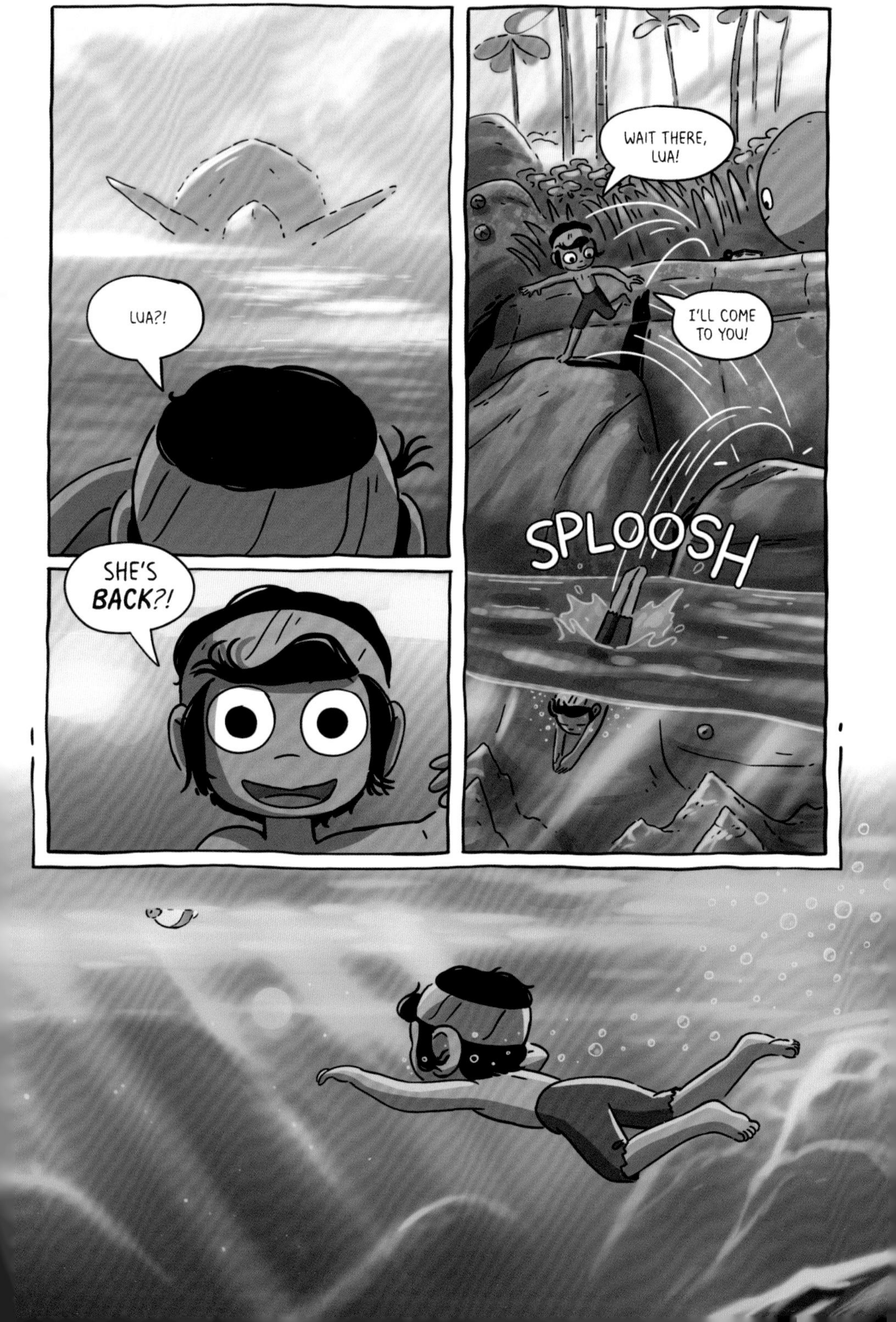
LUA?!
SHE'S BACK?!
WAIT THERE, LUA!
I'LL COME TO YOU!
SPLOOSH

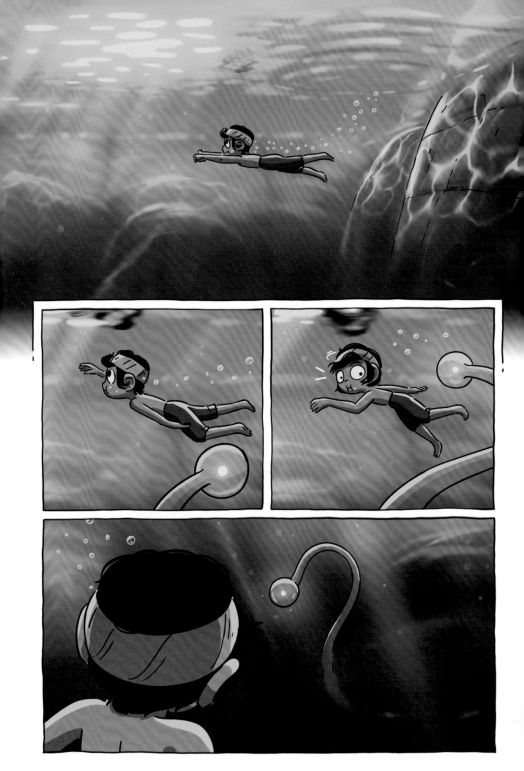

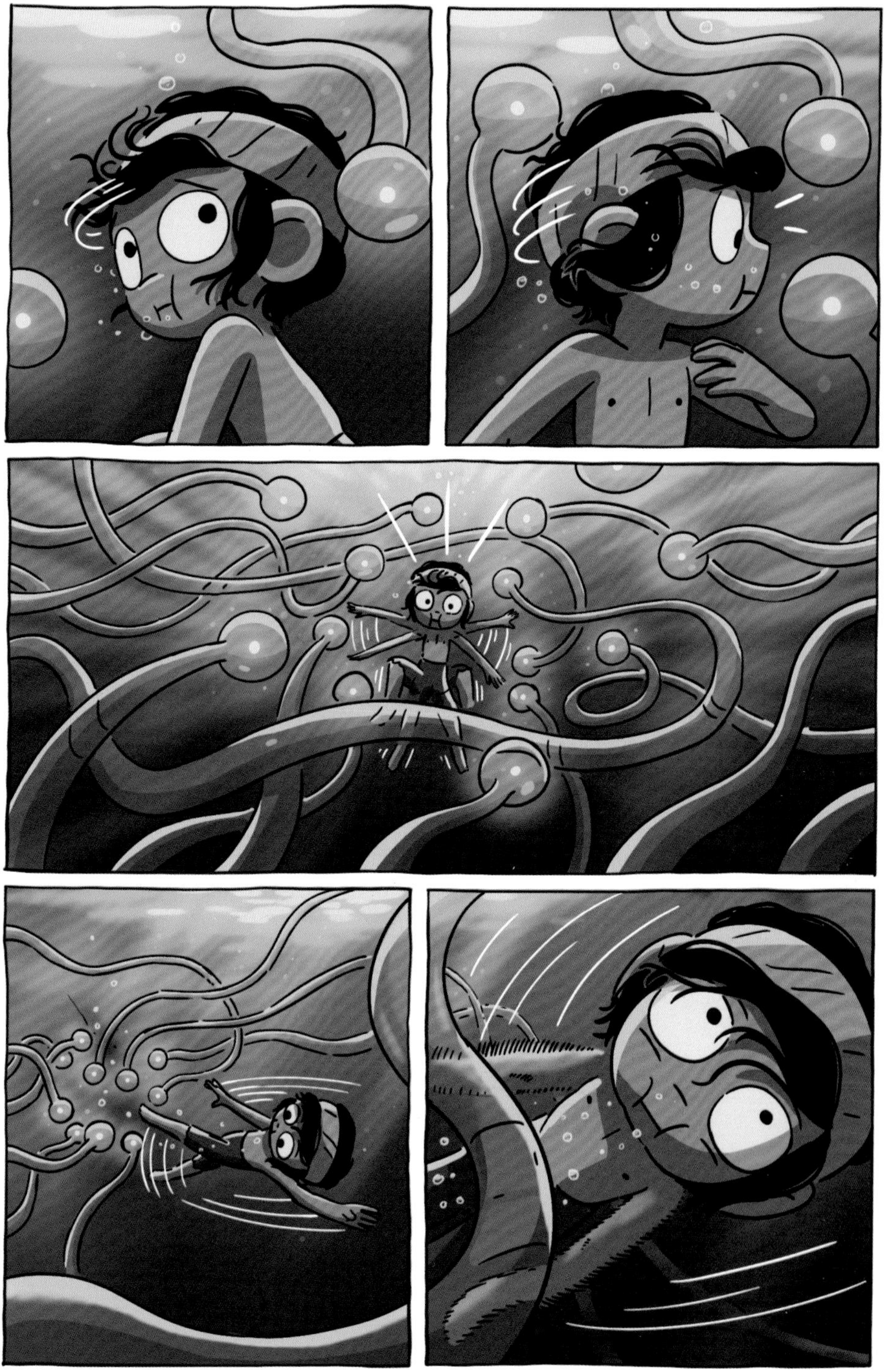

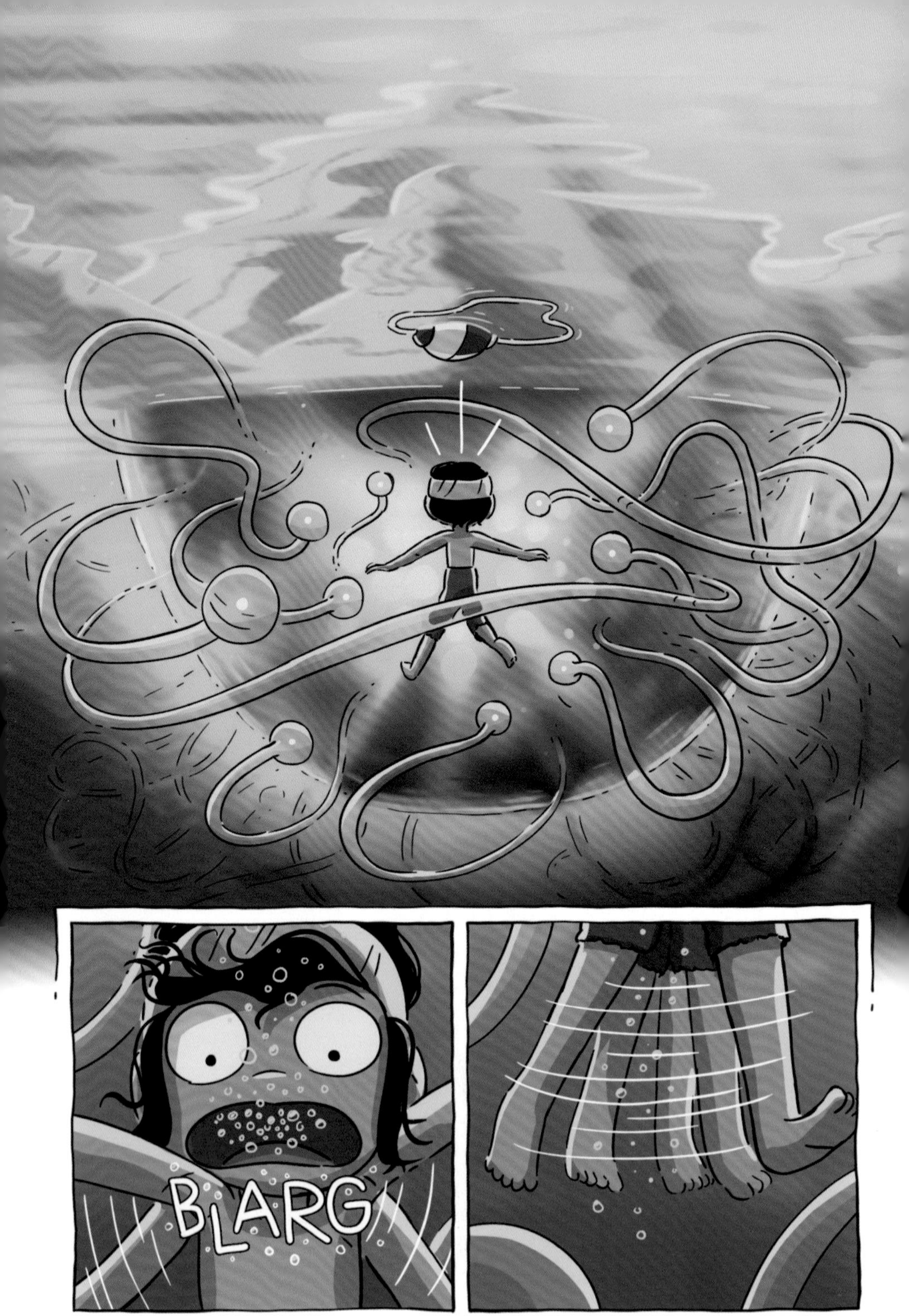
BLARG

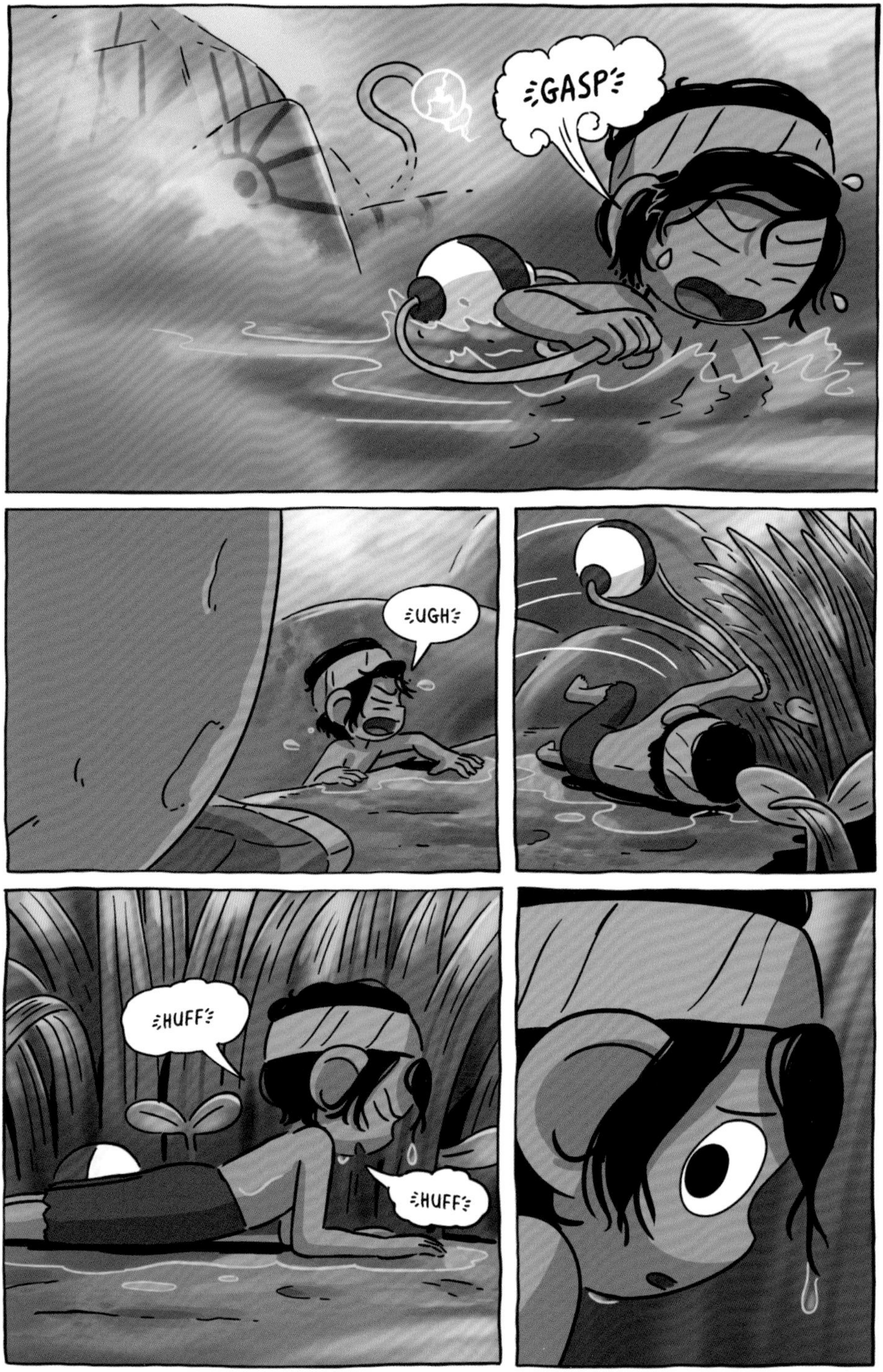
GASP
UGH
HUFF
HUFF

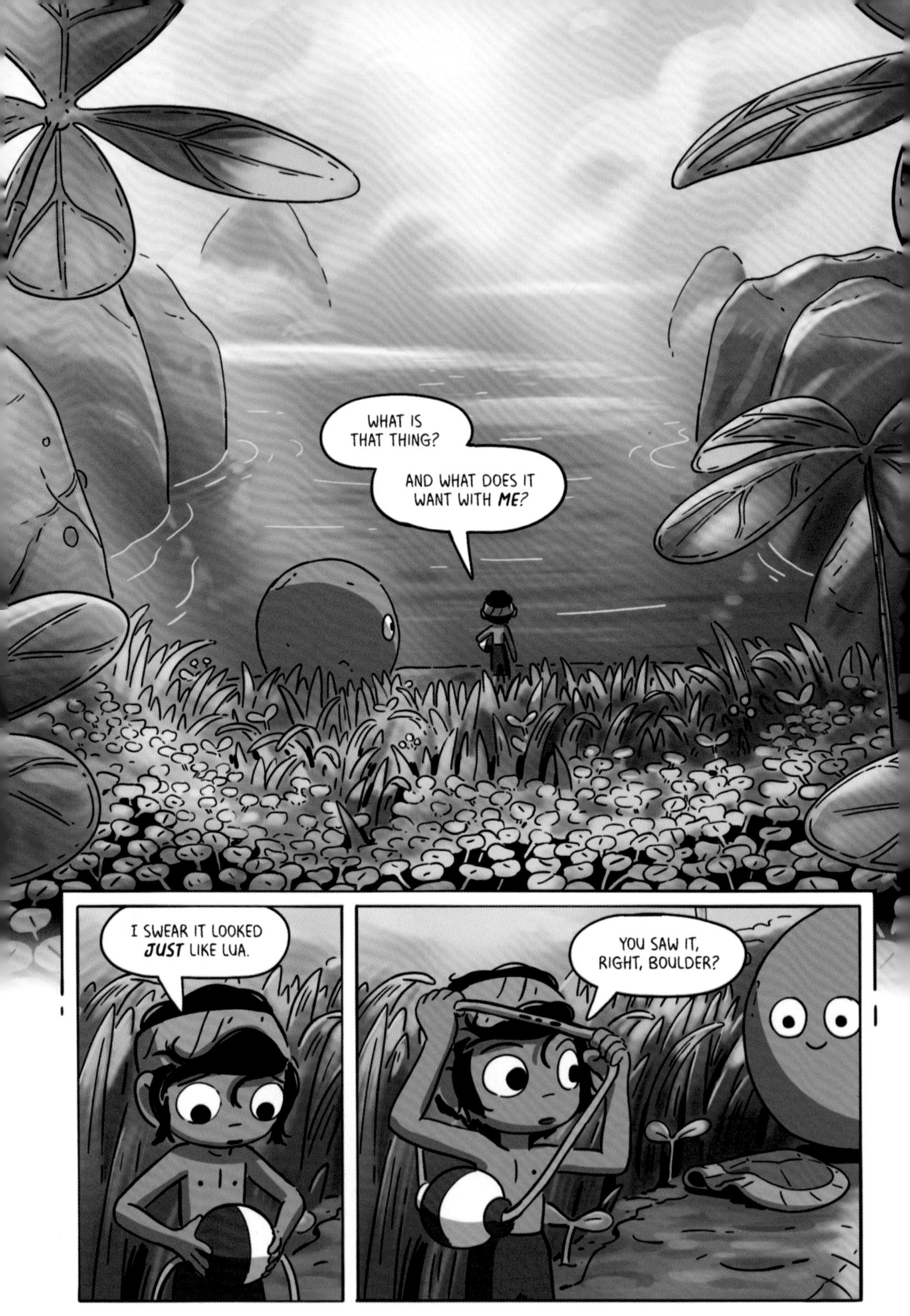
WHAT IS THAT THING?
AND WHAT DOES IT WANT WITH **ME**?
I SWEAR IT LOOKED **JUST** LIKE LUA.
YOU SAW IT, RIGHT, BOULDER?

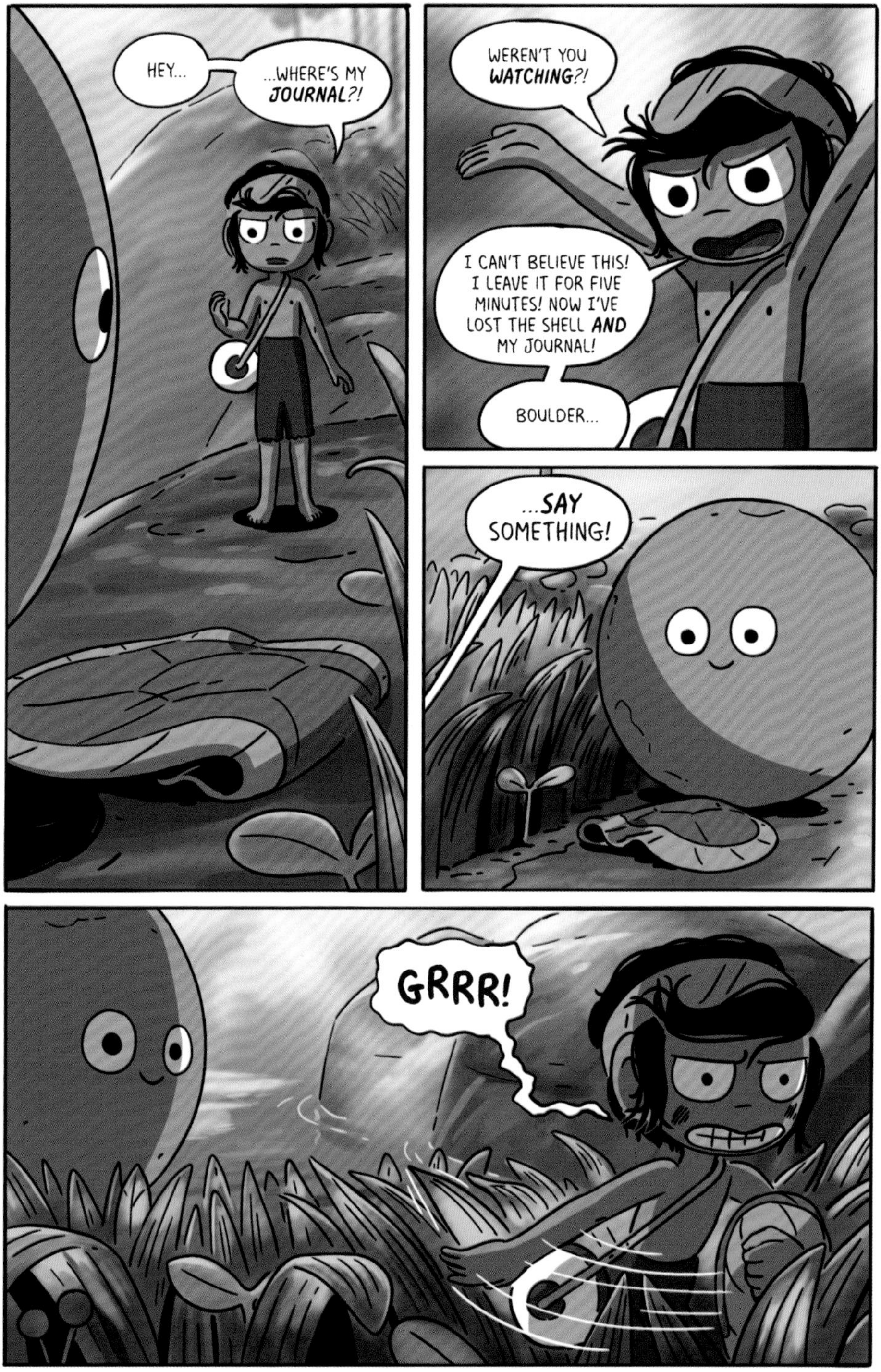
HEY...
...WHERE'S MY JOURNAL?!
WEREN'T YOU WATCHING?!
I CAN'T BELIEVE THIS! I LEAVE IT FOR FIVE MINUTES! NOW I'VE LOST THE SHELL AND MY JOURNAL!
BOULDER...
...SAY SOMETHING!
GRRR!

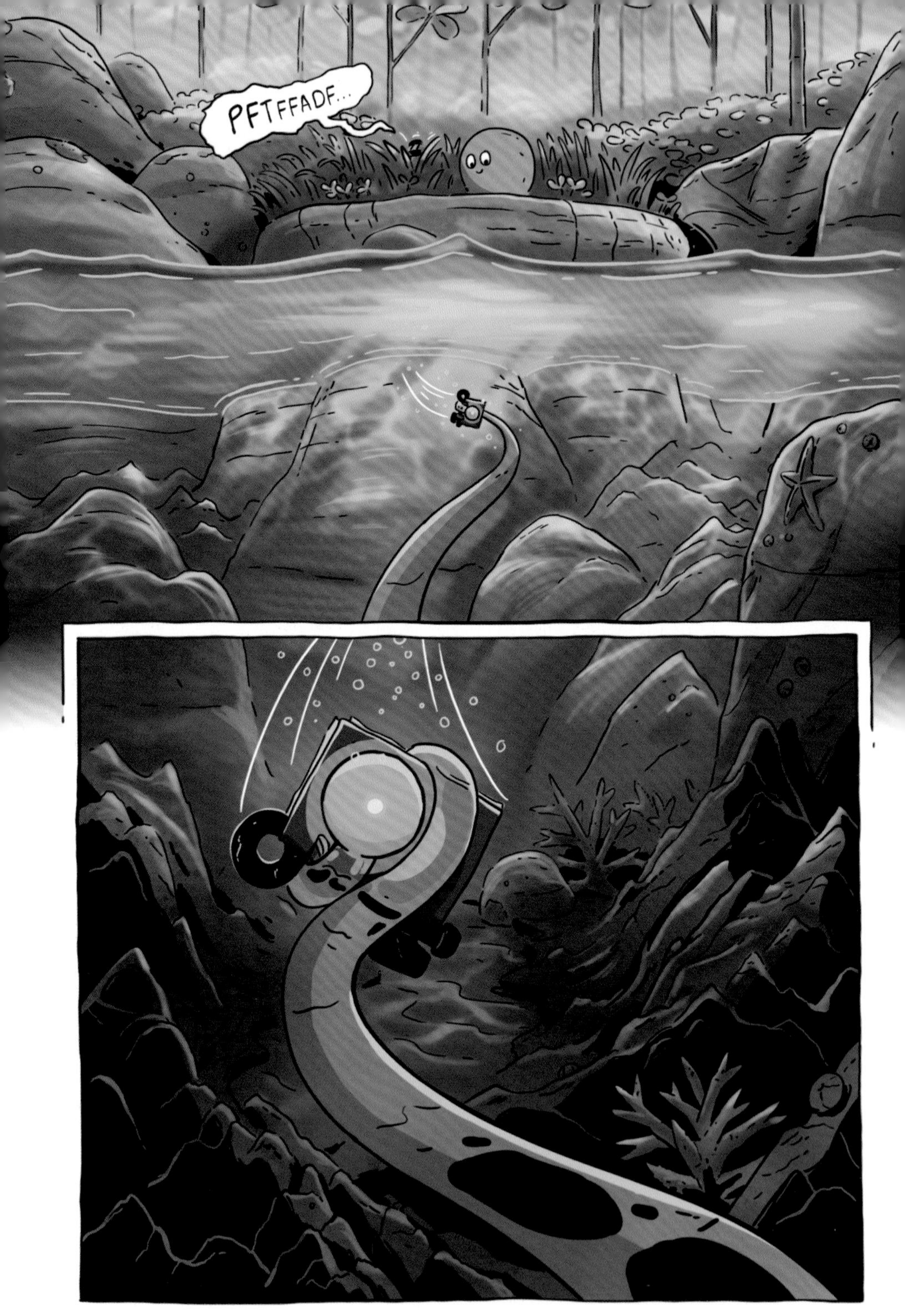
PFTFFADF...

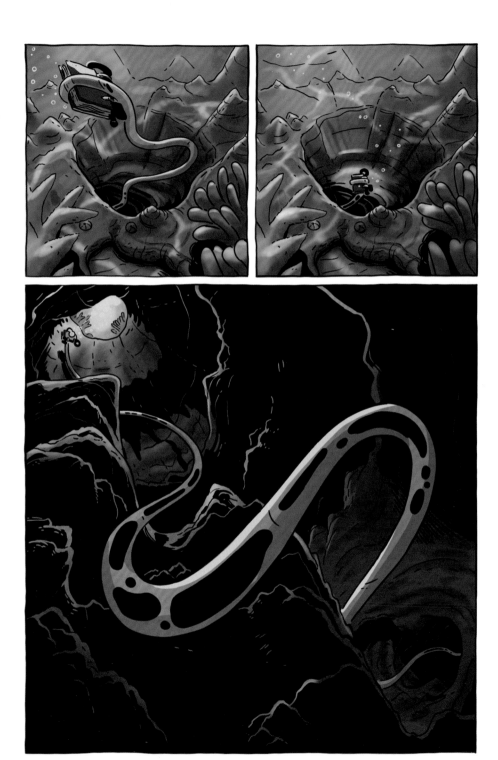

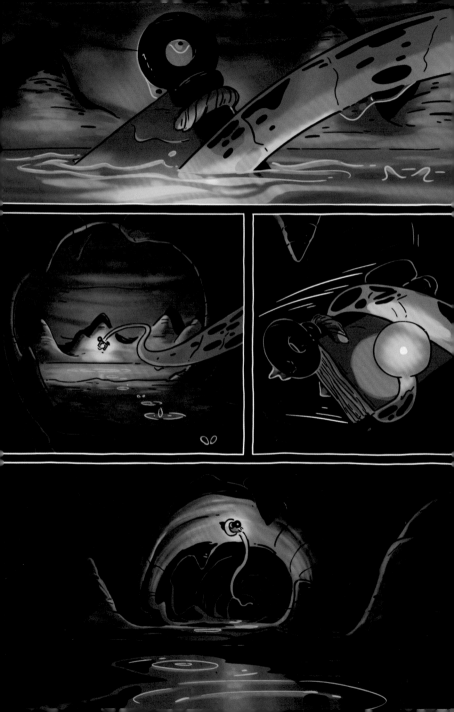

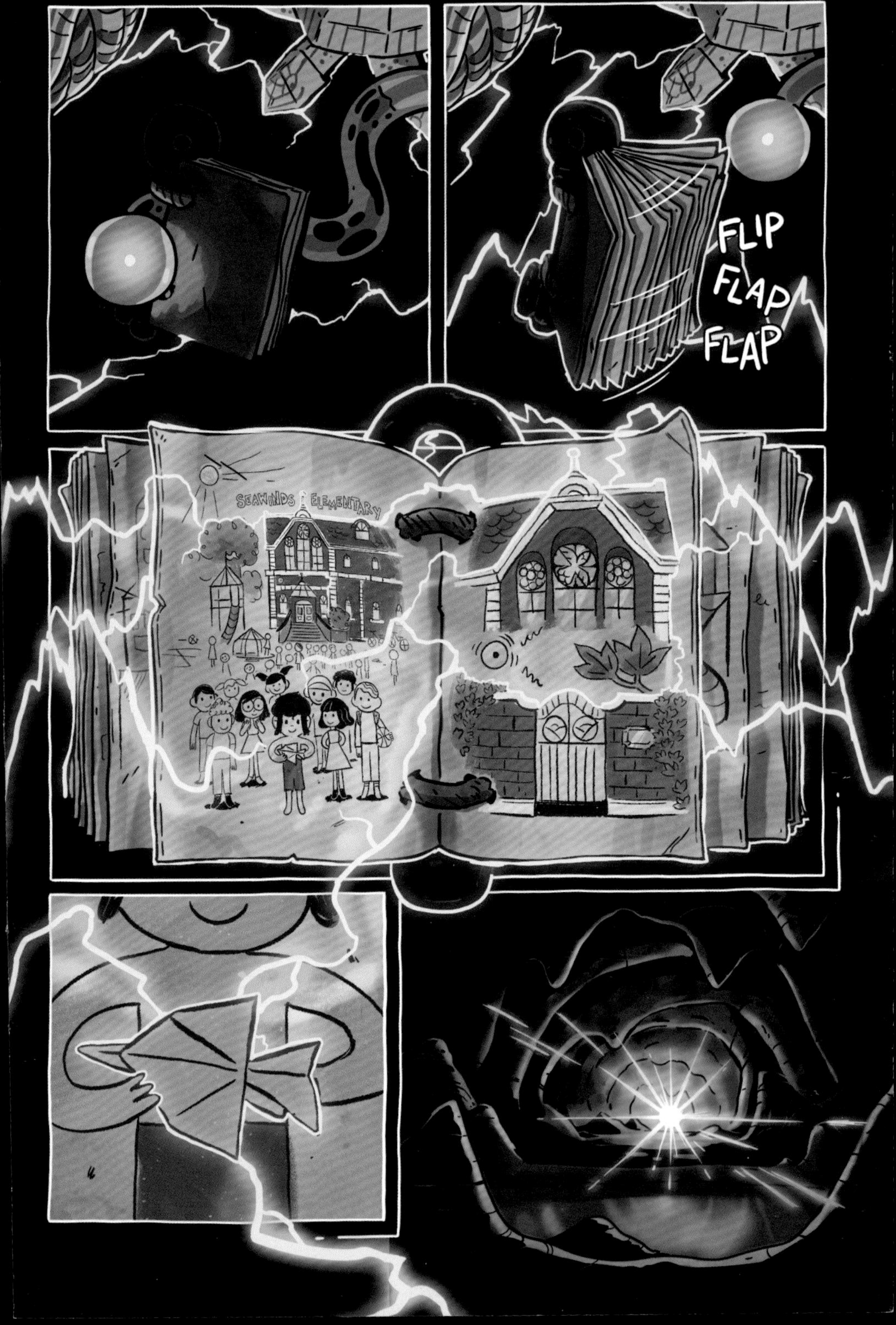
FLIP
FLAP
FLAP
SEAWINDS ELEMENTARY

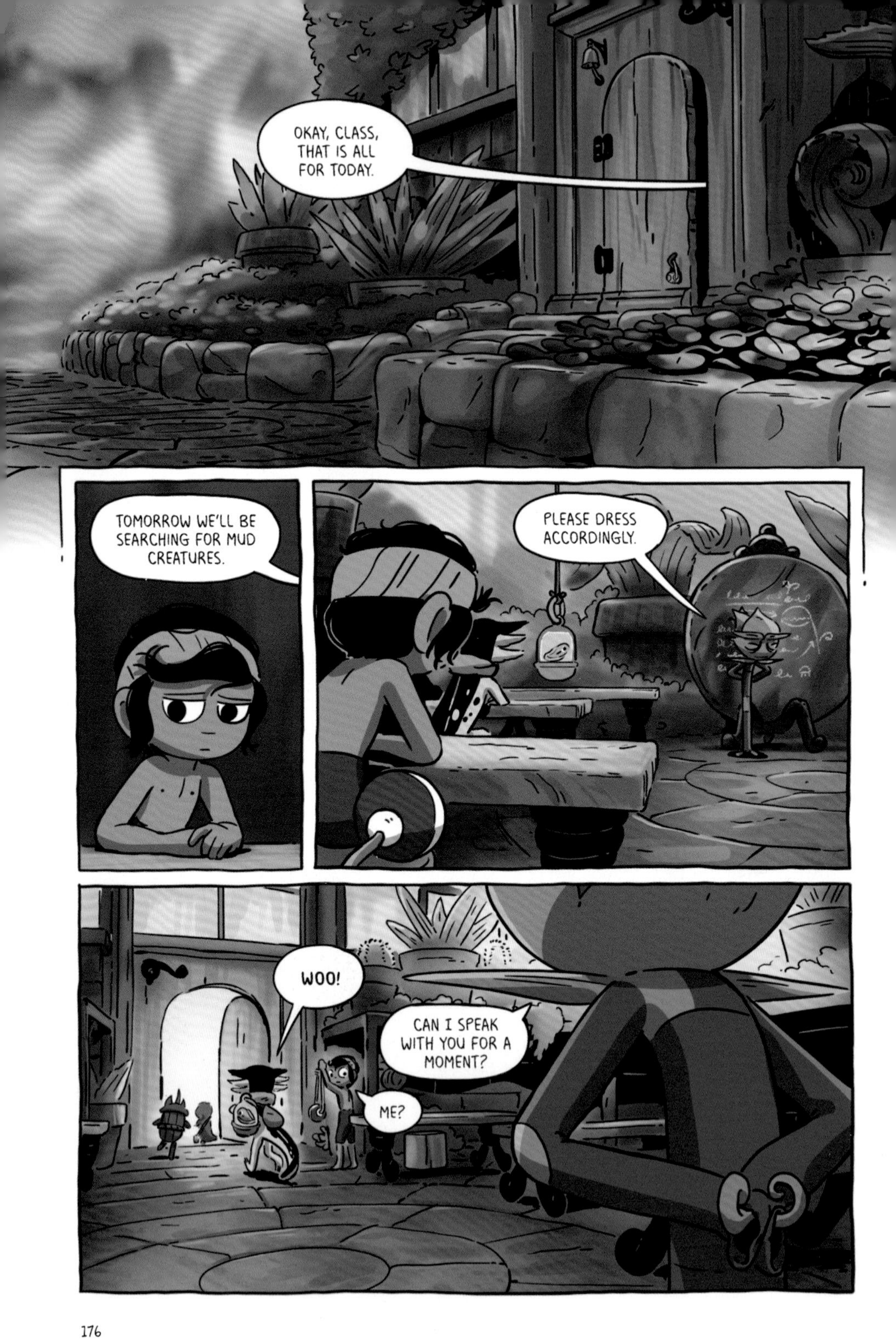
OKAY, CLASS, THAT IS ALL FOR TODAY.
TOMORROW WE'LL BE SEARCHING FOR MUD CREATURES.
PLEASE DRESS ACCORDINGLY.
WOO!
CAN I SPEAK WITH YOU FOR A MOMENT?
ME?

I CAN SENSE THAT YOU'RE HAVING DIFFICULTIES SETTLING IN, EMBER.

IT'S JUST... THIS PLACE ISN'T HOW I IMAGINED. AND THE OTHER KIDS DON'T SEEM TO LIKE ME AT ALL.

IT IS ALWAYS A CHALLENGE BEING THE OUTSIDER.

YOU MAY BE SURPRISED TO KNOW THAT, WHEN I WAS JUST A SEEDLING, I TOO STRUGGLED TO MAKE FRIENDS.

MY CLASSMATES SAID THAT I HAD NO SENSE OF HUMOR. THAT I HAVE A "COLD AND MENACING DEMEANOR."

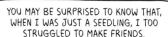

AND *NOW* LOOK AT ME!

NOW I *TEACH* THE CLASS!

AHEM. YES, WELL, ANYWAY...

THE POINT IS TO STICK IT OUT AND GOOD THINGS WILL HAPPEN.

OH. AND EMBER...

BEFORE. SUNRISE.

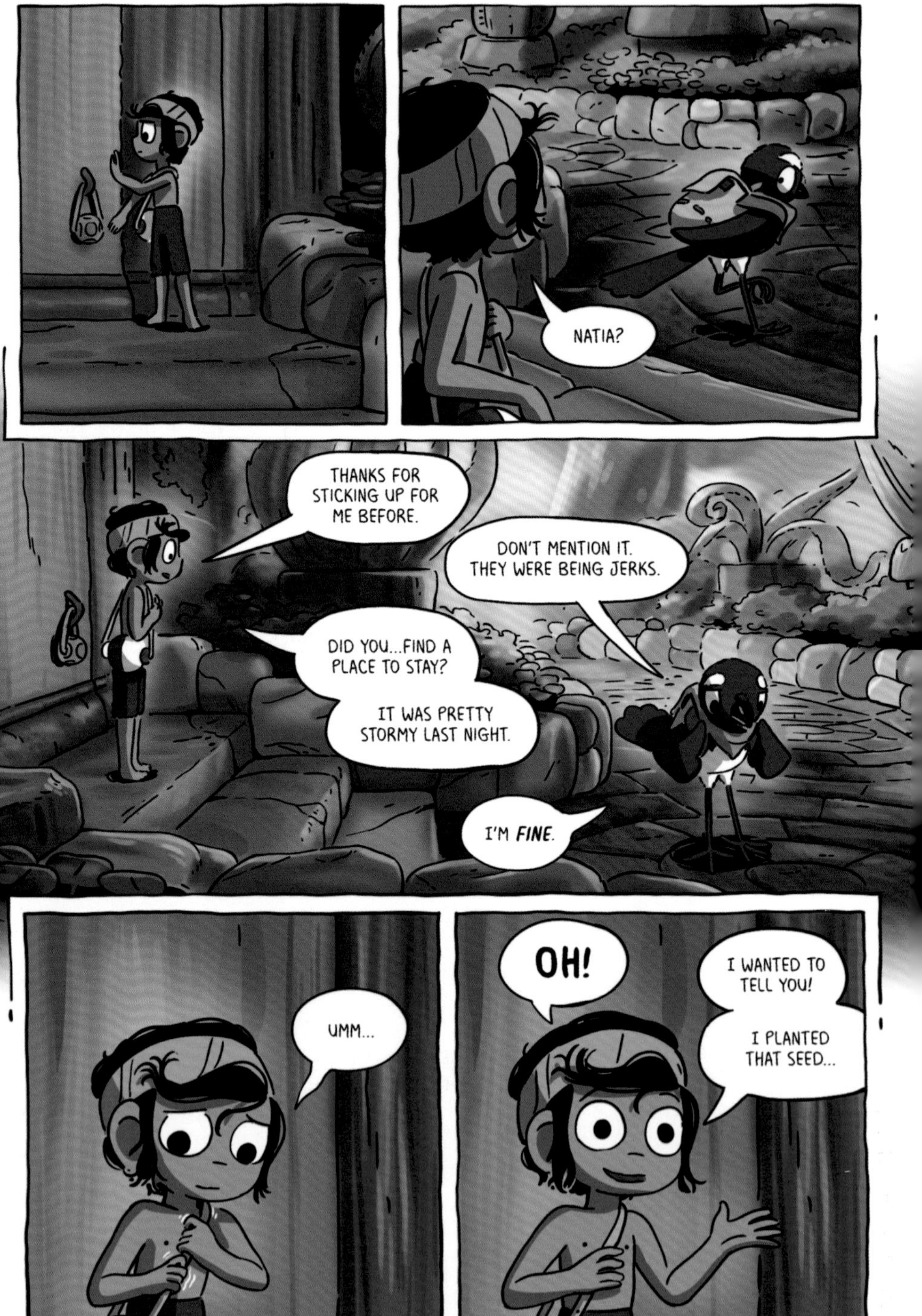
NATIA?
THANKS FOR STICKING UP FOR ME BEFORE.
DON'T MENTION IT. THEY WERE BEING JERKS.
DID YOU...FIND A PLACE TO STAY?
IT WAS PRETTY STORMY LAST NIGHT.
I'M *FINE*.
UMM...
OH!
I WANTED TO TELL YOU!
I PLANTED THAT SEED...

...AND IT SPROUTED THIS MORNING!

ALREADY? WOW.

DO YOU...

...WANT TO COME SEE IT?

I PROMISE I WON'T ASK ABOUT YOUR SECRETS! Y'KNOW...

...ABOUT YOUR FAMOUS PARENTS OR THE THING YOU DROPPED ON THE BEACH OR THE PELICAN OR WHATEVER!

DON'T TALK ABOUT THAT!

ABOUT THE PELICAN?

GOOD*BYE*.

I...

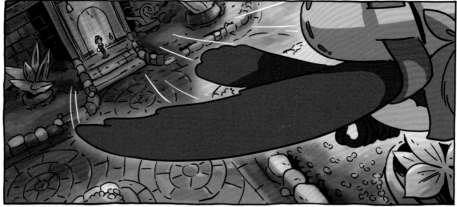

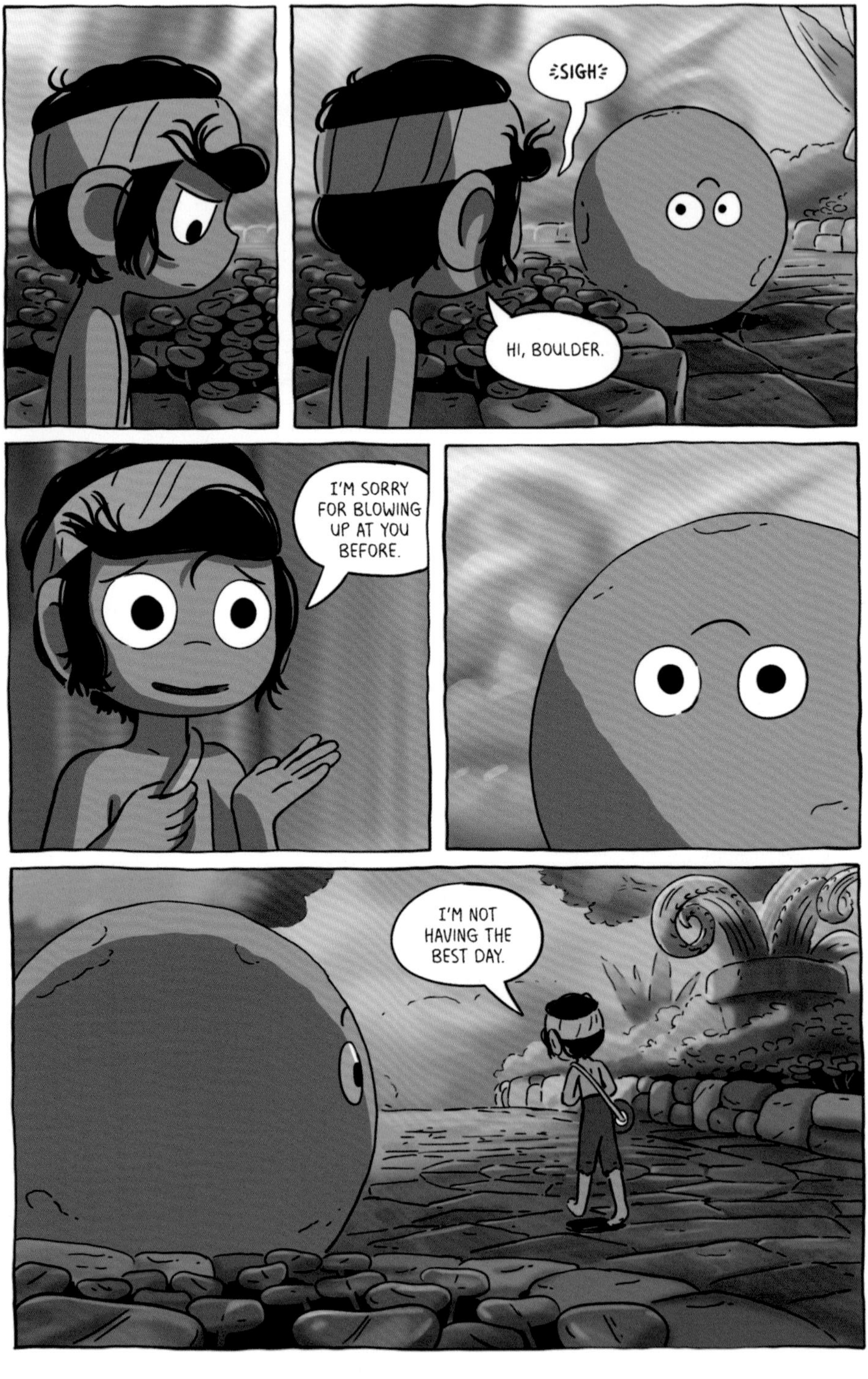
SIGH
HI, BOULDER.
I'M SORRY FOR BLOWING UP AT YOU BEFORE.
I'M NOT HAVING THE BEST DAY.

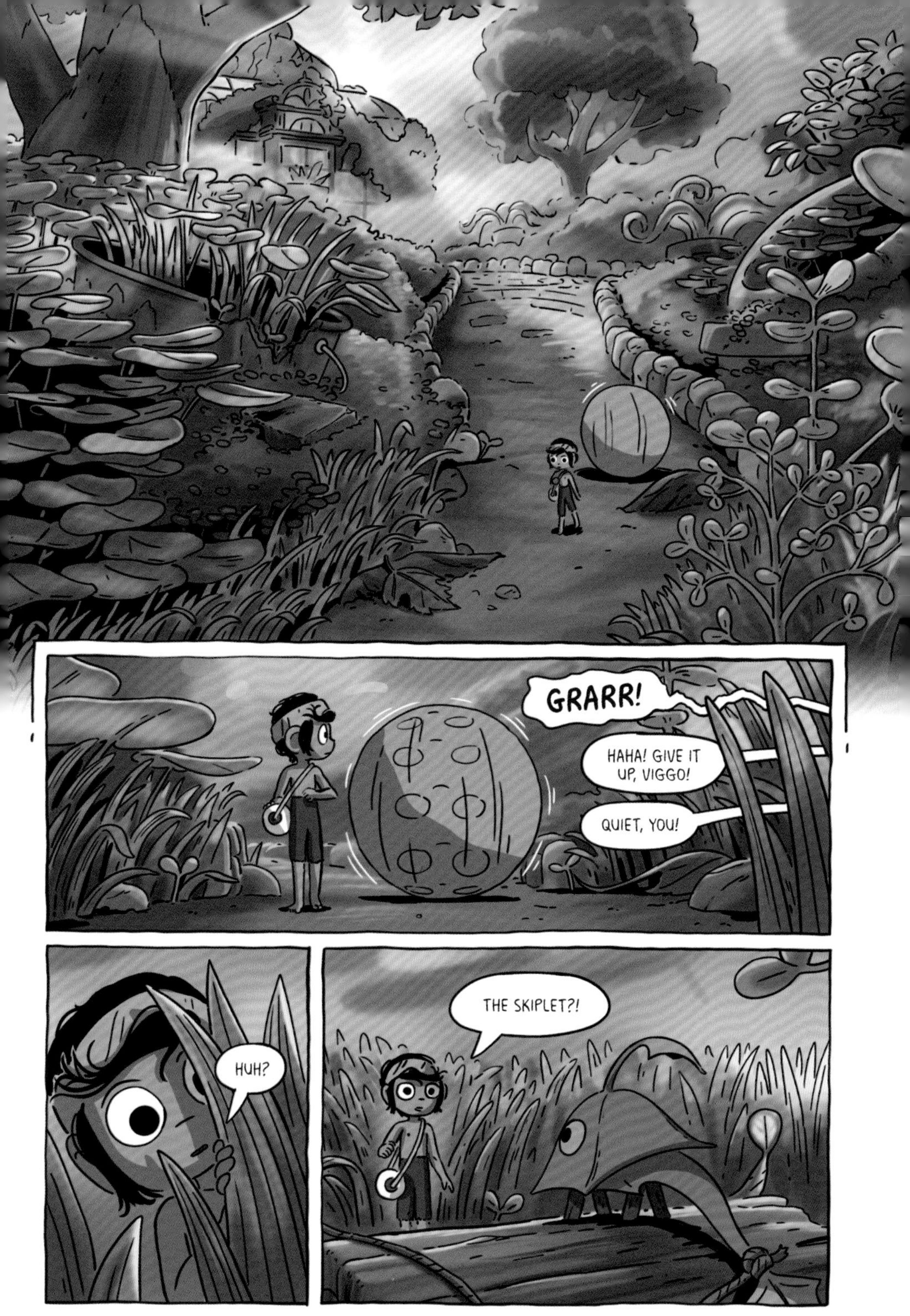
GRARR!
HAHA! GIVE IT UP, VIGGO!
QUIET, YOU!
HUH?
THE SKIPLET?!

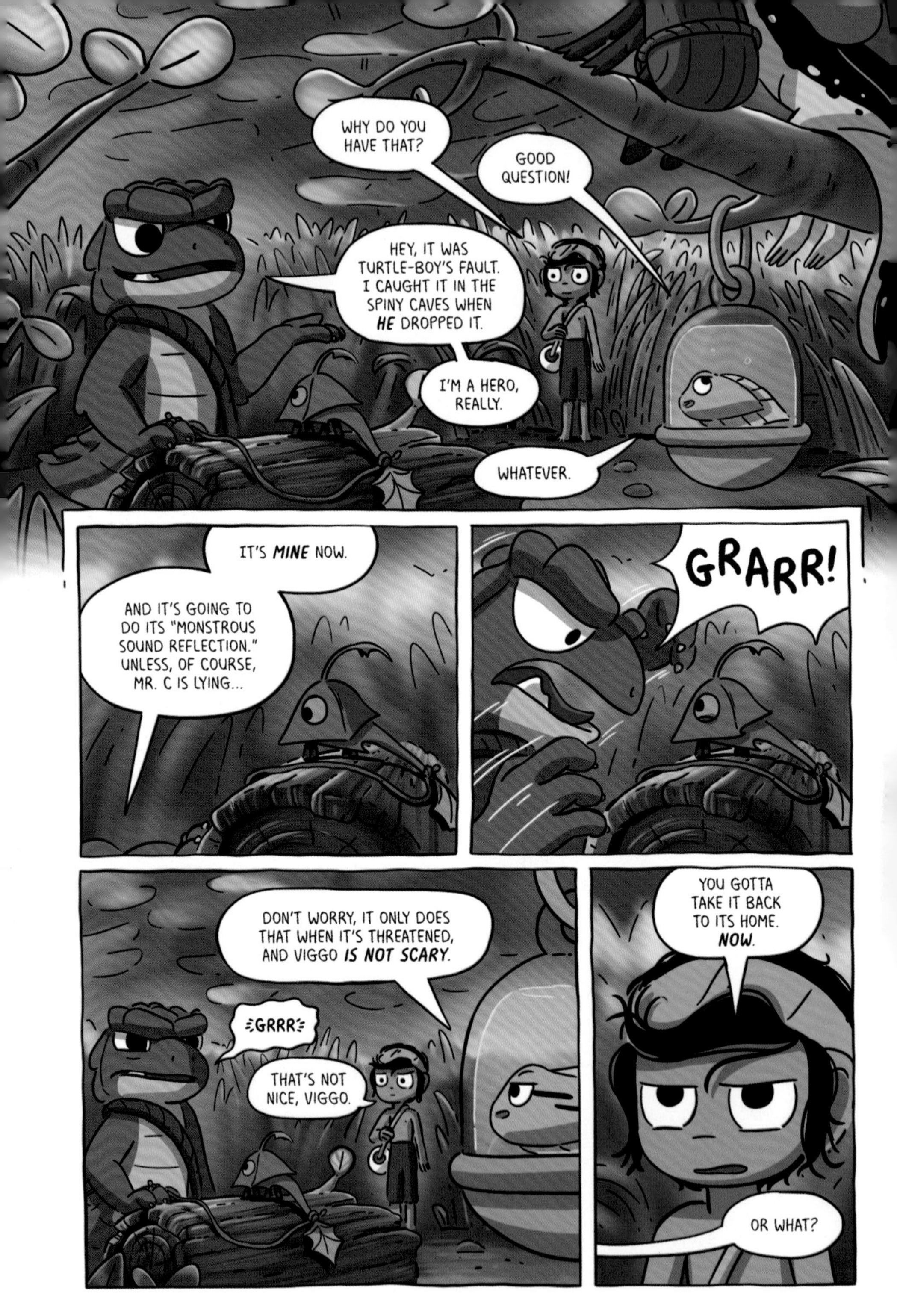
WHY DO YOU HAVE THAT?
GOOD QUESTION!
HEY, IT WAS TURTLE-BOY'S FAULT. I CAUGHT IT IN THE SPINY CAVES WHEN **HE** DROPPED IT.
I'M A HERO, REALLY.
WHATEVER.
IT'S **MINE** NOW.
AND IT'S GOING TO DO ITS "MONSTROUS SOUND REFLECTION." UNLESS, OF COURSE, MR. C IS LYING...
GRARR!
DON'T WORRY, IT ONLY DOES THAT WHEN IT'S THREATENED, AND VIGGO **IS NOT SCARY**.
GRRR
THAT'S NOT NICE, VIGGO.
YOU GOTTA TAKE IT BACK TO ITS HOME. **NOW**.
OR WHAT?

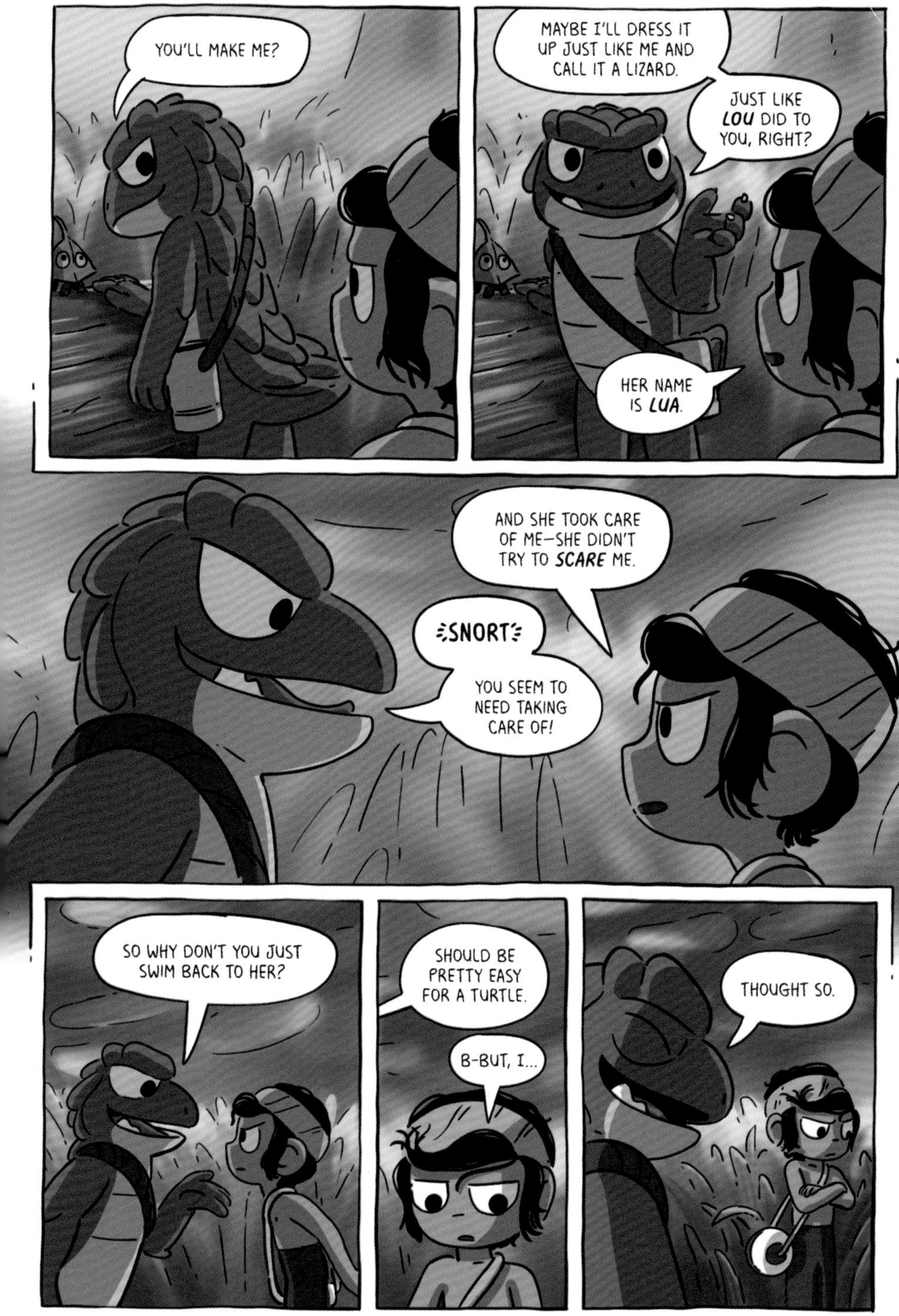

YOU'LL MAKE ME?
MAYBE I'LL DRESS IT UP JUST LIKE ME AND CALL IT A LIZARD.
JUST LIKE *LOU* DID TO YOU, RIGHT?
HER NAME IS *LUA*.
AND SHE TOOK CARE OF ME—SHE DIDN'T TRY TO *SCARE* ME.
SNORT
YOU SEEM TO NEED TAKING CARE OF!
SO WHY DON'T YOU JUST SWIM BACK TO HER?
SHOULD BE PRETTY EASY FOR A TURTLE.
B-BUT, I...
THOUGHT SO.

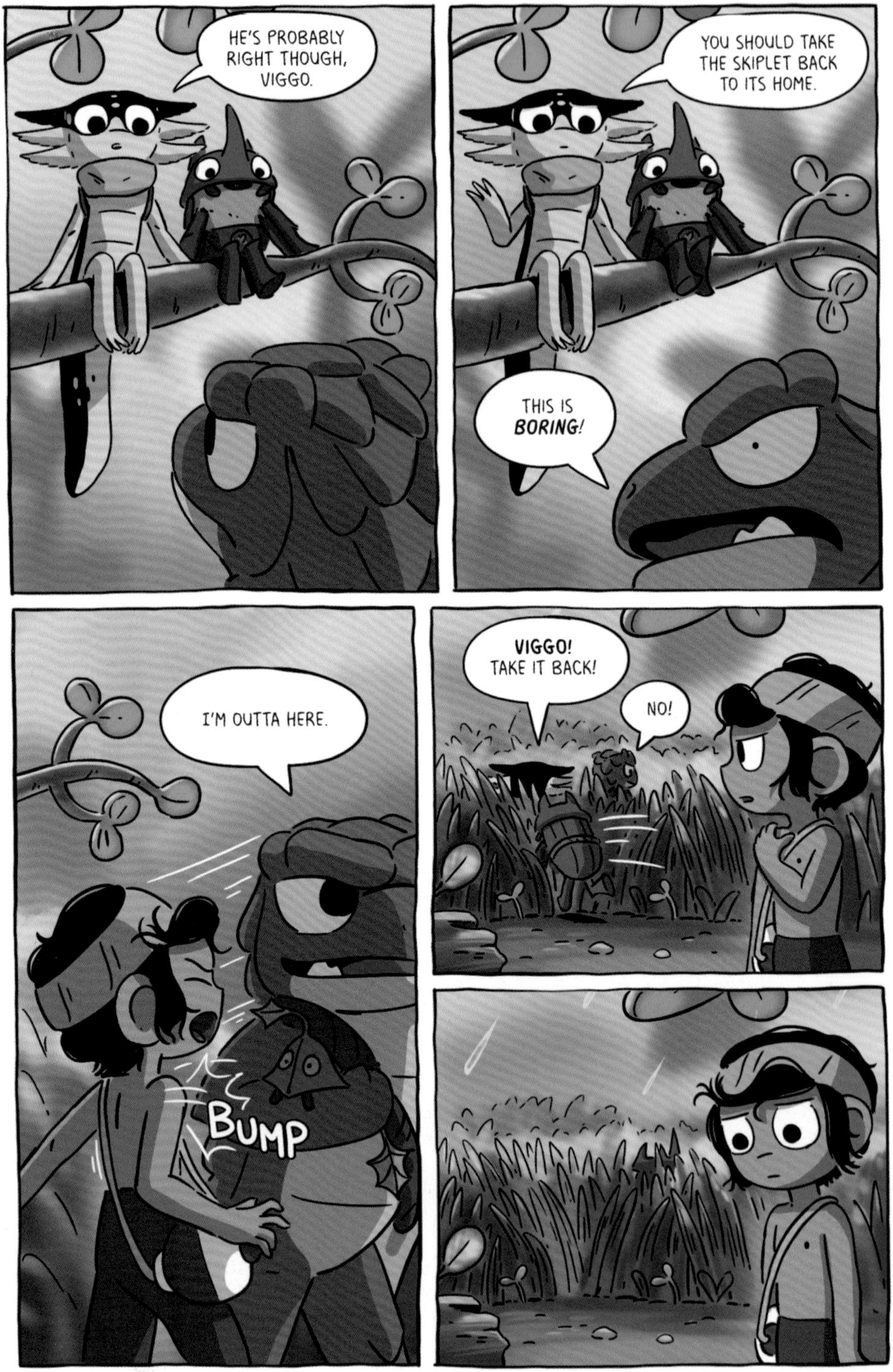
HE'S PROBABLY RIGHT THOUGH, VIGGO.
YOU SHOULD TAKE THE SKIPLET BACK TO ITS HOME.
THIS IS BORING!
I'M OUTTA HERE.
BUMP
VIGGO! TAKE IT BACK!
NO!

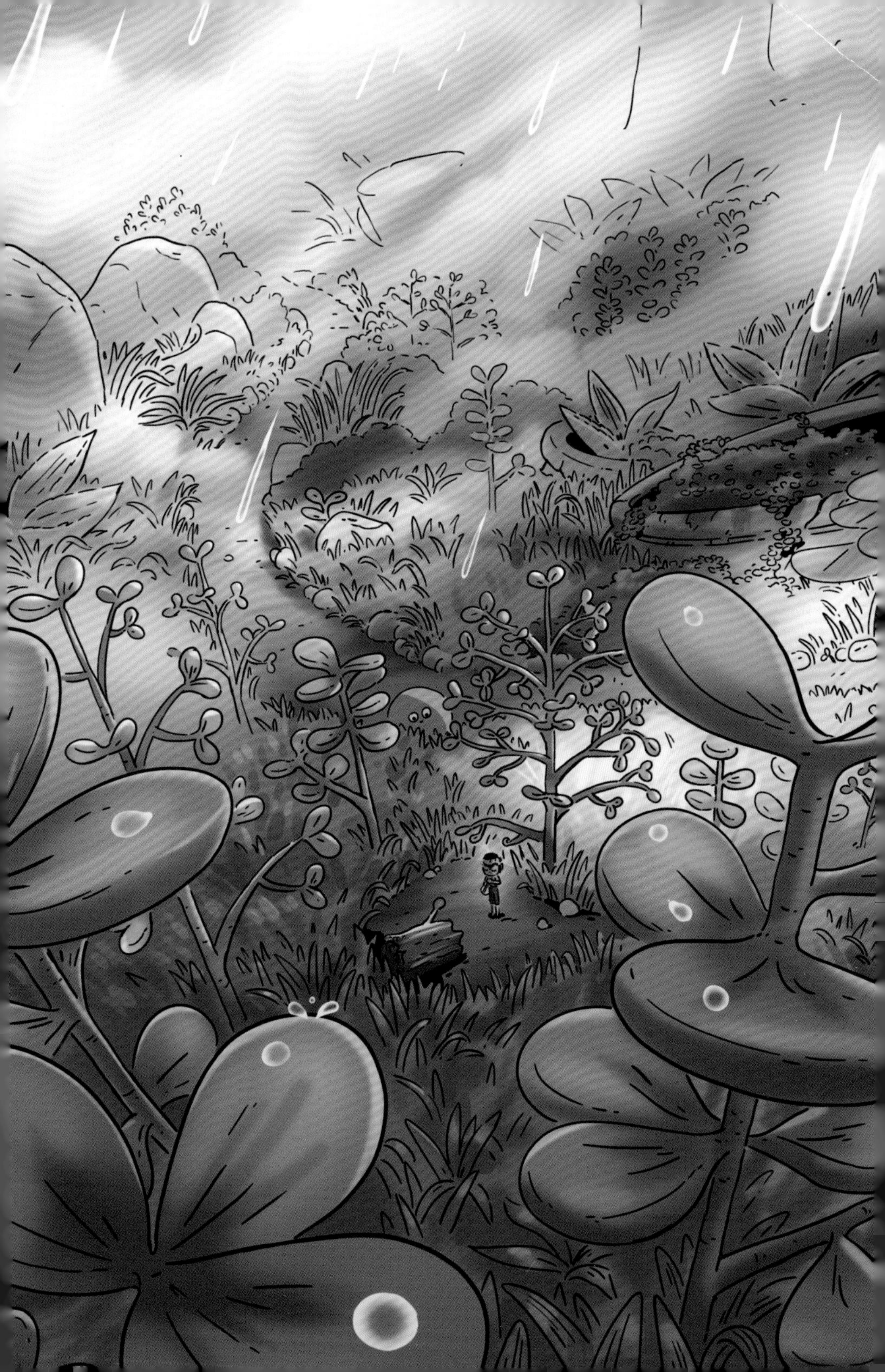

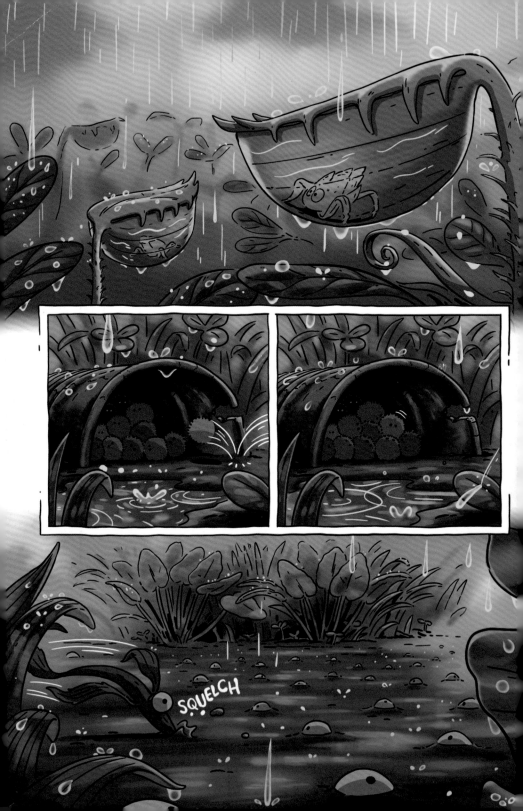

SQUELCH

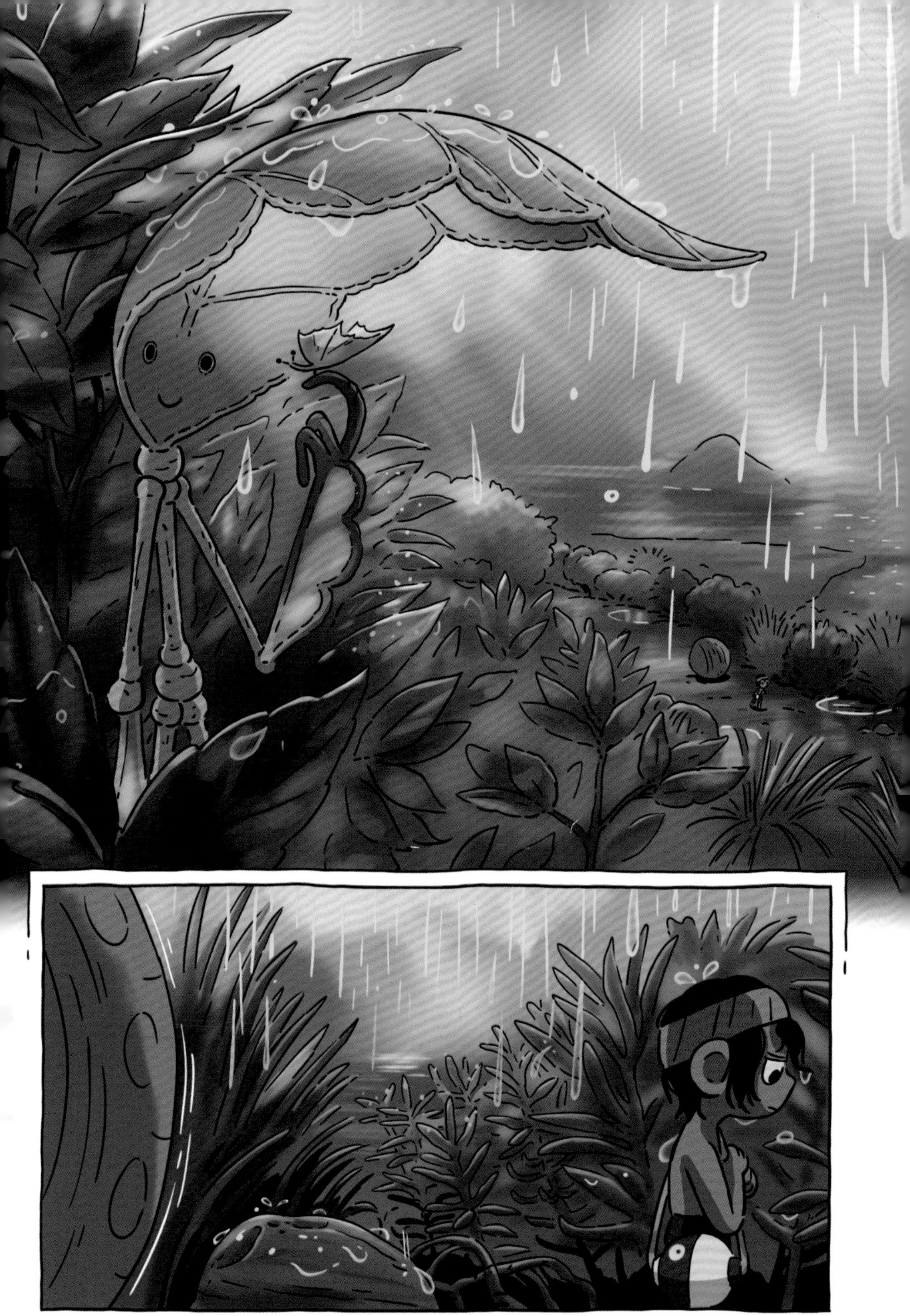

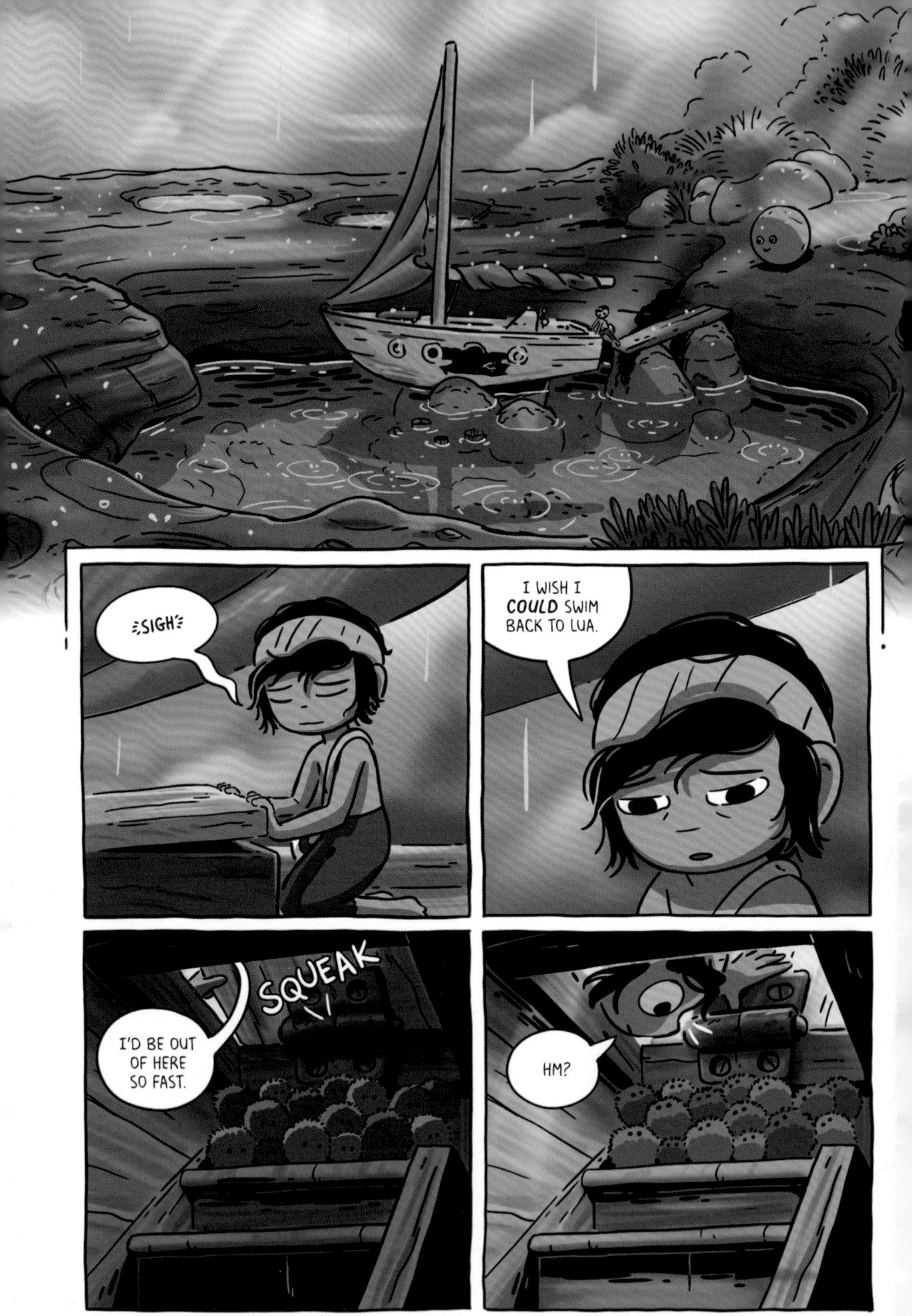
SIGH
I WISH I COULD SWIM BACK TO LUA.
SQUEAK
I'D BE OUT OF HERE SO FAST.
HM?

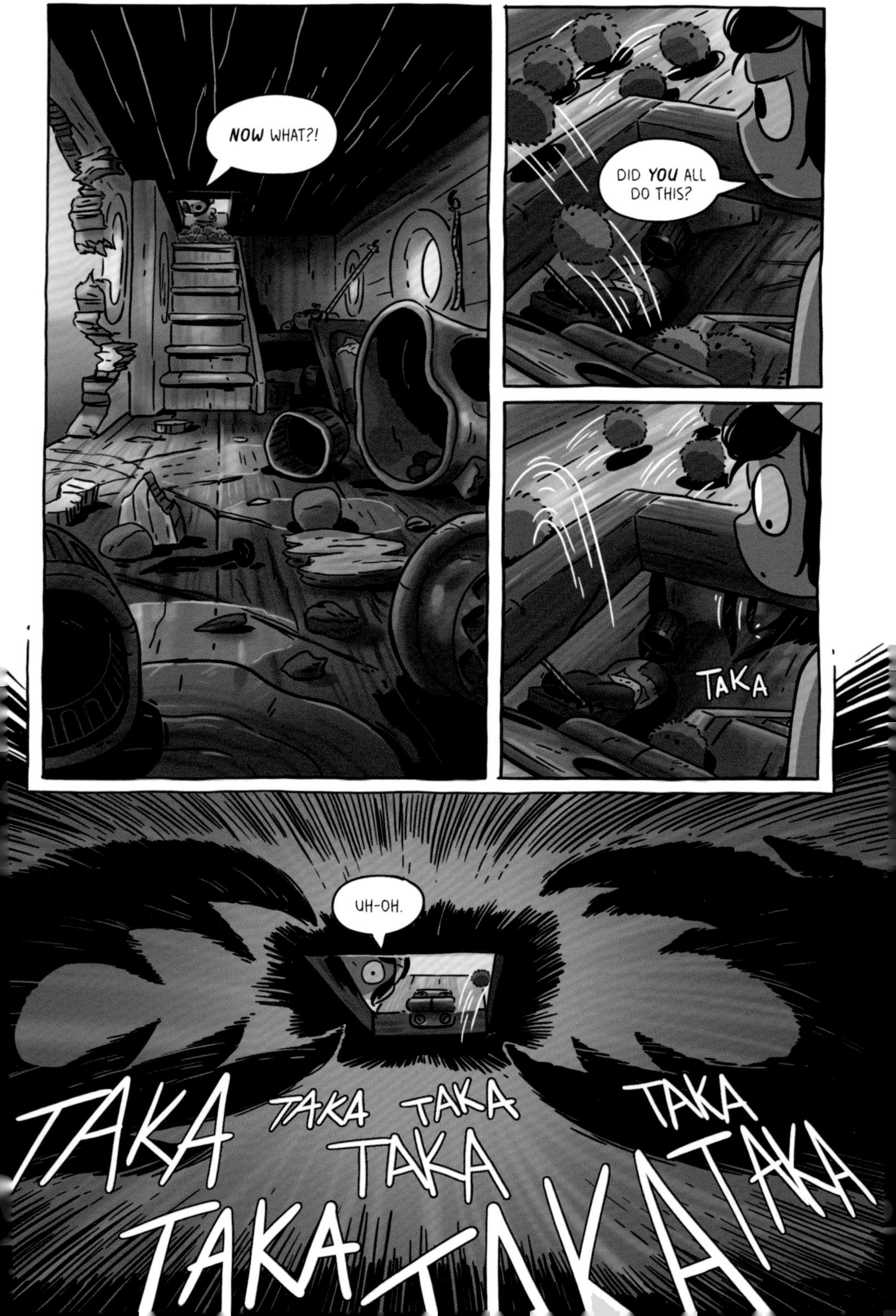

NOW WHAT?!
DID YOU ALL DO THIS?
TAKA
UH-OH.
TAKA TAKA TAKA TAKA TAKA TAKA TAKA TAKA TAKA

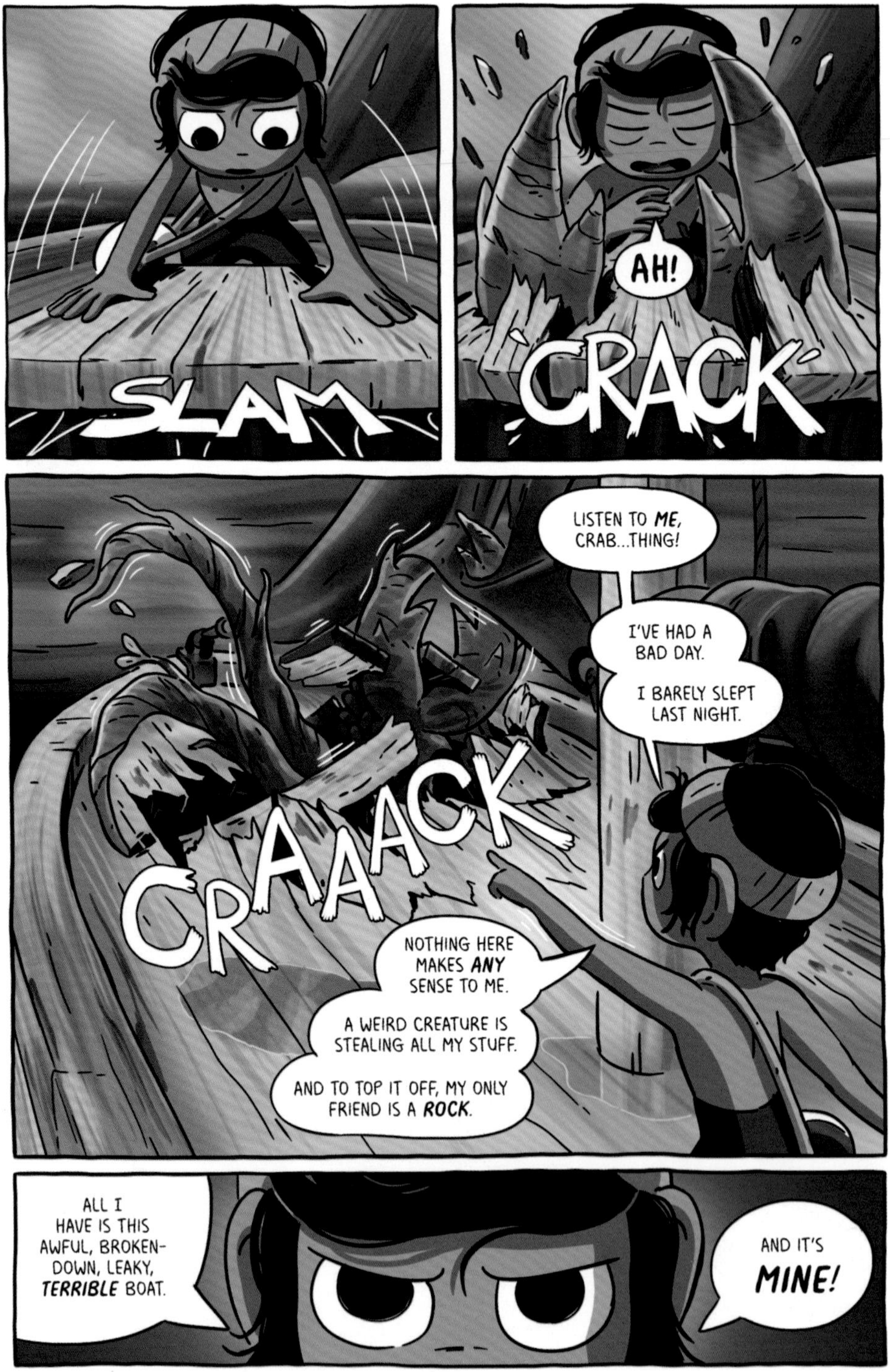
SLAM
AH!
CRACK
LISTEN TO *ME*, CRAB...THING!
I'VE HAD A BAD DAY.
I BARELY SLEPT LAST NIGHT.
CRAAACK
NOTHING HERE MAKES **ANY** SENSE TO ME.
A WEIRD CREATURE IS STEALING ALL MY STUFF.
AND TO TOP IT OFF, MY ONLY FRIEND IS A **ROCK**.
ALL I HAVE IS THIS AWFUL, BROKEN-DOWN, LEAKY, **TERRIBLE** BOAT.
AND IT'S **MINE!**

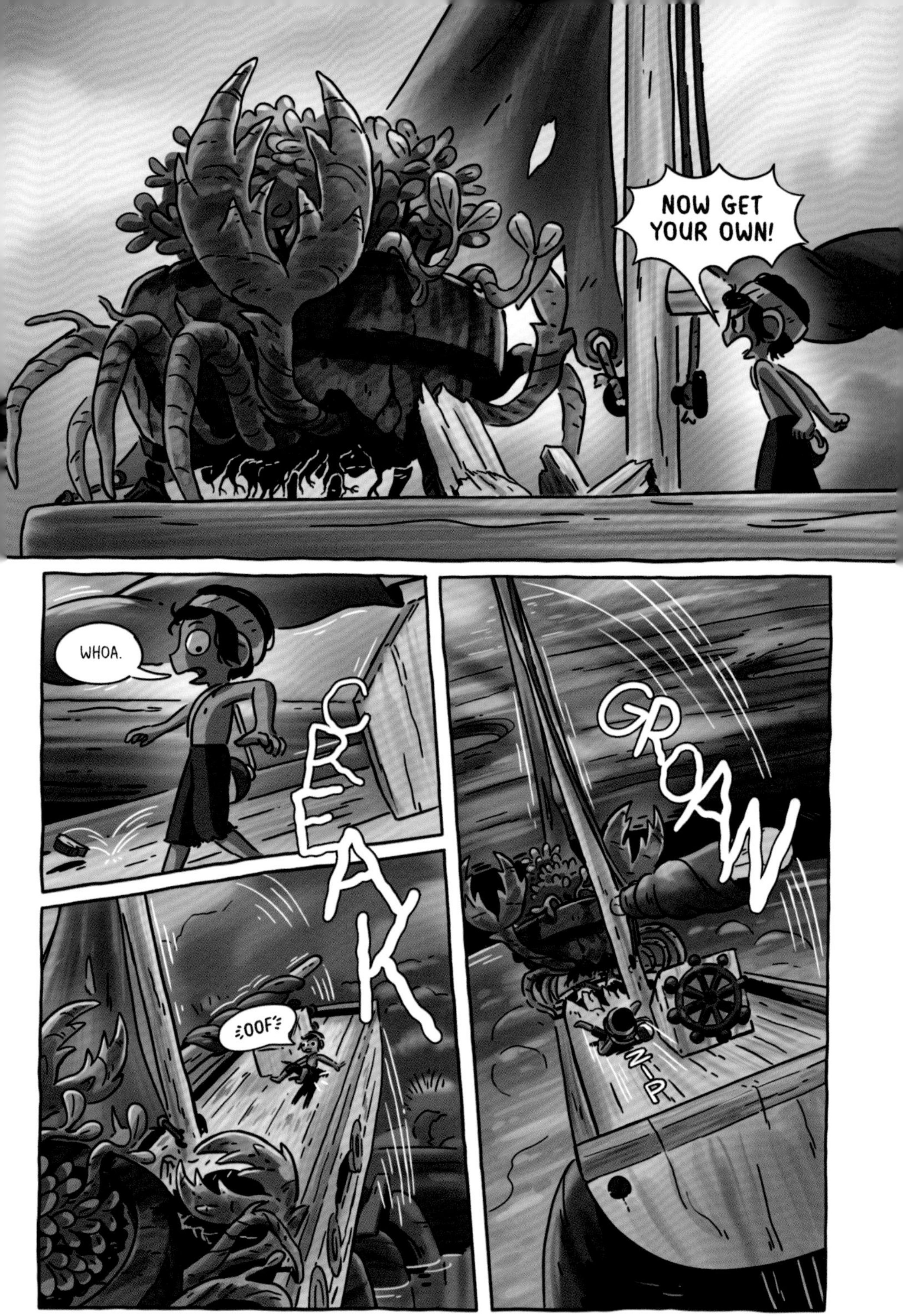
NOW GET YOUR OWN!
WHOA.
CREAK
GROAN
OOF
ZIP

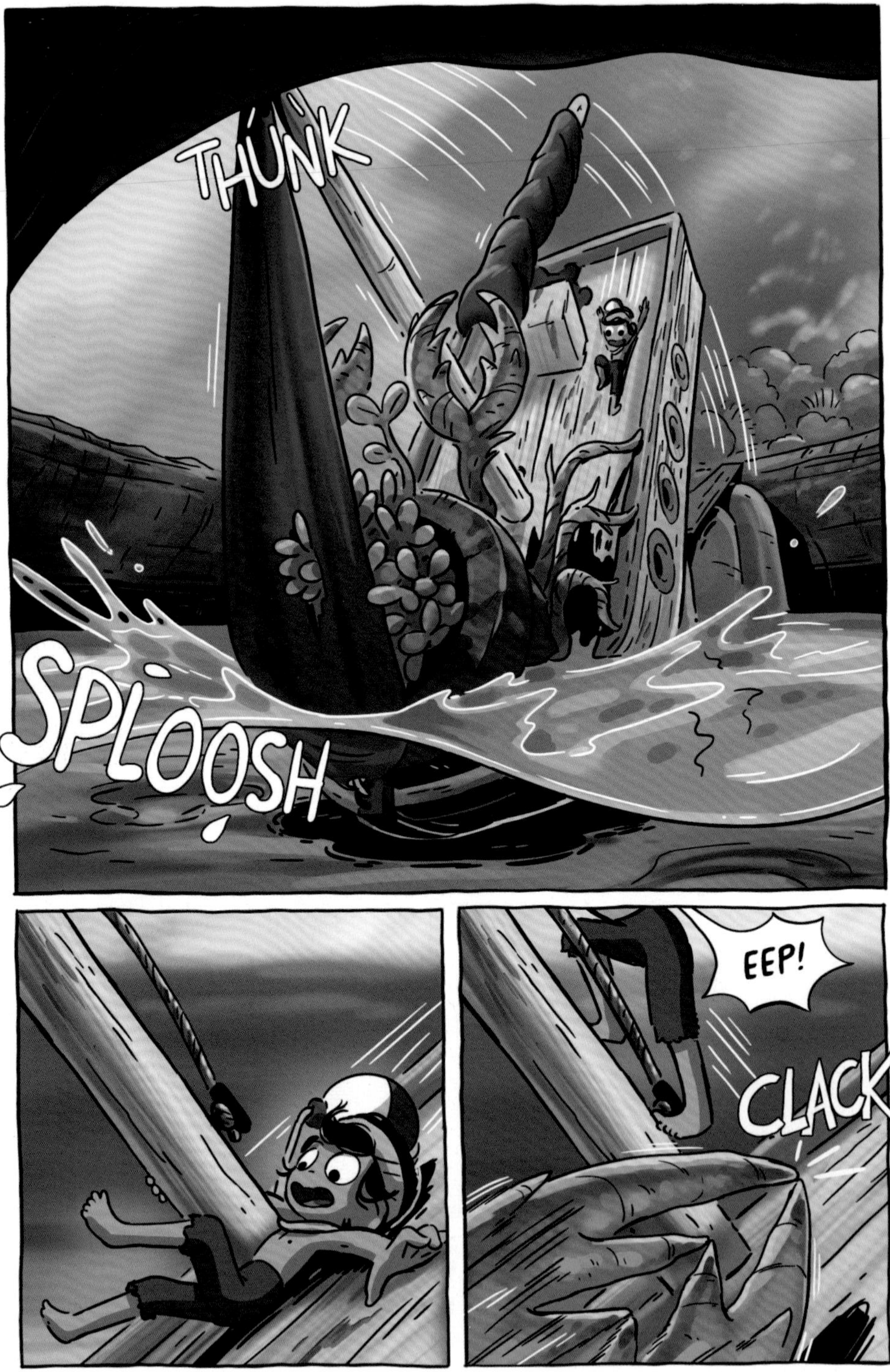
THUNK
SPLOOSH
EEP!
CLACK

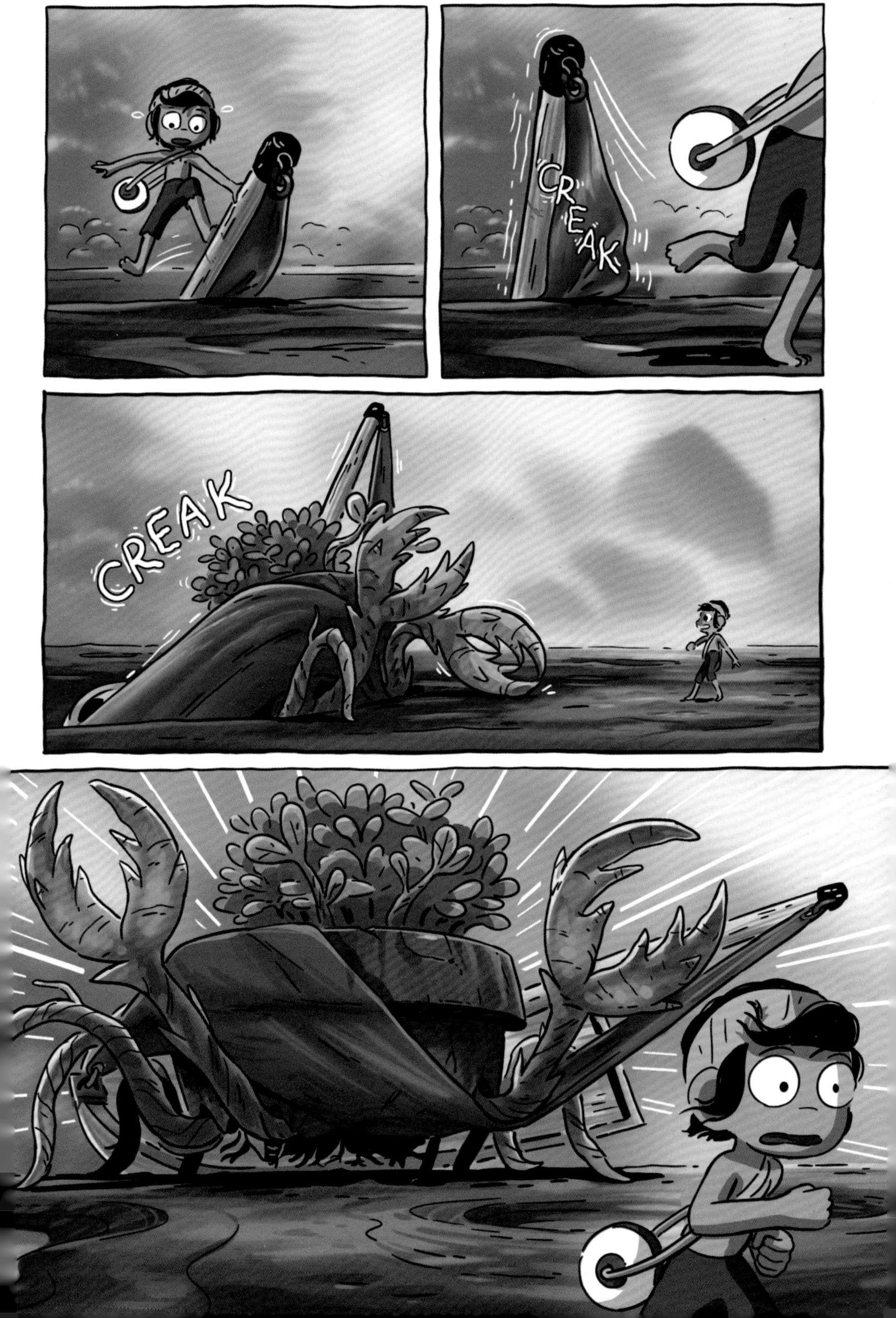
CREAK
CREAK

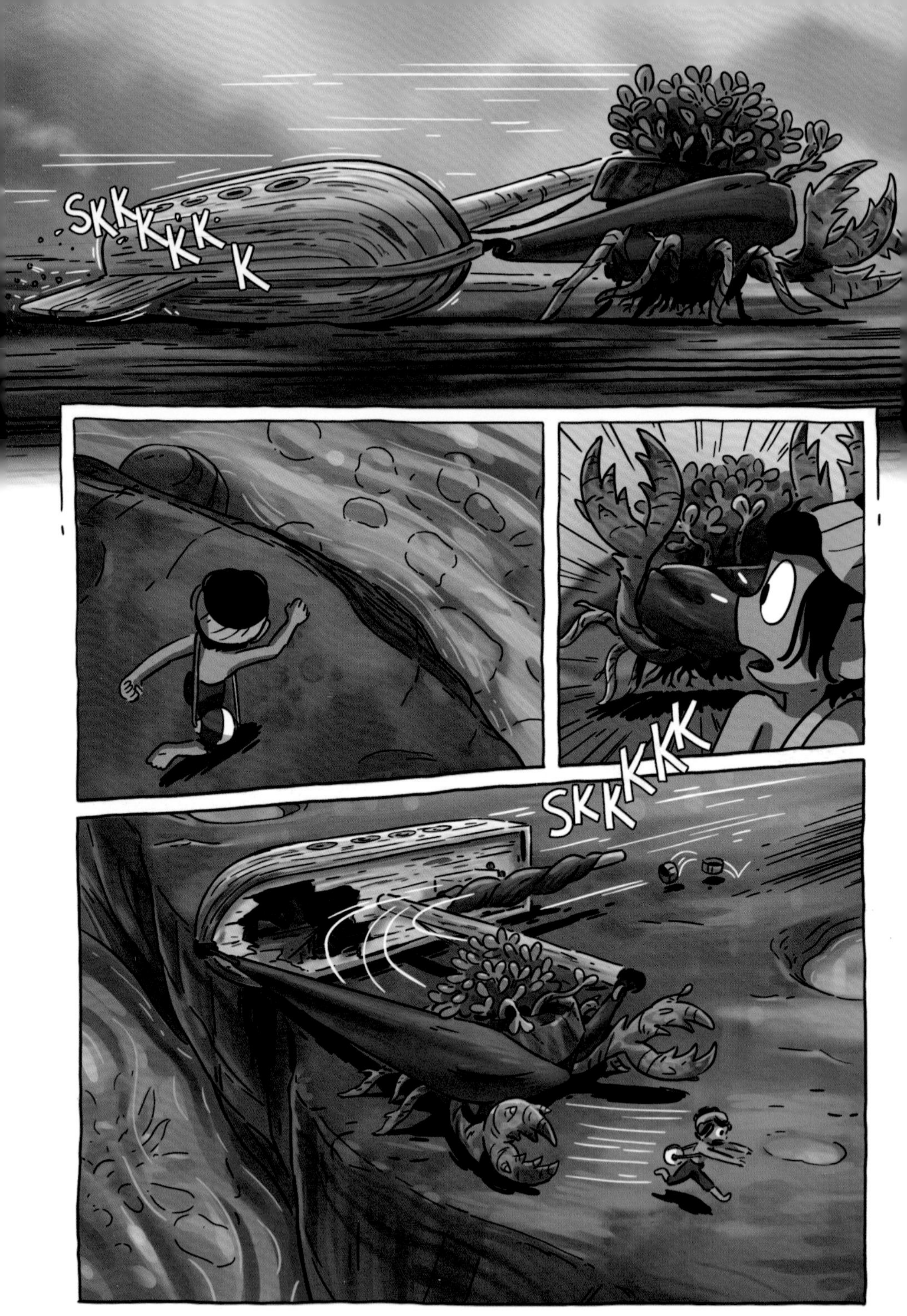
SKKKKKK
SKKKKK

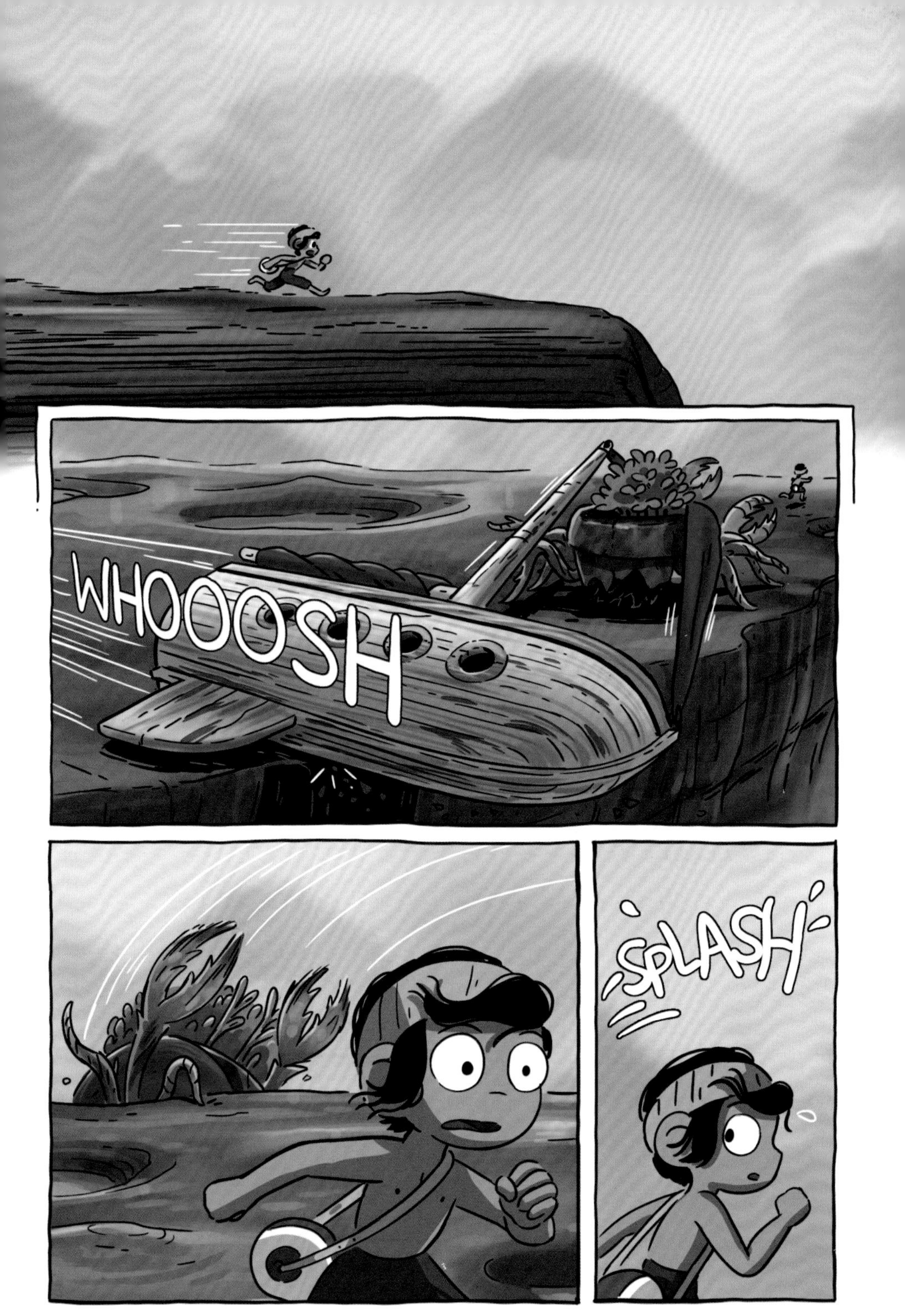
WHOOOSH
SPLASH

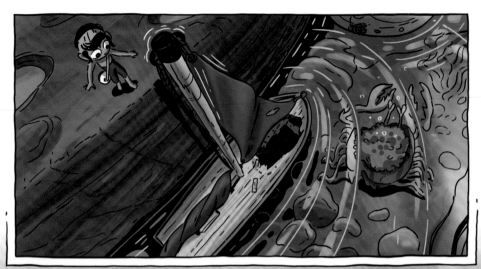

ZIP

IT'S IN THE
OPEN OCEAN!

I CAN SAIL
AWAY!

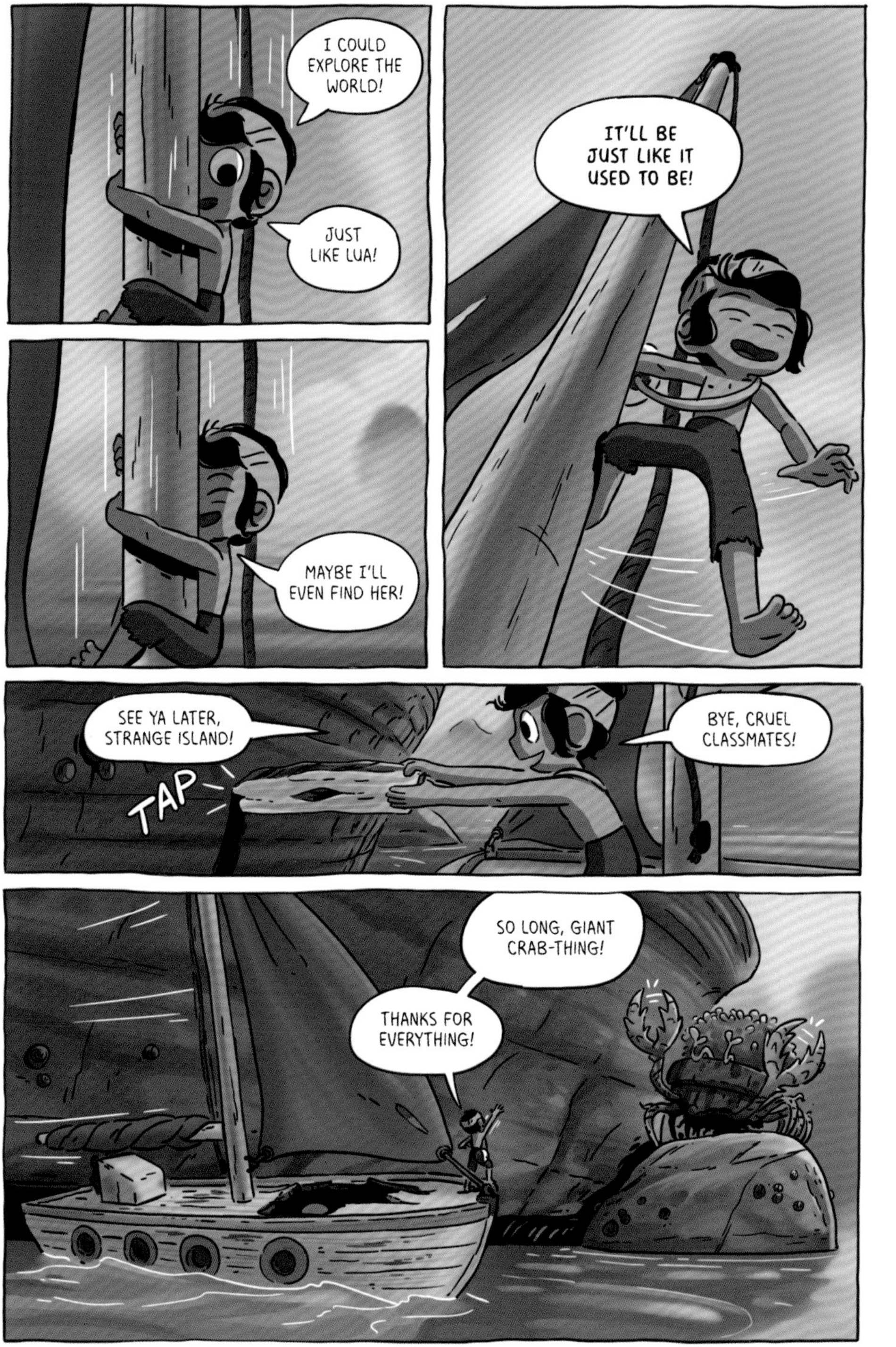
I COULD EXPLORE THE WORLD!
JUST LIKE LUA!
IT'LL BE JUST LIKE IT USED TO BE!
MAYBE I'LL EVEN FIND HER!
SEE YA LATER, STRANGE ISLAND!
TAP
BYE, CRUEL CLASSMATES!
SO LONG, GIANT CRAB-THING!
THANKS FOR EVERYTHING!

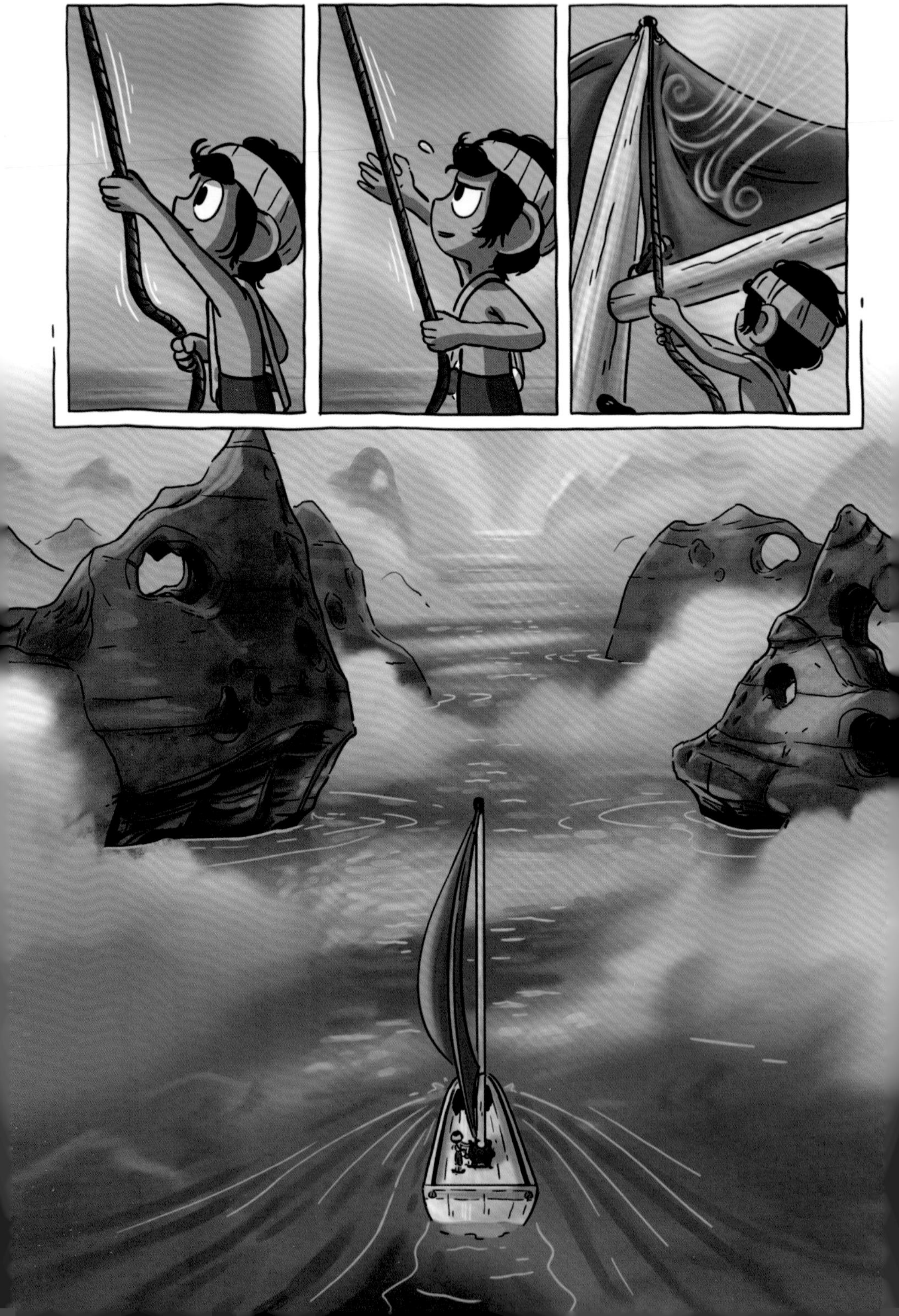

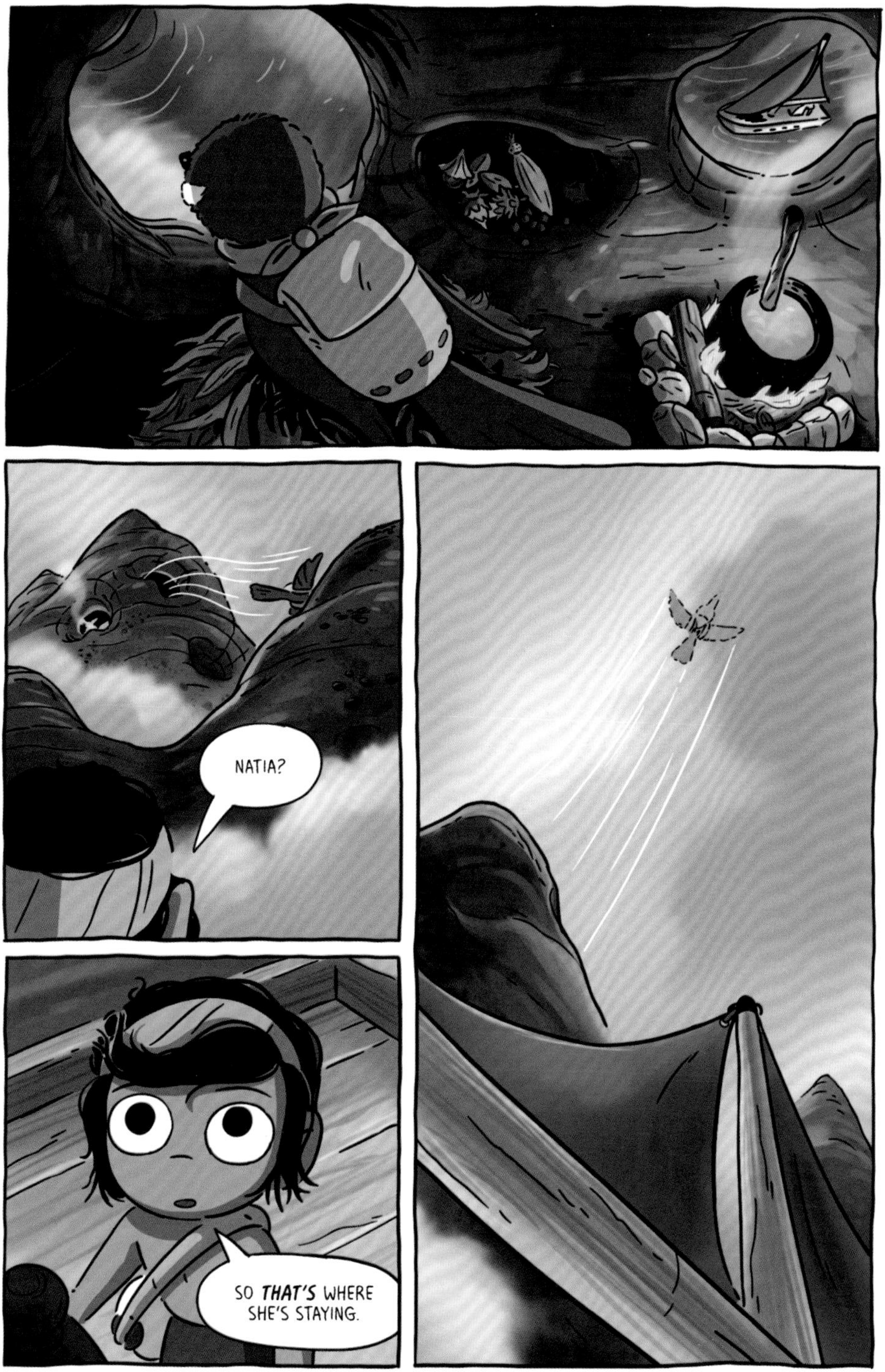
NATIA?
SO THAT'S WHERE SHE'S STAYING.

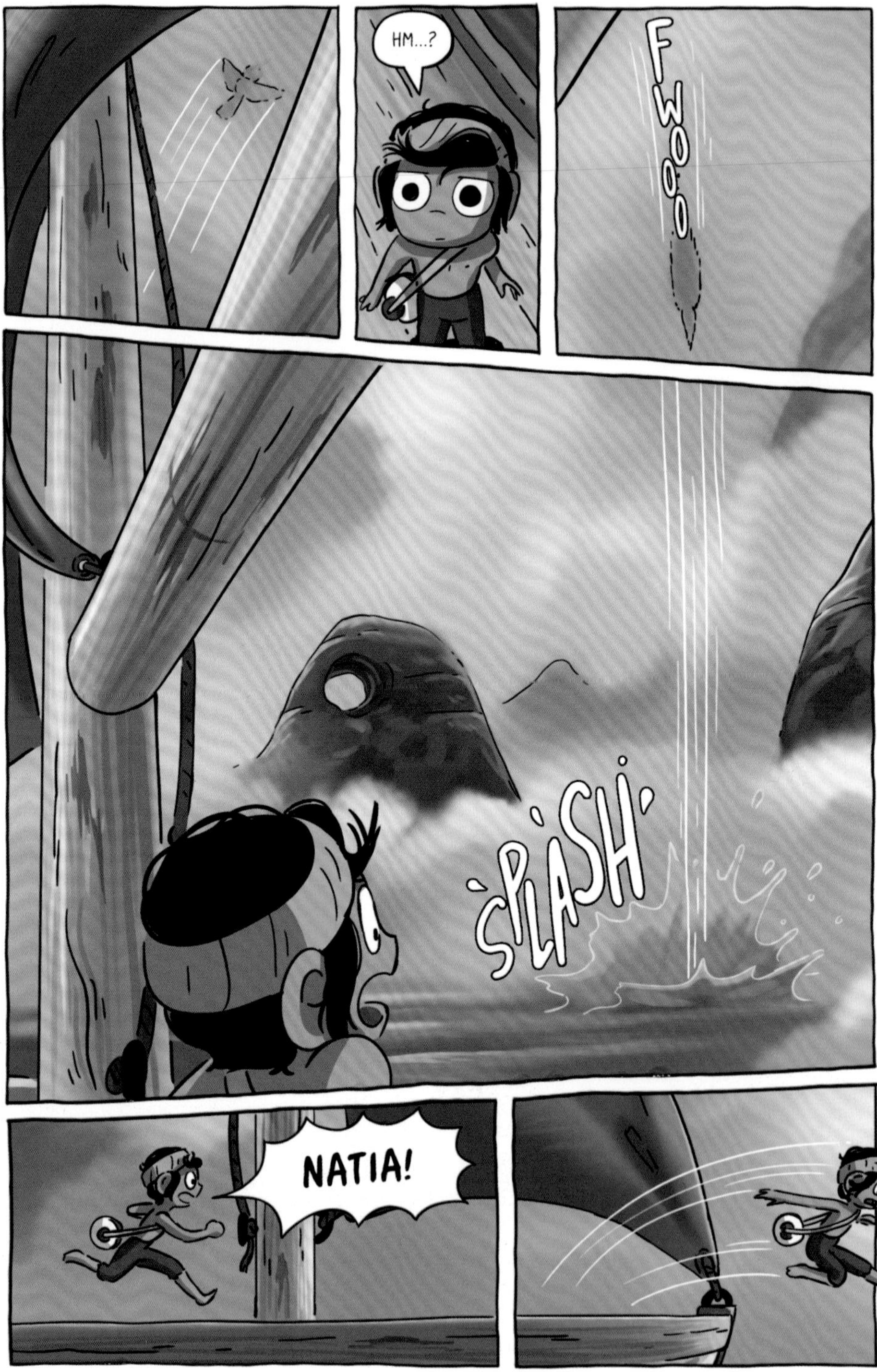
HM...?
FWOOO
SPLASH
NATIA!

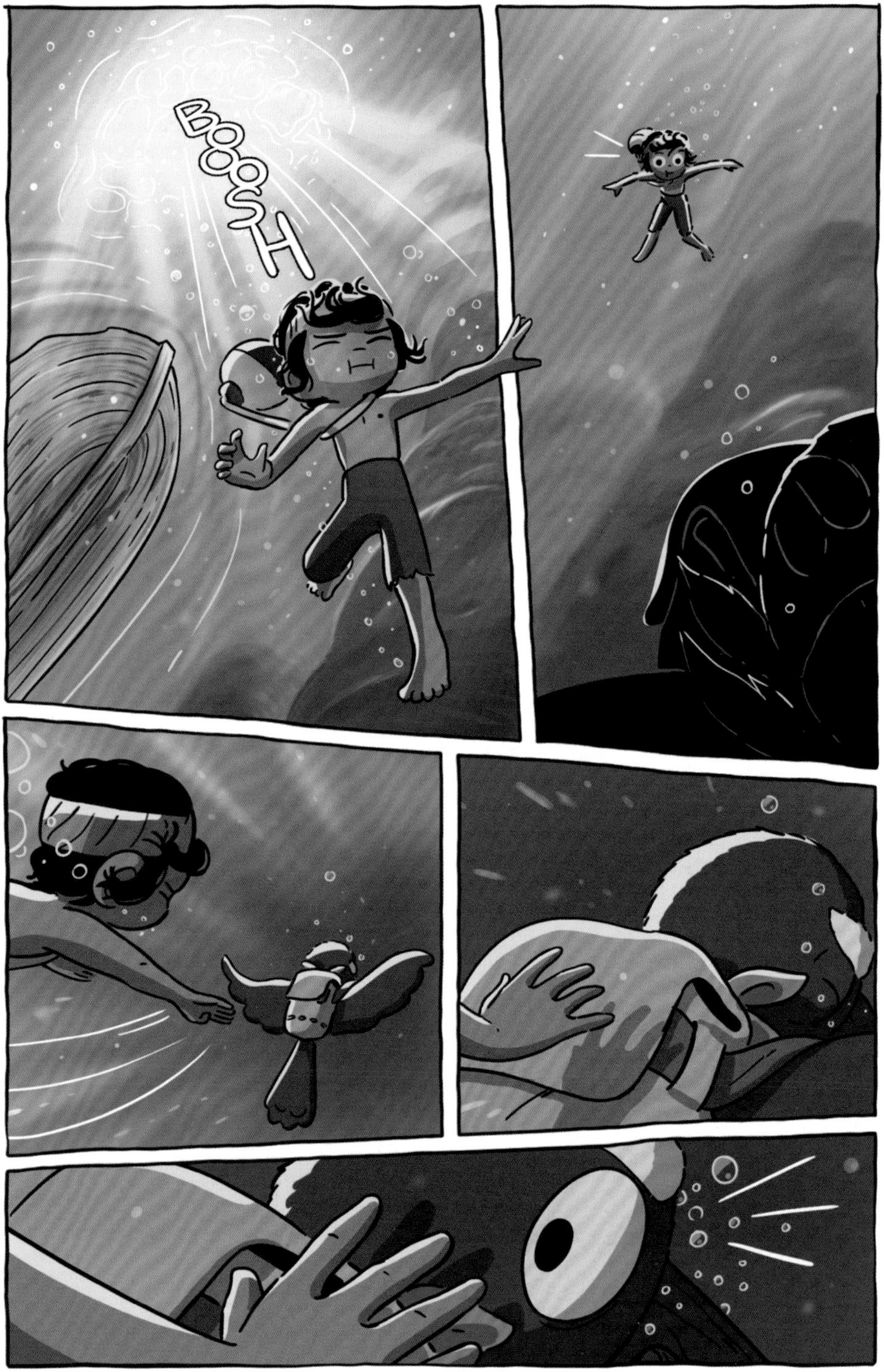
BOOSH

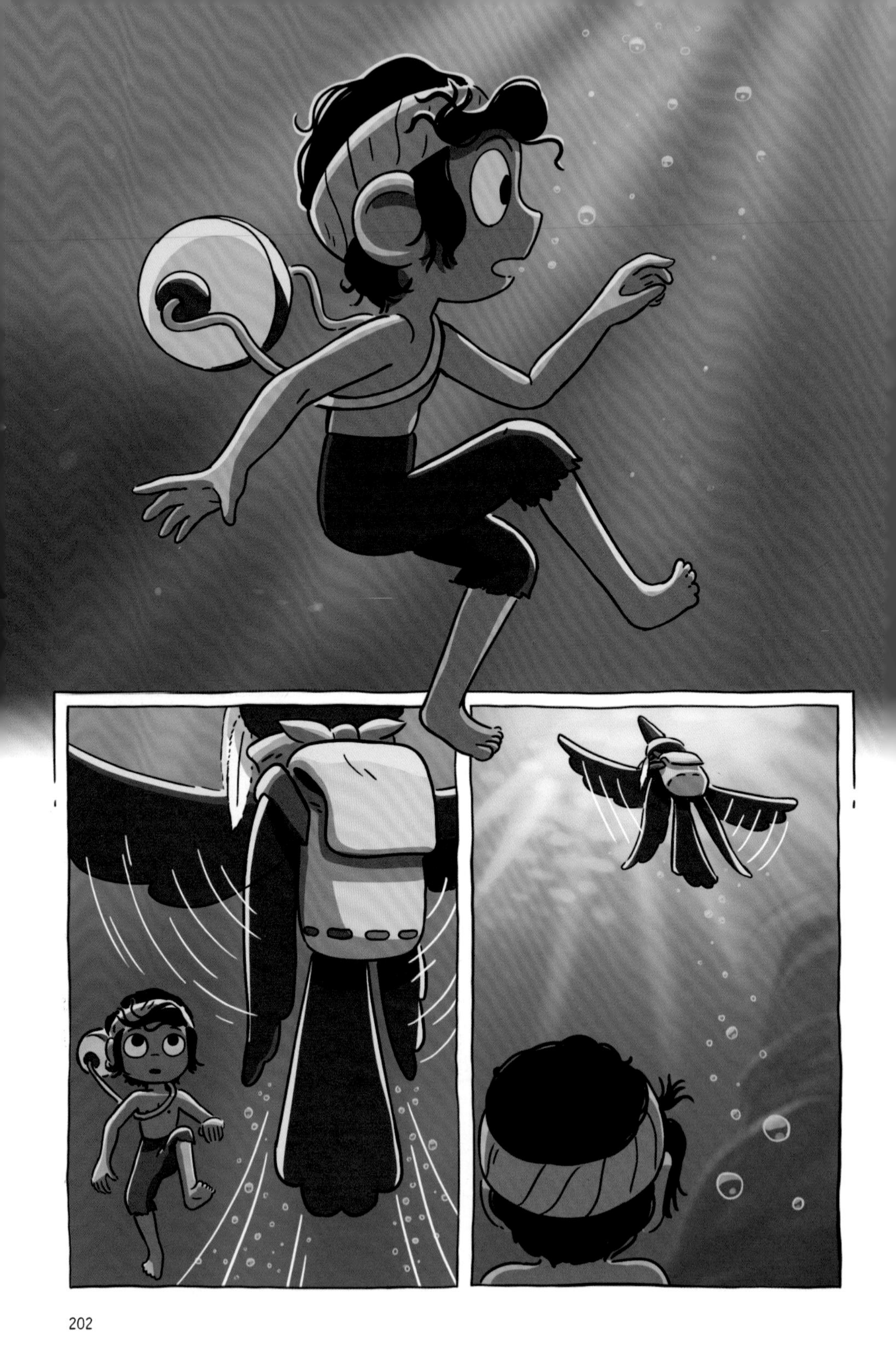

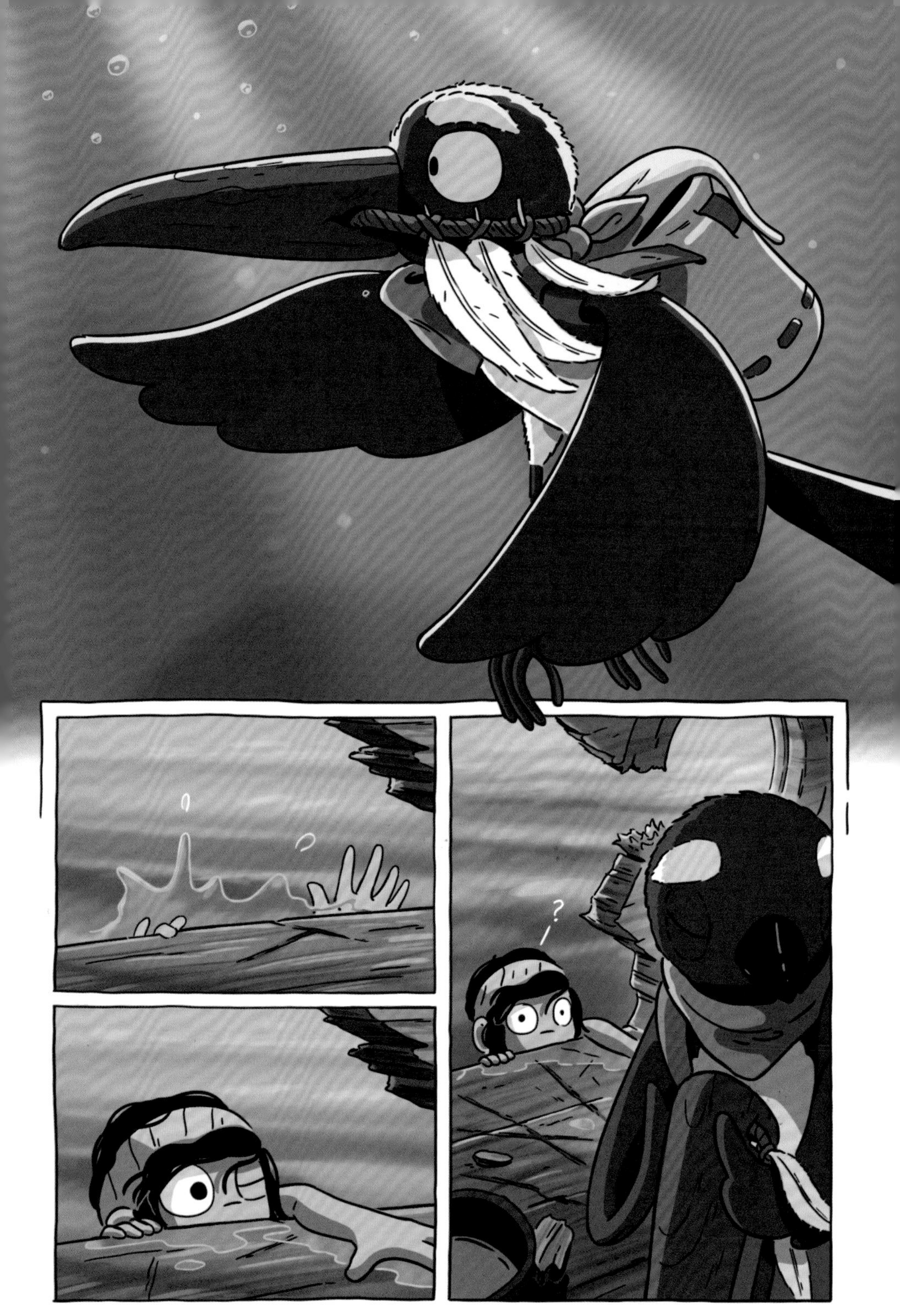
?

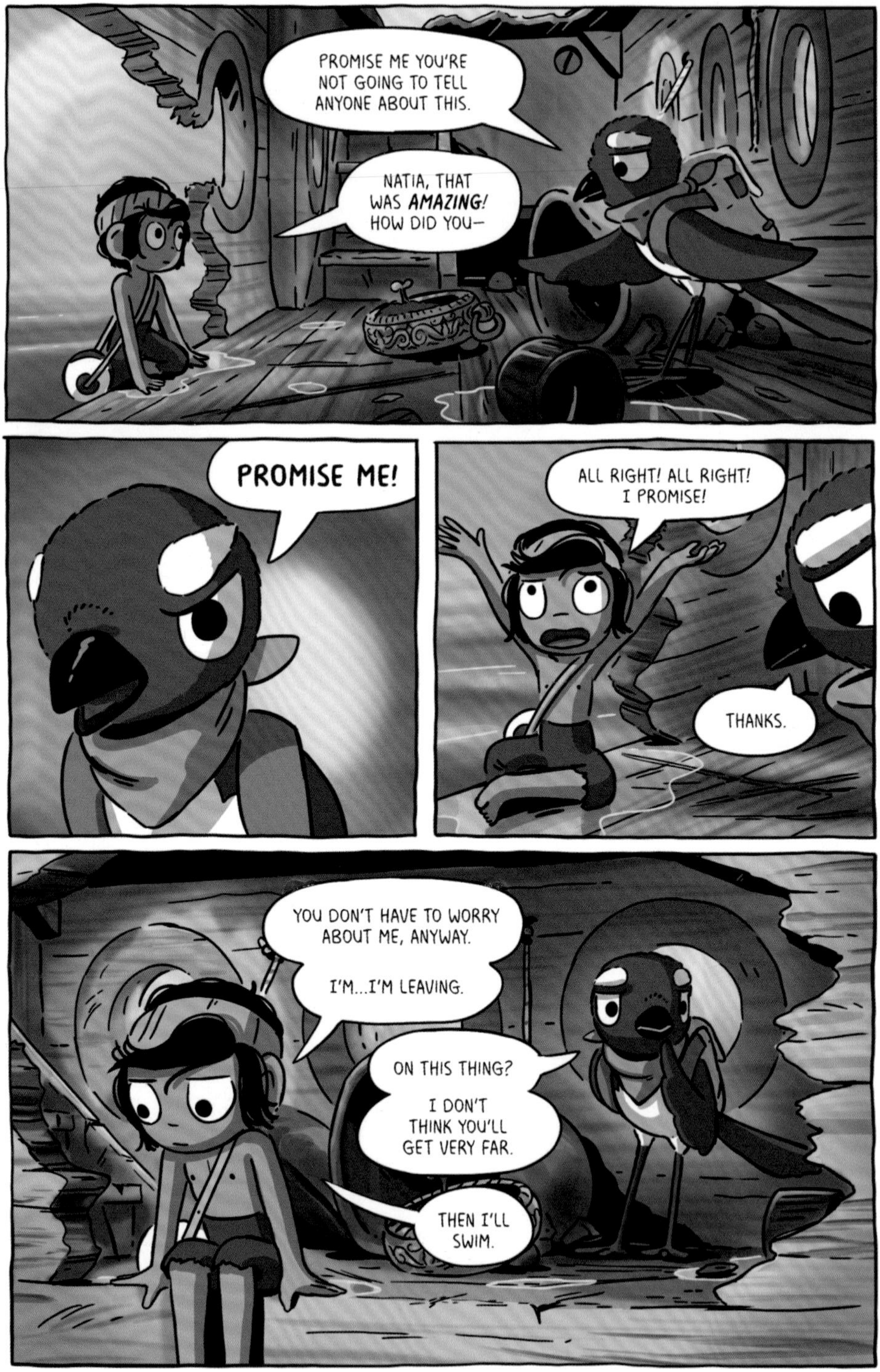
PROMISE ME YOU'RE NOT GOING TO TELL ANYONE ABOUT THIS.
NATIA, THAT WAS **AMAZING**! HOW DID YOU—
PROMISE ME!
ALL RIGHT! ALL RIGHT! I PROMISE!
THANKS.
YOU DON'T HAVE TO WORRY ABOUT ME, ANYWAY.
I'M...I'M LEAVING.
ON THIS THING?
I DON'T THINK YOU'LL GET VERY FAR.
THEN I'LL SWIM.

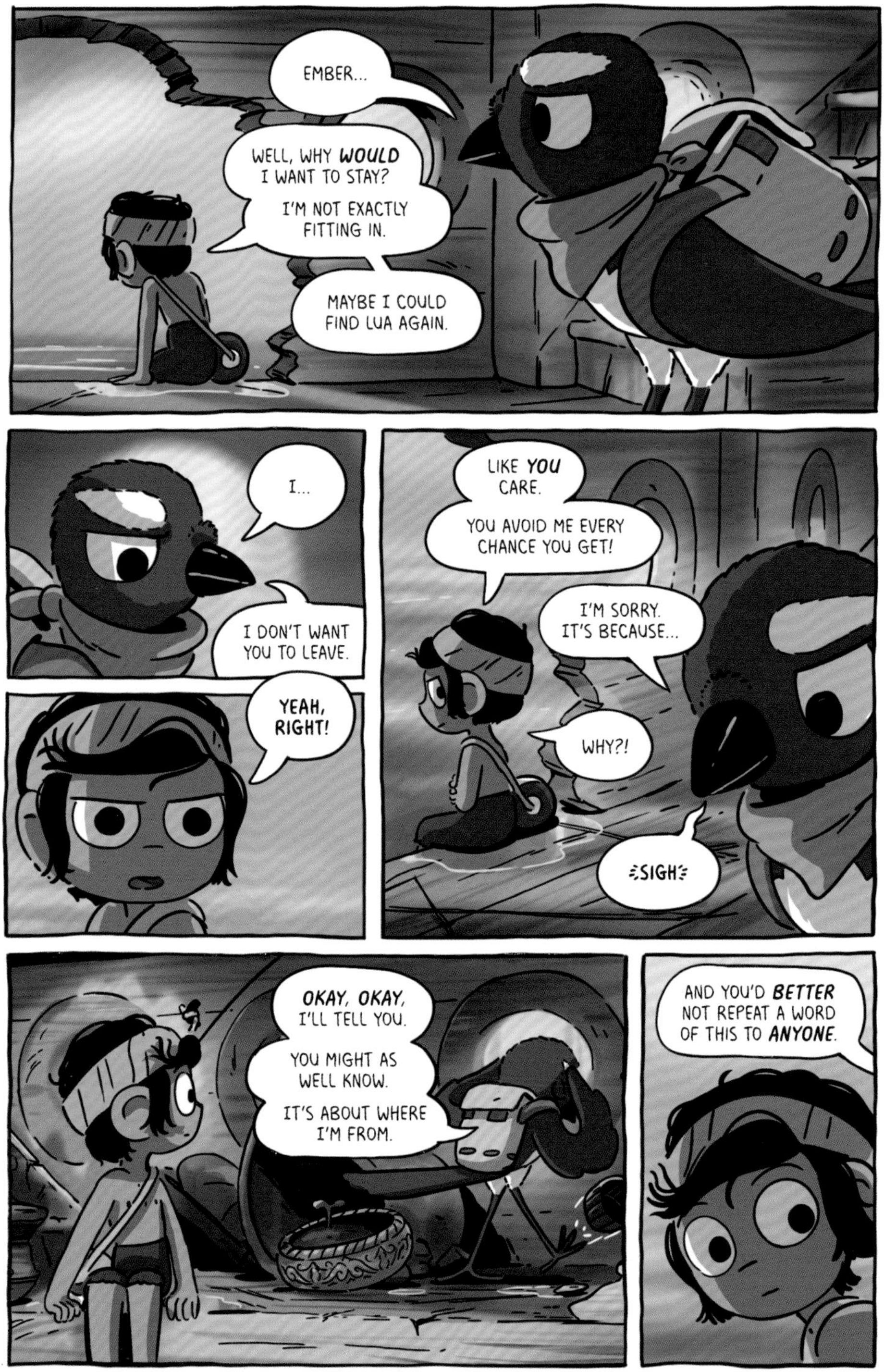
EMBER...
WELL, WHY **WOULD** I WANT TO STAY?
I'M NOT EXACTLY FITTING IN.
MAYBE I COULD FIND LUA AGAIN.
I...
I DON'T WANT YOU TO LEAVE.
YEAH, RIGHT!
LIKE **YOU** CARE.
YOU AVOID ME EVERY CHANCE YOU GET!
I'M SORRY. IT'S BECAUSE...
WHY?!
SIGH
OKAY, OKAY, I'LL TELL YOU.
YOU MIGHT AS WELL KNOW.
IT'S ABOUT WHERE I'M FROM.
AND YOU'D ***BETTER*** NOT REPEAT A WORD OF THIS TO ***ANYONE***.

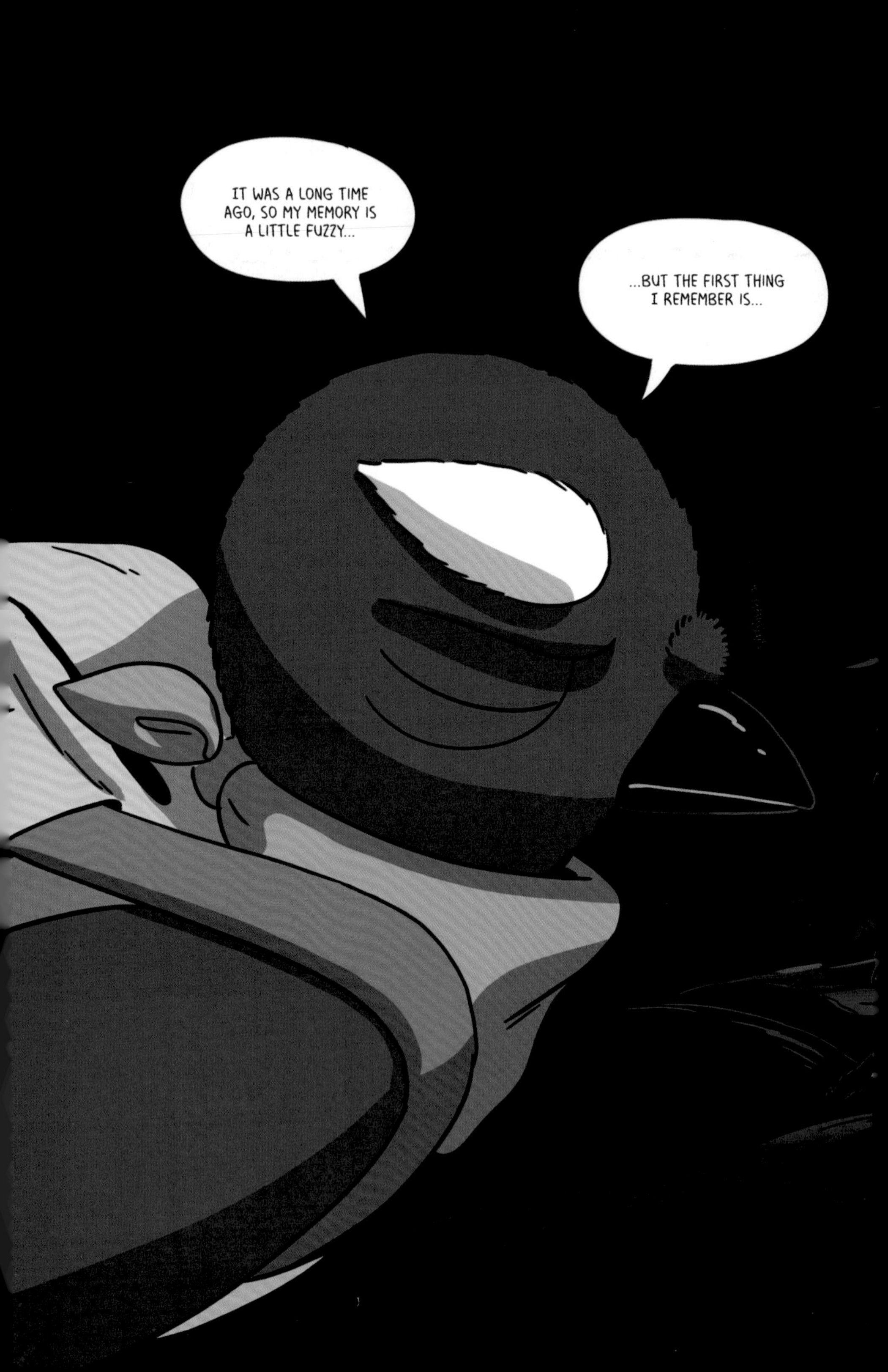
IT WAS A LONG TIME AGO, SO MY MEMORY IS A LITTLE FUZZY...
...BUT THE FIRST THING I REMEMBER IS...

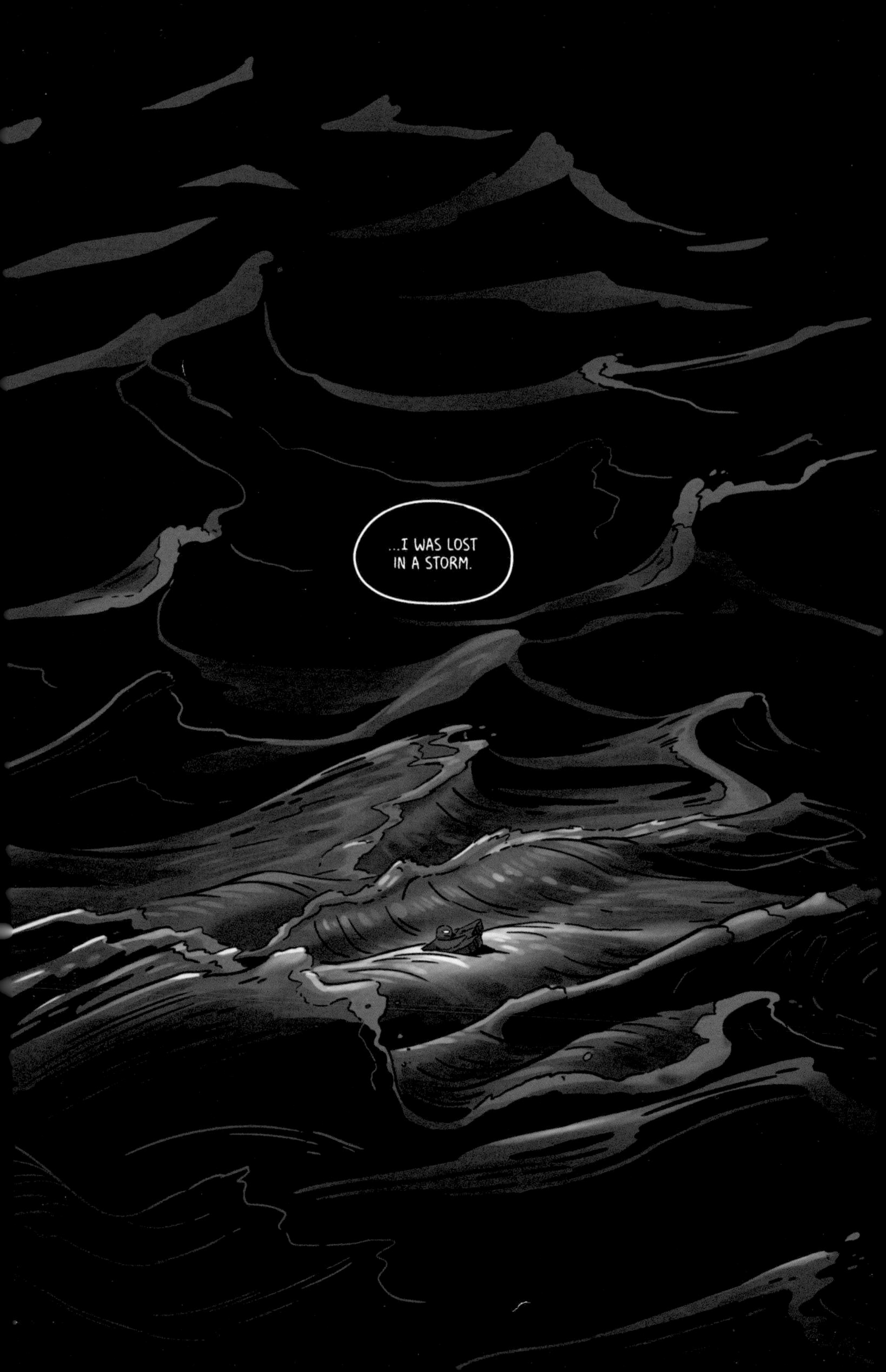
...I WAS LOST IN A STORM.

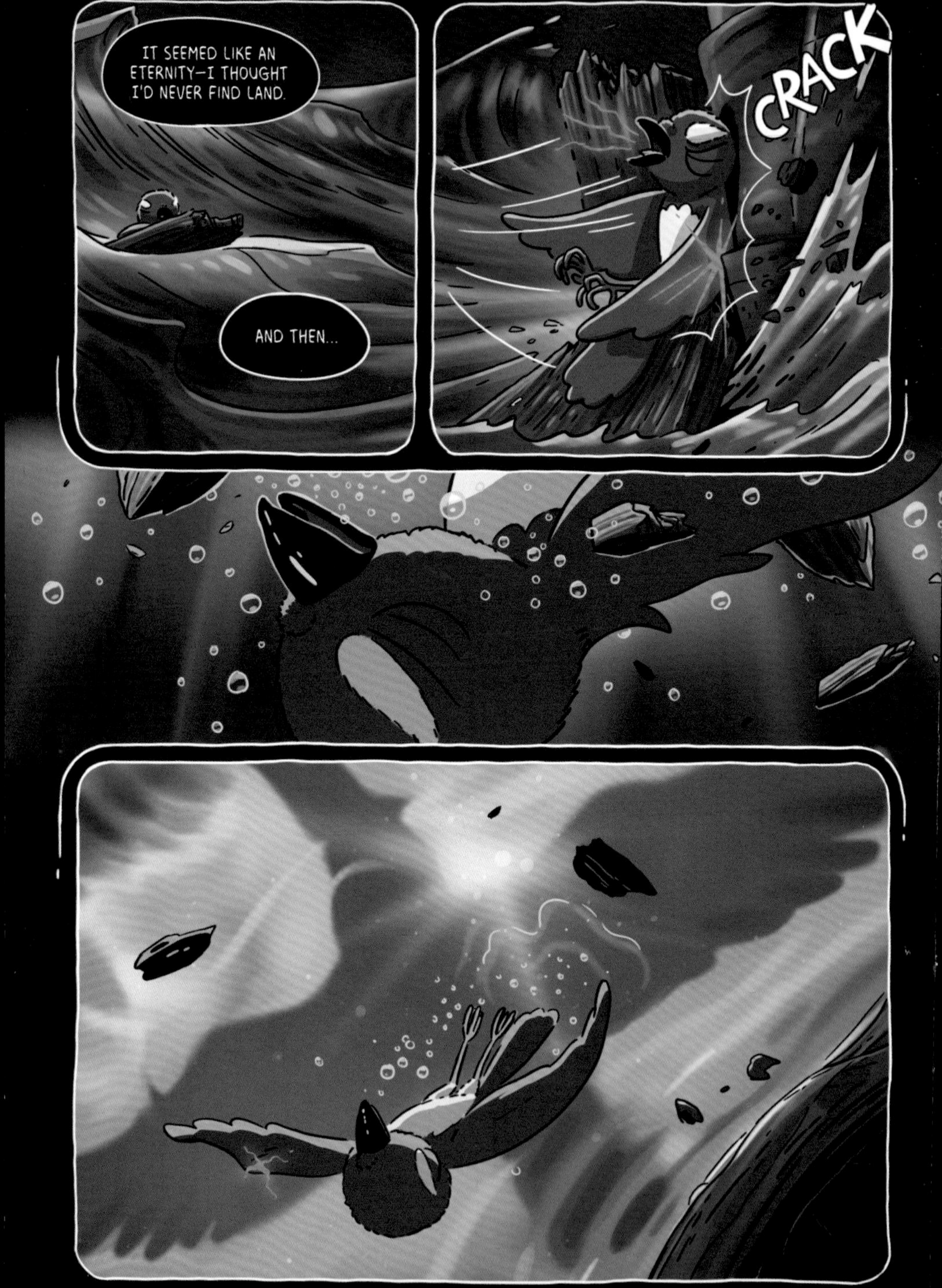
IT SEEMED LIKE AN ETERNITY—I THOUGHT I'D NEVER FIND LAND.
AND THEN...
CRACK

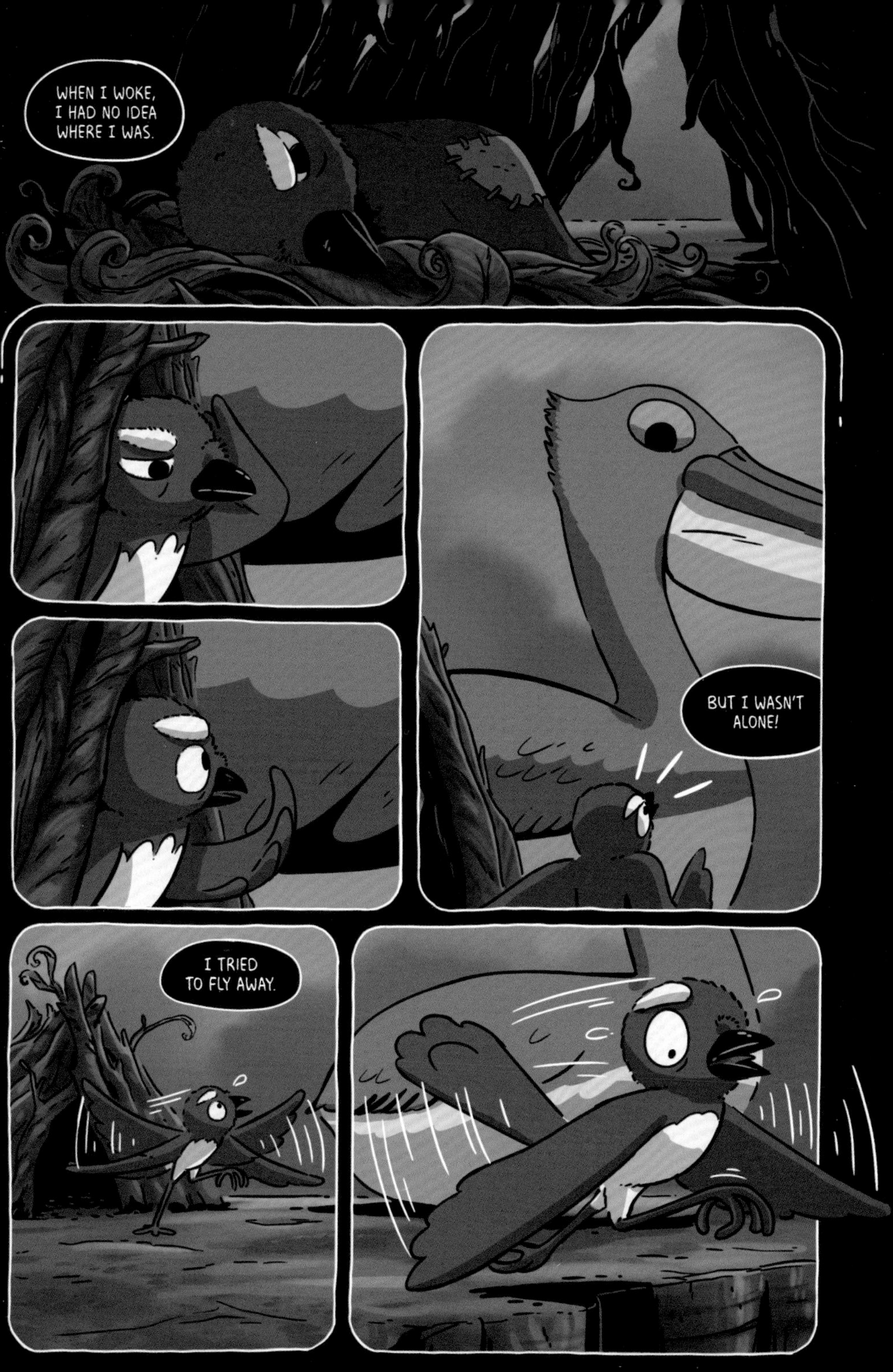
WHEN I WOKE, I HAD NO IDEA WHERE I WAS.
BUT I WASN'T ALONE!
I TRIED TO FLY AWAY.

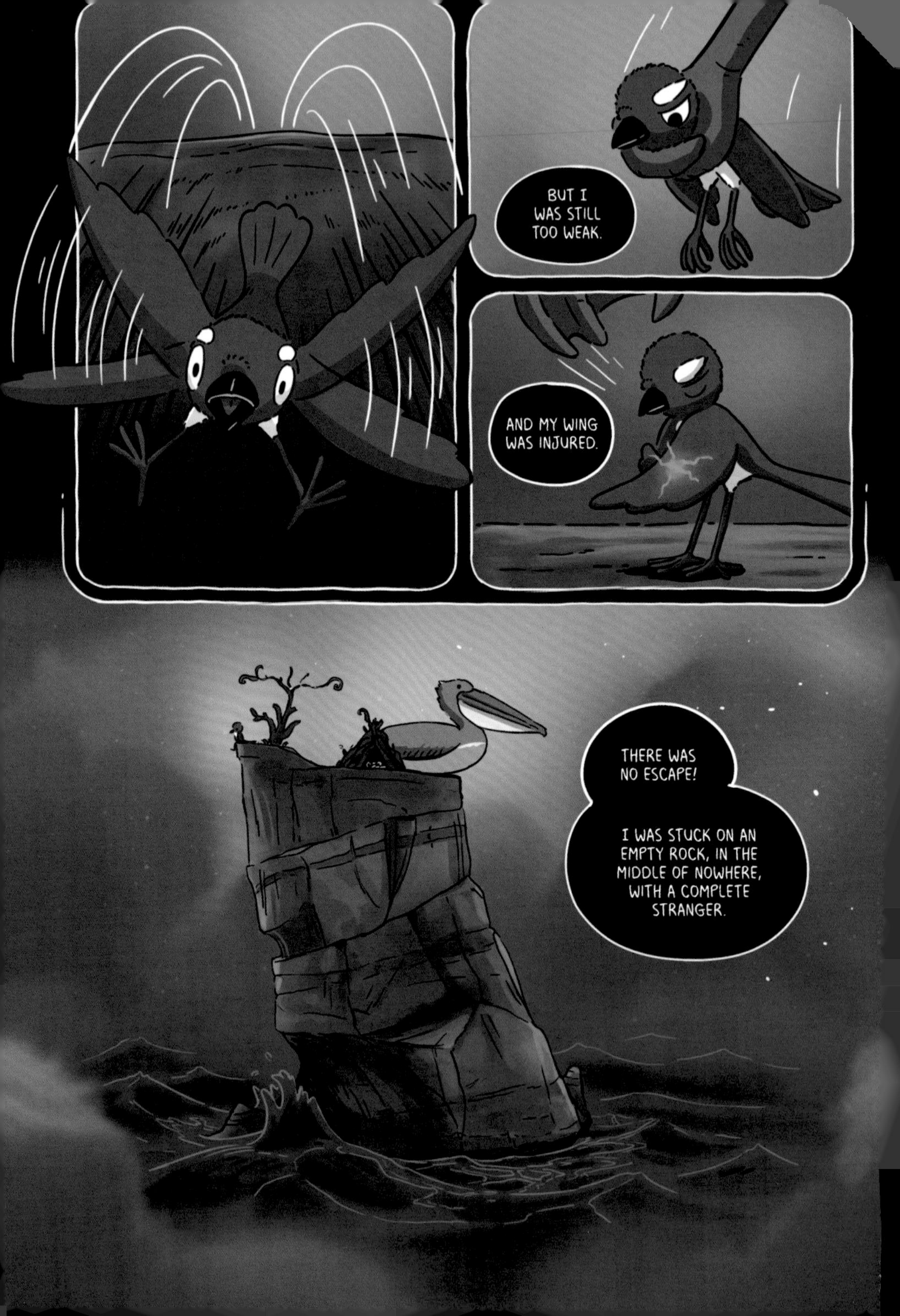
BUT I WAS STILL TOO WEAK.
AND MY WING WAS INJURED.
THERE WAS NO ESCAPE!
I WAS STUCK ON AN EMPTY ROCK, IN THE MIDDLE OF NOWHERE, WITH A COMPLETE STRANGER.

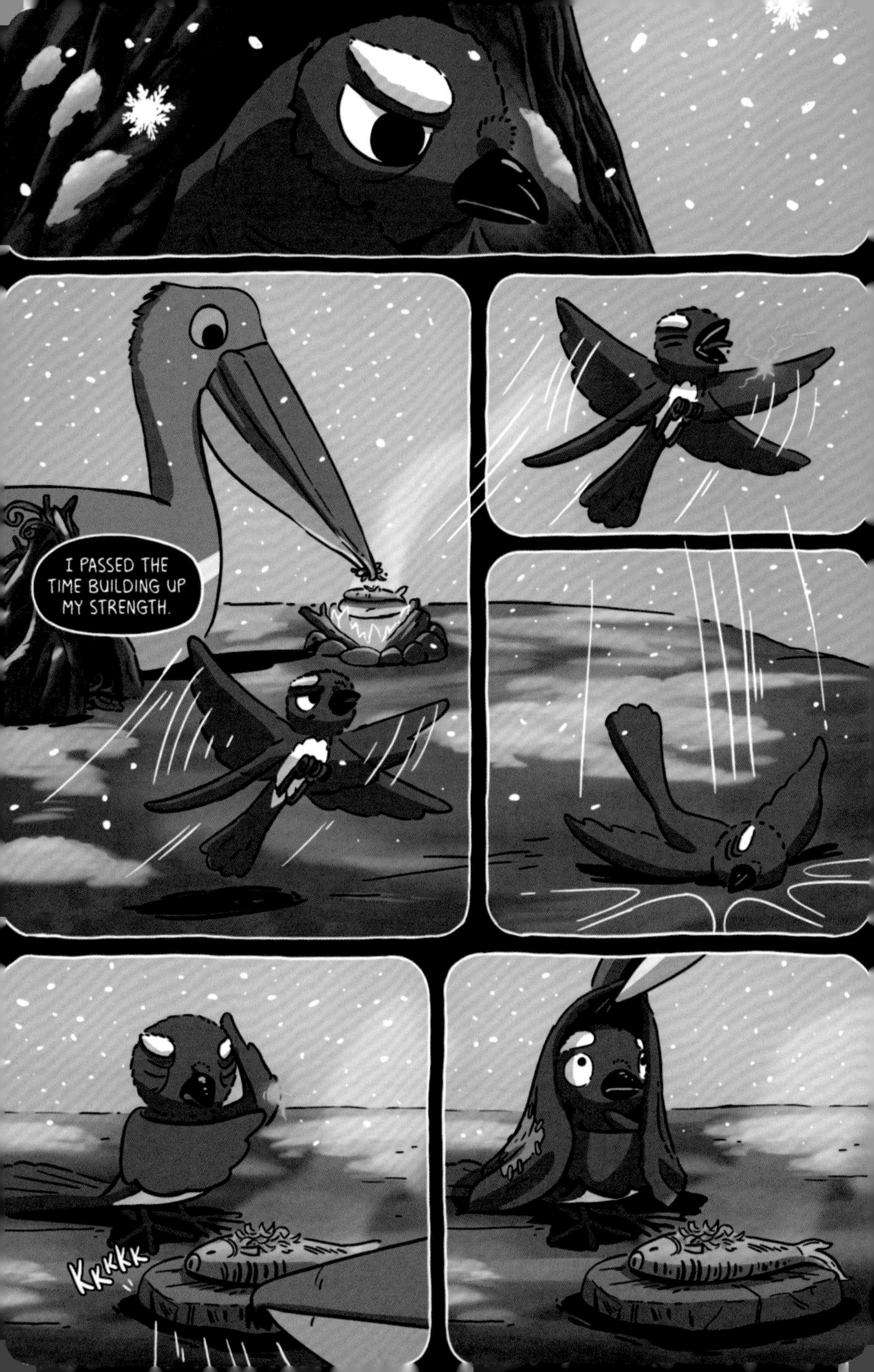

I PASSED THE TIME BUILDING UP MY STRENGTH.
KKKKK

IT TOOK A LONG TIME...

...BUT BY SPRING, I FELT STRONGER.

SOON I'D BE ABLE TO LEAVE.

TO GO WHERE? WHO KNOWS.

AND THAT'S WHEN I SAW IT...

THE STRANGER FLEW HIGH OVERHEAD.

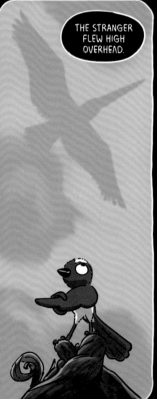

WHOOOOOSH

THEN, ALL OF A SUDDEN, HE JUST FELL TOWARD THE SEA!

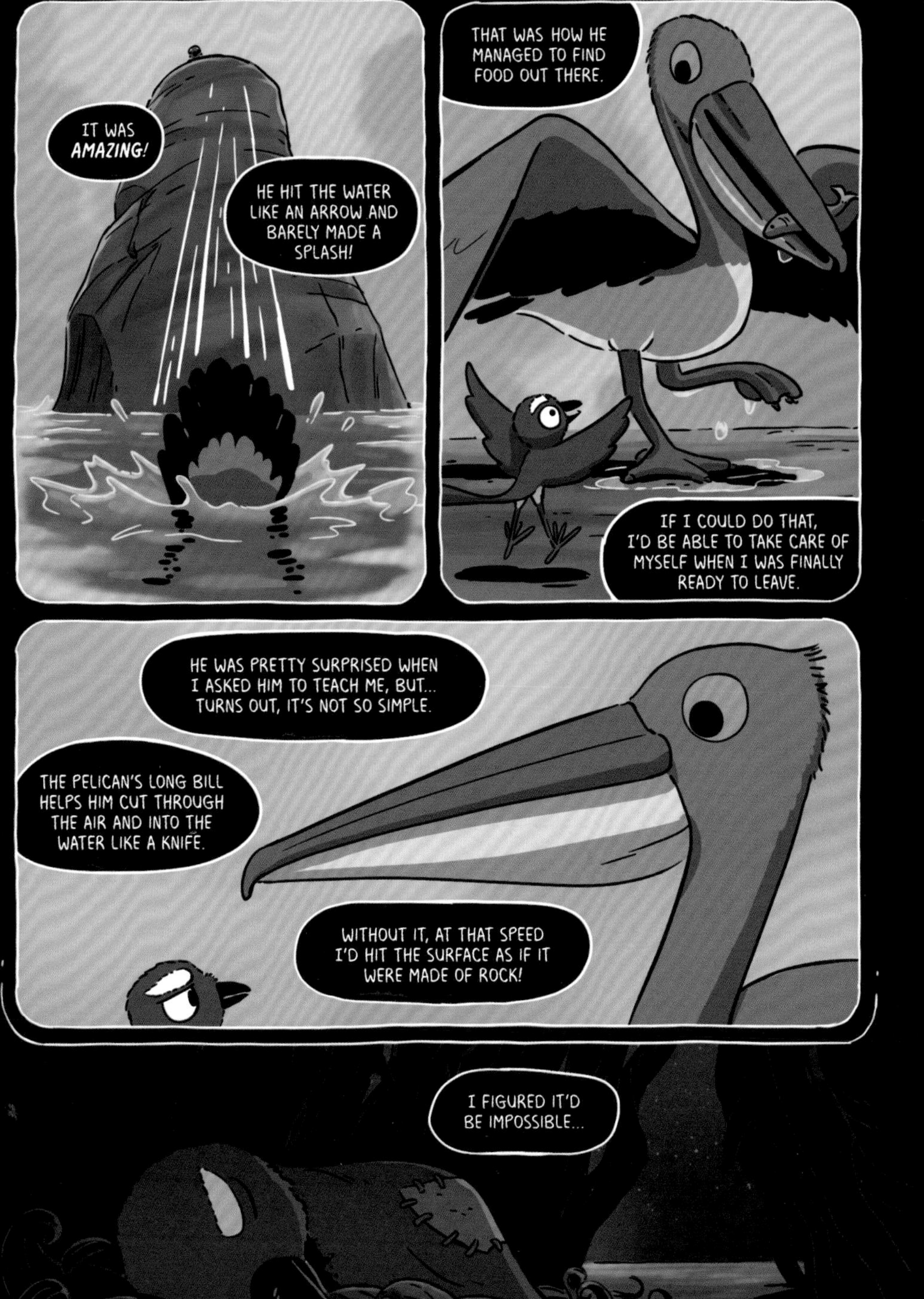

IT WAS *AMAZING*!
HE HIT THE WATER LIKE AN ARROW AND BARELY MADE A SPLASH!
THAT WAS HOW HE MANAGED TO FIND FOOD OUT THERE.
IF I COULD DO THAT, I'D BE ABLE TO TAKE CARE OF MYSELF WHEN I WAS FINALLY READY TO LEAVE.
HE WAS PRETTY SURPRISED WHEN I ASKED HIM TO TEACH ME, BUT... TURNS OUT, IT'S NOT SO SIMPLE.
THE PELICAN'S LONG BILL HELPS HIM CUT THROUGH THE AIR AND INTO THE WATER LIKE A KNIFE.
WITHOUT IT, AT THAT SPEED I'D HIT THE SURFACE AS IF IT WERE MADE OF ROCK!
I FIGURED IT'D BE IMPOSSIBLE...

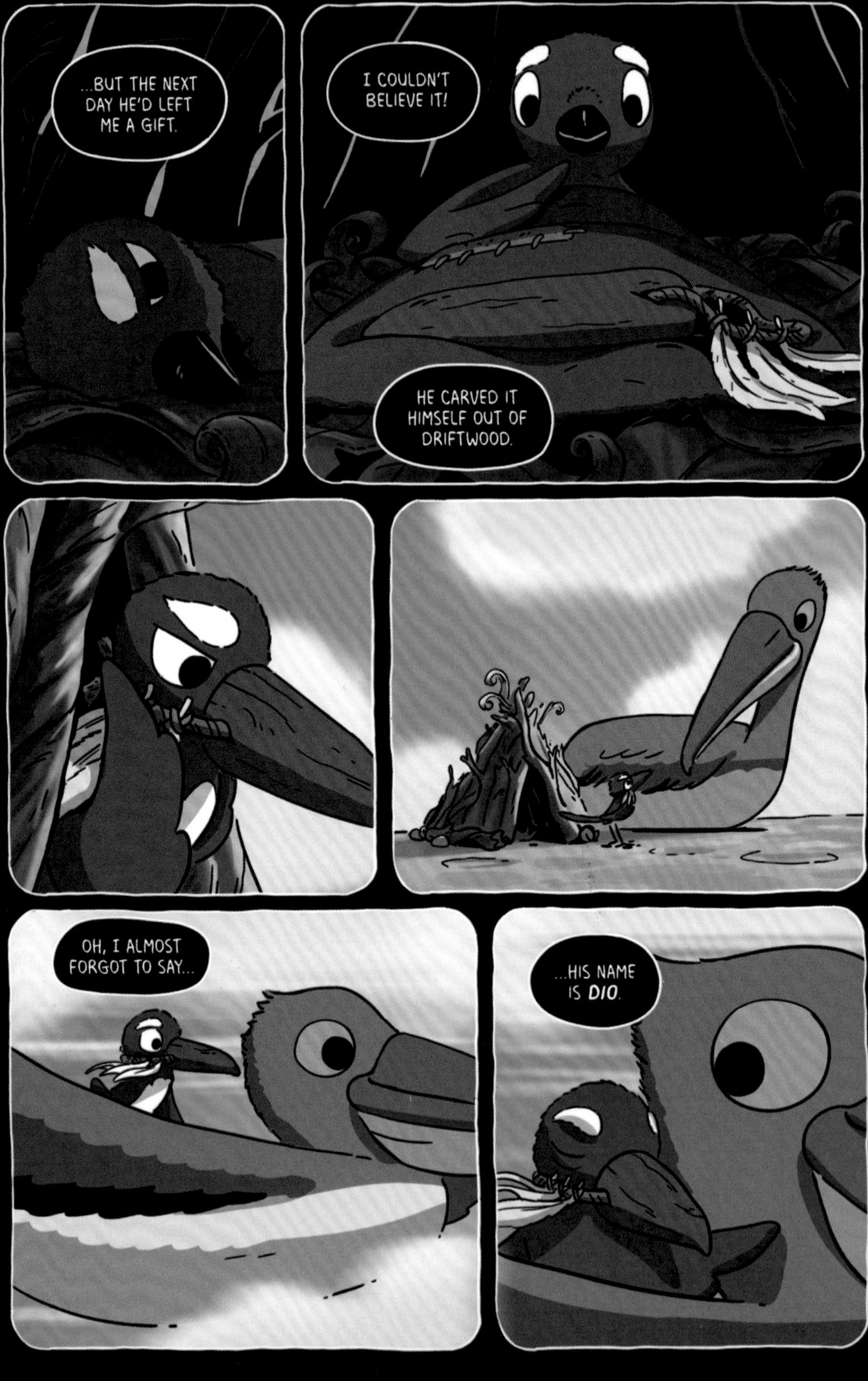
...BUT THE NEXT DAY HE'D LEFT ME A GIFT.
I COULDN'T BELIEVE IT!
HE CARVED IT HIMSELF OUT OF DRIFTWOOD.
OH, I ALMOST FORGOT TO SAY...
...HIS NAME IS **DIO**.

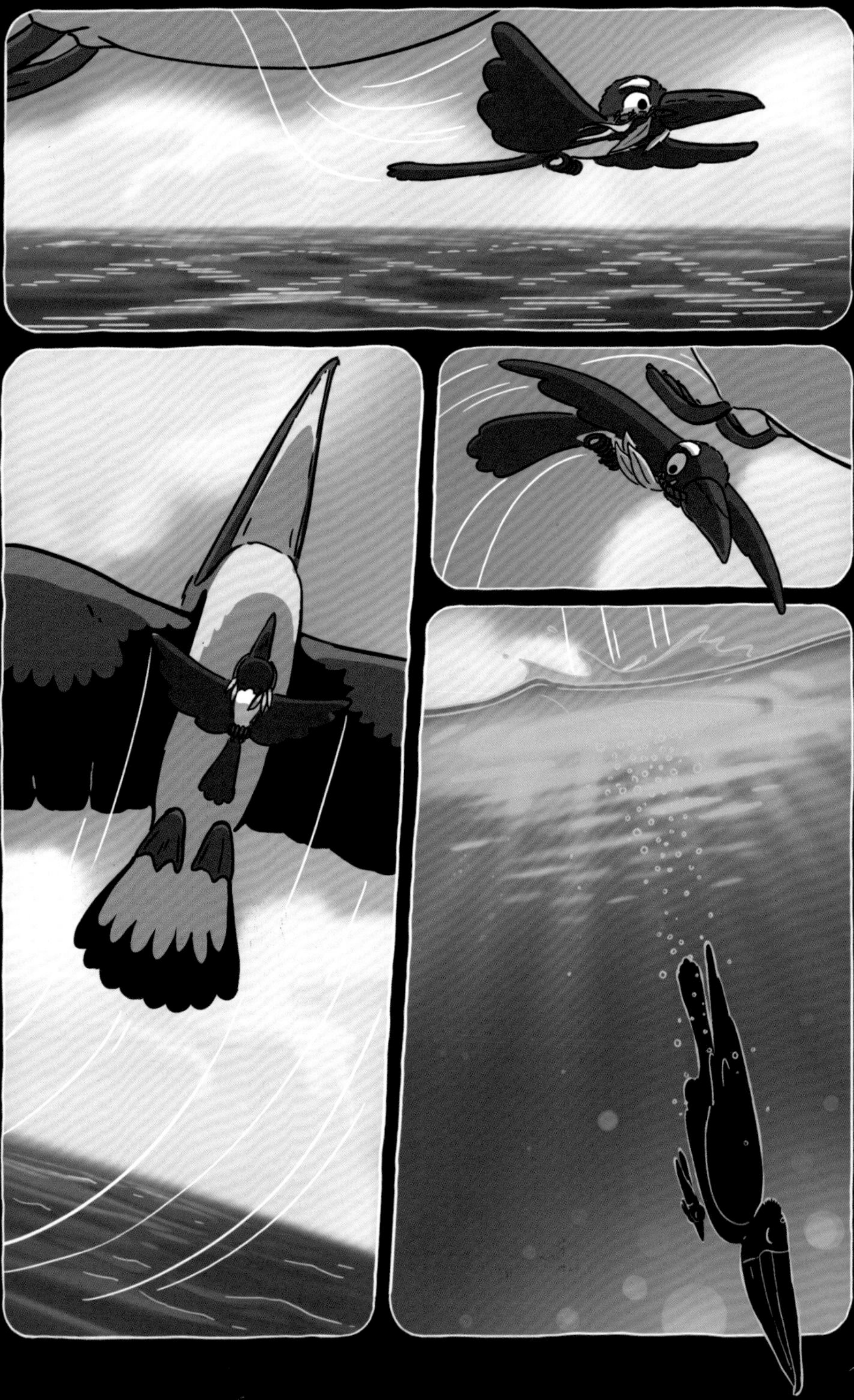

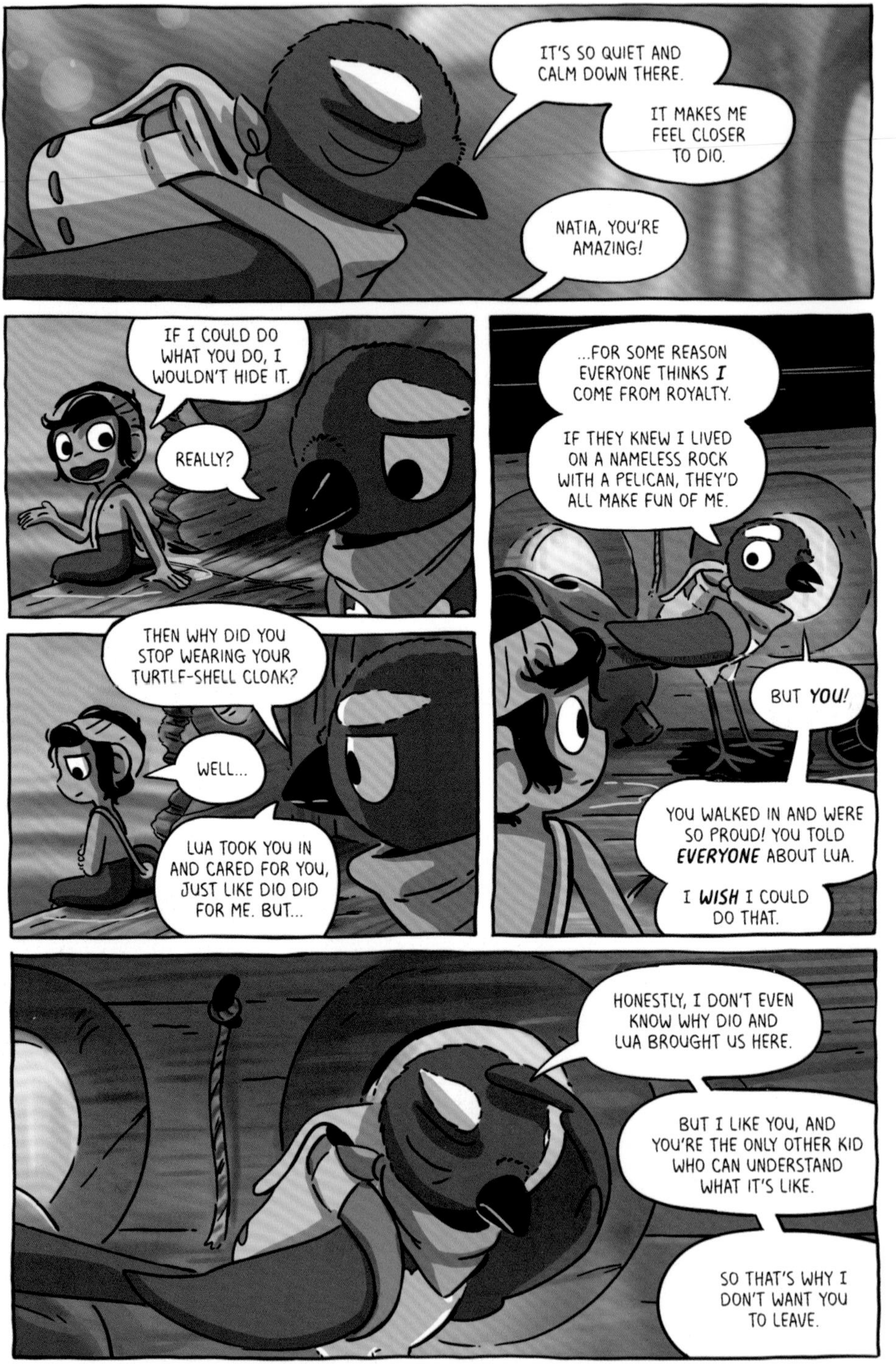
IT'S SO QUIET AND CALM DOWN THERE.
IT MAKES ME FEEL CLOSER TO DIO.
NATIA, YOU'RE AMAZING!
IF I COULD DO WHAT YOU DO, I WOULDN'T HIDE IT.
REALLY?
THEN WHY DID YOU STOP WEARING YOUR TURTLE-SHELL CLOAK?
WELL...
LUA TOOK YOU IN AND CARED FOR YOU, JUST LIKE DIO DID FOR ME. BUT...
...FOR SOME REASON EVERYONE THINKS *I* COME FROM ROYALTY.
IF THEY KNEW I LIVED ON A NAMELESS ROCK WITH A PELICAN, THEY'D ALL MAKE FUN OF ME.
BUT ***YOU!***
YOU WALKED IN AND WERE SO PROUD! YOU TOLD ***EVERYONE*** ABOUT LUA.
I ***WISH*** I COULD DO THAT.
HONESTLY, I DON'T EVEN KNOW WHY DIO AND LUA BROUGHT US HERE.
BUT I LIKE YOU, AND YOU'RE THE ONLY OTHER KID WHO CAN UNDERSTAND WHAT IT'S LIKE.
SO THAT'S WHY I DON'T WANT YOU TO LEAVE.

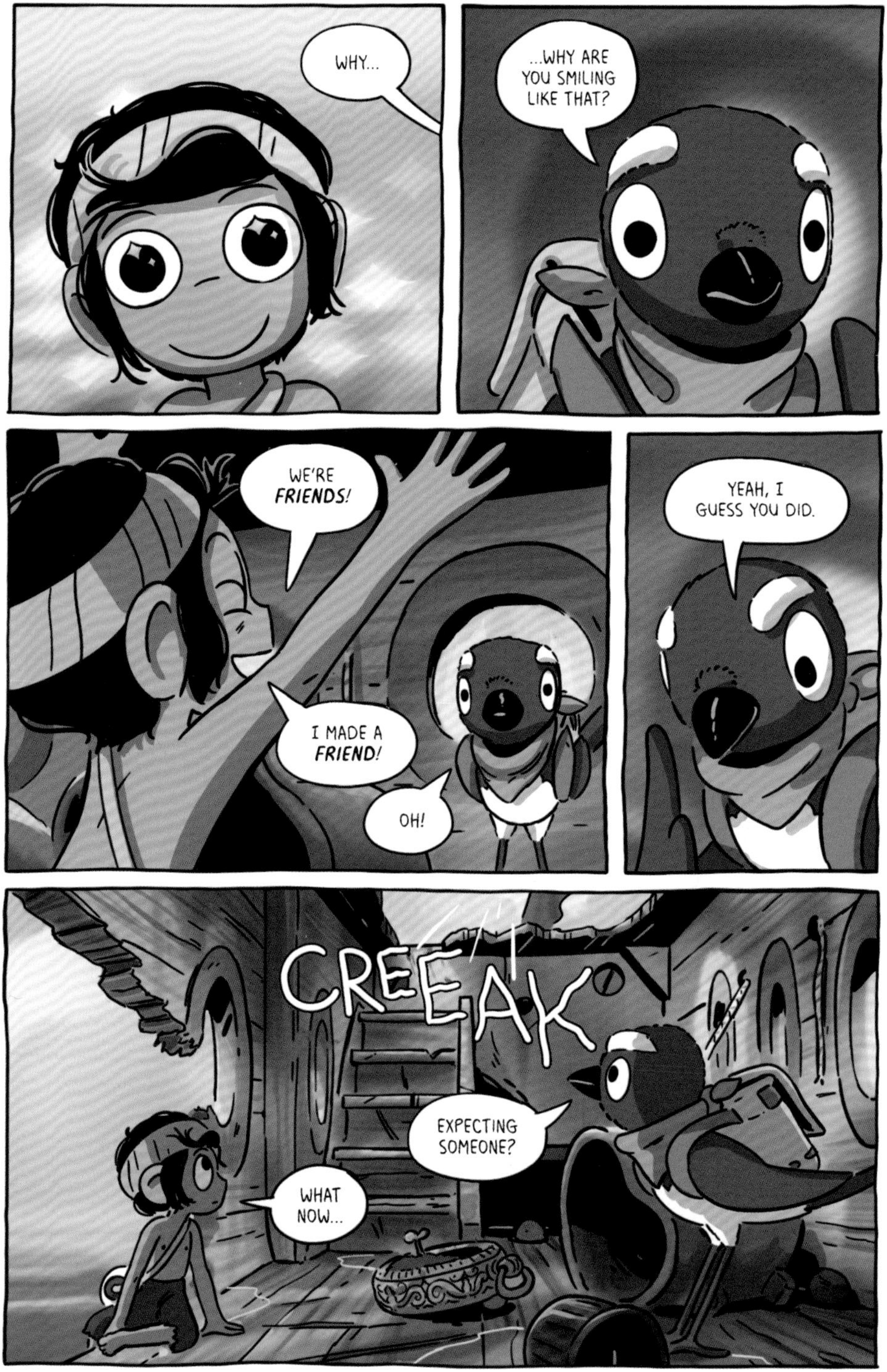
WHY...
...WHY ARE YOU SMILING LIKE THAT?
WE'RE *FRIENDS!*
I MADE A *FRIEND!*
OH!
YEAH, I GUESS YOU DID.
CREEAK
EXPECTING SOMEONE?
WHAT NOW...

THIS THING *AGAIN?!*

WHAT IS IT?

NO IDEA, BUT IT'S BEEN TAKING ALL MY STUFF.

HEY!

IT'S COMING DOWN HERE! **HIDE!**

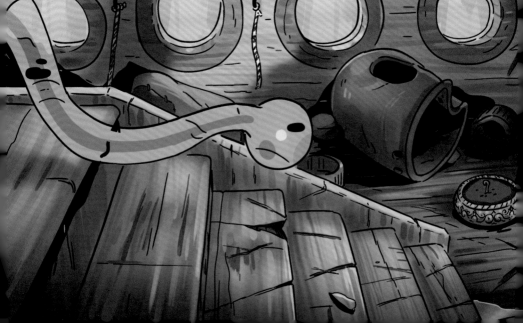

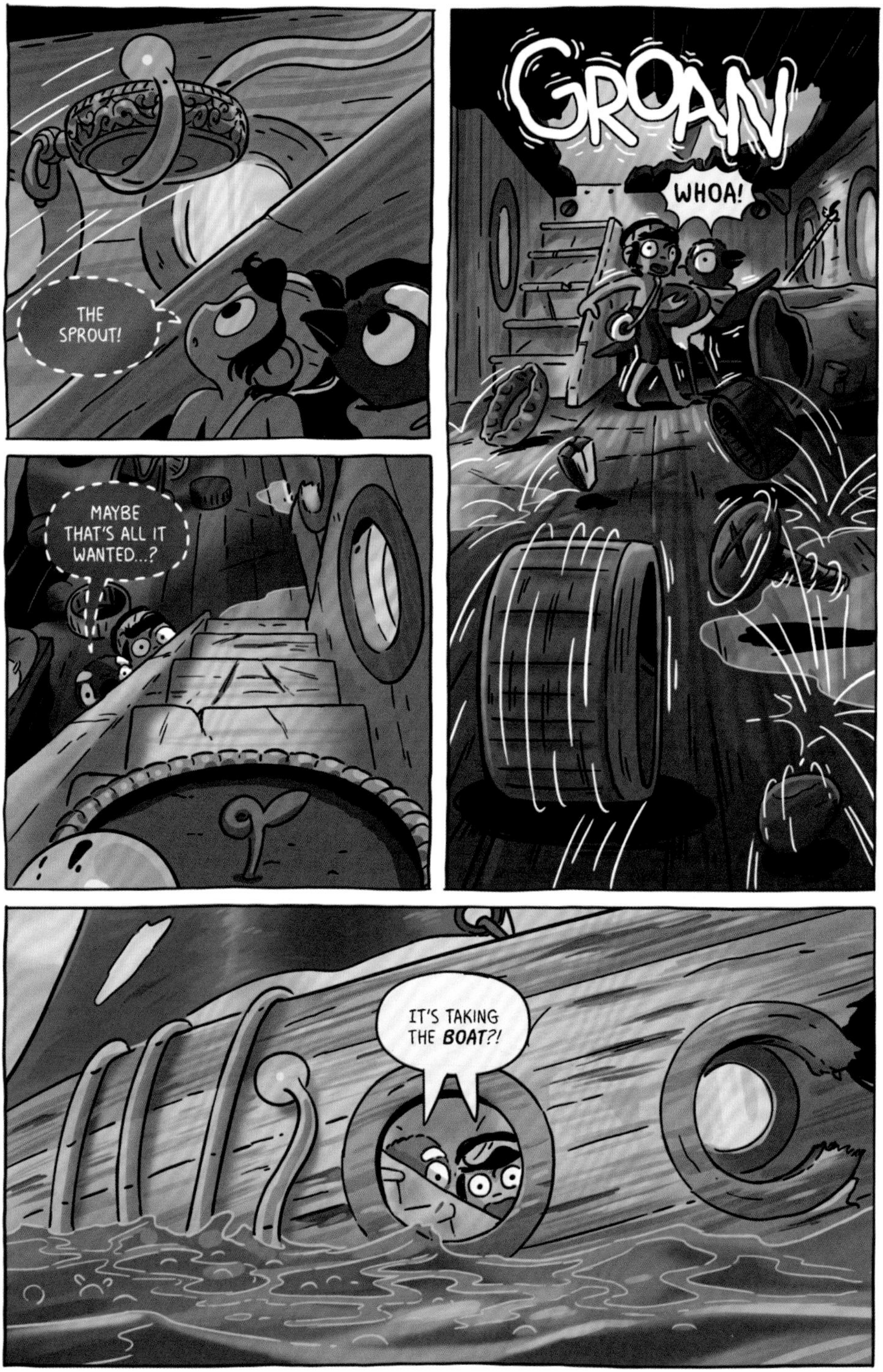
THE SPROUT!
GROAN
WHOA!
MAYBE THAT'S ALL IT WANTED...?
IT'S TAKING THE *BOAT?!*

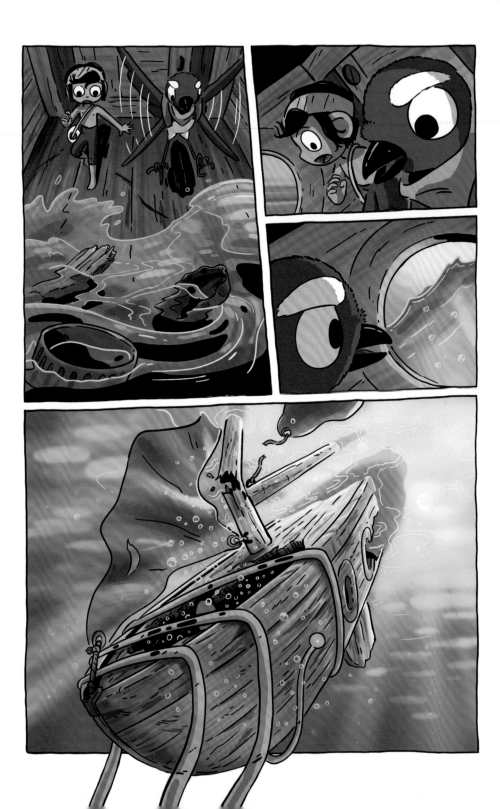

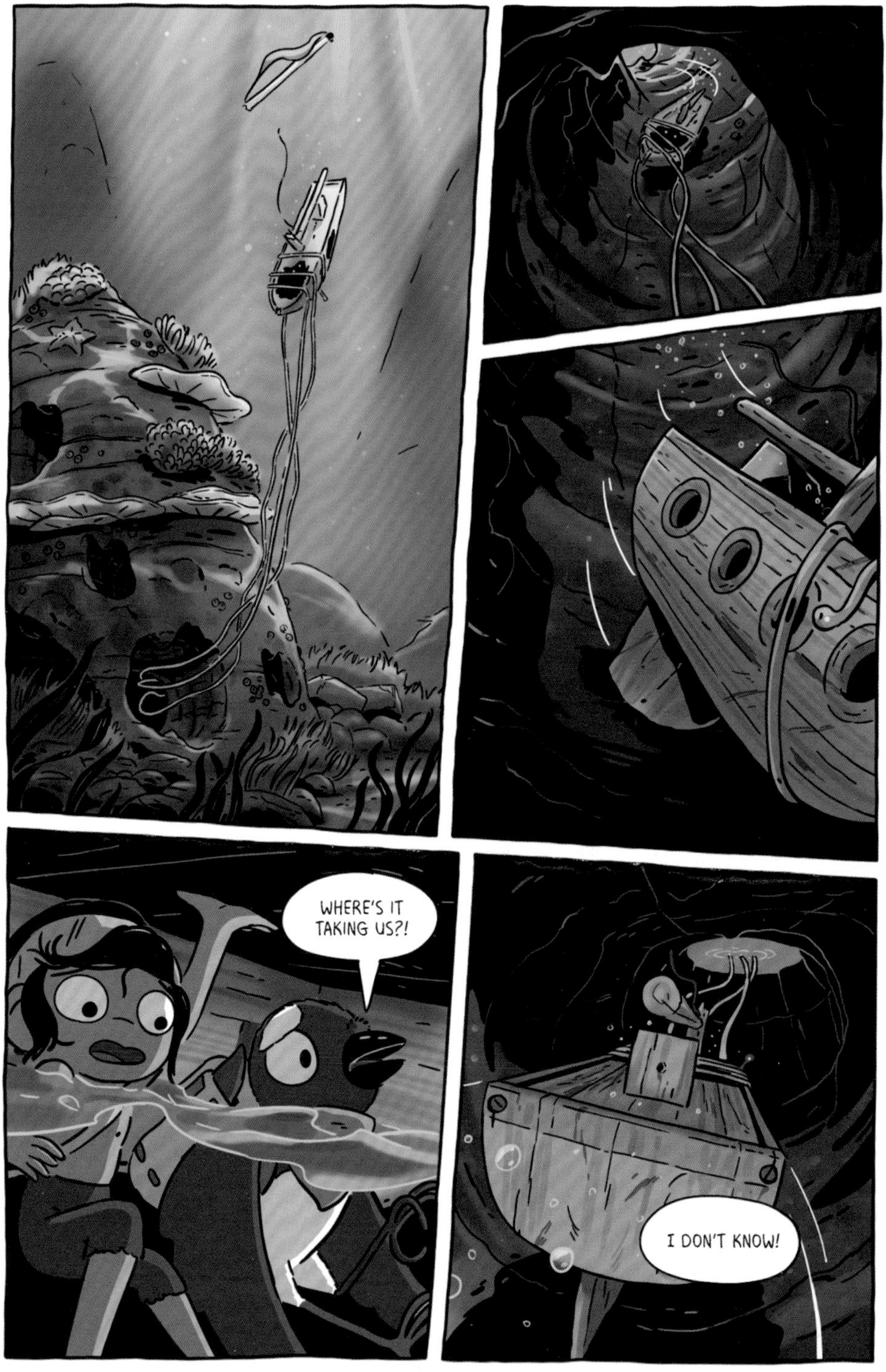
WHERE'S IT TAKING US?!
I DON'T KNOW!

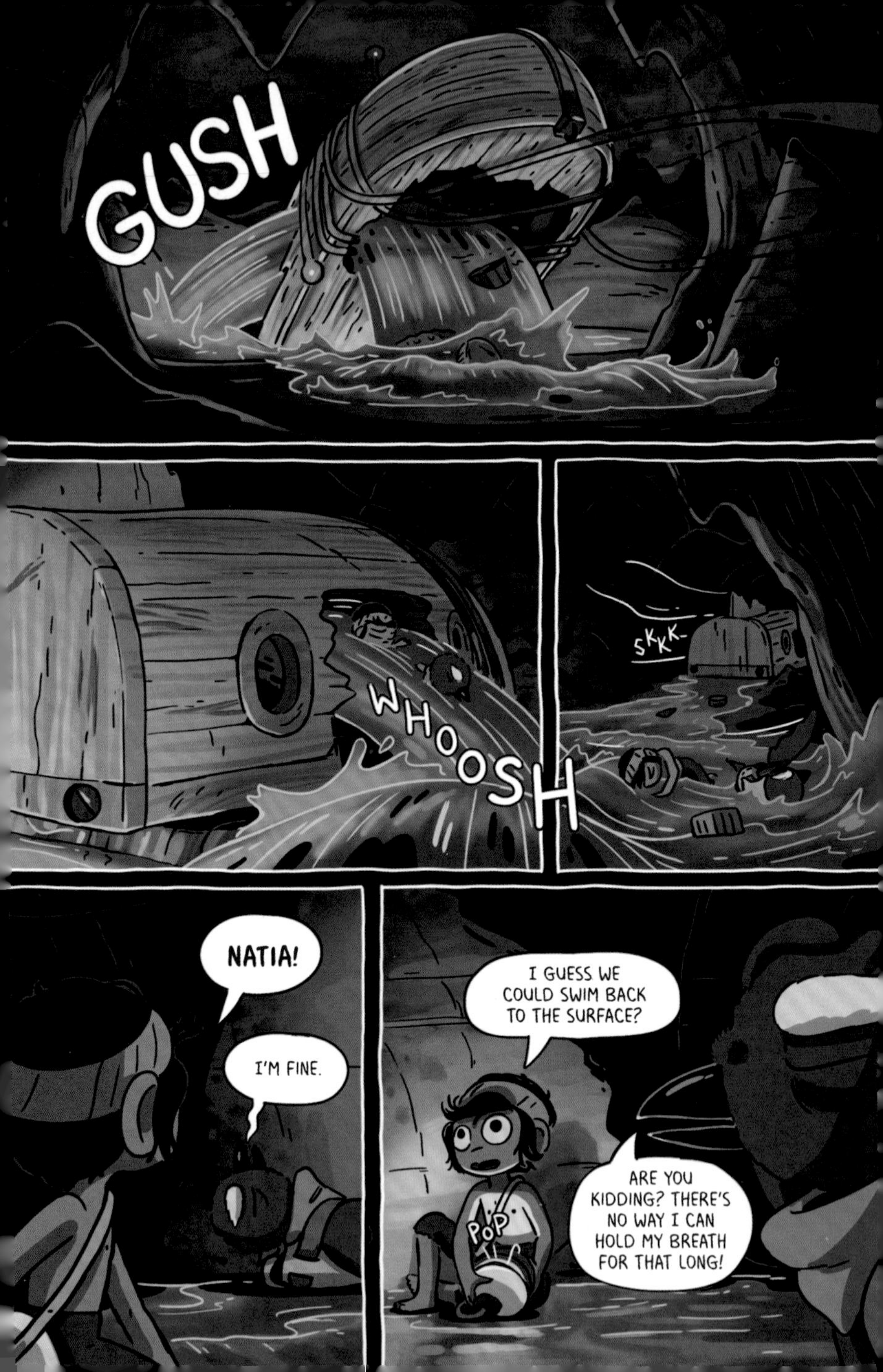
GUSH
WHOOOSH
SKKK
NATIA!
I'M FINE.
I GUESS WE COULD SWIM BACK TO THE SURFACE?
POP
ARE YOU KIDDING? THERE'S NO WAY I CAN HOLD MY BREATH FOR THAT LONG!

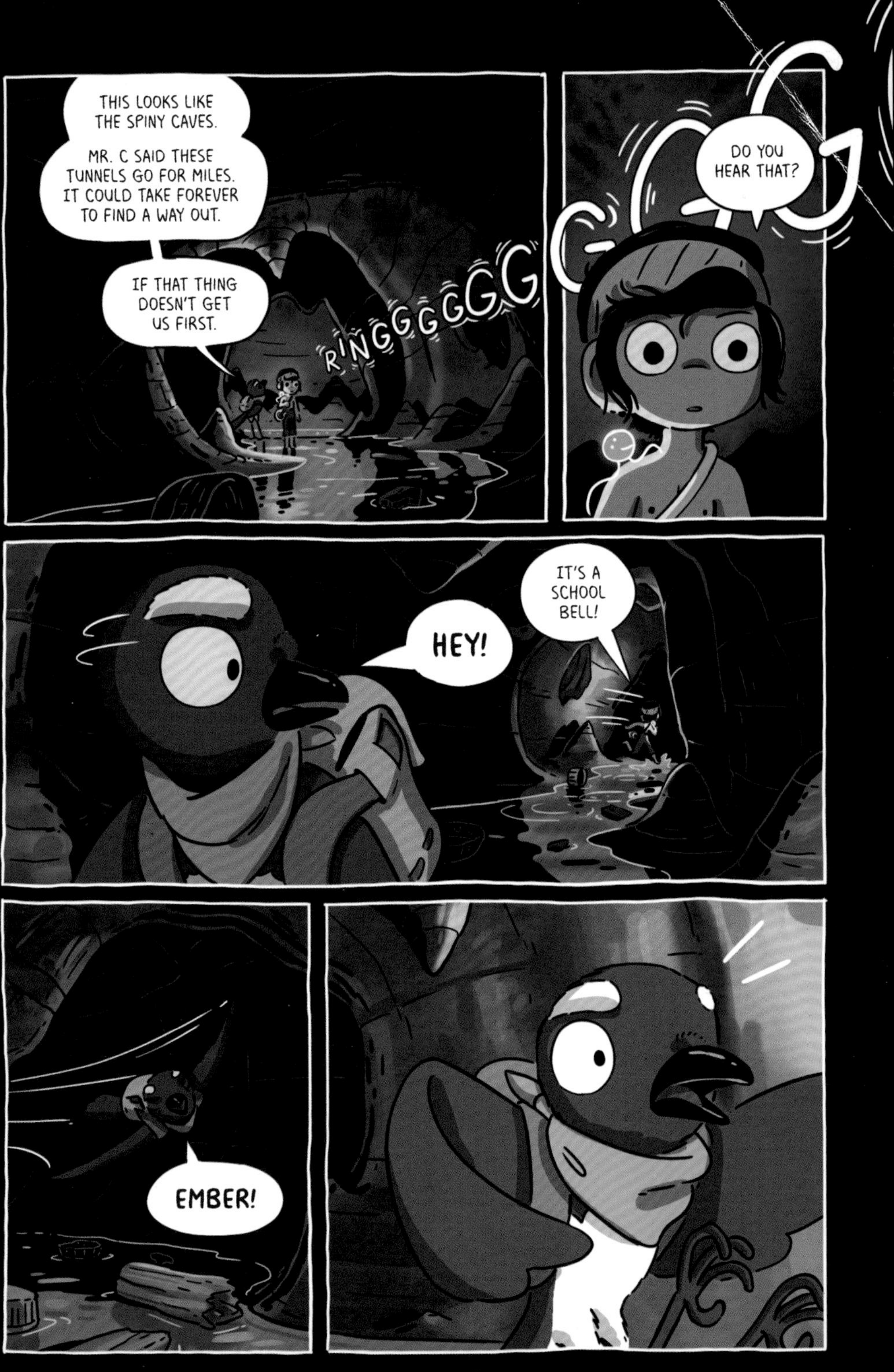
THIS LOOKS LIKE THE SPINY CAVES.
MR. C SAID THESE TUNNELS GO FOR MILES. IT COULD TAKE FOREVER TO FIND A WAY OUT.
IF THAT THING DOESN'T GET US FIRST.
RINGGGGGGG-G-G-G
DO YOU HEAR THAT?
HEY!
IT'S A SCHOOL BELL!
EMBER!

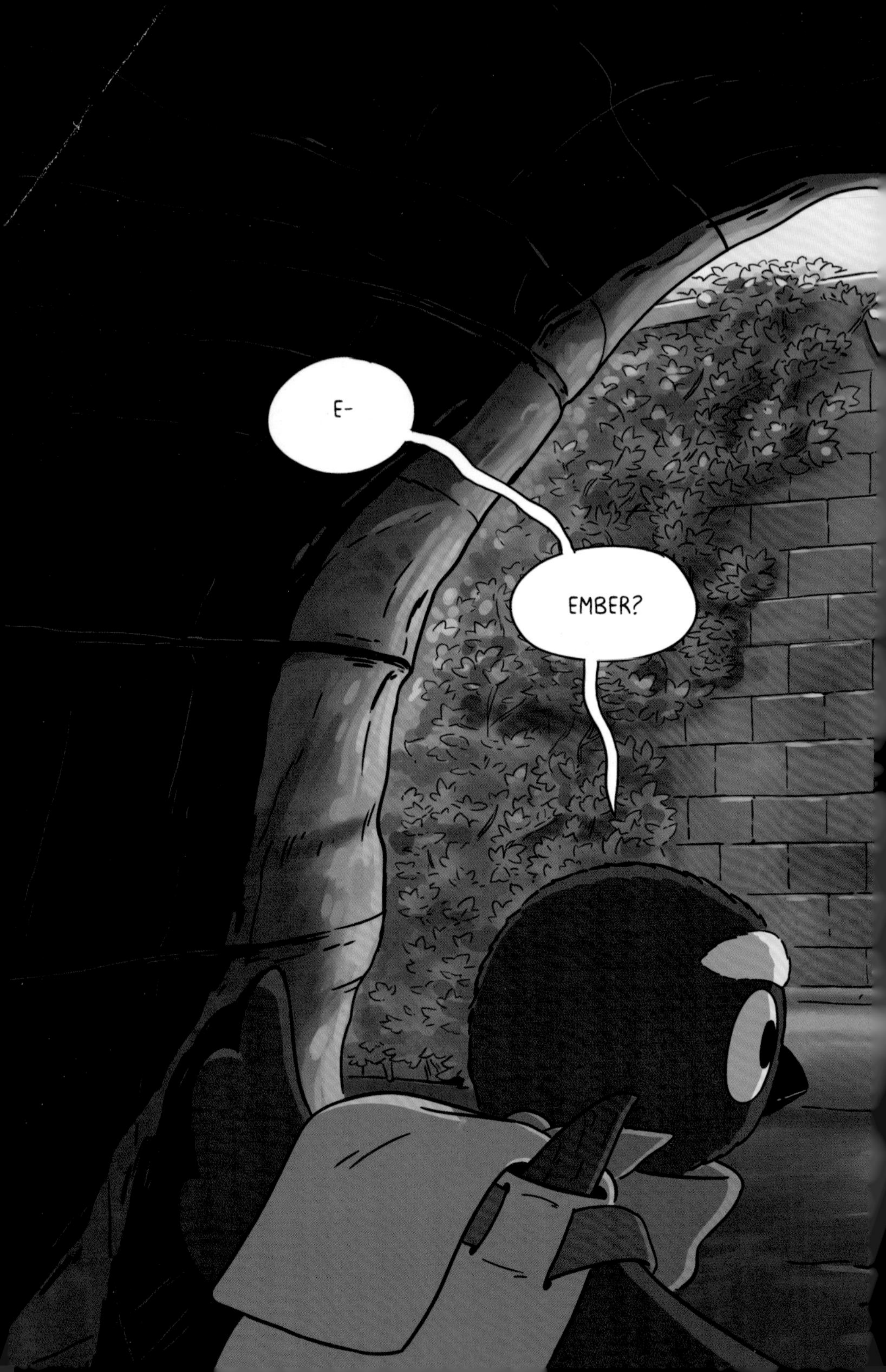
E-
EMBER?

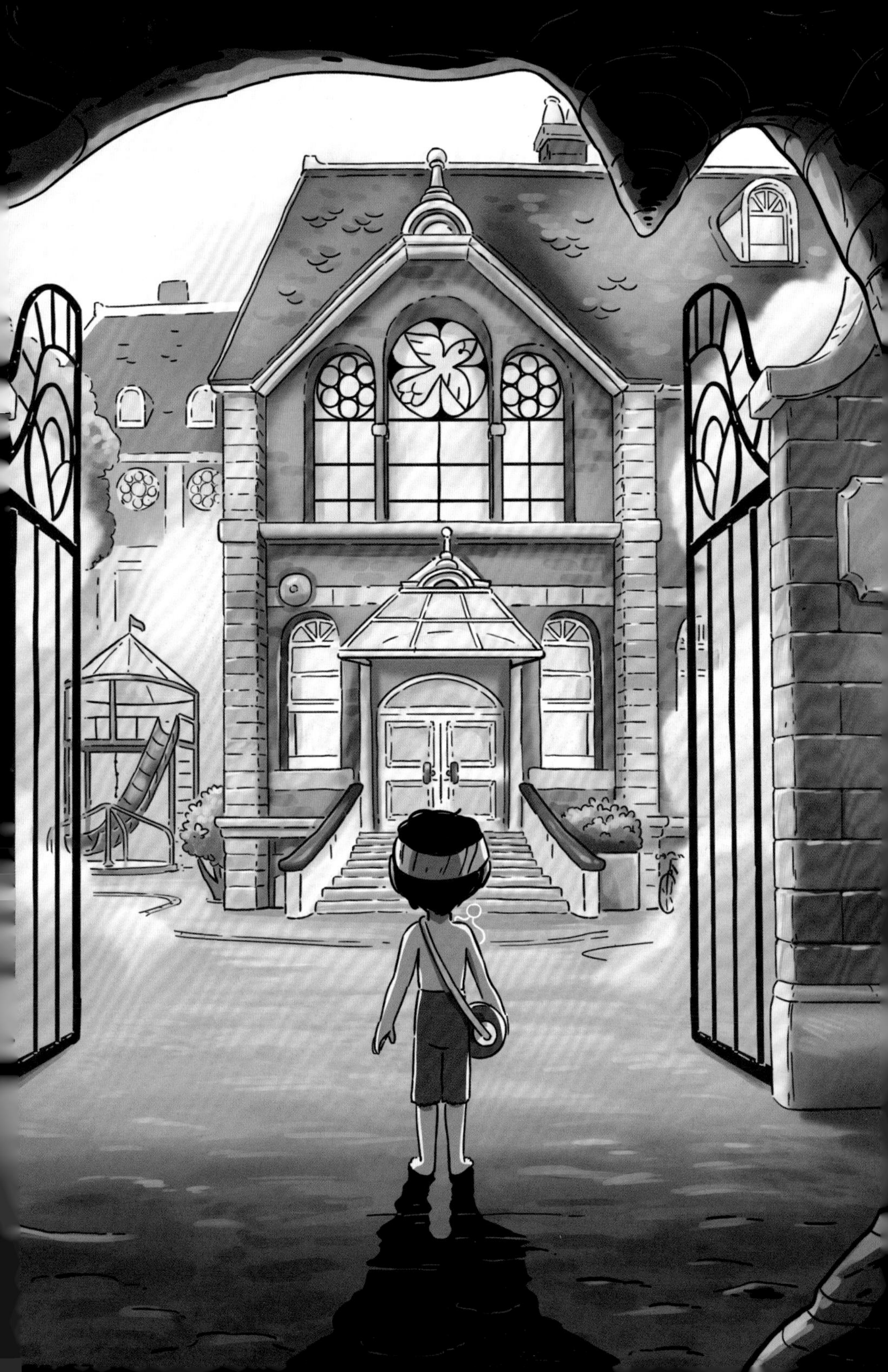

IT'S...IT'S THE SCHOOL FROM THE GIANT WORLD.

ONLY IT'S MY SIZE NOW.

BUT HOW...?

HEY, WHAT'S THAT?!

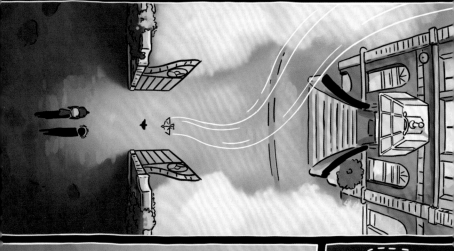

SKKK

MY PLANE...?

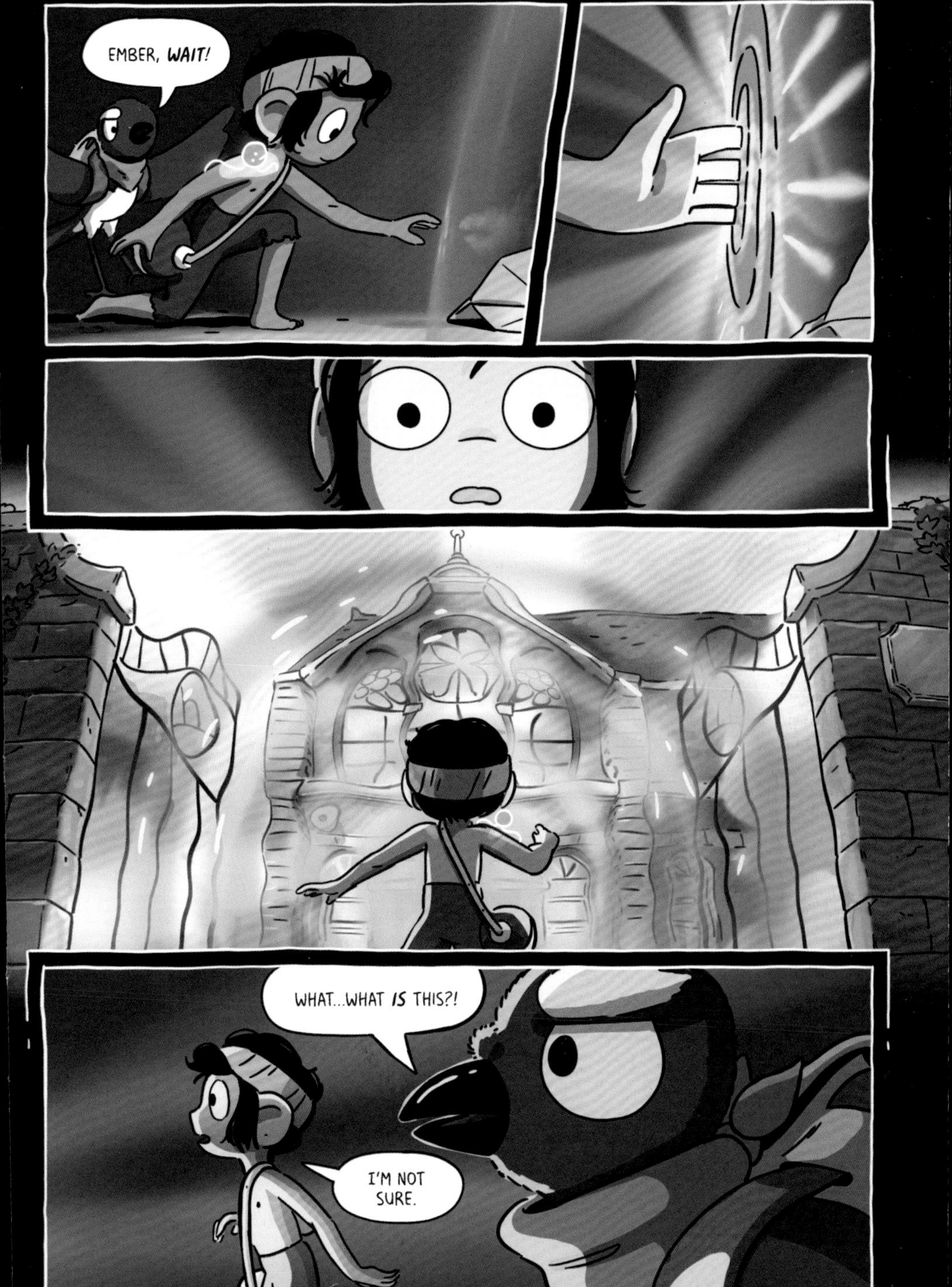
EMBER, **WAIT!**
WHAT...WHAT **IS** THIS?!
I'M NOT SURE.

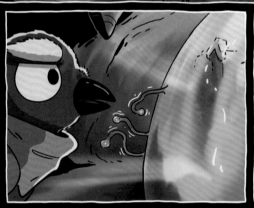

EMBER!

IT'S THAT *THING!*

WE'VE GOTTA GET OUT OF HERE!

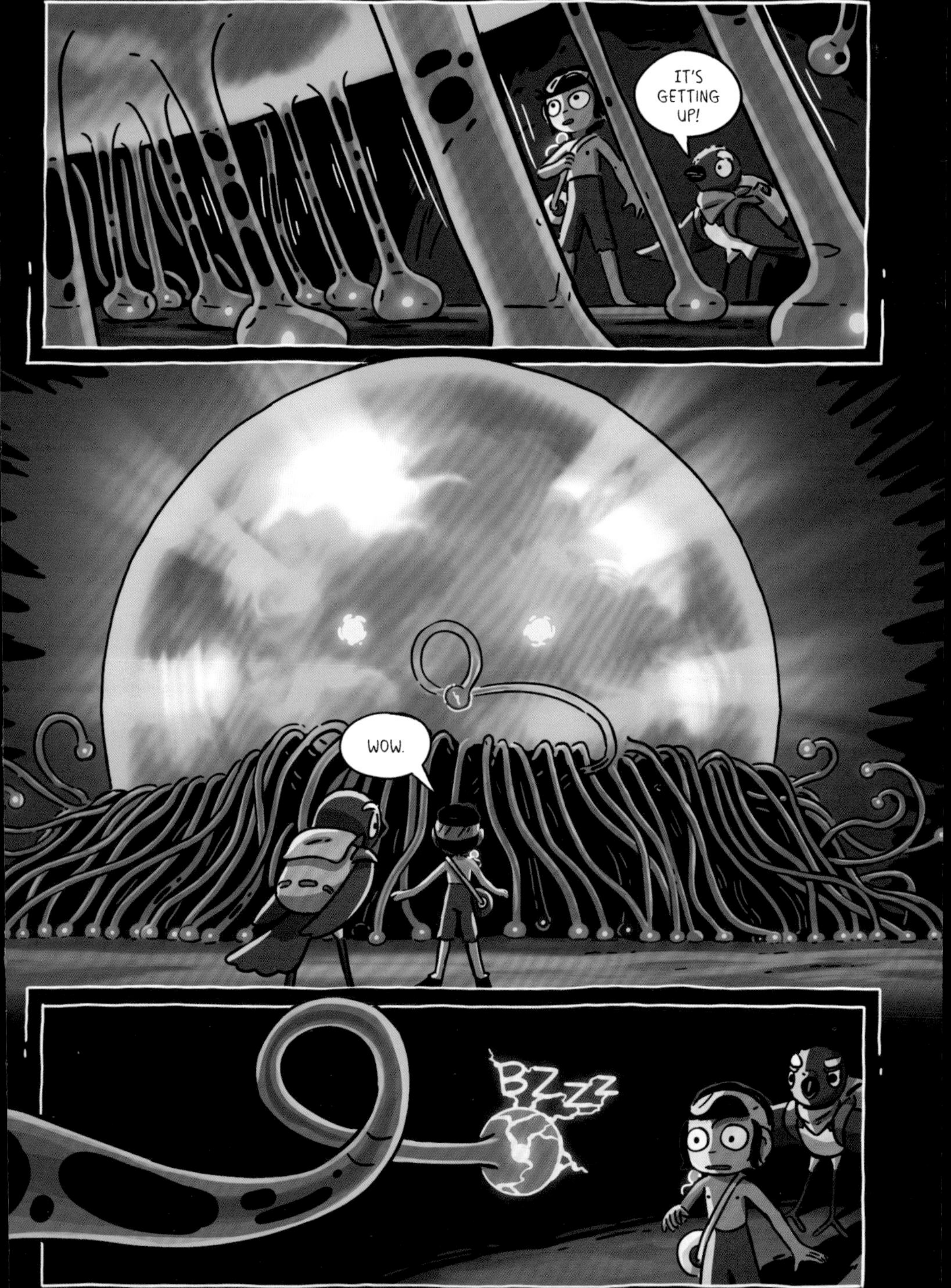
IT'S GETTING UP!
WOW.
BZZZ

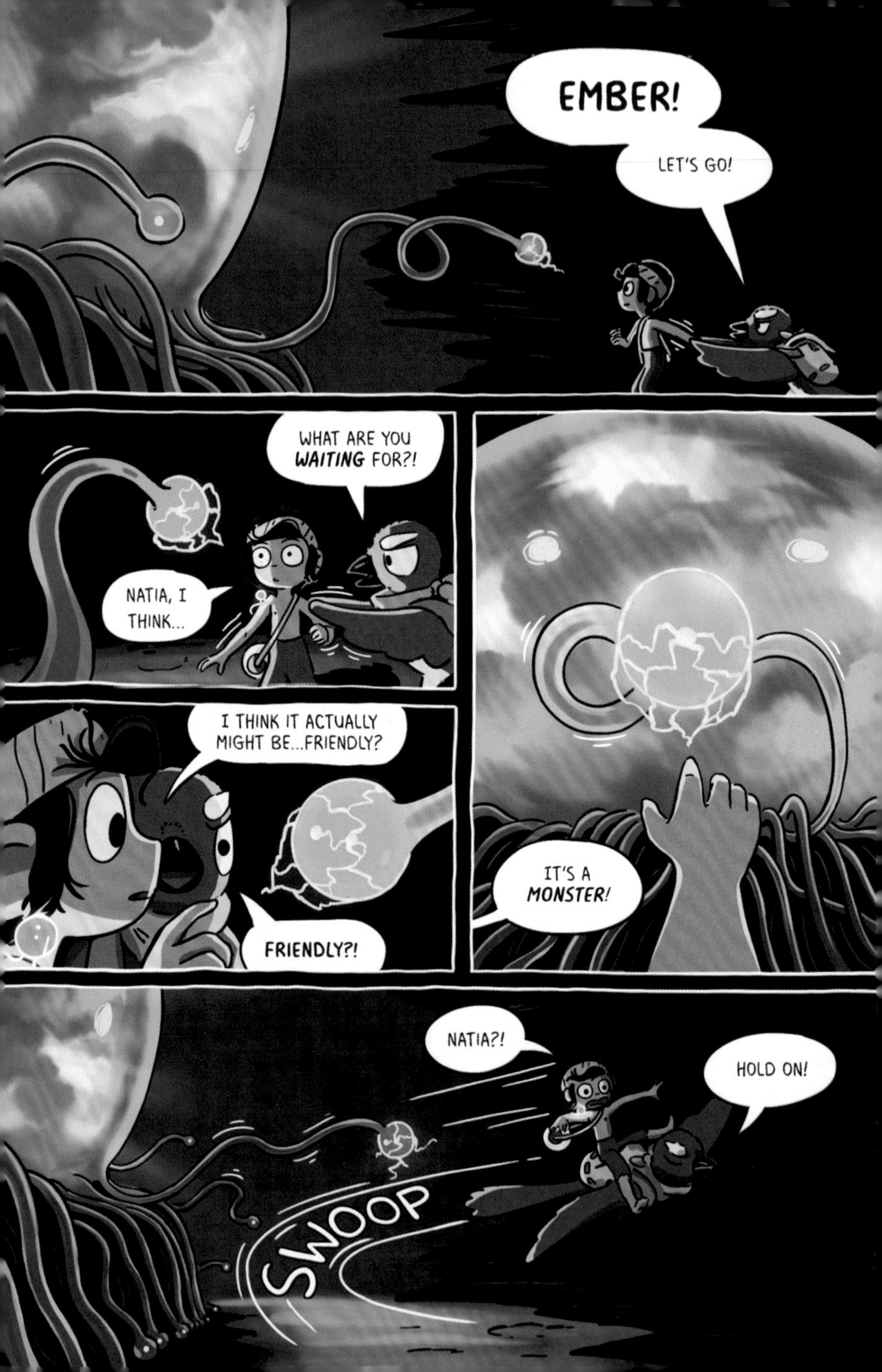
EMBER!
LET'S GO!
WHAT ARE YOU WAITING FOR?!
NATIA, I THINK...
I THINK IT ACTUALLY MIGHT BE...FRIENDLY?
FRIENDLY?!
IT'S A MONSTER!
NATIA?!
HOLD ON!
SWOOP

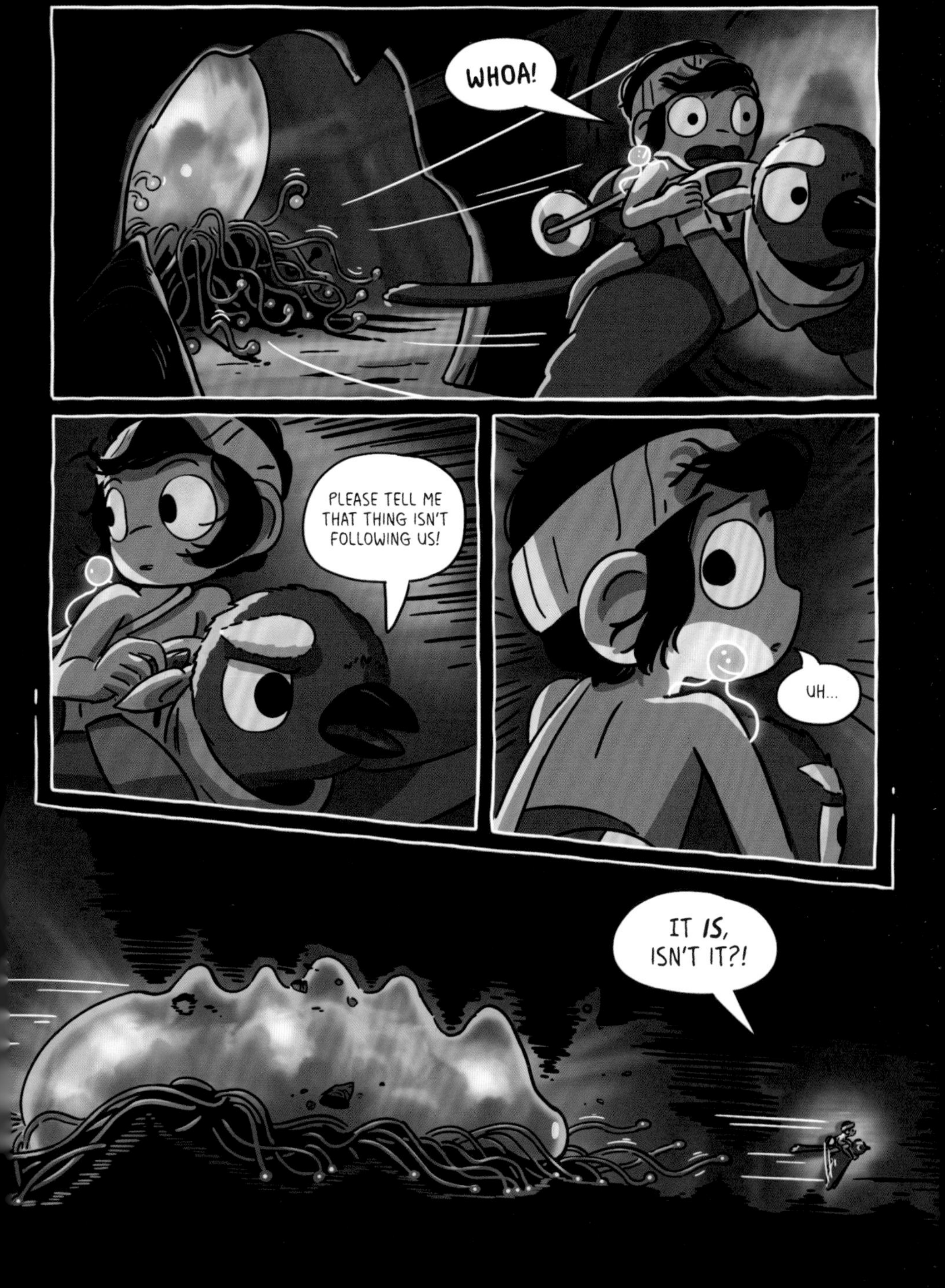
WHOA!
PLEASE TELL ME THAT THING ISN'T FOLLOWING US!
UH...
IT *IS*, ISN'T IT?!

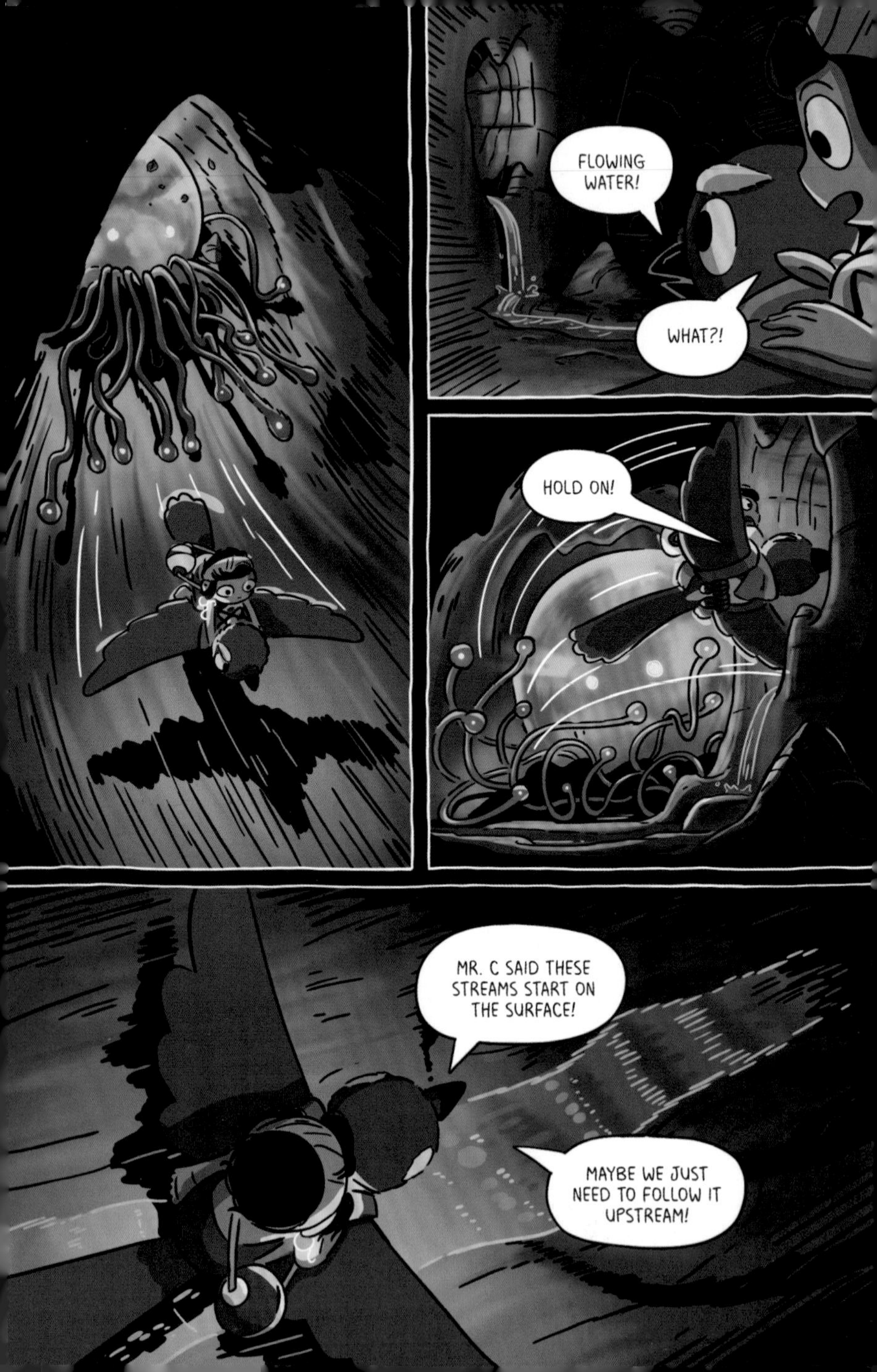
FLOWING WATER!
WHAT?!
HOLD ON!
MR. C SAID THESE STREAMS START ON THE SURFACE!
MAYBE WE JUST NEED TO FOLLOW IT UPSTREAM!

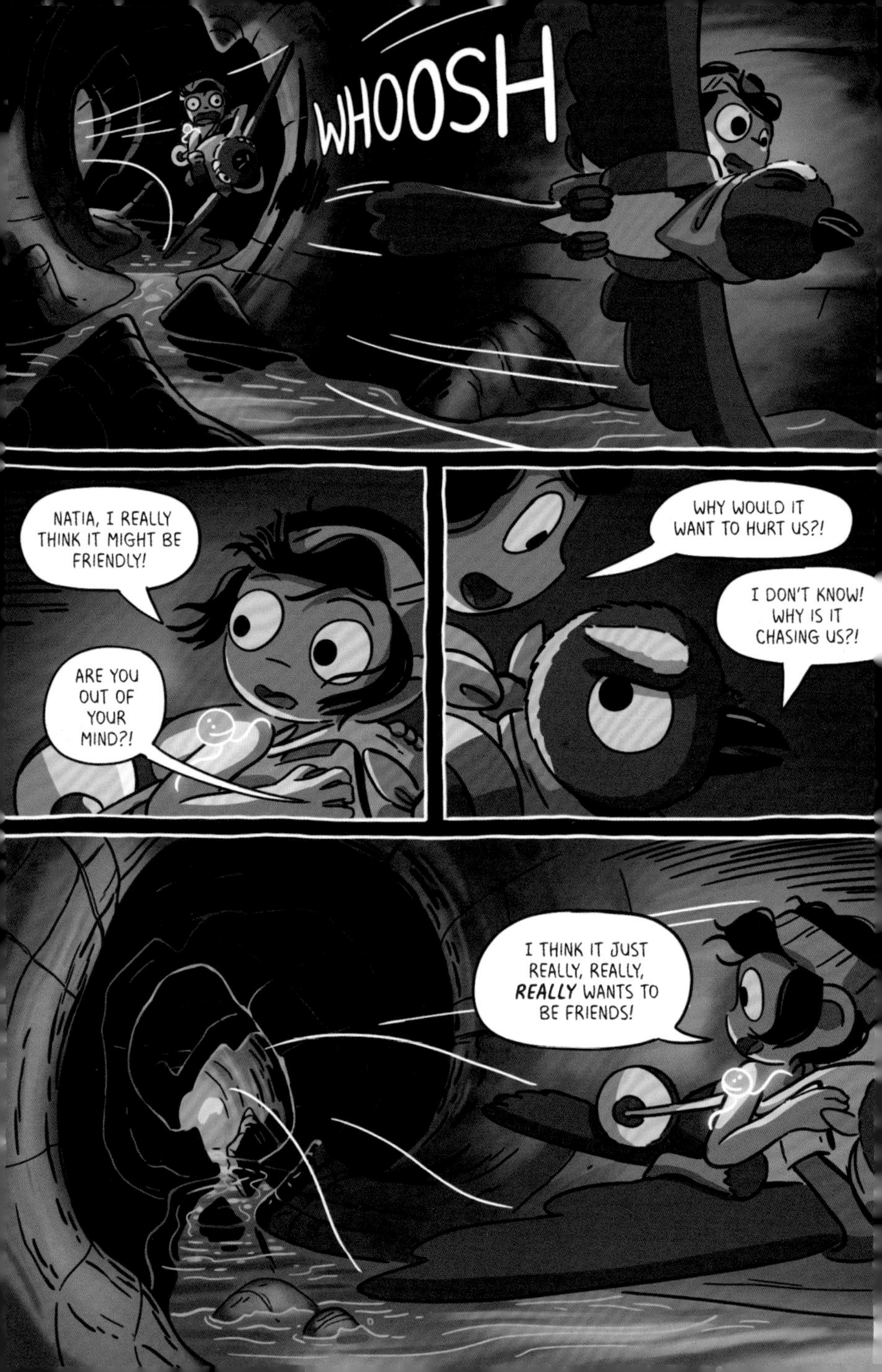
WHOOSH
NATIA, I REALLY THINK IT MIGHT BE FRIENDLY!
ARE YOU OUT OF YOUR MIND?!
WHY WOULD IT WANT TO HURT US?!
I DON'T KNOW! WHY IS IT CHASING US?!
I THINK IT JUST REALLY, REALLY, **REALLY** WANTS TO BE FRIENDS!

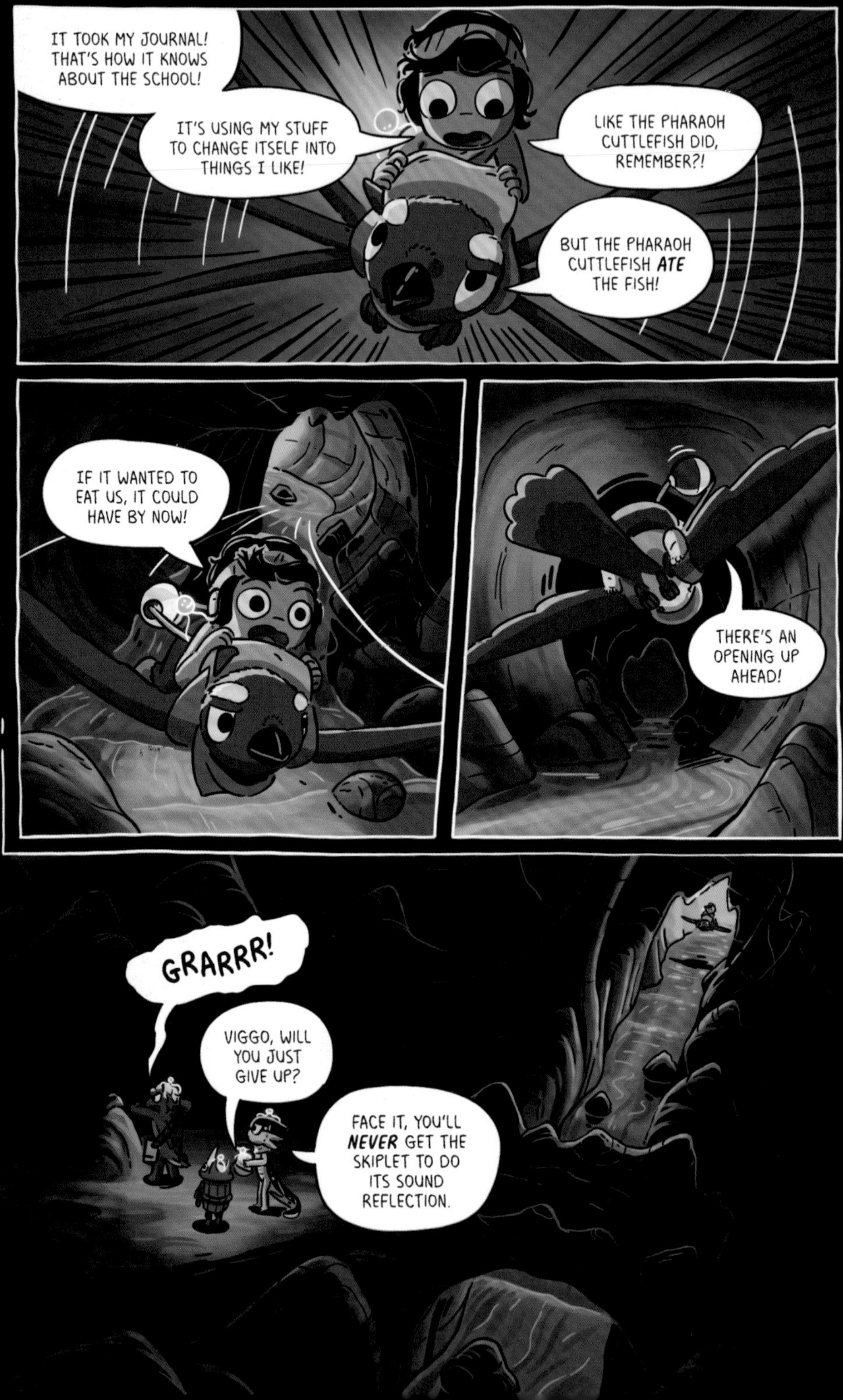
IT TOOK MY JOURNAL! THAT'S HOW IT KNOWS ABOUT THE SCHOOL!
IT'S USING MY STUFF TO CHANGE ITSELF INTO THINGS I LIKE!
LIKE THE PHARAOH CUTTLEFISH DID, REMEMBER?!
BUT THE PHARAOH CUTTLEFISH ***ATE*** THE FISH!
IF IT WANTED TO EAT US, IT COULD HAVE BY NOW!
THERE'S AN OPENING UP AHEAD!
GRARRR!
VIGGO, WILL YOU JUST GIVE UP?
FACE IT, YOU'LL ***NEVER*** GET THE SKIPLET TO DO ITS SOUND REFLECTION.

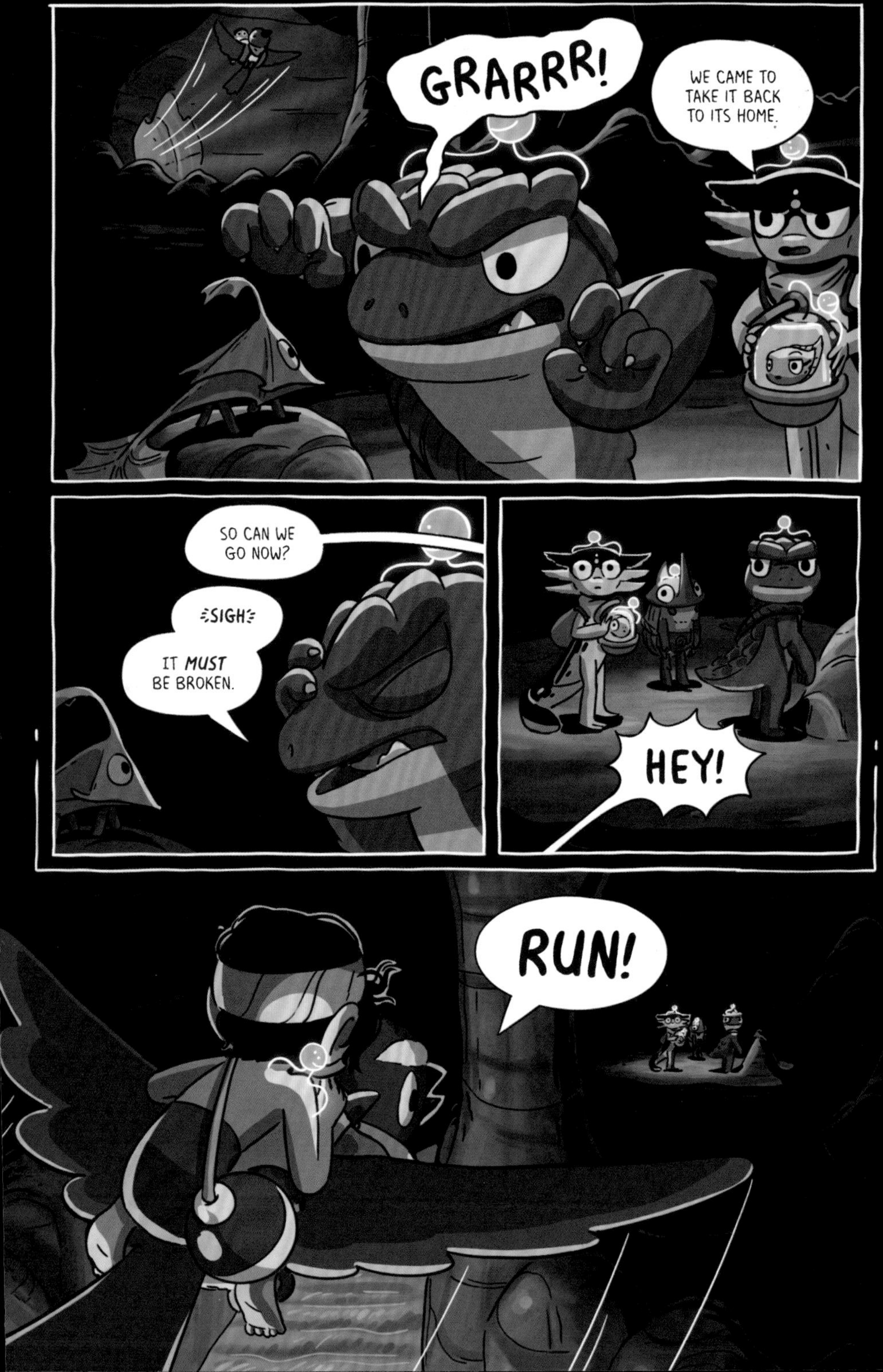
GRARRR!
WE CAME TO TAKE IT BACK TO ITS HOME.
SO CAN WE GO NOW?
SIGH
IT MUST BE BROKEN.
HEY!
RUN!

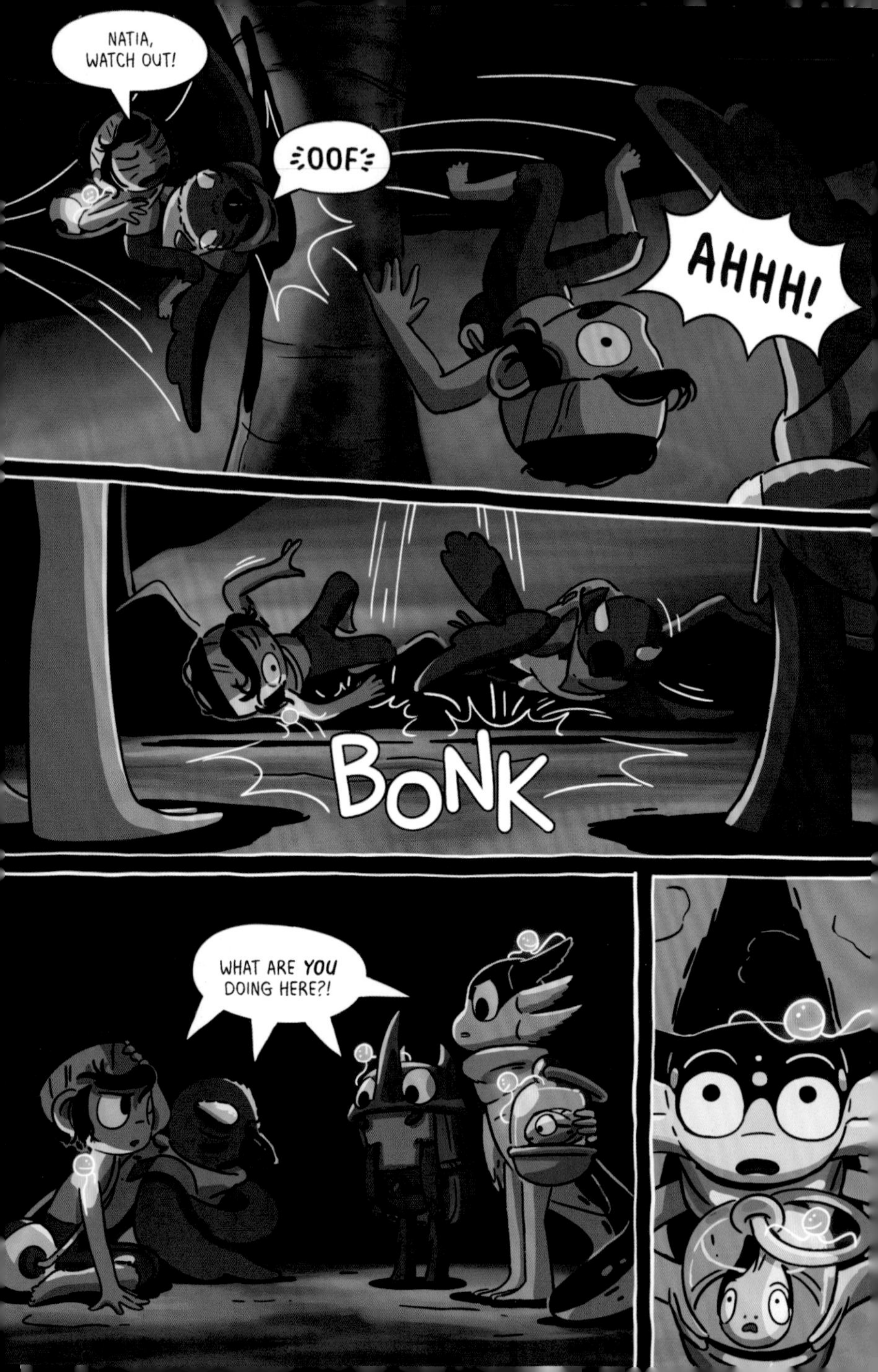
NATIA, WATCH OUT!
OOF
AHHH!
BONK
WHAT ARE *YOU* DOING HERE?!

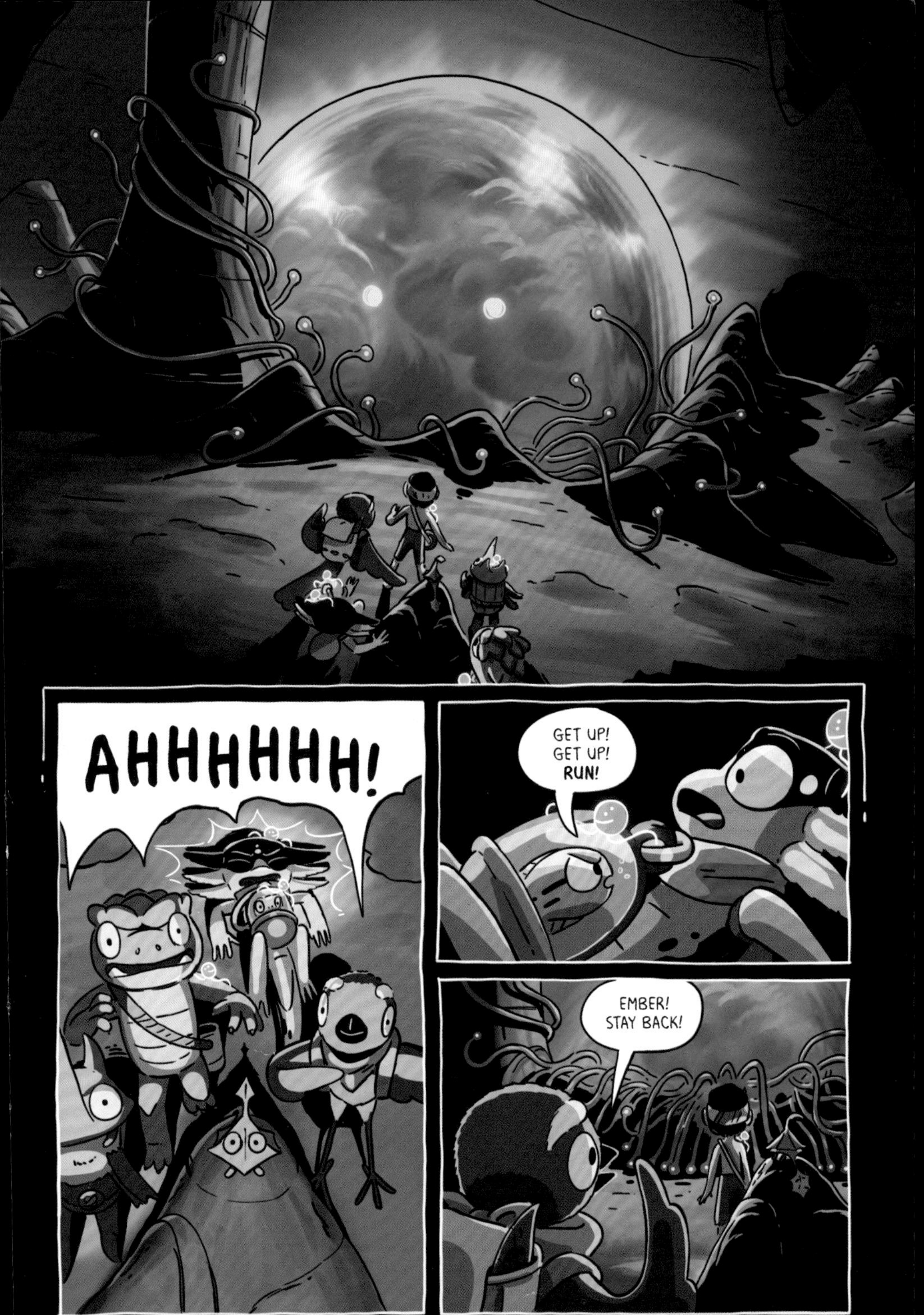
AHHHHHH!
GET UP! GET UP! RUN!
EMBER! STAY BACK!

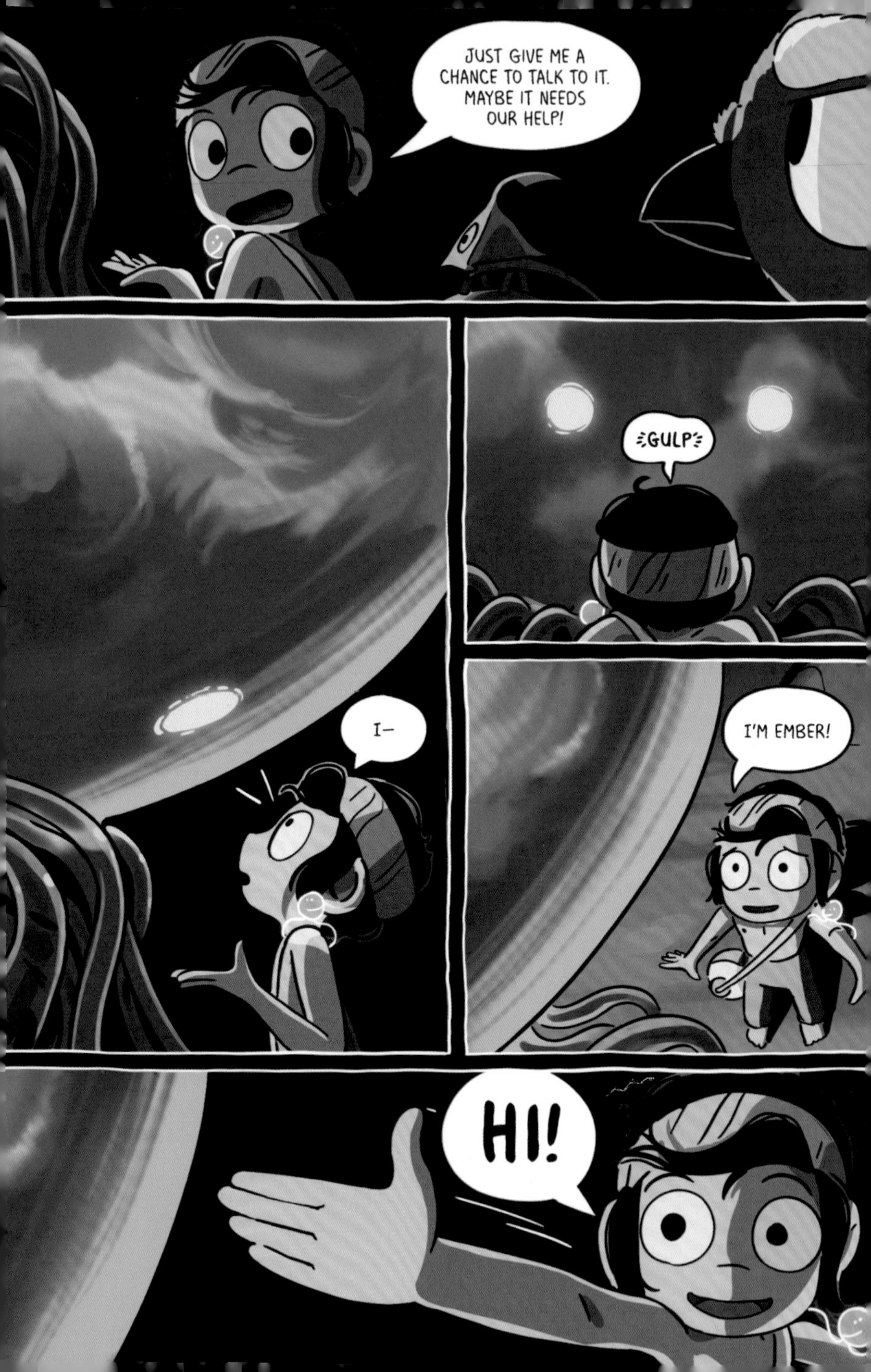
JUST GIVE ME A CHANCE TO TALK TO IT. MAYBE IT NEEDS OUR HELP!
GULP
I—
I'M EMBER!
HI!

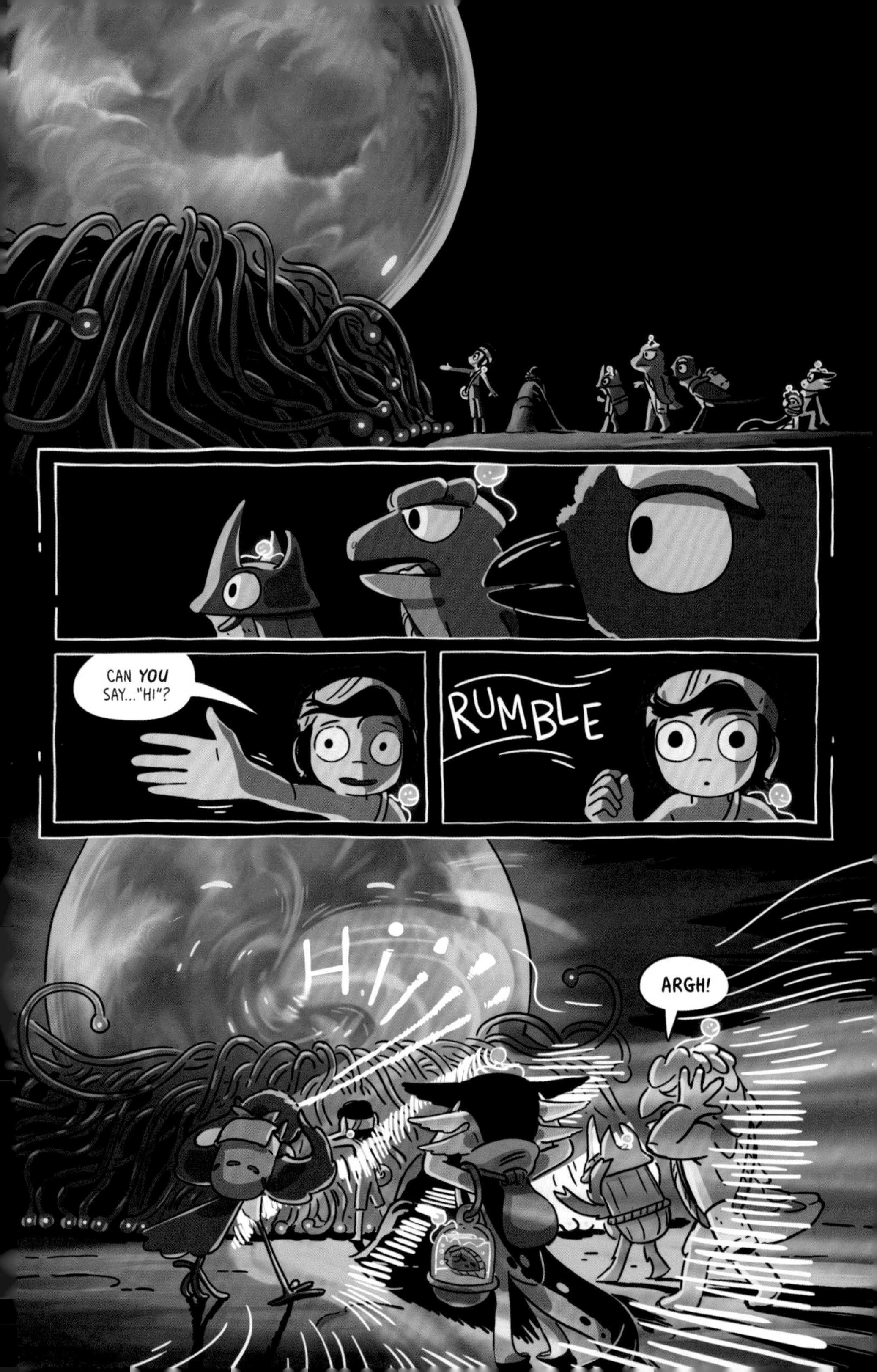
CAN YOU SAY..."HI"?
RUMBLE
HI
ARGH!

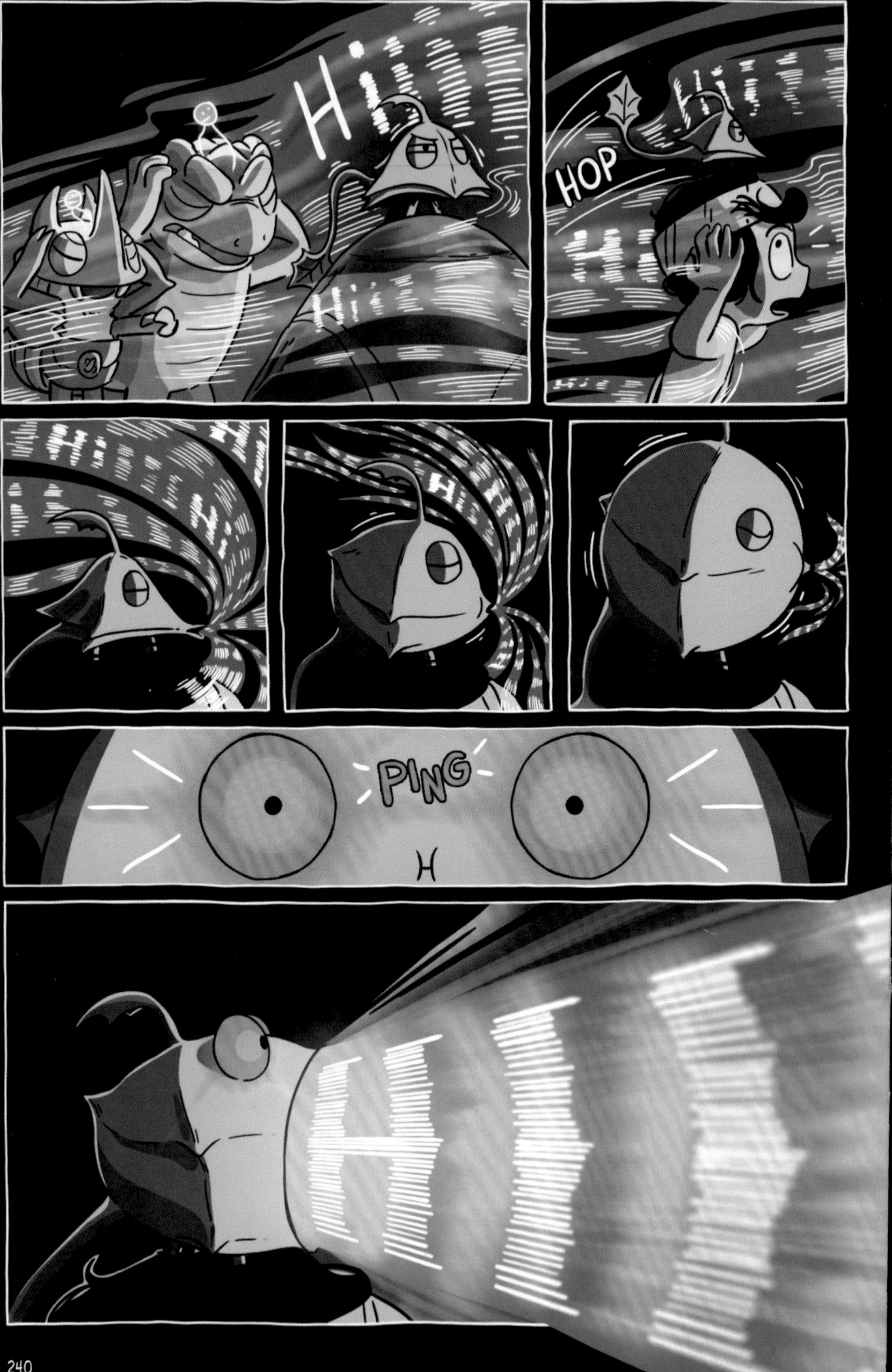
Hi
HOP
PING

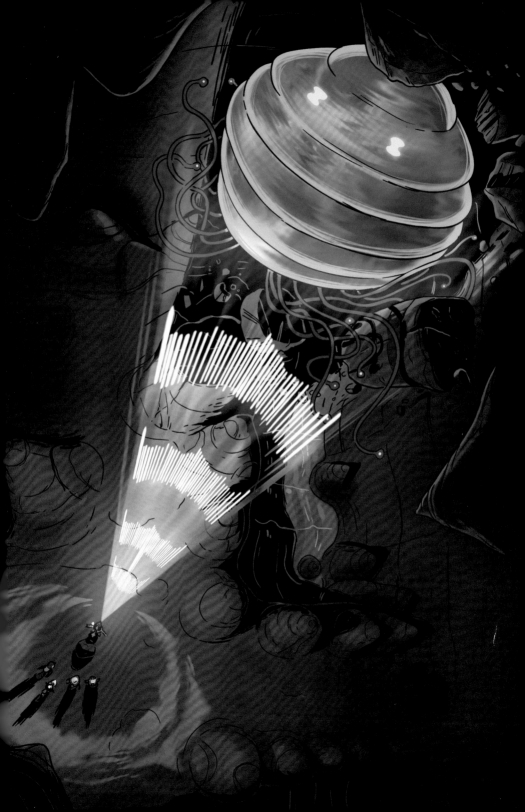

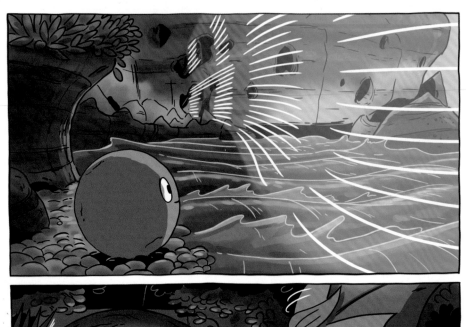

CRACK

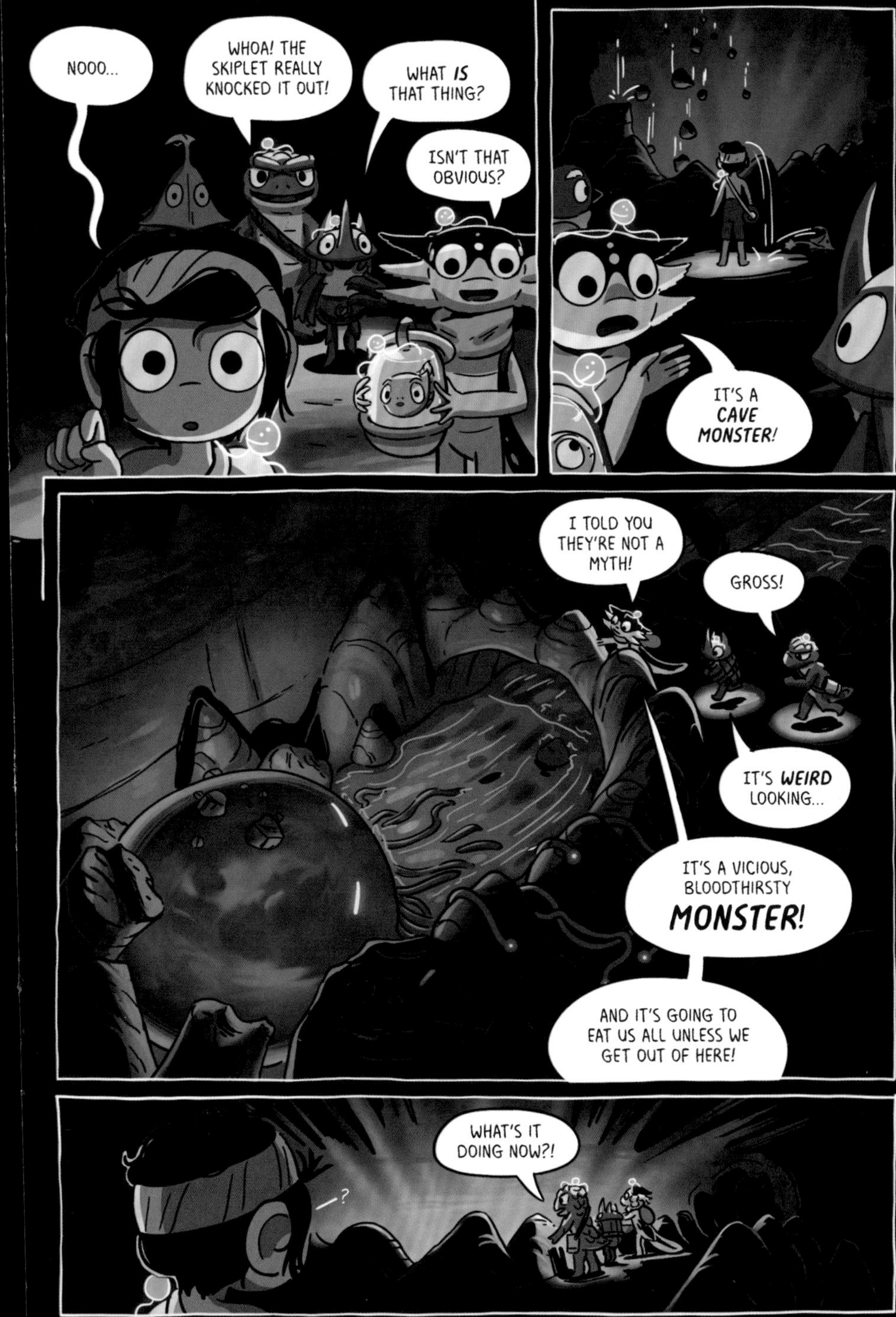
NOOO...
WHOA! THE SKIPLET REALLY KNOCKED IT OUT!
WHAT IS THAT THING?
ISN'T THAT OBVIOUS?
IT'S A CAVE MONSTER!
I TOLD YOU THEY'RE NOT A MYTH!
GROSS!
IT'S WEIRD LOOKING...
IT'S A VICIOUS, BLOODTHIRSTY MONSTER!
AND IT'S GOING TO EAT US ALL UNLESS WE GET OUT OF HERE!
WHAT'S IT DOING NOW?!
—?

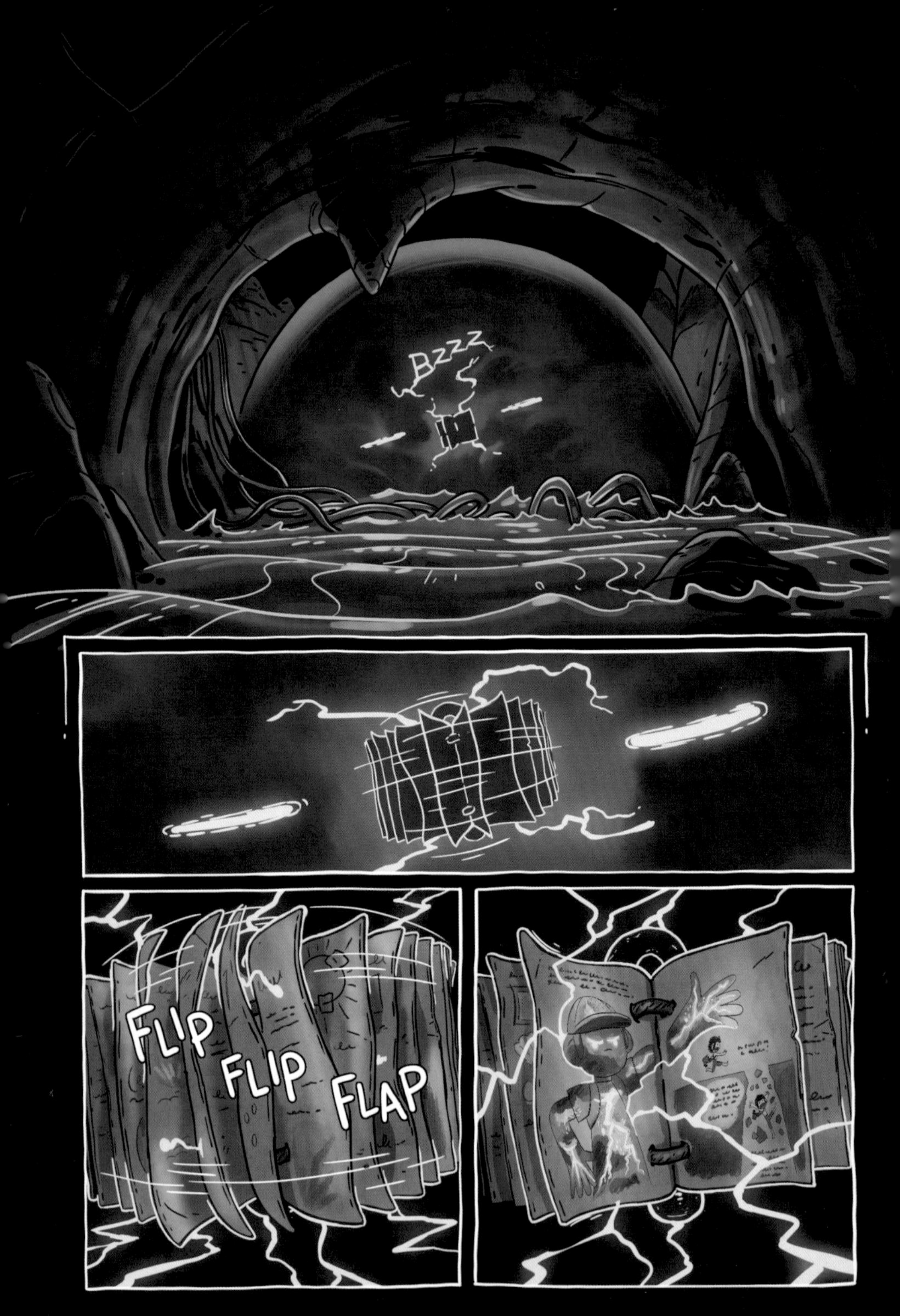
Bzzz
FLIP
FLIP
FLAP

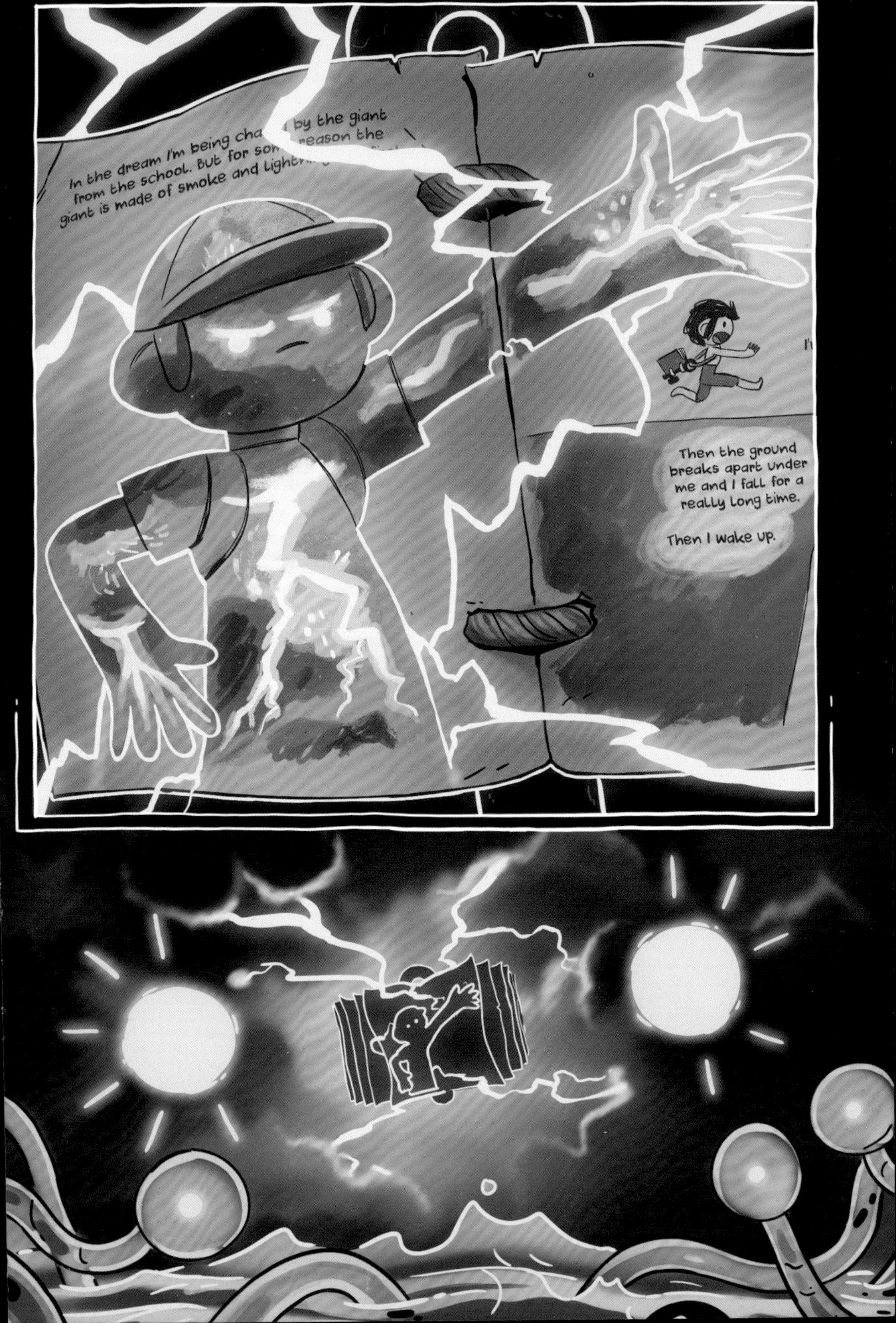
In the dream I'm being cha by the giant
from the school. But for som reason the
giant is made of smoke and lightn
Then the ground breaks apart under me and I fall for a really long time.
Then I wake up.

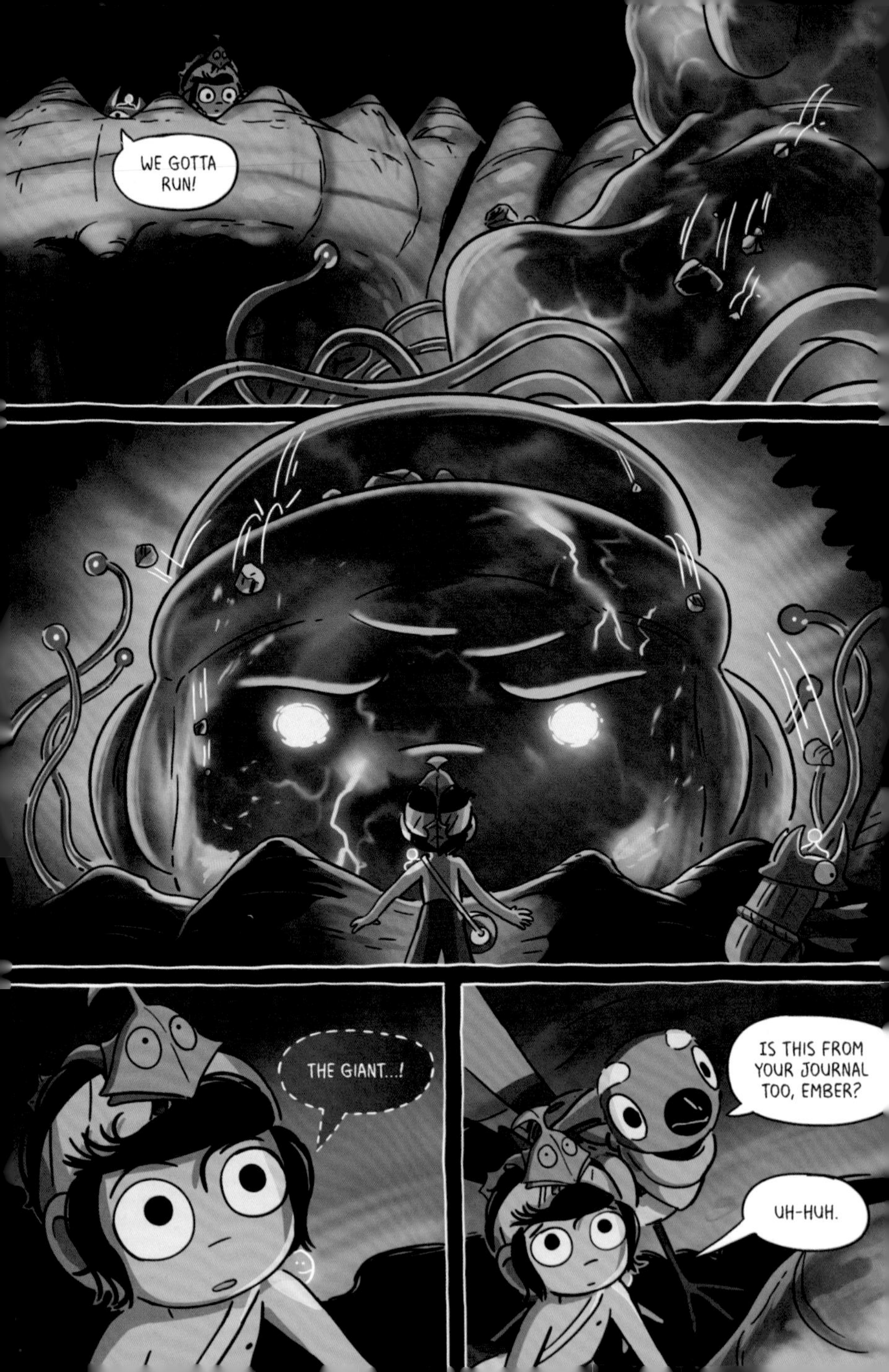
WE GOTTA RUN!
THE GIANT...!
IS THIS FROM YOUR JOURNAL TOO, EMBER?
UH-HUH.

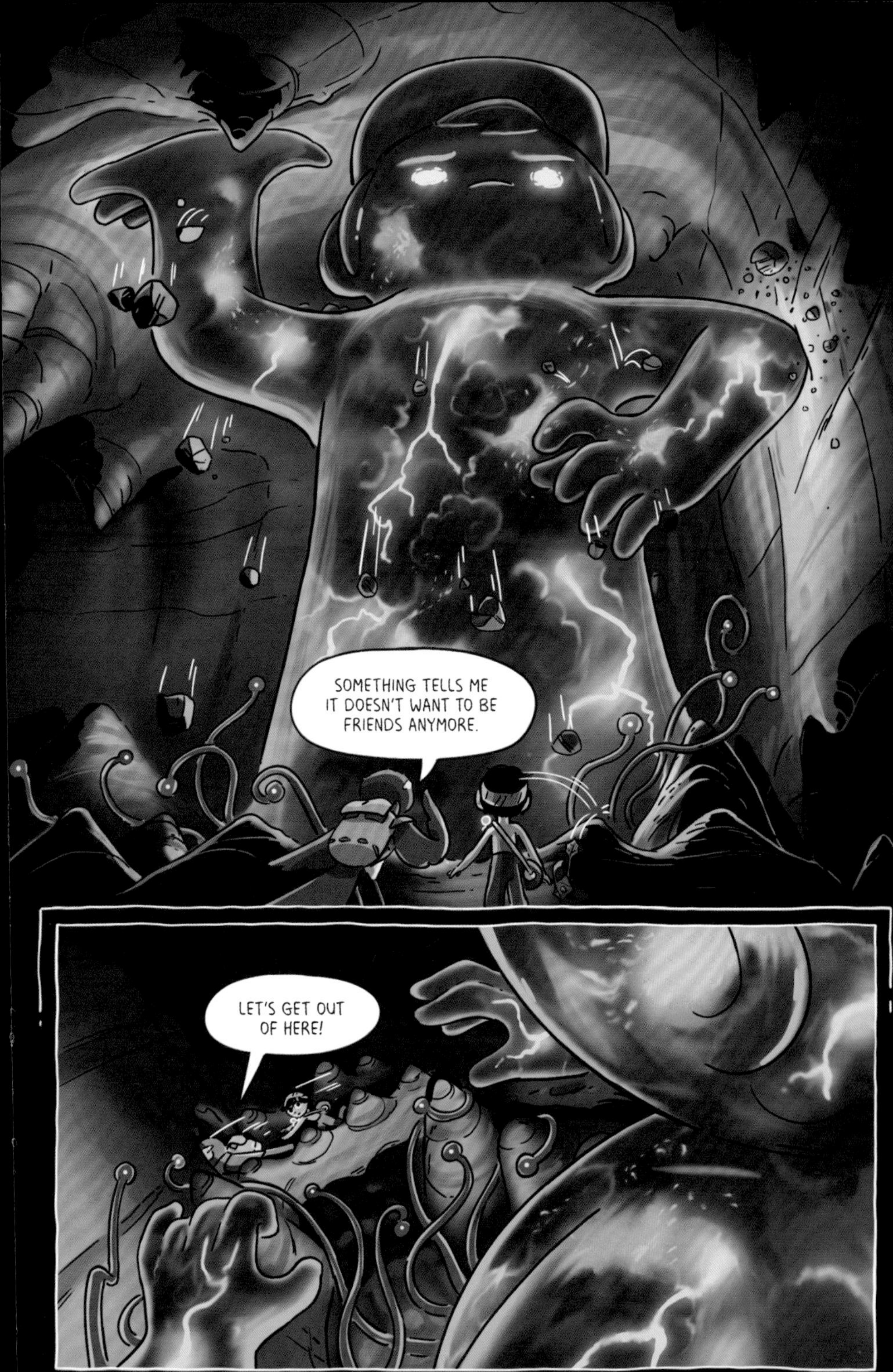
SOMETHING TELLS ME
IT DOESN'T WANT TO BE
FRIENDS ANYMORE.
LET'S GET OUT
OF HERE!

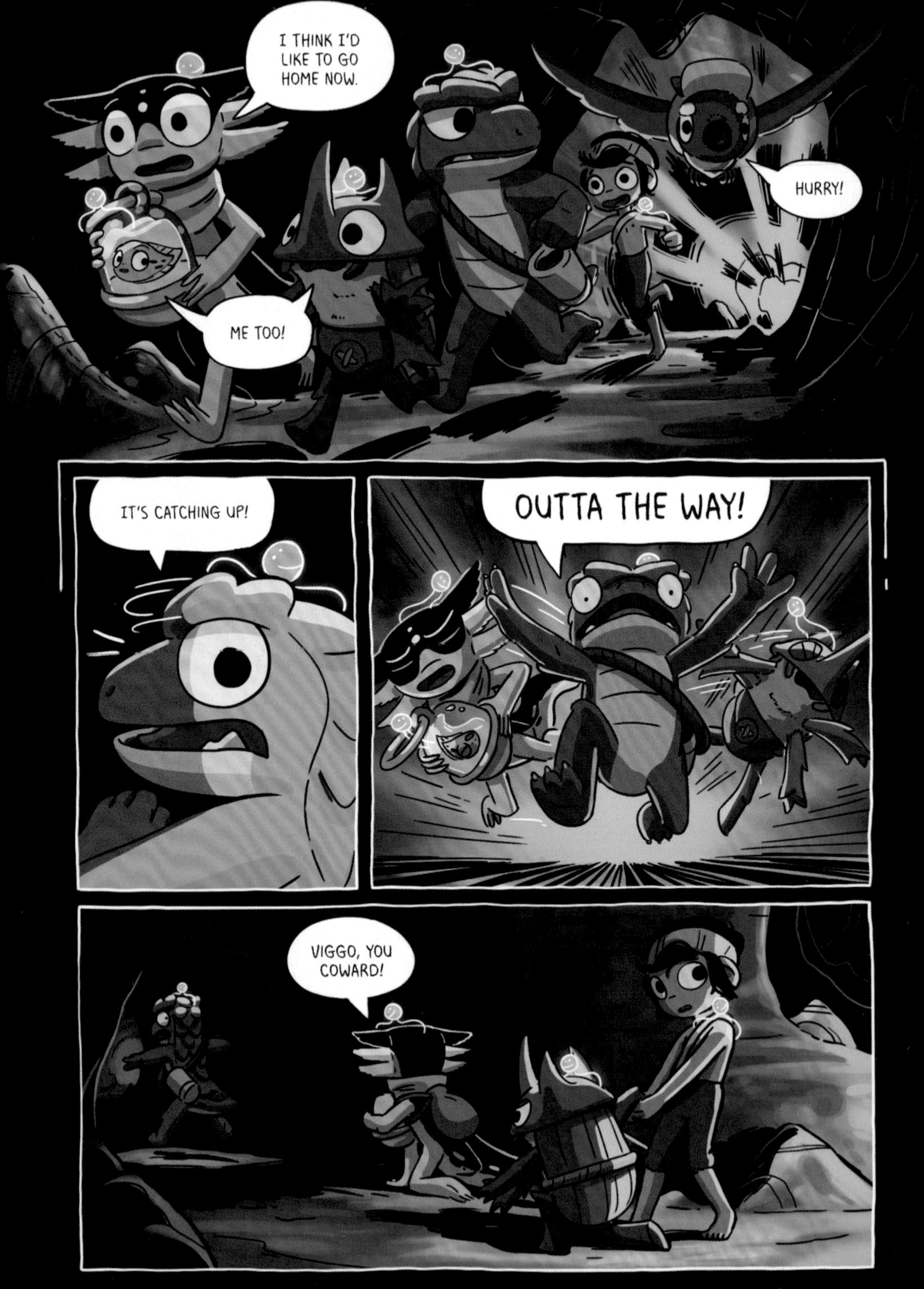
I THINK I'D LIKE TO GO HOME NOW.
ME TOO!
HURRY!
IT'S CATCHING UP!
OUTTA THE WAY!
VIGGO, YOU COWARD!

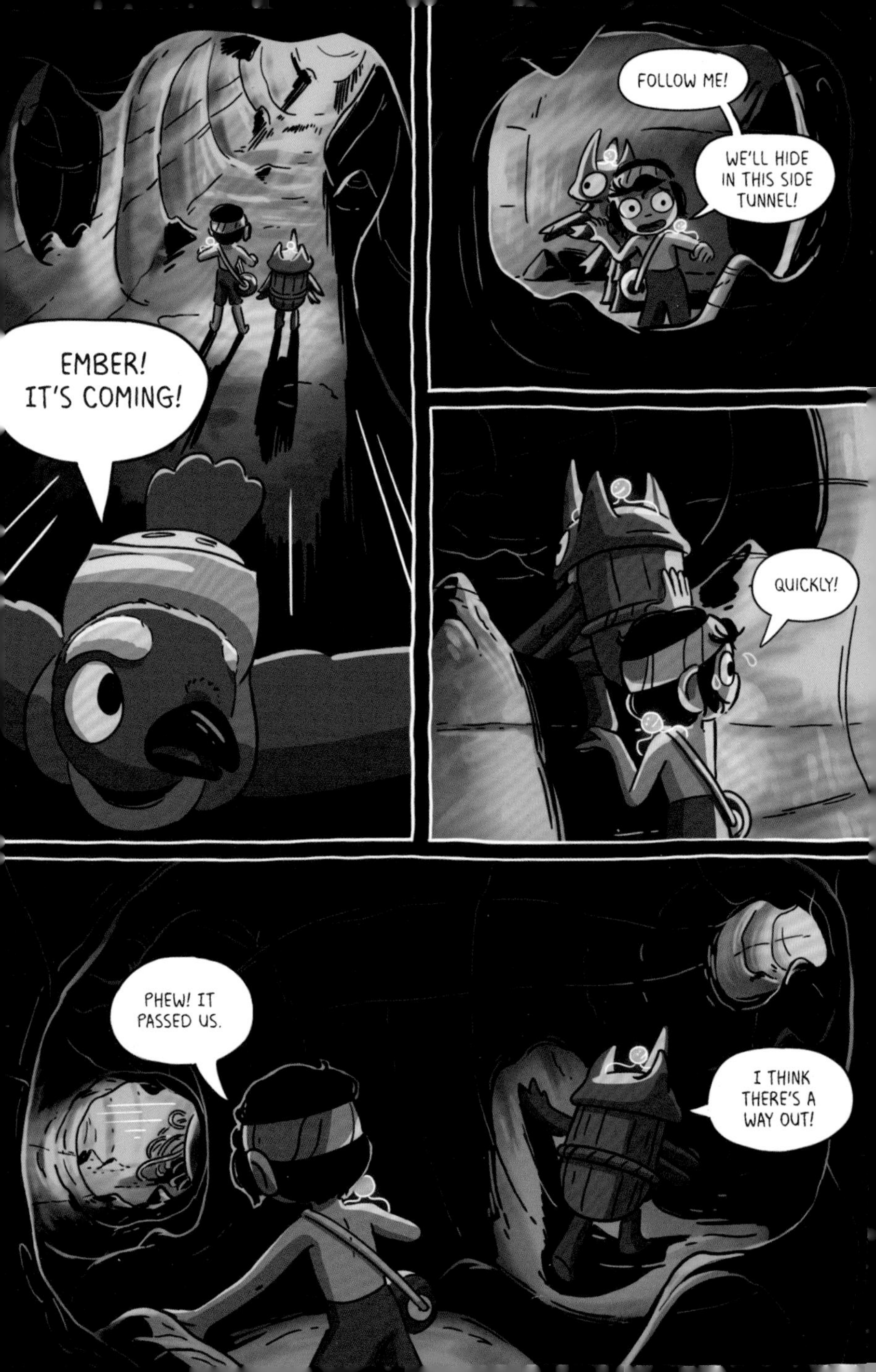
EMBER! IT'S COMING!
FOLLOW ME!
WE'LL HIDE IN THIS SIDE TUNNEL!
QUICKLY!
PHEW! IT PASSED US.
I THINK THERE'S A WAY OUT!

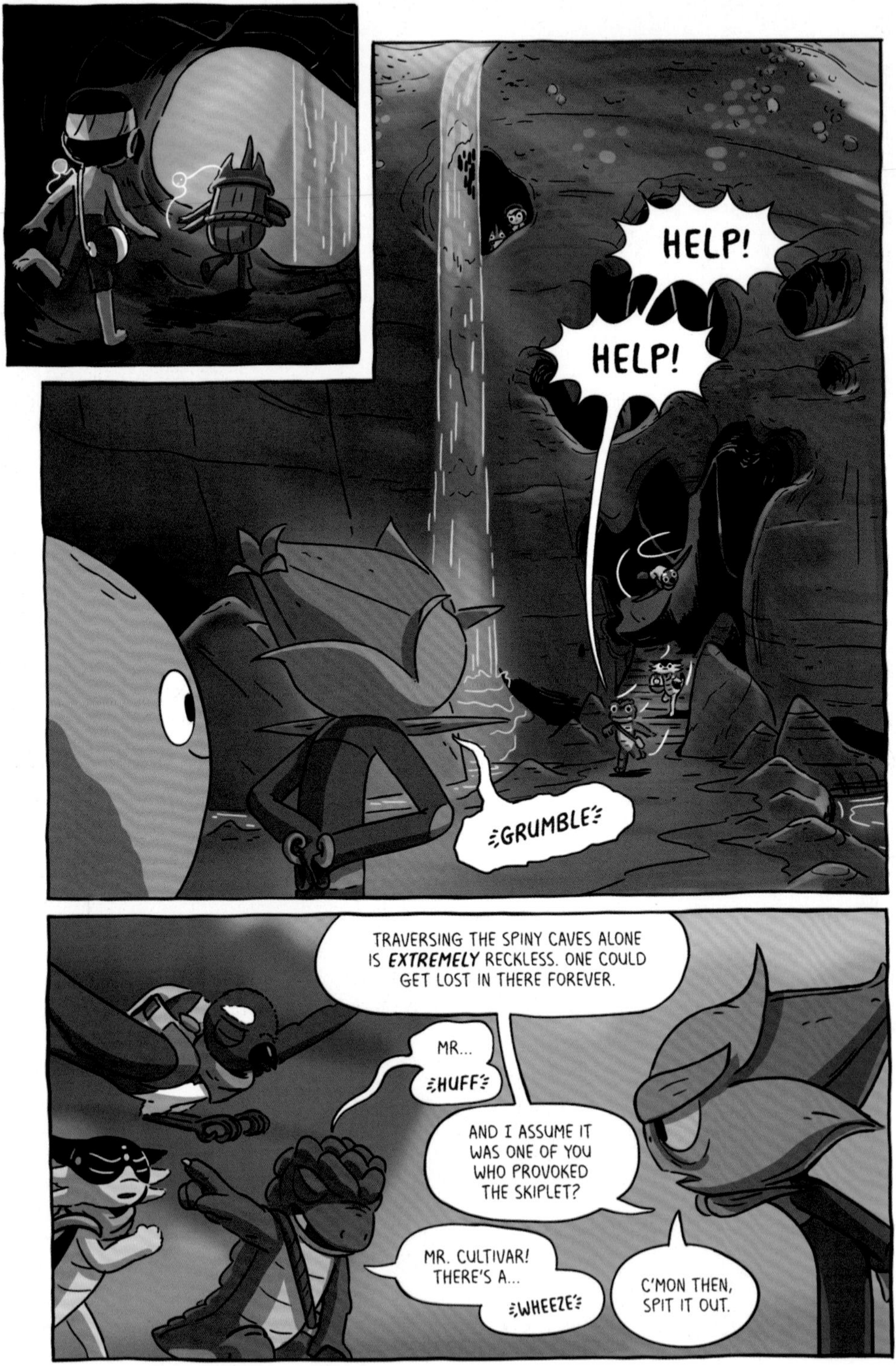
HELP!
HELP!
GRUMBLE
TRAVERSING THE SPINY CAVES ALONE IS EXTREMELY RECKLESS. ONE COULD GET LOST IN THERE FOREVER.
MR...
HUFF
AND I ASSUME IT WAS ONE OF YOU WHO PROVOKED THE SKIPLET?
MR. CULTIVAR! THERE'S A...
WHEEZE
C'MON THEN, SPIT IT OUT.

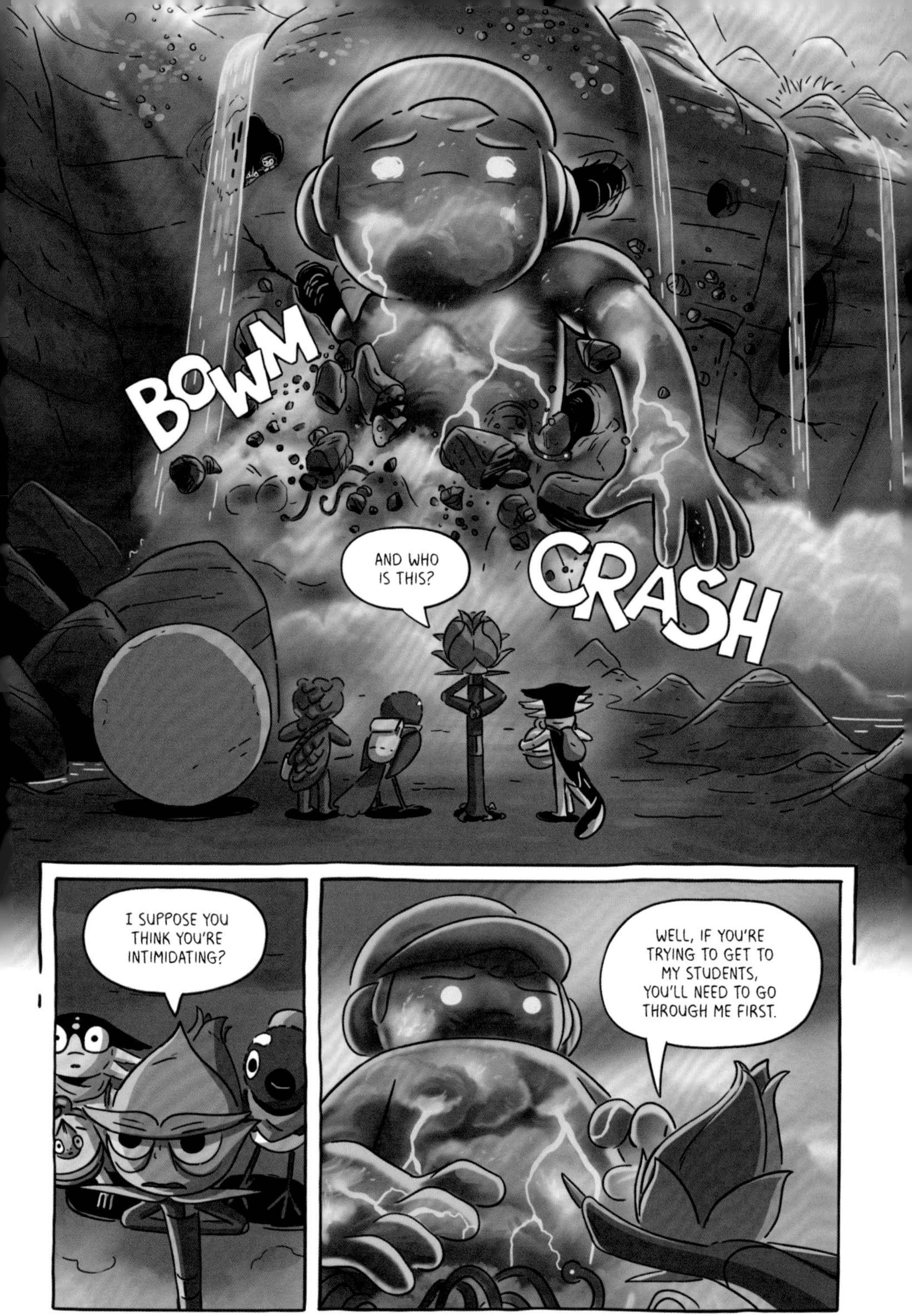
BOWM
AND WHO IS THIS?
CRASH
I SUPPOSE YOU THINK YOU'RE INTIMIDATING?
WELL, IF YOU'RE TRYING TO GET TO MY STUDENTS, YOU'LL NEED TO GO THROUGH ME FIRST.

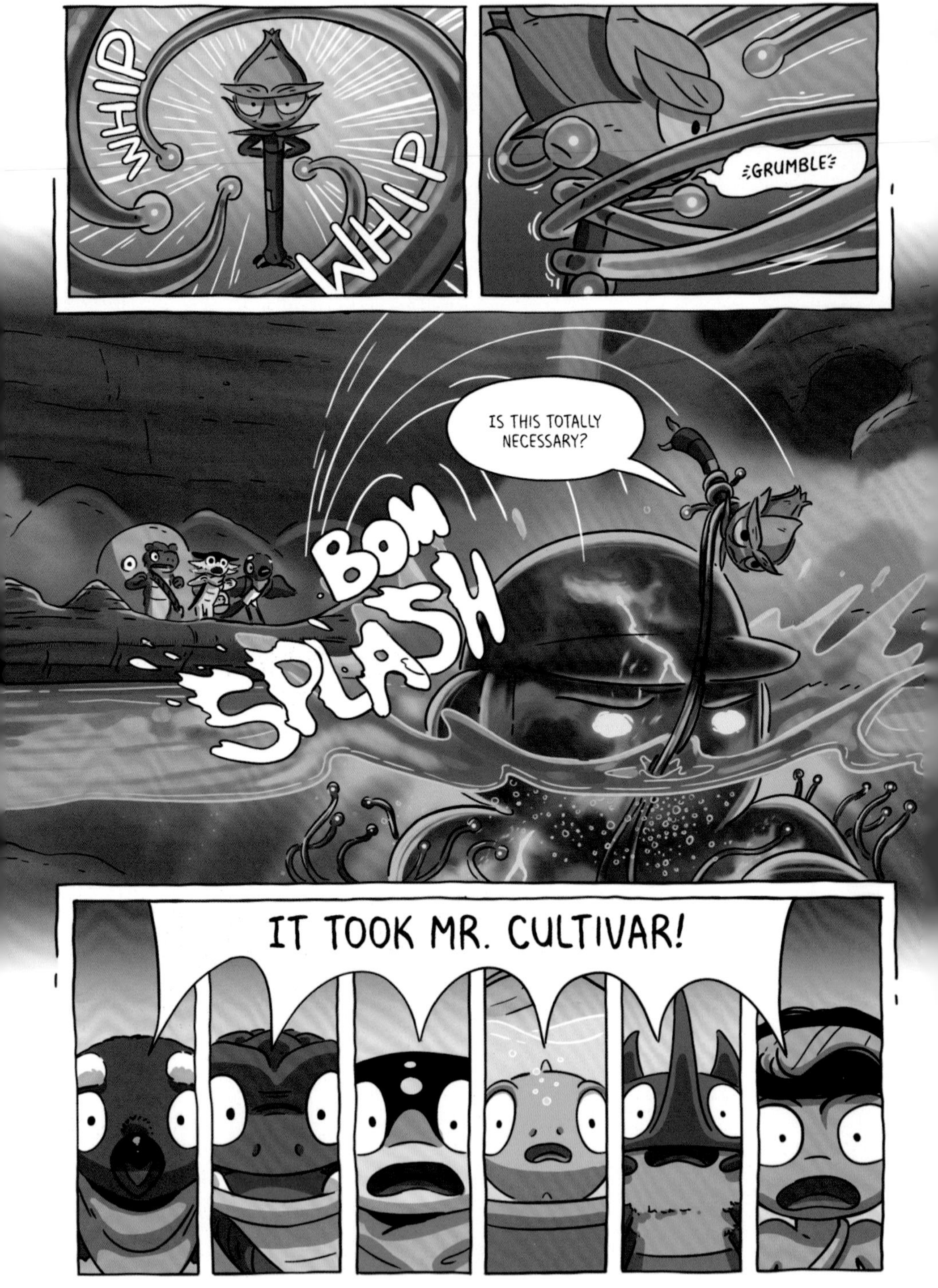
WHIP
WHIP
GRUMBLE
IS THIS TOTALLY NECESSARY?
BOM
SPLASH
IT TOOK MR. CULTIVAR!

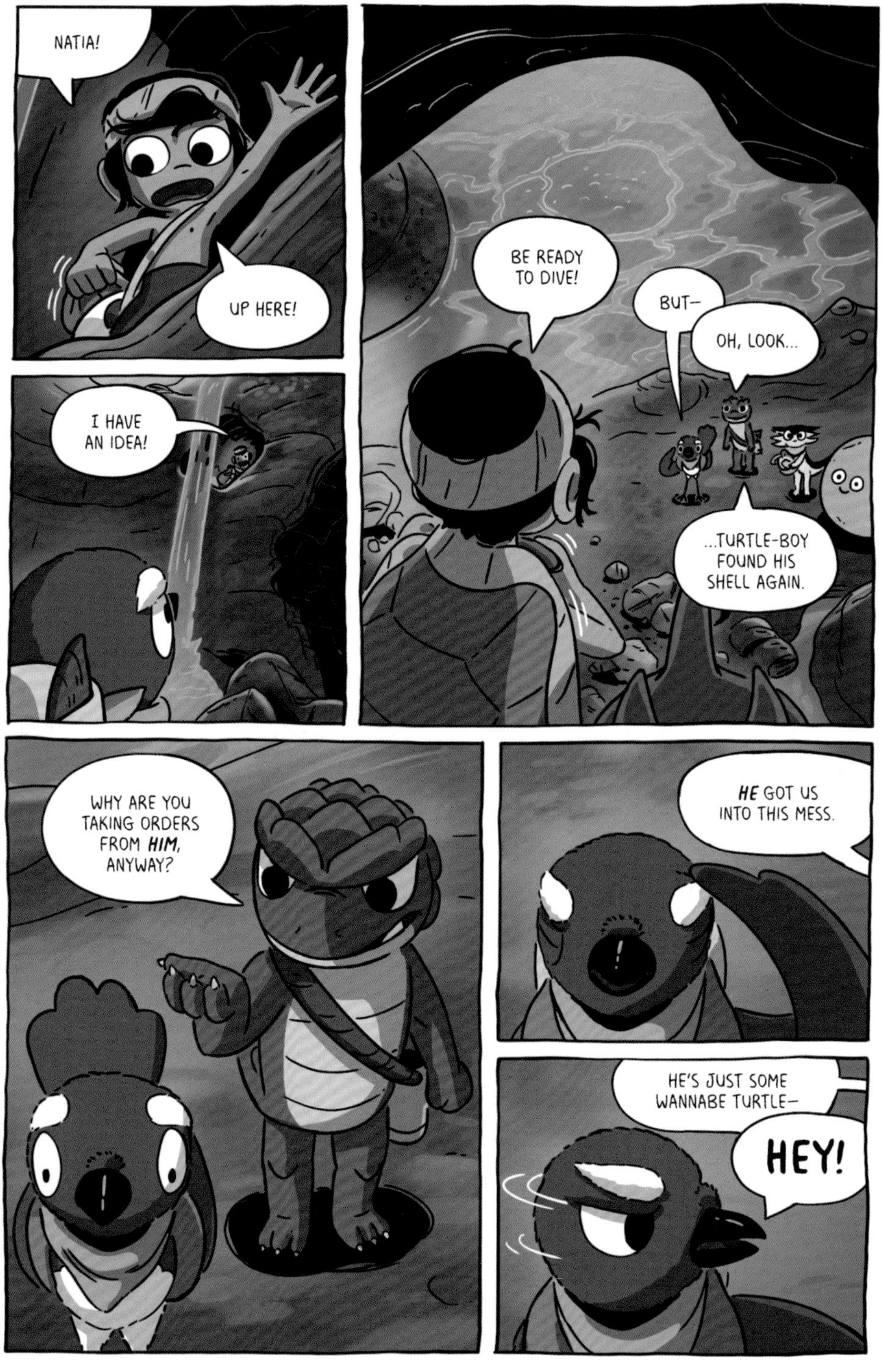
NATIA!
UP HERE!
I HAVE AN IDEA!
BE READY TO DIVE!
BUT—
OH, LOOK...
...TURTLE-BOY FOUND HIS SHELL AGAIN.
WHY ARE YOU TAKING ORDERS FROM **HIM**, ANYWAY?
HE GOT US INTO THIS MESS.
HE'S JUST SOME WANNABE TURTLE—
HEY!

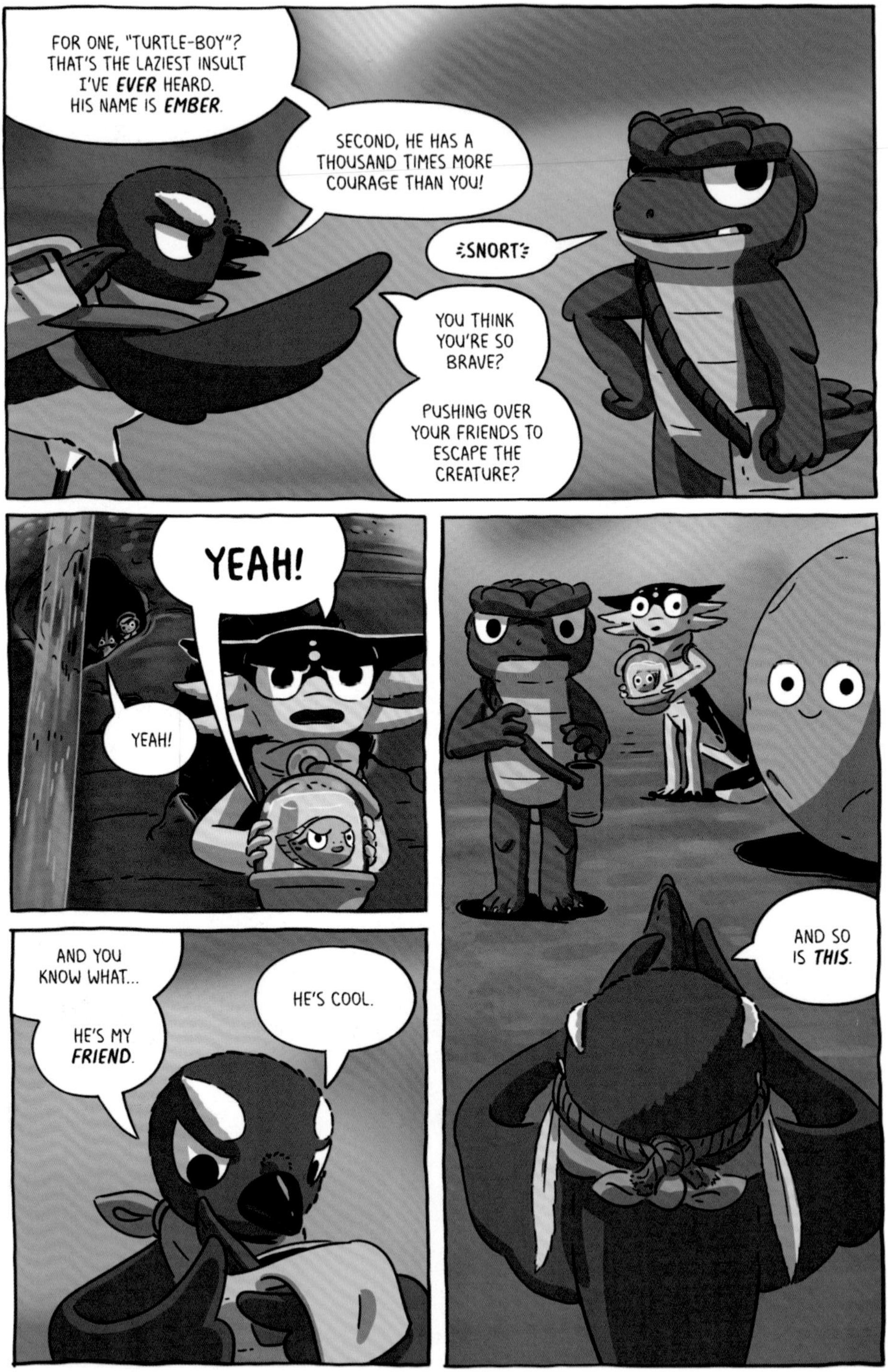
FOR ONE, "TURTLE-BOY"? THAT'S THE LAZIEST INSULT I'VE EVER HEARD. HIS NAME IS EMBER.
SECOND, HE HAS A THOUSAND TIMES MORE COURAGE THAN YOU!
SNORT
YOU THINK YOU'RE SO BRAVE?
PUSHING OVER YOUR FRIENDS TO ESCAPE THE CREATURE?
YEAH!
YEAH!
AND SO IS THIS.
AND YOU KNOW WHAT...
HE'S MY FRIEND.
HE'S COOL.

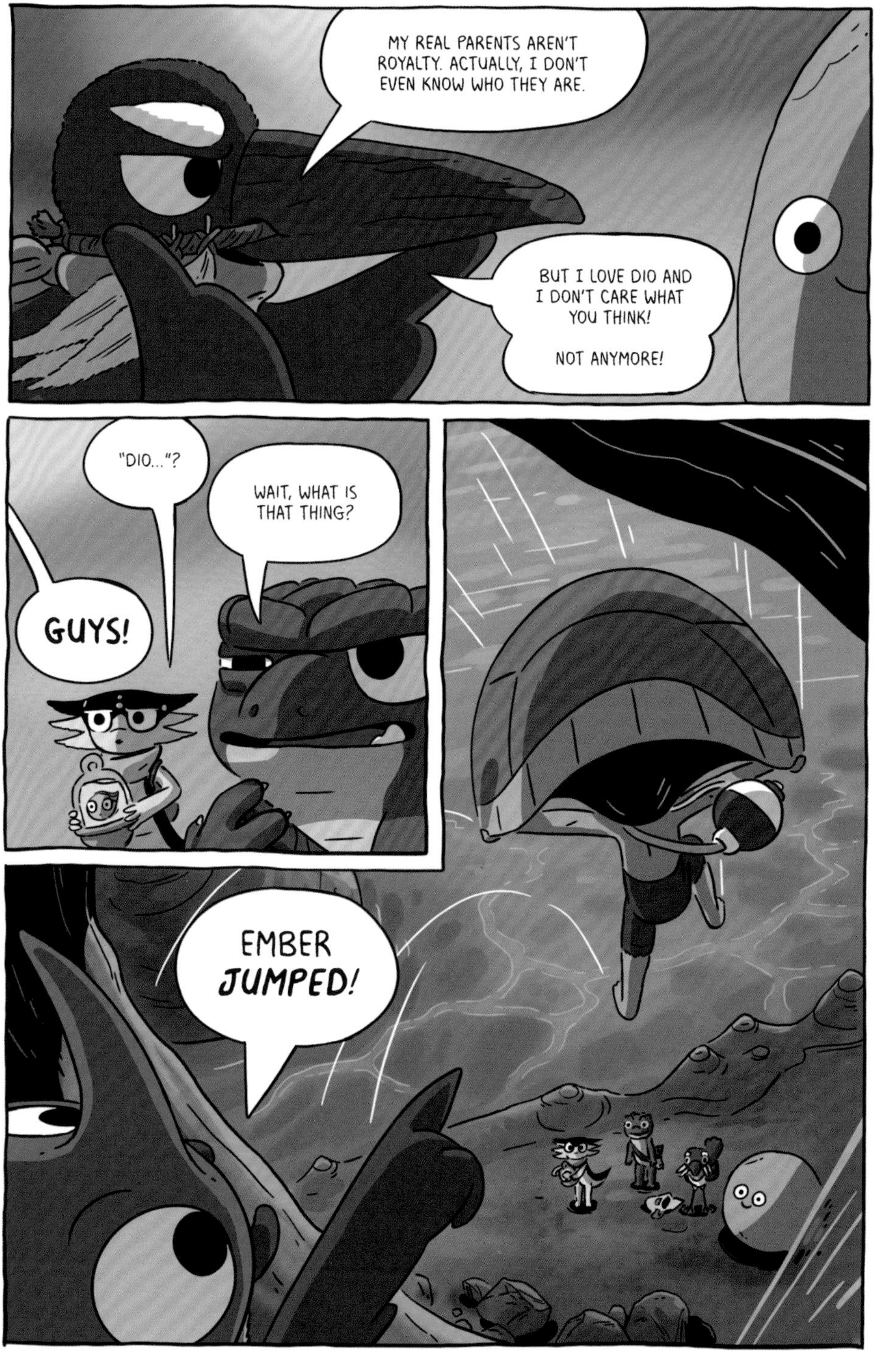
MY REAL PARENTS AREN'T ROYALTY. ACTUALLY, I DON'T EVEN KNOW WHO THEY ARE.
BUT I LOVE DIO AND I DON'T CARE WHAT YOU THINK!
NOT ANYMORE!
"DIO..."?
WAIT, WHAT IS THAT THING?
GUYS!
EMBER JUMPED!

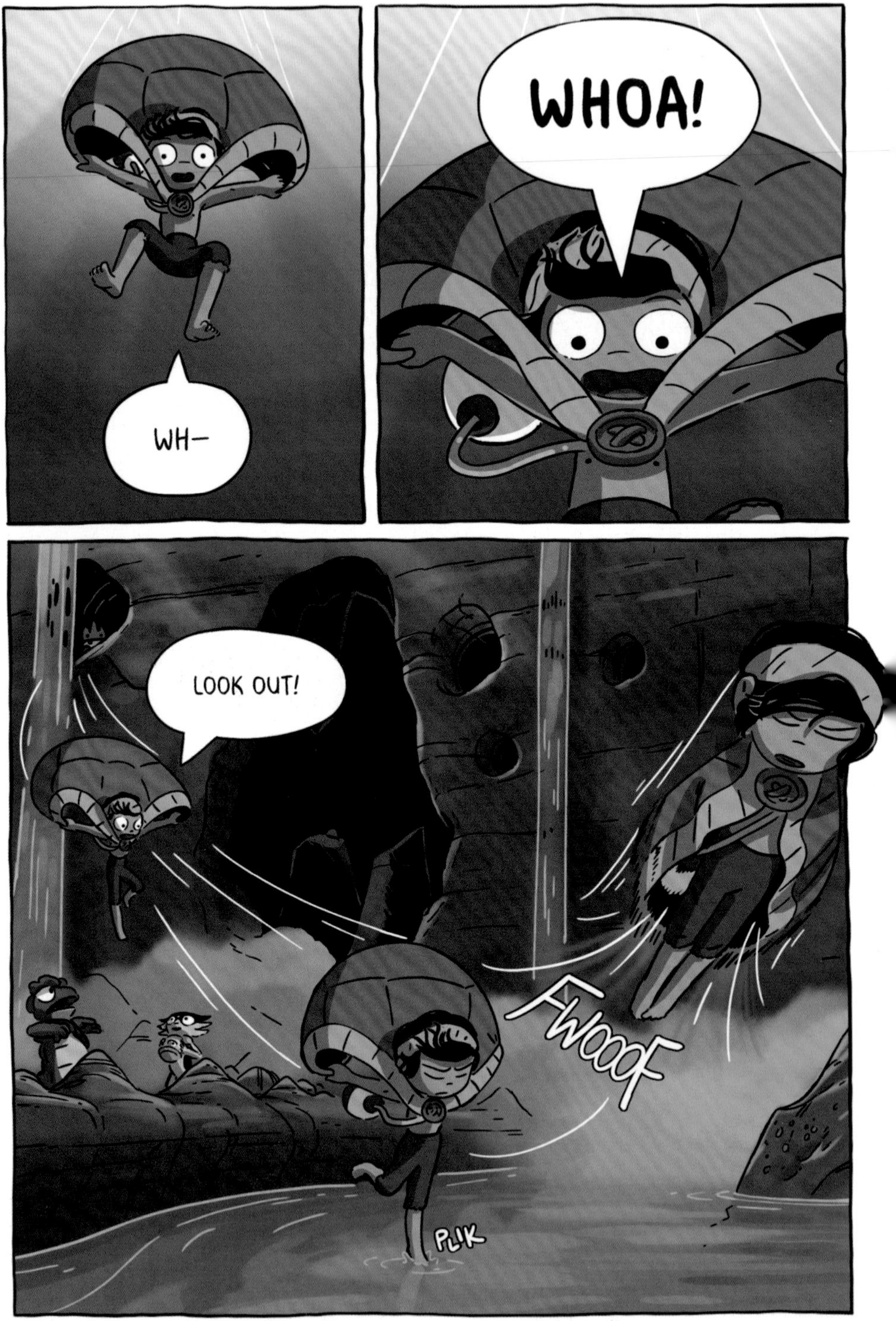
WH–
WHOA!
LOOK OUT!
FWOOOF
PLIK

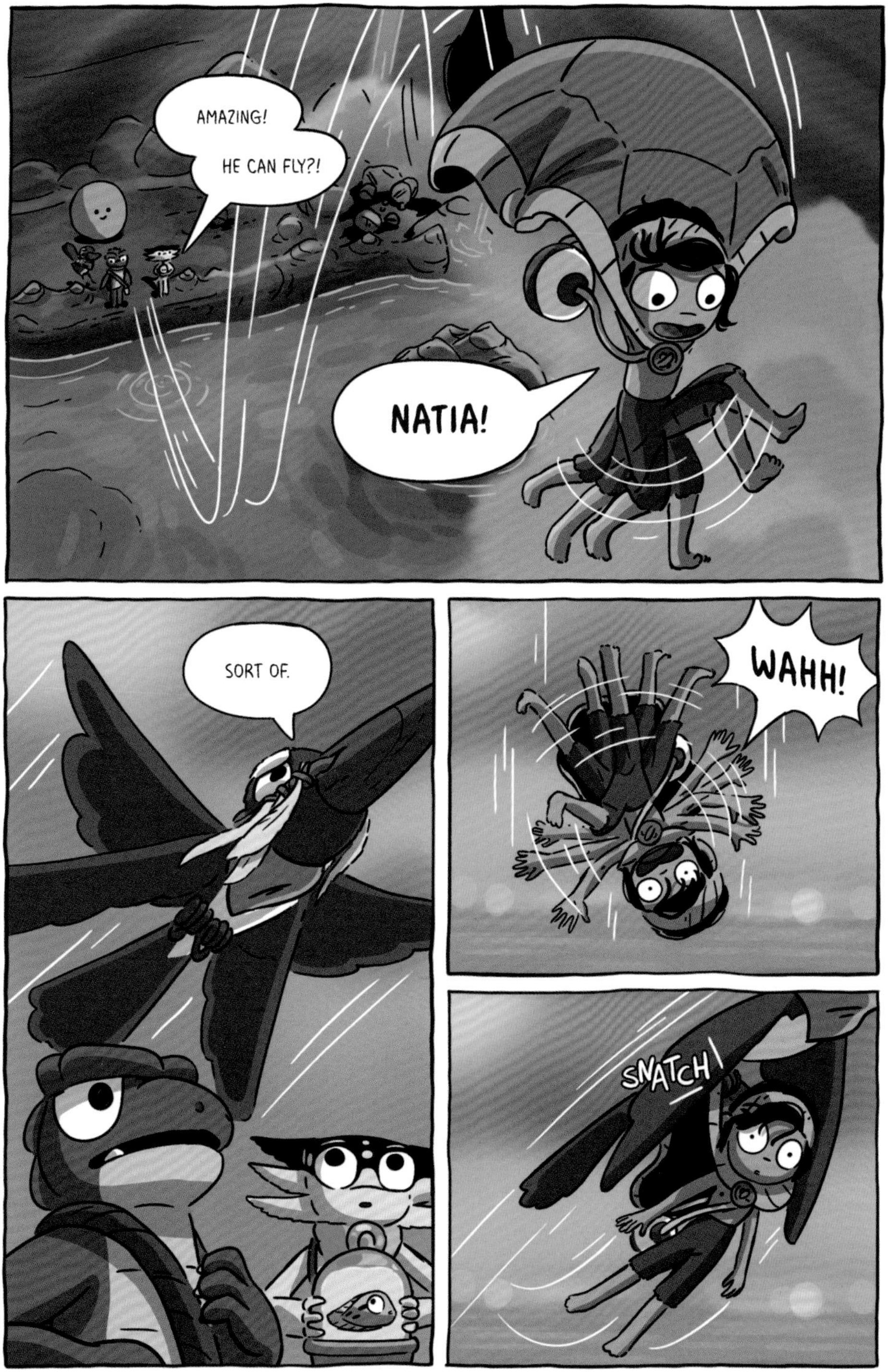
AMAZING!
HE CAN FLY?!
NATIA!
SORT OF.
WAHH!
SNATCH

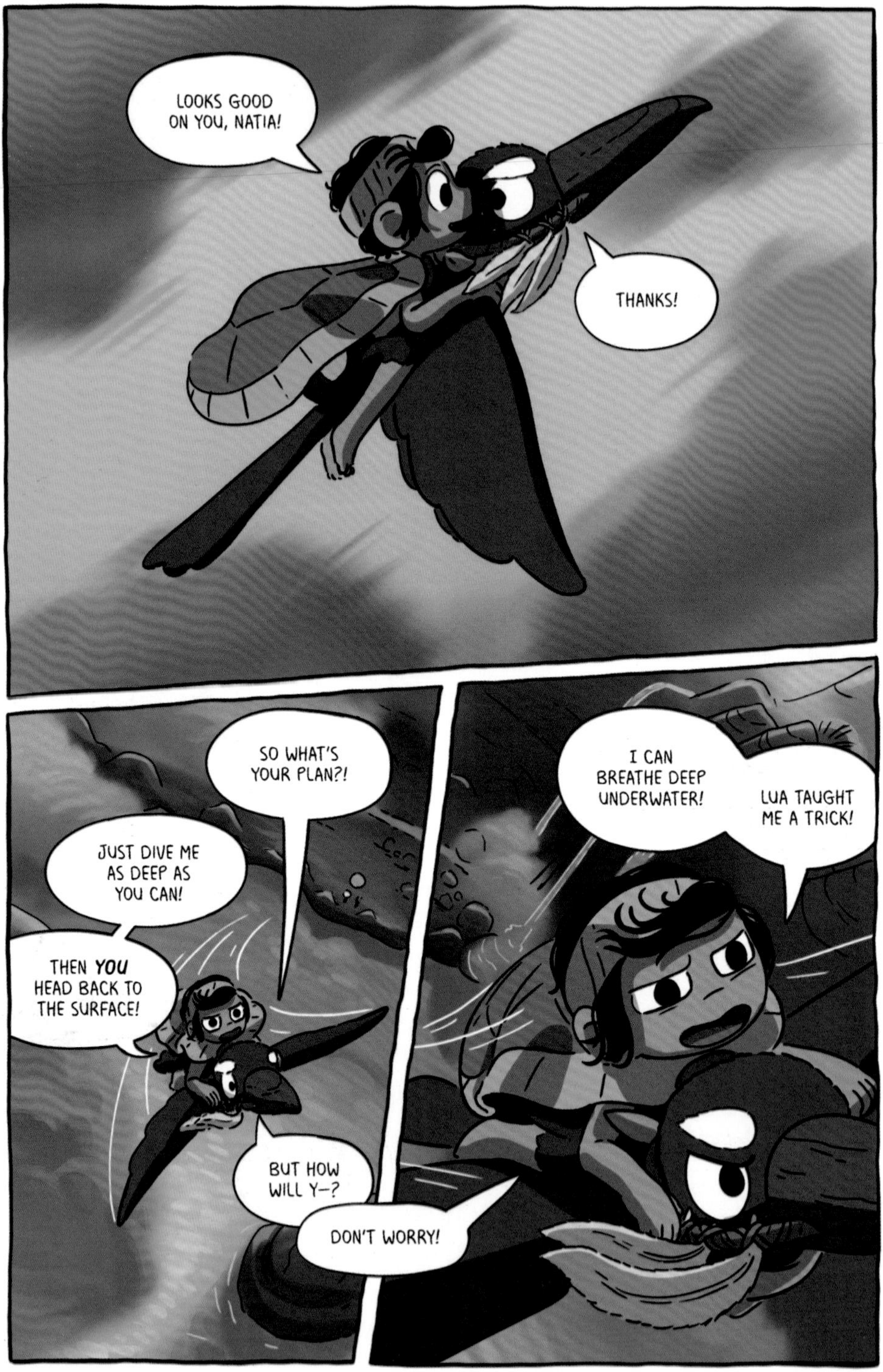
LOOKS GOOD ON YOU, NATIA!
THANKS!
SO WHAT'S YOUR PLAN?!
JUST DIVE ME AS DEEP AS YOU CAN!
THEN YOU HEAD BACK TO THE SURFACE!
BUT HOW WILL Y–?
DON'T WORRY!
I CAN BREATHE DEEP UNDERWATER!
LUA TAUGHT ME A TRICK!

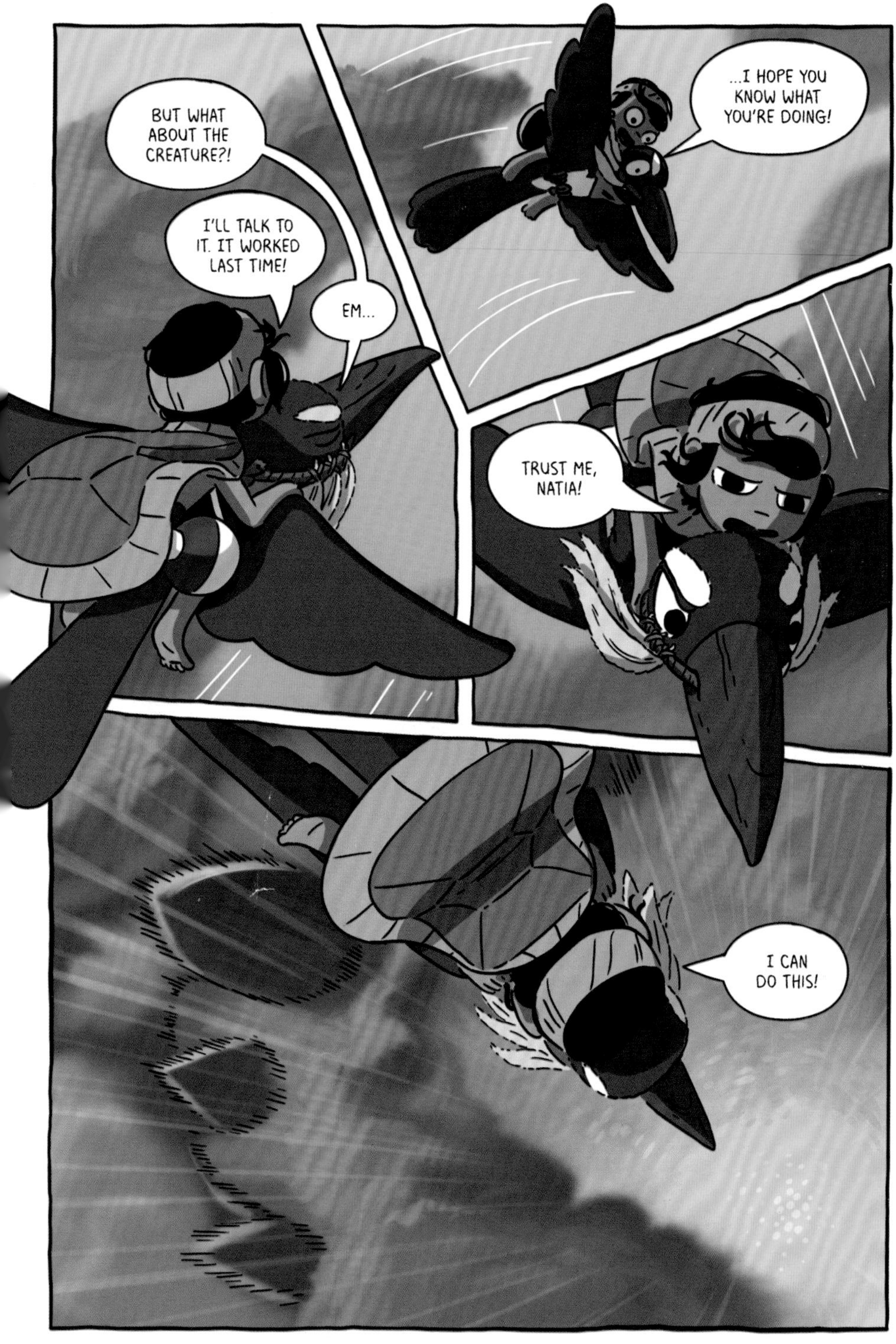
BUT WHAT ABOUT THE CREATURE?!
I'LL TALK TO IT. IT WORKED LAST TIME!
EM...
...I HOPE YOU KNOW WHAT YOU'RE DOING!
TRUST ME, NATIA!
I CAN DO THIS!

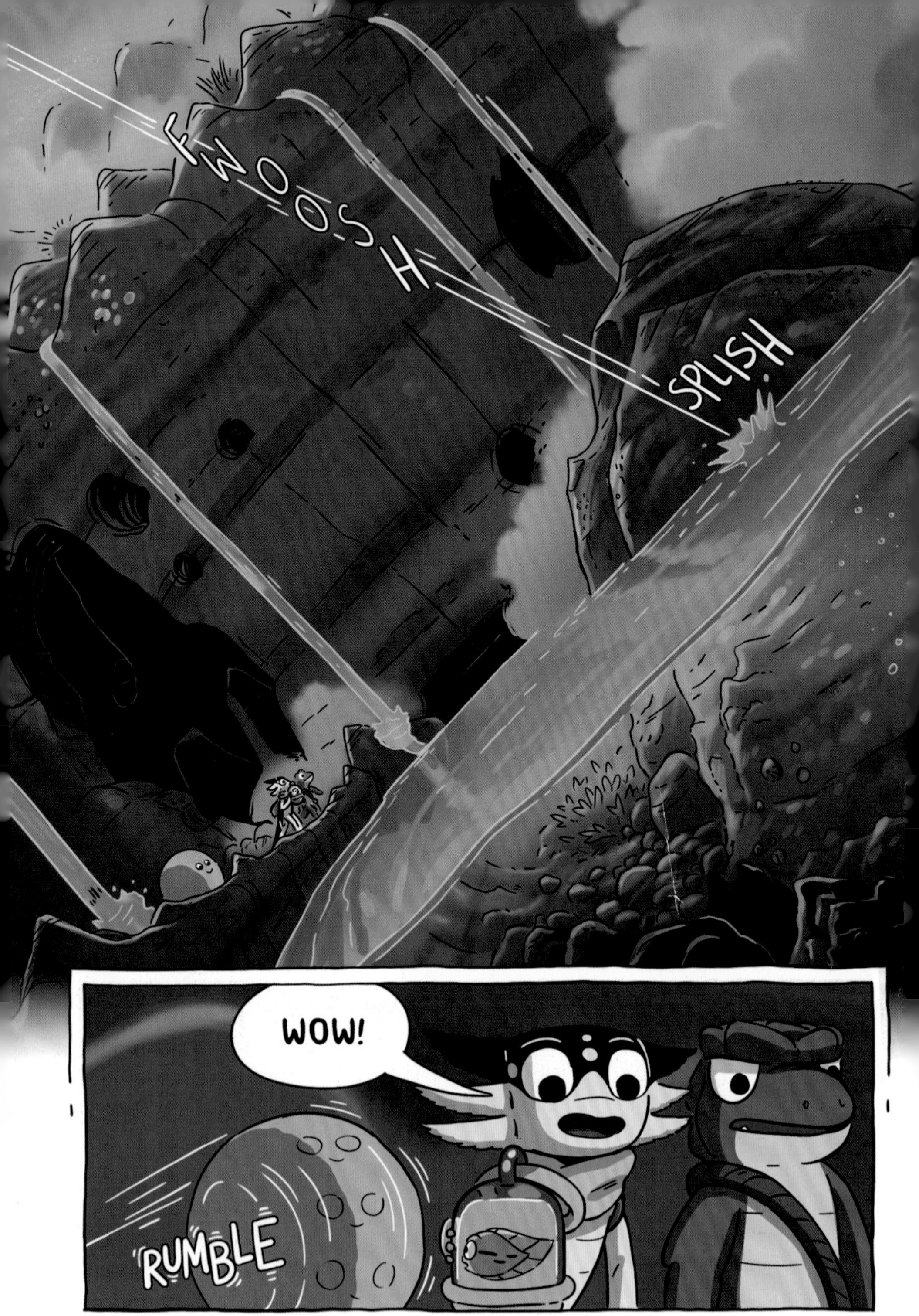
FWOOSH
SPLISH
WOW!
RUMBLE

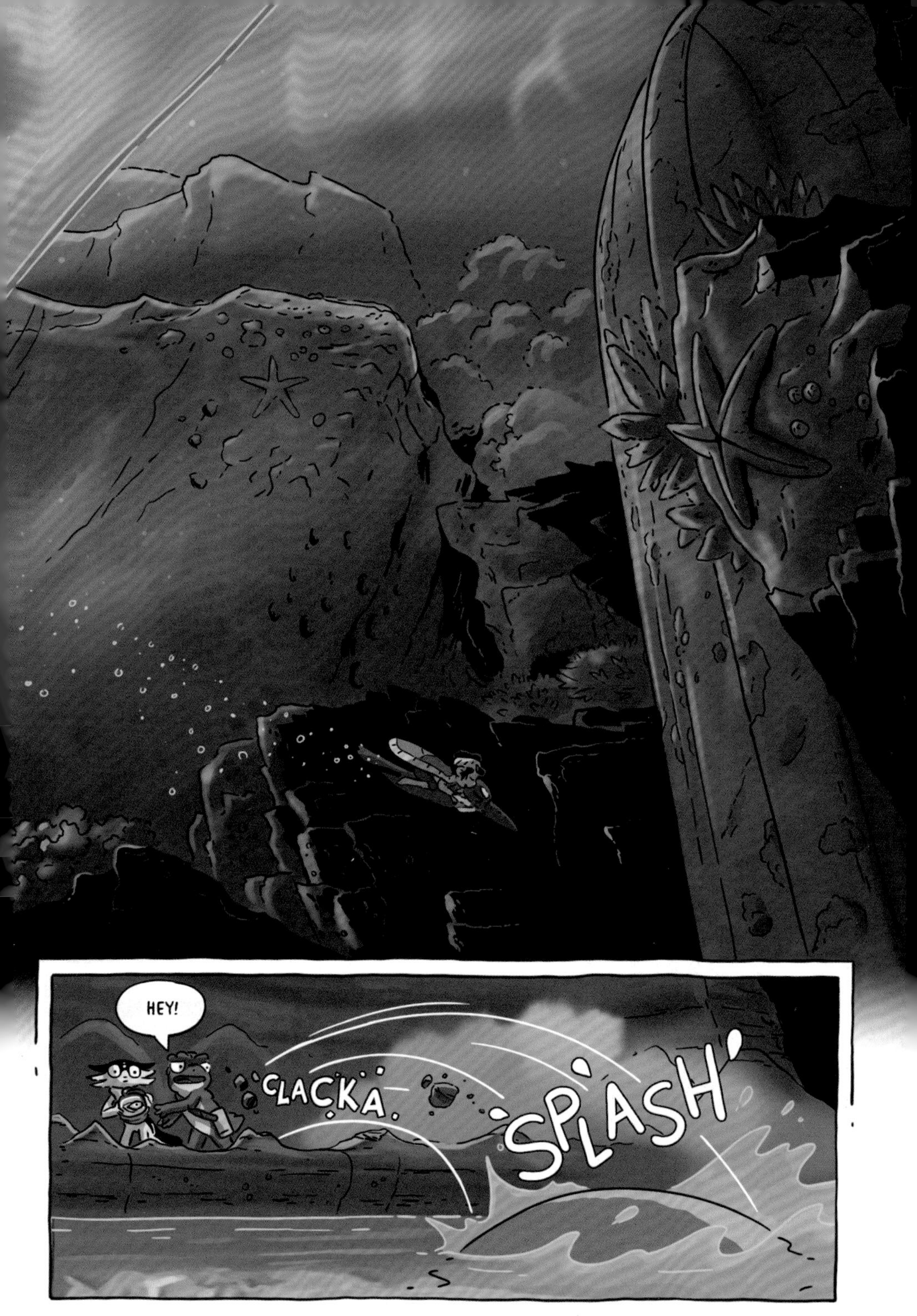
HEY!
CLACKA
SPLASH

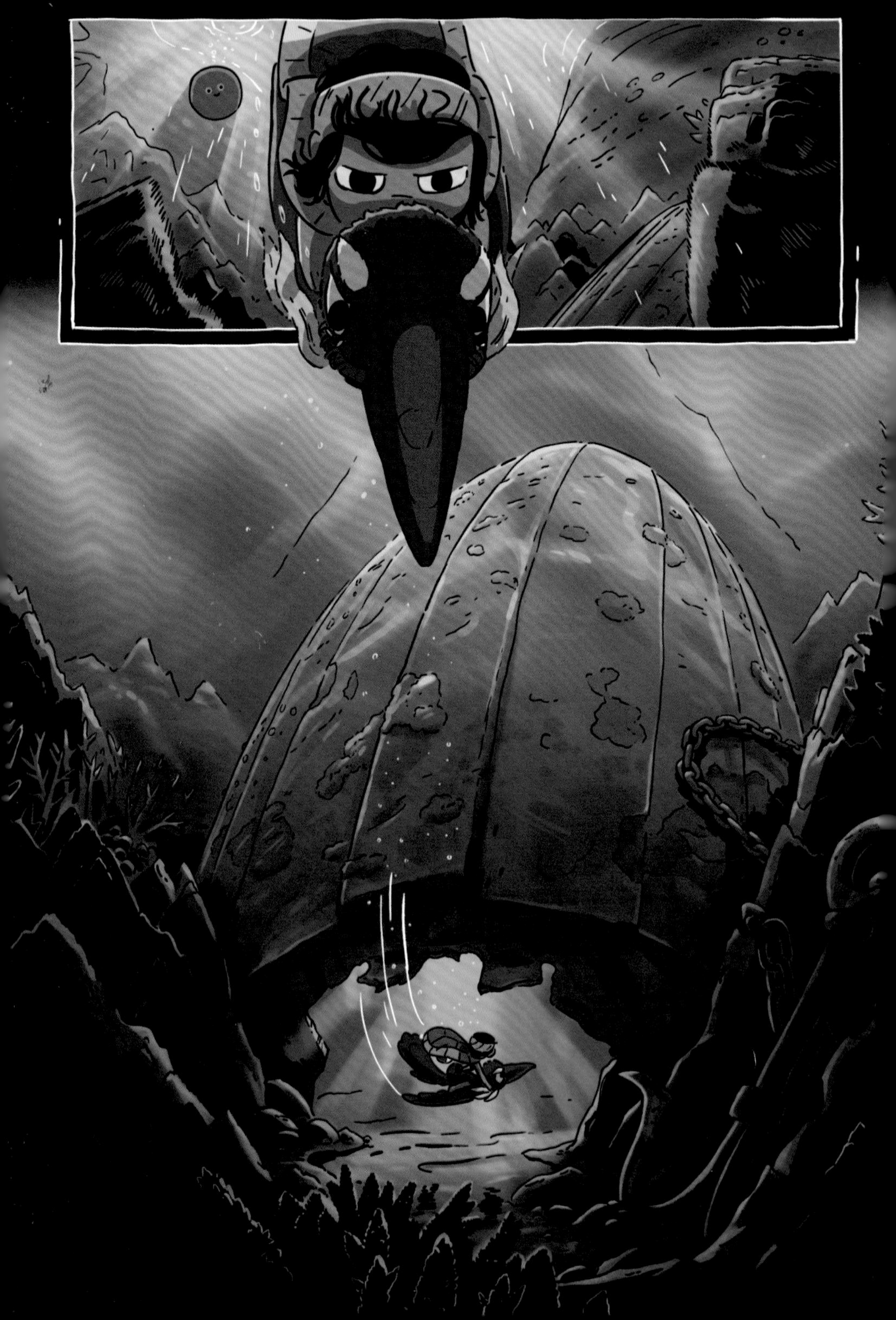

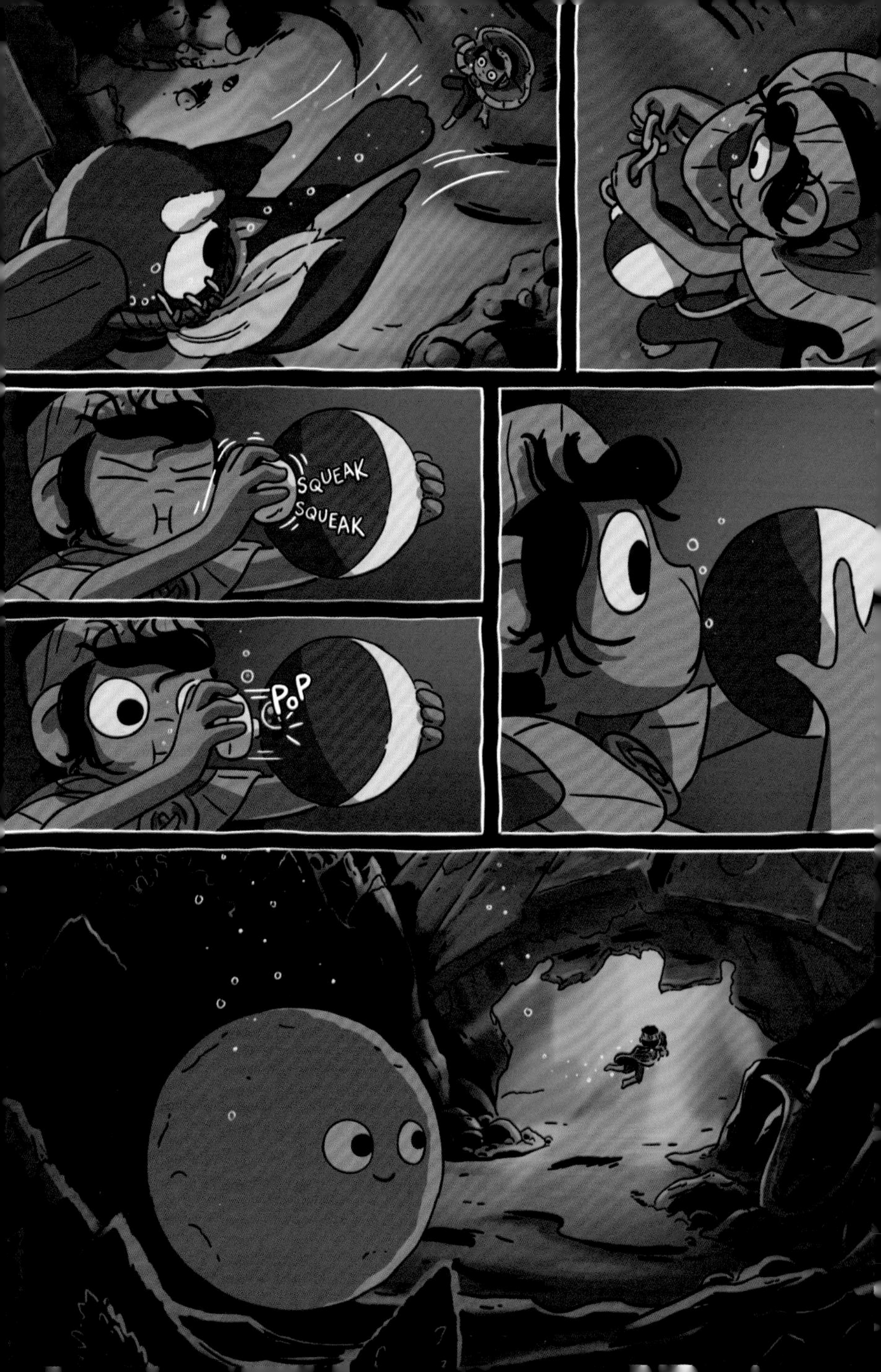
SQUEAK
SQUEAK
POP

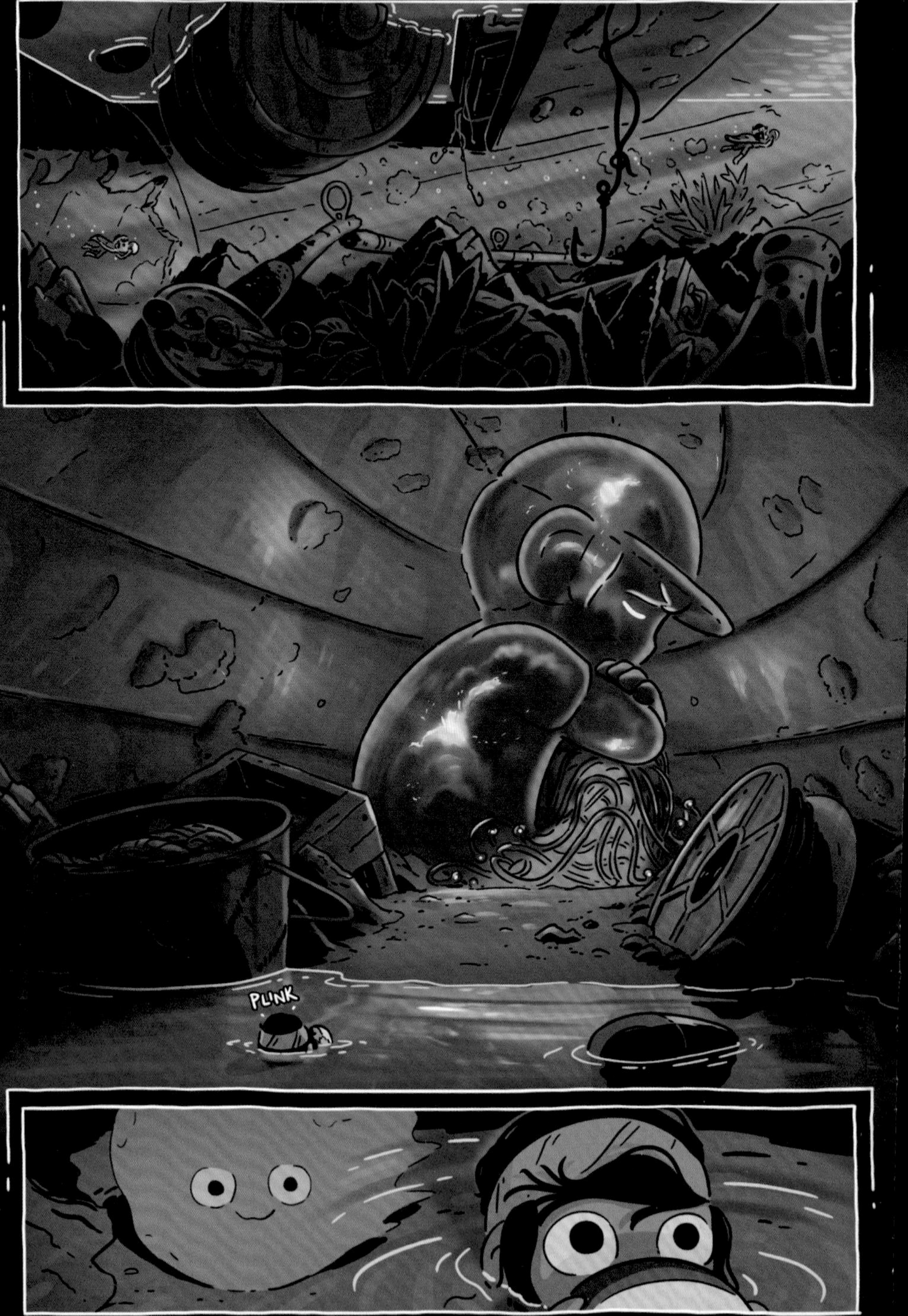
PLINK

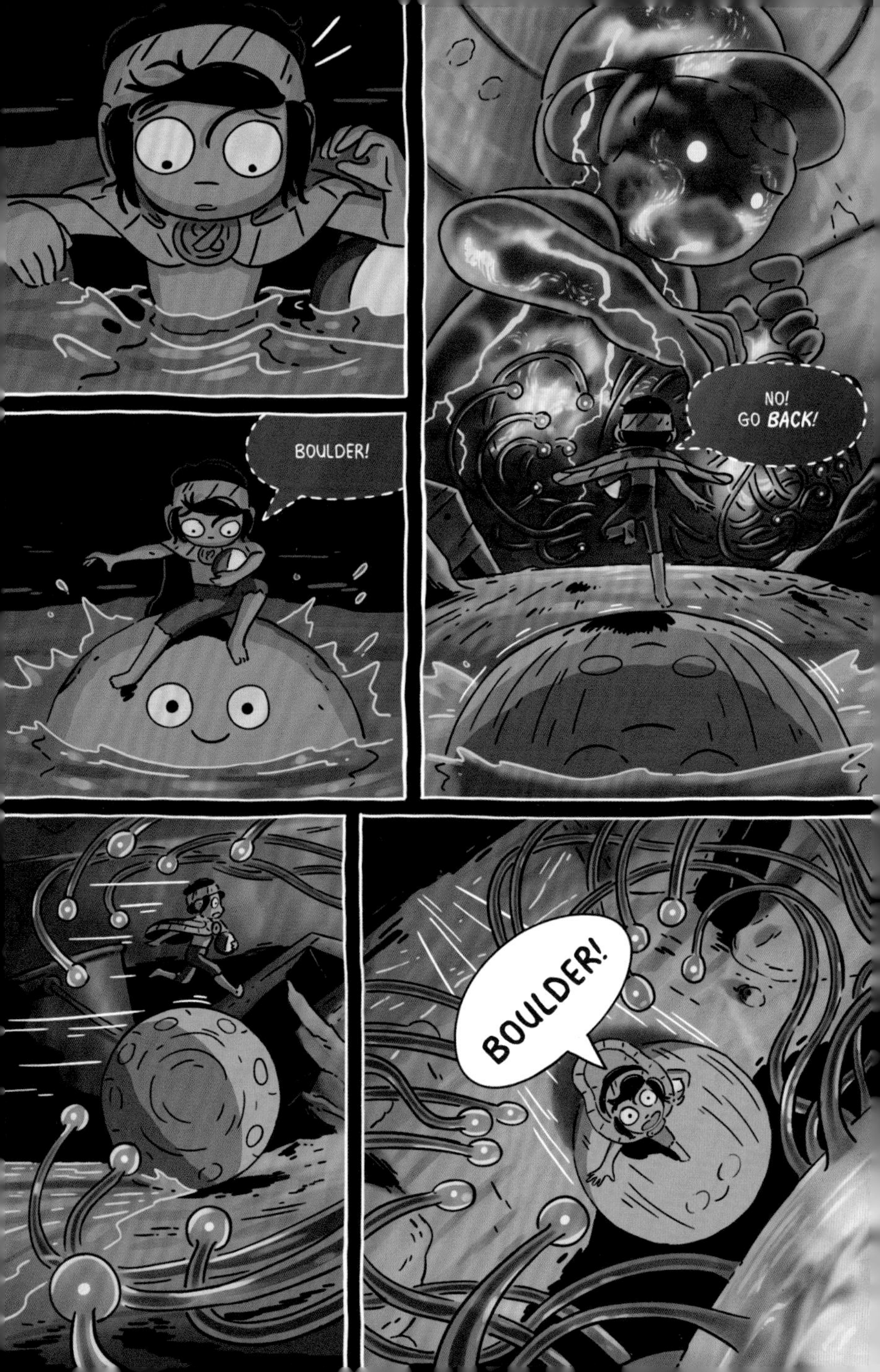
BOULDER!
NO! GO BACK!
BOULDER!

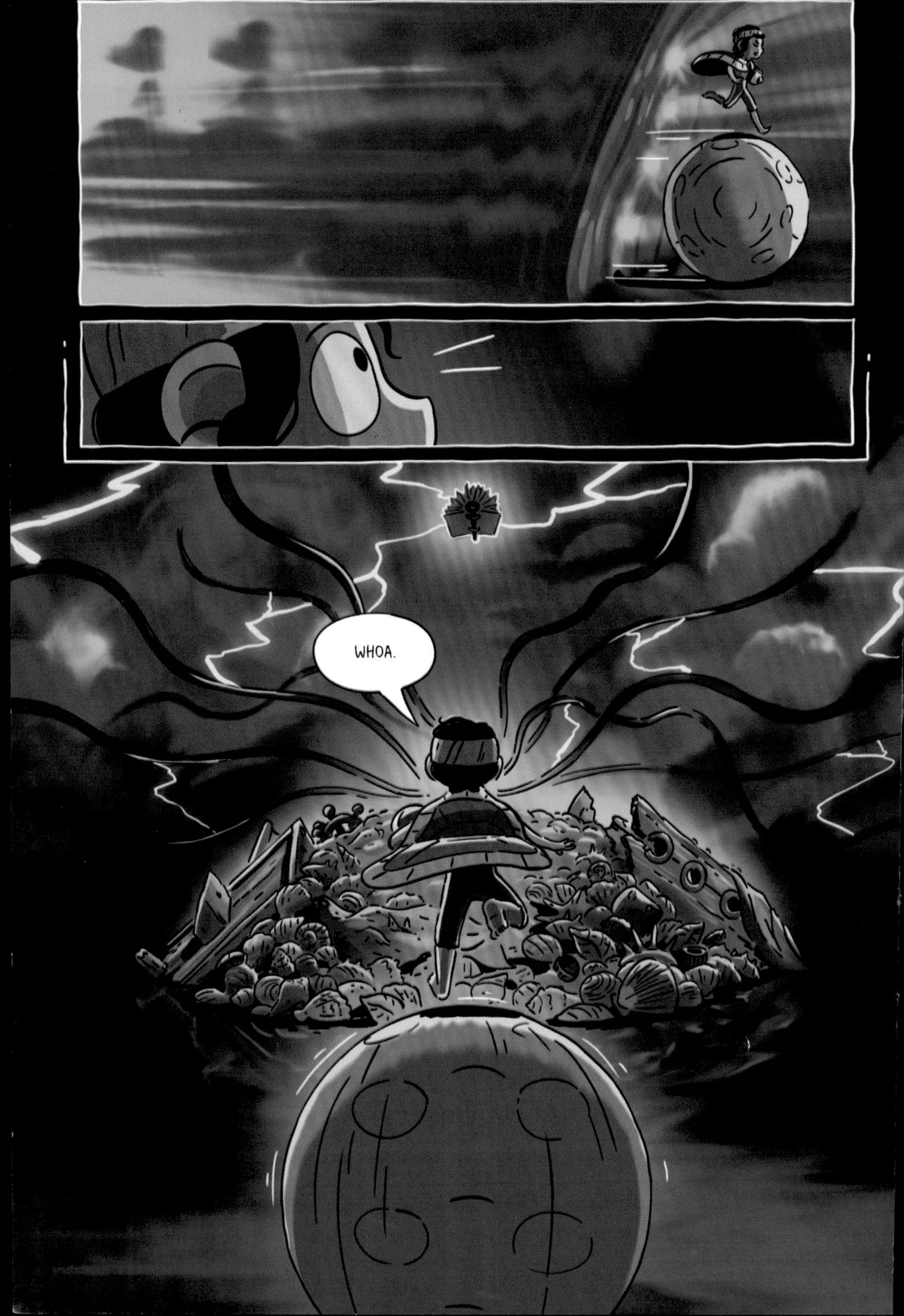
WHOA.

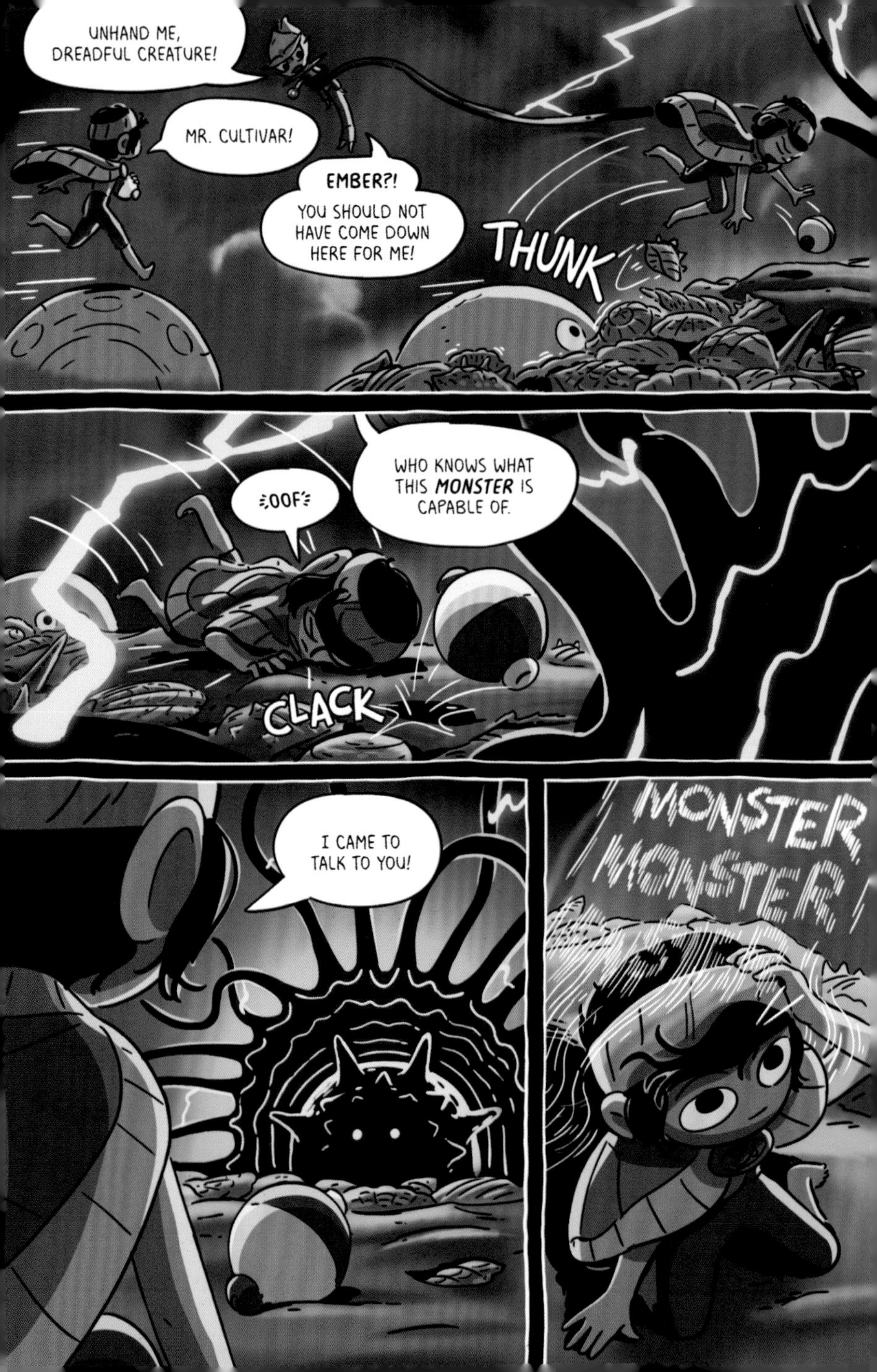
UNHAND ME, DREADFUL CREATURE!
MR. CULTIVAR!
EMBER?! YOU SHOULD NOT HAVE COME DOWN HERE FOR ME!
THUNK
OOF
WHO KNOWS WHAT THIS MONSTER IS CAPABLE OF.
CLACK
I CAME TO TALK TO YOU!
MONSTER
MONSTER

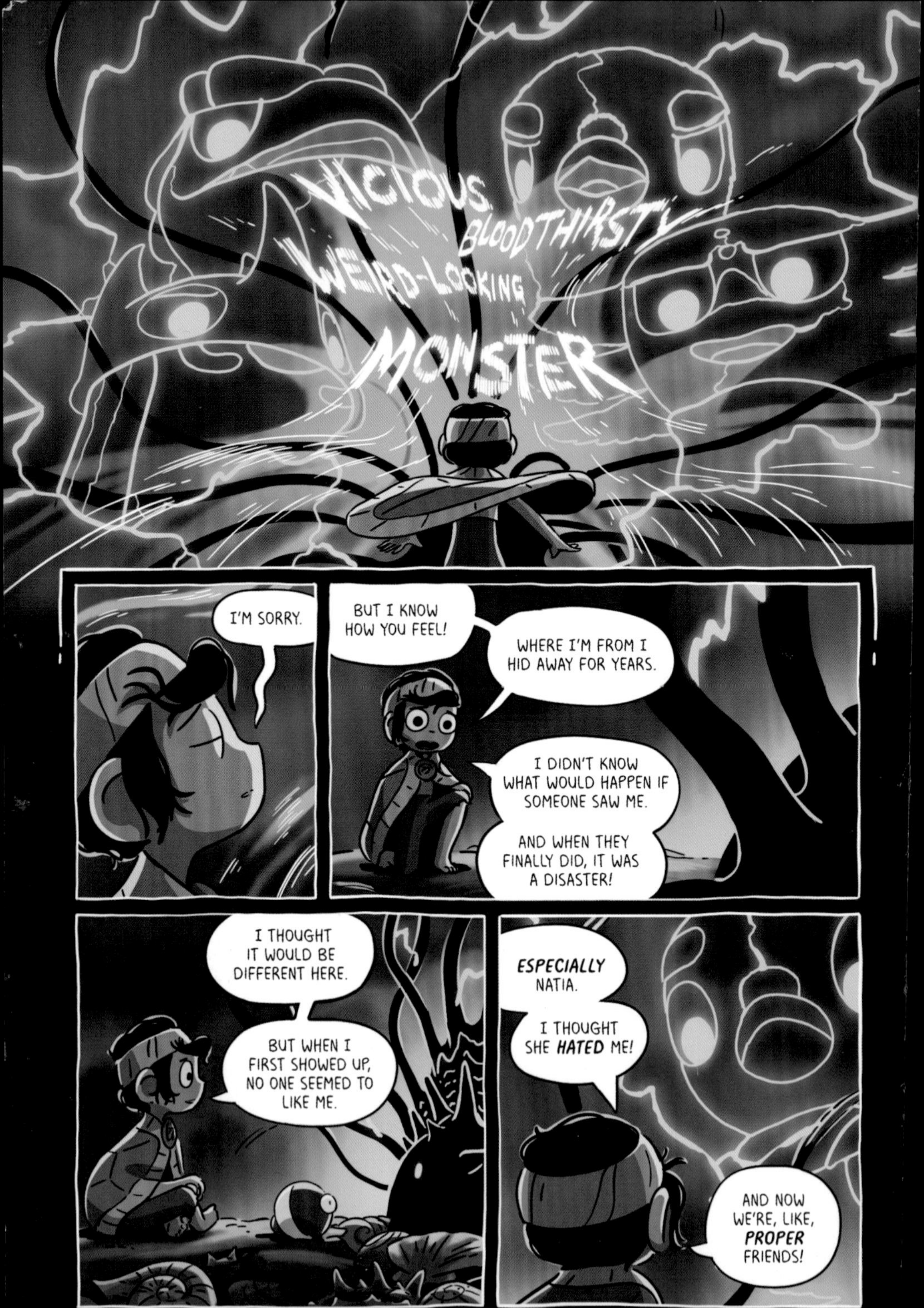
VICIOUS
BLOODTHIRSTY
WEIRD-LOOKING
MONSTER
I'M SORRY.
BUT I KNOW HOW YOU FEEL!
WHERE I'M FROM I HID AWAY FOR YEARS.
I DIDN'T KNOW WHAT WOULD HAPPEN IF SOMEONE SAW ME.
AND WHEN THEY FINALLY DID, IT WAS A DISASTER!
I THOUGHT IT WOULD BE DIFFERENT HERE.
BUT WHEN I FIRST SHOWED UP, NO ONE SEEMED TO LIKE ME.
ESPECIALLY NATIA.
I THOUGHT SHE HATED ME!
AND NOW WE'RE, LIKE, PROPER FRIENDS!

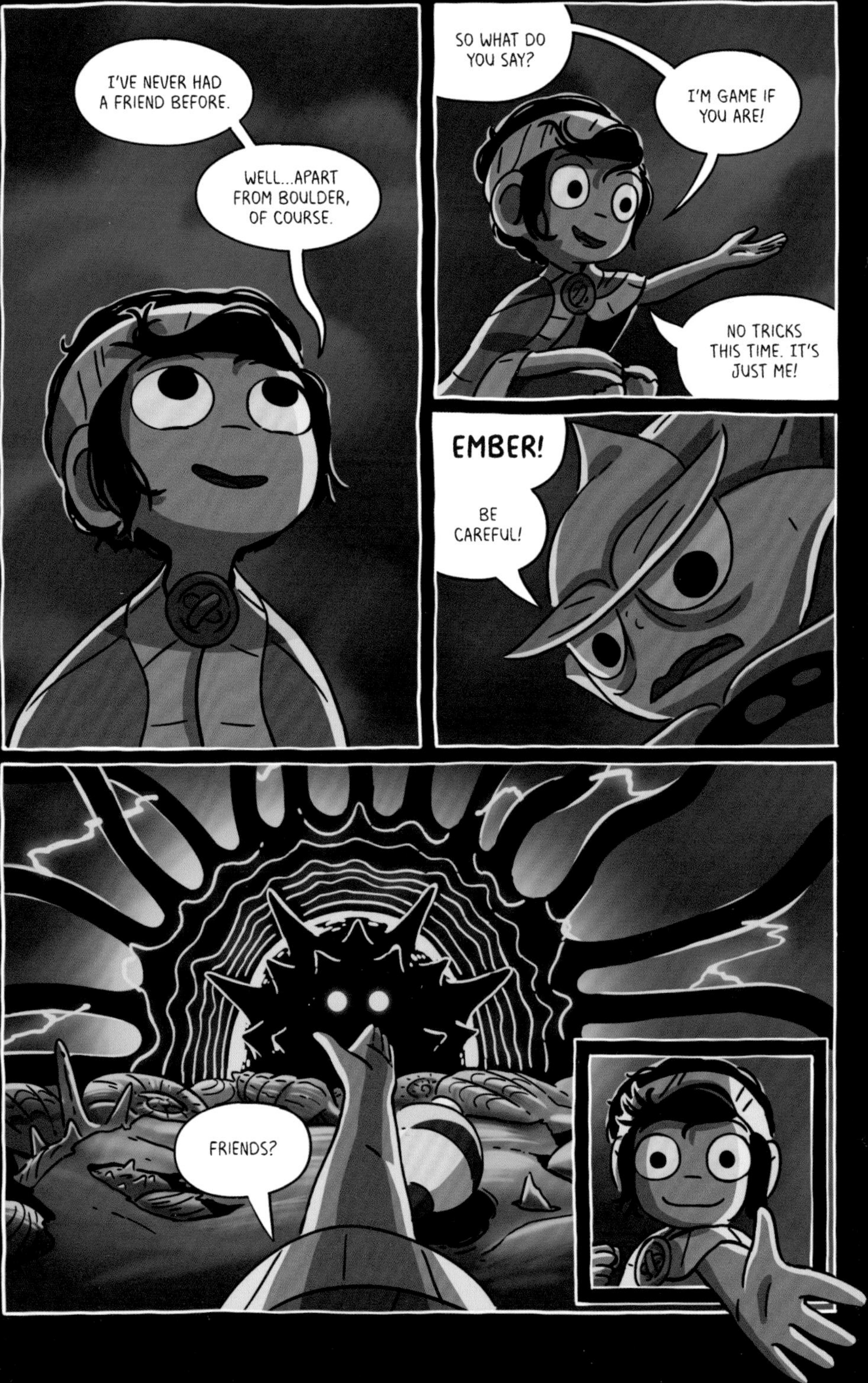
I'VE NEVER HAD A FRIEND BEFORE.
WELL...APART FROM BOULDER, OF COURSE.
SO WHAT DO YOU SAY?
I'M GAME IF YOU ARE!
NO TRICKS THIS TIME. IT'S JUST ME!
EMBER!
BE CAREFUL!
FRIENDS?

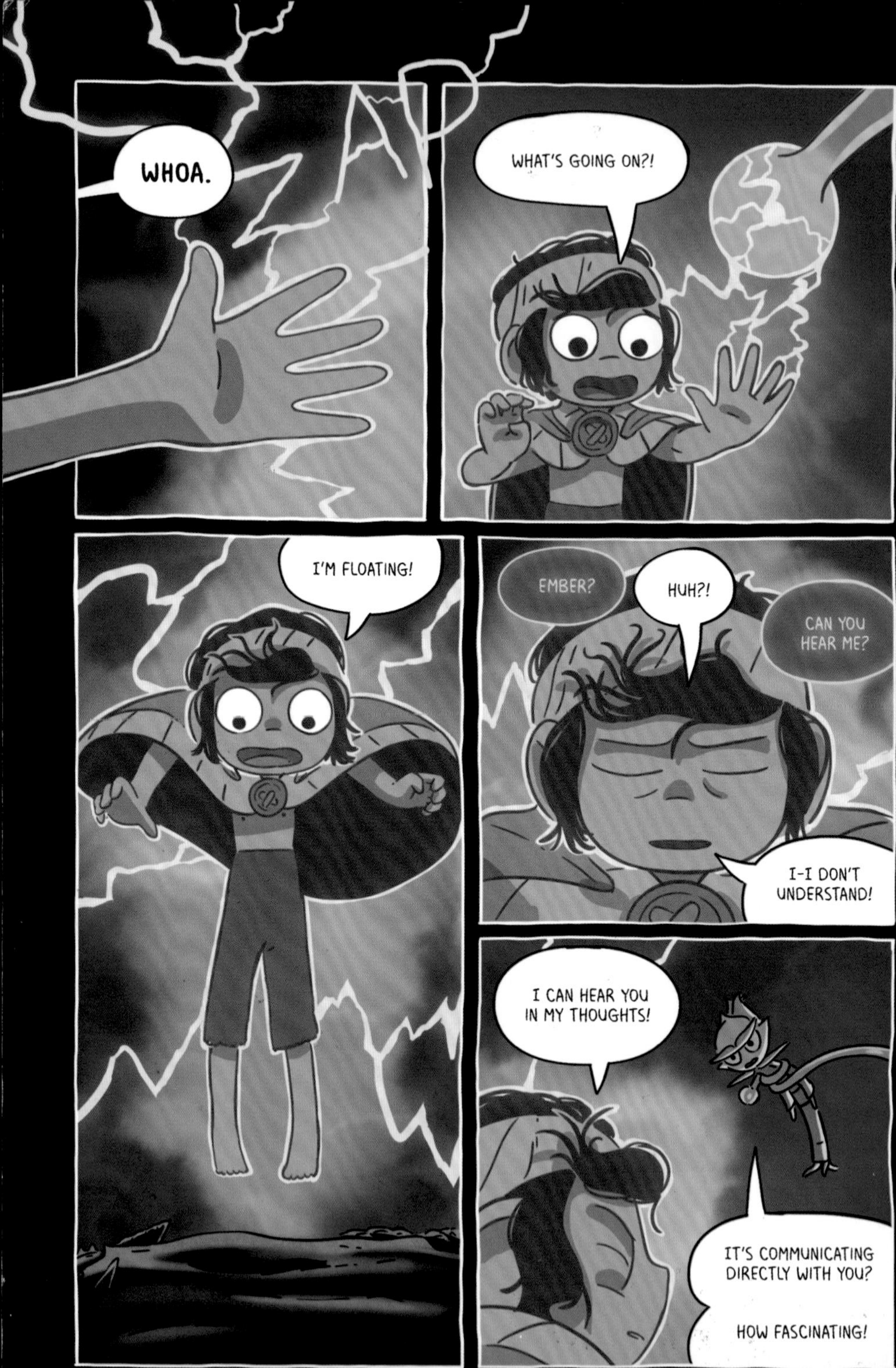

ZAP
WHOA.
WHAT'S GOING ON?!
I'M FLOATING!
EMBER?
HUH?!
CAN YOU HEAR ME?
I-I DON'T UNDERSTAND!
I CAN HEAR YOU IN MY THOUGHTS!
IT'S COMMUNICATING DIRECTLY WITH YOU?
HOW FASCINATING!

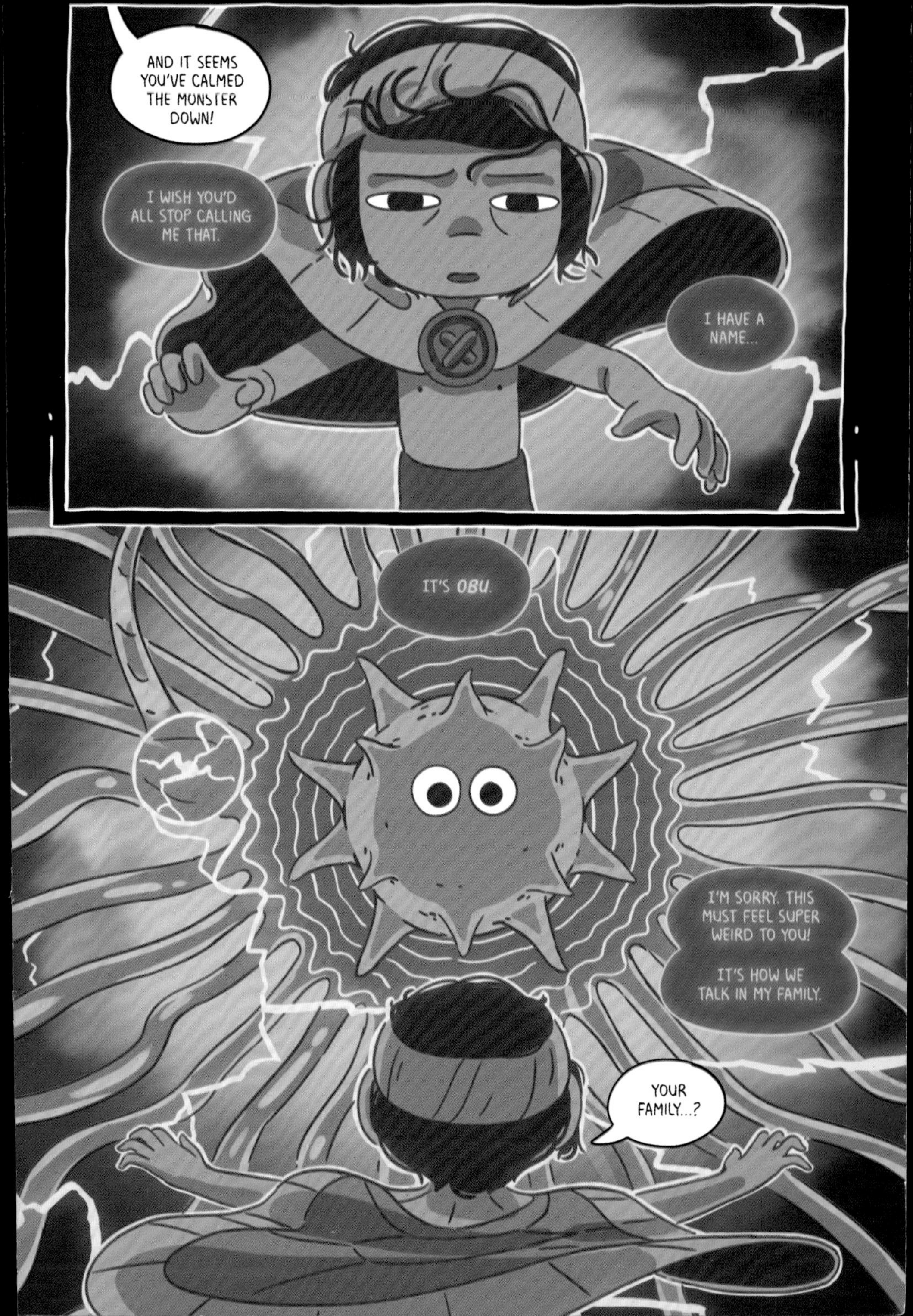
AND IT SEEMS YOU'VE CALMED THE MONSTER DOWN!
I WISH YOU'D ALL STOP CALLING ME THAT.
I HAVE A NAME...
IT'S OBU.
I'M SORRY. THIS MUST FEEL SUPER WEIRD TO YOU!
IT'S HOW WE TALK IN MY FAMILY.
YOUR FAMILY...?

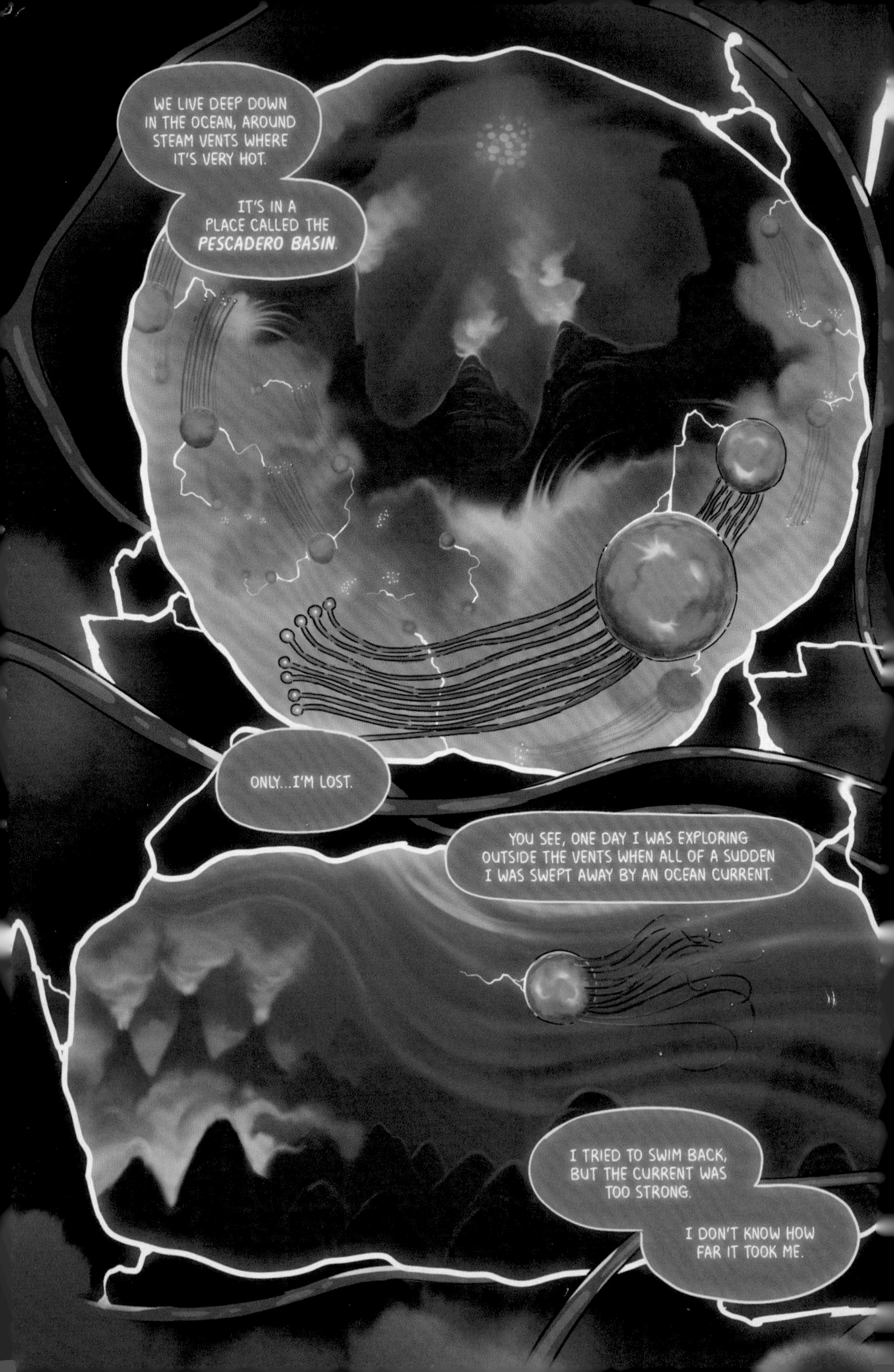
WE LIVE DEEP DOWN IN THE OCEAN, AROUND STEAM VENTS WHERE IT'S VERY HOT.
IT'S IN A PLACE CALLED THE *PESCADERO BASIN*.
ONLY...I'M LOST.
YOU SEE, ONE DAY I WAS EXPLORING OUTSIDE THE VENTS WHEN ALL OF A SUDDEN I WAS SWEPT AWAY BY AN OCEAN CURRENT.
I TRIED TO SWIM BACK, BUT THE CURRENT WAS TOO STRONG.
I DON'T KNOW HOW FAR IT TOOK ME.

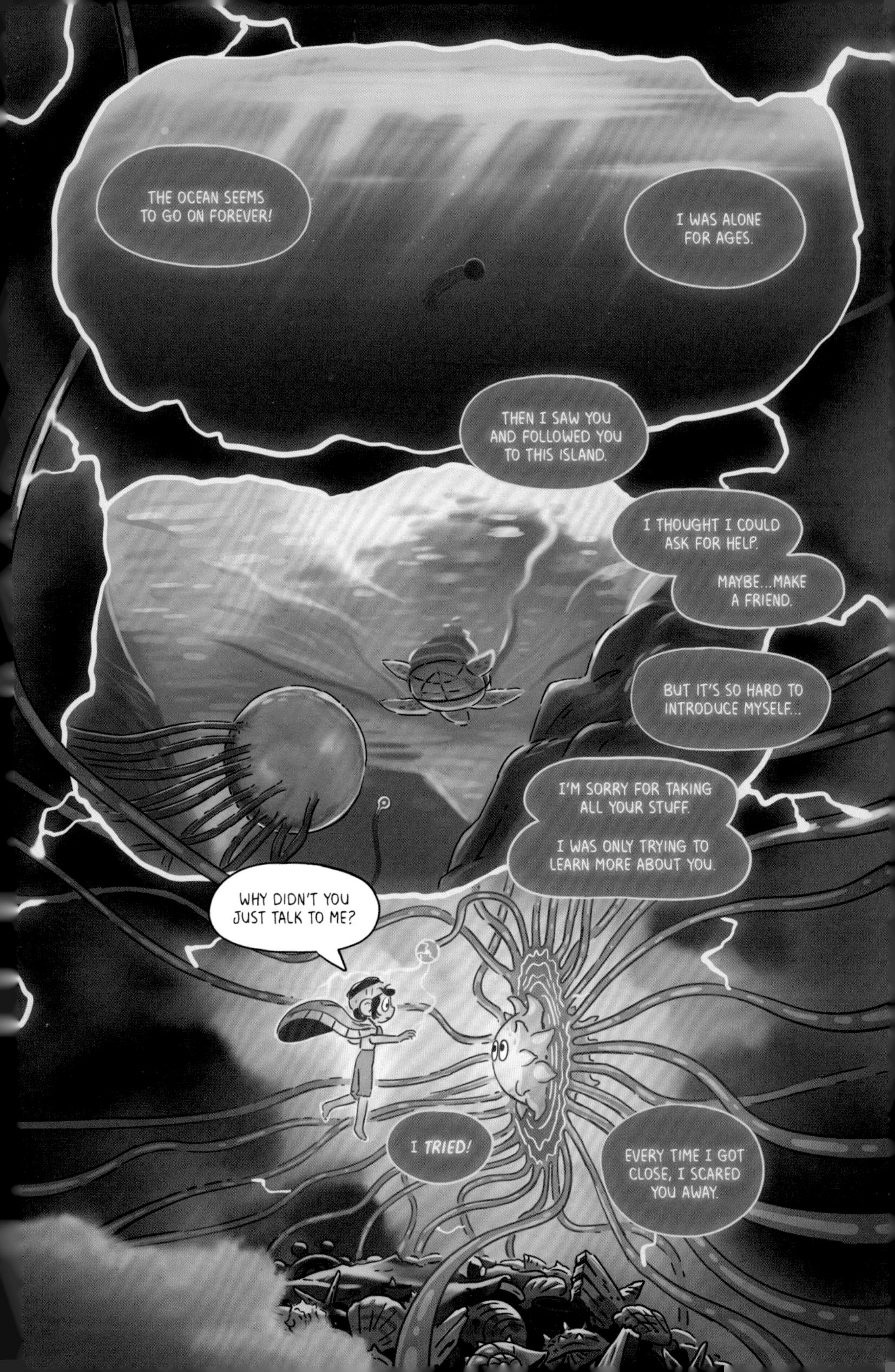
THE OCEAN SEEMS TO GO ON FOREVER!
I WAS ALONE FOR AGES.
THEN I SAW YOU AND FOLLOWED YOU TO THIS ISLAND.
I THOUGHT I COULD ASK FOR HELP.
MAYBE...MAKE A FRIEND.
BUT IT'S SO HARD TO INTRODUCE MYSELF...
I'M SORRY FOR TAKING ALL YOUR STUFF.
I WAS ONLY TRYING TO LEARN MORE ABOUT YOU.
WHY DIDN'T YOU JUST TALK TO ME?
I *TRIED!*
EVERY TIME I GOT CLOSE, I SCARED YOU AWAY.

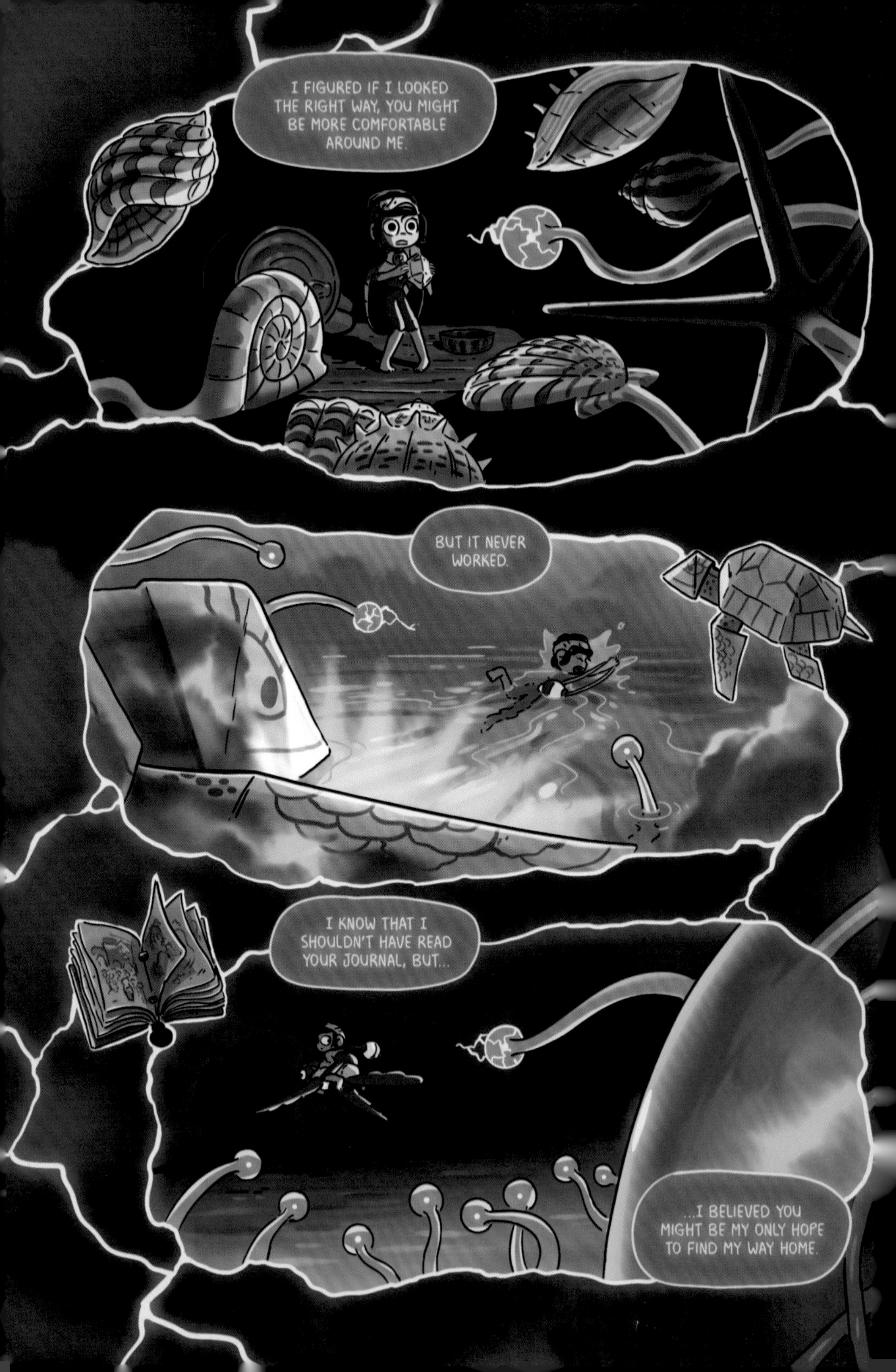
I FIGURED IF I LOOKED THE RIGHT WAY, YOU MIGHT BE MORE COMFORTABLE AROUND ME.
BUT IT NEVER WORKED.
I KNOW THAT I SHOULDN'T HAVE READ YOUR JOURNAL, BUT...
...I BELIEVED YOU MIGHT BE MY ONLY HOPE TO FIND MY WAY HOME.

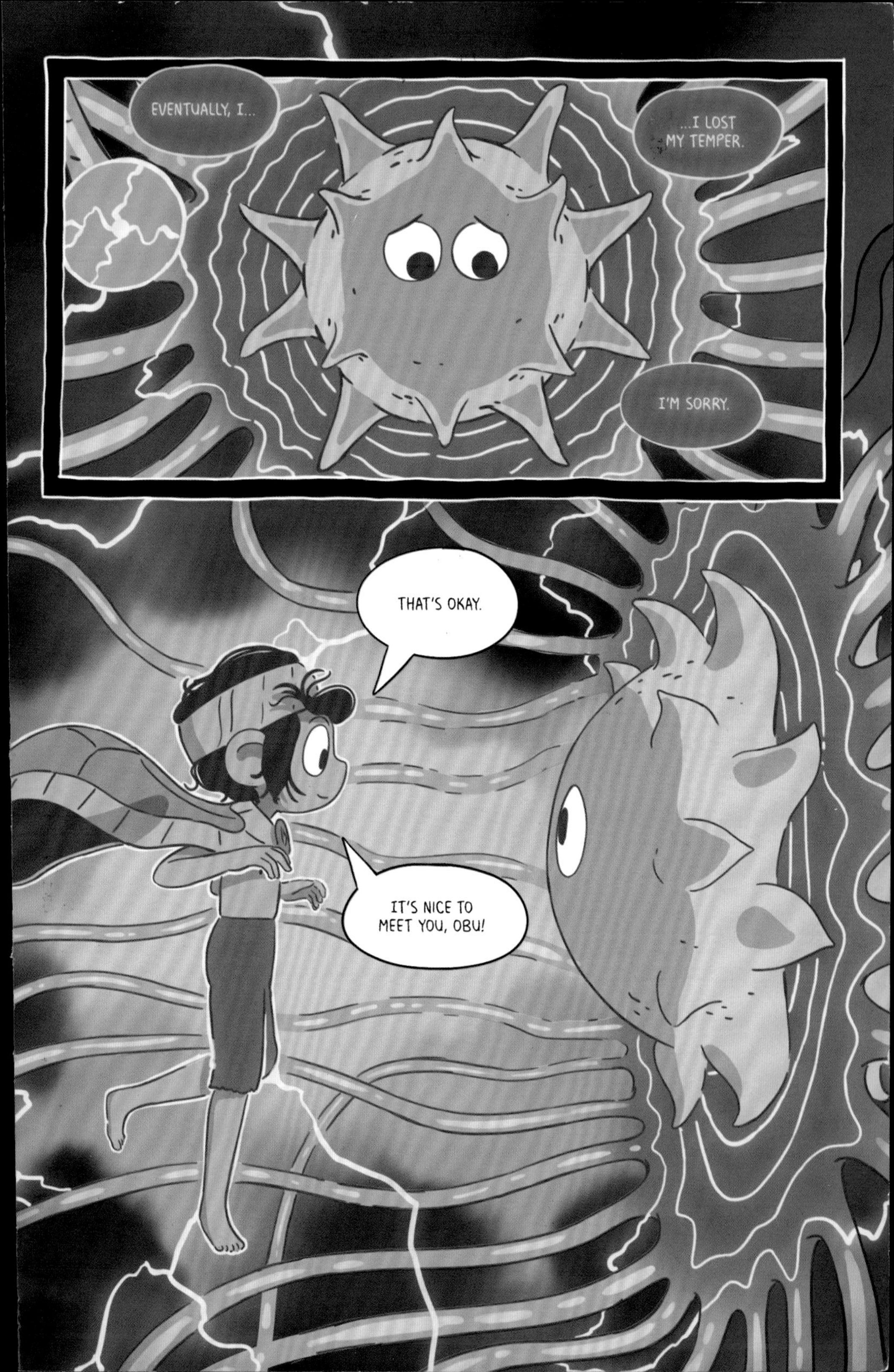
EVENTUALLY, I...
...I LOST MY TEMPER.
I'M SORRY.
THAT'S OKAY.
IT'S NICE TO MEET YOU, OBU!

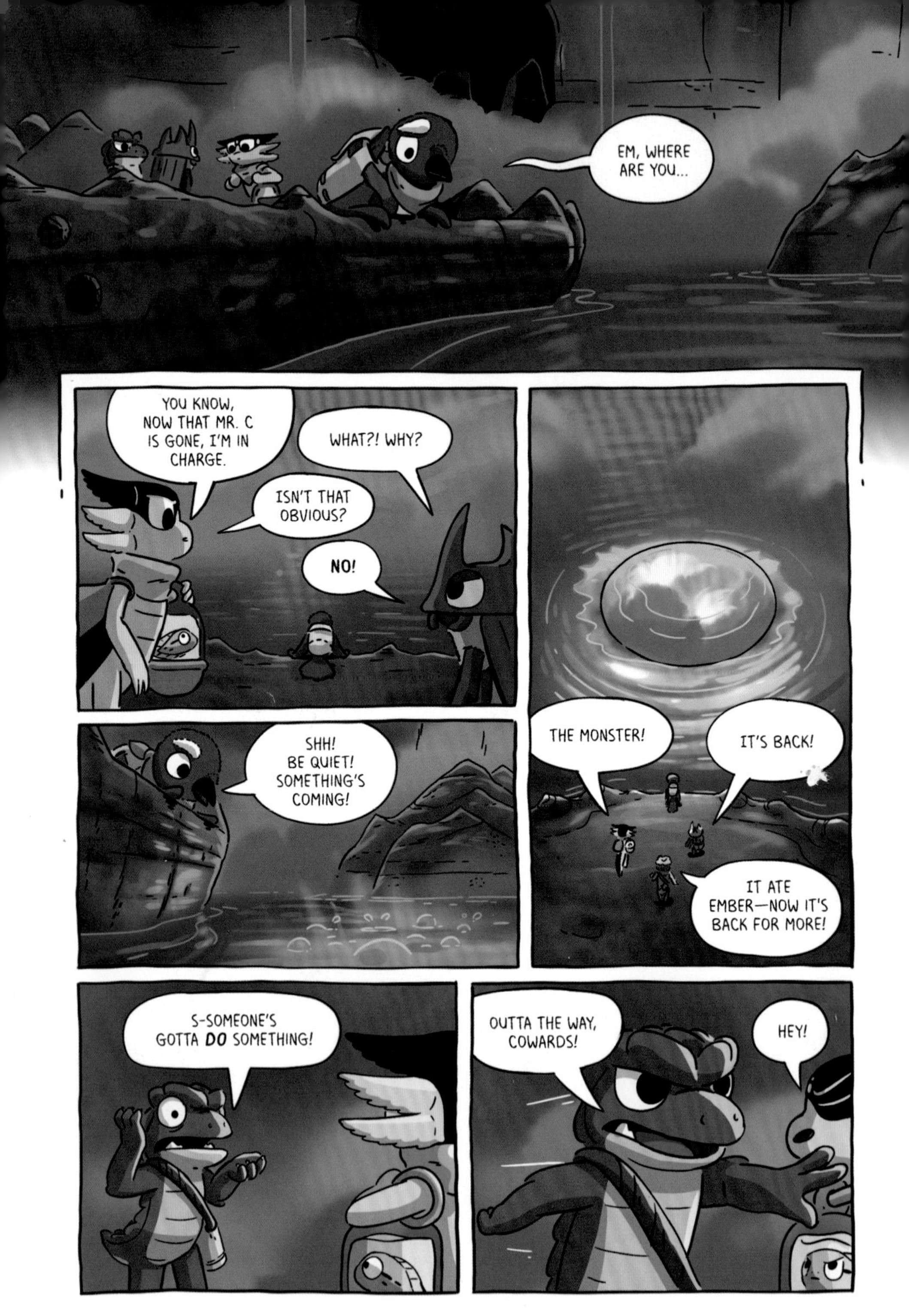
EM, WHERE ARE YOU...
YOU KNOW, NOW THAT MR. C IS GONE, I'M IN CHARGE.
WHAT?! WHY?
ISN'T THAT OBVIOUS?
NO!
SHH! BE QUIET! SOMETHING'S COMING!
THE MONSTER!
IT'S BACK!
IT ATE EMBER—NOW IT'S BACK FOR MORE!
S-SOMEONE'S GOTTA **DO** SOMETHING!
OUTTA THE WAY, COWARDS!
HEY!

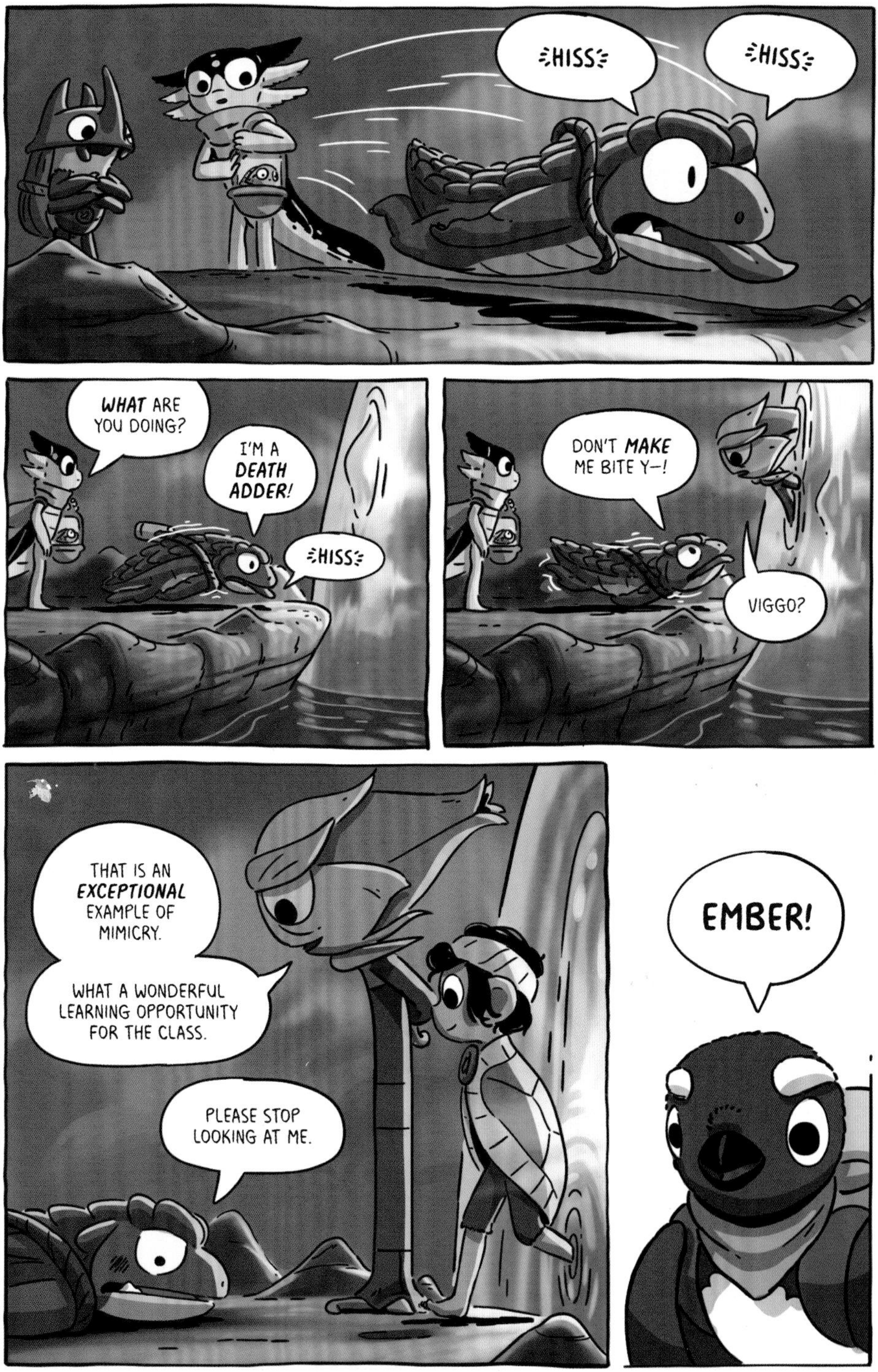

HISS
HISS
WHAT ARE YOU DOING?
I'M A DEATH ADDER!
HISS
DON'T MAKE ME BITE Y—!
VIGGO?
THAT IS AN EXCEPTIONAL EXAMPLE OF MIMICRY.
WHAT A WONDERFUL LEARNING OPPORTUNITY FOR THE CLASS.
PLEASE STOP LOOKING AT ME.
EMBER!

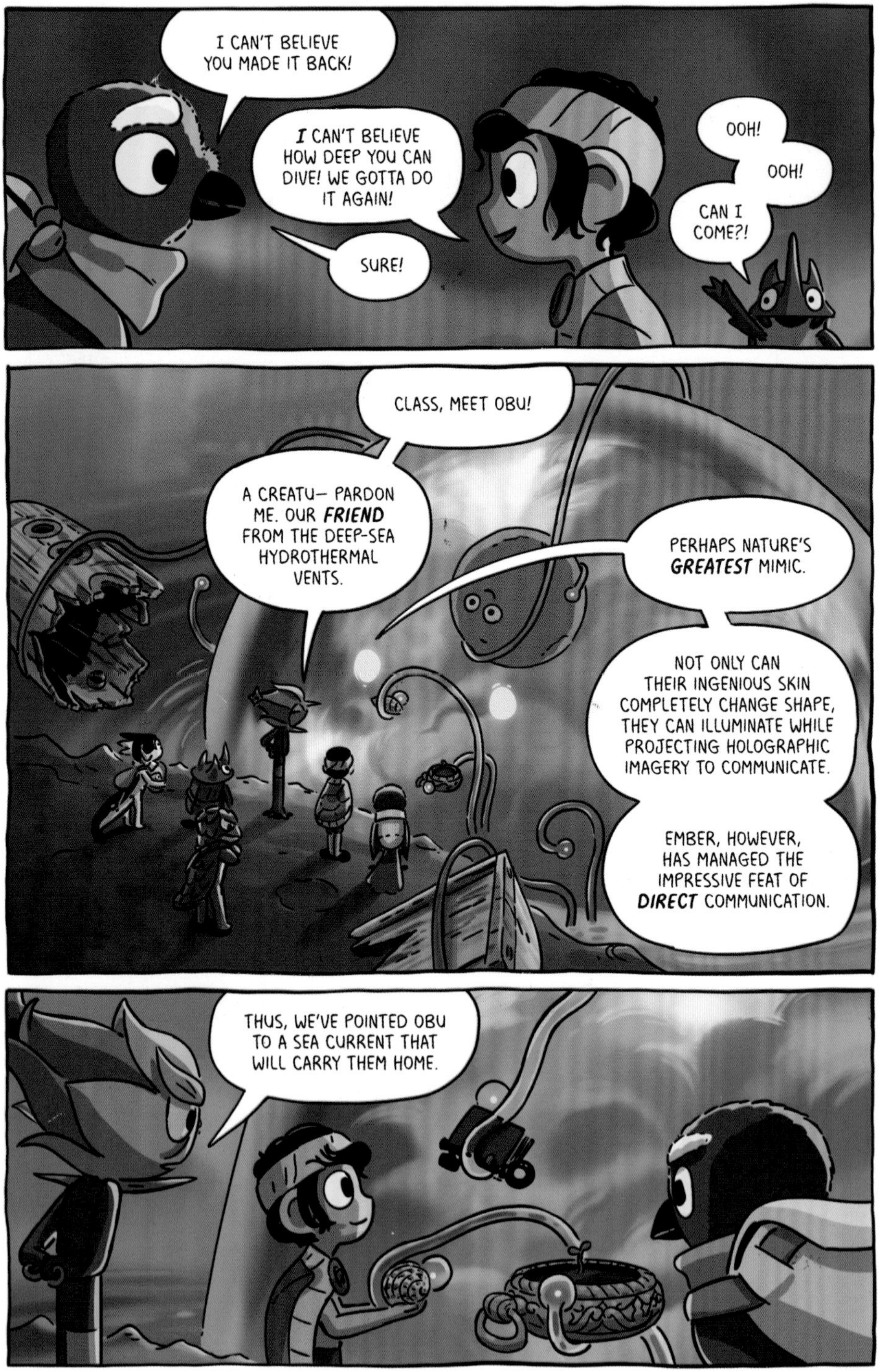
I CAN'T BELIEVE YOU MADE IT BACK!
I CAN'T BELIEVE HOW DEEP YOU CAN DIVE! WE GOTTA DO IT AGAIN!
SURE!
OOH!
OOH!
CAN I COME?!
CLASS, MEET OBU!
A CREATU— PARDON ME. OUR FRIEND FROM THE DEEP-SEA HYDROTHERMAL VENTS.
PERHAPS NATURE'S GREATEST MIMIC.
NOT ONLY CAN THEIR INGENIOUS SKIN COMPLETELY CHANGE SHAPE, THEY CAN ILLUMINATE WHILE PROJECTING HOLOGRAPHIC IMAGERY TO COMMUNICATE.
EMBER, HOWEVER, HAS MANAGED THE IMPRESSIVE FEAT OF DIRECT COMMUNICATION.
THUS, WE'VE POINTED OBU TO A SEA CURRENT THAT WILL CARRY THEM HOME.

OBU HAS A LONG AND ARDUOUS JOURNEY AHEAD.

BUT, WITH ANY LUCK, THEY WILL SOON REUNITE WITH THEIR FAMILY.

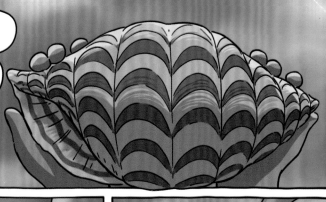

≶SIGH≷

HERE.

TAKE IT, OBU! I WANT YOU TO HAVE IT.

I *KNOW* YOU'LL TAKE GOOD CARE OF IT!

IT WAS GIVEN TO ME BY LUA, AND GIVEN TO HER BY SOMEONE SPECIAL, TOO.

IF YOU'RE FEELING LOST OR LONELY ON YOUR WAY HOME, MAYBE IT WILL REMIND YOU OF ME?

OBU MUST BE EAGER TO GET BACK TO THEIR FAMILY NOW, SO WE MUST SAY GOODBYE.

BYE, OBU!

GOOD LUCK.

DOES THIS MEAN WE'RE *NOT* IN TROUBLE FOR GOING IN THE CAVES?

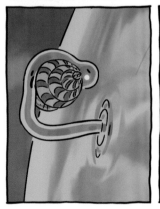

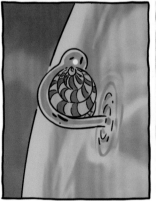

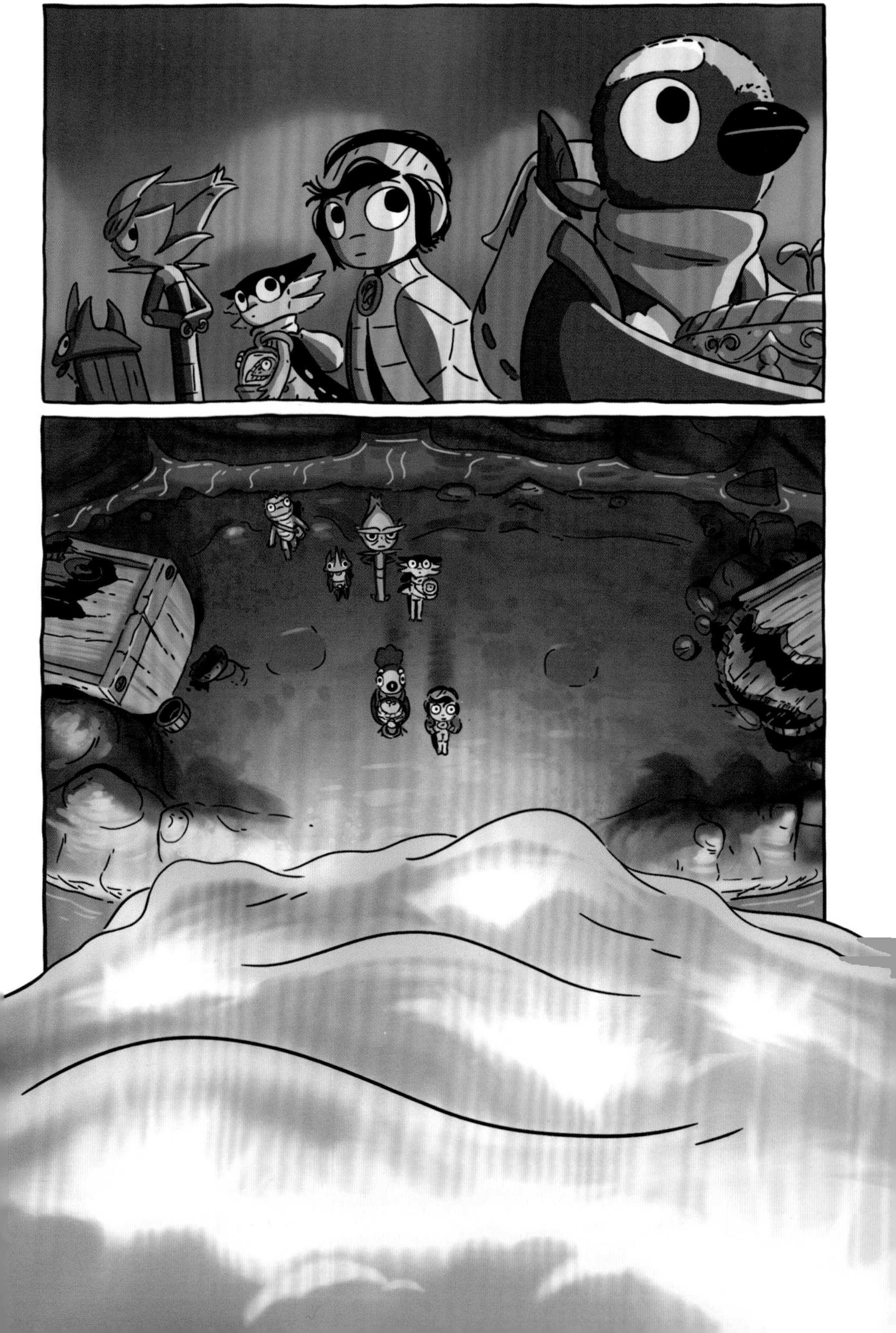

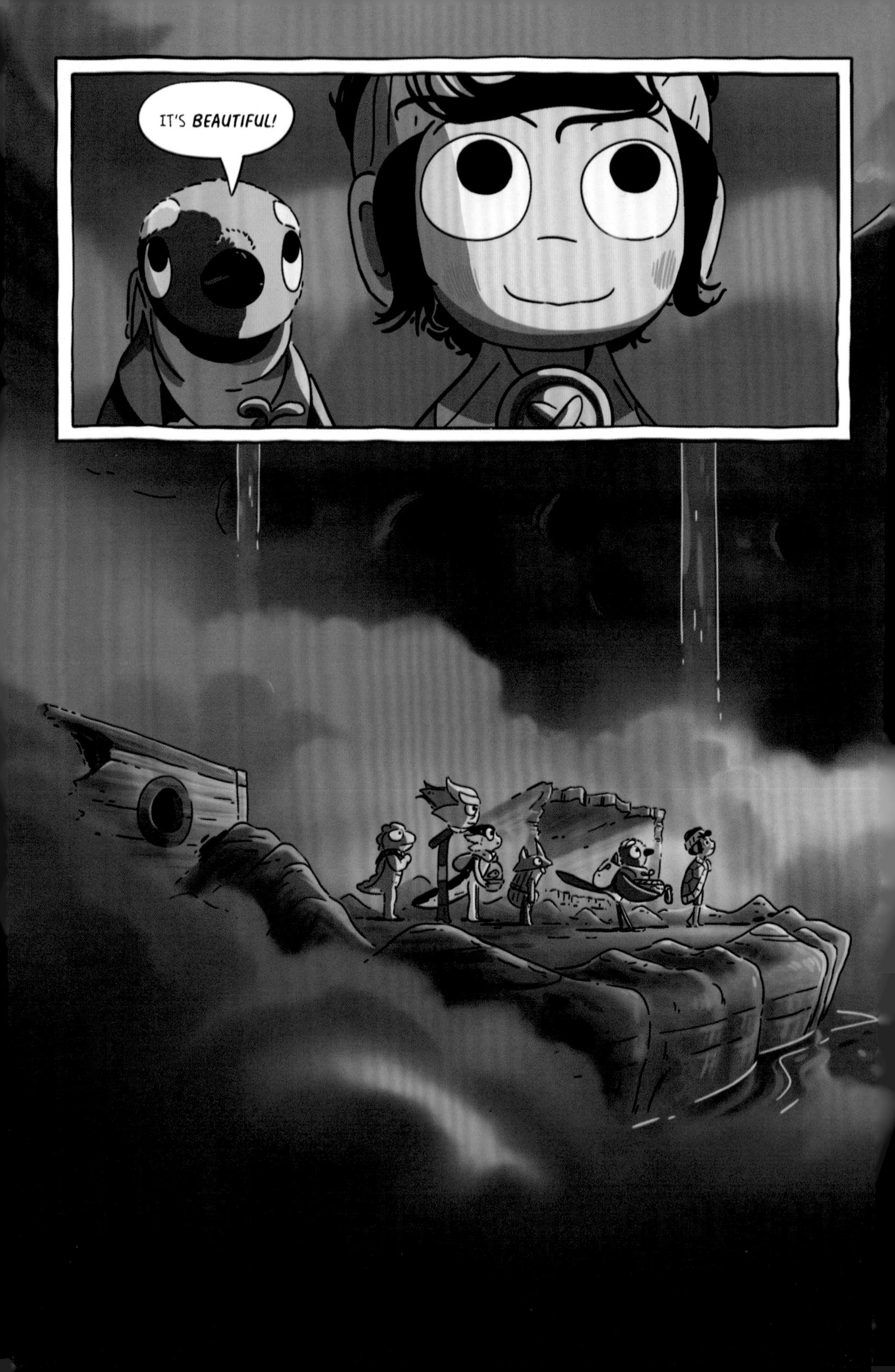
IT'S BEAUTIFUL!

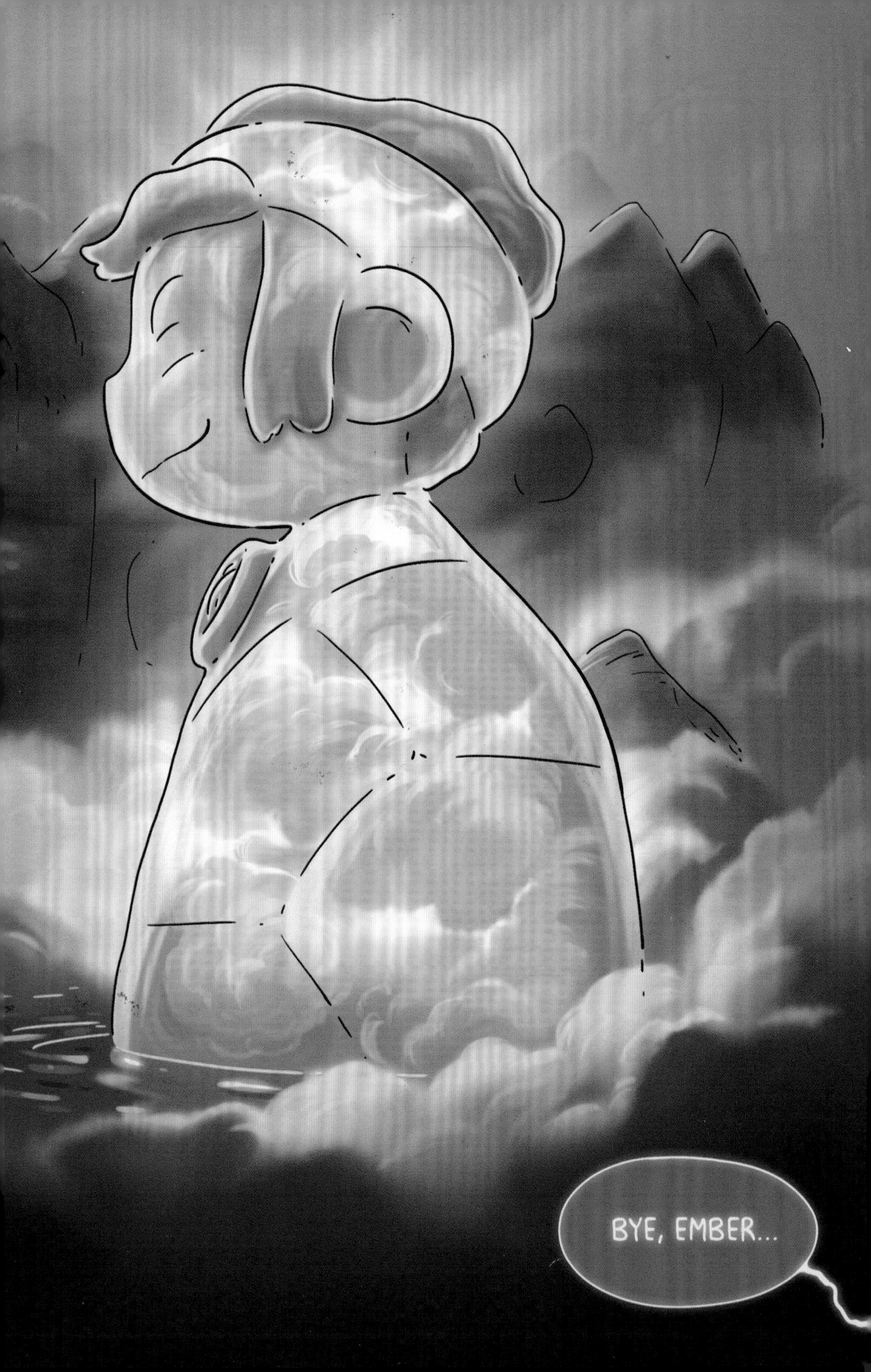
BYE, EMBER...

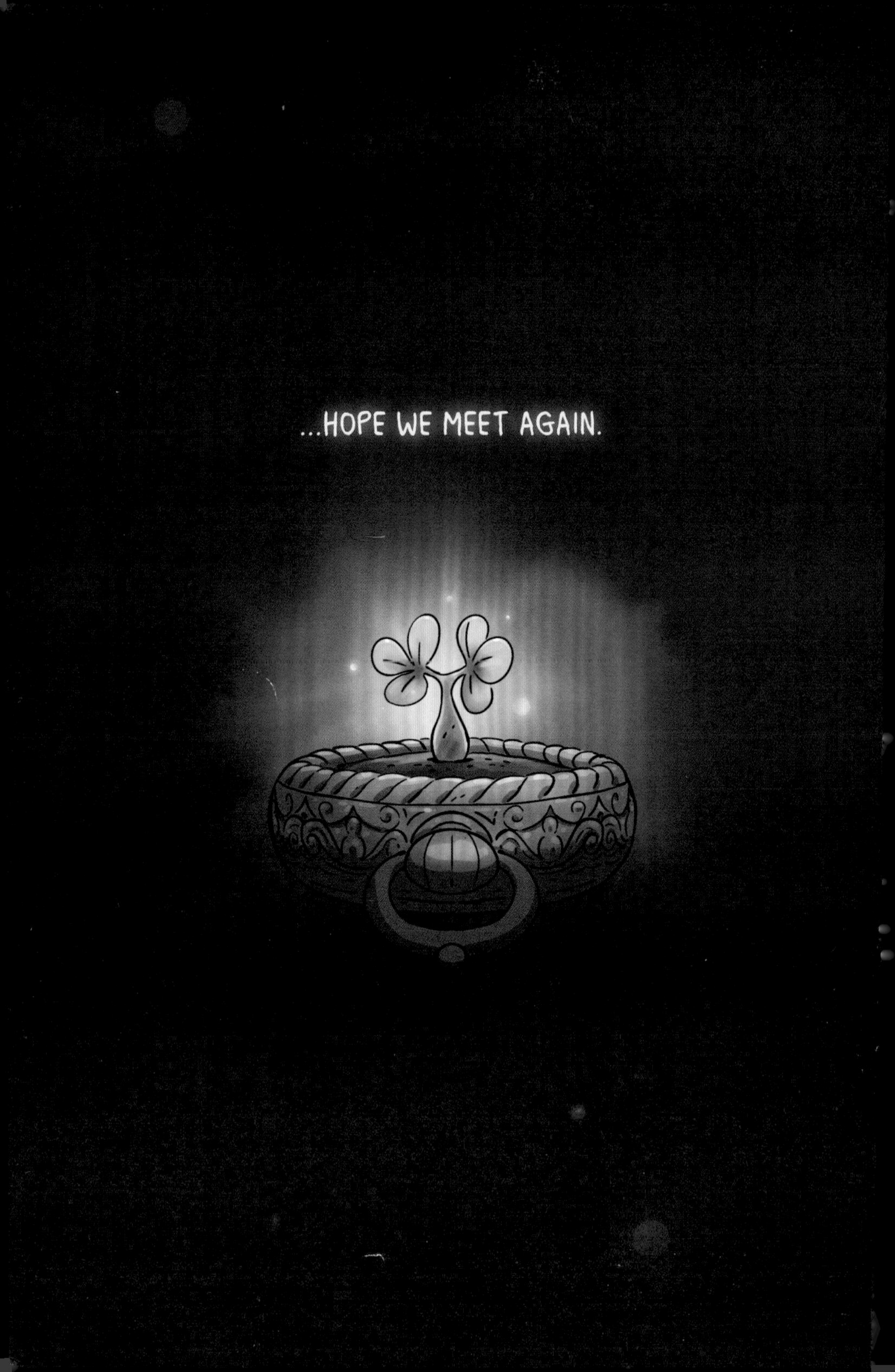
...HOPE WE MEET AGAIN.